—THE HERETIC'S GUIDE TO—
HOMECOMING

—THE HERETIC'S GUIDE TO— HOMECOMING

BOOK II: PRACTICE

SIENNA TRISTEN

MOLEWHALE PRESS

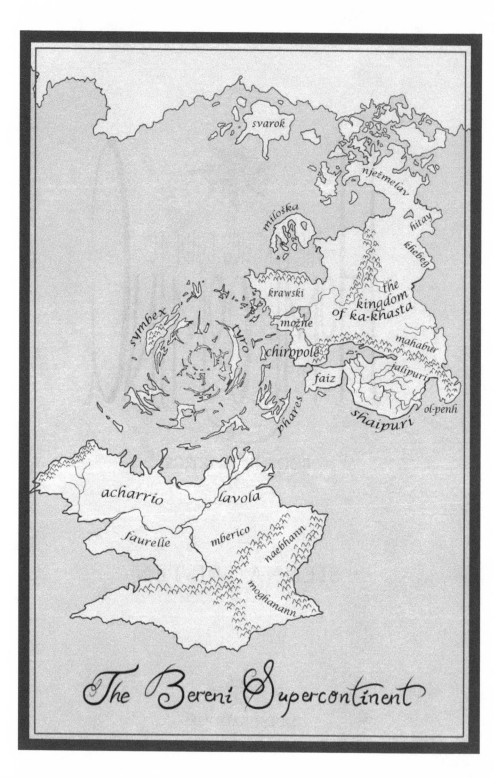

The Bereni Supercontinent

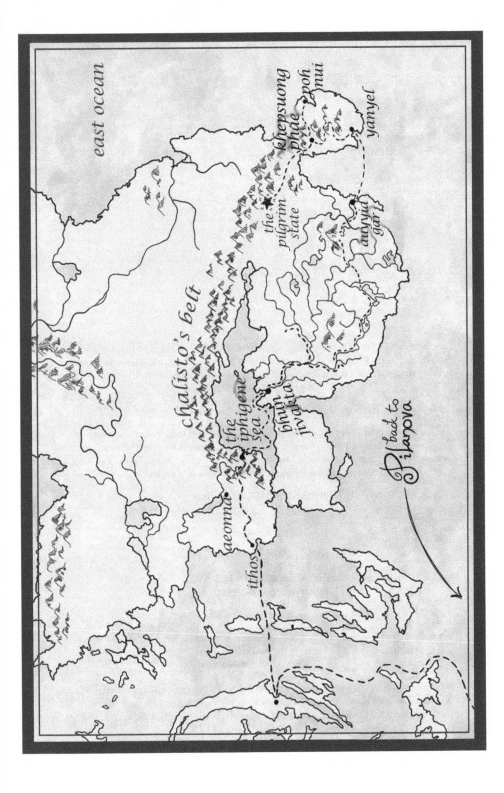

Published by Molewhale Press
www.molewhalepress.com

First Edition

Print edition ISBN: 978-1-7752427-6-5

Cover art and interior illustrations by Haley Rose Szereszewski
haleyroseportfolio.com

Maps and book design by Sienna Tristen

The author gratefully acknowledges the creators of the following typefaces, which were used in designing the text of the book: 'Gentium Basic', 'Garamond Pro', 'Lucida Calligraphy'

Content Warnings: war, violence, references to human trafficking, culturally contextual ritual murder & suicide, near-death experiences, on-page death, attempted murder, deep explorations of depression, substance abuse, existential terror & crises of faith

For Pico, and Santiago, and that pepper merchant's son.

Part Four

HER KISMET DISPROPORTIONATE

*G*ATHER 'ROUND, *my little demons. It's time for a bit of history.*

In the long-last age, two turns of the Great Wheel ago, the boundaries between the overworld and the underworld were not holding. Brittle, easy to break through by accident—or on purpose. The whole rainforest was thrown into chaos. Creatures in the prime of health would drop dead overnight; creatures that were long-dead came back to the overworld at random, warping the environment around them. Creatures that were supposed to die kept on living, even when you stabbed their hearts, even when you cut off their heads. Seasons shifted unpredictably; crops would spontaneously wither and sprout. They say even day and night became unstable, distended as time bled between the worlds.

Now, when you have overworld and underworld spirits mingling all over the land, some outlandish things are going to come of those mingles. Strange little havocs to be wrought, you know. They say a lot of the new gods sprang from this age, when life and death coupled and gave rise to things that were tethered to neither. This is where she came from.

Some say her father was the shiyalshandr, others say her mother, but everyone agrees the mother was the jaguar. Some say the child herself looked like a normal child, perhaps with strange eyes or spots in the right angling of shadow; others say she was monstrous, girl with a jaguar head, cat with a human face. She emerged from deep in the woods, she-with-the-sharp-teeth, and saw the pandemonium caused by those mouldering boundaries, and knew that they had to be fixed.

The tribes each have their own version of what happened next. In essence, our little jaguar girl performed a certain number of magic tricks to separate the underworld folk from the overworld, resurrecting what should have lived, slaying what wouldn't die. The precise number is important, but different depending on who you ask. Some say it was seventy-two tricks, some say one hundred and nine; some say four hundred and thirteen, one for every day of the year, but my own mamu told me it was only three, and that's the version I like best. One trick

3

to bring back the living, one to send back the dead, one to force the things on the edge to pick a side.

And what of the tricks, you ask? Did she use Subindr jinju palm and heart-break clay to mold their likeness and bury them? Did she lie with them and brand them with Umujandr binding scars while they slept? Did she sing a song even the hymning, humming Millikindr don't know, a verse from that which set the Great Wheel turning all those endless eons ago?

I wish I could tell you, but even my greatest grand mamu's guess would be a lie. It's an old story, from an old, old age. Most of the true parts have crumbled away. But the bit we all remember is this: after her tricks were over and done, little jaguar girl climbed to the highest peak of the tallest mountain in the heartland and threw herself off. Her body broke apart on the forest floor, skin unfurling to stretch weblike over the stones, bones pushing through the soil to pillar the ceiling of the underworld below, tendons lacing tight the seams of the reality she had willed. Her pieces spread and sprouted until she had grown over all the old rotten borders between worlds, holding them in place. She became the sky for shiyalsha, the stable earth for us.

And the age of Chashakva began.

 ## ONE

"WHEN GREAT DEPHNOS HEARS that his son is being held hostage in that fortress of shadow, see how he gnashes his teeth in righteous fury! How he curls his hands into claws of retribution! He resolves that very evening to journey to the dread coliseum of the underworld, to pass the trials and gain entry, besting the demons there in order to emerge victorious, clutching his precious child to his—"

"I did mention this story is entirely plagiarised, didn't I?"

For the third time in as many minutes, Ronoah was wrenched out of the tragicomedy unfolding before him by Özrek's commentary. He leveled a warning look at the man beside him. When they had taken their seats for the show, he'd been perplexed as to why Özrek had chosen places near the rear of the theatre—he now understood it was so that he could annotate the play without annoying anybody but Ronoah, who had no choice but to listen.

On stage, Dephnos was preparing for the trials of the underworld, donning leather gauntlets and drawing streaks of blue along his cheeks. In the sharp afternoon light, Ronoah could just make out an accidental smudge of paint clinging to the edge of the hero's porcelain mask. He stalked around the inner edge of the platform, the briny, fishy air of the marina stirring his dark warrior's plait.

"It's the coliseum," said Özrek, who wasn't done. "That's what gives it away."

Ronoah only barely suppressed a sigh. "Gives it away as what?" he whispered, unable to continue ignoring the verbal rib-nudging. Dephnos was pounding on the garishly-painted prop door at stage left, demanding to take on the coliseum's trials in exchange for safe passage through the underworld.

"Come on, little archaeologist, surely you can give it a guess."

This time the sigh got away from him. "I guess ka-Khastan," he hazarded. "Didn't the Chiropes learn that kind of architecture from ka-Khastan engineering?"

"Got it in one," purred Özrek, giving a satisfied wiggle. "But not just *any* ka-Khastan story, oh, no, they've only gone and pilfered from one of the most enduring epics put to parchment. This is a thinly-veiled tale from the Aspenheart Chronicles, which is itself a compilation of supernatural tales sieved from ka-Khasta's Prophetic Collection. This encounter happens about a third the way through, I'd wager story number fourteen? Fifteen?"

"Out of how many?" Ronoah asked, curious despite himself.

"There are thirty-nine chapters in the Aspenheart, as the canon goes—but there's centuries of bickering about whether this text or that should be added or removed from the compendium. The legend of the Prophet Evin is not one cohesive story, you see, but rather a constantly shifting collection of fables and fragments pulled from just about every mouldered bit of parchment the librarians at Aç Sulsum could scrounge up. That's what happens when your library burns half a dozen times." Ronoah winced in sympathy, but Özrek only shrugged a shoulder, recrossing his legs. "Frankly not a bad track record, for nearly four thousand years. Not like it's hard to recover the accounts—every region in ka-Khasta has its Evnist stories, its local legends about ancient days when the Prophet came to town. Half of them are false, but it's only religious devouts and archivists who get in a huff about it—there's a long tradition of fictionalizing Evin's life, that's not unusual. The unusual part is how *campy* this is." The man tilted his chin at the melodrama occurring on-stage between Dephnos and the demons. "ka-Khastan renditions of the Prophetic Collection are romantic stories, you know the kind, full of integrity, take themselves very seriously, so not only have the Chiropes filched a cultural cornerstone, they've subsequently decided to *parody* it. Kharoun would be scandalized. That, or she's their source."

Özrek had been like this—restless, fidgeting, chatting Ronoah's ear off—since they left the monastery beneath Chalisto's Belt. Much the same way their surroundings had gone from quiet gloom to burgeoning bright, Özrek's mood had ballooned to the boisterous, exuberant high that Ronoah remembered from their early days. The creature's elation at being free of the caves had him leaping around like an overexcited dire wolf, dragging Ronoah out of the mountains in only a week's time and slingshotting them down the path to the Iphigene Sea, to the trade port of Scybia clinging to the coast. They had tried every street food in sight, played every public game of *aephelys*, danced to every busker's tune. It was clear just how much Özrek was relishing his return sunside, how much he was reveling in the bustle of civilization. He was in his element.

By contrast, Ronoah was having some trouble adjusting. Under the mountains he had become his own unique creature, grown used to moving unnoticed, to speaking aloud to himself without anyone to look at him funny for it. He had gained some of the unselfconsciousness that comes with solitude; he had settled into that intense look Sophrastus had once made fun of. If anything, he had become even more socially inept than before, only now he was less agonized about it.

Less, but not entirely unfazed. While Özrek basked in the brash rays of the overworld, Ronoah was finding he sort of needed to squint against the glare of life, against the stares of the living. It had actually taken him aback, how unnatural it felt to interact with other people. Until he'd found out how long they were down there for.

"Hand up, little pilgrim."

"What?"

"They're looking for volunteers on-stage, up you get."

"Özrek, no, *no*, you're not getting me to—!" The rest was cut off in a whooshing exhale as Özrek whacked Ronoah's back, knocking him right to his tiptoes. Not one but both arms went into the air as he flailed, trying not to reel into the spectators in front of him.

There were other hands up—after all, this was Chiropole—but no one else had leapt to their feet and yelped like a street dog, and so of course, after a moment of surprise, they picked him. "Come on then lad, seeing as you clearly missed your calling, we'll give you a taste of it," one of the Tellers called, waving him down to the main platform while people in the audience tittered. Ronoah bristled.

"Come now," came Özrek's voice to his left, low and yet impeccably clear under the chatter of the crowd, "this may well be the last Chiropolene play you ever see. Make it something to remember."

"I'd remember it perfectly well just watching, and you know it," Ronoah replied in an indignant undertone, pulling his hands to his sides. The man chuckled in response.

"I'd say the time for sitting back and watching life is over, wouldn't you? Besides," Özrek said, giving the back of Ronoah's arm a gentle pinch with his bronzed hand, "nothing says *birthday boy* like being the centre of attention for a minute. Have fun."

So Ronoah, fighting his own traitorous smile, edged into the aisle and walked down to the stage, reminding himself to keep his chin up and his shoulders back, to not get distracted by the looks people gave him as he passed.

In Chiropole, the year was split into sixteen months. Ronoah and Özrek had lived under Chalisto's Belt for seven of them.

Only today had they found out how long they had spent in the mountain's underworld. Once they'd reached Scybia's docks, Özrek, who wasn't shy about asking weird questions, had cornered a sailor and inquired about the date. The answer had shocked Ronoah. Time had gone strange down in the caves, sure—he'd felt it viscerally, as he'd slowly come unstuck from a sense of calendrical order. But he hadn't expected a sum like that. Seven months. A harvest come and gone. His birthday had passed unnoticed; when he realized, he'd tried to backtrack, out of queer curiosity, to see if he could remember what it was he'd done that day. He could not peel the days apart enough to tell.

When he'd mentioned this to Özrek, the man had demanded they find someplace to celebrate the belated occasion. "It's an unpredictable world out there, you know as much by now—no run around the sun is guaranteed," he'd said as he tugged Ronoah away from the shore, back into town. Ronoah could not quite tell whether he was teasing, but was touched that Özrek had decided to make such a big deal of it.

So here they were, celebrating his continued survival with a trip to the theatre. Naturally, he was about to render the whole thing null by publicly croaking from stage fright.

As Ronoah passed the front row, one of the Tellers pulled him into the wings while Dephnos—while Evin—gesticulated wildly at the gatekeepers of the coliseum's first trial. "You'll need this," she said, looping one end of a blue-dyed rope around his wrist, "and you'll need to come up with an answer pretty quickish to a question."

Ronoah balked. "What—what's the question?" he asked, clutching the rope in both hands.

Beneath the awning of her porcelain mask, he saw her eyes appraise him, one quick flick down and up again. "Why not, you look like you'll need the advantage. *What transforms every gain into a loss?*"

Before he could ask anything further, she spun him around and pushed him on-stage.

Scybia was large enough to have its own entertainment district, a corner of the marina where bards and dance troupes performed on stages interspersed among vendors' stalls. Smack in the middle of that district—arcing over the water itself, from one jut of rock to another—was Scybia's archway, one of the stone gates Chiropole was known for. Never a people to be deterred, the Chiropes of Scybia had constructed an amphitheatre on the water, floating a few feet above the waterline. Seated in the audience, or skirting the stage, it felt solid enough; it was only as Ronoah approached the centre that he saw the sea beneath it, the well in the wood they had uncovered for his scene.

"When the challenger of the first trial appears, he is fierce and mighty indeed!" cried the Teller narrating the story, while Ronoah stood there squinting and looking neither of those things. Dephnos was taking a position on the other side of the well. "The task as the demons explain it to noble Dephnos is naught but a simple tug-o'-war." Of course, because they were demons and this was ka-Khasta-by-way-of-Chiropole, the tug of war was held over a 'pit of oblivion', and the rope provided was not a rope but a magical snake with a head at both ends. As the contestants heaved and hauled, their head would ask them a question. If they answered wrong, the head would latch on with its fangs and drag the contestant over the edge.

Trust these people, Ronoah thought, to put tests inside their tests inside their tests.

"Hey, *myros*," murmured the Teller as she passed him to give Dephnos his end of the rope, "don't pull too hard, eh? Go easy on him." She patted Ronoah on the arm and left him to wonder why anyone would feel that was something they had to specify. Likely it was a general warning—it was a play, after all, not a real contest. There was probably no need to actually tug hard. More important was the answer to the question. *What transforms every gain into a loss?* What could invert abundance that way? What had that kind of alchemical power?

Dephnos pulled on the rope-snake, and Ronoah, startled, dug his heels in and shifted his weight, trying to balance between not pulling the Teller off the stage and not plunging headfirst into the well himself. He could see it between them, the water shifting and swelling between the struts. The pungent smell of the sea spiralled up from beneath.

If it had been Özrek who'd asked, Ronoah might have jokingly answered the riddle with his own name. For so much of his life he'd worried about every good thing that came his way, until it was worried down to nothing. He'd sabotaged every opportunity that was offered him. Every compliment into an insult; every suggestion into a warning. Gain to loss, unnecessarily. His life had not been perfect, but it had been full of generosity, and a bounty of kindness, and he was only now beginning to recognize it in full.

"What transforms every gain into a loss?" asked the snake at his wrist. Ronoah looked at it, and then up at the waiting crowd, scanning until he locked eyes with Özrek.

"The wrong perspective," he called out, his most exultant apology to date.

He had just enough time to register that the crowd liked his answer before he was yanked into the pit.

It was a shallow pit, but he was a fast thinker. He thought all kinds of things on the way down, like *wait no fair I didn't get to hear Dephnos' answer* and *happy birthday you stupid idiot* and *Özrek you brazenfaced ass*. This last he actually yelled aloud, but the splash muffled the sound.

He spent the rest of the play sulking soaking wet beside an offendingly-amused Özrek, an unconvincing demon dripping annoyance and also literally dripping.

"It was 'time'," the man said once the Tellers had taken their bows and everyone was getting up and rubbing their backsides and talking about getting chowder. "The real answer. I figured you'd want to know."

"Time?" Ronoah echoed, scratching behind his ear where salt water had dried into an itchy film.

"Indeed. Think of it from the perspective of the City of the Dead: even though Dephnos succeeds in stealing his son back from the underworld, it is a temporary victory. No matter what treasures you claim in this life, eventually they will disappear from your side. Whether it takes minutes or years, all is simply a matter of when."

For once in his life, Ronoah had been thinking too abstractly.

"I liked yours, though," Özrek added, gesturing for Ronoah to leave the aisle ahead of him. "In fact I liked it better. There's determination in a comeback like that. There's daring."

When they went to congratulate the Tellers on their performance, the Tellers in turn expressed their appreciation of Ronoah's quick wit. "Honestly, we'll likely be stealing it," laughed the woman who had tied the rope around his wrist. "Thanks, *myros*."

"Stealing it for what?" Ronoah asked.

"In case the other guy guesses right." She wound the rope in tidy loops around her elbow, round and round. "The answer's important, sure, but not as important as Dephnos passing the trial. If he lost, the play would be over, you see?"

"I do," said Ronoah, who now understood that Özrek had not volunteered him for theatre as much as for a good dunking. For his part, Özrek did not even attempt to look innocent about it.

Crossing the boardwalk back toward the entertainment district, something occurred to Ronoah that distracted him from brooding about his up-close-and-personal preview of the Iphigene. "I don't know that word," he told Özrek, who raised his eyebrows in question. "What she called me? She said it before, too, when she gave me the rope …"

"What did she call you?" Özrek asked, ready to help.

Ronoah grimaced. "Myros?"

Suddenly Özrek's expression went very still and controlled.

"Oh, gods, what does it mean," groaned Ronoah, who knew the man well enough by now to see the smirk hiding in the straight face. The Chiropes were famous for their insults, so any part of him was up for grabs—his scars, visible on his arms and face, his skin, so much darker than most of the townsfolk, his ridiculous wide-eyed owlish look, his accent—

Özrek shrugged his massive shoulders, a snickering exhale coming out his nose. "It means a couple things, depending on context," he said, and when Ronoah pointed out that this was not a serviceable answer, he added: "Dearest Ronoah, you've essentially been pegged as a *hunk*."

Ronoah nearly walked right off the docks.

"*What*," he spluttered post-stumble. "Absolutely not, you're bluffing. I am *not* the sort of person people say that about."

"I am not. And you might be." Özrek inclined his head at Ronoah's sceptical look. "Times change, little pilgrim. In Ithos, I'd agree, nervous little squirt like you could only catch a mortal eye if you'd accidentally gouged it out first—"

"Thank you."

"—but my, how you've grown. You don't even realize it yet, you're barely out of your chrysalis, but wait and see. You might find the world suddenly treats you different from before."

It hadn't yet struck Ronoah that the changes in his personality were going to have repercussions on his relationships. Oddly enough, of the hundred directions his mind had gone wandering while they'd descended Chalisto's Belt, it hadn't wandered there. Perhaps the solitude of the monastery had wiped it from consideration; perhaps he hadn't factored friends into the equation. Perhaps he just didn't believe he had changed enough for anyone else to notice—after all, he was still getting comfortable with his own responses to things, fresh and fledgling as they were. Before the monastery he never would have backtalked Özrek, never would have joked about his own insecurities so lightly, so resentlessly. He felt oddly inexperienced with himself, ungainly in his newfound confidence. A little awkward yet. How could the world know how to treat him, when he hardly knew how to treat himself?

He felt a whisper of warmth in his chest, a ghostly knock on the back of his head. A reminder to ensure that no matter what anyone did, they treated him kindly.

"All right," he said, looking up at the mythical man beside him with a faint twist of a smile. "We wait and see."

Özrek gave Ronoah a tap under the chin with the backs of his fingers, made noises about chowder, and together they resumed their promenade.

Two

THE DOCKS OF SCYBIA were an imposing affair. In mid-afternoon, the boats crowded so close together you could cross from one pier to another by simply jumping the decks between them. Their masts formed a forest, bobbing up and down in slews and sways. Merchant companies prepared their vessels as townsfolk came to peruse the shells arrayed on the vendor's blankets, the decorations made of driftwood and sea glass, the stalls selling freshly-breaded fish patties. The planks of the boardwalk were ringed with salt, winged with pungent seaweed. Seagulls perched proud on fenceposts, anticipating an easy meal. And beyond it all, the glistening Iphigene, colourful, coralful, spread out like a second sky.

"There are several notable Chiropolene trade centres along the edge of the Iphigene," Özrek was saying as he led them down the quay. "But Scybia is the largest by far, being that the route via Phys is so easily accessible. It's got character, this place. It's got history. There are ruins a ways out of the commercial centre, back where the ancient port used to be before the water levels changed and it dried out—some say they're the leftovers of Thesopole, that capital of Chiropolene myth, upended and jettisoned and left to pique the curiosity of everyone who comes a-touring." Curiosity thusly piqued, Ronoah turned to look—and the man grabbed his hand and tugged him along. "No time for that now, we've already spent our afternoon sponging up the local culture. Tide's out in a couple hours. We have a ship to find."

The plan was set before they'd left the monastery: they had harvested the goods that would garner a price at the markets, spices and fragrant woods and glowing crystalroot, and then brought them to the nearest trading post to swap for local currency. Turns out seven months' worth of 'a little saved for later' added up—after some shrewd haggling, a taste test, and a not-quite-untrue story about the crystalroot maybe belonging to a mountain god, they'd acquired enough credit to purchase a tiny, serviceable sailboat.

For a moment, in the shade of the general store, with the appraiser going wide-eyed at the crystals' aqua light, Ronoah had felt a little like his mother. Arriving windswept and mysterious, months off-schedule but with enough wondrous bounty to make it all worthwhile.

They found the boat docked in the west side, among ketches and cutters and colourful sloops. Ronoah read the name on the side as Özrek passed their papers to the boatman: *Aventina*. Lodestar. "Lead the way," he murmured, laying his hand on the wood, and it may just have been the swell of the water below, but it rose to meet his touch.

In the next hour they rigged the sails and secured their supplies under the benches, and then, as they unmoored from the docks and manoeuvred out of the marina, Ronoah took up residence in the corner created by the headsail and watched Scybia—watched all of Chiropole—fall away. He'd forgotten how surreal it was, to watch land cede to sea like this: one moment you were surrounded by hills and buildings and people, and then at some point you looked away, to check your course or to tighten a knot, and when you next looked back it was all gone. Nothing but a vague, raggedy landscape, an uneven line like a strip of torn paper floating in the wine-bright blue.

His heart tugged as if some part of it were still connected to the land, unready to let go of everything that had happened within its borders. He'd said he was, in the monastery, said he was prepared to take the next step forward, but—it was different, out in the sun, seeing all of those untaken chances and unmet friends disappear with the shore. Those seaside towns, so abrupt and jostling; those winding trade routes, sprawling unruly through the countryside. Those mountains, so quiet, so proud.

Maybe it was going to be like this everywhere he went. You were never truly done with a place, were you? There was always one thing more. The trick, he was learning, was to choose what you wanted over what was readily available. Good enough wasn't good enough. Not anymore.

He watched Scybia disappear, trying to will a proper goodbye into his gaze. When the last lip of land slipped beneath the waves, he wiped his eyes on his sleeve, took a deep breath, and turned in his seat.

"So how do we do it?" he asked Özrek. "How do we get to the Pilgrim State?"

"It's not very complicated," the man replied, leaning against the tiller. "The edges of the Iphigene are littered with port towns and outposts, plenty of harbours to overnight in. We'll hop-skip our way through until we reach the port town of Ay Hang, which is a stone's throw from the road to the Pilgrim State. From there, it's a straight shot."

"How long until Ay Hang?"

"A month, maybe two if the season catches up to us. We should skirt the worst of the storms, but there's no guarantee we can outrun the Maelstrom's nasty attitude forever. Ay Hang and Scybia are diametrically opposed." Özrek lifted a hand to point full-fingered at the horizon. "To reach Ay Hang is to cross the entire length of the sea."

Ronoah hummed a soft acknowledgement, glancing underlash at the eastern horizon. Conflict was brewing in his body. On one hand, he was apprehensive about such a long voyage; Özrek phrased it like a quest that would take years, like something big and grand and full of danger. It made him go still, as if even slight movements could convince the boat to tip. No doubt Özrek would connive an escape if anything tried to wreck their vessel, but the wind's grabbing fingers caught and pulled nervous at his ribs. He knew from experience that to cross the sea was no easy feat.

And yet.

And yet distance and danger aside, it was now within reach, the end of their pilgrimage. The steps could be counted on half a hand. It went like this: a boat ride, a hike, and done. So easy he recoiled.

All those months ago, under Hexiphines and Kourrania's roof, he had looked inward and asked what Genoveffa wished from him. And Genoveffa had answered, bright and sharp and clear. She wanted him to go to the Pilgrim State. Everything he'd been through—Hexiphines and Kourrania, the Tellers, Bazzenine and Jesprechel, Özrek himself—it was all in service of this one command. He had built himself on its foundations; he had warmed his heart with the purpose of it, the destiny.

But what would become of him, when it was all over? What then?

"Hey, *myros*." Ronoah opened his eyes at Özrek's chuckle. He hadn't realized they were closed. "Mind hiking over portside?"

Ronoah stood and grabbed for the ropes, braced one foot against the hull and leaned over the side to counterbalance. For that moment, he existed more outside the boat than in, hovering, liminal. He scanned the dark hide of the sea, and thought about how far down it went, and over the sound of the spray he called, "At least if I get tossed in, I've had some practice, right?"

It came out more like a jab than a joke.

"You're still annoyed about that?" Özrek called back, a lilt of surprise in his easy voice. No, Ronoah thought, he was just deflecting, distracting from that terrible sense of foreboding—

And then he realized that actually *yes*, he was still annoyed, and the realization caught him off-guard. Really? Over something that trifling?

"You—!" The boat crested a swell and he got a faceful of brine. He spluttered, feeling it sear a stinging line along the inside of his cheek where he'd bit down. "You didn't even know if I could swim," he said, coming back into the boat as it finally rebalanced.

"I will point out that you spent a month on a boat before I ever met you."

"Lots of sailors choose not to learn how to swim." The ocean was unforgiving, and ships were hard to turn around. If you went overboard, your chances were slim enough that swimming was seen as prolonging the agony of drowning.

"And you spent a year in a coastal town full of cozy, family-friendly beaches before that. Besides, if you couldn't swim you'd've died down in the caves."

"Did you ever think maybe being shoved into bodies of water might be a *little* nerve-wracking after that near-dying thing?" Ronoah surprised himself a second time with the sharp shape of this accusation. With how it stung to say aloud. "Maybe?"

The man tilted his head, wisecracking silenced. "I did not," he eventually said, and to Ronoah's appeasement, he sounded thoughtful. "You were so calm in the face of catastrophe that I figured you'd chalked it up to just another part of the adventure. You had your week of shivering, and then you shook it off entirely."

"I was kind of distracted?" Ronoah pointed out. "By the—by everything in the Echo Chamber."

"Fair enough." Özrek leaned forward, arms rested on his knees, and pinned his gaze on Ronoah. It was every bit as burrowing as it had always been. "This is about more than a bit of unwilling volunteerism, isn't it," the man said, at the exact moment Ronoah discovered that, in fact, it was.

"You do this a lot," he answered, testing the sureness of his claim, its accuracy. Like stringing a bow, checking its flex. "It's not just this once, it's— this is sort of a pattern." Riding supplyless into the Chiropolene countryside. Trading stories for room and board. Walking head-on into an underworld with no idea what long dark awaited there. "You throw us into all kinds of trials and, and I know that's what I signed on for, you made it clear from the beginning that's the kind of adventure this was going to be, I just ..."

He searched for words, failed to find them, sighed in frustration. After a moment, Özrek made a little offering gesture. "You know I only put you to the occasions I have faith you can rise to," he said. To Ronoah's ears it sounded almost like a defence.

"And I am flattered by your faith," he replied, the spread of warmth in his chest reminding him how true that was, "but also, also couldn't you—can't you just think *less* of me once in a black sky?"

It wasn't really what he wanted. An arrow, overshot. He sighed again, wringing his hands, trying to pull a better answer from his joints. He started over. "You know, I thought I would be lonelier. In the monastery. I guess, it wasn't—we weren't really alone, were we? All those echoes, all those mysteries, Bazzenine and Jesprechel . . ." Their names still caught in his throat. He swallowed. "Maybe it's the history left behind there, those imprints, maybe it's my, my *empathy*, but it felt like there were always people around."

Özrek was silent, watching Ronoah work his way through it. Somewhere above them, a lone gull cried. Ronoah took a deep breath.

"I'm surprised it didn't bother me more. I'm—I'm really glad that it didn't. But it could have." He planted his hands down, leaning forward on the bench. He let the arrow fly. "Seven months is a long time, Özrek. It's a really long time."

A twitch of a smile at the corner of the man's lips.

"A long time for *me*," Ronoah clarified, fingertips coming to his breast. "For any human. I can't get any of it back."

"Do you want it back?"

"*No—*" Ronoah pressed his hand more firmly to his heart. "It was important time. Useful. But there was a chance it could have all gone wrong—"

"Not much of one, you're easier to predict than you—"

"—and I want you to acknowledge that it *could* have," Ronoah continued, raising his voice pointedly. Özrek quieted, and a flurry of nerves fluttered at Ronoah's throat. It was so strange asserting himself like this. But it felt good, despite the discomfort. It felt like growing. "I want you to give me some indication you understand there was a *possibility* you could have miscalculated, that just maybe sequestering a human being in a cave for half a year isn't the best or, or *kindest* of ideas." He bit his lip, tasting salt. "And I'd sort of like an apology for it."

Özrek leaned into the tiller as he reflected on this request, turning his face to the wind. Ronoah stared him down, trying to calm the furiously buzzing instinct to take it all back. It had been so long just the two of them that he'd almost forgotten to quail before this creature. It was partly thanks to the gargantuan caves, how they had made even seven-foot Özrek seem small at times. But in human-scaled Scybia he'd had the chance to measure Özrek against other people; in Scybia, it had struck him anew just how commanding Özrek was, how arresting. World-shaker, warrior king, four-thousand-year-old demigod. Was Ronoah fit to demand apologies from a being like that?

"Very well." Özrek nodded in concession. "I'm sorry for any suffering I caused you. Goodness knows you didn't need more of it."

Perhaps it doesn't matter, a voice said in Ronoah's head, as long as he apologizes anyway.

"Thank you," he replied. A spark of warmth flicked him in the back of the head, and he added, shyly: "Me, too."

Özrek's eyes widened a fraction. Something shifted—the man's aura drew closer, dampened the din of the ocean around them. It was the kind of feeling that had an almost geographical substance, like Özrek could generate his own weather system, small enough to encompass them alone.

"No need," he finally said, and it was perhaps in that simplicity of reply that Ronoah recognized his fellow stranger's sincerity.

"I'm grateful." Ronoah scratched the scruff of his cheek, feeling vulnerable despite the cradle of the mainsail. The cocoon of it. The thought of Özrek saying *chrysalis* echoed in his ear. "That you hold me in such high regard. It's—it's an honour."

"It is the way of things."

The sea lifted beneath them, surging, stomach-dropping. Ronoah fixed his gaze on its rise and fall, on the silver dunes they skimmed. "Why?" he asked.

"Because your actions have proven you trustworthy. Cruel or not, the caves served their purpose; coming out of them in one piece, on your own authority, has earned you an equal hand in this grand adventure. No more tagging and dragging along, no—now, you shape the course as I shape it. We make and face our choices together. We throw the rules out the window. Congratulations, Ronoah," Özrek said, and he rose from his place at the stern and took hold of the mainsheet, adjusting the tension, trimming the sail anew. "You are more than just another human."

And just like in the monastery, when Özrek had called him considerate, Ronoah felt the hairs on the back of his neck stand up. It was the potential of the words, how they unfolded in the ensuing silence, revealing layers and depths and hidden compartments. More than one thing at once. A compliment. A warning. An apology. A promise.

You get to choose, said a voice in his head. You have a say in your future, in your destiny. Your godling's approval and your fellow stranger's friendship.

For as long as this lasts.

"Good," he murmured, eyes on the east. The sinking sun threw long shadow on the water.

THREE

RONOAH THOUGHT A LOT about power in the following weeks. Power, and perspective. He and Özrek sailed the leisurely Iphigene, skirting the southern coast. They crossed paths regularly with the Faizene fishers, eel-slim and viper-strong, who would dive into the shallows and resurface minutes later with armloads of rosy mussels plucked from the sands. The first time Ronoah let them try to teach him, he couldn't force himself to open his eyes underwater; the second time he managed it, and caught a glimpse of a different kind of underworld, swaying and silent. He looked up and saw the undersides of their boats garlanded with barnacles and algae, and something about seeing them from that creeping angle made his lungs tighten and he swam fast for the surface, a single mussel clenched in-hand.

Whenever they drew near a potential berth, Özrek would ask him, "This one? What do you think?" If Ronoah didn't have enough information to decide, he would request it, and Özrek always obliged. It was polar opposite to what he'd grown accustomed to, the constant game of wait-and-see he'd been losing for almost half a year—he'd always known Özrek as coyly mysterious, and the present dedication to equality threw off the internal balance he'd been trying so long to cultivate. This new balance might've been a better one, but it was still new, and he wasn't yet sure where the boundaries lay.

From what he could tell, Özrek wasn't sure either. Perhaps that was the point.

The only time Özrek reverted to his commandeering ways was at the island. They banked hard for it one blue-skied morning, and Ronoah couldn't for the life of him see why: it was equally uninhabited and unremarkable. Memories of the farmer's markets and splashing, flashing watermills of their last stop were still fresh as bread in his mind, and eager not to let that excitement grow stale, he was perhaps a bit impatient when he finally asked, "Why this place—why dock at all, when we just restocked? There's nothing here, Özrek."

"There's sturdy anchorage, and a clear lookout, and that's enough. It's not a question of where we are—it's a question of when we arrived."

Only once the shield of the cliffs cut the wind did Ronoah realize what a foreboding, electric wind it was. The back of his throat tingled with it. "The Maelstrom's coming."

"Indeed." Özrek swept a hand at the scrub-covered promontory above them. "And now we have mezzanine seats for the show."

It took until after midday for the storm to swell. Ronoah and Özrek dangled their legs off the rocky point facing the open sea, and the afternoon sun warmed their backs even as the northward sky turned black. A shape emerged, a force whose colossal outline recalibrated his eye to see everything as miniature in comparison. A shelf cloud, Özrek called it—such a mundane name for something so magnificent, so divinely terrifying. Ronoah watched it advance, roiling and wind-torn, saw the way it stretched across the heavens like a road, like another Highway.

It felt like watching the dust storms approach Pilanova. Or like confronting the all-consuming inferno of the Ravaging, blistering and bright, with its starblocking smoke, its animal roar. The Maelstrom blossomed the same forbidden feeling inside him: lachesism, the longing for disaster to finally strike. The texture of the different bands and stripes of the shelf cloud, the colours that whipped and churned beneath it, murky and green and ethereal—he saw a flash of sheet lightning illuminate deep within the mass and gasped, quietly, with the same eager relief he had always carried and never understood.

Perhaps this, too, was the burden of an empath, to crave the breaking of tension no matter how destructive the snap.

There had only ever been one time he had felt this catastrophic awe with no disaster in sight, one instance where the ghost of it alone was powerful enough to shorten his breath. A cliff like this, overlooking a sea like this, a lifetime ago.

"Is this what it looked like?" he heard himself ask. "The Shattering?"

They had talked about it before—almost. The day on the hill, the Tellers eating and reading and minding their business, and Özrek, Reilin then, giving Ronoah a hint. Ever since he'd failed to pick up that hint in time, he had spent many a late night—under the stars of Chiropole, under the stones of Mount Rheta—picking it up in retrospect, handling and polishing it under his scrutiny until it became so smooth as to destroy all identifying markings. Once the treasure hunt in the monastery had reached its fever pitch, Ronoah had begrudgingly set down his musings about the Shattering in lieu of the more demanding task at hand, accepting that he could deduce nothing without another one of Özrek's intimations.

That kind of secret was hard-won. It had taken a trip across the Chiropolene plains and into the bowels of a mountain just to learn that Özrek was *not* a shalledra; it had taken seven months of puzzle-piecing to discover Bazzenine and Jesprechel's story. The story of the Shattering was a prize beyond anything Ronoah had earned, and he knew that. He wasn't asking for an answer; he was just thinking aloud, pondering in the face of the Maelstrom, sitting with his newfound tolerance for the unknown.

So it was something of a surprise when Özrek replied: "Worse."

Ronoah opened his mouth. Closed it again. Turned to Özrek with enough bemused incredulity to singe the sedge behind them. And Özrek evidently mistook the source of his shock because, Vespasi wake, he began to *elaborate*: "This supercell is isolated to the southwest quadrant of the Iphigene Sea. We are far enough away that you can see where it ends and begins. If this were the Shattering, you'd have to sail all the way back to Lavola to find the other side of the cloud—and the ashfall would cement your lungs solid before you got halfway. Ten leagues above you and still you could bake in the heat of it." The man tilted his chin at the storm before him, colossal and pitiful in comparison. "Fearsome though she is, the Maelstrom, in the end, is a *natural* disaster. The Shattering was anathema to nature itself."

"I—I don't know which is more amazing," Ronoah sputtered said through a baffled laugh. "The image or the fact that you're giving it to me."

"The Shattering is not a secret," was the man's rationale, which was either a bad joke or a petty semantic sticking point, given it absolutely definitely *was*. "Everyone knows that it happened."

Semantics it was, then. "But no one knows what *it* actually was, Özrek, apparently no one—"

"But me. I know." There was a lack of something in that reply—coyness, or charisma—that stifled Ronoah's retort. Instead of pressing with words, he just waited, allowing his curiosity to bloom from the thorns of his exasperation like the flowers on a cactus. The storm was less patient; thunder growled out from the north, and Özrek returned a long sigh. It changed him in some indistinct way, gave him an air of forbearance, of long-suffering intimacy with the topic at hand. "I don't tell this story often, but it's got nothing to do with hoarding secrets or retaining knowledge for the worthy." He leaned forward, arms crossed over his knees. "I just don't enjoy the telling."

This was such a simple thing, delivered with such devastating indifference, that Ronoah actually gripped the ground tighter as a wave of vertigo overtook him. Dissonance rang harsh in his ears: the glittering fanfare he'd expected in learning of the Shattering, clanging against the unadorned truth of it.

Dissonance, and maybe a little shame. It had never occurred to him that there were stories Özrek just didn't *like* telling; subconsciously, he had elided Özrek's right to that kind of autonomy. Cast him less as a librarian and more as the library itself. "So why...?" he asked, his question burdened with new care.

Of all things, Özrek shrugged. "Because you asked, and it seems important to you."

Another gust of light-headedness blurred the edges of Ronoah's vision. "You'll just—tell me," he said, the dawning of it making his tongue clumsy, "if I want to know?" He knew the answer before Özrek nodded, but that didn't make the confirmation any less astounding. The origins of the Shattering, that greatest mistake of the shalledrim—secret or not, it was one of the biggest *mysteries* on the planet. This was something archaeologists and cartographers and historians had been trying and failing for centuries to uncover, something people had dedicated their entire lives to in vain, and here he was, not one hundredth as deserving of the answer, but able nevertheless to receive it at a word? To have it proffered so willingly, so *casually*, without having done any of the work?

His analytical side laughed at that. Waved it away as absurd, unjust, impossible. But the part of him that was wide-eyed and wild-hearted, that yearned for truth and craved understanding, the part of him that heard *you shape the course as I shape it* and believed it—his better angle, it sensed that this story could be something far more subtle and complex than a trophy, if he let it.

When he reached for it, the garnet tucked in his pocket was warm. Genoveffa's lodestone brushed against the base of his palm and said, *ask*.

"If you don't mind telling it the once," he said, "it would kind of change my life."

"Yours more than many, it would seem," Özrek replied, and suddenly the man's voice held a resonance, a vibration which seemed to accelerate the air around them. The hollows of Ronoah's own bones buzzed with the frequency, a pitch so exquisite it was nearly unbearable. He leaned in, garnet clutched between clasped hands, waiting for it. And then it came.

"It was a war." A pause; then, "Disappointing, after all that conjecture, isn't it? Just a bit of war."

A chill wind skimmed the isle. Ronoah's body shivered against the invasive cold, but Özrek was preternaturally still, focused as if he were persuading the story to allow itself to be told. Eventually, it yielded. "Once upon a time, all was not well with the Shalledrim Empire. The king and his brother were at odds; each had their soft spots, their secret depravities, and each thought the other repulsive for his vice. One day, those secrets got out." He tilted his head, glancing at Ronoah out the corner of an ink-black eye. "What did I tell Hexiphines, in the coffeeshop? In the end, a shalledra always has to share."

Ronoah nodded, mouth gone dry.

"Of course, they were only helping—they thought an intervention would help to set everything straight, bring their poor deluded brother back into the fold. Each felt he was perfectly within the right. You can imagine how appalled they were, to discover their magnanimity had been ill-received. Revenge was taken—petty, at first, and then very grave indeed. Sides were chosen, or else enforced. Before long, people were dying for it, human and shalledrim alike."

"Over a sense of wounded pride," Ronoah murmured, repeating what he'd heard from Özrek back on the Chiropolene plains. He'd racked his brains about that scrap of a sentence so many times. "What does a shalledrim war even look like?"

"Exactly like a human war. To begin with, anyway." Of course. All those tens of thousands of human slaves, why wouldn't the shalledrim pit them against each other rather than risk their own lives? "But eventually that resource ran its course, and the shalledrim found themselves needing to pick up the fight where their servants left off. That's when the damage passed the threshold of what is acceptable." Özrek didn't need to look at Ronoah to know the face he was making; darkly, the man chuckled. "It should hint at the scale of the issue, that I am writing off a genocide-by-proxy-war so easily. Loss of life is tragic, but new life will always rise to replace it. Unless it can't."

Ronoah's mind went unbidden to Acharrio. To the desert, which once was bountiful and green before the aftermath of the Shattering sucked the marrow from the land. A cycle of life, disrupted forever. As if he could sense Ronoah trying to make sense of it, Özrek elaborated: "There are certain structures that keep this planet in balance, that keep it *habitable*, and those structures were threatened. What does a shalledrim war look like? Like all the forces of nature you never wanted to see, colliding on ground too fragile to bear the strain."

Far out to sea, a bolt of lightning hit the water. Steam exploded around the point of impact as the filament burned itself out of the sky.

"Of course, that wasn't the worst part."

Heartsore already, Ronoah braced himself and asked: "What was?"

"When it ended." Özrek rearranged his seat, leaning back on his hands.

"One cloudy day, a battle was pitched that the king was not prepared for. He'd grown overconfident—arrogance was his greatest mistake. He was slaughtered by his brother, whose greatest mistake was impulsivity. Or perhaps just poor aim." The man smiled, toothful and mirthless. "You've seen the imprints left by ragged, barebones shalledrim. Our shalledrim king had power to rival the sun."

All of a sudden, the sunlight hitting the back of Ronoah's neck made his skin itch. He reached to scratch it away, his shoulders hiking instinctively.

Özrek was watching the Maelstrom with apparent dispassion. "It shone like a star on the earth," he said. "The blast. It killed a battalion of shalledrim in an instant—and then *they* went off, and on it goes, a chain reaction sweeping the centre of the supercontinent. A constellation of death throes; a people going nova. When it was done, all that was left was that twisted middle mass. And those structures I mentioned, those delicate life-giving systems, were well and truly fucked."

Ronoah should have asked something seeking, something shrewd, like how the shalledrim had avoided this chain reaction until then. He should have brought up Acharrio, to show he understood the consequences Özrek was talking about.

But something wasn't right. Özrek's face, his tone, the way he explained this mass destruction—it was missing a piece, and that piece was so distracting that when Ronoah realized Özrek had left an opening for him to respond, all he bumbled out was, "What—what do you mean?"

Perhaps equally surprised by this blanket question, Özrek turned to Ronoah, eyebrows lifted. "I mean that cloud we spoke about was an inconvenience compared to what followed. The discharge from the explosion didn't just go up, it also went *down*. Drove a rail spike right into the carefully-arranged mosaic that floats atop the planet, dashed the whole thing out of place, and then ..."

The man paused, and before he began again something changed in the flow of Ronoah's bloodstream, some great creeping coagulation that piped him full of dread. His heart was finally getting involved in what his mind was learning.

"Fire spilling up, fire spitting down. The wind screamed like we'd killed its mother. We didn't see the stars for a while; we barely saw the sun. We worried the sky would rip away entirely. A surge like that could have severed our moons. It could have done anything."

We.

That's what it was.

"You were there," Ronoah breathed, and Özrek did nothing except flip one hand palm-up on his knee in acknowledgement. "You were *there*, you—you don't just know this because you know everything, you saw, you *survived* it—"

A scoff, sardonic, from a blessed miraculous more-than-*five*-thousand-year-old throat: "I do not know everything. How dull that would be."

"How did you survive?" Suddenly Ronoah was shaking. A heat at the base of this throat, a furious tingling all through his palms. Like an ancestral memory, something that had clawed its way through his bloodline from all the way back when this catastrophe was fledgling and raw. His question came out a strained whisper: "How did anyone—how did we survive it?"

Özrek turned his face up to the sky. Perhaps it was the angle, the slant of sunlight on his cheek, but the man looked more gaunt than Ronoah had ever seen him. Slowly, Özrek closed his eyes.

"You're welcome," was all he said.

Ronoah stared, stunned beyond reponse—and then all that petrified grief flash-melted, sublimated into something squirming and surging and irrepressible. He grabbed for Özrek's arm, and Özrek let himself be yanked close, let Ronoah smush his face into the man's shoulder and hug him tight and weep like a child. He wrapped his hand around Ronoah's wrist and squeezed, once, and Ronoah heaved sharp shaking sobs of pain and amazement and gratitude, and right there they re-enacted the whole thing in miniature: one sensitive, delicate life-given system crying the cries of the planet he represented, and the protector of one and the same holding vigil, one more time, until the worst of it passed.

Eventually the squalls died down—on the Iphigene, and in Ronoah. When he was ready, he sniffed, gave an extra forehead press into Özrek's collarbone for good measure, and opened his eyes to the thinning clouds. The world looked different now. Sharper, richer, more impatient. Alive in a way he could not access before. Genoveffa's garnet burned pleasantly in his still-clenched hand like ceramic, like a teacup fresh-filled with boiling liquor, and he wondered whether his godling was taking a moment to look through his eyes.

"You know the part that always made me angry?" Özrek asked in basso murmur. "How easily it could have been prevented. No great effort necessary, only a little tolerance, a little grace. Those two abhorred the idea that anything could be beyond their understanding, least of all their own family. If they could have embraced that fact instead, each would not have provoked the other so much trying to force him into recognizeable shape."

Now this, Ronoah could relate to. He noticed it all the time: Sophrastus' family disowning their son for loving a boy; Hexiphines unable to face the water because he couldn't fathom its motives. Ronoah's predecessor, elder sister the exile, sent to die in the dunes for a violation nobody could name. He had followed her of his own accord, fled Pilanova to escape a life of constant contortion to others' expectations. So many tiny Shatterings, every day, for lack of clarity. Lack of compassion.

He'd done it himself, not too long ago. Been careless with his assumptions of another.

Once in a while, being what we are, we are going to experience things differently. We will express those experiences accordingly.

He bit his lip. "I'm going to run the gauntlet."

Özrek nudged him off his shoulder so they were face to face. "Come again?"

"The gauntlet of Truth. I'm going for it." He looked upon Özrek's face, sharp and bronze and almost cruel unless you knew where to look for the care tucked inside. "I hate that the world nearly ended because two people couldn't see eye to eye. I hate how that thoughtlessness repeats itself everywhere. I want to learn the truth about as much as possible, about everything, so that—so that I know how not to hurt anyone." He swallowed. "You said once that Truth doesn't yield very easy. I'll trip and fall on my face a lot, probably. I don't care. I'll trade bruised knees for an open mind."

He hoped the man understood. He hoped they had done enough reaching for each other's truth already for this desire to make sense, this wish that Pilanova had misjudged and that Padjenne had failed to satisfy and that Genoveffa had made with all the ardour and will of a wildfire. He hoped it was clear to friend and god alike how devoted he was to bridging the gap, to making the leap.

He'd need a running start, with five thousand years between them. But he wanted to try.

Özrek tilted his head. The smile that appeared—clamorous, devious, charmed—seemed to creep up even on the man himself. He nudged Ronoah's foot with his own, aiming a playful kick at *Perseverance*, and for one floating moment Ronoah knew with absolute certainty that the feeling was mutual. "On your mark, little one."

The Maelstrom moved on, and so did they.

Four

*T*HEY ISLAND-HOPPED FOR ANOTHER TWO DAYS before returning to the coast and its harbours. Özrek hadn't bothered to pretend at humanity since the monastery, so on nights where the man didn't require sleep, they didn't dock anywhere at all—they just kept on through the silky midnight blue, with Ronoah curled atop their softest supplies, watching Pao and Innos pulse through the gaps between mast and sail until his eyes closed for the night.

Eventually, though, Özrek made a big show of stretching and yawning when there wasn't a port in sight. They bore south and reached the shoreline by sundown. Ronoah moored the boat, watching his companion stalk off over the dunes in search of a comfortable nest. By the time Ronoah walked inland to find him, Özrek was already asleep, snuggled in a blue-blonde patch of sea oats like some great sand dragon.

Ronoah watched the man for a while—the stillness like landscape, the pretense of breathing abandoned—then unrolled a blanket and settled in with him, back-to-back. It was habit by now. When his thoughts scattered too far, he'd found that proximity to Özrek brought them back into alignment. Under the awning of that energy, fear-beyond-fear could not find him; he could safely face what scared him. He could snare the rabbits of his anxiety, get a proper look at them, and then loosen the noose and let them go with grace. *Had he been insensitive in telling Kourrania to go south to Lavola? Had they properly resealed the ossuary to preserve Bazzenine and Jesprechel? Was Gengi still alive and healthy?* Little things, big things, ridiculous things, each had their turn. They came back a little tamer every time.

Except the ones who were not anxieties so much as inevitabilities.

Like the fact that, inevitably, this journey was coming to a close.

They were halfway across the Iphigene. Ay Hang and the straight shot were mere weeks away. There was only so much mussel-diving and stormchasing they could do until they were just—there.

When his time with the Tellers was ending, Ronoah had been unsure whether he wanted time to slow, or skip ahead. The fidgeting liminality had felt unbearable then, but he'd never chosen how to handle it, and ultimately the fork in the road had appeared and chosen for him.

No such quibbling this time. He knew what he wanted. He wanted more time so badly he could scream.

But he was silent tonight, like he was silent all the others. That desire was too tangled in the doubts surrounding it to be given voice. Why didn't he feel ready to set foot in their destination yet? Hadn't he been so convinced when he chose to leave the caves? Why did he believe so persistently that asking for a little longer—from Özrek, from Genoveffa, from anything— would only spoil the magic somehow, that it wasn't possible to be upfront about these hesitations? Could he even put a name to them?

He couldn't. The best he could get was a deep, start-over sigh, and an answering sound from somewhere inside Özrek's heart, like the echo of a knock.

Nightbirds cooed and warbled beyond his line of sight. Beyond the scrag, the waves shushed in and out. It was a testament to his growth, that it only took an hour to fall asleep.

And perhaps his wanting didn't need words, because the Universe had a response for him by morning.

He was slow to wake; that much in itself was unusual. Perhaps it was the radiant warmth of the beach, or perhaps it was the seductive nature of his dreams, full of floating rocks and tea-coloured springs and mermaids with the rippling ribbontails of eels. Groggily, almost unwillingly, he opened one eye.

A woman was sleeping beside him.

He bolted upright, barely suppressing a squawk of surprise; the woman snoozed on unbothered. *Özrek.* It's Özrek, yawned his brain at him—this isn't the first time this has happened, you've seen it before. You shouldn't be so caught off-guard the second time.

As if he could help it, when that fleeting magic suddenly made itself real in front of him like this. Both eyes wide open now, he took in the sight of his unexpected bedfellow.

The first thing he noticed made his heart skip: she was Acharrioni. The same flared nostrils, the same apricot-kernel cheeks, the same thin, wispy eyebrows that were hallmarks of his people. Her head was freshly shaven, as if she had just undergone a coming-of-age, though Ronoah couldn't think which one—perhaps a new child ceremony. She seemed around the same age as Diadenna when she'd borne Lelos. Her body was lean, compact, with a strength that came from density, a proportion that was equally harsh and handsome. She was elegantly articulated, put together in a way that made Ronoah want to cup her joints in his hands.

Which was odd, when he thought about it. Özrek's change in form did not catch him nearly so off-guard as the gut-deep feeling for the new form itself. It was *fondness,* immediate and instinctual as if he really were looking upon his mother—upon either one.

As Ronoah watched, the woman curled in tighter, her brow contracting, then opened her mouth wide in a catlike yawn, revealing a thin pink tongue. She settled back down, nuzzling her cheek into the crook of her elbow. A crop of pink yarrow had sprung up around her overnight.

Every bit the awed toddler, every bit the archaeologist, Ronoah caught himself with his fingers laid in wonder just above the ridge of Özrek's ear—and Özrek opened one eye and caught him in the act.

"Am I a pottery fragment you've found in the dirt, little archaeologist?"

Ronoah recoiled so fast he basically lunged backward, face flooding with heat, and landed heavily on his backside in the sand while Özrek laughed. Served him right for letting himself get so wrapped up in curiosity.

Özrek sat up and reached overhead in a luxurious morningtime stretch, arching her back until something popped with startling loudness. "Only teasing," she grinned in a voice sleek as candle smoke. "Go ahead, poke around if you like."

Infuriatingly, being given permission made it even more embarrassing. Or perhaps he'd just lost his nerve. Özrek saw his hesitation, tisked, and before he could move she slid forward in space and nudged her head into his still-outstretched hands. He felt the closeness of the shave, the scratch of barest stubble on her scalp—and then an entire life of Pilanovani propriety kicked in and he snatched his hands back with a look that only made the woman laugh. Determined not to back down, he wrapped his hands instead around her own, giving the palms a gentle probing squeeze.

"Is this—is this Özrek's body?" he asked. But the name didn't sound Acharrioni, didn't sound like any of the Southern tongues he knew—

"Come on, Ronoah," Özrek chided, "that's just a *smidgen* too obvious."

"Then who? Anyone I'd know?" He'd asked this last time, but then it had been layered thick with sarcasm. Now it was genuine. A face like that could belong to any number of Acharrioni folk heroes.

But Özrek merely shrugged her perfectly bony shoulders. "We made something of an odd pair," she said, fluttering her fingertips against Ronoah's wrists as if to illustrate how well they now matched. "The further east you go, the more you stick out. I figured we might as well present a unified front."

She smiled and met his gaze, blue on cobalt blue, and in dwelling on that mirror image Ronoah could not help but wonder if there was more to it, somehow. Perhaps this was not so much a *front* as something deeper: an allegiance, a kinship. A will to bridge the gap, displayed in the astoundingly material way only Özrek could do. Maybe he was just projecting, but—but also he remembered the unguarded affection on Özrek's face, when Ronoah had declared his lofty goal. He hadn't imagined that delight.

Özrek was also thinking about the Maelstrom, though apparently a different part of the conversation had caught her interest. "So listen," she began, "our stormy little heart-to-heart gave me an idea. All that talk of war, it's reminded me of a *thing*, a little local history in the area, something I'd been meaning to check in on eventually, and I figure seeing as we're so close by, it wouldn't bother you too much if we popped in to have a look?"

Ronoah blinked. "An errand?"

Özrek lifted one hand out of his and wiggled it.

"A side trip," Ronoah corrected, raising his eyebrows.

"Not a long one, swear on whichever gods you like—just a day or two, some sightseeing here, some nosepoking there, try the local delicacy for kicks and we're on our way. Reasonable?"

Ronoah appraised this notion. Özrek smiled a winsome smile.

"…Where is it?" Ronoah asked. Recent commitment to equality or not, he wasn't going to agree without a little more information than *that*. The caves had taught him better.

"Just down the coast. It's one of the biggest ports on the Iphigene these days—and the only port for leagues this way besides." She waited the requisite beat, then: "Tell me. What do you know about the trade city of Bhun Jivakta?"

She indulged Ronoah's blank look for a few seconds, then grinned. "You may not have noticed, but yesterday we crossed a borderline. No more Faizene fishermen for us, oh no, for we have passed into the land of Shaipuri. It is home to the sweet-smelling frangipani, the two-striped tarsier, and the largest river system in the world, the Shaipurin Basin. It is also home to a half-million people who have collectively decided to prop up a sign which reads 'KEEP OFF THE LAWN', with a nice neat fence of severed heads on pikes to really drive the message home." Blithely ignoring Ronoah's horror, Özrek waved her hand across an imaginary landscape. "It's a mystery land, a misty enigma that never learned how to play well with others. If you're not Shaipurin, you don't bother with Shaipuri. That is, unless you visit Bhun Jivakta."

She looked at Ronoah, waiting to see if he was intrigued yet. Truthfully, he'd been hooked by the name of the city alone. Such was Özrek's power, as always, to make everything mouthwatering. "Why the exception?" he asked, frowning.

"The Shaipurin Delta sits at the mouth of the Sanaat River, which is the largest tributary in the system. Straddling that delta is the relatively-welcoming Bhun Jivakta, the only settlement amenable to visitors in the northern half of the region. It's a floating emporium, a grimy little paradise on stilts, marketing some truly magnificent deals on some truly magnificent items—as long as you know who to talk to and how to ask. At some point, the coastal tribes sussed that there was more profit to be made opening their doors to the public, given they had sole access to all the goodies buried in the heartland, so they built a place to do business with curious outsiders without having to invite them into their living rooms. All the thrill for half the threat."

"Okay," Ronoah said. Fascination was gaining on him, except— "Speaking of threats, you mentioned *war* had something to do with this?"

"Oh, it's nothing dangerous, the worst of it happened centuries ago." Özrek rolled her neck and the stretch produced another loud pop; Ronoah thought he saw a spasm of starlight branch from the realigned juncture, but it was too bright out to know for sure. "It was tribal war deep in the rainforest, nowhere near the delta. It was an intense period, I'll grant you that, there were eighteen different territories involved, but they'll have had their victor for decades now. I just haven't had time to check in and congratulate the winners."

The way she said it, like it was a footrace or a baking competition, was a little disquieting. Ronoah remembered all the trouble Özrek had gotten into in her life, all the mishap and mayhem she caused—and suddenly this side trip didn't seem quite so innocuous. He gave her a hard look, trying to weigh his curiosity against his common sense.

"Come on," Özrek whined, pushing at his shoulder, "where's that adventurous spirit? It'll be fine—it'll be *fun*. Promise."

She's *asking* you, pointed out a voice in his head—even for the big things, she's asking. To her credit, Özrek wasn't just dragging him off to the delta without giving him a choice. She was tempting him instead, which meant that if he said no, the no would be honoured. She would politely wait to visit Bhun Jivakta until—until after they'd reached the Pilgrim State. After they'd parted ways. She'd get him there, and wave goodbye like the Tellers had, and she would go on her adventure without him.

It made his stomach hollow, the image. It welcomed all of last night's apprehension back.

But here was a solution, a forestalling—she was asking *him* for more time, and for some ill-defined reason, that preserved the integrity of it all. That made it okay. If he was completely honest with himself, his other concerns paled in the presence of that possibility.

He took his time to answer anyway, and Özrek let him have it—and if she knew already what his answer was, or that he was only pretending to deliberate for the sake of the game, she let him get away with that, too.

"Fine," Ronoah said at last, to a gleeful whoop from his companion and a guilty unclenching of his heart, "all right, let's do it."

They breakfasted, beat the sand from the blankets, made their way back to the boat. The Iphigene was a blaze of rose and turquoise, the angle of the morning sun turning the water into one brilliant, ever-undulating sheet of light. When they made it into open water, they set course for the promise of adventure, for the unknown shores of the Shaipurin Delta.

And in Ronoah's mind, the ghost of Ay Hang took one step back.

FIVE

*T*HE NEXT DAY, the water started changing colour. The sea behind them was blue as always, but the waters up ahead were olive-tinted, getting greener with every passing mile. Ronoah had never seen anything like it, but Özrek only smiled.

"Nearly there," she said. Sure enough, if he squinted shoreward, Ronoah could make out the rough shapes of a settlement, the tall-masted statuettes of other boats on the water. It was still far enough away to remain indistinct, but from what Özrek had said, there were no other open ports this side of Shaipuri. It had to be Bhun Jivakta.

Ronoah had spent most of the voyage wondering about their destination. In all his farfetched dreams of library research trips and archaeological digs, never had he envisioned himself landing in Shaipuri; he could point to its general vicinity on a Bereni map, and that was where his knowledge ended. The words Özrek had uttered—*tarsier, frangipani*—tasted like spells to him, foreign and mystical and full of potential. Translation was futile; having never seen the tropics before, Ronoah had no reference point for their flora and fauna, for their geography, for anything. He heard *delta* and the closest he could conjure was the fig trees and reeds of Padjenne. It was all he knew to imagine.

So it was all he could do, to gape like a child at the world that emerged on the coast.

Bhun Jivakta. A city on stilts, propped up in the deep mud of the marsh; a riot clothed in paradise green. As they steered away from the trade docks, joining other small vessels in navigating the boardwalk-bordered waterways, Ronoah was confronted with an explosion of colour and vibrancy. The quays were crammed with noise, the shout of sailors, the rolling of cart wheels on planks, the plop of stones in the shallows as children heaved them over the sides trying to startle the pink birds that perched one-footed in the silt. Dockworkers stacked crates under walkways canopied in broad banana leaves; flayed eels lay drying on wooden racks while fishermen blew salt over their shimmering bodies. What snippets of conversation Ronoah could catch reminded him of his time in Tyro—sentences like pomegranates, each word a glistening seed ready to pop between your molars. He understood none of it, but felt its substance heavy in his hands, dripping between his fingers.

They had only just moored the *Aventina* when they were descended upon by a swarm of twiggy, topknot-bearing boys. "Faizene?" they asked with eager grins, elbowing each other out of the way, "Mahaburin? Ol-Penher?" Ronoah had just enough time to hear a boy fumble out an uncertain "ka-Khastandr?" before Özrek promptly swatted one in the head and they all tumbled away, off to waylay the next group of itinerants.

Ronoah was ready to admonish the woman for needless physical force—when an uncomfortable reality dawned on him. "Özrek," he asked, "do they—do they *speak* Chiropolene in Bhun Jivakta?"

Özrek laughed outright, which was all the answer he needed.

"How can you blame them?" she said matter-of-factly to his disappointment. "It's on the other side of the sea. It's not exactly a common tongue in these parts—Chiropole's not a major player in north Berena to begin with. It'd be like expecting an Acharrioni to know Chiropolene."

Ronoah stared at Özrek rather pointedly.

"We're talking typical, normal people here," the woman replied without missing a beat, "shepherds and glaziers and somesuch, not a renegade academic with a near-perfect memory and an ancient know-it-all at his disposal."

"I thought you said you didn't know everything."

"See what I mean?" Özrek stepped onto a rope bridge, hands trailing the intricate latticework in the side netting. "Can't even let me self-deprecate without pointing out inconsistencies. Your debate opponents at Padjenne must have hated you."

Ronoah heard the smile in Özrek's voice. He was grinning himself when he replied, "I never entered any debates at Padjenne. Too busy learning Chiropolene."

Özrek cackled. Some greater power—the ghost of an affronted Padjenne, or a summoned Chiropolene deity, or perhaps even Genoveffa herself—decided not to let Ronoah feel too suave about it, as he lost his footing immediately, stumbling on the sway of the bridge. He struggled upright as Özrek continued on ahead, her voice lilting over her shoulder: "Distance aside, the Shaipurin are loathe to use anything other than their own languages. That indignity is reserved for the suckerfish. Can't have it both ways, after all—got to talk in order to trade." She indicated a conversation happening on the nearby promenade, between a Shaipurin woman and the merchant from whom she was accepting cargo. At the merchant's side hovered another topknotted boy. "But I daresay we're shark enough to sniff out our own blood."

Ronoah frowned. "Meaning?"

"Meaning I shall translate for you." Özrek stepped onto solid planks again, turning and offering a hand to help Ronoah down. "And it shall be as it was in the old days."

The old days was putting it rather dramatically, they'd met less than a year ago—but Ronoah was charmed by the sentiment anyway. It managed to be grandiose and utterly silly all in one, and though he'd developed a resistance to Özrek's glamour over time, he let it tickle his fancy now. After all, said a voice in his head, this is what you came here to do—to be swept up, to be dazzled, to have fun. No point asking for more time if you don't relish the moment.

He put his hand in Özrek's and let her tug him off the bridge and into their side trip.

Wood-paneled houses sat hemmed in by the criss-crossing boardwalks, dark burnished buildings lifted high on piles where the Bhun Jivaktandr entertained foreign emissaries on their porches. Potted palm trees and ornamental limes stood guard at the base of every flight of steps; the roof-tops sloped steep and proud as the bows of Lavolani barques. Squeezed between these larger edifices were scores of street food carts, where local cooks were flipping flatbread and stirring deep pots of broth under red-and-green striped tents.

At the first whiff of spiced steam, Ronoah's stomach refused to let them go another step without sampling something. Özrek led them to a stall where fish soup was being sold in coconut shells. She ordered, tipped a small handful of ivory chips into a shallow dish for payment, and then engaged the server in conversation while a fresh batch was stewed.

Ronoah peered into the shade of the stall, watching the cook slide chunks of fish and whole shrimp sizzling into the round-bottomed pot. Then the vegetables—that looked like pepper, those ones maybe yam?—then the liberal splashing of coconut milk. By the time two bowls were ladled and garnished with lime juice, Özrek had finished her conversation looking less pleased than Ronoah had expected.

"He doesn't know," the woman said in between slurps of soup, answering Ronoah's unspoken question as they walked on. "More accurately, he asked *What war?* Which I should have expected—like I said, Bhun Jivakta had nothing to do with the war, plenty of folks here won't have the faintest what I'm talking about, especially the younger generation. It was a long shot, but no matter—we'll eventually run into someone old enough to remember the stories come out of the heartland."

Their search led them to a canal where a group of oarsmen were smoking in their boats. Özrek produced a few more ivory chips and hired a lean, leathery man to ferry them through the commercial centre. Ronoah ogled the sights while the woman chatted with their rower: the multilevel houses and their elaborate engravings, the layers of footbridge and rope, the damp cloth of the humid air polishing everything to a dull pewter shine. Around one corner, two labourers carved a colossal shark, laying sections of meat onto a mat while a third supervised from the shade. Their boat passed close enough for Ronoah to hear the rasping clatter of the handfuls of teeth they poured into a jar.

Once they reached the place where the canal opened up to the sea, Özrek stood to disembark, and, wobbling a little, Ronoah went to follow. Instinctively he thanked the oarsman in Chiropolene, but he received no reply, just a look that was impossible to decipher.

"Two for two," Özrek tisked, pursing her lips as their guide rowed away. "Is memory so short in Bhun Jivakta? Or are men just as entirely clueless as ever here?" Ronoah raised his eyebrows, and Özrek sniffed a laugh. "Don't think I ever mentioned—Shaipurin societies are quite aggressively matriarchal. It's their women who write the contracts and keep the treasuries."

Ronoah cast a critical eye on Özrek, on the way her old tunic draped differently on this new body, the curve and swell of the fabric. "You took that into consideration, didn't you?"

"Of course! I could've boosted Reilin another six inches, made him brawny as sweet Dephnos himself, given him a pair of scimitars for all the Shaipurin would care—they'd still only take him half-seriously." Özrek snickered, smoothing her hands over the sharp jut of her hips. "But this is a skin they will respect. I just need to find a lady who'll meet me on equal terms."

Ronoah thought for a minute as he watched a cargo ship departing for the Iphigene. Thought about how power manifested in a trade centre. "You could try a clerk at one of the administrative headquarters," he pointed out. Now it was Özrek's turn to look surprised. "You know, the trade offices, or the—it's the *house of figures* in Lavolani, where imports and exports are managed?" He held out the empty coconut shell he was still carrying. "The ginger flowers in this soup didn't come from ka-Khasta, right? They came from—"

"Upriver." Özrek appraised the waterway in question. "Can't run an operation without knowing your terrain, ai?" She turned back to Ronoah with an appreciative smile. "I never would have thought to go in that direction. Let's try it—see if Bhun Jivakta's brokers have any intel for me."

It wasn't difficult to find the offices for Bhun Jivakta's trading company: they towered a full storey above the other buildings, and the carvings of fish and flowers that embellished their porches and walls spoke to the wealth that flowed in turn through their doors. Inside was one large, open-concept room, partitioned into booths by decorative privacy screens. The agents of the house walked briskly between booths, delivering folios, fetching assistants to mediate or record dealings with merchants. It was stifling in there, like the sweatiest afternoon in all Chiropole stuffed under one roof. Some of the other visitors to the office seemed to find it similarly oppressive: one merchant was rather desperately waving a wooden fan about his shining face as he squinted over a slip of parchment on the low table before him. By contrast, the Bhun Jivaktandr clerk opposite him sat perfectly at ease as she twirled her stylus between her fingers, ready to etch some new amendment into their agreement. Environmentally-speaking, it was clear which side of the negotiation had the advantage.

The clerk who waved Özrek and Ronoah into her booth was no less intimidating. She held herself with the cool confidence of a falcon about to dive for a couple of rodents. A pair of ka-Khastan reading lenses perched on her forehead; she pulled them down to her nose as they sat, as if in preparation for examining their paperwork.

That composure was betrayed only by the slightest twitch of her colour-stained lips when Özrek addressed her. As the clerk returned the greeting she made a subtle gesture, and the assistant who had materialized at her side took his leave again, bowing out of the booth. Apparently no one had been expecting the clearly-foreign woman before them to speak fluent Shaipurin.

Özrek was swift enough to translate, discrete under the hubbub of the trade house: "We'd like to make an inquiry into the heartland."

"Which alliance do you represent?" was the clerk's answer. "Show me your Queenstoken and we can send your message to the appropriate contact."

Whatever a Queenstoken was, they didn't have one to spare. "Oh, we don't hail from any alliance," Özrek said, to the immediate eye-narrowing of the woman opposite her. It did not escape Ronoah, the suspicious sidelong glance she pitched in his direction as Özrek repeated herself in Acharrioni. "I'm not here to ask about jade production or the quality of this year's plumeria harvest. My question is altogether more historical in nature. I'd like to know the victor of the War of Heavenly Seeds."

The clerk's frown grew even fiercer. "This is a professional establishment, not a rumour mill."

"Indeed. I assumed such a respectable association would therefore possess accurate information—"

"You're probably unaware of this," the clerk said, with a sardonic look that swept up everything other about Özrek and Ronoah, from their dark blue eyes to the dyed linen they wore, "but the city in which you sit was founded partly to get away from that mess, ai? This association doesn't manage dealings with the interior—we deal in reliable stocks, with dependable partners." Özrek opened her mouth, but the clerk continued overtop her rebuttal: "Among the many fine goods Bhun Jivakta exports, *gossip* is not one of them. If you don't have an inquiry related to our business here, then free up the booth for someone who does."

Ronoah didn't know whether civil servants were allowed to be so brusque in Bhun Jivakta, or whether Özrek's line of questioning was just that offensive. The clerk seemed—almost *too* offended. Like that feeling was covering for something else, the heavy taste of honey and spice concealing spoiled meat. Ronoah inhaled, trying to separate the layers, to discover the base note beneath the affront—

The clerk said something sharply enough that Ronoah startled. Özrek didn't need to translate for it to be obvious what she wanted. Quickly, as they were standing up, he said, "Ask her who manages the supply chain from the heartland."

Özrek obliged—and to Ronoah's senses, she did so with just a bit of divine insistence, with a dash of five-thousand-year-old authority thrown in. Ronoah felt it like dizziness, buoyant and not actually unpleasant; he didn't know how it felt to the clerk, but he saw her breath hitch, saw her reach to clutch the cluster of pendant necklaces resting between her breasts. She gave her answer through a tight jaw. Özrek inclined her head in farewell and turned to take her leave. Ronoah waited until they were out the door before asking what she'd said.

"The respectable Lady Sansha'it is our next quarry—apparently, she's heartland-born. Came to Bhun Jivakta to manage inter-provincial affairs on behalf of the Trade Queen. Between her lineage and her line of work, there's no way she *isn't* intimately familiar with the details of heartland politics." Özrek paused her brisk walk to let Ronoah breathe the fresh air, cooler now that afternoon was mellowing to evening. "Our friend made it abundantly clear she wasn't optimistic that we'll get so much as an audience, let alone an answer. Whoever thought this would become such a closely-guarded trade secret, ai?"

She didn't sound discouraged. Far from it—Ronoah had watched every successive false start add to her vigour, her sense of gleeful mischief, until now she stood taut as a hunting dog, quick-eyed and prick-eared. He felt himself falling for it too, the allure of this mystery, the ever-deepening desire to unravel it. Incurable, unquenchable curiosity, consuming them both. In some things, they did not need to strain to understand each other.

"Where do we find her?" he asked.

"The other side of the city. Lady Sansha'it's office isn't on the delta—doesn't need to be. She deals not with the sea, but the river. But we're not going to make it today." The woman snickered at Ronoah's open impatience. "Be courteous, the sun's going down. Our visit will have to wait until business hours open tomorrow—for now, let's grab another bite and scout a place to overnight."

As light bled from the boardwalk and the torches were lit, Özrek and Ronoah made their way back to the quays, seeking a guesthouse for the night. They found one squeezed into the back of a restaurant, its single long hallway opening onto windowless rooms outfitted with low-swinging hammocks. The sounds of the kitchens drifted through the thin walls as they settled in, mingled shouting and the flashing hiss of fresh fish hitting hot pans.

After sliding the bolt home on the door, Özrek lifted her shirt off. Then, to Ronoah's surprise, she slipped out of her trousers as well. Stark-naked, she drew near the lamp-tree Ronoah had just finished lighting, holding her clothes up to the five clay lamps and scrutinizing them in the glow. She must have noted Ronoah's confusion, because a corner of her mouth twitched up. "I'm deciding how to dress for the occasion," she said. At length, she nodded and began tearing her clothes neatly by the seams, crouching to lay the pieces out on the floor. End-to-end, like a jigsaw, cannibalizing them into something new. Without looking his way, she held a hand up. "Tunic, please."

Bewildered though Ronoah was, he wasn't shy. He loosed the arm wraps of his own shirt and passed it to her with little fuss. His trousers went the same way, pressed into Özrek's waiting hand; their lovely indigo hue joined the patchwork of taupe and cream, a river through a sunblasted desert. It was when Özrek beckoned for a third time that Ronoah hesitated, biting his lip.

Özrek glanced up at him. Protectively, his hand went to his hip, to the red wrap he'd just retied around his waist. "My parents wove this for me," he said.

Özrek's eyes softened. Of all things, it was this acknowledgement that made him flush. "I only need another couple square feet," she said, her

gaze travelling further upwards. "Your bandanna ought to do just fine."
That was an article of clothing so essential Ronoah had completely forgot
he was wearing it. At his scandalized expression, Özrek pulled a wry smile.
"Head coverings aren't exactly local fashion, and tomorrow I'm trying for
every sign of respect. If anyone goes for your scalp, oh pious Acharrioni,
I'll bite their fingers off. How's that for—?"

Whatever else she said was lost under the horrified squawk Ronoah
made. She was still sniggering when he untied his bandanna and chucked
it at her, gruff in his haste to outrun any misgivings.

They spent a while in silence, Özrek bent to her work pulling stitches,
Ronoah watching, squatting so he wasn't in the way of the light. The
amber glow of the lamps reflected off the sheen on Özrek's skin; remarkable, how even though she didn't sweat, she remembered to attend to
these crucial human details. How though she did not breathe, her chest
rose and fell just the same. Her tattoo lay upon her chest, unmoving
sickle moon, sharp and dark as ever.

"Özrek," he said after a while, "tell me about the war." The woman
had named it in her conversation with the tradehouse clerk: "The War
of Heavenly Seeds."

"What would you like to know?"

"We're running all over town trying to find out how it ended, but why
did it *start*? What was it all for?" Chasing this mystery down was a thrill in
itself, but now he hungered for context. He wanted the rules of the game
they were playing, to properly savour the prize at game's end. "Why did
the heartland break out into fighting in the first place?"

"Well. You might not believe it," Özrek said as she pulled the last seam,
"but they did it to save the world."

The light from the lamp-tree flickered. Ronoah went and adjusted
the wicks, frowning all the while. By the time he set the tweezers back
down, he still had no idea what to make of the statement. "You're going
to have to elaborate."

"I have every intention." Linen and cotton had finally been laid in a
pattern she found acceptable; as Ronoah watched, she skimmed a hand
across the patchwork and threads began to entangle, warps and wefts
joining like root systems. Indigo dye seeped forth to follow her gesture,
bleeding blue through boundaries. As the landscape of their old clothing
marbled and mottled into something new, Özrek sat back on her heels,
opened her hands on her knees, and elaborated.

THE GREAT WHEEL IS TURNING. *That is what they say, in the heartland of* Shaipuri, *when the end of an era approaches. Not every generation gets to utter those words—the ages of the rainforest are governed by its gods, by what builds the karst and the marsh and the deepwood, and the tenure of such creatures runs long. Seventy years, two hundred, more: the length of an era is the lifespan of its god, the time for which that creator can pour its vitality into this world. But it is the first thing a heartland child learns to say, the first talisman stone they hold beneath their tongue, because you never know when that vitality will be spent, and the old god wither and die, and a new one come to take the world from its failing hands. When the last floating motes of life's exhale trickle out, in the great demon silence before the next inhale comes, in that reverent stillness they look to one another and say: The Great Wheel is turning.*

It takes preternatural skill to hear the faint titan creak of that Wheel as it sets to motion upon its axle. To guess where it will come to rest anew. For this, the heartlanders turn to the wisewomen.

Crafty, canny, the wisewomen live with one eye on their cosmic calendar, blessed and burdened as they are with its stewardship. Over two and a half thousand years they have learned how to predict these transitions, how to prepare for their arrival; this sacred knowledge makes them the midwives of this world, well-versed in the ways of swaddling and suckling a newborn era, in seeing those dawn days through their first bout of colic, of pox. Even fully-established, every creator has its quirks, its preferences and predilections—and the wisewomen learned to interpret these, too, and so characterize the many nights ahead for their people. In time, Shaipuri's heartland found a certain reliability in the turning of the Great Wheel, and insofar as peace lies in a land where even the flowers will hunt you for sport, it was peace that they found. Until a spoke broke.

One day, a few hundred years ago, a blight hit the rainforest of Shaipuri.

The canopy withered. The rivers burned. The beasts grew ragged and haggard and lean. The wisewomen had read the death of the old creator already, in the grey of the moss and the smell of the rot, but nothing had warned them of decay on this scale. A Council of All Tribes was called, and the wisewomen gathered from the six directions and practiced what haruspicy they could upon the entrails of the old world. By their combined power, they gleaned the terrible truth: the era being ushered in was governed by a young god, a sickly god, not yet strong enough to support the plenteous rainforest the old god had left to it. The world had been passed into shaky hands; if those hands could not be steadied, the world was sure to drop.

What do you do when your god doesn't have the power to hold you safe, you wonder? You help them attain it, of course.

With the help of the wisewomen, the sickly god hewed itself into eighteen pieces, eighteen supernatural beings who implanted themselves within each of the heartland's tribes. They were called the Stakes in the Ground, holding fast the land, or else the Taproots of God, placed there to milk the soil of its latent strength, but the name they came to be known by above all other was the Heavenly Seeds, because these words most accurately depicted their future.

The Seeds came down to the earthly realm to be fertilized, to be fed the necessary power to hold the world together—and it was by the sacrifice of the living that this power would be derived. It was by the sacrifice of the living that the creator would draw the might to make the rainforest flourish again.

So the heartland began its ritual war.

Battles were held—not solely martial in nature, for a creator needs more than fighting might to rule. Contests in reed flute and jumprope and poetry were equally revered, and harvested an equal number of losers. It was not such a bad thing, to lose in the heartland; it meant your life had reached its peak, its apex. It meant you were ripe.

Each of the Heavenly Seeds had imbibed a tribe with its essence, providing them with guidance, with a preferred offering and a name to invoke as the offering was made. The Seeds required different donors for different reasons—adults, children, birds, black caimans. The fertility idols Farhati and Gaam split the bellies of pregnant women to harvest the raw creative power inside; the river gods and rainmakers, Hunanun and Jau-Hasthasuna and Azm-ka-Habaur, devoured children for the purity of their lifegiving tears. The keeper of the sun and stars Baramsula needed sacrificial pyres to keep the celestial bodies lit. By the bloody mulch of mortality, the Seeds were nourished, Taproots fattening on the hopes of the slain.

And one day, those roots would push forth blooms. And one day, what once was split would splice. One day, when each Seed was sufficiently strengthened, these supernatural beings would battle each other, mirroring the sacrifice provided by humankind, and consume the bodies of the defeated until only one remained.

This Seed, fully sprouted, radiant with the willing pain of all Shaipuri, would transform into the heartland's new creator god, replacing its old sickly aspect with a resplendent reincarnation, preserving its Seedly name to honour the tribe who reared it.

By such means, the paradise of Shaipuri would be revived; by such means, the land would be resurrected, and its people find peace again. By the will of the wisewomen, by the War of Heavenly Seeds, the Great Wheel would turn once more, to an era more shining and bountiful than any come before.

*Ö*zrek stood up, gathering her newly-formed fabric as she rose. She tucked and wrapped the material around her waist to resemble the loose trouser-like garments the Bhun Jivaktandr sported. Then she looked down, and saw Ronoah still sitting there—Ronoah and the face he must have been making.

"It is a bit of a gruesome story, isn't it," she admitted.

Ronoah was clutching his arms so hard that it hurt when he loosened his grip. Swallowing a knife of nausea, he nodded.

"By now the story is all that remains. Don't hold it too close, little empath. It happened years and years ago."

"But it *happened*," Ronoah retorted. "It's not just a story, it's truth, it really happened—they really did all those, those ...?" The great wail of a dozen children crying. An unborn fetus, cored from the womb like digging the pit from a peach. The caustic smell of burning hair. He pressed his forehead to his knees, assaulted by the litany of sensations rising from the echoes of this ruthlessness.

"How did they ...?" he breathed. "How *could* they?"

Özrek tisked. It was not an unkind sound. "As I said: because they loved their world, and wanted to deliver it from ruin. Remember this wasn't shalledrim throwing lives away over pettiness, or the possessive conquest of my Torrene Empire. The War of Heavenly Seeds was—in a way—a community project. Not an injustice, but an honour."

"An honour?" Ronoah repeated, voice strained. His fists clenched in the soft cotton of his wrap—clinging instinctive, clinging in vain, to a land where even to speak of such deeds was unforgiveable. "How do you find honour in so much pain?"

"It is difficult for you, I understand. But for someone who grows up watching new trees spring from the rotten logs of their grandparents, who

43

toddles their first steps through a land where fungus pops jolly from the carcasses of beetles, it is quite a simple thing to grasp that death is required for new life. It is only a matter of time before that knowledge bears another piece of fruit: that their people, like the forest, are not individual organisms but leaves and branches of one sprawling plant. Sometimes pruning a plant is what keeps it alive." More gently, after Ronoah still had not raised his head, "They fed themselves to the earth, and in turn, the earth feeds itself now to their grandchildren. So goes the great consumptive cycle."

"I get it," Ronoah said. "I get the logic, I do. I get it in *theory*." He lifted his head, scowling defiantly. "But when the time comes to actually do the—to make the sacrifice, when someone's *right* in front of you and you both know what's about to happen, I just—that's where you lose me. I can't get to there."

Genoveffa was owed his whole soul, his heart and his breath and his every ambition. He loved her so much it could fill the ocean. But if she turned her candled countenance his way and told him he needed to kill another human being, he would call it all off. He would walk himself to the Salt Flats, lie down in the ageless tear tracks of his godling, and wait until either she changed her mind or took him as replacement. That was all there was to it.

Özrek's gaze flicked to the five pinch pot lamps on the lamp tree, considering. "I don't imagine it ever came easy for any of them. That would defeat the purpose. It's not a sacrifice unless it feels like losing something." One of the wicks was sputtering again; the woman rose and tended to it, ignoring the tweezers in favour of her bare fingers. Completely out of place with the conversation, a pang of jealousy resonated in Ronoah's own hands. "Ritual helped ease the emotional burden, scheduled dates and sacred sites to which this violence was confined. Perhaps more comforting was the assurance from the rainforest gods that the War's participants would be granted a place on the most glorious branch of shiyalsha, their underworld. In exchange for your pain, an eternity of feasting and dancing alongside creators of old. Not a bad trade." She looked over her shoulder at Ronoah. "But still, never easy, no. I don't think it was."

In a paradoxical way, knowing the War was hard on its warriors made it easier for Ronoah to handle. Perhaps that was unkind of him. He shouldn't have wanted these people to suffer any more than their gods demanded. He mulled it over as he spread his bedroll across the hammock and clambered in, listening to the kitchen four doors down still going full-swing.

Özrek pulled from her satchel the collection she'd amassed on the docks that evening: handfuls of smooth, rounded pebbles plucked from the shallows. Ronoah watched as she picked up each stone and polished it between her fingers. It was hard to see the process of change, small as the stones were, low as the light was, but when she set each pebble back in place it had burgeoned into a jade pearl, tumbled to a lustre like boiled sweets. A trick he'd seen before, in the monastery. The same small magic that had borne his garnet.

The gem in question was tucked into his bedroll, nestled close to his head. What did Genoveffa think, he wondered, of the War of Heavenly Seeds? Would those gruesome deeds have repulsed and affronted her as they would any other Pilanovani? Or did she come to it from the side of the gods, from a perspective nearer to Özrek's than his own? Ravaging firestorm as she could be, did his godling understand the sense in the great consumptive cycle?

You're going to have to learn to understand it, said a voice in his head—understand, or at the very least tolerate. Lady Sansha'it won't exactly feel eager to talk about her ancestors if you're standing there grimacing about them the whole time. If you really want to run that gauntlet, you'll need to learn how to jump this kind of hurdle with grace.

A heavy click from the table—Özrek was reordering her stones on the table. Like he had many times before, Ronoah distanced himself from the spinetingling unease of his thoughts by watching his companion's work, her keen expression as she examined the jade procession before her. Materials in order, she withdrew—from her own hand, her own phalange—a sliver of starlit bone, a needle fit to pierce reality itself. In comparison, the jade didn't stand a chance. Özrek picked up the first pearl, brought it to point. She punctured the stone easy as a grape. And the next, and the next. The last thing Ronoah saw before he fell asleep was the cord she pulled from her bag, the lampshine on the first bead of the necklace as she slid it home.

Six

OFFENDING LADY SANSHA'IT WAS NEVER something Ronoah needed to worry about. Apparently, he wasn't even going to get the chance.

"I told you," Özrek was saying to the two guards posted outside the woman's estate, "we've come together."

"We know," came the translated reply a moment later, accompanied by a pair of judgmental looks that suggested they didn't need telling to infer as much. "But you don't represent any known partnership, and the rules of engagement for strangers are clear: *one at a time*."

Amazing, how Özrek managed to convey even the guards' condescension in her tone—the hallmark of a creature who understood tone to be a human thing, Ronoah supposed, or at least the way they made use of it. She reverted to her own cadence now, lightheartedly irate: "Heartland operation, heartland rules, of course they would—but I guess it's for the best. If they're this stern at the front door, the inner sanctum will have even more restrictions. Chances are I won't be able to translate for you without putting myself at a disadvantage."

Shame stung Ronoah's nape in a way it hadn't for a while. A conviction he'd been trying to shake since the monastery: that Özrek couldn't be herself because Ronoah limited her freedom. He slowed her down. In the caravans; in the caves. Seven months in the monastery just to grow him a backbone. Deep down, he discovered, it could still wound him, thinking he was in her way.

But Özrek caught the scent of that self-blame in an instant and scoffed loudly, waving her hand like she could shove Ronoah's guilt straight into the canal. "Ah, how very *possible* I must be in your mind. Not so for others. In my time dealing with humankind I've been able to sort you all into roughly two groups. The first is full of people who fall head over heels for what I represent; the second takes one look at me and wants

46

absolutely nothing to do with me." Ronoah couldn't imagine wanting *nothing to do* with something as exquisitely alive as Özrek. His affronted, protective expression said as much, and Özrek laughed, endeared. "You make plain where you fall, little pilgrim. Not everyone has your greed for the marvellous—keep well shy of glory, keep well shy of trouble, as the ka-Khastans used to say. My point is, it is very difficult for me to charm anything out of group number two, and it has nothing to do with the companion at my side. It has nothing to do with you."

Ronoah let that sink in. "It's about whether Lady Sansha'it is like me or not," he tried, and Özrek inclined her head just so, and he had to admit, it appeased something in him. Restored that fledgling equality.

"I would've liked you standing at my shoulder, to hear the thing as one. But we lose that particular pleasure, it seems, in exchange for our learning." The woman stooped and scooped a tiny hermit crab from the planks, deposited it in Ronoah's palm. "So be it. Soon we will arrive in a land where your curiosity is welcomed as it should be. Sit tight, make a friend, I won't be long in the asking."

Özrek ascended the stairs with the sort of pleasantly menacing word to the guards that Ronoah could only assume was a *watch him for me*, and then Ronoah was alone. Mostly. Compulsively he cradled the crab from the wind, fidgeting his weight from foot to foot, the subtle supple creak of the planks undersole. He clapped eyes on the bridges and waterways, scattered with palm fronds and splattered with droppings, populated by ibises and salamanders and the humans who walked among them—and for lack of anything else to do, he took to studying the private life of Shaipuri.

Even this far from the docks, where they need perform for no one, the Bhun Jivaktandr carried themselves with a certain swagger. People kept themselves busy weaving mats and mending nets, tending to cooking fires on the damp rocks under their stilted houses while they chattered idly with neighbours. Children chased each other down, vaulting the water on long poles for sport. They had dark, silky hair, cut and tied into fashions that reminded Ronoah of water in all its forms: tide pools, fountains, waterfalls. Their skin, too, was reminiscent of the rivers their city stood upon, a pale brown that went ruddy in the sunlight and oddly greenish in the shade. Bare-chested, sandal-shod, the denizens of Bhun Jivakta slowly but surely squeezed the sweet golden juice from their day as Ronoah watched, and his mind wandered.

He was wondering where he and Özrek would go once they were finished here. Whether the people in Ay Hang spoke Chiropolene. Wondering—first absently, then with sudden gripping urgency—whether he was making the most of *his* day, whether he was enjoying these hours, these precious minutes, as much as they were worth. Was enough happening? Was the right *type* of thing happening? Was he participating enough in this side-trip, was he reacting right, was he dwelling fully present in this moment?

Did asking these questions defeat the point altogether?

Maybe he should suggest another side-trip once Özrek emerged with the answer to the heartland's war. Afford himself a second try. Figure out how to stall, how to steal more days like this from their journey—or maybe, he admonished himself, you should use this time to build up the courage to be plain. Find the words to tell Özrek that it's not that you don't want to *go* to the Pilgrim State, it's that you're afraid of what will happen once you arrive. Afraid that what will happen is nothing at all.

Because that was the problem, wasn't it? That's what was keeping him from leaping eagerly towards the end. He had a destination, but he didn't have a goal. He'd made the decision to follow Özrek—follow Reilin—on impulse, in an instant of divine command. Özrek had a reason to visit the Pilgrim State: she was meeting someone there. She had something to do. Ronoah had begun this pilgrimage to prove himself to Genoveffa, but it wasn't—*enough*, was it, to simply go there? Did arriving in a place mean anything on its own? The notion felt insubstantial. Incomplete. He couldn't just *be* there. He had to *do* something.

A skitter on his index finger—the hermit crab nearly fell out of his hands and he yelped and caught it midair before it tumbled. Be careful, he thought; you shouldn't be holding it if you aren't going to pay attention. He set it back on the boardwalk and watched it crawl away, disappear under the banana-leaf fringe of a tiny building erected to the side of Lady Sansha'it's front gate, an ornately carved cabinet adorned with chunks of coral and branches of frangipani and a wooden bowl piled with limes. A pale jade icon of a shark was affixed to the back wall. It was a shrine—perhaps to Bhun Jivakta's deities, perhaps to the heartland's, to the Heavenly Seed Özrek was in the process of identifying. Lady Sansha'it was a bond between the two locales, so both were possibilities.

Would there be a shrine to Genoveffa in the Pilgrim State?

The thought struck him in the almost insultingly obvious way that all thoughts do which you should have thought long ago. He'd never considered it. The belief had always sat unexamined that he would find Genoveffa in the Pilgrim State in a purely metaphysical way. But what if he found her physically, literally? The Pilanovani may have been loathe to travel outside their lands, but Pilanova was only one of Acharrio's city states. Maybe someone else had gone before him to the Land of a Thousand Temples, however long ago. If his own improbable journey was anything to measure by, it wasn't out of the question. If he could find an Acharrioni shrine, if he could kneel at the foot of Genoveffa's fire and lay his journey down as offering—that would give him a sense of completion. Of ritual. A repository, a place where he could lay his pilgrimage officially to rest, instead of watching it dissipate insipid in the Pilgrim State's breeze.

And if there is no shrine? asked a voice in his head. It is on the other side of the world. No guarantee your gods ever made it that far.

Then, he thought, with an updraft of energy inside him that set his bones ringing like windchimes—then I'll build one myself.

Now *that* was a worthy objective. Giving Genoveffa one more window with which to look upon the world. He was an adult, and by Pilanovani standards that meant he was allowed to build, had been taught to lay bricks and lacquer walls. If he'd completed his training as a priest, he would have been granted the right to consecrate spaces, to create sanctity where none had been before. Perhaps at the end of this road, he could grant that right to himself. It would be a pretty Genoveffani thing to do.

There you go, he thought, watching a palm leaf blow loose from a tree and land with a splash in the river. You've figured it out. Nice job. That's been bothering you for ages—now you should have no problem moving forward. You should be ready.

Only he—wasn't? He wasn't. This new plan was fitting, and it was a comfort, for sure, it allayed his fear of not knowing what to do with himself once they made it to the Pilgrim State, but…his stomach still squeezed when he imagined getting in their boat and setting sail for Ay Hang. Now properly vexed, he asked himself in grumbling Acharrioni: "What's wrong with you? Why can't you finish this?"

The answer came gazing at the undersides of the Shaipurin houses, the shade and the stones, their own tiny personal underworlds. The answer came rebounding back from the Chiropolene caves, from the monastery, from a room lit up like an observatory by Özrek's internal galaxies: *You need no more telling what is wrong with you. You need telling what is right.*

Revelation bled into his awareness inevitable as the dawn. There wasn't anything wrong with him for wanting to continue journeying. It wasn't fear of inadequacy that was keeping him from the Pilgrim State. It wasn't fear at all.

It was enjoyment.

He was—oh, gods, he was just having too much *fun*, wasn't he? Especially since leaving the monastery, everything with Özrek—the birthday play in Scybia, the voyage on the Iphigene, the Maelstrom, this treasure hunt of history in Bhun Jivakta—this was the kind of life he'd longed for in Pilanova, the kind he'd read about so hungrily in Padjenne.

Traversing the planet, discovering myths and mysteries, pulling secrets from the earth like wild carrots in the Chiropolene countryside. Having someone to share those secrets with.

It was the best he'd ever felt. This pilgrimage, selfishly, meant more to him than pilgrimage, more than granting Genoveffa's wishes—it had become dear to him for its own sake. It had become a way of life, one he was enamoured with, one he didn't want to let go. He *loved* this. It was that simple.

Simple, but not easy. Did Özrek have any interest in travelling with Ronoah beyond what they'd already agreed upon? What if she already had other plans, other adventures in mind? What if she was preparing to take some other fellow stranger on-side—or just wanted to be on her own, what if she grew tired of masquerading as mostly human with Ronoah and wanted to go back to being the sort of thing that could quell the Shattering? It felt wildly egotistical, it felt like attempting to swallow the sun, but he couldn't stop himself from wondering—could he convince her to keep doing this with him, at least a little longer? Could he persuade her to stay? What could he do, what could he say to pique her interest?

Something about lemons and lychees might get the point across. Or the glorious unknown, that trademark way of thinking about the world that Özrek possessed and which Ronoah was beginning to share. But he never decided precisely which convoluted metaphor would form the backbone of his appeal, because then the gates of Lady Sansha'it's office swung open and Özrek stalked out.

And a dense disturbance swept out with her, and all of Ronoah's fervent scheming froze. She looked more perturbed than Ronoah had ever seen her.

"I got my answer," Özrek said as she reached him.

Three seconds passed. Four. Five.

"...And?" Ronoah looked askance at the woman, searching for clues in the crescent of her face. "Who was it? Who's the god of the heartland?"

Özrek frowned, turning in the direction of where delta became river, where the water snaked from the lush jungle crowning the mainland, and replied: "No one. Yet."

Without the sun moving an inch, the sky seemed to go darker.

"Wh—Özrek, what do you mean, yet?"

"I mean," Özrek said, her eyes glinting with a strange, disquiet light, "the War of Heavenly Seeds isn't over."

She brought one hand to her chin, fingers covering her mouth as she considered. Passersby gawked openly at her, this tall woman with skin like silt and muscle like sandstone, with her polished cheeks, her gleaming jade beads clustered about her chest, holding herself proud as a mountain, her eyes roving the shadowy forest like she was stalking something deep within its foliage, hunting something down.

"Ronoah," Özrek started, and instinct told him what was coming then. "My apologies for having lied, but this side-trip might take a little longer than I anticipated. This is—out of place. This merits an investigation."

Ronoah's breath caught, stilled. "You want to go into the heartland." Özrek nodded.

"Into the War—into everything you told me about...?"

"*Want* is an interesting way to sum it up, but essentially."

Ronoah looked away, into the water.

It should have been a harder decision than it was. It should have required careful consideration, risk analysis—it should have required more *data*, should have waited until Ronoah asked more questions like he'd asked about Bhun Jivakta itself, until he'd measured his own safety against the danger inherent in this choice, until he'd reasoned it out—

But he knew his answer, and reason could not touch it. "Sure. Let's do it."

Özrek paused. Tilted her head, ever so slight. "Ai?"

"Plenty of room," Ronoah quoted slowly, looking up into Özrek's eyes, the words a lemon burst upon his tongue, "for reasonable amounts of dawdling, right?"

Özrek opened her mouth—then closed it, exhaling a laugh through her nose. "Doing that godling proud, aren't you," she murmured, and it thrilled Ronoah almost immorally to hear it here, now, in this moment, choosing what he was choosing. Özrek turned to face south—there was something curious in the way she moved now that she was in this new body, head-first, the motion flowing down her spine like she was herself a river, or a snake—and planted her hands on her hips, nodding her agreement. "Then it's settled. Into the heartland we go."

And even though Özrek had suggested it in the first place, it was Ronoah who felt the almost-nauseous triumph of getting away with something. He put his hand into his pocket and squeezed his garnet in guilt, in apology. I'm sorry, he prayed, turning to the misty sun. I'm sorry. Wait for me.

"Not Özrek."

That was—what? Ronoah blinked the sunspots out of his eyes, frowning at the woman. "Sorry? Not...Özrek?"

"Mm. Not anymore." She jutted her chin at the palm trees. "Not unless I want to suffer a hundred snickering mispronunciations the second we set foot in the interior."

"What will you choose?" Perhaps it was the remaining dazzle in his vision, but he thought he saw not-quite-Özrek's skin flicker and fizz, right out in the open, as she contemplated. The woman sucked her teeth.

"Now let's see, what was it I used in those days ..."

The sounds of the outside world faded to make way for her, the clatter of vaulting poles and the chitter of monkeys gone mute in respect for this great thoughtfulness. The air drew close, intimate in that breathless way it did whenever this creature delved deep enough into memory. Ronoah held his breath alongside it.

"...Chashakva." A broad smile stretched her lips, slicing the tension like slitting a waterskin; her next words came out laughing, accented with something fleshy and tongue-sparkling as a mouthful of mango. "Ahai, that'll be the one, she-with-the-sharp-teeth, no doubt they remember *her* in the heartland."

An eerie relief braided itself up through Ronoah's spine. "And—and in Bhun Jivakta?"

She beheld the city all around them—Bhun Jivakta, brash and bold-faced and pulling no punches—and Ronoah *felt* it shrink before her, into what it was in her eyes: a tropical treehouse, and the children that played in it.

"Before their time," she said simply.

Even after all they'd been through, statements like that could still entrance Ronoah. His pulse quickened, and Chashakva grinned like she'd cut her newly-sharpened teeth on his unguarded heart.

"Now come with me," she said, catching his hand and whisking him away from Lady Sansha'it's estate, over a rope bridge, across the canal, away— "We have business in the market."

Ronoah half-tripped up and down steep wooden steps, feeling the spring in his soles. Gods, but he loved this. "We do?"

"Oh, yes. It was all well and good bumbling around in the ports, figuring it out as we go, but for a trip like this? We're going to need a bit of help." She pushed him through a long tight alley—his inhale jostling, her arm nudging his arm, the bubble of shade like the mouth of a cave—and out onto a boardwalk vibrating with pushcarts and pole-vaulters, paving the way back to the city's commercial centre. Linking her arm in his, she set her sights on the snapping flags of the west arcades. "I eat my words. It's time to find us a suckerfish."

# SEVEN

*I*N THE SOUTH-WEST QUADRANT of Bhun Jivakta spanned a boardwalk that stretched itself luxuriously out over the marshland. Thick bamboo posts formed a colonnade, overrun by ambitious passionflower vines; strong palm thatch kept the sweltering sun at bay, providing shelter for those who crowded underneath. Here the people of Bhun Jivakta sold themselves—either alone, freelancers standing on crates and proclaiming their many talents, or in groups, watched over by minders who sat drinking passionfruit juice and smoking cigars while their wares were inspected by patrons pinching biceps, checking teeth, seeking strength or beauty or cleverness.

Ronoah saw all of this through the metaphorical spaces between his fingers.

"Özrek—Chashakva, wait, no," he called, hurrying to the woman's side as she approached a platform. "We can't, this is, Vespasi wake, this looks like—"

"Like what?"

Out of breath, casting about for the most suitable way to explain, all that came to him was, "I studied the shalledrim for over a year. I read about the Trans-Bereni Highway, about the fairs. I saw the block prints."

His dark tone only made Chashakva swat his shoulder. "Ronoah, a request in honour of the ghosts you're talking about: if you're going to invoke their memory, don't skirt around it. If you mean *slave labour*, say slave labour." She pushed through the throngs, dragging a spluttering Ronoah behind her. "These aren't slaves, they're *kish kiriish*."

"Kish—?"

"Remora. The sharksuckers." Chashakva elbowed through to the front lines so they could see what—who—was on display: two boys, wrestling each other to demonstrate their strength. "In matters of work and wealth,

53

the shark is Bhun Jivakta's guide. Never ceasing, never still, productive and powerful—you've noticed shark teeth pass for local currency? It's a sacred animal." Eyeing Ronoah's horror, she added, "Oh yes, in the end the Bhun Jivaktandr are still Shaipurin: they know the best way to hold something sacred is to pull it to pieces. But back to the remora."

One of the boys managed to throw the other over his shoulder, standing proud above his defeated partner as interested patrons put up hands to bid.

"Bhun Jivakta modeled its social system off what it saw in the water. It's simple: if you've got enough teeth, you're a shark. If you're willing to eat shark shit in exchange for the protection provided by those teeth, you're a suckerfish. The kish kiriish find a patron and latch on, do whatever work needs doing—bodyguards, boy-toys, bounty hunters—get their way paid for, and detach once the current bends or the contract ends, whichever comes first." Ronoah managed one final glance at the winner of the match bowing his head toward someone's hand—attaching—before Chashakva tugged him away from the platform towards another.

"We need someone who can interpret for you in the heartland, someone to keep you informed when I'm busy. We need an oarsman to guide us through the Shaipurin Basin—preferably someone who's already done it, I don't want us going over a waterfall because of some overconfident sculler's geographical hubris." The woman paused, regarding two separate groups from a distance. She squeezed Ronoah's hand and a sizzle like butter in a pan flashed up his wrist. "And we need someone to keep you safe."

Right. The whole active-battleground thing was about to become a visceral reality.

Ronoah swallowed the thought before it could grow teeth of its own. "That's—that's a lot of people."

Chashakva laughed. "I intend to net one who can do it all. Welcome to the reefs, little shark. Here we shall hire our guide to the heartland."

Easier said than done, as it turned out: Chashakva was fiendishly picky about her labour. This one isn't strong enough, that one isn't fast enough, this one spooks too easily, that one's great but doesn't speak Chiropolene. They moved through the market scrutinizing people of all builds and backgrounds, and with infuriating nonchalance Chashakva dismissed them all. This one's too sullen, that one's a shrimp, this one speaks Bhun Jivaktandr and Chiropolene but doesn't know any jungle tongues, that one there's got all three and the biceps to match but is just *missing something*.

"What I really need," Chashakva mused, "is someone you'll *like*."

"Wh—*me*? Are you kidding?"

"Do I look like I'm kidding? No use finding the perfect candidate only to have you flail anxiously around them like so much bewildered flamingo. You'll be spending a lot of time together; you'd better get on well."

While most of Ronoah was aghast that his personal preferences were being seized as criteria in the purchasing-another-human-being-but-not-really-it's-complicated that he was complicit in—the analytical part of him had to admit it made practical sense. It wouldn't start their expedition well, if they were fighting before they even touched the rainforest.

This rationale didn't stop him from being loudly, squawkingly awkward when Chashakva asked for his opinion on the next round of suckerfish, of course.

Ronoah saw more people than he could have imagined on display: divers and dancers, fishers and flautists, the lovely, the literate, the unlucky. It wasn't just for hard labour that they sold themselves—there were kish kiriish hired to mind the children, to mind the books, to mind other kish kiriish. He started to wonder whether there might actually be more sharksuckers in Bhun Jivakta than there were sharks, whether everyone was, in some way, latched on to someone.

But their nets came up empty. After another unsuccessful tour of the arcade, Chashakva bought them a bunch of fresh, fleshy pink-and-green fruits she called guava, and they sat with their backs to a bamboo column to recoup. Between bites, Ronoah wondered aloud what they would do if they couldn't find someone suitable. "Come back tomorrow," was Chashakva's answer; "The current's fast enough that a decent percentage of what's available will have changed. And if that doesn't work, then I stash you somewhere safe for an evening and visit the trench market myself."

Ronoah swiped at a bit of juice on his chin. "Trench market?"

"I doubt it's something your sensibilities would be up to handling. It makes all this look delicate in comparison. Sharks who abuse their privileges tend to be blacklisted quickly—if your kish kiriish all swim back with injured fins, so to speak, you will quickly find that no one is willing to latch onto your cause anymore. What is a disreputable lout to do?" She waved her hand at the arcade. "Set up a market where those protocols do not apply, that's what. The reefs have a strong taste if you're not used to them, but they're clean enough. The trench is poison. You don't walk in there unless you've got a tolerance for toxin."

Coming from Chashakva, who could and would eat a hornet's nest for breakfast, this was saying a lot.

Ronoah was about to say as much when the woman lifted a finger for silence, gesturing with a moue of her lips at the arcade's interior. As Ronoah followed her gaze, she murmured, "Might not have to deal with that unpleasantness after all. Someone's looking confident."

A boy was walking toward them. He was a wiry, rascally-looking thing, somewhere in his mid-teens, with bowl-cut bangs and the simple topknot Ronoah had come to know as the mark of the kish kiriish.

He stopped close enough that Ronoah could've reached out and swiped at his shins. Ronoah craned his neck to see the boy's face—he was square-jawed, button-nosed, with long dark lashes fringing clever eyes. He crossed his arms, clearing his throat noisily, and it was then that Ronoah noticed the flurry of recently-healed scars across his right shoulder.

"Market says you've got hard standards to meet," he said to Chashakva, in accented but unmistakeable Chiropolene. "Sister, have I got a sweet deal for you."

Ronoah watched as the boy addressed her, speaking now in the language of Bhun Jivakta—then in something different, and different again, each sentence a new demonstration of his linguistic skill. Ronoah had no idea how many languages it actually was—five? six? they all sounded so close to his ears that it was only through guesses and gut-instincts that he caught the switchover, a rolled R here, a guttural sound there—but when it was done, Chashakva was smiling that reptilian smile of hers that meant she was extremely pleased. The boy finished his pitch, raising his eyebrows as if to ask the woman's opinion. Even not knowing most of what he'd said, Ronoah was impressed by the nerve it had taken to approach them at all.

"Go on, smooth-talker," Chashakva grinned, "it's a unanimous decision you need."

The boy looked at Ronoah with an expression that was—shockingly unimpressed. "Brother, something tells me she's saying that just to be nice," he said. He jutted his chin at Ronoah, who sat there completely taken aback. Beside him, Chashakva radiated amusement. "You're the reason Chirope's a must, ai?"

Ronoah had no idea whether he was being insulted. He didn't even know if that was allowed. "Right—yes, it's me, I don't speak any Shaipurin," he said, recovering himself. "I'd be happy to learn, though—"

"Ha!" The boy threw his chest out in one loud laugh. "Right, and I'll teach you to swallow the moons while I'm at it? Sorry, if you en't got it by now, with your lady speaking so precise, not a chance in *shiyalsha* you're getting it from me. Got no patience for teaching. Got good arms though," he continued before Ronoah could retort, flexing his biceps in a way that was comical enough for Ronoah to be distracted. "If you're seeking a raftsman, you found the best arms in port. I walk in the boathouse, all the oars fall off the shelves trying to be my pick."

"What's your name, little sharksucker?" Chashakva asked, finishing the last of her guava.

The boy bowed, apparently unironically. "I am Nazum," he said as he came upright again, his voice full of pride.

"And your purpose? Why have you swum all this way to see us?"

The boy named Nazum planted one fist on his hip, pointing the other hand full-fingered in Chashakva's direction. "Lady, I'm asking you the same question—no disrespect, but what you need to go upriver for? What treasure you seeking out? Clearly a sister of your disposition en't hurting for teeth," he commented, gesturing at her jade necklaces, "or for taste, might I say," he added, with a flattering wink. "And forgive me but you're both looking out of place to start."

"Ah. So it's curiosity that tugged you over here." Chashakva snuck a glance at Ronoah, laden with significance—look here little pilgrim, it said, we might have found our guy.

"Sure is." Nazum gestured graciously at Chashakva. "And I know *hulaat* when I see them."

A what? Ronoah was about to ask, but, absurdly, didn't know who to turn to—his companion, or the boy who was pitching himself as an interpreter. Nazum seemed about to explain, but he'd hardly opened his mouth before Chashakva was talking, in Acharrioni of all things, her grin still fixed in place.

"Hulaat. *Red*, as in red-tip shark, a species known for the impressive number of suckers it allows on its underside without getting tetchy. It denotes generosity. The kind of buyer who can pay handsomely for work, but lacks the nasty attitude that typically comes with such wealth. In short, easy money—although," she said, with a low laugh, "he'd be offended if he knew I'd explained it that way."

When she finished, Nazum let out a loud whistle. "Lady, you gotta have a forked tongue to hold onto that many lingos," he said, clearly impressed. "Where you from again?"

"A little all over the place," Chashakva replied, coolly amused. Ronoah was pleased to see how that gaze made even this charismatic boy trip over himself a little.

Carefully, he thought through what Nazum said he was capable of. He claimed he could steer a boat; he spoke all the right languages, fluently enough to have a sense of humour in each. And evidently he was not easily intimidated. That left one thing. "You've traveled the river before, then?" he asked. "You know the waters well?"

At this, Nazum laughed in a way that brought out all that roguish charm. "Brother, do I ever. Better than any of the guava-heads around here. Trust me, you go with Nazum, you get where you need to go. Which is ... where, again?"

Ronoah deferred to Chashakva—who simply leaned back against the bamboo pole, pointedly silent. Ronoah wondered whether she was keeping this information secret out of her habitual coyness, or whether it was a legitimate part of the way negotiations in Shaipuri worked.

Nazum took her silence in stride. "Ahai, quiet's another tongue you well-versed in. Fair enough—wherever it is, it's getting further from you every minute. Market closes soon—be a shame if you missed your chance." He inhaled, and as he straightened up, squaring his shoulders—one greenish brown and smooth, the other pink, wrinkled with scar tissue—some of his playfulness fell away. Without his smile, suddenly he seemed very professional.

"Buy my time," he said, lifting his arms to showcase himself, "and you won't regret it."

Toying with one of the beads of her necklace, Chashakva subjected Nazum to her scrutiny. Nazum stood there and endured it with the patience of someone who was used to being assessed. Ronoah wondered what Chashakva was looking for, whether she was hunting for some discreet layer in the boy the way she'd done with Ronoah.

At last, she knocked Ronoah's elbow with the back of her hand. "Well?" she asked. "Suitable?"

He swallowed. This *was* the first time he'd seen Chashakva refrain from outright *insulting* a suckerfish, so that was a good omen. And he had to admit, he was feeling less uncomfortable about purchasing Nazum's services than anybody else's—because Nazum had walked up to *them*, not the other way around. It felt more equal. Perhaps it was an illusion, but that's how it felt.

So he nodded, glancing up at the boy who was to be their guide. "Suitable."

Nazum puffed out his chest, cracking another dazzling smile.

"Wonderful." Chashakva rose to her feet, rolling her shoulders. She stood nearly a foot taller than Nazum. "To the notaries? You're a freelancer, no?"

"Ha! No, no, I'm with Lady Sikundhasma—"

"And she let you drift all the way over here?"

"I don't make a good runaway, sister. Too blindingly beautiful, impossible not to see me—"

They continued this flirtation until they arrived at Lady Sikundhasma's reef. She was a javelin of a woman, straight-backed and lean, sheathed in thick necklaces of shells. Chashakva struck up a conversation; they were negotiating a contract, Ronoah gathered, a price for Nazum's labour. Nazum stood to the side and made a show of not paying attention to this, bearing a self-satisfied smirk at his success.

The smirk slipped when Chashakva untied her necklace and slid seven swollen jade beads into Lady Sikundhasma's hand. For the first time, Ronoah saw what he thought was a flicker of doubt in Nazum's eyes. But then the two women turned to the boy, and Chashakva lifted her hand, palm-down; Nazum stepped toward her, pressed his forehead into her palm. Lady Sikundhasma watched approvingly, then gestured an assistant forward, who picked up her stylus and recorded the transaction.

It was done. In the eyes of Bhun Jivakta, Nazum was attached to them now.

"Right," Chashakva said breezily as she led them out of the arcade, "that's settled. Welcome to the team, brother."

"And what warm welcoming it is," replied Nazum, rubbing his nose in a parody of bashfulness. His eyes cut between Ronoah and Chashakva with a shrewdness that belied all his posturing. "So now that my soul's sold, what'll you be putting it to use for, exactly?"

Chashakva remained unforthcoming. "My demands are simple," she said as she stepped over the market's threshold, into the balmy afternoon of Bhun Jivakta. "You guide us where we need to go, you alert us to any dangers on the way, you interpret for my companion. In the event we are separated, you protect him to your last breath."

Nazum took the time to give Ronoah an exaggerated once-over. "You ask much of me," he said archly, and it took all of Ronoah's composure not to squawk in offense as Chashakva laughed.

"Perhaps," she replied, "but if you can manage it, then the favour of the gods themselves may just descend upon you."

Ronoah didn't know why that insinuation made him twitch, but it did, quick and sympathetic and strange. Nazum gave the woman a strange look of his own, but then he, too, crossed the threshold, squinting into the sun. Presumably Chashakva took his advance as an affirmative, because she continued talking.

"No time to waste. We need a craft that's river-worthy—poor *Aventina*'s not built for it, her mast would snag before we hit ten miles—we shall trade her at the docks, she'll fetch more than enough for a quality raft, presuming some urchin hasn't made off with her yet—"

"Or," Nazum suggested with a shrug, "you can just use one I already got."

Chashakva clapped. "Oh he comes with *accessories*, too—"

"Will it hold three people?" Ronoah asked, having seen enough of Bhun Jivakta's single-size skin boats to want to check.

"Sure is, brother, and well-weighted too, sturdy as a hippo and balanced as a hummingbird, en't nothing going overboard if we hit rocks. And there'll be no hitting rocks anyway."

"Very well," Chashakva said. She gestured for Nazum to lead. "To the river, little sharksucker."

Without hesitation, Nazum turned on his heel and started down the boardwalk; Ronoah caught the subtle motion of his hands as he cracked his knuckles. He fell in step behind the boy, with Chashakva taking up the rear.

While they were still surrounded with enough noise for Nazum not to hear, Ronoah slowed his pace until Chashakva nearly bumped into him. It was all he needed to do; she put her hand between his shoulder blades, an answer to his voiceless call.

"Why aren't you explaining anything to him?" he asked in Acharrioni undertones. Twice Nazum had asked to be let in on their plans, a request that was perfectly reasonable given he was now involved. "Won't it make his job easier if he knows what to expect?"

It took the entire length of a bridge before he received an answer: "Before I say what I am about to say, I would like to make it clear that I understand precisely how distasteful the idea will be, and also that I appreciate the effort it will take you to honour it convincingly."

The words felt like they were being conducted not through the air but through his bones—and so serious, so devoid of Chashakva's usual easygoing mockery, that any retort Ronoah would have made was cut short.

"I intend to play secretkeeper for as long as possible, and I request you do the same. Don't tell the boy anything about us or why we're here." And then, possibly even closer and more seriously, "Please understand it is a matter of safety. His and yours. What comes toward us now is a situation of unknown shape—we may need to stretch to fit its frame. The time for storytelling will come, but until we can get close enough for me to suss out what we must be to get our answers and leave in one piece, you must content yourself with living as a mystery."

She was right: Ronoah didn't like that. He was built for settling mysteries, not churning up more of his own. But he could feel a conciliatory sort of regret vibrating in the space between them, and knew that Chashakva meant it when she said she understood his unease.

And he remembered a truth he had known for years, a truth he had learned all the way back in Pilanova, in the seclusion of the temple, when he was training for priesthood—sometimes having the answers was even more burdensome than being ignorant. Sometimes knowledge cut up the hands trying to hold it.

He clenched his fists. He nodded his promise.

EIGHT

$\mathcal{T}$HE SANAAT RIVER FLOWED SLUGGISHLY this time of afternoon. It made it easier for Nazum to push out into the middle of the river and start rowing against the flow of the water, out of Bhun Jivakta and into the heartland. Away fell the boardwalks and canals, replaced by one wide waterway banked with reeds and ferns. Mountains rose in the distance, green straight to the summit, with cottony dabs of fog catching in the peaks. Slowly, as they wended their way further inland and the foliage built higher upon itself, the mountains disappeared. Ronoah didn't know exactly when it happened, but at some point they swept a curve in the river, and when he turned back to search for Bhun Jivakta he found that it, too, was gone. The rainforest had them all to itself now.

What an otherworld it was.

Trees bearing unripe and beautiful fruit drooped over the sides—speckled passionfruit, clusters of bananas, lumpy pear-shaped drupes that felt surprisingly dense when Ronoah passed his hand under one as they floated by. The reeds had given way to mangroves lining the river's edge, holding the land and the water apart. Flowers more ostentatious than Ronoah had ever seen flourished in the shade, flowers like dragons and scorpions and butterflies, lustrous and intricate. The noise was disorienting, all the million clicks and calls from the inhabitants of the jungle, the flocks of blue-chested birds, the pairs of monkeys loping from branch to branch, the solitary frogs twanging in the mud, the uncountable swarm of iridescent insects, the whine of their flashing wings.

The air was so thick it coated the throat like soup, like an inhale would produce an exhale of pure water. After so long breathing the glassy winds of the Iphigene, it was a change that took getting used to. Ronoah didn't have long, though, before Nazum called on him to help row. "Next mile or two's willful, and I figure you don't want to splash in circles. Your hand to the oar for an hour, and we'll cut the muscle of her nice and timely."

Chashakva was not rowing—mostly because Nazum wouldn't allow it. When Ronoah so much as looked back to ask the woman for help, the boy hissed loudly for his attention, making a face as if to ask *What the crap are you doing, lady like her don't row a boat, are you stupid or what?* Ronoah, who knew that Chashakva wouldn't mind—that under her influence the river would probably start flowing in the opposite direction, just for them—was reduced to grumbling internally.

But Chashakva didn't seem particularly smug about this preferential treatment. Once they'd come into the thick of the river she had retreated into herself, the sentinel crouched at the stern, moving only to occasionally dip her fingers into the water as if checking for a fever, or a pulse.

Her enduring silence left a lot of empty space, space that even the lush cacophony of the rainforest couldn't fill forever. And so, fighting the grip of the Sanaat one oar stroke at a time, Ronoah quietly began to refresh himself on how to talk to a person.

It was a short revision. The truth was he'd mostly *forgotten* how to interact with other humans. He'd spent seven months in a cave with nothing but Chashakva's cosmic oddness and a bunch of dead shalledrim for company, and his attempts at conversation *pre*-monastery had mostly gone so tragically wrong as to be nearly funny. He was more confident now, sure, more adventurous—but in appealing ways? Sociable ones? What did these improvements actually *look* like, held up to the light of another human being?

Nazum seemed similarly reluctant to start a conversation—although for different reasons. Ronoah caught the boy's eager, impatient stare more than once; he guessed that Nazum *would* ask if he knew he *could*, if he knew it was allowed.

It made Ronoah itch, that power difference. It made him push for equilibrium. "So how—how did you learn Chiropolene?" he asked, keeping his eyes on the dip and plunge of his oar in the murky water. "It isn't widely spoken in the region, right? Who taught you?"

"Heard it off an old shark," Nazum said. "The Rs sounded weird. I decided to give it a try—it's a mouthful, but a mouthful's what I get for knowing to speak it." He sounded pretty offhand about it—perhaps too much so. Especially given what Chashakva said about the Shaipurin being loathe to speak any language but their own. Why would Nazum just *give it a try*?

Nazum must have felt him staring, because he shot back with a "Brother, where did *you* pick up the tongue? You just find it lying around one day?" Ronoah blinked, and Nazum changed his footing so he could look over his shoulder at Ronoah, raising a short eyebrow. "En't no way you born with it, after all. Neither one of you. So?"

Don't tell him anything about us. What, exactly, did Chashakva mean by *anything*?

He had never needed to obscure his story like this. The closest he'd gotten was back when he and Chashakva had only just begun their pilgrimage, when she was still Reilin, and he was still reluctant to speak of himself. But even then, he had yielded in the end. How could he avoid doing the thing he was literally born to do—tell the truth?

What would Chashakva say, he thought, if you asked a question like this?

"...You could say I picked it up along the way." Try again, Ronoah, Nataglio help you. That wasn't mysterious, that was bland. Think enticing and infuriating. "A girl with a clay face and a jade tongue taught it to me." Much better. And true, what with Amimna's maskmaking past, her mythmaking present. The thought of what she'd say, being praised this far from her home, made him smile. It eased the discomfort at not being all the way honest.

"Right. And your clay-face girl, she teach you how, exactly? She a Chirope?"

Ronoah paused to think. "At the very least, she knew all of their stories," is what he settled on.

"Where are you *from*?" Nazum asked, finally bursting out with it in his impatience. Ronoah caught the boy staring at him again, abandoning his rowing temporarily. "What kinda place spits out a brother like you?"

"One that didn't like the taste of me much." This repartee was starting to get more comfortable, almost like a game—find the true thing that gives away nothing. "Not anywhere you'd know."

"Am I an infant? Try me."

"The other side of the world." Was that too far? He risked a glance at Chashakva; even without her directly facing him, he could tell from her posture, from the set of her brow, that what he'd said was satisfactorily opaque. He might even have caught a hint of a smile.

Nazum did seem pretty taken aback. Before the boy could recover, Ronoah tried another of Chashakva's tactics: redirecting, reflecting the conversation. "And you? Where in this land are you from? You say you know these rivers, these heartland languages. How did you come by that knowledge? What—what brought you to this profession?"

Nazum sighed as if he'd been expecting this. "Oh I see how it is—avoiding the most basic of queries and then asking my life story." He resumed his paddling, guiding them around a jut of rock dividing the river. "Fine, if you gotta know. I was born on the delta—lived my whole life there, skipping stones at the flamingos, helping my babu with the alligator skinning. Was gonna grow up to be a fisher like him, learned to mend the net and throw the spear and all. Plans got scrapped when a fever took my mamu—it happens, when you en't wealthy, happens a lot. She went to see *shiyalsha*, then babu, all busy grieving his lady, wasn't looking where he stepped one day and *snap!* the alligator got him back for all her cousins. She took his leg, but the swelling and the rot took his life—I put him out on the boat so he could die somewhere looking skyward. Took maybe a week, and then it was just me left, and the pantry got emptier every day 'till the only thing left in was the smell. Had to fend for myself, and there en't no other work for a shrimp as I was, none but this right here." He picked up his pole and swirled it at the rainforest around them. "Sold myself as suckerfish, and seeing's I was so small and sneaky they put me with the pickers and diggers, folk what ford upriver for exotic goods, the kind our lady's wearing round her fine neck. I been through here so many times the monkeys all know me—you watch, long enough they'll start throwing coconuts at me to keep me fed."

It was a lie. Every word of it. Ronoah could tell instinctively—but it was such a watertight story, delivered so easy and well-practiced, that he couldn't find a way to pick at it tactfully.

"That sounds really hard," was all he could say in the end.

"Not so much as you'd think. Like I said, hard luck's the norm when you're toothless and poor."

Ronoah nodded and turned back to paddling to hide his troubled frown. They stood there, on either side of the raft, stewing in the half-truths and untruths they'd told each other—the silence somehow even more awkward now that it had been polluted with suspicion—while Chashakva sat statuesque behind them, fixed upon another realm entirely.

That is, until she broke her stasis to inform them: "At the split in the river, we turn east."

She rose from her crouch and approached them, her face set in one of her kaleidoscopic expressions, irked and concerned and satisfied and conniving. Ronoah had just enough time to register all these conflicting sentiments before Nazum—sighting the junction in question—made a loud, doubtful noise.

"You sure, lady? You know what lies thataway, ai?"

"Ahai."

"That's Subindr territory."

Ronoah felt something flickering off Chashakva's skin—anticipation, winking like sparks, gathering around her like bee-flies. "So it is."

64

Nazum stared hard at Chashakva, wiping the sweat off his brow in a long streak on his forearm. It didn't do much, given the rest of him was just as damp. "Fine," he said eventually, "but we're gonna have to move to a real tricky beat. Stay off the river some hours, make camp further in the bush, keep our heads low so's we're not found by the locals."

Having lost this game before, Ronoah could guess what was coming before he even heard the woman scoff. "Found by them?" she said, incredulously. "I intend to walk up to their front door."

Nazum choked. The boy had visibly paled, the pink tones draining from his cheeks and giving his skin an even greener tinge. Then he laughed. "You are one hilarious sister, y'know that."

Chashakva's eyes narrowed—playfully, Ronoah could tell, but to Nazum it probably just seemed critical. "I am the type to laugh at my own jokes, yes. Do I look like I'm laughing now?"

There was a loud *plunk* as Nazum swept his oar out of the water and planted it on the raft. "S'cuse me for presuming, I didn't know the thing you sought in here was DEATH," he scowled, with an accusatory sweep of his arm. "If that's the case, just step off right up around the corner here and I'll be on my way—you get to kill yourselves, I get a nice easy float back downriver, and you can pass me a croc eye off your baubles for pay, though you might as well sling the whole string 'round my neck 'cause you en't be needing it for long."

Chashakva took none of the boy's allegations seriously. "Don't be dramatic, little sharksucker—what's the harm? All the cannibals in the jungle are just stories, intimidation tactics to keep the overly-nosey away. I wouldn't go so far as to call them *gracious*, but the tribes of the heartland are honourable—they don't go around slaughtering indiscriminately. We avoid doing anything to offend them, and we should have no problem."

Nazum was looking at Chashakva like she'd grown another head while he wasn't paying attention. "Okay lady, I don't know where you got your intel from, but things aren't—like—that—anymore." Three stamps of the oar on the raft served to emphasize his words. "Maybe in my great grandmamu's time you could pull shit like that off, but these days there en't *no* telling what they'll do to you—"

He drew up short at the look Chashakva was giving him. That sudden focus of hers, that keen gleam of piqued curiosity. "What's a delta boy like you know about the politics of the heartland?"

Nazum threw his head back and groaned. "*Chuta ka saag*, probably more than someone who *just showed up*," he said, plunging his oar back in the river. "What you even going there for? What's so important you'd risk a traditional Subindr welcome for it?"

"I'm going to speak to the wisewoman." That cut Nazum's griping short. Chashakva raised a sardonic eyebrow and added, "They still have *those*, don't they?"

Nazum said nothing. He just sucked his teeth and returned his attention to paddling, muttering defensively to himself in Shaipurin all the while.

Before dark, Nazum scouted a suitable place to dock for the night. With the first step onto land Ronoah felt his foot sink into the saturated ground; even off the river, they weren't out of the water. They dragged the raft under the canopy, far enough inland to be invisible from the banks. From their supply cache Nazum retrieved a coil of cord, a large bundle of cloth, and a hefty-looking knife. "You know how to string up a hammock?" he asked his patrons, regarding them with the mild scepticism that was rapidly becoming the norm.

"Actually, I do," Ronoah said. He'd learned while he was aboard the ship between Lavola and Tyro. Nazum made a pleasantly-surprised noise, then tossed the bundle and rope into Ronoah's startled arms.

"You can be doing the rigging then, while I throw together something to cook on. And..."

"I'll be finding you something to cook," Chashakva finished. Nazum nodded; Ronoah saw the boy peer after Chashakva as she stalked into the woods, going so far as to get up on tiptoe to crane his neck and get a last glimpse of her before she melted into shadow.

It might have been the shifting mud beneath them, but Ronoah thought he saw Nazum rock back and forth, once, like he was deciding whether to stay or go. Like he was fighting an instinct to heave the raft back into the river and leave. But the boy caught Ronoah looking, and smiled a conspiratorial smile, wide and sly, and disappeared off in another direction, swinging his machete with an easy roll of his wrist as he went.

At night, the rainforest became a different beast. The landscape was lit by luminescent fireflies, by phosphorescent moss, glowing gentle chalky green while mushrooms sprouted from their depths like clusters of lighthouses. Bats slalomed through the trees, discernable only as a compression of the darkness, as a firefly suddenly blowing out. Nearby, a spider as large as Ronoah's hand rested on a trunk, the fine fur of its body visible in the mosslight. The thrum in the air felt more guttural, more predatory; the noise hit a different pitch, a new nocturnal frequency. The symphony of the crepuscular, repeating endlessly.

After the vast absence of the monastery, the quiet and the void and the vertigo of negative space, this was like being thrust into the fist of life itself, hot and immediate and pressing and surging and constant, constant, without reprieve. The dark somehow made it even more pervasive. It made Ronoah tremble. It was nearly too fruitful to stand.

"Hey," came a voice from the other side of camp. Nazum was minding the small fire he had miraculously managed to start. The low flames flickered on the boy's throat, hollowing out his cheeks. He looked older than he was, in the dark. "You mind if I ask your names? That a thing I can do?"

They had never even named themselves, Ronoah realized. Neither he nor Chashakva. He saw Nazum sitting there, whittling at leftover pieces of bamboo for something to do with his hands—and anxiety puckered in him like a gulp of lime juice, nerves on behalf of this boy who was with two people he didn't know and didn't trust, fording a river he didn't want to be on.

Softly, he sighed. What harm could it do?

"She is Chashakva," he said, nodding to the woods. Nazum's eyes got wide.

"Oh-kay," he said, leaning back in his seat, "no wonder she's such a terrifying sister. That's a *name*," he added in response to Ronoah's curious frown. "That's the kinda name you give your kid when you want 'em to grow up to be a world-destroyer."

Of course it was. "I didn't know," Ronoah said, leaving the hammocks to come and sit opposite the boy, eyes on the fire. The poor flames seemed bedraggled in this waterlogged environment. For a brief moment, he longed for the knife-dry air of the desert. For the burnished orange tones, the heat like the point of a needle, the grit of sand stuck in the web between his fingers.

"Well?"

Ronoah blinked, looked up. Nazum was waiting for something.

"I asked you for your one," the boy clarified, after a few seconds of mystified silence.

"My name," Ronoah confirmed. The smoke from the fire tickled his nostrils. "Ronoah Genoveffa Elizzi-denna Pilanovani." It had been so long since he'd spoken it aloud. Strangely, it didn't feel quite so cumbersome anymore. It was more natural; more comfortable. More like it used to be. It stirred all sorts of things inside him, as if the words were a breeze that had set his soul aflutter.

His moment was interrupted by Nazum laughing.

He laughed like a crow, harsh and a little nasty. Innocently malicious, if such a combination existed. "Yeah, good luck getting me to say *any* of that," he said. "That's a ballad of a name. What was the first bit?"

"Ronoah," said Ronoah, slightly embarrassed, and annoyed for allowing himself to be embarrassed.

"Ro-no-ah." Nazum rolled the sounds around, testing them out, then smiled a scrunched-up smile like he didn't appreciate the taste. "Right. Well, don't go seeing this as me being rude or nothing, but we need to find you a new name."

"What? Why?"

"Where we're going en't no one gonna say that one. No offense, but it'd be like asking 'em to put a clod of dirt in their mouths."

"Thank you," Ronoah said, leaning on his sarcasm as heavily as he could. Nazum put his hands up placatingly, and from his posture Ronoah knew that, insulting as it was, the boy really didn't mean it as an insult. It was just the reality of the situation. For some reason that hurt more.

Nazum just whittled his bamboo cane, occasionally glancing at Ronoah before returning to his work with a dismissive head shake. Maybe ten minutes later, he spoke up: "How about *Runa*? S'close enough."

"Runa?" Nazum shrugged in a that's-what-I've-got sort of way. Ronoah repeated it soundlessly, lowering his eyes to the fire. "What does it mean?"

"It's like a, like a jungle cat—kinda puny, but big moony eyes, and black marks all over like you got."

Quietly, Ronoah exhaled. Well, he thought, why not? If what Nazum says is true, it's either pick yourself a name now, or soon someone else will pick for you. "Okay," he said, and then, because it felt like the right thing to do, "Thanks."

"Just looking out for you, brother. S'my job from here on out, en't it?"

Ronoah met Nazum's eyes. For the first time since meeting him, he thought he saw a glimmer of a real smile hidden under the exaggerated smirk.

The rains came and went, so suddenly Ronoah yelped in surprise—in a heartbeat it was all around them, shearing down with incredible volume, drowning out all else. Nazum had raised a frame over the fire, and so together they sat beneath the thatch, watching silver glints appear and disappear in the mosslight. Chashakva slipped back into the camp, carrying two fresh-dead monkeys and no discernable way of having caught them. Nazum took them and prepared a meal. Ronoah noticed that, though the boy now knew Chashakva's name, he did not use it. Perhaps he didn't want her to know he had asked.

After they'd eaten, Nazum tossed the remains into the river; once he'd returned, he declared that he would take first watch. "Cause there's gotta *be* a watch, if we're gonna stake out in Subindr territory," he said, with heavy emphasis. He remained under the cooking frame, stirring the coals, while Chashakva and Ronoah each picked a hammock.

It was kind of ridiculous, Ronoah thought: Nazum staying up even though Chashakva was probably only pretending to sleep and Ronoah was too on edge to get any rest himself. Of the three of them, the boy was probably the only one who'd make good use of a hammock. But there it was. He curled up as much as he could, trying to get the cloth to envelop him, so he felt less exposed.

Softly, inaudible over the chitter and growl of the rainforest, he uttered his new name. When they met the Subindr, he wanted to be used to it already, to not be caught off-guard when they called it. Runa. Little spotted jungle cat.

On one hand, he was still smarting at the way Nazum had tossed his given name into the mud. His name represented so many of the things he held dear—his godling, his family, even his memories of Pilanova. As long as he could remember, it had held him together, had kept all of his disparate parts working in some semblance of harmony. To strip him of his name was to strip him of his story.

But on the other, there was Chashakva. Chashakva, who was once Özrek, who was once Reilin. Ronoah remembered the day in Ithos where the creature had picked a name for the occasion—that meant she was using a different one in the hours before Ronoah asked. Technically, that meant he didn't know the name he'd met her by. Ronoah doubted he would ever find out—that name, or the rest, or which one had come first.

But they all still belonged to her, didn't they? They all *were* the creature now known as Chashakva. They just described different aspects, or moods. Like the seasons. There were eight seasons in Pilanova, eight names to describe the land in different states. But it stayed the same land.

He pulled his garnet from the folds of his wrap, held it close to his cheek. Perhaps, he thought, this was not so much a loss as a gain. Perhaps this was a gift. He only had to look at it right.

He shifted, and the hammock swayed. Another rain shower filtered through the woods.

 NINE

NAZUM WAS TWITCHY THE WHOLE NEXT DAY as they paddled further into Subindr territory. He did a commendable job of hiding it; evidently, after realizing his fate was sealed, he had decided to squash any misgivings under a brave face. Ronoah could only tell that Nazum was less calm than he seemed because, when they got close enough, he felt a crackle of agitation leap like sickly green static between them.

At one point Ronoah made the mistake of asking about the Subindr. "What are they like? Which Heavenly Seed is theirs?"

"It's Subin," Nazum said, as if it were obvious. "They're named after her."

"And—sorry, she, Subin, she is ruler of...?"

"The sky." The words came from both Nazum and Chashakva. They looked at each other in mild surprise, and then Nazum ducked his head and gestured for Chashakva to take the lead. "Subin is a weather god, presiding over the winds and the winged things of the woods. She is also an agricultural god, given that the bulk of Shaipurin plantlife reproduces through airborne pollination. Vultures are sacred to her, beehives are seen as her blessing, and before you ask the question I know you're hesitating to ask, she has them strangle people." Guiltily, Ronoah winced, and Chashakva smiled a little too keen for his liking. "Legend has it that Subin is perpetually running out of breath as she huffs and puffs the winds across the sky. That's where she gets the name—*Subin*. Blue-Face." The woman stretched her arms above her head, fingers interlaced. "If she runs out completely, the winds will stagnate. So they give her the air from their own lungs. Well—not their *own*, specifically. But you catch my meaning."

"You hear all kinds of stories," Nazum added. "Some say they braid ropes out of special vines and wrap 'em around your neck; some say they take you to a sinkhole on a clear day, so the water's reflecting the sky, and they drown you for all the bubbles what come gushing out your mouth. But mostly they use *ki'itni*, it's a poison moss, they press it on your face and you breathe in and your lungs go pop."

Ronoah was starting to understand why Nazum would rather stay clear of the Subindr.

"Are you sure they'll be able to answer our questions?" he asked under his breath in Acharrioni, nudging Chashakva's elbow. "What are you going to tell them when we get there?"

"I'm still figuring it out," was Chashakva's answer. She didn't sound overly concerned, but Ronoah knew that easygoing tone for what it was: the vague pleasantry Chashakva employed when she was busy checking calculations, when you caught her mid-scheme. The lack of a plan was unnerving—but oh, the thrill of watching it come together. It was absurd to be excited about being here, but Ronoah could not deny how he loved to watch Chashakva think.

It was not obvious when they arrived.

Late that afternoon, Chashakva directed Nazum down another, narrower branch of the Sanaat. They floated through a thicket of palms, a bamboo grove, a stretch of water shallow enough for Ronoah to see the yellow crabs tiptoeing the sand at river's bottom. The air darkened and the rain came like a wall, dousing everything for twenty minutes before evaporating. The river curved tight around a tree draped in vines, and to Ronoah the land on one side of the tree was exactly the same as on the other, there was absolutely nothing to suggest that they were in any more danger than they had been five minutes ago—except Nazum and Chashakva both suddenly stood differently. Alert; prepared. It was only when Ronoah noticed that stance that he realized they had reached their destination.

"How do we find the village?" he asked, stepping closer to Chashakva. She scanned the treeline, inscrutable.

"The villagers," she replied, "are going to have to find us."

"How long until you think they do?"

Chashakva just stared out at the impregnable forest and said, "They already have."

Ronoah followed her gaze, looking into the trees, and saw nothing. A chill pinched his shoulder blades.

The river split, and again they took the smaller tributary. Their progress was eerily uninterrupted; Ronoah could do nothing but stand in the middle of the raft and wait, trying to shake off the dread that came of knowing someone out there was watching them. It felt like the entire jungle was holding its breath.

Then, up ahead: a half-rotten log lying clear across the waterway. "That'll be the place," Chashakva said. Nazum made a noise of agreement. The log was just a log, a toppled trunk from a storm seasons ago—the fact that it was so mundane made it all the more disturbing. Not knowing how to prepare, or even what he was meant to prepare for, Ronoah sent a prayer to Genoveffa.

And six women walked onto the log and stood silent, waiting for them.

"All right, little sharksucker," Chashakva murmured, "time to teethe a bit on those interpreting skills of yours."

Nazum pulled his oar out of the river and stepped back so he was side by side with Ronoah. Close as they were standing, Ronoah felt the boy square his shoulders. They freefloated within a few feet of the log before their forward momentum was quelled by the current, and they stalled, and Chashakva began to speak.

"We come seeking Subin's wisewoman," Nazum said in Ronoah's ear, his voice surprisingly low and unobtrusive. Gone was the posturing and complaining, replaced by a discretion and a seriousness that caught Ronoah off-guard. "We come bearing tidings and gifts."

One of the scouts asked a question. "What sort of gifts?"

"Ones that are befitting of her—honourable spirit." Nazum glanced at Chashakva, brow furrowed. "They are not for your eyes to see."

"And for what reason do you come all this way to deliver them to her?"

"There is a matter of great importance we must discuss with her. It concerns the fate of her most glorious tribe, and of all tribes in Shaipuri."

"What matter is this?"

Ronoah saw Chashakva smile with a regret he could tell she did not feel in the slightest. "It is not for your ears to hear."

The scouts stared at Chashakva, hard and long, like they were trying to figure her out. At last, one of them gestured to the banks.

"Come," Nazum translated as the woman spoke, "we will bring you to her holiness."

The boy bent to pick up his oar, leaving Ronoah disconcerted at how they had been welcomed so quickly. He'd assumed it was going to be much trickier than a statement of intent and some presents. What presents, exactly, were they going to give to this wisewoman anyway? How had Chashakva gotten away with not volunteering them for inspection now?

He looked up as Nazum rowed them to shore, and saw one of the scouts staring right at him. He was surprised to see a mote of caution in her expression.

They had only just hopped off the raft before two of the scouts confiscated it, hoisting it onto their shoulders and bearing it away into the woods. Whatever was coming, there was no escaping it now.

Of the four remaining, the woman who had invited them to shore took the lead. Chashakva was motioned to follow, with another scout falling in step behind. Ronoah was next, with a third woman at his back, and Nazum was made to walk behind her, with the final member of the party pulling up the rear. Interspersed like this, even the most surreptitious whisper was impossible, neither in Chiropolene nor Acharrioni. Ronoah made the journey in fretful silence, trying to control his mingled fear and fascination at the prospect of seeing one of the heartland tribes up close.

After a half-hour's worth of brisk hiking, Ronoah heard the blue shout of rushing water. Their party circumnavigated a hill and emerged onto an expanse of clear, tamped-down earth, the first Ronoah had seen—and then he looked up from the path and nearly tripped into the woman in front of him.

The valley spread open like a gasp. At first all Ronoah could see was a breathtaking blanket of green, but then came detail, came differentiation, and he noticed three trees breaking free from the canopy, interrupting the smooth green swoop of the slopes. In the nadir of the valley was a river, brown and twisted like a worm—a spray of cold droplets splattered Ronoah's cheek and he turned and saw the river's source, the cavernous opening in the hill, invisible from the other side, where the waterfall frothed out over the rocks. Without slowing their pace, the women began the descent along a very narrow, very slippery footpath cut into the rock face. Ronoah's silence intensified as he renewed his efforts not to trip.

As they made their way down the cliffside and into the valley, the first of the villagers came to watch them. Dozens of people in grass skirts with ornaments around their ankles, with curious, glittering eyes. A man passed by shouldering a bunch of bananas; in a shallow dirt pit, a boy was showing off to a group of children by walking on his hands. He tumbled over into a somersault, to the laughter of the others, and then one of the children noticed the procession, and they all turned and watched them go by with eerie solemnity.

Eventually they came to the base of one of those giant trees—and Ronoah's knees went weak at exactly *how* enormous it was up close, the fact that a living thing could reach that size. All the water in Acharrio to feed something like this; Subin the god of growing things, indeed.

Their party's leader grabbed a leathery vine and scaled the trunk with a series of simple, graceful acrobatics. Chashakva followed suit. When it was Ronoah's turn, he readied himself to embarrass the lot of them with his clumsiness—then surprised himself yet again when he found he was able to climb with ease. He looked at his arms as he climbed, noted for the first time that they were shaped differently from how he remembered.

They reached a wooden platform, then continued spiraling upwards by way of terrifyingly railing-less rope bridges. They were so far above ground that the very atmosphere changed, the air breathing drier than it had in days. Ronoah was immensely grateful for the foliage obscuring the world below.

First came the buzzing, then came the treehouse. Resplendently ornamented with braided vines and bamboo windchimes, it wrapped in a torus around the trunk, so large Ronoah was astonished it stayed put. The architecture was remarkable. Flowers nestled like hummingbirds amid branches that were curiously boled, misshapen lumps clinging to the bark. Only when he caught the swarm of movement upon the boles' surfaces did he realize they were beehives.

"In there," Nazum said, arriving at Ronoah's side. Ronoah looked to one of the scouts, who was indicating the house's entrance. "In there she will greet you."

And then quietly, he added, "Where we'll all be launched into the godsforsaken sky, no doubt."

Ronoah glanced at Nazum, but the boy's face showed no sign of complaint, no sign of anything at all. That they were all so impassive made Ronoah worry he was doing something wrong, gawking over everything he came across. Trying to smooth his expression, he advanced with Nazum to Chashakva's side, and together the three made their way to the entrance.

"They're just going to let us walk in alone?" Ronoah whispered. "After all this caution? Aren't—aren't they worried we'll do something to the wisewoman?"

"It is my guess," Chashakva replied, "that the wisewoman can take care of herself."

Two curtains of beads formed an antechamber; they slithered through Ronoah's hands as he brushed them aside. The first was dark, lissome, made of dried seeds and nuts. The second was fashioned of tiny bones.

Inside burned hundreds of candles, wax dripping in rippling stalactites down the sides of stands and tables, filling the house to the rafters with the fat, creamy smell of honey. How the place had not burned down long ago, Ronoah had no idea—maybe even this high up, the wood was too damp for a flame to gather purchase. The golden glow wrapped around everything in the room: plants, live and dried, potted and hanging and climbing and creeping; bottles and jars cluttered on tables and swinging from rafters; an armoire, massive and ornate, boasting a long and pitted mirror.

A lady straddling a branch of the tree.

Ronoah noticed her just as he heard Nazum's sharp intake of breath, as he felt a rumble of satisfaction resonate through Chashakva's body. The lady paused what she was doing—something with a flower, or maybe those were feathers?—and leaned over the side to peer at them. Her hair draped over her shoulder like a slick of oil.

Then she dropped off the branch and touched down with a glass-rattling thump that made Ronoah fear for the candles all over again.

"Visitors," she said, straightening and sweeping her hair away from her face, "I hear you brought me presents."

The wisewoman was built like an ox: wide-hipped and chunky-calved, with dimples in her knees peeking out from the fringe of her elaborately braided grass skirt, with a belly that was at once flabby and slate-strong. She had a square jaw, wicked eyes, and a full mouth made even fuller by the grin it was sporting. Around her neck and breasts she was wearing a braided rope.

"But before you give them to me," she continued, "who in the five realms of shiyalsha are you?"

"It's funny you mention," Chashakva said—and then she said something else, but Ronoah didn't catch it because Nazum cut himself off, breaking his stoicism to gape at Chashakva. Not wanting to be rude, but knowing how quickly Chashakva could talk once she got up to speed, Ronoah gave Nazum a nudge, asking with a quirk of his brow what had been declared. Nazum looked at him with fresh eyes, newly lit with confusion, and translated:

"We have come from the underworld."

It took all of Ronoah's power not to balk. Or to burst out laughing. No wonder the scouts had allowed them passage, if *that's* what Chashakva had implied.

The wisewoman's eyes were wide—not with Nazum's bewilderment, but with a milder surprise, as if she had been expecting this but she'd been expecting it two weeks from now. She put her hands on her hips and puffed out an exhale. "Well shit, I wasn't expecting a drop-in from the shiyalshandr—would have put the tea on." She was taking this remarkably well. Maybe it was more of a believable cover than Ronoah thought. "Come then, give me the news. Are all souls well in shiyalsha?"

"No, actually," Chashakva answered, "they're not. That's what we're here about." She eyed the treehouse, the bees flitting in and out of the window slats. "We'd like to discuss the War of Heavenly Seeds."

The wisewoman blinked. Then she put her hands to her cheeks. "Ai, me, there aren't enough sacrifices, are there?" she said, rubbing at her jaw. "It has been a little dry this year, I admit—but no need to worry, we're planning on rounding up another batch before the year's out. We've been planning a raid for the coming weeks, actually, it's looking to be quite the success. Lots of honoured souls coming your way soon."

It became real then. The war, the sacrifices, everything. Despite Chashakva saying so, despite this journey into the heartland, it had still somehow remained a gruesome story in Ronoah's mind—but here, now, it was real. And handled so casually, so offhand. It was some combination of shock and raw survival instinct that kept Ronoah's stomach from betraying him.

Chashakva, on the other hand, had gotten over her initial concern about the War. It had sloughed away with her old name, replaced by that hunter's relish, that harbinger's pleasure in breaking bad news. He heard it evident even under Nazum's translation: "Yes, see, this is the thing. We don't need more sacrifices, we need less. Specifically none at all."

That, too, was a sentence the boy tripped over.

The wisewoman was similarly astonished. She cocked her head to the side. "…Right, I know a trick when I see one." Her eyes narrowed and her grin returned, a vicious, malicious grin, a grin that absolutely meant harm. "Whose tribe are you from?"

"The one under your feet," Chashakva replied without missing a beat. "This battle has dragged out for centuries. The fifth branch of shiyalsha is overpopulated with sacrificial souls. It is crowded and unpleasant—with all respect, you're disturbing our peace down there, and we're getting annoyed." The woman narrowed her own eyes. "So I come on high authority, to investigate this latest distortion in our boundaries."

"Authority, huh." The wisewoman considered this. It seemed her want to one-up another tribe's trickery was warring with her want to avoid offending any actual underworld agents. "… All right," she said at length, sweeping her hair back again, "I hate to be this girl, but before I discuss a matter of that sensitivity, I'm gonna need proof that you are what you say you are. Surely a small display of your provenance en't an offense to ask?"

"Not at all," Chashakva replied. She turned and caught Ronoah's eye, and in that instant she invited him to share a private moment of humour, a laugh at what they both knew was about to happen, and he could not help but crack a smile.

All at once the woman's skin flickered to life like Ronoah had only ever seen in private, patches of vivid starlight showing through the walnut wood of her skin—clustered, precise, like a pattern, like—spots? *Little jaguar girl*, Chashakva had called herself. Her profile morphed, just for a second, into something resembling a cat's muzzle—and Ronoah heard a curse fly out of Nazum's mouth, too muffled to make out the specifics. Chashakva spread her arms and smiled, and he thought he saw a ghostly whisker twitch.

Undeterred by this display of ferocity, a bee alighted on her wrist; gently, she took a moment to shake it free. Lilac-blue light kaleidoscoped across the walls at the motion of her arm, then faded as the spots were re-absorbed, back into the visitor who had now undeniably asserted herself as demon.

The wisewoman was clapping delightedly. Nazum was looking at them like he'd been personally wounded, his wide-eyed glare equally fearful and accusatory. The boy struggled for words when the wisewoman started speaking again; her breathless excitement mingling with his bristling tension produced a strange emotional dissonance in translation. "Ooh, that is *magnificent*," she was saying, "like something right out of the stories, ai me, a pleasure and an honour to have you here—but what about you, silent one?" To Ronoah's horror, the wisewoman bore down on him, gesturing eagerly. "What little miracle will you perform for me?"

Ronoah had no miracle to perform, except perhaps vomiting spontaneously in fear. But Chashakva was prepared for that, too. "Alas, he will not be performing any miracles today," she said, a hand held up to graciously fend off the wisewoman's disappointment. "Unless you wish to divulge your dearest secrets to a stranger, or be moved to weeping in public. For he has it in his power to pick your emotions like berries, and he always knows a lie."

The bottom of Ronoah's stomach dropped out. *Sketas naska*, he thought, you're really going for it now.

"He has accompanied me as an emissary," Chashakva explained. "A representative of the lower realms and their interests. He was born in the glorious fields of the fourth branch, far beyond any of the conventions that keep the overworld together—your world is as abstract to him as his is to you. He cannot speak the language of the living, cannot even take mortal form without a host—hence the servant, whose beating heart ensures his safe containment." Ronoah saw the wisewoman's gaze level on Nazum for a moment, the first time she had acknowledged his presence. "To ask for his true face would be to touch burning coals to your own eyes. But as a gesture of goodwill, he will bless you in the language of our people."

Chashakva angled herself toward Ronoah, giving a slight bow, and in Acharrioni she said, "You're doing an excellent job not contradicting me, little demon. I will tell you all you need to know to play a convincing part later, but now is the time to kneel and bless the ground she walks upon. I'm sure you won't fail to impress."

Unable to adequately communicate his exasperation, Ronoah stepped forward. Before the wisewoman could discern the hesitation in his eyes, he knelt and laid his hands on the planks a few inches away from her toes.

He noticed the two littlest ones on her left foot were bandaged together.

With a deep breath, he opened his mouth and put his mother tongue to use.

"I have no idea how to bless people," he began, "seeing as I'm not actually a demon or a denizen of the underworld. My power is limited—if not laughable—but we're here and it's what I have, so it will have to do. Your god—your Seed, she frightens me with her violent demands, but she is divine, and you represent her, and a friend once told me that I needed to respect the customs of others, so—so here I am. Trying to do that."

It was dawning on him that she was taking this rambling seriously. She and Nazum both. They really had no idea. As long as he was convincing enough, he could say anything.

"You frighten me too," he said, "but you haven't thrown us out of this tree to die yet, so I am grateful. For whatever reason, you seem inclined to believe the absolute dunghill my companion is feeding you—" he raised his voice slightly at this "—which in my opinion makes you very generous. Please, keep being generous. Please keep having faith in this, because maybe if you do we can—we can figure out why you're all still dying for this battle when you're not supposed to be. You're not supposed to be," he repeated, and a pang in his chest made his fingers curl reflexively. He caught sight of her toes twitching in tandem, like a static shock had passed between them. "So for what it's worth, I bless the ground you walk upon."

He got to his feet, eyeing the wisewoman for a reaction. She seemed pleased. Grinning her wide grin, she said something to him.

"It tingles," Nazum translated from behind. Surprised, but not all that surprised, Ronoah offered her a small smile back. She put her hands on her hips again, and Ronoah saw that the two littlest fingers on her left hand were bandaged like her toes. "Okay, shiyalshandr, for better or for worse you have my interest. I will have your names in recompense."

"Our emissary is Runa," Chashakva said, placing a hand on Ronoah's shoulder; through it, he felt a vibration like a chuckle. "His servant is Nazum. You may call me Chashakva."

At this, the wisewoman's smile turned rueful. "Mayn't I. Welcome to the overworld, shiyalshandr; I am Chabra'i Subindra, interpreter of the will of Subin, doctor and warrior at your service." She strode to the table and pulled out a chair, spinning it on one leg before pushing it in their direction. "Sit and eat with me, and we shall discuss the War of Heavenly Seeds."

TEN

Chabra'i sent for a meal, then bustled around grabbing dried herbs from bundles and jars, lighting them in a clay brazier with one of her innumerable candles. The others seated themselves at a table in cushioned wicker chairs. That is, Ronoah and Chashakva had chairs—Nazum crouched on the floor next to Ronoah. Ronoah was forcibly reminded of the social hierarchy he'd tried to forget back on the river. It didn't feel right—wouldn't a shiyalshandr's aide be afforded more hospitality than this? He leaned over to ask if Nazum wanted something to sit on, only to receive the boy's hand on his side pushing him back upright.

"You can pity my sore hiney later, demon boy," he hissed under the table. "You offer me a seat, she *will* take offense. Now en't the time to get misty-eyed."

Oddly stung by this rejection, Ronoah shifted in his seat. *Demon boy.* That was who he was now: unearthly being on a field trip from the fourth realm of the Shaipurin underworld. He had no idea whether Nazum believed Chashakva's story—did he have much choice, after seeing her transformation for himself?—but either way, the boy didn't seem about to leak any incriminating details, like *we're speaking Chiropolene* or *they hired me in Bhun Jivakta, not in shiyalsha.* Perhaps, like Chashakva, he saw it as a matter of safety to keep silent.

Safety from whom, though, was impossible to tell from this angle. Ronoah swallowed his questions, his feeble assurances, and waited for their table to be set with something more appealing.

Men came bearing supper: braided loaves of bread, a steaming clay pot of bamboo shoot and taro root, a whole baked catfish stuffed with herbs. The three of them tucked in. Nazum reached for nothing, which concerned Ronoah even more—but after everyone had cleared a first plate, Chashakva broke a hunk of bread off the loaf and passed it to the boy, and Ronoah knew it was okay to feed him henceforth. He piled crispy catfish at the edge of his plate, nudging it in Nazum's direction. He thought he caught a grateful glance—but as the second course began, so did the conversation, and Nazum had to eat his food in stolen snatches between translating.

"All right," Chabra'i said through a mouthful of fish, "explain this to me again. You want me to call off the sacred practice we've partaken in for centuries for the sake of a little breathing room down below?"

"I do." Chashakva sipped the broth from her soup, then proceeded to wave her spoon around like a baton. "Beyond that, I want to know *why it is still happening in the first place*. You began this warring out of a united sense of responsibility, a need to save the world you live in. Unless I am missing something, your world is saved. What in Subin's sweet teeth is keeping you from putting an end to it? And come to think, what did you mean by planning a *raid*? That's not the way of the War."

"Damn, you people don't check in on us much, do you?" Chabra'i picked a fishbone out of her teeth. "Two things, sister. First, the way of the War's changed—the old rules were thrown out generations ago. En't no one left alive who remembers doing it like the legends say."

"Thrown out." Ronoah traced the contour of heavy scepticism in Chashakva's tone. "Thrown out by *whom*?"

"Who else? By the gods." Chabra'i reached for more bread; she kept her two bandaged fingers lifted delicately as she worked a chunk free. "One day the Heavenly Seeds decreed that there needed to be a change in how the war was conducted. The premeditated nature of battle was stripping sacrifices of the visceral emotions the Seeds need for fuel—fear, anger, righteousness, passion. It's not *really* a sacrifice if you come in expecting it, you know?" She popped a tuft of bread into her mouth. "If you're planning for it, that gives you time to separate yourself from it, to be at peace, and peace makes for low-grade fertilizer. They needed the war to stop being fake, so it became real."

Ronoah had to stop eating for a minute, trying to swallow the cold hard stone Chabra'i Subindra had just set on his plate. It made it difficult to want to pick up his spoon again.

"It's a *ritual* war, not a fake one," Chashakva said. "The point of your sacrifice has never been fear or revenge; the power comes of devotion. It comes of love."

"Trust me, sister, I'm with you on this one." Chabra'i's mouth turned down in a genuinely mournful grimace. "Personally I think it's a waste. Never saw the honour in ambushing people while they're unprepared—there's no satisfaction in it, no art. How I covet the pristine battlegrounds of my ancestors. But Subin told my great grandmamu to change things, and we en't the only ones. Unless Subin tells us to change *back*, it's beyond my power—if I go against her wishes, if I tell my people to back down, d'you know what happens to us?"

She picked up her knife and flicked it into the catfish, spearing it in the head. "We all go down to shiyalsha ourselves. Just like the Vashnarajandr."

There was a moment of silence. Nazum took the opportunity to eat his fish.

"Ai?" Chashakva said slowly, regarding the wisewoman with resharpened interest.

"Ahai." Chabra'i dipped her fingers in the soup and flicked the broth at Chashakva playfully. "Surely you know at least *this*, Chashakva? They must have come down in droves, what, three or four years ago?"

Chashakva was silent. Ronoah had the feeling she wasn't going to ask out loud, so, hoping this wouldn't be the precise moment he choked on a fishbone, he asked for her. "What happened?"

"The Vashnarajandr tried this years ago. The whole *return to tradition* thing. They refused to attack unannounced, I think they even called for a Council to reinstate a battle almanac—and then they were murdered, every single one of them. The whole tribe wiped out of existence." The wisewoman sucked her teeth in distaste. "They went back on their promises to their Seed, and they paid for their stubbornness. That, or someone took a chance when they saw it—hard to tell these days, what's for the gods and what's for your grudges. No one will own up to that massacre, so nobody knows."

Beside him, Chashakva had gone still. Ronoah understood. Neither of them had been prepared for a story as horrible as this.

"This," Chashakva eventually said, "is exactly the sort of sweeping extinction your people are supposed to be avoiding. We have gotten off-point: I'm not here to convince you to return to almanacs and artful combat, Lady Subindra, I'm here to make plain that your fighting should cease entirely. An end to the War at last."

Chabra'i snorted. "And this is why I took you for a huckster," she said. Chashakva's expression didn't shift an inch, but Ronoah felt the crackle of irritation snap off her skin. "I just told you an entire tribe was slaughtered for fighting fair—can you imagine what would happen if we went as far as declaring total ceasefire? How can you expect us to take that kind of risk?"

"Because I'm quite certain you people would rather host your jumprope competitions and practice your reed flutes and sip your mango juice *without* the concern that at any point your loved ones could be taken and slain by the arbiters of a neighbouring Seed."

"Ah, sister, what a world that would be, but it's simply not possible in this age."

"Why?" Chashakva demanded, pointing accusatorily with her spoon again. "Why is it not *possible*?"

Ronoah had it before anyone else could speak. "Two things," he said, looking at Chabra'i. "You said there were two reasons why the War isn't over."

For the first time, Chabra'i lost some of her easygoing arrogance. Her full mouth settled in a hard, unhappy line. "There are." She sniffed the air, then stood and went to the brazier, adding a pinch of this, a stem of that. "Stay the night, shiyalshandr," she said. "I will show you tomorrow. It's too dark to venture out now." When Ronoah looked out the window, he realized the air had gone mauve with encroaching darkness. Night pressed in on the treehouse. It made the interior feel flimsy, somehow.

Chabra'i brought them to a hut nestled a level lower than her house, perched in the fork of one of the tree's limbs. As they crossed the rope bridge, Ronoah heard the wisewoman calling orders to her retinue. He also heard Nazum's sharp inhale as they neared the threshold of the hut, felt the boy stiffen behind him.

"What's wrong?" he asked in hushed Chiropolene, but Nazum said nothing. It didn't take long for Ronoah to find out; once they were all gathered in the hut, Chabra'i patted the wall and said a jovial few words which the boy grimly translated:

"This is usually where we keep the sacrifices," she told them cheerily, "before the ceremony happens, you know."

"I did notice the detachable rope bridge, yes," replied Chashakva, with a mild smile of her own.

Ronoah's stomach clenched, but his fear was apparently unfounded; Chabra'i was laughing, putting a hand to her throat. "I'll make sure everyone knows not to come smother you in the night," she grinned. "It'd be a real embarrassment on their part. And you wouldn't even count anyway."

She bid them goodnight as a serving boy lugged in a chest of blankets and reed mats. He set up their bedding, then bowed himself out and hurried across the bridge—the bridge, Ronoah realized, that could be rolled up at any point, leaving them trapped.

Chashakva seemed to trust that Chabra'i Subindra would keep her word. Nazum very obviously did not. Ronoah didn't know where he stood—he trusted Chashakva's read on a situation, but she'd been misinformed once already. What if Chabra'i wasn't as welcoming as she seemed? What if she'd seen through their story and was preparing them to be sacrificed even now?

The worry followed him to bed, circling his mat as he tried unsuccessfully to block it out. After some internal inquiry, he discovered it was actually less a worry that they were in danger of dying—he trusted Chashakva to keep them bodily safe, regardless of what else happened—and more a worry that they were in danger of being found out. Chashakva had told a series of complicated lies, woven a web of falsehood and mystery that Ronoah didn't know if he could maintain. He remembered her apologizing in advance for this.

He rolled over, face to face with the woman; she had her eyes open, waiting for him. "You're right," is what he said in quiet Acharrioni. "It *is* going to be an effort to be convincing."

Chashakva's eyes glittered. "Not as much as I worried," she replied. "Not once we get you caught up on some things."

Into the dark, dense inches between them, she spoke the great tree of shiyalsha. She explained how it hung inverted in the void, its branches growing down towards infinity, its roots tangled with the root web of Shaipuri's overworld in the great woven mat that separated the mortal and immortal planes. She described the five branches of the tree, each a world unto itself, with its own laws and native inhabitants: the first branch, closest to the overworld in character, where regular mortal souls spent their afterlife; the second, more bountiful, more fanciful, built for *the prime cut of life*, for jaguars and wisewomen and the souls of banyan trees. "By Bhun Jivaktandr standards, you would find dead sharks there, too," said Chashakva; "by heartlander standards, you would *not* find dead Bhun Jivaktandr." Ronoah couldn't help but stifle a laugh.

According to myth, the third, fourth, and fifth branches stretched so far away from the overworld that they began to abandon earthly logic—became increasingly conceptual in nature, more symbolic, more impossible to define. Spirit worlds, demon worlds; these were not lands that a human being could understand, let alone inhabit. The exception, presently, being the fifth branch, where the Shaipurin gods resided: as reward for the War of Heavenly Seeds, sacrificial souls were allowed in on the basis of having essentially lent their life essence to a god and thus become pseudo-divine themselves.

"As a visitor from the fourth, you have perfectly acceptable reason not to know how anything works," Chashakva murmured. "By all means, ham it up if you like—next time you see a vase, put it on your head, everyone's too scared to tell you it isn't a hat."

Ronoah's smile at this was more subdued. "I don't want anyone to be scared of me."

"That's beyond your control." Before Ronoah could protest, she continued, her brow arched in fond condescension: "I got the idea from you, you know. For the underworld thing."

"What?"

"*From the other side of the world*, wasn't it? What you told Nazum? That doesn't track for a Shaipur, even one from Bhun Jivakta. In Chiropolene those words mean one thing, but there's only one other side to the world in Shaipuri." She gestured with her eyes at the planks beneath them. Below.

Something shifted then—some agency, some blame. Ronoah wasn't sure how to describe it. Into his disquiet silence, Chashakva cited her sources: "You *are* a blood-and-bone lie detector, thanks to that godling of yours, and you're disturbingly sensitive to other people's feelings if Bazzenine and Jesprechel have anything to say about it. It's true that you wouldn't last long here without Nazum and I to safeguard you—and it's true too that if someone broke that mortal form of yours, I would bring a Maelstrom's worth of fury down on them, and who's to tell the difference? The story's not ultimately a lie. I just gave them a leg-up in understanding it."

Ronoah glared an admonishment at this glib list. "This is what you do, isn't it. You take real things and you twist them into something so farfetched that the original facts are unrecognizable. Or irrelevant."

Chashakva pulled the sheets up to her nose, peeking out impishly. "I'm not the only one, Firewalker."

Sighing as loudly as he dared, Ronoah turned away from Chashakva; once they got into coy one-uppances, the conversation was over. He laid his hand flat on the mat in front of his face, straining to see five fingers branching away in the dark. Wondering, with an aching heart, how many people the Tellers had told that story to by now.

Chashakva nestled into him, the concave of her chest fitting the contour of his spine, her strange twinkling heartbeat against his back. So warm she almost felt cool, so cool she almost felt warm. Slowly, the exhaustion of a long day caught up.

But through half-lidded eyes Ronoah saw Nazum, awake and fretful, sitting on his mat and watching the house's entrance. Bristling, vigilant, seemingly unsure whether it would be worse to receive a visitor or remain untroubled. To be interrupted, or left alone.

ELEVEN

THE MORNING GREETED THEM—all still alive—in a slurry of rain like shattering glass. The downpour continued all throughout the jungle hike Chabra'i Subindra led on the way to her demonstration. Peering from beneath a banana leaf parapluie, Ronoah saw one wonder after another: a cluster of jewel-coloured frogs half-concealed in a patch of mud; a monkey drinking water from the hollow of a bell-shaped plant, little black hands grasping the stem like a goblet; a shelf of fungus growing out the side of a tree, large enough to sleep on.

When they reached the riverbank, Chabra'i retrieved a boat stashed in the reeds and they clambered in: Chabra'i at the front, Chashakva at the back, Ronoah and Nazum wedged in the middle. As they paddled their way downriver, Chabra'i began an impromptu lesson on her Seed.

"Part of Subin's bounty is the medicines she grows," she said over the plashing of rain on the river. "This world is unforgiving by nature. Snakes, spiders, stingers and suckers, demon fever, poison—you make a wrong move, the land will make mulch out of you. Subin cures us of our ailments. Through her gifts we remedy our mistreatment, our stupidity, our bad luck."

She pointed out a bank growing tufts of tubular grass, dusty blue-green in colour. "Dawn grass, good to chew on when something sharp's cut your mouth. Numbs the pain, keeps the bugs out." A willowy tree dripping over an outcrop: "Shouting tree, whose bark is so upsetting to the stomach. Boil it and drink the broth, and whatever rotten thing you ate will be out of you harmless in no time. And there." She stood up in the boat, waving at something Ronoah could not see. "Blue fishfruit, mushrooms that grow low near the jinju palm, a good cure for a sore heart." She did not specify whether she meant it emotionally or physically. Perhaps it was both. "Legend says that when the old age died, the medicines died with it. The rainforest collapsed, crumbled into ruin. No goodness, no green—just the body of a dead creator, rotting off the bones. Centuries of sacrifice brought the land back, species by species, but before the War of Heavenly Seeds began, all of this had disappeared."

"That is…it's hard to imagine," Ronoah said. All this intimidating liveliness—to imagine it culled and curdling was something even his disaster-happy brain was having trouble doing. It felt like it belonged to the myth, not the actual happenings of the War.

Chabra'i laughed. "Won't be so hard in a minute or two," she said, oddly bitter. "Just you wait."

Mystified, Ronoah waited. And a minute or two later, the rain stopped, and he looked ahead, and understood.

They'd rowed into a wasteland.

The canopy thinned until there was more sky than tree. The lush ferns on the riverbanks dwindled in size and then disappeared altogether, abruptly, as the river emptied into a lagoon gone rusty at the edges with algae. The water was torpid, stifled; no skittering bugs, no shimmering fish, just cloudy brown-green bordered by slimy piles of decomposing vegetation.

There was no noise. Ronoah registered it after a confused minute trying to figure out what was making his ears ring—the cacophony of the rainforest had simply stopped at the border, unwilling to follow them in. Only a few brave birds perched atop the crumbling stumps. In the air, the fetid malodour of unnatural decay—not the sweet rot of hay or ripened fruit, but the nose-tingling, lung-itching stink of something dying of disease.

It felt parasitic. It made him want to scrub his skin raw.

"What," Chashakva said, her voice filled with a weight Ronoah had seldom heard before, "is this."

"This is why the War's not over, sister, and why your claims of ending it are hard to believe." Chabra'i used her pole to prod at a mound of limp reeds tangled on the surface of the lagoon. Nazum's voice sounded about as grim as she looked. "Because the world en't fixed yet. When we send out scouts, I get reports of patches like this as far as Rugakashndr territory." She sifted through the reed pile as if searching for signs of movement. Finding nothing, she tipped it into the water. "There's probably more all over everywhere."

Ronoah thought of this blight perforating the rainforest, punching it through with sludgy yellow holes. A part of him, equally empathetic and analytic, could see why all the sacrifice had gotten started. Why a people would resort to anything to prevent something like this from spreading.

He looked to Chashakva—and a shiver shook him from the inside out.

It was the first time he'd seen her truly angry.

"What's—what is causing this?" he asked Chabra'i, peering out at the muggy lagoon with his eyes squinted half-shut. Vespasi wake, his body protested even the sight of it. "Where does it come from?"

"You tell me, shiyalshandr. I was kind of hoping you would recognize it as something from your side of things." When Ronoah shook his head, the wisewoman sighed. "Worth a try. Way I see it, the Seeds still en't up to multitasking. Letting things slide in one place while they attend to another—you know, like when you put the kettle on the fire and then get so distracted you forget it's there, until it starts screaming and spitting boiling water all over the place?" She spread her arms. "Welcome to the kettle. We're all going to boil alive in here if we don't do something."

"But it—it *has* to be sacrificing people?"

"It's the only thing that's ever worked before."

Chashakva made a noise somewhere between amused snort and agitated growl. Everyone looked, waiting for her to speak, but she said nothing. She remained silent for the rest of the ghastly tour, prickling with intensity. It made Ronoah worry what would happen when she finally opened her mouth.

As they left the deadzone and re-entered the rainforest, he was hit with relief so palpable it left him lightheaded. The thousand sounds of the jungle, previously overwhelming to him, were a comfort after that eerie silence.

It took them another hour to row back upriver. When they climbed onto the bank, Chashakva put her hands on her hips and said, "Congratulations, wisewoman, you have officially made this my problem."

"Ai?" came Chabra'i's voice from among the reeds as she stowed the boat.

"Ahai." Chashakva looked out at the river, as if she could see the deadzone from here. "It's time for this all to end."

"You say it like it's so easy, I'm nearly offended." The wisewoman emerged from the reeds, one cynical eyebrow raised. "How are you planning to fix this, shiyalshandr?"

"I'm calling for a Council of All Tribes."

The weight of the words chilled Ronoah—but Chabra'i and Nazum both started laughing. Chashakva stood and waited for them to be done.

"Sister, no one goes to Councils anymore," Chabra'i finally said, regaining herself. "S'got *mystique* when you say it, like it used to be—but no. We've had, hm, maybe three in the last hundred years? All failures. I don't think even half the tribes showed up to the last one, and that was about the Vashnarajandr."

"You don't think?" asked Chashakva, unnervingly even. Chabra'i shrugged, unabashed.

"Didn't go. Sent a representative. It's real worrisome what happened to the Vashnarajandr, but there's no point in going and leaving *my* tribe vulnerable. Everyone else apparently felt the same—and if they wouldn't even show up for the destruction of a whole village, what makes you think they'll answer *your* call?"

Chashakva tilted her head. "Are you saying you won't go?" Ronoah had the urge to take her hand—to hold her back, to pacify the dangerous rumble in her voice that perhaps only he could hear.

"I'm saying I'll need convincing, Chashakva." Chabra'i chin-pointed in the direction of the river. "And so will everyone else."

At this, Chashakva relented. A change came over her, a sense of finality. Ronoah saw her settle into it, saw her next steps resolve in the upturned corner of her lips. "So be it," she answered.

Three puny words, but they shocked him deep in the bones; they stood in for a commitment as wide as the heartland itself, a promise made in the same titanic tone as the Great Wheel turning. *This side-trip might take a little longer than I anticipated.* Not a few days, not a few tribes, not anymore. Chashakva intended to visit every single one of them, all—how many again?—all eighteen tribes of the heartland, to persuade them to put aside their distrust and come together to solve the War. To end it.

Seventeen, a voice corrected him. Seventeen tribes. The Vashnarajandr won't be solving anything.

It didn't seem like Nazum was taking this development in stride. He was stony-faced the whole way back to the Subindr village, only opening his mouth when he needed to bounce words back and forth. He caught Ronoah looking, and gave him a glare of such helpless frustration that Ronoah was, absurdly, shamed into looking away. It must have been a blow to learn how long he was going to be away from Bhun Jivakta—that, or he was still smarting about having his soul tied to a parasitic demon.

Now who's the shark, that same voice asked, *and who's the suckerfish?*

It needled him, the look on Nazum's face. It needled him all the way back to Chabra'i's village. Upon their return to the treehouse, Chashakva and Chabra'i began rifling through cabinets—searching, Chashakva explained quickly, for tokens to indicate the wisewoman's goodwill. The two spoke in such rapid, muffled Shaipurin that Nazum eventually gave up on translating and just sat with Ronoah on a bench—and Ronoah felt his throat constrict in sympathetic resonance with Nazum's tension, and decided he couldn't leave the boy isolated any longer.

"Nazum, I'm sorry," he said quietly, as they watched the house get ransacked. "What Chashakva said about, about us being, about you and me—"

"Don't wanna hear it," was the boy's reply, his eyes fixed resolutely on the back of Chashakva's head. "What was it your lady said? *Favour of the gods themselves?* Funny joke. Hoping I can trade it for at least a few jade beads when this is over."

"But it wasn't—" Setten and Ibisca, but it *sounded* like. It sounded like they had set this up from the beginning. Nazum must have been kicking himself for getting tricked that way. "Nazum, I understand this is how you make your living, but if it's, if it's really something you cannot stand to do—"

"Then I'm gonna have to suck it up and do it anyway, *shiyalshandr*," Nazum said, and there was a sneer to the word when he said it, a derision that took Ronoah aback. The boy scratched irritably at the scars on his shoulder. "What, you think you can just unlatch and let your poor host go back to Bhun Jivakta? You don't understand a damn thing about this place. The deal's been made *for* me. Lady Sikundhasma sold my whole bond to you— not a day's labour, not a month's, not three years. My whole fucking life."

What? Ronoah frowned. That wasn't …Chashakva hadn't told him—

"It's true," the boy said flatly, clearly interpreting the look on Ronoah's face. "It's on record. I been sold to your jaguar lady for as long as she needs me to take care of *you*. When that's done, shit, she has every right to drag me down to shiyalsha with her. I so much as show my face in Bhun Jivakta without her officially returning me, no one'll ever believe I didn't just run."

That explained it—the confidence with which Nazum had approached them, the way that confidence had faltered the moment Chashakva and Lady Sikundhasma had agreed on an exchange. The boy had been expecting to sell his service, not his soul.

But wasn't that all the more reason to want to know who he'd been sold to? "I'm sorry, really, I'm trying to explain—"

"And I told you I don't wanna know." The boy allowed himself one terse, restrained snort. "It doesn't matter who you are or *what* you are— the important thing is you own me, demon boy. Explanations en't gonna make that any easier."

It was like running into an invisible wall; it just didn't make sense. The not-knowing would have tormented Ronoah, in Nazum's place. But before he could say something about it, Chashakva turned around, and Nazum stood up roughly and went towards her. Wrestling with the feeling that he'd somehow made the whole situation worse, Ronoah followed suit.

Three orange gemstones nestled in Chashakva's hand—at least that's

what Ronoah thought they were, until he noticed the dark shapes floating inside each stone. Were those—bees? "Amber," Chashakva called
it, which made him blink. He'd seen amber in Lavola's incense shops,
but it was opaque, crumbly like fudge, nothing like the glassy eggs in
Chashakva's palm.

"Very rare amber," came Chabra'i's disgruntled correction. She was
standing with her weight thrown into one hip, arms folded. Apparently
she wasn't eager to give them away. "The kind of gift that'll signal how
committed I am to Lady Chashakva's plan. A sacrifice in its own right, if
you ask me."

Chashakva slipped the amber into a satchel with a long drawstring and
put it around her neck, where it settled among the clicking beads of her
jade necklaces. "Right. No time to waste. It will likely take three or four
weeks to reach all of the quadrant's villages and make our case—I shall do
my best to speed my return, but you can't rush negotiations like these."

Ronoah's stomach went cold. "Your return?"

"Did you think you were coming with me? No, no, you're staying here
with the wisewoman until I get back."

It seemed this was news to everyone but Chashakva herself—Ronoah
and Nazum both made inelegant, involuntary noises, and even Chabra'i
raised her eyebrows. "Why aren't—why aren't you bringing them?"
Nazum translated for her, tripping over words in his own distress. "You
ask much of me already, sister, and now I've extra mouths to feed on top?"

Chashakva was rubbing dirt off a knuckle. "You know how it goes," she
said; "Seventy-two tricks, and all that. Or four hundred thirteen, however
your mamu taught it to you. I am not cowed by the chaos of your overworld;
in fact, I am built to bring it to order. But our fourth-branch representative
is still finding his living legs. He's here to learn, and who better to learn
from than the servant of Subin, teacher of health and wholeness?" In case
this flattery wasn't quite enough to win Chabra'i over, she added, "Once
I return, you won't be bothered by us again—until the Council happens."

"If it happens," Chabra'i countered. It wasn't argumentative; she genuinely just seemed sceptical of success. The wisewoman sucked her teeth,
then said through a sigh: "I suppose it is an honour, to put up with an
exalted being for a few weeks. But you won't be getting no reverence
from me, shiyalshandr, not without earning it. If you're staying here,
you're pulling your weight."

Ronoah nodded, too distracted to pay much attention to what he
was agreeing to. He'd felt the foreboding of the deadzone, the inevitable
approach of a tipping point, but in all his concerned catastrophizing, he
hadn't prepared for this.

"Can I—can we talk for a moment?" he asked Chashakva. "Before you go?"

He led them to the edge of the room, beside the door. His heart was pounding so hard he could feel it in the roof of his mouth. "You never said we'd split up," he said in Acharrioni. He was trying, really, he was doing his best to live up to all that he'd promised—he was trying to be adaptable, to be flexible, to run the gauntlet and understand, but— "You never said I'd be in this place *alone.*"

"You're not alone," the woman replied. "You have Nazum with you."

Ronoah let his expression convey exactly how little that comforted him. Chashakva rested her hand on his shoulder. "We got lucky with Chabra'i. She is endeared by you."

"Is she?" Ronoah asked, laughing a slightly desperate laugh. "I hadn't noticed."

"Call it culture clash. Or a brash personality. Either way, it remains valuable to us. She is inclined to share her shelter and her table, which is apparently a stroke of good fortune. If what she's said is true, then not every wisewoman will take so flippantly to a pack of strangers waltzing into their territory—even magical ones. You really are safer here."

Again with the safety. He didn't remember her ever being so concerned before. Maybe she'd done it all along and hadn't bothered to tell him; maybe the situation really was that much more threatening. Maybe she had just come to care about him enough to warrant the worry.

"I'm safe with *you*," he muttered, feeling at once childish and justified.

Chashakva smiled one of her manifold smiles, lifting her hand to push playfully against his forehead. "That's never been true."

"What—" He swatted at her while she chuckled. "What do I do until you get back? What do I tell people, how do I explain—?" Nazum's glare flashed in his mind's eye. He bit his lip, fighting a flutter of anxiety. "How do I make this work?"

"Vase for a hat, remember?" At the unfettered dismay on his face, Chashakva tisked. "Oh, Firewalker, just *be yourself*. With your clove bones and garnet heart, your stories of the ocean and the desert, your fellow-feeling for the monsters that walk this earth—you're a strange enough human to pass as a different creature altogether. If you ever get truly stuck in it, then call on that mother of yours." She lifted her eyes to the hundred honeyed flames illuminating the room. "I'm sure she'll have an idea or two."

As if in agreement, a spark of warmth flared deep in Ronoah's gut. In the way that kindness can crack a dam, it only made his emotions well up stronger. He swallowed, hard. He put his hands on Chashakva's arms, aiming a look straight into her eyes.

"This is scary," he whispered. Saying it any louder would make his voice break.

Gentle light glinted under the woman's skull—sapphire magenta mauve, a smattering of stars peeking out before veiling themselves again. Transparency, as literally as she could show it. "I know, little brave," she answered, leaning in to kiss the top of his head. "I know."

She had never used that name before. Ronoah closed his eyes, savouring the fact that he'd earned it. Savouring the sense of security that surrounded him, trying to store it up for when he might need it.

"Granted," she continued blithely, "most of the time when *you* go in scared you just come out slightly embarrassed."

Ronoah nearly headbutted her on instinct. She dodged, laughed again, and hearing the unwavering confidence in that laugh made him feel a little more confident himself. He gave her the richest glare he could muster, full of exasperation and anxiety but also faith and good humour. He trusted her to catch every layer.

"That's more like it," she said, cradling his face affectionately with one hand before giving it a lighthearted little smack. By the time he'd blinked away the sting, she was out the door. He followed her through the swinging bead curtains, leaning over the ledge to watch her diminishing form as she descended the tree, as distance dissolved the sight of her into nothing but a silhouette, nothing but a smudge, nothing at all.

He sent a prayer after her. Just in case.

Behind him, he heard Chabra'i speaking. A staggered moment later, Nazum's voice joined in: "So the first thing you're gonna do is help me put my house back in order."

Squaring his shoulders, Ronoah turned and began.

TWELVE

*T*HE LIFE OF CHABRA'I SUBINDRA was a busy one. Ronoah found this out over the next few days as he and Nazum worked to earn their keep. She did everything with a vigour, a grinning briskness; she rose early and retired late and thought naps were for the weak. The first thing she did in the morning was hike the length of her tree, down and back up, checking on her dozens of papery beehives—listening, she said, for Subin's will in the rhythm and pitch of the bee-buzz. After that came the patients. Some would arrive at her door bearing small offerings, a cake wrapped in banana leaves or a new candle; others, Chabra'i would journey to herself. Ronoah and Nazum got lots of exercise on those mornings, as she used them to fetch instruments and ingredients she needed and hadn't thought to pack.

When she wasn't mending the ills of her village, Chabra'i was training. She would practice for hours, sparring against the other Subindr warriors, testing and besting them at hand-to-hand combat and all manner of weaponry, ropes and knives and a thin but vicious quarterstaff she was fond of.

At first Ronoah squirmed to see it, twitching every time he heard a grunt of pain or a crack of the staff. But Nazum saw him flinch and looked at him funny—*sure you're from down below?* asked that frown—and so in order to avoid arousing suspicion he made it into a challenge for himself, to watch without reacting. If he framed it a certain way he could understand it as the art form Chabra'i claimed it was: a tradition perfected by necessity, a gift passed down generation by generation. That made things easier.

In the precious hours the wisewoman had free of her obligations, she went on excursions into the rainforest, returning with baskets of blue fishfruit, of shouting tree. Enough to last until the next flush, no more. "Most are hard enough to pick when you show up at the *right* time, let alone walking in and ignoring their preferences," she'd say, threading a needle through her mushrooms and stringing them up to dry. "You want the medicines to work for you, you gotta respect what they're willing to give and when they're willing to give it—which means I go whenever I have a second, or tomorrow's rashes will go untreated for my laziness."

Much to Chabra'i's amusement, Ronoah asked if he could help on these excursions. "Runa, you're cute, but the last thing I need is some—" Nazum snickered, then continued "—some overeager stampcrab trampling my bushes. You stay right here."

Which left Ronoah feeling thoroughly expendable. Apparently the cover story of being a fourth-branch demon was working *too* well: Chabra'i didn't expect him to know how anything important worked, or to be any good at it, which meant she only assigned him the most menial of tasks. Power came with tight limitations—even illusory power. When Chabra'i went on her journeys, Ronoah would wander the walkways of the massive tree, and sulk, and miss the days of the monastery, when every single thing he'd done had built towards something bigger, even if he hadn't known it at the time.

Eventually, like a vine climbing a hundred-foot tree to reach the sun, his need to help in a meaningful way reached Genoveffa. Eventually, like the rays fighting a way through the canopy, her answer came rebounding back. One day Chabra'i returned from a gleaning with hands and feet that were shiny and swollen with bug bites. "With me, shiyalshandr," she grunted. "Turns out there is something you can do."

Something turned out to be giving the woman a foot massage.

Chabra'i was seated by her armoire, mixing together two creams and a powder into a little dish. Ronoah was on the ground beside her, trying to shove down his mounting embarrassment.

In Pilanova, the bottoms of the feet were considered an incredibly intimate area. It was one reason why getting them tattooed was a rite of passage—beyond just demonstrating your patience and discipline, you were submitting to the collective power of the community. With the exception of family members, asking someone to rub your feet was the kind of thing you only did after a lengthy courtship.

Chabra'i spoke; Ronoah looked up to see her handing him the dish, now filled with a pale orange cream. He set it beside him, and then he sat there like a fool trying to figure out how to approach this. Which foot did he start with? How much pressure was too much? If he tickled her by accident, would he get kicked in the face—?

"In case you're wondering, it's not spreadable," the wisewoman quipped. Nazum spared Ronoah a look as he translated that was nearly sympathetic. Apparently he did not envy Ronoah his task.

He wanted to shake himself for his discomfort. Come on, he thought, it's only weird if they know it's weird. And they don't. They have no idea that she may as well have propositioned you. Just go for it.

With only a slight heat in his cheeks, he started to massage Chabra'i's right foot. She made a stifled snarl of discomfort, and he asked, "Does it hurt?"

"It's starting to," was her answer, delivered with another self-directed huff. "The biters numb the skin when they break it, so it takes a few hours before you notice how pocked full of holes you are."

So different from stark Acharrio, where the things that hit you—sand flies, scorpions, sidewinders—hit fast and hard. Even Shaipuri's insects planned sneak attacks. Ronoah kneaded at the arch of Chabra'i's foot. Her toes curled in response.

"I'm ashamed of myself," she continued, sounding completely unashamed. "What an embarrassment, limping in so ungraceful-like when there are underworlders present. This never happens—I've known since I was a kid when and where to go to avoid bloodsuckers." She sucked her teeth. "Serves me right for getting greedy."

Ronoah smoothed cream up to her ankle, working at the bones. "Greedy?"

"Walking where I normally don't, taking what I usually leave alone. There are places in the forest where no bug can touch me, and places where I'm just another warmblood lolloping around. I've been intruding and this is what I pay for it."

"Why the change? What's—there must be a reason?"

"Overharvesting," came Chabra'i's unhappy reply, accompanied by a slightly happier grunt as Ronoah pressed his thumb into the bottom of her heel. "Maashava root, specifically. I keep needing to run further afield to gather enough without completely stripping my regular patches. It's time consuming, and clearly not pleasant work"—she withdrew her foot from Ronoah's grip, pointing and flexing as if to demonstrate—"but alas, I have no choice."

She recrossed her legs and offered him her left foot to tackle. Ronoah was about to ask what was so special about maashava root when the wisewoman made a sudden, remembering noise, and pulled her foot up over her knee. She unwrapped the bandage around her two little toes, and Ronoah saw something he didn't expect.

"What happened to your toes?" he asked instead.

In place of two toes was one mass, crooked and a little shriveled, with a lopsided, double-capped nail that tipped him off to the fact that it was, in fact, two toes fused together.

"Oh, I was born like that," Chabra'i said, wiggling the appendages in question. "Got 'em on two paws out of four, see?" She unwrapped the two smallest fingers of her left hand—smallest finger, perhaps, he thought, wondering whether it counted as just one.

"I thought you had—injured yourself, before we arrived," he said, embarrassed to admit it. Chabra'i's physical dexterity was not something to underestimate. "Why do you keep them bandaged?"

"Same reason I dress them with honey every day." She twisted to root around in the drawers of her armoire, as if mentioning it had reminded her. "Because otherwise stuff will—oh, gods, *ew*—stuff'll *burrow* in there. Fungus, bloodsuckers, you name it. *Chuta ka saag.*"

Ronoah raised his eyebrows at Nazum. The boy waved a hand in apology, eyes squinched shut.

"What can I say? I'm a high-maintenance lady." The wisewoman uncorked a bottle with a punctuating flourish. She poured a honey so clear it passed for water onto a cottony tuft of fibre and dabbed at her fingers. "And there's no taking the economical way out. If I cut them off and sent them to shiyalsha, the tribe would be scandalized."

"Why?"

"Because they freaking named me for them, you foolheaded demon," she laughed, sneaking a teasing glance at him through the mirror. "*Chabra'i*: She of Nine Toes. This is how I got the job—at least in part. There's magic in these little uglies. They're sacred."

A voice rang in Ronoah's head—his own, insistent and echo-fringed by the vast open spaces of the monastery. *Where I am from, the body is the soul.* One of the oldest Acharrioni tenets; one of the few organizing principles he'd brought with him from Pilanova. Here, too?

It made him smile—so they shared some things after all. Maybe they went about expressing it differently, but the underlying philosophy was the same. He could connect.

Carefully he smoothed cream over the cleft in Chabra'i's fused toes, reverent over this most holy part of her. In some deep-seated place, he felt his Acharrioni propriety loosen and relax as he attended to the wisewoman's irritated skin with all the focus of date-picking, or coffeemaking, or weaving a red wrap.

When he was finished, Chabra'i anointed her toes with honey before dressing them in fresh, dry bandages. She rolled her ankles with a grimace. "It's not ideal," she said, "but we don't waste our time waiting for the ideal to appear. We'll give it half an hour for the cream to set, and then we should be okay for training."

Suddenly her irritation made more sense—the bites were going to compromise her agility while fighting. "Do you have to train today?" Ronoah asked. "You practice every day for hours at a time—surely you could rest for one afternoon? To let yourself heal?"

Chabra'i scoffed. "If you only practice when you're in good shape, what happens when the real thing comes? You gonna pass just because you've got a runny nose or a headache? Besides, the training en't for me. I don't need three hours of practice a day—I'm fast like an adder, strong like a boar. It's for the rest of those blundering klutzes, Subin bless their lungs. I'm captain, so I'm in charge of teaching. And with the raid coming up, they need all the teaching they can get."

"The—sorry, the raid?" Ronoah blinked. "What are you...?"

Too late, it came back to him. A throwaway comment, delivered flippantly on their first night here, before any of their grand plans had been set in motion.

"...You're planning on capturing sacrifices," he said slowly. He wanted so badly to be mistaken.

"Sure am. Been planning it over a month now." Chabra'i uncorked another jar sitting by the mirror and dabbed some oil onto the splash of acne scars around her chin. "Got a couple weeks of prep left. Should be a good haul."

She said something else, and Nazum translated, but Ronoah didn't hear. All the sound had been sucked out of the room, replaced by a dull ringing.

How could he have forgotten?

It had just never been brought up again, and he'd never thought to ask, never thought to question what it was that Chabra'i and the other warriors were training *for*. Or perhaps he'd had the vague understanding that it was for an attack but had just never assumed it was scheduled to happen *now*, while he was here in the village to witness it—perhaps he'd assumed their arrival would put things on hold. How egotistical of him. How naïve.

"But—" No, not in Acharrioni. He stopped himself, switched languages: "But doesn't that, won't that undermine Chashakva's negotiations?"

Chabra'i was rummaging through the cabinet again. "Runa, first of all, Chashakva's negotiating to call us to Council, not to stop us from sending honourable souls your way. That gets decided *at* Council, if we make it that far. And second of all—" She closed the cabinet and swivelled in her seat to face him pointedly. "Second of all, because I have a generous heart, I'm already pushing the raid back an extra week to give your lady time to return. It's very inauspicious, you have no idea how confused everyone is that I'm making the call. But I'm making it. If Chashakva returns within the three weeks she proposed, and with a favourable response, then I'll be impressed enough to follow her lead until the Council meets. If she doesn't, I'm going to assume she's either been banished back to shiyalsha or eaten by those fucking banshees down south." She shrugged. "And then I'll run my raid."

So the only thing stopping Chabra'i and her warriors from swinging down into a neighbouring tribe and exploding everyone's lungs in their chests was...Chashakva's sense of timing?

Ronoah felt like he might throw up.

"My—she, my companion is a little, a little overzealous with her estimates," he said, hoping Nazum's confident tone would mask his panic. On some things—a synchronicity here, a bit of weather prediction there—Chashakva's sense of timing was impeccable, but on anything human in scale her track record was so hilariously bad, her frame of reference so askew, that Ronoah regularly amused himself by making her guess people's ages. He didn't think Chashakva knew what a week *was*. "I think she might have meant an approximate date, not three weeks exactly—"

"Then she should've said so," Chabra'i countered, reasonably. "I didn't know you were so against this, Runa. Are a few more souls really gonna break the banks of shiyalsha?"

"That isn't—" With a start, Ronoah remembered that was the story Chashakva had spun: a story about balance and displeasure and the whims and wraths of gods. A story the Shaipurin could respect. "That isn't the point," he said quietly.

"Ai? What, then?"

His own version of things, tender with pathos, might not be so convincing. But he had to try.

"If Chashakva is right," he began, "then you're—you're killing people for *nothing*. That isn't sacrifice, it's murder." He suddenly wished he were still massaging her foot, that he had something to do with his hands. "I thought the death of all people was what you were trying to *avoid*. What's the point if you end up just destroying each other?"

The wisewoman inclined her head in an acknowledgement that somehow failed to be encouraging. "I like people—a lot. I care about my village, my kin. But people aren't what I'm defending, shiyalshandr. It's the rainforest itself. I don't enjoy the idea of killing for no reason, but you saw the deadzone. If the War keeps that from spreading, I wage the War, simple as."

"And what if it's making it worse?"

That earned him a look sharp as a bee sting. He steeled himself, followed through. "Chashakva saw the deadzone, too—it was only *after* she saw it that she decided to take this so seriously. You have to consider that they're connected, in a different way than, than you were taught." And maybe it was the thought of Chashakva, that brazen confidence of hers worming into him by proxy, but he made a split-second decision and pushed even further: "You said Subin hasn't told you to back down. Have you *asked* her?"

Chabra'i's face creased in an affront that seemed—off. It reminded him of something, though he couldn't identify it. "I commune every morning with her messengers, if you haven't noticed."

Another smoke-wisp of Chashakva's influence floated into his mind: *and he always knows a lie.* "With respect," he said, meeting her gaze, "that isn't an answer."

He noted the tightness around the corners of Chabra'i's mouth as she replied. "Subin hasn't communicated a change of heart since she spoke to my great grandmamu. Runa, the fuck are you doing trying to get between a wisewoman and her Seed?" Ronoah blinked; that wasn't a translation. Nazum had delivered it flawlessly covert, but it was the boy's own opinion, his own warning. The first time he'd pitched in for days.

Far from dissuading Ronoah, however, this only added more kindling to the fire of inspiration. Ronoah hadn't thought to even argue this point— it felt risky, bold in a way that made his palms sweaty, but—but Chabra'i's second answer was indirect as the first, and Chabra'i Subindra was not in the habit of being indirect. In a snap it came to him: her reaction reminded him of the clerk in Bhun Jivakta's trade house, performing heavy offense to mask something beneath. Uncertainty.

So he latched on and bit down. "If the killing *is* making it worse, maybe Subin can't communicate like she used to. Maybe she can't get through to you." Something truly dangerous shone in Chabra'i's eye and he rushed to finish before Nazum's job got infinitely harder— "I'm not from your world, I don't know your rules or your methods. But I'm—a good conduit." He thought of Jesprechel's voice finding him in the caves; of Özrek calling him a prism, a butterfly net. Of his own body hurtling through a city ablaze. "I'm good at talking to gods no matter where I am, it's a fourth branch thing."

Chabra'i snorted—but she replied, which meant she was still entertaining him. "You want to intercede. Not a chance, shiyalshandr. I'd never know it if you tricked me."

"You would if I could prove it to you," he insisted. "Tell me what I must do. Tell me how I prove she's on my side."

The sound of his own voice sent a tiny shudder through him. He had to admit, he would pay attention too, if someone sounded that intense.

Chabra'i growled something that Nazum didn't repeat. By its rough edges, he took it to be a curse. "I've been overharvesting maashava root for a reason," she finally said, her mouth puckered as if she disliked the taste of the situation. "There's a sickness going around. You've seen glimpses at my housecalls—dry cough, high fever, nasty rash. I've been softening symptoms with maashava tinctures, but the medicine I need to actually purge the disease is ... out of season."

"Which medicine?" Ronoah asked.

"Guguri." The word came out of Nazum's mouth a moment after Chabra'i's—the same word. Exactly the same.

Ronoah swiveled to Nazum. "That's not Chiropolene."

"No? Well shit, I don't know what to tell you." Ronoah's stare intensified, and Nazum threw up his hands. "I'm not a damn codex, demon boy, the Chirope I learned didn't prepare me for a career in herbalism—it's *guguri*, that's all I got for you."

"Look, shiyalshandr. Here's what you can do." Chabra'i was talking again, and any further protestations Nazum might've had were cut short as he resumed his translating. "I need this plant. Right now it is withheld from me. If you can produce even *one* guguri bud, I'll take it as a token of Subin's favour."

And the raid would be called off. The possibility glimmered to life, bright as a tiny sun inside him.

"Where does it grow?" he asked, and saw the grim smile resolve on Chabra'i's face and knew the answer coming was a trap sprung, something defeatingly self-evident, something like—

"It used to grow in the deadzone. That's where the mature trees were. I've only ever seen seedlings elsewhere, too young to flower."

One of these days, Ronoah thought, I'm going to be given a challenge I'm actually equipped to handle.

But the challenge had been issued. And that meant he had a chance, however slight.

Thirteen

$\mathcal{A}$ WEEK LATER, Ronoah realized that 'slight' was a generous description of the size of his chances.

It would have been hard enough, tracking down a plant that even the local wisewoman couldn't find. It transcended difficulty and became pure absurdity when you factored in that he didn't even know what it *was*. He attacked this challenge from all angles: he quizzed Nazum right to the end of the boy's patience, and then a little further; he spoke to the villagers, asking if anyone had any guguri stashed away in their cupboards. (His reputation as an underworld creature must have spread, because they all tended to avoid him, and to be quick and suspicious in their responses when they were cornered.) In his frustration, he even braved a return to the deadzone, rowing alongside Nazum into the stagnant lagoon and poking around the edges, sifting through muck for a miracle.

He wished desperately that Chashakva were here—if she were, she could probably just conjure the guguri from thin air. Then again, a voice reminded him, if Chashakva were here, you wouldn't be running around looking for mystery medicine anyway.

Chabra'i reserved a hut on ground-level as a quarantine for victims of the illness. Ronoah and Nazum watched her minister to the sick, easing their suffering with her hard-earned maashava root, talking them through their shakes with an easygoing confidence that was in stark contrast to her actual words:

"There's only two ways this goes, brother," she'd say, blotting some-one's brow or measuring out a tincture. "Either you live and you get to play and fight and die another time, or you chuck it now, and head down to shiyalsha where none of this nonsense will bother you no more."

Amazingly, this seemed to genuinely comfort the villagers. For Ronoah, it only added to the urgency of his search—if he could find enough guguri, not only would the raid be called off, but the people of Subin would be cured.

Whenever he felt like the task was about to overwhelm him, a memory would surface instead. *You know, I only put you to the occasions I have faith you can rise to.* Come on, he'd say to himself—if you can survive seven months looking for something that didn't even physically exist, you can sniff out something that does in a couple more weeks. Chashakva wouldn't have left you if she didn't believe in you; she wouldn't give you a problem without a hint on how to solve it. It's what she's always done before.

Still, it took until mid-way through the third and final week of his allowance that he resorted to the woman's advice:

If you ever get truly stuck in it, call on that mother of yours—I'm sure she'll have an idea or two.

Genoveffa wasn't Subin, but she was a god nonetheless. Perhaps, from one god to another, she could pass a message along.

It was logistically both very simple and very tricky, to consult Genoveffa. All Ronoah needed was a fire, and ideally some salt and cloves, both of which he still had from the monastery. The *what* was easy—it was the *when* and *where* that posed a challenge. After all this time, he still didn't feel comfortable communing with Genoveffa in front of people, and he was with either Chabra'i or Nazum every moment of the day. He doubted Nazum would allow it if he asked to be left alone—after all, his life depended on Ronoah's safety. The boy stuck to him like a particularly snarky burr. The only way to catch ten minutes of privacy was to wait until everyone was asleep.

For once he considered it lucky that he slept so poorly. It meant he could go to bed trusting he'd be up in two hours' time, when the rest of the village was slumbering.

In the dead of night, Ronoah retrieved his ingredients and stole from the hut, circling up to Chabra'i's treehouse. There were plenty of braziers to choose from on those tables, and besides, he figured if he wanted anyone to catch him mid-prayer, it would be the wisewoman. She'd take it for shiyalshandr magic. He slipped into a version of the treehouse he'd never seen before: in shadow, the candles unlit. Cautiously he chose a clay brazier and loaded it with kindling. He struck a spark, cast his pinches of salt and clove into the gathering flames, and took a seat on one of Chabra'i's bolsters. With a deep breath he searched within himself, sought the eloquence he could sometimes summon when he prayed.

"Oh Genoveffa, daughter of Pao," he began, remembering with a pang the way Chashakva had called upon his godling back in the caves, "blade of truth and wisdom, sunskinned lily queen, oh errant, perfect firestorm—oh mother mine," he prayed, bowing his head to the fire, "I ask your counsel, if you have a minute."

The heat wicked away the stickiness of the rainforest. It caressed his cheek, and he took it to mean she was listening.

"So I know this is completely outside your usual dominion," he said, grimacing in apology, "but could you talk to Subin about something? Her people need this, this plant, only they can't find it anywhere, and if I can find it then I can save them—and also the others, I can save the people they're going to sacrifice. If Subin can show me where they are, the guguri, that—I could do something big, with that." He bit his lip as something else occurred to him. "And if she's really not strong enough to grow them, maybe, maybe Setten and Ibisca could help?" It was unlikely that the sibling godlings of agriculture and livestock held any sway here—but then again, Genoveffa had come this far with him, hasn't she? He'd once heard it right from the mouth of a priestess that *gods travel the same way people do.* Maybe all they needed was an invitation.

So he invited them. He invoked them, coaxing them with fragments of poetry and supplication, murmuring his thanks and praise until the undulating flames and the enveloping smell of cloves lulled him into another space, another state. He felt like he was suddenly viewing this crisis from a distance, from the seat of something so huge and so old it could see back to before this war had begun, and forward to a time long past its end. That was how he knew his prayers had been heard.

It struck him in the midst of this cosmic objectivity just how miraculous it was, that he was sitting here and making the pleas he was making. It hadn't been in his plan to visit Shaipuri at all until Chashakva brought it up. All this war and secrecy and suffering—he would have sailed right past it without a second thought, on the way to the Pilgrim State. It was hard to imagine. Now that he was here, feeling the pain of the rainforest in his own bones, it was amazing that there was a version of him only a few weeks younger that hadn't cared at all.

Plans changed, with or without your permission. Priorities shifted. Ronoah pleased himself by realizing he wasn't fighting it this time, wasn't trying to lock down the uncertainty of unfolding events. Perhaps this was a lesson he had finally, finally learned.

"Hey, look," he said quietly, smiling down at the ramble of flames. "I'm finally doing something right."

At the very least, the fire winked back, you are doing *something.*

It was at this point that Nazum burst through the curtains like a brick through a window.

"Nazum!" Ronoah yelped as Nazum squawked "RUNA holy shit you're alive" and collapsed to his knees, hands to his heart like it was about to explode. "I woke up and you were gone, I thought they'd choked you for sure—"

Ronoah cringed with guilt. "Ah, no," he managed. "Sorry for worrying you—you were worried?"

"Of *course* I worried," Nazum snapped, which lifted Ronoah's heart until the boy continued, "if anything happens to you then your lady's gonna turn me into charcoal, doesn't matter if you get killed from your own stupidity—"

"Well I'm fine," Ronoah said acidly, gesturing at the embers before him. "So you can go back to bed."

"Nah, thinking about my impending doom got me wide awake." Nazum waved off Ronoah's attempt to regain his privacy, taking in the scene with an expression that shifted from relieved to confused to sceptical with remarkable agility. "What are you *doing* up here?"

"I was just—looking around?" It was a poor excuse, but Ronoah wasn't about to explain to Nazum, who had laughed off Ronoah's name before he could ever so much as say Genoveffa's. "I, ah, I wondered if maybe Chabra'i still had some guguri that she forgot about—"

"Ye gods, if she catches you lurking around her stuff you'll frigging die." Nazum squinted. "Again. I don't know, I don't know how it works."

To Ronoah's dismay, the boy ambled over and sat down, rubbing one eye with the heel of his hand. His hair was mussed from sleep; free from its topknot, it was about as long as Ronoah's, a choppy black curtain brushing his bony shoulders. Brushing his scars, ridges flaring ruby in the firelight.

The silences between Ronoah and Nazum were never comfortable, but what with the intrusive quality of the boy's arrival, this one felt doubly awkward. So Ronoah was relieved when, after a long silent side-by-side, Nazum stifled a yawn and asked, "You sure are serious about finding that stuff, aren't you?"

"Of course I am," Ronoah replied. "Why wouldn't I be?"

He only realized his voice had an edge when Nazum put his hands up placatingly. "Don't mean anything by it, brother, it's mighty impressive, that stubbornness. Got plenty of it myself. I figured you were just looking for something to occupy yourself with while your lady's upriver. Like a distraction from all the creepy stares and the constant possibility of getting strangled, ai?" The boy plonked his chin on his knees, looking at Ronoah; Ronoah noted, startled, that the look was a soft one. "Guess I was wrong. You really do care about everyone staying alive, or whatever."

Nazum had never admitted fault before. It gave Ronoah pause. "I really do," he agreed, slowly. Nazum hummed in acknowledgement, letting loose another yawn. Heartbeats passed while they both stared into the brazier, and then Nazum spoke up again:

"Why?"

Ronoah was baffled. Why did he care about saving people's lives? He didn't have the faintest idea how to answer. That caring was not a thing to be questioned—it was fundamental as breathing, obvious as the sky.

The sky is obscured by the canopy here, said a voice in his head. *Their house, their rules.* Cast off the mantle of your judgement. Come into it curious instead.

"You want to know why I care about people?" he ventured, hoping it didn't come out dismissive.

"It's not a given, you know? You being—you're shiyalshandr, why would you care about the lives of overworlders? We don't expect you to, we're none of your business. Your lady, she seems like she cares too, but in a different way?" Nazum grimaced, his button nose scrunching as he tried to explain. "She's coming in and trying to put a stop to the whole War, and honestly brother, you come off a bit like her sidekick if not her pet"—Ronoah didn't even have time to retort—"but between the two of yous, *you're* the one that gets all cut up when people are actually in danger. I just wondered why that is."

Ronoah lifted his eyes to the flickering bones of his fire, praying for clarity, for words. For the right kind of honesty. The air shimmered and creased with heat, and as if it were a curtain blown aside by Genoveffa herself, he saw a glimpse of his city, his Pilanova, in the fold of the mirage.

A queer smile came to his lips. It's sort of an underworld, he thought. It's due south. It counts.

"Where I am from," he began, "a war like this is unheard of. We'd never even consider it—the considering alone would make us sick. Violence towards one another is—it's shocking, it's unnatural." Denne and Ngazze, sent out of sight until they could be civil. His elder sister the exile, thrown to the desert. Even when violence was inevitable, Pilanova found a way to keep its hands clean. "To destroy another is the highest sacrilege."

"So what do you do when there's famine? Or locusts, or plague?"

"We dance," Ronoah said. "We sing. We share—we endure together."

"What about when someone's unfit to stay with the tribe? When they really mess things up?"

The fire climbed its kindling. A twig popped and sparked. "We find a way to forgive them."

Nazum shook his head, seemingly in wonder. The boy let out a great big scoff of a sigh, dangling his wrists on his knees. "Damn. So everything they say about shiyalsha's actually true. Really is a paradise down there, huh?"

Ronoah had caught glimpses of Nazum's pensive side, but never anything like this. The boy's loud, brash energy was compacted to something stonelike, pressurized. Ronoah saw, and then without fully understanding, he probed, and felt a flutter of feelings like a dove against his cheek—the muted tones of sorrow, the strange, airy freedom of bitter-sweet relief. Involuntarily, he wondered how many times Nazum had seen someone die. How many times he'd nearly died himself.

Still caught in contemplation, Nazum brushed his hair back from his face. Ronoah's attention was snared by the motion, by those scars. They were on the same shoulder as Ronoah's darkscarring. He returned his gaze to Nazum's face—and saw with some alarm that whatever the boy was considering, it was actually hurting him.

It was too bizarre, to see Nazum in pain. So he took a chance. "Those scars look recent," he said, his voice uplilting, like a question, like a peace offering. Please, he thought, let this be the right thing.

Nazum shifted his shoulder instinctively, the same automatic response Ronoah always had. Then the boy uncurled from his slouch. He gave Ronoah a once-over, stopped at Ronoah's ribs, and replied, "So do those."

Ronoah couldn't help but smile in relief at the boy's tone.

"They are. They're—still a little tender," he said, hoping the admission would sound like divulging a secret and not like confessing a weakness. "It was on my way here. I was walking through a cavern and I lost my light. I tried to find my way out in the dark, and I stumbled into—an angry spirit." That sickening surprise, that shocking instant when he'd expected his foot to stop and it had just kept going. It wasn't a lie; Jesprechel's echo had been repeating that frustration for nine hundred years. "I nearly got sent right back where I came from."

"Not every branch of shiyalsha so flowery as yours, then," Nazum observed, squinting at the tough, dark skin splattering Ronoah's side. He whistled, short and low and—maybe?—impressed. "How you get outta that one?"

"Chashakva saved me. She found me and carried me out. I—I still don't know how she knew where I was."

Nazum looked out the window as if he knew what direction Chashakva had gone, as if he could see a thread connecting them, some spider silk gathering dewy beads of information, becoming visible only as the glob-ules accumulated. "Well," he said eventually, "if she en't told you already, I doubt she's gonna tell you ever."

Ronoah prodded at the embers of his fire. A breeze sieved in cool across his brow. Outside, the susurration of the leaves.

"Mine's from the long-last job," the boy continued. "The job before the job before this one." He rolled his shoulder with a fine sort of tightness to his face that hinted he was still getting used to how the skin pulled. "I'm sent up a tree, real big guy, harvesting bark for spice. I got a handsaw what's made for shaving bark off the branch, I got a basket to put it in, and I got a rope attached to the basket for pulleying up and down. Basket's come up, and the branch is bare, so I'm climbing for a new perch and I've got the rope coiled 'round my shoulder, for safekeeping. Once I sit my butt down somewhere sturdy I put the pulley back together. Only I don't get that far. Skin on that tree's real baggy by this time in the season—I put my foot down, the bark slips, rolls right off the branch, and I go tumbling maybe ten feet before this rope on my shoulder squeezes tight like a frigging python, and I get a bit debarked myself but at least I'm not dead."

"Who came to get you?" Ronoah asked. Nazum smiled in an aren't-you-funny sort of way.

"Brother, no one comes to get me. I get myself down." He waved his clenched fist in the air. "Still got a handsaw, don't I? So I try wiggling to get loose, because I'm an idiot and clearly I en't ever seen a python suffocate a lemur in my life, and of course the rope's just getting tighter and cutting deeper. And I figure if it's a toss-up between losing an arm and splattering all over the jungle floor, I'll take the splattering—suckerfish don't get jobs with one fin—so I cut the rope and by some dumb luck I don't cut the bit keeping me secure, just the bit keeping me tangled. I grab the nearest branch and shimmy down that tree faster than a gecko what's just had his tail popped off, which in a way I guess I almost was."

He shrugged again, but there was a tug of a smile on his face, a lessening of scepticism. Ronoah found himself smiling back, sincere and relieved to be sincere. "I'm glad you made it down," he said. Nazum grimaced, but it was a good-natured grimace.

"Course you are," he said, with the return of his lazy lackadaisy, "if I didn't then there'd be no one to keep you from losing your nose when you go sticking it places it don't belong."

Ronoah made an affronted noise, and Nazum grinned his shark's grin, and normalcy was restored. How odd, that distance could feel affectionate. That discomfort could be comforting.

Nazum sat with Ronoah for the length of time it took the creatures of the rainforest to switch shifts, late-night frogs swapping with early morning insects. Eventually the boy stifled another yawn and asked, "How much longer you gonna sit up here?"

"A little longer," Ronoah said, biting his cheek to hide his own replying yawn. He had been surreptitiously pinching his thigh to keep himself alert. He wouldn't feel right without giving Genoveffa the proper thanks and acknowledgement before he released her attention. Especially after asking her to meddle so directly, it struck him as disrespectful to just up and leave.

This tenacity won out at last, as Nazum clambered to his feet. "Well I'm done. Being up here without the wisewoman's permission freaks me out." He knocked his knuckles lightly against the top of Ronoah's head. "Don't die."

"I'll do my best," Ronoah said, not without a certain wryness.

Nazum started towards the exit, but paused midway. "And keep your weird feeling powers off me," he added, half-turning to glare at Ronoah. Ronoah's shoulders hunched in the guilt of getting caught. "You want that guguri so bad I can smell it. Like literally smell it right in this room. Stop that."

"I—sorry?" Apparently satisfied, Nazum exited the treehouse, leaving Ronoah to boggle at the boy's parting statement. Chashakva had confirmed that Ronoah could pick up the subtle emotions and memories of other people and places, sure, but never had she implied he could push them the other way. He didn't even know what guguri smelled like, so how could he imprint that scent on Nazum? He didn't smell anything unusual. The only smells were the assorted earths of Chabra'i's hut, the clinging odour of damp, living wood, and—

Oh. Oh god and gods alike.

Ronoah turned back to the brazier, inhaling as full and deep as he could. He thought they'd all burnt off, but there, floating amidst the fragrances of the unfamiliar, was the sharp spice of home. There, in the bottom of the bowl, glowing like an answered prayer, sat the winking eye of one clove bud burning.

FOURTEEN

"*B*ROTHER, I GET YOU'RE SHORT ON OPTIONS, but why you making us try something we already tried?"

"Because that something changed," Ronoah answered, taking the stairs to the treehouse two at a time. "Hurry, we want to catch Chabra'i before she starts work—"

Nazum grunted with the effort of keeping astride Ronoah's longer legs. Ronoah didn't slow down. His heart was galloping in his chest. The logistics of his plan were ruthlessly self-refining in his mind, smoothing their rough edges until they could interlock as a viable whole.

There were a few ways it could go wrong, sure. But he was pretty confident he could handle them.

He took in a deep breath as the curtain of seeds slid across his shoulders, let it out as the curtain of bones parted to make way. Chabra'i was sitting cross-legged at her table, enjoying a breakfast banquet of fruits and fatty insects.

"Wisewoman," he said, with Nazum only a step behind, "your Subin has heard me out."

"Mm?" Chabra'i looked up, licking juice off her fingers. "Did she now, shiyalshandr? And what did my Subin have to say? Got turned down politely at least, I hope?"

Ronoah allowed himself a smile—a smile like Chashakva, cryptic and foreboding. "She agrees with me, Chabra'i. She thinks the time is now to focus on healing what's around you, not destroying what is afar." Chabra'i frowned, probably about to counter how that wasn't the right way to look at the War, but whatever she had to say was lost with Ronoah's next announcement: "And she's giving you the tools to do it. I'm going to the deadzone. And when I come back, it'll be with handfuls and handfuls of life."

For a moment, no one spoke. Both Nazum and Chabra'i were looking at him like he was a new creature entirely. Ronoah dared not move, dared not even twitch, for fear he would shatter the brittle sense of foreboding he had managed to impose.

"...You do that, Runa," Chabra'i said, her expression smoothing its worried creases. She shrugged one shoulder, a hint of her smirk on her lips. "I'll see you at lunch, I guess."

Ronoah nodded. Then, before anything could go wrong, he turned on his heel and strode from the treehouse.

The cloves, hidden under the folds of his red wrap, prickled at his hip like a hundred fire ants.

When he'd solved the mystery of the guguri last night, it had taken every ounce of his wisdom not to jump up and go running for his supplies. The helper in him, the wide-eyed, kind-hearted novice, it wanted to press the cloves into Chabra'i's hands that very moment. But the adventurer in him said *wait*, and he waited. The shrewd, analytical part of him, the one that had survived seven months underground, it was taking a moment to mull things over.

You can't just hand them over, it said. You have to make a show out of it. If you say you had them all along, what kind of divine favour is that? It could be written off as coincidence—or worse, as intentionally stealing or hiding medicine from the wisewoman. You need to make it look like a myth. Like a miracle. That's the only way you'll get the respect you need to have your way.

He thought of Reilin the Conqueror, blazing his way up the Alvyssian continent, slashing down anything and anyone in his path. *I fashioned myself the embodiment of their ideals; I changed my ways according to how they would respond to them. And once I had captured not only their allegiance but their faith, then I changed their ways.*

He needed to be a bit of a Conqueror himself.

The plan had taken the rest of the night to form—Ronoah had removed all trace of his ritual, and then returned to lie wide awake on his mat in the sacrificial hut, scheming until the scheme was pristine.

Chabra'i had said the guguri grew in the deadzone. So the deadzone was where he would find it.

"You gonna let me in on when *this* happened?" Nazum griped as they pushed their way through the rainforest. "Last I checked Subin hadn't so much as sneezed on you. Now she's backing your weepy nonviolent credo?"

Ronoah was so focused that he didn't even take offense at being called weepy. "It happened after you went to sleep," he said, bending a branch back and slipping underneath. "That, um, that fire was—"

"A magic fire!" Nazum hissed in distaste as they came upon the riverbank, searching through the reeds for a boat. "I should've known, I should've known you were up there doing shiyalshandr woo, but *no*, sleepy Nazum's got no self-preservation, *clearly*, sleepy Nazum was sitting there wondering whether we'd be roasting newts for late night *snacks*." The boy found the boat, hauled it into the water. "Such an idiot."

"I don't know, I think sleepy Nazum's okay."

"Get in the boat, Runa."

The mist rolled in ghosts on the bank. Thin shafts of morning light penetrated the fog; by the time they reached the edge of the deadzone, the sun had gained enough strength to burn it away, to banish the obscurity of the rainforest. They rowed across the threshold, and Ronoah felt with renewed sensitivity the cloves scratching at his side, and willed the excited tightness in his chest to recede. Nervous energy was welling in his body, a bizarre mix of stage fright and existential terror. They had arrived. There was only one thing left to do: make it believable.

He spotted a soggy little island near the interior, with a great grand tree trunk splintering through. That seemed like the kind of once-sacred place he could perform his sleight of hand.

"Over there," he directed Nazum, and together they pulled up to the side of the island. The banks were slushy and untidy; when Ronoah stepped gingerly out of the boat, the ground gave and sprang beneath him. Unstable. Waterlogged. He'd have to be quick, lightfooted. Like he was more spirit than flesh.

"Tell me I get to stay in the boat," said Nazum, eyeing the island.

"You get to stay in the boat."

"Thank Subin," the boy cried, flopping back onto his seat. "You en't sacrificing me for no magic medicine, that's for sure."

Ronoah left the boy to his complaints—they seemed to calm him down, and in this eerie, sour land, calm was difficult to find. If Nazum was in the boat, it would make it all the simpler to return with the cloves.

He padded over wads of wet grass and decaying matter until he reached the tree trunk. Up close the bark was swollen with rot, covered in blistering irregularities. It forced a shiver through him. He wanted to touch it, to reach out in comfort, in wordless apology, but an equally strong instinct told him to avoid touching things if he could. Clever trick or not, Ronoah, this place is not for lingering. Just because you're playing a deathless creature does not mean death cannot find you.

The air was cloying, but he forced himself to breathe evenly while he retrieved the sachet of cloves tucked into his wrap. He remembered making the bag in the monastery, pounding and drying the barkcloth, sewing the pattern, filling it with buds he'd plucked and dried himself. He had hoped it would last him all the way to the Pilgrim State. If they'd never stopped at Bhun Jivakta, it just might have.

He upended the bag into his hand. It would be too strange, too convenient, if he came back with them all wrapped up neat like that—they had to come from his hands, raw and wanting and real. Stashing the sachet away again, he cupped one hand over the other, forming a protective globe. He took a breath, and turned for the boat.

Then the weeds gave way underneath him.

The only thing he thought to do when the water hit was to brace his hands as tight as possible—if he lost the cloves then he would have nothing, truly nothing, and so he held on as if holding on could shove him back to the surface. He'd been too surprised to scream, so luckily he found himself with full lungs. Not only did that give him time, it gave him a sense of direction—up was the way his body tugged.

He forced his eyes open a fraction, just to find light, to double-check, but the lagoon stung like it had claws, like it was scraping at his eyeballs, and he scrunched them shut again, gritting his teeth to keep from shouting.

He couldn't swim up. Chances were he'd get blocked by that mat of weeds, thick enough to stand on. No breaking through that with his arms occupied. He had to swim out from under the island.

There was no current to fight against, but it was thick, muddy water, sluggish and slow-going. Ronoah swam as best he could, trying to release his air in timed streams, enough to lessen the pressure in his chest but not so much that he would run out. Weeds brushed his exposed skin, shoulders and sides and the tops of his lashing feet.

And under the water, he sensed the presence of something that scared him more than drowning, more than dropping all the cloves into the deep. Under the water, in the silent, undulating gloom, some great and ancient malice passed him by.

No one's here to get you this time, he thought frantically, so you better keep kicking.

He wedged his eyes open again, just enough to tell by the colour and clarity of the water that he was out in the open lagoon. He changed direction, blasted to the surface by a fierce drive of willpower. Breaching the water he gasped for new air, spluttering out the slime that got in his mouth. "Nazum!" he called, but the boy had already seen him, was already rowing with all the swiftness his wiry arms could muster.

"What," the boy yelled as he arrived, "the actual fuck, what the *kulim putrash* just happened, what are you—!"

"Short visit to the underworld," Ronoah's mouth said, quicker in this instant than even his rabbit of a mind. "Please—please help me up."

He leveraged an elbow out of the water, kicking so hard his legs seared. Nazum grabbed hold of it and hauled him, with lots of bumping and scraping and swearing, into the longboat. "Why the fuck," the boy said again, not yelling but still loudly, "aren't you using your godsforsaken hands?"

Hold, said a voice in Ronoah's head. He will look at you differently after this. Life will tilt on its axis. Savour whatever strange relationship you had—it is about to be upturned, unraveled into something new.

He savoured it. He took his moment to enjoy the sweet sensation of air in his lungs, the burning satisfaction of pulling a perfect victory from an unforeseen obstacle. And then he opened his hands, and Nazum shouted loud enough to startle what few brave birds perched in the deadzone.

"Like I said," Ronoah panted, "handfuls of life." The spikes of the cloves had pockmarked his palms, dozens of indents and pinpricks. The marks of a job well done. "Come on, little shark. Let's go give our host a present."

And if Nazum thought it impetuous of Ronoah, to use a pet name that Chashakva had coined, he did not say so now. He set to the oars, and he rowed them back, and not a word of complaint slipped his mouth.

They found Chabra'i administering maashava root to the fever-stricken patients in the quarantine hut. Ronoah caught the wisewoman's eye, then stepped back outside, waiting under the awning. Rain was beginning to hit the thatch in dull pats and thwaps. To his ears, the sound sparkled.

"Welcome back, shiyalshandr—got caught in the drizzle on your way?" The wisewoman edged out between the hangings, slicking her hair back from her face. "Another of Nalaya's girls caught fever, so I'm stuck here waiting out her shakes. You can send for lunch yourself, if you're hungry..."

She trailed off as she caught the glint in Ronoah's eye. Wordlessly, he held out his hands; warily, she reached forward with her own, pulled one of his palms away like opening an oyster, gasped at the small pile of pungent, priceless pearls sitting within.

"By my mother Subin," she said in a low, intense voice, looking at the guguri, then at Ronoah, "how—how in the world did you—?"

"Rinse them well," was all Ronoah said. "And call off your raid. You have patients to doctor."

Chabra'i searched his face in amazement. For the first time, Ronoah noticed the lines under her eyes. She was so formidable, so much larger than life, so tired of losing this fight.

Lovingly, he parted his fingers and let the cloves slip into her waiting hands. Their scent wafted up, and he took it as a farewell—he was giving every last one to her, to the wisewoman and her people, and he did not know when he would come across another bud again, when he would next be able to cast them into the fire and feel his home surround him. They passed to her, a sacrifice, an offering: I have granted your miracle, Chabra'i Subindra. Now grant me mine.

He left her with her medicine, left the hut and walked into the open air of the village, into the burst of rain springboarding off every surface, rain somersaulting and pirouetting and falling in festoons from the sky. It washed him clean of the lagoon, of its heavy dread, its helplessness. He reveled in the downpour.

Just you wait, he thought, tilting his head back and letting his grateful tears mingle with the rainfall. Just you watch. I am changed; I am changing. No more cowering from me. I will find lemons in lychees as many times as I have to.

And if the responding surge of jubilation he felt wasn't life swooning, he didn't know what it was.

Fifteen

*I*T WAS ANOTHER THREE WEEKS before Chashakva returned to Subindr territory, and in that time Ronoah's place in Chabra'i's community changed dramatically.

News of the guguri spread as quickly as the fever it cured, and the wisewoman wasn't shy about crediting its source. All of a sudden, as if moved by their leader's approval, the same villagers who had avoided Ronoah wanted to invite him to try their honeyed ants or show him how to stand in a canoe without tipping it. A small child brought him a gift, a thank you for helping to cure his mamu, and a brave girl only a few years younger than Nazum dared to touch him, to put her hand on his shoulder in passing. She was casual as she did it, but Ronoah heard her talking fervently with her friends only moments afterward.

Chabra'i herself viewed Ronoah with renewed respect. She taught him how to prepare medicines, listing off their uses while he ground shouting tree or shaved slivers of blue fishfruit. She even let him shadow her foraging excursions so he could get a sense of *where the land coughs up all these cures.* Maybe she was hoping he would disappear on one of those outings, return with another handful of guguri; he hadn't exactly heaped them upon her.

But even though no more miracle buds found their way into her hands, she kept her word.

The day the raid was meant to take place, the entire village gathered at the base of the massive trees of the Subindr village and watched Chabra'i and her warriors compete in a tournament. They fought to first blood, demonstrating their practice, their prowess, and then they picked each other up from the mud and cleaned each other's wounds.

Sometimes, in a rare quiet moment, Ronoah lingered just outside the hangings of the quarantine hut. He'd catch the flashing scent of clove, and a small smile would pull at his lips, and then he would move on.

But those weeks passed, and one day the three of them—Chabra'i, Nazum, Ronoah—were hiking up to the treehouse with baskets of maashava root on their backs, wondering aloud which of them had been stung the most and whether anything terrible would happen to the bugs who'd bitten the shiyalshandr among them, when they ducked through the curtains of seed and bone and a voice wafted through to greet them:

"A few of your candles blew out, so I relit them. Hope you don't mind."

There she was, swarthy and cunning and capable, sitting on the edge of Chabra'i's great table with a bouquet of trinkets and talismans in her hands.

"See?" smiled Chashakva, jostling her collection. "Presents. Just like I said we'd have."

In all the days they had been apart, Ronoah had never worried for Chashakva. But only in seeing her did he realize just how much he'd missed her. It took all his strength not to run to her.

"You're late," is what he said, before anyone else could get a word in. Chashakva's mouth twitched.

"The rainforest grows at exactly the speed it will grow, and no faster," she said, eyeing their party as they slipped the baskets off and set them on the ground. "It is not up to us to decide when the vines will flower, or the jinju palm bear fruit, or the termites pile their stacks. All we can do is be there for the harvest, sickles in hand." She inclined her head at Chabra'i, who walked over to inspect the offerings—a deep blue tailfeather, a polished bronze mirror, a braid of silk thread, a small corked bottle of some unidentifiable substance. "Is my crop to your satisfaction?"

Chabra'i took the bundle, saying nothing. She picked through the peace offerings, lips pursed in consideration. Ronoah knew enough by now to know her answer was already set. It was just Chabra'i's way, as a wisewoman and as a person, to make it seem like a fight.

"You got me, shiyalshandr," she sighed at length, landing herself in a chair and kicking her feet up on the table's edge. She shook her head in something between pity and wonder. "You took the kettle off the heat. I'm with you. For now."

"For now," Chashakva allowed.

And then she hopped off the table and faced Ronoah, eyes sparking with successful adventure. "Did you not miss me at *all?*" she taunted. She only had to lift her arms a fraction. This time Ronoah did run.

They spent all morning discussing and adjusting Chashakva's plan for the Council of All Tribes. Three other territories had consented to meet: the Gaamndr, the Ra'ushandr, and the Dandakhti-Kashndr. "I'm working a fourth as we speak," Chashakva said, rolling a leaf between her fingers until it released its fragrant oils. "Plus you, that makes five. The whole northwestern quadrant, ready to hash things out. Imagine."

"I am imagining," replied Chabra'i, with a hint of a sour pucker at her mouth.

Soon enough, Ronoah discovered the many problems and pitfalls of these arrangements. Given the number of tribes yet to enter into agreements, and how long it would take to locate and persuade them, and the length of time it would take for each tribe's wisewoman to travel to the meeting place, which had to be selected in a way that couldn't be perceived as advantageous to any one tribe—they were looking at meeting another five, six months from now.

Then the seasons were brought up, by Nazum of all people. Much of the Sanaat became impossible to navigate during monsoon. It wasn't worth it to risk the safety of the wisewomen on willful waters. Six months became ten. And months were counted differently in Shaipuri than they were in Chiropole, or Acharrio for that matter—ten months to Nazum and Chabra'i were thirteen to Ronoah. Three shy of a year.

Faintly, a voice in Ronoah's head made some barbed comments about daytrips. He ignored it.

At last, the time and place were set: the first days of prewinter, when the constellation of Jassam Tai the Mushroom Picker was overhead; the Sasaupandr Plateau, an escarpment from which plummeted Sasaupta Falls, one of six main sources which fed the Sanaat. It was uninhabited, laid claim to by no one. When Ronoah asked Nazum why, the boy replied in an undertone: "You'll know just by looking. Place like that en't for human beings. That's a place only gods call home." Perhaps it was irreverent of him, but Ronoah looked forward to witnessing it. Even if it was going to take a year to get there.

It fell to Chabra'i to send out messengers to each of the northwestern tribes, to inform them of these coordinates. While the wisewoman was dubious, Chashakva assured her no harm would come to anyone's go-betweens. "But leave the Jau-Hasthasndr to me," she added. "They're not a guarantee just yet."

The Jau-Hasthasndr, Ronoah guessed, was where they'd be heading next.

"I've gotta hand it to you, sister," said Chabra'i as she rose from her chair, "I've heard stories since I was a girl all about the devious, tenacious shiyalshandr, but even for you folk, this is mighty bold. Chashakva always has her way in the end, ai?"

"Ahai," said Chashakva. Her sharp teeth glinted in the candlelight.

"Well." The wisewoman ticked her chin at the doorway. "Now I've got to go deliver the news to my village that our centuries of war are possibly at an end."

"Will they take it well?" Ronoah asked. Chabra'i looked at him with the arrogant grimace that he had come to understand as a sign of her fondness.

"Sure they will. I got a tongue smooth as dolphin skin—no one'll take issue with it if it comes from me. The trouble's going to come finding messengers brash enough to actually *make* the housecall."

"We'll leave it in your hands," said Chashakva, rising from her own seat. "It's as good a time as any to take our leave. You have what you need to guide your people, and we're scheduled to arrive at the Jau-Hasthasndr village within a few days. The Great Wheel is turning."

"Who knows what mysterious age it will land us in," murmured Chabra'i. Ronoah saw Nazum duck his head as if in agreement, acknowledgement of this force that governed their world. For a moment—flitting, flashing—it struck Ronoah that maybe it was unwise to meddle with it.

But it was too late to back out now. The meddling had set them in motion.

"I'll see you at Council, Runa." Ronoah looked up just as Chabra'i reached him, landing a light chop with the side of her hand between his ribs. "If you talk to Subin again between now and then, tell her my bees are the mightiest in all the rainforest. Better than they've ever been."

"Which is wisewoman-speak," Nazum added snickeringly as Chabra'i left, "for 'tell her I'm sore she spoke to you and not me'. Gotta hurt, when you find out you been ignoring your god's wishes."

First, Ronoah didn't understand what Nazum was implying. Then it connected, and a dizziness swept him like he was standing at the very top of the tallest tree in Subindr territory, looking all the way down. The vertigo of perspective—and the dawning horror, that too, because—

Chabra'i's faith was shaken?

Because of him?

That was—Setten and Ibisca, no, he hadn't meant for *that* to happen, that was never what he wanted. It wasn't his place, it wasn't *right* to make Chabra'i question her connection to her god—if their roles were reversed, if he knew Genoveffa was conferring her secrets and wishes upon someone else, someone not even serving her, it would be agony. It would feel like being tossed aside.

With a jolt deep in his stomach, he realized he hadn't actually seen Chabra'i make her morning rounds of the beehives since he gave her the cloves. She wasn't reading them anymore.

He nearly ran after her right then and there to come clean—but he couldn't. His toes curled with the effort of keeping him in one place, but he couldn't undo what he'd done. He'd tricked her. Worse.

For the first time possibly ever, Ronoah Genoveffa Elizzi-denna Pilanovani had told a lie.

Told a lie and got away with it.

The implications of this followed him down ninety feet of wooden walkway and rope bridge, out of the village, through the jungle, all the way back onto the Sanaat, back onto a river wide enough to see the sky. The rusty crescent of Pao, faint as a topaz in the daytime, hung watchful in the south. An eye narrowed in condemnation. It prickled between Ronoah's shoulder blades as they paddled the other way.

In order to reach the Jau-Hasthasndr, they needed to double back on the tributaries that bore them to Chabra'i. Watching the same scenery from six weeks ago appear in reverse—now transformed, as Ronoah could name so many of the plants, understood their wiles and wisdoms—he couldn't get rid of the thought that he had earned that knowledge by deceit. Stolen it, almost. An old feeling roused itself in him, a curdling, clawing thing, all the more painful for its silent attack: the warning signs of fear-beyond-fear, prickling his bones. He helped Nazum with the paddling to give his hands something to do, needled Chashakva for stories of the other tribes to occupy his mind. She didn't let him down.

"The Gaamndr made me walk on coals," she told them, "which honestly isn't a very effective trial, anybody can do it given proper training—but the Dandakhti-Kashndr, oh, they were *wonderful*. Had a whole feast prepared when I arrived, full of all the things a demon's meant to eat, blue clay and gold and scorpions, and I got to sit and chew through it all, ten hours at a banquet table fit for the dead while they played shakers and drums and musical bows—ever heard of a musical bow? Well, they look like archery bows, but you take a gourd and—"

The thrum of her voice, the wonders and dangers it carried—it exposed how selfish his worries were, laid his anxieties at the feet of a much bigger picture. Reminded him that there was far more at stake here than his own petty personal creed.

What does it mean to *be* something, anyway, he thought as they pulled the raft ashore and made their way down a portage trail. You haven't stopped being a desert boy just because you're on the water, right? You can still be honest after this. It wasn't even really a lie, it was—a story, like Chashakva said. What was that line of hers, back in the caravans? *Fictional details to depict an essential truth?* You're still you, just—better at storytelling. Doing what you have to.

Downslope the rapids churned and scoffed. He kept his eyes on the trail ahead.

Chashakva's reaction only confirmed how silly his discomfort was. "And what of your stories?" she asked a few days in, tapping him on the cheek. "You went from hapless imp to revered spirit in the span of six weeks. How." He told her the official story and she nodded along, keen as a child at a street magic show; later, as Nazum slept, he confided the truth of it in hushed Acharrioni, and she practically crowed with pride.

"Oh what a *sneak* you can be," she gushed, while Ronoah tried to shush her before she woke Nazum and the three closest tribes along with him. "You marvellous, clever, resourceful—you've worked a real miracle here, they'll talk about this for *years*."

Her admiration was infectious—and reminded Ronoah that, just a few days ago, he too had considered this a triumph and not a moral failing. He wanted that lightness back, that self-assurance. Wanted it enough that he pushed his worries into the underbrush, let Chashakva's praises revive his good mood. He wanted it enough that, when Chashakva's smile vanished—"you fell in the lagoon?"—he was quick to gloss it over, told her that while something had felt maybe a little strange under there he'd probably just been projecting his own fears again, reliving the shock of the underground river, old habits, memories, you know how it is. There were more interesting things to talk about anyway.

"Do you think my empathy goes more than one way?" he asked. "Nazum said that I pushed the scent of cloves into his mind, and that isn't what happened, but it made me wonder about...what's possible." He reached for the poker to rearrange their blackened logs. "There were moments in Chabra'i's village, or back in Bhun Jivakta with that clerk at the trade house. I don't know."

"Are you putting your heart in other people's heads, little demon?"

"No, and I wouldn't want to. I just—" Ronoah bit his cheek, seeking language he'd never been given. It was like trying to piece clouds together. "I don't mean it—*assertively*, like that. It's not that I've been pushing my feelings into anyone, it's that I'm sort of choosing which feelings push their way into me? Sometimes now it feels like I can—tap into it, instead of having it *invade* me."

All his life he'd endured random bursts of it, fickle and unpredictable visitations roaring in and razing the tender architecture of his heart. But ever since they'd left the monastery, Ronoah's empathy had felt less like a typhoon and more like the Sanaat: still willful, but moving in a direction he could see. Could sometimes even ride, when the current allowed it.

"New knowledge of old power can feel like new power entirely," Chashakva offered. A log popped sparks in agreement. "You have named the thing that has controlled your life, and in naming you gain a container for it. A skin, if you will, overtop what used to simply be naked nerves grated raw." Ronoah winced, and Chashakva looked at him like the wincing proved her point. "You're asking whether one day you might also grow it bones, structure it enough to manipulate at will, to reach out and touch whatever effervescent truths take your fancy. You're asking whether you can learn to command that which commands you."

She fell silent. She was considering, weighing all she knew against all she saw; Ronoah could practically taste the granite of the grindstone milling her mulling into conclusions, into potentialities. While he had always been aware of Chashakva's complexity, now he felt it geographically, like a point on a map he could travel to if he approached from just the right angle, a temple he could enter if he could only find the one open window.

But before he could try, she cut him a look that said *don't get overzealous*, and reluctantly he reconsidered the possible consequences of crawling into a five-thousand-year-old head unprepared.

"Going for the oil painting before you can sketch a circle," she said, half-chiding, half-charmed. "You sensitive types are all the same. Give it some practice—give it some *time*, heavens—but yes, I think you very well could learn the art of interfacing with that affective plane."

The encouragement seemed to thrill that reality into being, a landscape at once intangible and attainable, someday. "Really?"

The blue notes in Chashakva's eyes flashed in the firelight. "It has happened before."

Then, "But aren't you serendipitous, bringing this up just when I was going to." Ronoah's brow quirked, and she continued: "I'm glad you're interested in exercising this sense of yours, because there's a situation that calls for it. The Universe gave you a role in securing Lady Subindra's cooperation; I may have given you a role in securing Lady Jau-Hasthasndra's. She needs your help while I'm wrangling the rest of the northeast."

"Help? With what?" If he'd learned anything from Chabra'i, it was only through absolute flukes of luck or destiny that he could be helpful to a Shaipurin wisewoman.

"You share certain tendencies," was all Chashakva said. Ronoah wasn't liking the increasing obscurity of these responses. "Don't glare at me like that, I'm not *trying* to keep you in the dark. It's tricky to explain without being there. It requires a visual." A smirk slunk across her lips. "Well. It requires a lot of things."

After a beleaguered moment Ronoah sighed, massaging his brow. "As long as you give me the visual before you disappear, I can handle it. Probably."

"Most probably," Chashakva agreed, and she said it with a vigour Ronoah hadn't expected. "You've done so well already in an emergency—I can only imagine what you'll achieve when you're not on the backfoot."

Heat flushed Ronoah's cheeks. The praise, so genuine, so convinced—it jittered in him like one glass of coffee too many, instilled both giddiness and glimmering confidence. He *was* capable. Chabra'i's test had proven it. And luck and destiny had been on his side once already.

The next day they helped Nazum pack the camp and travelled on down the Sanaat, on course for a new tribe, a new wisewoman. Another puzzle to solve; another god to persuade. The canopy undulated above them, vaulted green unfurling to sky, weaving shut, unfurling again. The river quickened, thickened, splattered with rapids. Choppy, frothing. Quelling. Calm.

One last secret revealed, the morning before they arrived: "Chashakva?"

"Mm."

"The cloves. They used to grow here—in the rainforest."

"Mm."

"How did they end up here? I know the tree in the monastery was a gift, it could have come from anywhere on the Trans-Bereni Highway, but here..." It just seemed so unlikely. So much like coincidence. Like another nudge of fate.

Chashakva was winding the hammocks up in cord, her arm travelling swift spirals around the bundle. "A friend of mine came here once, a long time ago," she said. "She came bearing a great satchel of seeds, everything that was left of her land, which had ceased to exist."

Her fingers flickered through the motions of tying the knot. Her eyelids looked bruised with dusk in the dawn. Around them, everything was breathing in together.

"She planted the most delightful garden," she said.

SIXTEEN

*J*AU-HASTHASNDR RAIN WAS DIFFERENT from Subindr rain. The rain in Subin's territory was a volley, punching through the dartboards of the leaves, stinging like the Seed's beloved bees. But in Jau-Hasthasuna's land the rain was pulverized, turned to mizzling blue mist falling in diaphanous layers, encrusting everything with a crystal patina of dew. In Subin's territory the rainforest had jostled constantly with the rebound of boisterous raindrops, but the foray into Jau-Hasthasuna's was still, and cold.

Trees switchbacked up from the marshy lowlands, shingled with bark in thick, resinous scales like they were sheathed in alligator skin; pale vines webbed the canopy like roots in reverse, drinking the vitality from the air to feed some deep and ponderous flower underground; a tribe of great apes observed from a distance before turning and dissolving into the fog. None of it was deadzone as far as Ronoah could tell—it was just the way the land lay. Lissome, elegant. Uncanny.

"There are two kinds of water to the Shaipurin," Chashakva was saying as they floated through the fenland. "Water of the land, and water of the sky. Jau-Hasthasuna is a land-water Seed, a rivermaker, responsible for the movements of the Sanaat, its seasonal flood and fade, lord of sinkholes and cenotes and all the watery entrances to shiyalsha. He is partial to the heron, the lotus, the snake."

Ronoah saw a pair of pythons resting on the branch of a mangrove, dove grey and intestinal pink, flickering liquorice tongues. "What do they do to appease him?" he asked. Better to know beforehand than to be surprised.

Chashakva hissed a sigh between her teeth. "What is water but a collection of tears?"

"They drown the shit out of you," said Nazum, who had apparently decided accuracy was more important than delicacy. "Throw you in a well or a sinkhole, and then they scoop out your eyes for good measure, just to squeeze the last tears outta those babies."

A memory surfaced, unconnected yet insistent: Jesprechel's mummified body, the way her eyelids still swelled despite there being nothing left behind them. Ronoah gave a thin shudder, and Nazum nodded with satisfaction.

"Speaking of babies, they mostly do it to kids, so we should be fine." The boy cocked his head, scrunched up his nose. "Probably. They're hardcore, the Jau-Hasthasndr, I hear the wisewoman herself gets chucked into one of those cenotes and spends a night treading water before anyone accepts her authority. Some initiation, huh?"

The boy sounded awed even through his irreverence. Ronoah understood the feeling. He swallowed. "And the wisewoman, she...how does she feel about her traditions?"

"Oh, Pashangali's as dedicated as they come," Chashakva said airily. "If there's a custom, you can bet she's upholding it. Or trying to."

It was Pashangali that Chashakva had visited last, after gaining the trust of the other tribes in the northwest; it was Pashangali who had required Chashakva to double back and fetch Ronoah and Nazum. While Ronoah was encouraged by their welcome status in the Jau-Hasthasndr village, he was unnerved by the fact that they needed to return a second time at all.

He wasn't the only one. As they drifted over the swamp and the village materialized, rope bridges and thatch huts on stilts like a miniature Bhun Jivakta, Ronoah saw villagers standing sentinel on docks or floating in skin boats, saluting Chashakva's return—and he felt the tang of their tension sure as he saw it on their faces. They weren't hostile, but they weren't exuding friendliness either.

All of a sudden, it occurred that sometimes having your reputation precede you was a bad thing.

They came upon a great weeping willow whose fronds formed a protective curtain. A scrawny dockhand hooked the fronds with a pole and drew them back, permitting their craft to pass. Unencumbered, they slid into the rustling amniotic bay.

Chashakva spoke to the boy who had run to help secure the raft; Nazum took a moment before picking up the translation. "I would have thought your Holiness would be here to greet us formally."

"She—she is in her sanctuary," was the boy's reply, his hands trembling even as he tried to clasp them still. Again, the words were slow to come in Chiropolene—Ronoah glanced at Nazum, who he could tell was concentrating hard because his face had lost its expressiveness. Perhaps this was a heartland tongue their interpreter could not wield so deftly.

"Then we shall conduct ourselves there instead."

"Please," said the boy, evidently terrified of the message he had to deliver, "no one is meant to see the wisewoman today. It is—you are—it is—"

"Is what?" Ronoah asked, edging his way in front of Chashakva and trying to keep his voice sweet. If he thought he was going to be any less frightening, he was mistaken; the boy's shoulders shot straight to his ears, eyes wide like two waxing glassy moons. Nazum's description of the Jau-Hasthasndr sacrifices echoed in Ronoah's mind, and he looked away, at the boy's fidgeting hands.

"Bad timing," the boy finally squeaked out.

"Not for me it isn't," proclaimed Chashakva, reaching out and clapping the boy on the top of his head. She did it gently enough but he still looked ready to keel over into the bay. "You know who I am, what I have come to do. I am never late to the party, because the party is me—!"

Ah, there was Nazum's stifled snort of laughter. The speed at which he settled into each dialect really was impressive.

"Please," insisted the boy, "we will, we will feast your return, we will make arrangements for your rooms, but you really mustn't see the wisewoman right now."

"No," insisted Chashakva right back, "I really think I must."

And she stepped around the boy, loping lithe as a jaguar up the docks. Trading looks, Ronoah and Nazum followed after her, out from the womb of the willow and into the village proper.

The dockhand wasn't the only one intent on dissuading their party. In the few minutes it took to traverse the delicate web of wood and thatch suspended over the swamp they were intercepted by no fewer than four villagers: a weaver, a warrior, a wife and her husband. All with the same warning: no one should see the wisewoman today. Chashakva brushed past them all, and they let her, let her pass with their heads bowed in respect and their eyes staring hard at the ground in concern. It got to the point where, as they neared Lady Jau-Hasthasndra's dwelling—a wooden cabin gone black with the damp, only a few ghostly torches daring to break the sense of oppressive peace and quiet—Ronoah started to get a little concerned himself.

"Chashakva," he whispered, for this place begat whispering, "maybe we should just wait—"

A bone-chilling noise stopped him there, a low, keening wail.

"You know, contrary to what the villagers fear, this is actually the perfect time for us to drop in," Chashakva spoke into the shuddering silence that followed. "This way you can see what you're getting into." Ronoah felt the sweat on the back of his neck mingle and go cold with the dew. Chashakva simply made her way to the entrance.

"What the fuck kind of demon pact did she make for you," whispered Nazum at Ronoah's side, and he cracked a surprised smile, immensely grateful for the boy in that moment.

"One I can handle?" He lifted his eyes to the cabin, heart somersaulting in his chest. "I hope."

They mounted the steps just as Chashakva was opening the door. "Pashangali, dear," the woman said, poking her head into the darkness, "is this any way to treat your guests—"

She ducked under the teapot thrown at her head. Ronoah yelped as the clay smashed against the door.

"—and it was such fine earthenware, too," Chashakva tutted. With a pitying glance spared for the remains of the pottery, she entered. Steeling his nerves, Ronoah plunged in after her.

The wisewoman's cabin had the kind of stillness that made it feel preserved, the kind of bareness that made it appear excavated. There were no candles lit in Pashangali's home, no clear-flamed lanterns, no jars of fireflies. The only illumination came from the blue-grey afternoon, dim light tumbling in with the mist. Shapes hinted at themselves in the alcoves and the corners, a curve of crystal here, a twist of driftwood there, a bale of bundled herbs hanging high like a child swinging her skirts from the rafters. The weight of the air, the symmetry of the design—it was nearly shrinelike.

And there in the middle of the array, set back near the wall like any good icon would be, lay the silhouette of a young woman, curled and panting.

"Pashangali Jau-Hasthasndra," said Chashakva, her voice concedingly low, "I have brought what I promised."

The wisewoman's head came up from the crook of her arm: disheveled hair plastered to a pale face, the sharp nub of a cheekbone, an eye like black wildfire. Her hand gripped the edge of a stone bowl; something thick and pulpy sloshed inside it as she slid it behind her, out of sight, and then she was staggering to her feet. She walked like a spectre, too light and then too limping—Nazum, usually so cocksure, took an actual step back, and Ronoah felt a selfsame revulsion in his gut, a horror and a nausea that came on too quickly for it to belong to him.

Pashangali Jau-Hasthasndra wiped her mouth on her forearm. "In the name of the Great Wheel, it had better work." Her voice was roughened, as if one of the rounded jade beads had fallen from Chashakva's necklace and chipped, gaining a cutting edge in its injury. This close, Ronoah could tell she was fighting not to shake.

"Come," said Chashakva. She stooped to support Pashangali, a shadow bracing a ghost, wrapping an arm around her waist and guiding her to the suggestion of a stool in the gloom. "Can your eyes take a candle?"

The wisewoman slid onto the seat, doubling over with her face in her hands. "Yellow's too sickening," she said, or he thought she said—Nazum had an uncertain lilt in his voice as he translated, as if he wasn't sure he was getting the words right.

Chashakva cast a seeking hand across the darkened table. "That is not a difficult request to manage," she said, retrieving what appeared to be a clay oil lamp. She dipped her fingers into the fuel pooled in the recess, then pinched the wick alight—and it came to life like no ordinary flame, blooming an eldritch blue that shifted and stabilized into a green like cucumber sauce. Just as soothing, too, if the relieved slump of Pashangali's shoulders was anything to go by.

She was younger than he was, and taller by a handspan, slender and smooth as a young eucalyptus, fluted and fine-boned and furious. Thick bands of dark body paint delineated limbs, circling the rounds of her shoulders, the knobs of her elbows and knees, clustered like rings around each of her fingers. With a curious frown, Ronoah noticed a rope wrapping around her ribs and shoulders, almost the same as Chabra'i had worn except the knots and twists were different. Her round face, framed by her straight black bowl cut, had something keenly animal about it: perhaps it was the upward arch of her lip, reminiscent of a rabbit, or the flare of her nostrils, suggestive of a snake.

"Our Lady Jau-Hasthasndra," Chashakva said by way of introduction. She locked eyes with Ronoah, added in Acharrioni: "A visual."

Chashakva had some pretty high hopes if she thought he knew what to do with this.

Lady Jau-Hasthasndra was still too sickly to speak, so it fell to Chashakva to give Ronoah and Nazum context for what they were seeing. "Pashangali was born *third-minded*. As far as Jau-Hasthasndr philosophy goes, most animals have one mind—sensory, instinctual, concerned with the realm of the material. Human beings have a second one, which lets you ponder and plan and generally reflect on your own existence. But once in a while a heartlander will be born with a third mind, one that overlaps and overtakes both of the others, amplifying their qualities—and aggravating them, too."

Pashangali's third mind allowed her to experience the world through an array of outlandish senses—smelling colours, tasting sounds, feeling the pricks and pings of human speech in her own limbs. The kind of enigmatic, associative logic that meant she could tell truth from lies by whether she felt a statement in her skull or her toes, or detect illness by sniffing behind a person's ear.

"In exchange for this power, our wisewoman is besieged by all manner of physical ailments—cluster headaches, chronic nausea, enough muscle tension to make rocks feel soft in comparison." Chashakva left Pashangali's side to fill a cup with water from a basin. The soft slosh cradled the harsh reality of her words. "Not all of those sensory chimeras are friendly. Sometimes the overload is enough to completely incapacitate her, leave her useless until she can crawl into some dark, quiet place to recover."

"That sounds awful," Ronoah murmured. Pashangali shifted in her seat, and he wondered whether the sound of his voice did something, whether it hurt. He hoped not.

"People learn to cope with these things." Chashakva pushed the cup into Pashangali's hands. "She has her assists, her little strategies. No, from what I've heard the *real* trouble started when she was made wise-woman. Something about the role—the intensity of the initiation rites, the pressure of fulfilling her new responsibilities, perhaps even the bless-ings of her Seed—something birthed an entirely new ability from Lady Jau-Hasthasndra's third mind."

Ronoah looked again at Pashangali. She could only have been a few years older than Nazum, eighteen, nineteen at most. He wondered how long ago she had stepped up as the Jau-Hasthasndr wisewoman, and suppressed an anxious jab in his chest. "What was it?" he asked.

"Mirroring. A very rare and totally involuntary sensation of touch that matches anyone she sees in front of her. When a child scrapes its knee, the sting runs up her own leg; when young lovers kiss, she feels it on her lips, the breath, the brush and press." Chashakva's eyes flicked up to meet his. "It's a particularly vicious kind of empathy."

Every desire and discomfort of her people, reflected in her body without her control. Though Ronoah had no third mind, he suddenly understood completely. Kinship sparked green as a flame at his breast— alongside an unexpected protectiveness. No one should have to suffer that.

But the similarities didn't end there. "She'd hate to hear me say this," Chashakva said, facing Ronoah and Nazum, "but the mirroring isn't actu-ally the biggest obstacle. It's the guilt. It's the fear." Ronoah heard the implication in his head, in a voice halfway between Chashakva's and his own: *the fear-beyond-fear.* "Lady Jau-Hasthasndra is pious as they come. The thought of failing her Seed is unbearable—and she spends so much time fighting it that she leaves herself no strength for marshalling that third mind. It undermines her, she cannot perform her wisewomanly duty, and *zam*, prophecy self-fulfilled."

"And then it happens even worse the next time," Ronoah breathed, peering at Pashangali's tense form hunched over the table. She was in such pain, and yet he couldn't help but behold her with a sort of awe. There was someone else. Another person who battled the same self-criticism he battled, who could spiral to such extremes. He hadn't known.

Chashakva dipped her chin. "Just so."

In the silence that followed, the wisewoman roused herself, bracing her hands on the table and taking a measured breath before speaking. She kept her eyes closed. "I hear this gift is common among your people, shiyalshandr," came Nazum's translation a staggered moment later, and Ronoah realized she was addressing him. "Ai?"

Oh. Right. *He has it in his power to pick your emotions like berries.* In this story, in this role, it turned out he *did* have a third mind. "Ahai," he said softly.

"Then you know the secret to wielding it, to controlling its might." When Ronoah did not immediately reply, she reached across the table and found Chashakva's arm, squeezing hard enough that Ronoah saw the paling of flesh beneath her fingers. "That *is* what you promised me, Chashakva."

The green flame flickered; by the time it settled, Ronoah understood the shape of the plan, the help he was supposed to give. "You want me—to teach you," he said, trying to inflect it simultaneously like a statement for Pashangali and a question for Chashakva. He wasn't sure he managed either correctly, but Chashakva met him halfway.

"Pashangali needs someone to guide her through emotional regulation," she said in Chiropolene. "Someone to teach the difference between making a mistake and being one." Those words were still precious to Ronoah, pearly with his own personal connection to them. They made him straighten up, square his shoulders. "Once her anxiety's under control, you can try exploring ways to skin her empathy over, like yours—who knows, you might discover a trick or two for yourself along the way. When she feels she is able to appear at the Council of All Tribes as a wisewoman worthy of the name, she will come."

"That's...that's it?" Ronoah frowned. "Just—tell her how to be kind to herself?"

Chashakva indulged him with a darkly amused smile. "It's harder than it sounds." Then, more seriously, "And there is a time limit."

"The—before pre-winter, right?" No, that wouldn't give Pashangali time to make it to Sasaupta Falls. It had to be— "Before monsoon?"

"Earlier. In order to secure Pashangali Jau-Hasthasndra's support, we need to heal her relationship to her powers before Orchid Ten. The start of the second week of the second month of spring."

Nazum scoffed, so abruptly that Ronoah actually jumped. "Right," the boy said, the single word absolutely dripping with scorn. "Sister, not so sure Runa's cut out for work like that."

The lack of faith stung. Hadn't they moved past Nazum's low opinion of Ronoah after the guguri? Before he could ask, Chashakva met Nazum's stare, cut it down with a genial menace of her own. "I don't remember asking you, remora mine."

Nazum stiffened, his face a limelit mask of displeasure. Ronoah bit his cheek; while he was grateful for the defense, that was a cruel way for Chashakva to frame it. "I can do this," he said to Nazum, trying to redirect. "Really, it's—it's exactly my sort of thing."

Nazum looked at him with seemingly inexhaustible scepticism—which made it all the more impressive that Ronoah didn't feel discouraged. If anything, he was excited. Tentatively, respectfully, but excited nonetheless. He could see why Chashakva had thought to bring him; it was an oddly perfect assignment. Another touch of destiny.

He approached Pashangali, who was massaging her face like she'd just woken from a long sleep. She looked like a life-size marionette, with those night-black bands of paint around her joints. Like a series of segments. "It's an honour to meet you, Lady Jau-Hasthasndra."

She peeked through her fingers, staring at him with eyes that were equally haughty and suspicious. Maybe, like Chabra'i, she had inherent distrust of shiyalshandr; maybe she just thought no one could help her. But Ronoah saw beneath that, down to the deep weariness, the want to be helped, to be better. A half-smile crept onto his lips. Mirror indeed. "I will teach you everything I know."

SEVENTEEN

LADY JAU-HASTHASNDRA NEEDED THE REST of the day to recover, so Chashakva took the lead in showing Ronoah and Nazum around the village. They traversed wooden trackways through the swamp, visiting the weaver's workshop and the warrior's training grounds, the tannery, the brewery, the smokehouse. The library where codices snuggled in alcoves, history inked into delicately-veined vellum; the furnaces on the outskirts of the village, where the Jau-Hasthasndr smelted choice morsels of iron from ore fished from the bogs. In Subindr territory everyone ran and climbed everywhere, exuberant and brisk, but the Jau-Hasthasndr took their time. Perhaps it was to do with the treacherous ground they walked, pocked with peatland, ready to cave under their weight.

Chashakva's tour was not solely for their benefit. While she made sure to introduce Ronoah and Nazum to the places they would be spending most of their time—banquet hall, baths, plumeria-garlanded guesthouse—more than half of the walk-around was spent presenting them to the people they would be spending that time *with*.

"The river runs," Chashakva would say, the customary greeting, and receive "The forest grows, sister," in return, coloured with nervousness or relief or awe depending on how ready someone was to meet a bona fide demon that day.

Everyone seemed far less suspicious of Ronoah than Chabra'i's people had been; nobody shied way or made excuses to avoid them. Maybe Chashakva had laid the foundations for a good first impression after all. At the very least, she had apparently informed everyone of Ronoah's purpose here, because within minutes of meeting they told him their hopes and prayers for the wisewoman, wellwishings for Pashangali Jau-Hasthasndra peppered with accounts of their own challenging encounters with her.

"I have to hide this arm if she is to see me," said one of the librarians, holding up an arm layered with the deep red rash of an old burn scar.

"I keep fresh water lilies in my house in case she walks by—I think it's something about how I smell?" said the tallest of the warriors, gesturing to a threshold awash with blossoms.

"When she visits to consult with my wife, I cannot speak." The track-layer's husband brought a hand up, touched his chin almost tentatively. There was nothing about his voice that Ronoah thought noteworthy, but the man insisted, "It makes her nauseous. I used to sing in the choir on feasting days but ..." He looked away, and Ronoah's heart twinged.

The Jau-Hasthasndr villagers approached Ronoah furtively, respectfully, in a way that reminded him disorientingly of prayer. It couldn't be further from Chabra'i's jibes and playful ridicule. In Subindr territory he'd been seen as a trickster, a potential danger, or else a slightly naïve spirit; here he was a chthonic guardian come to assist a tribe in its woes. That realization settled extra weight into his step, extra care into how he held his face. This wasn't illusory power anymore—somewhere between Chabra'i's treehouse and Pashangali's cabin, it had transformed into something real.

The consequences would be just as real if he messed it up.

"Do you really think I can do this?" he asked Chashakva that evening, the last private moment they had before she left for the rest of the northeast. "It's not just Pashangali, it's—the entire village is in disarray, in conflict. I can feel the fault lines." Emotional fractures webbed the Jau-Hasthasndr village like a second layer of trackway, rifts of guilt and disappointment. Unspoken questions drifted just under the swamp surface: what good was a wisewoman who could only see two thirds of her villagers? What kind of villager would cause their wisewoman so much grief? How could you reconcile, when with every movement or every sound, one of you is wincing?

"Don't get ahead of yourself," Chashakva replied as she crouched to untie her boat from the docks. "I did not ask you to fix a village."

Around the edges of the bay, the willow fronds stirred. "I know." Ronoah frowned, hugging his arms. "I just ..."

Chashakva huffed a laugh through her nose, and he knew she'd caught the thing curled delicate under his tongue, the thing he still didn't quite know how to say aloud. "You didn't know one person's anxiety could wreak so much communal havoc?"

Ronoah's stomach tightened, trussed by his own sudden guilt, but he dipped his chin. "Mm."

"Humans are porous creatures," Chashakva pointed out, tossing the mooring rope into the craft. "Sure, there aren't many empaths of your calibre, but everybody feels everybody else to some degree—you're all interconnected. For better or worse." She leveled her gaze at him, stark in the lamplight. "All the more reason to concentrate on Pashangali. She is at the center of this web. Remedy her relationship with herself, and she'll see to her relationships with the others all on her own."

"They'll still—" He bit his tongue, faces flashing in his mind that belonged to no one in Shaipuri. "...want her, when she's feeling better? As wisewoman, I mean."

Chashakva smiled. "I believe they will."

And Ronoah let himself be comforted. "Have you figured out anything about the deadzones?" he asked, and Chashakva's smile stayed exactly the same but the air about her grew sombre nonetheless. "I'm glad so many tribes are already agreed to come to the Council, but does that change anything if the rainforest is still in danger? Could their gods really still need...?"

"I have a guess or two. But my guesses are proving themselves intriguingly difficult to track down."

"How long do you think you'll be away?"

"Difficult to say—I thought I was conservative in my estimate last time, and yet." She considered him. "Are you asking whether I'll return before Orchid Ten?"

His deadline. The date that would decide whether the Jau-Hasthasndr came to Council too. Ronoah reached for Chashakva's hand; it burned cool, tingled with bottled lightning. "Please try. I'm going to do my best, but—but just in case," he said with his own sheepish smile, "I'd really appreciate you swooping in at the last minute to save me from anything stupid I've done."

Chashakva squeezed his hand, not in acquiescence but acknowledgement. A whirlwind of tingles in the cradle of space between their palms. Ronoah pulled her in for a hug.

"Good luck," he said as he stepped away—and, as a queer instinct took hold of him, "Good hunting."

"Likewise, little demon."

And then she was leaving, ducking under dripping willow as she rowed the craft away. Ronoah saw her off like he had in Chabra'i's hut, watching until the mist disappeared her from the world.

According to Nazum, Orchid Ten was almost three Shaipurin months away, closer to four in the Chiropolene calendar. Three months was plenty of time. Sure, it had taken six for Özrek to teach Ronoah these lessons, but Ronoah considered himself a tougher nut to crack than Pashangali. Özrek had to resort to some extremely finicky, over-the-top pageantry with Ronoah; he wasn't planning on sticking Lady Jau-Hasthasndra in a sinkhole until she self-confidenced her way out of it. He didn't need to.

Fear-beyond-fear was an opportunistic feeder. It devoured whatever was within reach, transfigured any mild concern into calamity. Anxiety cast all your mundane worries like bones and read from them the ruin of your life. It would scare a banquet out of you, and then eat its fill. Ronoah had spent enough time laid on the table of his own fear to know this. He knew the helplessness, the harrowed, haunted feeling, the frustration of being held back by something invisible to everyone else. He could trace that downward spiral in his sleep.

But he had also traced himself a new tributary, carved a new river of thinking by hand. He had learned to pick himself up, to forgive himself, to distinguish between mistakes and catastrophes. He had strategies—human-shaped strategies, ones that wouldn't take half a year of spelunking to impart.

"For the last time, shiyalshandr, that *isn't going to work.*"

A few days in, Ronoah realized he had also grown a new power: the ability to overestimate himself.

"I understand it's, it sounds illogical at first," he was saying, trying to sound convincing heedless of Pashangali's glare, "but it really does work—if you accept your panic then it frightens you less."

"It doesn't *frighten me.*"

"And it's okay to admit that you're frightened! This isn't your fault, you're not failing anyone just by feeling scared—!"

Pashangali hissed something Nazum didn't bother to translate; Ronoah knew a curse when he heard one. "I do not feel *scared*, shiyalshandr, I'm useless but I'm not pathetic. I cannot let these sensations rule over me, you're suggesting I just lie down and let them win—"

"That isn't what I'm saying," Ronoah said, but he felt her inflexibility like an iron rod in his hands. He sighed, lifting his eyes to the rafters of her cabin, where hopefully some extra patience lay shelved among the bales of herbs. "It's not *about* letting anything win, it's about not *fighting* so hard that you—"

"Not fighting?" the wisewoman cried with a laugh like acid. "How soft *is* the underworld? Fighting is how I get through every moment of every day."

"Including this one, I see," Ronoah snapped, then sighed again, massaging the hot strike of irritation out of his brow. Clearly extra patience was beyond him today. "Take some time to breathe, Lady Jau-Hasthasndra. I'll return later."

This had become a pattern by now: showing up, talking it out, hitting a snag, spiralling until either Pashangali or Ronoah himself got frustrated enough to call it a day. He was having second thoughts about being the more stubborn one in the room—Pashangali wasn't just resistant, she was flat-out obstinate. She was easily annoyed when asked what she deemed stupid questions, and when Ronoah asked non-stupid questions she was still reluctant to answer. Maybe, like Ronoah, she worried that speaking was summoning—given she could literally feel words, that seemed a legitimate fear. Maybe it was simply difficult to explain.

It was certainly made no easier by needing Nazum as an intermediary. The boy had never experienced any of the sensations Ronoah and Pashangali were trying to communicate, and so their sessions were protracted by his pauses as he tried to find a suitable translation. More than once, Pashangali slapped the boy upside the head for taking too long or asking her to repeat herself a third time; the violence made Ronoah bristle, which added friction to the already-strained proceedings. But Nazum forbade him from making a fuss about it.

"Brother, leave it lie," he said, re-tying his topknot after the end of another ill-fated session two weeks in. "It's not like I get some perverse enjoyment from it—s'just that it's either me or you, and you remember what our lady said. 'Human shield' is in the job description." The fact that he'd smacked Ronoah in the arm when Ronoah suggested admonishing Pashangali was, apparently, an exception.

"We can just *not tell* Chashakva, it's okay—"

"Runa, have I mentioned lately that you're kind of a wimp? She'd give you one good whack and you'd have to take the day off." He ignored Ronoah's scowling, leading the way to the baths. "You en't allowed a day off, shiyalshandr. The faster you fix yon cranky lady, the sooner we leave this place behind. I can soak away the bruises until then."

The public baths were one of the busiest locations in town. Jau-Hasthasndr villagers washed daily as part of their water Seed's worship, and Chashakva had warned Ronoah and Nazum that they would be looked at funny if they didn't follow suit. The two arrived and swerved into the men's side of the baths; as Ronoah eased into the water, his feet instantly tingling from the temperature, he saw a servant carefully heaving heated stones in. They hissed as they hit the surface.

"Why are there baths if they live on the river, anyway?" he asked Nazum, his irritability lingering. "I never asked Chashakva."

Nazum had sunk down to his chin, hair gone frizzy in the heat. "Beats me. Maybe they like showing off."

"Showing off to who though?"

"It's a joke, Runa." Nazum brought his hands up to splash water on his face; his fingers had bloomed pink. "I dunno. Kinda stupid that the worshippers of a river god don't think the river's good enough for 'em."

"That's not what I—" Ronoah exhaled evenly through his nose, slumping a little further in the water himself. "Sorry." It was nice to hide in the steam, to let himself be shrouded from everyone's curious, hopeful stares. Underwater, Nazum elbowed him. *No hard feelings, demon boy.*

Except there were. Not between Ronoah and Nazum, but between Ronoah and himself. He couldn't understand what was wrong with him. It wasn't that he was making a less-than-impressive start as Pashangali's emotional tutor—he was dryly surprised he had expected anything else. It wasn't even that his own empathy tended to clang against Pashangali's in jarring ways. These things had reasonable explanations; they didn't upset him.

What upset him was how *annoyed* he was by Pashangali.

Ronoah had thought he would be a good mentor to Pashangali Jau-Hasthasndra, given they experienced so many of the same extremes, the same *tendencies*, as Chashakva put it. He could relate to her, understand what she was going through. Nothing had prepared him for just how unsympathetic he actually felt in practice. Watching her clam up, hearing her say something self-deprecating or say *nothing* and feeling the defeatist undercurrent hidden in the silence—knowing what she was thinking didn't make him kinder to her, it made him want to shake her until she stopped. He'd believed he was a better person than that.

Slowly, the bathwater leached the pent-up agitation from his body, drained him of both Pashangali's malice and his own. He washed water up his arms, returning the cordial nods of some of the bathers—and noticed something that made his stomach flip.

"Nazum, did we go the wrong way?"

"What? No, why?"

"We—" No, they'd turned right, like they always did. So it was just that— "Some of the men have breasts."

"Oh." The boy bobbed up from the water, squinting. "Oh, yeah. It's a thing. Some tribes sort out men and women by the lumps and bumps on your body—others sort it by the ones on your personality."

Weirdly, that was grounding. Here was a place whose concept of social role was a little more fluid, less like Chiropole's and more like Pilanova's. Here was something he related to and understood without baggage. Ronoah leaned his head back on the stone lip of the bath, feeling even through the curtains of steam that a part of him had become unhidden.

"I wish my personality was better suited to this," he confessed, to the sky and to Nazum. "I think maybe I was wrong."

"I know," Nazum said, and Ronoah cut him as withering a glare as he could manage. As per usual, it bounced right off. "Seems like it's really gnawing at you though."

"I just didn't expect it to be *this* difficult. She won't even *try*—I'm doing everything Chashakva taught me and it's just not getting through."

"With respect, brother, things sound mighty more impressive when they come outta Chashakva's mouth."

Ronoah covered his face, groaning in renewed irritation. Didn't he know it. "So is it *my* fault, then?" he asked through his fingers. "Am I just a rotten teacher?"

"*Chuta ka saag.*" Ronoah looked up just in time to get splashed in the face as the boy threw water at him. "If you're looking for advice, ask. I been ferrying your words back and forth for long enough to have an opinion." Rubbing bathwater out of his eyes, Ronoah nodded. "Far as I can see, all your ideas are good and sound and sane enough—you're just framing them all wrong. It en't your material, it's your *tone*. She's right, you know," he said in response to Ronoah's confusion, "calling your underworld soft, and you along with it. You always take the, the *nice* road, going on about kindness and patience and *embracing vulnerability*—maybe she doesn't need kindness. Or maybe—gah, maybe her kindness looks different to yours. Like being told to get over herself already."

Ronoah's mouth fell open. "I really don't know if that would help," he started—but then he stopped, as a memory overtook him. Özrek, in the monastery, confirming all of Ronoah's self-obsessed sabotage before listing his more shining qualities. Usually Ronoah avoided reflecting on the first half of that conversation—Özrek himself had called it redundant—but maybe those words had their place. Maybe Pashangali needed that blunt honesty.

Nazum picked at the rope scars on his shoulder. "I'm just saying sometimes people don't need pity, they need perspective. Remember what Chabra'i used to say to her patients? *Either you get better or you die?* Might be a shock to you, but that's what kindness sounds like here. Think about it—does this tribe seem like the kind where normal people are allowed to criticize the wisewoman to her face? Asides from Jau-Hasthasuna himself, you and Chashakva are probably the only ones with the authority to tell her what's a problem and what's a piss-fit. She's already getting praise and comfort and whatever from her people— and honestly, the praise'll be worth more from them, because they didn't just show up two seconds ago."

"It's—a stronger approach, than I would think to use." Ronoah bit his lip. "I wouldn't like it, if it were me."

"Yeah, well. You can't always talk to someone the way you'd wanna be talked to. People learn all kinds of ways, and fancy feelings demon or not, you en't in a position to begrudge 'em that."

Ronoah was not prepared for this level of profundity from Nazum. He never was. The cocky, constantly-complaining persona the boy fronted was so pervasive that it was easy to forget another side lurked beneath, something thoughtful, measured. Like Ronoah, Nazum had a soft under-world of his own. It was worth listening to when it surfaced.

"I'll try it," he said at length. It felt dangerous—but so did repeating the same mistakes while Orchid Ten drew ever-closer.

Later, lying awake on his reed mat, Ronoah sifted through the things he might tell the wisewoman if he spoke to her like he'd once spoken to himself. Scared himself, a little, with how cruel he could still be. Tried to find a more constructive way—a more Chashakvandr way—to say it all. Firm, but fair. Approached with care. Kind like the sun could be kind, shedding light on even the ugliest things so you could work with them. Truthful.

In the morning, by the time he and Nazum crossed the threshold of Pashangali's cabin, he thought he had something to work with.

"The river runs, wisewoman," he called, words he'd heard so often he knew exactly how to say them in Shaipurin. He said them in Chiropolene anyway.

"The forest grows, shiyalshandr." Even though it was a ritual greeting, Pashangali always said it with the weight of hours worrying that the forest would, in fact, grow no more. She beckoned the two of them over to her low tea table. "What trick are you trying today?"

Ronoah didn't budge. "I'm not trying anything." Nazum translated, and Ronoah watched as Pashangali's black eyes widened. "Not until you decide to meet me halfway."

The wisewoman's shoulders stiffened. "What do you mean, meet you half—"

"Pashangali, you had sixteen weeks to get this right. Nearly three of those weeks are now gone, and absolutely nothing has changed. We talk every day, and every day you scoff at my theories, and you shoot down my suggestions without so much as considering them. I am—" His throat tightened. Here it was. "I am forced to wonder whether you actually want to get stronger, or whether you're just—just determined to keep being helpless."

It was so strange, hearing words like this leave his mouth. They had only ever been directed inward, in malice, in contempt. But perhaps the same words with a new tone could be used for good. A weapon made tool.

"I don't believe you *enjoy* being miserable," he continued before she could say anything, "but I think you are comfortable in your misery, because you know how it fits you. It is a—familiar pain. And perhaps my ways are strange and unknown and that represents the possibility of unfamiliar pain, of something you don't know how to deal with, but—but you have *obligations* to fulfill, Lady Jau-Hasthasndra, and if you keep going like this it will be impossible for you to fulfill them. This is about more than your personal embarrassment. It's bigger than you."

Pashangali took in what he was saying, opened her mouth—then closed it again. The faintest quirk of her brow, not a crease of anger but of...worry?

"So what am I supposed to do? Try some reckless thing and ruin any control I have?" Astonishingly, underneath Nazum's Chiropolene he thought he heard a quaver of dismay.

"Come to my lessons without a cenote's worth of pessimism," he said. "Accept that the control you currently have is—meaningless, in the face of the control you want. Humble yourself before Chashakva, who gave me to you for the sake of these teachings. Trust that I—I actually have your best interest at heart, that I'm not waiting for you to slip up so I can mock you for it." That was verging on *kindness and patience and embracing vulnerability*, so he added, "I have better things to do than laugh at you."

Again, he worried these judgements were too uncharitable, but again Pashangali gave his words a consideration she never had before. "You are brusque today, shiyalshandr," she said, though she didn't sound offended at his lack of warmth. If anything, she seemed almost a little cowed. "You speak as if I have no faith at all."

"I think you do have faith in us." Ronoah leaned against the doorframe, one hand reaching discretely for his garnet tucked in the folds of his wrap. For backup. "In shiyalsha, in your gods, in Chashakva and me. But I think you lack faith in yourself, and that kind of self-disgust is poison in the well here." Pashangali's hand came up to cover her mouth, a jerky half-aborted gesture. It was hard to find out someone else could see your deeper layers so plainly. "I think you need to allow yourself a possible reality where this *works*, where you show yourself mercy, before you can start to see results."

Pashangali closed her eyes. She was silent for a long time. When she finally spoke, it was in a muffled grumble that Nazum squinted at. Pashangali repeated herself just loud enough to catch: "And what if that reality *doesn't* exist? What if even the shiyalshandr can't fix—this. Me. What pains me." Her hand still shielded the lower half of her face, as if in a vain attempt to keep this dread from spilling out. "If I try your methods, and they *don't* work, then all I have is proof that even underworld magic cannot make me a worthy wisewoman."

There it was, fragile as splintered glass: the desire to grow that Ronoah had seen on day one, the yearning so desperate it calcified thick scales of cynicism to protect itself. The deep, dark fear that once you used up the last resort, there would be nothing for you.

"I don't believe your god would abandon you that way," he blurted—and then paused, caught himself on the edge of being too honest, too himself, too *human* for this particular answer. Out of sight, he squeezed the garnet for strength. "You are devoted, disciplined, you are hurting yourself every day trying to appease your Seed, to save him—that dedication does not go unnoticed." With his free hand, he gestured to the row of spears leaned against a slightly dusty corner of the cabin. "You're the latest in a long line of wisewomen. Do you really think the spirits of your predecessors below *aren't* supporting the ground you walk on?"

Something changed in the air, the electric tone between them. Got her.

"I come from shiyalsha," he said, tasting the words' power on his tongue, "and I know the dead still care for the living. Draw on their strength, call on their protection, and—and don't disrespect their faith in *you*. You're a worthy wisewoman because they chose you to be one. Because—they wished it. It's that simple."

Nazum finished speaking, and Pashangali locked eyes with Ronoah. His breath caught in his chest at the energy that rolled like mist between them. The lack of scorn in the wisewoman's features, the slump of her shoulders. The wince as the lance of her headache drove into her, ringing sympathetic behind Ronoah's eye—and the shaky sound as she inhaled, marshalling her ire into something softer, something raw.

"I only hope—I pray for the grace never to do that." It was more a confession than anything Ronoah had ever heard from her. It actually threw him a bit. "Disrespect their faith, I mean."

"Pray with your heart, but pray with your head and your hands, too," he said, coming to sit across from the wisewoman. "I know you have that grace. Help me prove it to you."

For the first time in three weeks, they spent a whole session without snapping at each other. Pashangali listened to his explanations, his theories, even agreed to try out a few affirming phrases in the privacy of her cabin. Ronoah could hardly believe it.

"I'm shocked," he said to Nazum later, eagerly scarfing down dinner. "That went so well, that was, gods, I thought it would take more than one try? She's usually so stubborn, but that just—wow. Wow, you were right. All it took was some perspective. That was amazing."

Nazum was listening to his rambling unusually patiently. The boy's cheek was dimpled in a smirk. "What is it?" Ronoah asked, and Nazum's smirk cracked open into a grin.

"You did good work, brother," Nazum answered, taking a slurp of bogberry wine. He set the cup down, swiveled it this way and that. "Much better than I expected. But I might've taken some liberties with your wording." He looked up, trickery in his eye. "Not my best tongue, you know. Gotta get creative sometimes."

"Vespasi wake," Ronoah swore in Acharrioni, with a vehemence that Nazum raised his eyebrows at.

"That a sneeze, demon boy?"

"What did you *say* to her?"

"Most of it's the same! Except that end bit about devotion and ancestors and stuff." Nazum swirled his finger in his bowl to pick up the last crumbs. "Summed up, I told her that worst comes to worst, she's right, and nobody can fix her, and she fucks up and fails and her Seed gets et by some other stronger Seed. Boo-hoo. That's how it's supposed to work."

Ronoah made a noise like a gerbil being stepped on. Nazum took the opportunity to swipe a piece of lotus bread from Ronoah's bowl, completely unabashed. "I also told her you said to appoint someone as replacement wisewoman, just in her own head, so she has an out if she's too weak to rise to the challenge. Sometimes knowing you've got the out is why you don't take it."

Cold, unsupportive, seemingly uncaring—and yet exactly what Pashangali needed to hear. These were words Ronoah could never have said, if only because he lacked the cultural attunement to imagine them. Nazum had done more than translate words; the boy had dug deep into his intention and interpreted that as well.

Ronoah startled them both with a bout of stunned laughter. "Thank you," he said.

Absurdly, it was only once gratitude was on the table that Nazum thought to look sheepish. "Yeah, whatever," he said, rubbing his neck. "Long as you don't mind me putting words in your mouth, or whatnot." He was so stiff all of a sudden, so awkward—and Ronoah caught that awkwardness like a contagion as they both apparently realized at the same time that this could have been misunderstood as sabotage, as deliberately stepping out of line.

"No—I mean yes, yes it's fine, you're fine, you're good." Gods, he was beginning to *sound* like Nazum, tripping over niceties. Where was his Pilanovani politeness when he needed it? "You know these lands better than I do, you have—more perspective. I would really appreciate your input." He paused. "Maybe just warn me beforehand so I know not to put too much effort into whatever useless thing I'm saying."

Nazum cracked and laughed. "You say a lot of useless shit. But sometimes you nail it, Runa. And you got me to save your butt until you get good at it."

So it was that Nazum became even more integral to Ronoah's task than he already was. More integrated. So it was that Ronoah began to suspect the boy was now, possibly, finally, truly on his side. So it was that, as the days wore on, Chashakva's promise to Pashangali showed the first possibility of being honoured.

EIGHTEEN

$\mathcal{A}$T THE END OF ANOTHER MONTH'S TUTELAGE, it came to Ronoah's attention that he was now a woman.

He found this out through Nazum—specifically, Nazum's sputtering surprise at some subtle change in the grammar the villagers used when they spoke about Ronoah. Somewhere along the line he had been bestowed the feminine; his progress with Pashangali had earned him the title of honourary wisewoman.

To Ronoah, this was both a sign of nearly embarrassing respect and a warning. You have their trust now, it said—do not squander it. Follow through.

"This is giving me headaches," Nazum groused as they went on one of their walks together. "You don't get it, your whole social standing just got bumped up, I gotta start talking in the feminine and I'm not used to that—and what does that make me? They gotta look at me and see girl even though I'm barely half boy to them, unless it *does* make me a girl, since I'm basically part of you."

"That does sound confusing," Ronoah offered. Nazum spat morosely into the water.

At least a few of the boy's questions were answered when, a few days later, Pashangali stiffly invited both of them to the baths.

"I usually go alone," she said by way of explanation, "but today is Rain Two, and it is good luck to spend Rain Two with company." She led the way from her cabin; Ronoah noticed the tensing of her shoulders as they walked by the tallest warrior talking to one of his comrades, but Pashangali lifted a hand in greeting and passed without incident. When they reached the vestibule that divided the women's bath from the men's, Ronoah felt the first physical impact of his new stature—he had to consciously turn left to follow Pashangali, instead of going where his instincts took him.

There was apparently a pool near the top of the cascade which was reserved for the wisewoman. The village women nodded greetings as they ascended, a few calling wellwishings for the holiday, and not a single one showed surprise at Ronoah being there.

"Would you—tell me about Rain Two?" Ronoah asked as he slipped into the pool. To him, the most surprising thing of all was that Pashangali Jau-Hasthasndra wanted to spend time with them outside their prescribed sessions. He wasn't sure how to interact with her here; hopefully asking about local custom would be an innocuous start.

Pashangali had procured a scraping shell and was now working the blunt edge into her left arm. Already the steam was flattening her black bowl-cut. "It is the second day of spring," she said. "Yesterday was Rain One, which is identified and confirmed by Jau-Hasthasuna's wisewoman. She goes on a ritual walk to check for signs that the new season has begun."

"What kind of signs?"

Pashangali held the shell at arm's length, scrutinizing. "There is a certain tree. If you can see it clearly from a certain perch, then the winter mists are lifting and will soon be cut by rain." She resumed her scraping, switching to the right arm. "There is a certain valley, on the edge of the swampland. If the orange lilies are blooming there, the rest of the spring flowers will soon follow. There is a certain place on the Sanaat, where the watersnakes make their nests. If the nests are empty, it means they have gone to join Jau-Hasthasuna as he sweeps a warm tide through the river."

It reminded Ronoah of Sweetwood Day. Go to the northernmost edge of the city, walk a day further, look to the east. If you see clouds above the mountain, the time has come to journey. It was one of the easiest moments to identify in the Acharrioni calendar—many of the others were signified only by slight alterations in the texture and direction of the winds, how dry they were, whether they drove from the west or the southwest. It was the job of Nataglio's wishgranters to learn the whims of the winds, to predict them accurately. Like Pashangali, scouting for signs of a season to come.

It also reminded him of a question he still had floating in his mind unanswered. It was the mention of the Sanaat that prompted him, the vision of the river. "These baths," he started. "Pashangali, your whole tribe takes baths every day in ritual, but why don't you do this in the river?"

Suddenly Pashangali's face was overcast. Chuta ka saag. Trust him to stumble into sensitive territory two turns into a casual conversation. "We did," she said, "until I ordered the bathhouses built. I am Jau-Hasthasuna's wisewoman; by his grace I am granted the power to divert the Sanaat as I wish."

Ronoah frowned. "Why did you give the order?"

"Because I am prudent enough to prepare in advance for the cruelty of others."

Suddenly there was a sharp sensation in Ronoah's chest, itchy and thick. He sat up straight again. "What's—is there something wrong with the river?"

Her nostrils flared, and Chabra'i's deadzone flashed through Ronoah's mind. But after a moment she shook her head. "There's nothing wrong with the river," she said. "I just don't trust the rotten tribes that live on it. Not after what happened with the Vashnarajandr."

Even in the warm steam, the hairs on Ronoah's arms stood up. Chabra'i had told them of the Vashnarajandr's demise, but she'd had no further details to offer. "You know what happened to them?"

"Of course I do. Some slimy tribe of oathbreakers went and took them all, probably killed Vashnarajan himself with what they did. Throwing everything off balance—that's already enough to punish them, whoever they are, but they didn't stop there." Ronoah's heart rose in his ears as he waited for her to elaborate—one beat, two beats, three. "They threw poison in the river," Pashangali finally said, her voice tight with fury. "They tampered with the sanctity of the Sanaat, they soured the water in Vashnarajandr territory, and everything it touched it touched with death."

That sounded exactly like a deadzone. "How do you know that's what happened?" he asked. Pashangali exhaled sharply out her nose, taking her scraping shell and getting to work on her ribs, her breastbone.

"Because we went to that Council. The wisewoman before me, she went to pay tribute. We heard the report. The tribe downriver from the Vashnarajandr got sick out of nowhere. Not just the people—the animals and the plants, too. Anything by the water. So they sent scouts up the Sanaat to investigate, and they found Vashnarajan's whole tribe dead in their homes."

"That's—that's horrible." He hoped the quaver in his voice wasn't audible under Nazum's measured translation. He took a deep breath, trying to steady himself. "That's—"

"It's thoughtless is what it is," Pashangali snapped, plunging the shell underwater with a splash. "It's thoughtless and excessive. The Sanaat feeds us all—they endangered everyone, they went directly against the wishes of the Heavenly Seeds. What use is it, to wipe out a god's entire people? What divine purpose does that serve? They're not trying to nourish anything, they're just satisfying their own bloodlust. They're probably the same ones who started all the ambushing, too."

Ronoah remembered Chabra'i talking about this as well, but he remembered her version differently. "Didn't," he began hesitantly, "didn't the—weren't the gods the ones who ordered a change in how the war was waged?"

Pashangali outright scoffed, casting a derisive look at Ronoah that he hadn't received in a while. "No, shiyalshandr. I've read four hundred years' worth of our wisewomen's words and nowhere does it say that the gods demanded this. It was an act of revolt, plain and simple. There's a tribe out there who wants the rest of us gone, who thinks they're the only one who should survive this. I'm sure of it. There's a tribe trying to *sabotage* the War."

Her voice tripped on the last sentence, and it hit Ronoah all over again just how young Pashangali Jau-Hasthasndra was to be trying to save the world from apocalypse. She was his sister's age; trying to imagine Lelos forced to hold such heavy tragedy made his heart ache.

The possibility that someone was intentionally trying to make it *worse* was unthinkable.

"Can I ask how you came to be Jau-Hasthasuna's wisewoman?" Ronoah hoped it wasn't a disrespect to ask. "Were you—what happened to the wisewoman before you, the one who went to Council? Did she also have a third mind?"

Pashangali hesitated, then sighed. She set the shell down and levered herself up to sit on the edge of the pool, resting her elbows on her knees in a posture that was painfully reminiscent of Chashakva. "I am the first of my family to become wisewoman," she said, "though we are third-minded in different ways. My father could taste sounds as I do; his sister could see them. I believe my father's mother was third-minded as well, but I cannot say how, for I never met her. We are traditionally bringers of good luck, helpers to the wisewoman of the tribe. We are often brought on war campaigns to sway the favour of the gods. So we die quickly."

Pain clenched in Ronoah's chest at the same time that Pashangali curled her fists. He wondered whether those deaths were the result of sheer statistics, or whether there was something more intentional to them. Maybe, in becoming wisewoman, Pashangali had switched one kind of sacrifice for another.

"I began life as a boy," the wisewoman continued, "but when I reached adulthood I grew breasts, and I bled, and the tribe realized I was—was *lua-mujakti*."

Ronoah glanced at Nazum, who had stumbled over the translation. The boy returned the look with the little grimace he wore when attempting to demystify a new concept. "It's like, well, it literally means 'perfect form', but it's also kind of a pun because *lua* is close to *laua* which is 'two'

146

but *mujakti* is formed in the singular—so it's like two things in one, which makes the one ideal? It's a regional thing, don't ask me for details," he said, waving any further explanation away. "Basically, twice the parts, twice the power."

Growing up in Pilanova, Ronoah had been taught that roles and responsibilities were determined by whether your godling was more in alignment with Pao or Innos, Chaos or Order. All godlings were a little bit of both—the only ones who were fully chaotic or orderly were Pao and Innos themselves, and they made wishes incredibly rarely. But Pashangali would be classed as something even more miraculous, in Pilanovani terms—a child of Eje, the transformative source that contained both Pao and Innos while still remaining a separate entity. He didn't think he'd ever heard of a wishgranter like that existing, not even in legend.

Granted, the oracles didn't rely on the shape of a body to determine a person's godling, so that wasn't necessarily true. He had to sort of swivel the concept sideways to have it make sense, but it helped him to understand where the Shaipurin were coming from with the *lua-mujakti*. Perfect beings. Twice as powerful.

"I didn't know someone could be both at the same time like that," was all he said. Pashangali nodded.

"The tribe took it as a sign that divinity surrounded me. Yet another sign, that my third mind was so much more powerful than my family's. When my parents had gone, fed to the gods, and it was my turn to be brought to the battlefield, the wisewoman named me as her successor instead of taking me with her. She never returned."

"She could do that?" Too late, Ronoah thought of how Nazum had told Pashangali to pre-emptively appoint her own replacement. "I mean—it's not a community decision? She has the power to just point and choose?"

"She does. I don't know about the other tribes, but here our wisewomen actually hold the wisdom they are named for." It nearly made him laugh, Pashangali's haughtiness interrupting even this intimate story. "We put our faith in them entirely. We put so much faith in them that when new wisewomen are named, they are barely trained. They are not confirmed until their predecessor dies."

"If they aren't trained, then how does the knowledge get passed on?"

"Our wisdom comes not from the overworld, shiyalshandr, it comes from the gods. Any knowledge worth preserving is transcribed into the library. There is a codex with the words of every wisewoman since the beginning of the war—which is forbidden to anyone but the wisewoman herself," Pashangali added, catching Ronoah's eager lean-in. "Every new wisewoman's first task, after the drowning, is to read it. They recopy it into new parchment, and then they sacrifice the original. So the wisdom of the gods becomes their own."

It was a beautiful practice. It carried a weight, lonely but meaningful. It still appalled Ronoah that Pashangali had endured so much so young—but suddenly he wondered whether that affront was patronizing, whether it did a disservice to the ways Pashangali had persisted and survived. His city had burned when he was fifteen; some would say he shouldn't have suffered that, either. And yet.

"So this is how you learned to look for orange lilies in the springtime," he said.

As Nazum finished translating, Pashangali blinked. She shook her head and said something with a tone he had seldom heard from her—admiration. The words came a moment later: "You have a sharp memory, shiyalshandr. It is enviable."

"It has its drawbacks," Ronoah quipped without thinking. Nazum said the words before he could take them back—and to both of their amazement, Pashangali actually laughed, a small, low chuckle that changed her face entirely.

"Doesn't every gift?" the wisewoman asked. Under the water, Ronoah felt Nazum's hand dig into his thigh, silent shorthand for *holy gods I thought if she smiled her head would pop off.* "You know, I don't think I've said so before, but the colour of your skin—that mottling—it smells faintly of lilies."

His shoulders dropped in astonishment. Orange lilies. Desert lilies. She may as well have said she could see Genoveffa standing behind him.

"Perhaps springtime will be my lucky season," mused the wisewoman, swishing her long legs in the pool.

It took another nudge from Nazum to get Ronoah to reply. "I—I hope so," he said. He took Pashangali's shell and worked it into his own arm for something to do with his hands, feeling water stream in rivulets down his lily skin. "I really hope it is."

Pashangali gave him a strange look, like she wanted to smile but wasn't sure how to do it under the circumstances. She slid back into the water, disappearing up to the shoulders. "I think it…might be," she confirmed, and Ronoah wasn't sure why she sounded so tentative about it until she added, so quietly Nazum almost didn't catch it, "I should thank you."

Pashangali had never expressed even a hint of gratitude to him—when she wasn't pronouncing his tutelage a waste of time she was quietly gritting her teeth through it, as if even speaking to him was a chore. Finally it struck Ronoah why they were here, why she had invited them, what this whole excursion was meant to demonstrate: her thanks.

"Are you—" Ronoah reined himself in before he could stumble over his own success. "Do you…think you'll be following your predecessor to Council?"

"I think so," came Pashangali's ever-cautious reply, and it was all Ronoah could do to keep from shouting in relief and delight. "I—this is so shameful, I shouldn't even…I only ever actually *made* one sacrifice, my very first, and ever since my weakness has kept me from performing another, I haven't been able to care for Jau-Hasthasuna in over a year, but—" Pashangali peeked over her knees, real hope brightening her eyes "—but this has made me stronger. You have made me stronger, shiyalshandr. I think I can do it now."

Ronoah's joy froze over.

"I really believe I can," Pashangali continued, mistaking his silence for lack of faith. "Last time I was unprepared, she was very small and my eyes were—" She brushed the rim of her eye socket almost curiously with her fingertips, and dizziness hit Ronoah like a storm, fast and howling. He struggled to hear her over the noise growing in his ears. "—maybe I'm too optimistic, maybe I'm overconfident, but I've called for a raid. Jau-Hasthasuna has starved in my care, but this Orchid Ten, I think he may finally eat his fill."

Her cheeks flushed pink with shy determination. She had never looked so proud, so happy. Ronoah could not reach for a single thing to say to her.

Somehow, his lying mouth found the words anyway: "That's—that's great, Pashangali." His stomach clenched. He held his voice steady. "I'm really happy for you."

That evening, the women of Jau-Hasthasuna's village—Ronoah and Nazum included—took a flower from Pashangali and together they followed her into the croaking, chirruping gloom of the swamp at dusk. Single file their procession picked its way under fallen rotwood, over middens of reed, through the dry brush of cattails until they found solid ground. Soon enough, a sinkhole appeared. One by one they tossed their flowers into the passage to the underworld, an offering for Rain Two. When Ronoah approached, he heard the rushing of water in the dark, amplified by the distance, and the dreadful familiarity of the sound rattled him deep inside. He cast his lily into the abyss, and backed away quickly.

NINETEEN

Springtime uncurled purple trumpet flowers on the pale vines of Jau-Hasthasuna's territory. It withered the bogberry patches and replaced them with ripening jackfruit trees, sent the white fowl toward cooler climates and ushered the alligators in. With a village so isolated, you didn't need the wisewoman's codex to tell you when the seasons changed—you could tell by what was on your table.

The send-off banquet for Jau-Hasthasuna's warriors was full of such spring delights: alligator and lotus root, cattail shoot and water chestnut, piled in trenchers made of massive mushroom caps. Spirals of incense crumbled throughout the evening, keeping mosquitoes at bay; lanterns full of fresh-netted fireflies were set about the perimeter to cut the gloom without resorting to the yellow torchlight that so often gave Pashangali headaches.

The wisewoman seemed determined to enjoy herself, symptoms be damned. She sat at the head of the long table and allowed her villagers to approach her with their congratulations, taking the praise with a solemn austerity that vibrated nonetheless with pleasure. She ate a little of everything, took a second helping of cattail shoots. When she blessed the gathering, she didn't wince even once. She couldn't be described as *social* by any means, but Ronoah reached a tendril of empathy out to her and felt that, in her way, she was having a wonderful time.

After the main meal, palate-cleansing treats: tufts of sweet lotus bread, cups of bogberry wine, clear crimson and tart like a knife to the tongue. Then came the songs. The first were ritual songs, hymns for the water and the strength of women, a lament for the alligator, a thirty-three-verse chant for the glory of Jau-Hasthasuna that left Ronoah tingling with its intensity. When Pashangali took her leave, the musicians played on—folk songs used in the field, for digging iron and nailing trackways, for rowing up difficult river. Nazum relaxed enough to add his voice to the calls and responses, and Ronoah was surprised to discover it was one of the most beautiful voices he'd ever heard. The others noticed as well, and for once Nazum's status as Ronoah's shadow was erased. Telling from the boy's grin, he relished the temporary freedom.

Ronoah did not join in. He floated in a strange space, adjacent to but apart from the festivity, sipping his bogberry wine and watching the Jau-Hasthasndr as they sang. Watching them refill each other's cups, retrieve bone flutes and hand drums, rouse the gathered for a big, swaying circle dance. He watched them with their arms around each other's shoulders, stepping left and springing right, swinging the little ones off the ground.

It was hard to remember these people were murderers.

These people, scoffed a voice in his head—an old voice, one that hadn't given him trouble in a long time. You say it like you aren't one of them now. Like you aren't the reason this is happening. It's not *hard to remember*, it's everywhere—how many times have you heard people mention sacrifices and just pretended you didn't hear?

He refilled his cup at the communal bowl, taking another sip and holding onto the fierce flavour, the warmth in his throat. He didn't know. He didn't know how he'd missed it, how he'd somehow managed to prepare someone to drown a child without ever stopping to think about it. No one had ever mentioned it to him—Pashangali hadn't brought it up until the baths, Nazum had never pointed it out, Chashakva had said he was helping Pashangali but she'd never *specified*, never told him what he was helping her to *do*, if she had he'd—

Don't go blaming Chashakva, the voice said, and it was cruel, but it had its point. She brought you to help a wisewoman; wisewomen sacrifice people for their Seeds. That's arithmetic so simple you could have solved it on day one. Nobody tried to hide this from you—you hid it from yourself.

Orchid Ten was eight weeks away. Orchid Ten and the second week of the second month of spring. One of three weeks in the Jau-Hasthasndr calendar where sacrifices were traditionally made. He could have found that out in the library. He could have been more curious about the reason for that deadline. All these could-haves, all these do-overs—all of them useless to him now. There was only one thing left to ask.

Seeds or not, Council of All Tribes or not—could he bear to continue the work, now that he saw what it meant?

No answer came that night. He went to bed fuzzy-headed from the bogberry wine, blood thrumming from the songs. When he woke groggy the next morning, the warriors had gone, and he was summoned to the cabin to deliver a very eager wisewoman her lessons.

And he went to her, because he couldn't see another way.

Time streaked together after that, dissonant and detached. Fuelled by her own deadline, Pashangali made considerable progress with her third mind; she mastered the act of breathing through her lesser discomforts without spiralling into worries about greater pains. On good days she even left the cabin door open to the villagers, that they might seek her counsel. Delicately, the village's mood bloomed, an orchid in its own right.

The more confident Pashangali grew, the more Ronoah seemed to take on her queasiness, her unease. Questions plagued him more pervasive than any headache, more galling than any nausea: was he capable of this? Could he live with knowing he was responsible for such violence? What kind of person did that make him? He couldn't expose his distress to the Shaipurin, not even Nazum, so he did the only other thing he could think of, the thing that worked last time—he built a fire. He cast his salt into the flames, turned his garnet over in his hands, but Genoveffa felt far from him. Perhaps it was because he was distracted, hearing Nazum and the other villagers in the distance; perhaps it was because he had given away the cloves, and their connection was weakened.

Perhaps she was just turning away her gaze while her wishgranter did terrible things.

Chashakva wouldn't turn away. Chashakva would have held this impossible thing with him, if she were here—she would probably prevent it from happening at *all*. She knew Ronoah, knew the gentleness of his heart; there was no way she had set him up as Pashangali's tutor without a deeper layer to the plan. She was preparing something out there, some shiyalshandr trick to reveal at the last moment.

She just had to come back in time.

Pashangali's lessons made Ronoah queasy, but missing Chashakva made him hurt, a great deep ache in his throat, in the hollows of his arms. When it got unbearable he would escape Nazum's watch, go to the edge of the village and call her name into the woods—all of her names, one after another, wondering which, if any, could summon her. She was probably three tribes away, probably embroiled in all sorts of danger, but once she had told him that she could hear a volcano on the other side of the continent. There was no such thing as too far to hear him.

"I really, really meant it," he whispered, to the willows and the cattails and the rain, "about saving me from the stupid things I've done."

But his pleas to the woods went unanswered, so he was left to find a way through those weeks alone.

Fortunately, his imagination was actually on his side. While some nights he suffered the bouts of sweating and shaking engendered by thoughts of *you are actively participating in ending someone else's life* or *what if Pashangali asks you to be there with her when she does it*, most of his daytime mind was occupied with discerning solutions. Maybe he could find some other way for Pashangali to satisfy her Seed, a sacrificial substitute—Chashakva had said sometimes the Shaipurin offered rare plants or animals to their gods. Or maybe there was a way to convince the wisewoman she should attend Council before she killed anyone, just in case it was no longer necessary. Maybe, he thought, the Jau-Hasthasndr warriors just won't come back with anyone, and you can avoid the problem altogether.

Feeling strangely traitorous, he began to hope for it, hope that the campaign would be unsuccessful. Pashangali couldn't perform her rituals without a victim, after all, and it wasn't like the Jau-Hasthasndr would sacrifice their own children.

"They could, in a pinch," commented Nazum on the day Ronoah came to him about it. The boy shrugged his mismatched shoulders. "Nothing in the rules that says offering your own en't allowed."

"But wouldn't that be—could you imagine sacrificing your child?"

Nazum laughed, hands on his hips. "I could do you one better," he was saying, and that was when they heard the cries outside. Cries from voices they'd not heard in weeks—the raiding party, returned home at last.

They were not cries of triumph.

With barely a look between them, Ronoah and Nazum fled upvillage to Pashangali's cabin—they had just enough time to startle the wisewoman from where she was resting before they heard the voices of two warriors at the threshold. They sounded panicked.

"They're saying they need help," Nazum said, even as Pashangali elbowed past to open the door. "They were—oh shit."

"What?" Ronoah asked, a guilty thrill in his gut. Maybe—

"They got the kids but one of the warriors, the tall guy, he's injured." The boy scrunched his face up, trying to keep pace with the frantic exchange. "Like two arrow shafts in the gut kind of injured. They brought him back but he's bleeding out in the healing tent right now—"

One of the warriors was crying. The crescent of Pashangali's face was pale under her body paint. The clench of her flustered fingers, the tight winch of her shoulder blades—she was unprepared. But she threw a satchel of herbs together and waved for the pair to lead her, and she disappeared down the stairs and into the rain.

Gods. This wasn't what he'd wanted.

Ronoah made to follow Pashangali—but Nazum caught his arm and yanked, nearly sending him sprawling.

"Wh—"

"Hang on. Wasn't it the Baramsulandr that Pashangali ordered that raid on?"

"I don't know, does it matter?"

The boy sucked his teeth. "Those arrows are totally poisoned. They fucked up his chances by moving him over so much ground—between the venom and the inside bleeding, he's a goner."

It hit like a cold stone, his matter-of-factness. It made Ronoah tug his arm away. "So what, we just—wait here? Leave Pashangali to do this on her own?"

Nazum looked up with an expression that chilled him. "If you want to go with her, be my guest, shiyalshandr. I'm not in the mood to see somebody die today."

The choice was obvious. Ronoah turned on his heel and fled. He ran towards the source of the commotion, louder with every vibrating footfall: the healing chants, the wailing. Everything Chabra'i taught him about medicine rushed through his mind, every possible tool he could use to fix this, to prove Nazum wrong. He raced across a walkway and around the library and down to the infirmary, pushing his way inside.

What he saw forced the breath from his body in one hard burst. The tallest warrior, laid out on a blood-soaked mat; six members of the war party running back and forth trying to organize linens and tinctures and clean water; a pair of unfamiliar children standing eerily still in a corner of the tent, holding hands; and Pashangali, heaving on her knees by the warrior's side, doubled over with her hands pressed desperately to her own abdomen.

Nazum would not be proven wrong. One look at that room and he knew. There was no question as to how this was going to end.

But he stayed anyway, he stayed and stepped forward and when he heard the warriors cry his name—*Runa! Runa!*—he became what he could for them, became wisewoman of the moment, getting down by the sickbed, holding arrow shafts still, a young woman with all the grace of the underworld behind her. Runa held the tallest warrior down as the wounds were enlarged and the arrows twisted and pulled. Runa chose the right wads of grasses to staunch the bleeding. Runa felt the pain humming in the dying man's bloodstream, creaking in his clenched jaw, and tried to send out waves of calm to soothe him. To prepare him.

The tallest warrior tilted his head to Pashangali and said something, faint, tremulous, tinged with the humour reserved for one's final moments.

In response Pashangali barked a sound that was half-laugh, half-sob. It was not until later, when the man's body lay cooling on the mat, when Runa could be Ronoah again, when Nazum found him in the baths all alone staring at nothing, that he found out what was so terribly funny.

"What were the sounds?" the boy asked. "Do you remember at all?" And Ronoah did the best he could to repeat it, fuzzy with shock though it was, and even cold-hearted Nazum had to swallow a hollow laugh before he managed, "Damn, that's—that's kind of badass."

Ronoah turned his gaze to the sky. "What did he say?"

"Bury me with water lilies," Nazum intoned, "or I'll stink up the whole grave."

Ronoah choked out a laugh. It dissolved so quickly into tears. He scraped the warrior's blood off his arms, crying freely while Nazum sat there and didn't say a word about it. He stayed until the sky changed colours, until the steam made him so dizzy he could hardly breathe. Then, he got up and took a couple shaky inhales and beckoned Nazum to come with him. He started on the path to the wisewoman's cabin, unsure of what he was going to do but sure he had to do something. If he felt this rotten, he could only imagine how badly Pashangali was taking it.

Until he walked through her door. Then he didn't even need to try imagining—it pierced him like a whole quiver of poison arrows.

He staggered from the energetic blow, and it was a good thing too, because he heard the smash of a teacup against the wall behind him, heard Nazum swear loudly in surprise. Such good earthenware, he thought woozily, trying to feel into the confusion of pressure inside the cabin.

Pashangali was on the ground, carelessly, as if someone had flung her and left her there, the paint crying down her rigid limbs. Within reach lay the rest of her teacups, presumably the only things she could grab in time, half-full of bile. The sight made his own stomach roil.

"Pashangali," he started hesitantly, but she cut him off with a snarl of Shaipurin that he understood perfectly even without the language.

"Get out," Nazum translated, stepping to Ronoah's side. The boy's arm brushed Ronoah's, hot against his suddenly clammy skin. Ronoah was about to obey that command, except something in her tone hooked him and kept him there.

"Pashangali," he tried again, "it's not your fault—you, you weren't ready. It was such a bad wound—"

Again, the wisewoman snapped over Nazum's translation, her volume rising. "Oh, for fuck's sake—do you really want to know what she's saying?" Nazum asked, and Ronoah should have said no but something had riled him enough to say yes, so he said yes. "Well, she's—ah, shit—"

Pashangali yelled something and they both jumped. The wisewoman had propped herself up on her elbows, glaring like she wanted them to evaporate. "You're useless! Useless, evil—you have done nothing for me, you have solved NOTHING."

"That's not true," Ronoah said, ignoring Nazum's warning look, "you've been making real progress, we just didn't—"

Another shout, this time a word Ronoah knew: *no*. "You've—ah, lady, really—you've tricked me into wasting my time while Orchid Ten draws ever-closer, you've ruined any chance I have to give Jau-Hasthasuna his strength, he will be *eaten* because of you—"

"That's *not true!*" Any good conscience he had was curdling. Pashangali was hauling herself to her feet, murder in her eyes. "It's not your fault and it's not my fault either, it's just, he, Pashangali he was *poisoned* there wasn't anything you could do anyway—"

"If your tricks and your strategies cannot even prepare me to look at a punctured gut, what do you think will happen when I have to—"

"*But why do you even have to do it?*" Now Ronoah was yelling. He did not want to hear the end of that sentence. He couldn't get the two children in the tent out of his head, the stoic faces, the green-brown eyes. "Why, Pashangali? To feed some vicious god that Chashakva said should have disappeared long ago? To try and save a forest that's dying anyway? Or just because you want to prove to yourself that you *can*?" They were three paces apart. He saw her collarbone rise and fall with her hard breathing, and it just made him think about how those two children were going to stop breathing soon and how they weren't the first, they weren't the first. "If it hurts you so much and you're so angry about doing it, if it upsets you this much every time someone dies for the sake of the war, then either stop the fucking war or call on your *replacement* and let her deal with it. Then you can finally follow the rest of your family onto the battlefield and be useful!"

He gasped in a breath that scraped the sides of his burning throat. Pashangali was yelling back at him, rancour dripping from her words—but what were the words? What was she saying? It dawned on him sluggishly that Nazum wasn't talking. He turned on the boy and saw him looking at Ronoah with apprehension, uncertainty alight in his face as he searched Ronoah for, for something, for what?

For language. He'd spoken in Acharrioni.

"Nazum," he said, feeling suddenly faint, but then Pashangali shouted something and Nazum held up a hand to stall her and she lunged and smacked his hand out of the air and then snapped back to deliver a brutal backhand to the boy's head and Ronoah's patience reached its absolute final limit. He stepped into the empty space created by Nazum's reeling form and lashed out and caught the wisewoman right in that heaving collarbone, shoving her so hard she stumbled into the table. Hand to her throat, she stared at him in shock—and then the stare changed, and just like with Feris all those months ago, Ronoah was permitted a fleeting preview of just how badly he'd messed up.

The beating that followed was quick, at least. A whirl of black hair, an explosive point of contact somewhere near his ribcage, and he was on the floor. Three sharp kicks, his kidney his ribs his shoulder all suddenly blossoming with feeling and all his idiot brain could think to offer was that his lessons *must* be working if she could kick him that hard without recoiling. He tried to roll over but another kick cracked into his diaphragm and knocked him flat. He inhaled, coughed, inhaled again.

And then in a furious bolt of green-brown, Nazum was above him, one of Pashangali's neglected spears in his hands. He swept one end down near her toes like a viper strike and Pashangali cried out and hopped back; he stepped forward, swept again, shook her footing so that she staggered and then crumpled, landing heavy on the cabin floor. Ronoah felt the aftershocks through the planks.

"Get up, Runa," Nazum said, dropping the spear. The boy looked over his shoulder at Ronoah; his eyes were flat, expressionless, and yet Ronoah swore he saw something burning in them. "We're leaving her to pull her shit together. Now."

Even if all the fight hadn't already gone out of Ronoah, he couldn't have argued with that tone. With difficulty he picked himself up and followed Nazum out of the cabin, leaving Pashangali Jau-Hasthasndra alone to her outraged, heartbroken sobs.

TWENTY

*I*N THE GUESTHOUSE, Nazum sat Ronoah down and circled him, inspecting his injuries by the light of a platter of clustered candles. It was like being in Chabra'i's treehouse again, the same yellow light. "Ayyeesh," Nazum griped, placing two cool fingers on the back of Ronoah's neck, "it's already bruising. Could have knocked a spinebone outta place. Don't you have stuff for this lying around?"

It took Ronoah an extended moment to register the question. "Oh—" was all he managed before his diaphragm went funny and a coughing spasm took him over. When he could draw breath, he wheezed out "gold-spice, in the drawers" and Nazum went rummaging for it, leaving Ronoah to sort himself out.

He had never been beaten in his life. He was still too astonished to be upset, too numb from surprise. He was barely in pain, no matter what Nazum could see. But surely that would come later. The pain and the panic, it would all come later, like it had after the Echo Chamber, after the Ravaging. For now all he felt was hazy wonder at the fact that he'd been hit, and the fact that he'd hit back. That he'd said what he'd said.

Gods, the words out of his mouth. Nataglio quell his tongue. They were the kind of things that would have made him sick to even think of saying a few months ago—and honed so finely, so easily. He'd taken every private admission of Pashangali's, every morsel of history, and used it to wound her. Was he the kind of person, now, who aimed to hurt people when he was angry?

It wasn't *your* anger, a voice inside tried to assure him—you were already raw, frayed around the nerves, and her bitterness seeped into those open wounds and infected you. It's not your fault.

Amazing, how little those words helped. He could see why Pashangali had scoffed.

"All righty, I found your magic plants, but you're gonna have to deal with my totally-not-gentle hands." Nazum was back with a bowl of golden paste, crouching to attend to Ronoah's injuries. He made a big deal out of complaining and making irritated noises, and Ronoah saw again the way the boy had changed in the fist of the fight, how he had struck with such detached efficiency. Nazum had essentially risked his life by intervening, by daring to take a swipe at Jau-Hasthasuna's wisewoman. Even in defense of Runa, that was a punishable offense.

"Thank you," he croaked out when he'd recovered his voice. "I'm sorry."

"Yeah, yeah." Nazum was behind him, but he could hear a tightness in the boy's tone. A tenderness. "You and your sorries."

"I won't—" Again, Ronoah's voice failed him. He held his breath until his diaphragm stopped its trembling, exhaled slowly. "I promise you won't get in trouble with Chashakva for this."

"Shut up, shiyalshandr." Of all things, Nazum's hand came lightly swatting the side of Ronoah's head. "I didn't do it for that."

Ronoah did as he was told. He shut his mouth and let Nazum spread peppery, marigold-yellow paste on his damaged body in brewing silence. Nazum, who had always made it clear that he was saving Ronoah to keep his own nose out of the fire; Nazum, whose hands were far more careful than he claimed.

Frogs plucked and strummed in the swamp outside. Thunder stirred in the distance, just-waking yawn of the gods. The salve sank warm through his skin.

"This is so stupid," Nazum eventually said. "She never should have asked you to do this."

A quip from weeks ago welled up in Ronoah's memory: *not so sure Runa's cut out for work like that.* He'd thought Nazum was criticizing him at the time, but he was wrong. The boy had seen this coming. He'd been concerned.

"Chashakva does a lot of things without—checking if they're all right first." Ronoah grimaced. The first throbs of pain were coming through, hot and angry as the thunder, radiating from where his neck met his shoulder. "Like—like buying your contract. You didn't expect that, she should have asked you first. I'm sorry."

"This en't about me, you stupid—it's about you." Another slab of paste was smeared onto his skin. It hurt enough now that he flinched. "You were so damn soft, and she brought you up here and we ruined it. We ruined it for you." A scraping sigh as the bowl was pulled closer; a gutter in the candlelight. "Any chance you can just forget it all when you go back down? That a thing you can do?"

Ronoah tried shaking his head, but his neck felt stiff and tender. "No," he said quietly, "I don't think it is."

Nazum huffed. Ronoah felt the breath ghost his shoulder. "I just—it en't right to make someone suffer who didn't have to. Especially someone like you. You don't suffer with dignity, you do it ugly, you cry and you try to fix things and—" A sudden hitch in the boy's voice. A beat of silence. "You remind me how sad all this shit really is," he ended, softly.

"I didn't mean to," Ronoah said, a tremble in his voice, a tremble in his limbs, he was finally starting to shake from the shock, from the— from everything. He didn't mean to hurt Nazum. He didn't mean to hurt Pashangali. He didn't want to hurt those children. "I'm, I—I wish we'd kept you out of it, too, Nazum, I'm so sorry—"

"That's three sorries, that's all you get," Nazum said abruptly, coming around to point a finger accusingly in Ronoah's face. "You couldn't've kept me out of it if you'd tried, so get over it. *I'm* over it. I'm even over our lady buying me out—I'm *glad.* It's been a pretty easy life babying your stupid shiyalshandr ass compared to some of the stuff people have bought me out for," he said in response to Ronoah's wide eyes. "I don't have to wait for dinner scraps, I get a mat for sleeping same as you, and you get uppity whenever anyone sasses me which means they only do it a little. You ask for my opinion. You don't ignore me in the room. You frigging *apologize* to me for snagging my contract like it wasn't my own choice to swagger up and get all boastful in your faces in Bhun Jivakta. I had my time to be pissed and prideful, and now I'm done, so you gotta be done too. All right?"

But now Ronoah's brow creased in confusion as an old conversation from a sweaty afternoon in Bhun Jivakta resurfaced: "But don't—doesn't Bhun Jivakta treat you well? There are protections in place for *kish kiriish*, right?" Being underfed and bedless did not sound like protection. Why did it sound like these basic tenets of care had been denied? "Öz—Chashakva, she told me the buyers who abuse sharksuckers get blacklisted..."

"From the reefs, yeah." Nazum planted his gaze somewhere up in the rafters, expelling a breath like a battle lost. "Where do you think they go instead?"

Thunder rattled the floorboards beneath Ronoah's suddenly-slack fingers.

"You were sold in the trench market," he said faintly, and Nazum grimaced an affirmative. "But, but how—I thought you signed up on purpose—"

"We all gotta start somewhere, don't we?" the boy said archly. As Ronoah stared, he got up and started pacing across their small quarters.

"Look, my babu was no fisher and my mamu got no fever. It wasn't 'till they were long-dead that I ever saw the delta, and when I got there it wasn't by choice. There's people what'll snap up any body they find and sell it for profit in Bhun Jivakta. I just happened to be what got snapped."

"You're—from here? From the heartland?"

"Brother, how the fuck you think I know all these tongues?" Nazum waved his hands in a this-should-be-obvious-why-must-I-explain sort of way. "I was sick of all this, the sacrifices, the war—that happens, you know, plenty of heartlanders just get fed up and head for the coast where apparently things are less insane." He laughed his nasty crow's laugh, swivelling on his heel. "No less, as it turns out—just different. I got caught and then I got sold and I'm not gonna fuck with what soft bits of you are left by telling you what happened then. Eventually I clawed my way out and sold myself to the first agency I ran into."

"Lady Sikundhasma," Ronoah said.

"Have I ever mentioned your memory freaks me the fuck out," Nazum said, waving at Ronoah again—the offhandedness of it almost made Ronoah laugh. "Yeah, the lady took me in and from then on I've had a say in what I sweat over. Including this. All the blood magic and child sacrifice in the whole damn rainforest is better than one more day stuck with some pompous *chuta* on his Chirope trading ship—"

Heard it off an old master. A Chirope merchant, blacklisted for his transgressions. This is how Nazum had learned Chiropolene.

Ronoah cleared his throat. It was painful to swallow. "Nazum, I—"

Three sorries, Ronoah, that's all you get. "...You know Chashakva will release you, when this is over."

"I'm not thinking that far ahead, shiyalshandr." Nazum finally stopped pacing, turned his face to the unglazed window. "I'm trying to guess how we stay alive through tomorrow."

A breeze blew in warm and wet, flecked with rain. It ruffled Nazum's bangs, but the boy did not close his eyes against it. Cold-hearted Nazum, who cared enough to want to send Ronoah back to the world below to spare him from the one above.

Ronoah shook his head. Enough, he thought. Enough of this. "That's my responsibility," he said, standing up on shaking legs and receiving a squawk for his efforts.

"Don't stand up you idiot you'll collapse—"

"I owe so much to you," Ronoah continued, raising his voice above Nazum's protests. He limped to the window, gripping the sill for support. "So much. None of this would be possible without you. You've—you protected me, at the risk of your own life, just like Chashakva said you should, and you cannot know how grateful I am. But *that*," he said, pointing out the window in Pashangali's direction, "fixing that is up to me. Helping her is up to me. Making sure you all have a—even a chance to *talk* about ending this war you hate, that's why I'm here, and that was my choice, too. Maybe Chashakva shouldn't have asked, but she did—she asked, Nazum, she didn't force me, and I was the one who said yes, just like you. I made the choice, and I'm going to follow through."

Jau-Hasthasuna's village was a huddling nest of outlines and shadows. Above, the clouds pulsed with lightning that never touched down. "I will," Ronoah murmured, and for one moment the relief of making a decision almost fooled him into being okay with it.

Behind him, Nazum sighed. "You know, Runa, for what it's worth, I believe you," he said, approaching Ronoah and flicking his arm. "I've seen you do impossible stuff before. But you'll have a lot of trouble putting any plan to action when you're too swollen to move, so sit the fuck down and rest."

And between this and Ronoah's own body pleading exhaustion, he had to relent. He let Nazum retrieve dinner for them, let him bully Ronoah into lying flat on his stomach to ensure he could keep an eye on the bruising. Ronoah lay there semi-immobile, like he had all those years ago after the Ravaging, and thought about Chabra'i Subindra no longer speaking to her bees.

He had done that. In service of ending the War, he had lied to her—lied to everyone, even Nazum, manipulated their sacred beliefs to suit his needs. In service of ending the War, he had abetted Pashangali's murdering. In service of ending the War he had allowed himself violence. Just one good shove, but the difference between one and none was infinity.

A younger Ronoah would not recognize the person he was now, the things he had done. But he couldn't stop; for this to be worth anything, anything at all, Chashakva's Council of All Tribes had to happen as planned. Otherwise the War would continue, and all the horrible things he had become in service of ending it would be meaningless.

On the rooftop, in the trees, the sound of rain invading.

Twenty-One

$\mathcal{R}$ONOAH WOKE TO THREE PULSING, painful welts on his back, and to thoughts of his brother in his head.

Ngeome Vespasi Elizzi-denna Pilanovani was the kind of person who couldn't bear disputes or hostility. His godling Vespasi was the peace-keeper, guardian of elephants and soothing aloes; the Acharrioni invoked his name when something unnecessarily confrontational crossed their mouths or their minds. But Vespasi—or at least Ngeome's embodiment of him—was not simply a proponent of passivity. He was also a ruler of fairness.

Many years ago, Lelos' goat Gengi had chewed through a grass basket Ngeome had already spent weeks weaving. Usually Ngeome would have sighed in his harassed way and unwound the basket to its least-battered starting point, but this time he'd shocked everyone by demanding that Lelos redo the work for him. "You have to fix what you've broken," he'd insisted, and it didn't matter what their parents said, didn't matter that the goat was the one who'd done the chewing—Gengi was Lelos' respon-sibility, and it was equally her responsibility to make amends for any trouble caused by her charge. Eventually, even their obstinate sister had relented.

A teenage Ronoah had wondered why his brother, usually so concil-iatory, had made such a fuss about a basket. This wasn't long after the Ravaging; perhaps their shared lack of resources was weighing heavily on Ngeome's mind. Or else maybe the basket was for someone special—Ngeome had begun courting by then. But when he'd finally asked, his older brother had something altogether more philosophical to say.

"It's because I need to be okay with it happening again," he'd explained. "Lelos is free-spirited—" a word for careless, in Ngeome's mouth "—and Gengi is a goat. They were both just doing as the gods intended, and I can't ask them to promise it won't happen again. It probably will. Asking them to repair their mistakes is how I allow those mistakes to happen, over and over again, without losing trust in them. If I trust our sister will atone for her pet's mischief, then the mischief can't hurt me for long."

Even then, Ronoah hadn't fully understood. The concept of allowing for mistakes was foreign to him—indeed, he'd continued punishing himself for his own imagined misbehaviours for years afterward. Obviously he hadn't taken Ngeome's wisdom to heart.

But now, as he eased himself to sitting, he thought he could finally see his brother's reasoning clearly.

His bones felt panicky in the joints, as if they might cease to hold together if he moved wrong; the swellings on his back pulsed like foreign entities, like fungi growing off the trunk of him. Cautiously, he tried to reach back and probe, but the stiffness between shoulder and neck elicited a gasp of pain through his teeth.

The sound had Nazum up in an instant. "What's going on—" the boy said, flipping over and whipping off his sheet, but then he saw Ronoah and started laughing. "Ye gods, you can't even scratch your ass can you," he sighed, shaking his head. He got to his feet, combing his fingers through his hair before flipping upside down to gather it into his topknot. "She's gonna be real sorry she did that. Now she's gotta look at it all day and feel bad."

And Ronoah's mind went to his sister's fingers deftly re-weaving a basket, and the idea knocked into him like a goat headbutting his brow.

Nazum righted himself, hair tied in place, and said "I'll get water for a new paste thing" just as Ronoah blurted "She needs to do it." Nazum paused mid-step, and Ronoah tried to clarify. "The goldspice, the...the wound care, Pashangali—I need Pashangali to do it."

Nazum's face was all scepticism. "Why? So she has a better shot this time?" Fear slid oily in Ronoah's stomach, a new reflex he'd never felt before, and Nazum caught the scent of it because his teasing stopped fast. "I won't let that happen, obviously."

"I know." And he did. He wasn't sure he'd be brave enough to suggest this without Nazum at his side. "She just...has to fix what she's broken."

Nazum grimaced at him like Pashangali had kicked some of the sanity out of him, but his sigh sounded understanding. "Fair's fair," he relented. "So I pack the dried stuff then?"

When their supplies were clinking softly in Ronoah's bag and last night's dressing had been washed away, they left their lodgings, the would-be wisewoman and her voice, and made the long, familiar walk to Pashangali Jau-Hasthasndra's cabin. Fully expecting the rule of threes to be respected, Ronoah was surprised when he entered through

Pashangali's doorway and did not immediately have some sort of pottery slung at him. "The river runs, wisewoman," he said in greeting. No answer.

"You think she went and jumped in another cenote—"

Ronoah elbowed Nazum with his good arm. "She's here," he said. "I can tell." That cloying gloom didn't belong to the house, after all. "Pashangali," he said, raising his voice, "we need to talk." He stepped inside and sought her form, lying behind the table or curled up in a corner somewhere. She was nowhere to be seen. Just as he was starting to wonder whether the planks actually *had* sponged up the wisewoman's emotional turbulence, there was a creak behind him; he turned to see her on the narrow stairs that led to the second floor, a place he had never been permitted to access. She was leaned against the wall, glaring at him with eyes that drowned their guilt in their accusation.

A corner of his mouth turned up in a smile, even as his heart jolted sickly in memory of the night before. "Pashangali Jau-Hasthasndra," he greeted, and then, before he could lose confidence, he turned his back to her, baring his wounds. Her hiss of vicarious discomfort gave him an odd courage. "Behold your handiwork."

"I'm looking." She sounded stung. Nazum confirmed it, watching the wisewoman's face as Ronoah couldn't: "She doesn't seem too proud of herself, brother."

The knot in his gut loosened a little. That remorse would make this easier.

"You're going to fix it for me," he said. "Where I am from, you must heal the things you harm. You are responsible for restoring what you throw off-balance." He winced his way to the table, lowered himself with a grunt, withdrew the ceramic jar from his bag. "So I have brought you goldspice, and you will heat it with cracked pepper."

A few terse heartbeats of reluctant silence—and then another creak of wood as Pashangali approached him, as her black-lined fingers took hold of the jar of goldspice powder. She disappeared out of view to work; he heard the clink and scrape as she ground peppercorns in her mortar, smelled the rich dusty aroma of goldspice as it emulsified in the pan.

While he waited, Ronoah withdrew his garnet from his wrap. Then he pulled his half-empty satchel of salt from his bag, too. He held them each in one hand, smoothing his thumbs over their textures. He needed all the divine protection he could get for the next part.

Pashangali came and squatted down behind him; he felt the taut suspicion of her, the awkwardness. He squeezed stone and satchel both, staring determinedly at the wall of spears. One was still out of place. "Spread it evenly," he instructed. "Go on."

There was an audible intake of breath, a preparatory motion. Then the salve landed hot and clumsy on his mid-back and he flinched and so did she, her hand sparking back as if he'd shocked her. "It's okay," he said, focusing on the smell of the medicine to help him through the pain. "You're okay. Try again."

"I have dishonoured you greatly," came her voice, low and tight with dismay, like she'd been thinking it all morning. "This is—I have acted unforgivably, Chashakva will—"

"Chashakva won't," he said. Chashakva—didn't have to know, if it was going to compromise the Council. He could handle it himself.

"It is unforgivable," the wisewoman repeated, and her hardened tone told him she was using this to confirm all her worst ideas of herself. Of all things, that made him irritated. "It is shameful, but it won't—"

"Pashangali, don't promise me you won't do it again." He cut her off a second time and felt her go rigid in guilt or in shame or, hopefully, just in attention. "Show me you can fix it when it happens. Show me you are more interested in atonement than in abasing yourself, and I will decide what is forgivable."

From the easy way the words were coming out of Nazum's mouth, the odd shine in the boy's eye, Ronoah guessed there were no tone adjustments today, no cultural translation necessary. Good. After all, this was about more than his bruises.

He needed to trust Pashangali could do good things with her hands. It was the only way he'd allow himself to help her do terrible things with them, too.

The wisewoman puffed out a sigh, but soon her touch returned, cautious, delicate as dragonflies. She painted the salve on with fingers that were long-used to swirling circles of paint on her own limbs; Ronoah felt that muscle memory take over, the instant her focus ebbed away from her own failure and flowed into the task before her. The peppery heat of the salve soothed him enough that his shoulders slumped in relief. He heard her answering hum, content and involuntary, and knew her pain was subsiding alongside his own, and he was proud of her.

He *wanted* Pashangali to succeed, he noted with a stab of terrible fondness. He wanted her to feel capable of holding the responsibilities of a wisewoman. He just wished, with all the useless yearning of the moons tugging the tides, that those responsibilities were different.

The longer Pashangali spent tending to his injuries, the less she seemed reluctant to touch him. The last bruise was the worst—the one high up on his spine, near his neck—but she did not falter in her applications, did not twitch in phantom pain. Nazum watched the entire process, his eyes sharp and alight with something halfway between disdain and worry; Ronoah watched him in turn, for any signs of alarm, because it was a hard thing to do, to literally show your back to an attacker not a day after the attack. To keep trusting good would come of it.

At last, Pashangali wiped her fingers on the edge of the bowl. Ronoah's neck felt soft enough to turn slowly, so he glanced back at her and asked, "How does it feel?"

He thought he saw the wisewoman's hand go to the back of her own neck. "Better than I thought it would," she admitted in a murmur. "Even though the salve is yellow."

He looked down at his ribs, saw the careful streaks of goldspice she had drawn. They looked almost like—he faltered a moment, confronted with the unexpected sweetness of it.

Like lily petals.

He let that gesture sink in. When he was ready, he scooted around to face Pashangali, noticing how bright the whites of her eyes were this morning, peeking out from between her fringe and the black bar smeared across the bridge of her nose. He tucked the garnet back into his pocket, then made Pashangali's bright eyes go wide by taking her hand. "I forgive you," he said slowly, the words sombre and tender on his tongue.

Pashangali ducked her head—it was a hiding gesture, like she wanted to burrow somewhere and couldn't. She stayed there, her expression hidden from view, as she worked her mouth around the words that needed to be spoken. " . . . I thank you," she finally said, with equal weight, almost as if she knew the extent of what he was forgiving her for. "And I apologize. Fuck yeah you do, lady."

Ronoah choked back startled laughter and glared up at Nazum, who shrugged and grinned his shark's grin.

Then Pashangali spoke again, and the boy's face rearranged itself into work mode: "What is that?" she was asking. "In your hand?"

Right. He'd slipped his garnet away, but the satchel of salt was still in his other hand. He revealed it to Pashangali, the muslin gently crumpled but still tightly drawn. "It is . . ." He thought a moment. What was it, in the end? He eased the drawstring open, sifted his fingers in the salt. It had gone clumpy in the humidity, like a piece flaked from the Flats. "A bit of home," he said simply. He deposited a tiny pinch of salt into Pashangali's hand. She frowned, holding her palm at eye-level; as Ronoah watched, she pushed a finger around in the grains, feeling their scrub and roll, and then, after a preliminary sniff, she touched her fingertip to her tongue. Her eyes lit up with wonder.

"It tastes like tears," she said.

And all at once, Ronoah knew what he had to do.

"That's because it is," he said, the words coming to him almost faster than he could get them out, "it's—they are crystallized tears. From the underworld, from shiyalsha." A look crossed Pashangali's face like maybe she regretted her decision to eat them, but he was glad she'd done it, he was glad, just as he was glad that Pashangali's empathy was not the emotional type, for his gladness was rivalled by the ambushing anguish of what he was about to do, the unfairness the *loss* his heart whimpering *no* even as his mind shouted *yes*— "They are a gift. You, you passed my test, so I am offering them to you as an alternative to—sacrificing those children. Chashakva needs you at the Council of All Tribes, Pashangali, no matter what happens on Orchid Ten, and in my eyes you have already proven how devoted you are, how committed to seeing the heartland thrive, you are *worthy* already, so—so these are yours, now."

He took a deep breath, held it as long as he could. He tied the satchel's strings. He held out the bag to Pashangali.

"I offer you the sorrow of my people," he said. "Our grief that the War continues yet. I offer you the magic in our tears, wisewoman, and I hope it appeases Jau-Hasthasuna better than any human would."

She looked at him, and a hundred voices all clamoured in Ronoah's mind, demanding to have their say before he just gave up this essential piece of himself there wasn't even time to say *goodbye*—but he swallowed them down, and she plucked the bag reverently from his hands.

"I will consider it," she said softly, and he knew they were closer now than ever before, for now he, too, had switched one kind of sacrifice for another.

The next three days were spent honouring the tallest warrior. On the first day his body was prepared with charcoal and tree resin, garlanded with water lilies as stories were told about his deeds and his integrity and his knack for finding rare mushrooms. On the second, he was paraded to the edge of a bog and his fellow warriors waded him out into the deep peat and left him there, in the cradle of the cattails. All day the villagers stayed on the edge of the fenland, singing songs and prayers as his body slowly sank beneath the surface. Pashangali did a praiseworthy job of leading the procession, laying hands on the warrior's quiet wounds, sitting sentinel as the mud closed over his arms and legs, his chest, his nose. She saw him into shiyalsha with all the grace a wisewoman should have.

Sensing an opportunity to do the right thing, Nazum sang the dirges and farewells in Ronoah's stead, adding his sweet tenor to the send-off. Ronoah was proud to have such a heartbreaking voice, if only for a moment.

On the third day a funereal feast was prepared, and the aromas of roasting meat and rising lotus loaf could be smelled from dawn to dusk. Between the eating and storytelling, the tallest warrior's possessions were divided among the villagers: a set of pottery with burnished edges, a finely-tooled bone comb, a flashy sash made of a cat's pelt. Golden, dappled black. Everyone knew without speaking who that belonged with now.

Runa accepted the gift with soft thanks, folded and tucked it carefully aside during the feast, fingers absently rucking and smoothing the velvety grain of the fur.

Life regained its pace. Ronoah's bruises flattened and faded. The foreign children were given a special cabin and fed well. And then, on Orchid Two, a messenger arrived from the Naskarahandr tribe to the east, bearing the news that they would be ceasing sacrificial raids until the Council of All Tribes at Sasaupta Falls. Ronoah had to clap both hands over his mouth to keep from crying out when he heard.

Chashakva had finished her work. He knew it the moment the messenger appeared, knew it with a shaking, giddy relief that left no room for doubt—somewhere out there, stalking back through the heartland, the woman had completed her liaisons in this quadrant. She would be back any day, any moment—maybe she'd even show up before Orchid Ten. Ronoah had spent so long steeling himself to endure that day alone that he'd forgotten there was a possibility he wouldn't have to.

He had done everything he could to prepare Pashangali, to exonerate himself. There was always the possibility she would use his salt instead. But in the end, he still wanted to be long gone before she made the choice. He wanted it badly enough that he dug through his bag, seeking the last few fragile grains of salt stuck in the seams, and sprinkled them into a damp fire, and prayed in muttered Acharrioni for the better part of an hour.

"Please," he said, eyes squeezed closed, the warmth of the flames swatting his face, "please, please bring her back. Let me be far away in some other tribe before Orchid Ten." The garnet grew warm in his fidgeting hands. "I don't, I don't know how well you'll be able to hear me after this—there are so many gods here, it is so crowded, and I've, I gave away the things that call you to me, so I just wanted to—to ask before I can't. Please. Bear me away from this last responsibility."

And salt or none, Genoveffa heard his prayer.

When Chashakva returned it was past twilight, so late it couldn't be called late anymore. Shadows clustered and stuck in the rafters. Ronoah, half-awake from his fitful slumber, heard her enter the room: those footfalls, so precise, so graceful in their danger. That rarefied air that clung to her skin, the feeling of something always just about to happen.

169

She paused beside him, radiating strangeness and familiarity all in one. Classic Chashakva, waiting for him to make the first move. Heart fluttering, he pressed himself up to sitting, turned his face to hers. "Cha—"

The figure above him grinned, fierce and stark in the twilight. It wasn't Chashakva.

Get up shoved an instinct and he scrambled to his feet but already there were hands on him and he might've been smart and quick in the reflexes but he was no warrior—he was flipped, flung over one shoulder, and the impact knocked the wind out of him and the room blurred as he was carried outside—there were others, more forms waiting and he was tossed and tied and just as his breath returned a wad of cloth stuffed in his mouth cutting short his shout of terror—flipped again, nauseous headrush, choked inhale, jostling movement—a voice. Yelling.

Nazum.

Ronoah twisted his head and there the boy was, rushing after them, shouting down the gods and holding his wrists out in front of him. Heaving chest, urgency, panic. Barking words Ronoah couldn't grasp, couldn't understand. They locked eyes and his desperate, furious guardian volleyed a lance of Chiropolene his way, a lifeline, a battle cry—

"NOT WITHOUT ME."

The pack was happy to oblige.

They swooped down on the boy and he disappeared beneath them, manhandled just the same, and then they were off and running, whooping and cackling like demons, like the real true genuine thing. The village swung by in smears and streaking stars, bright swipes of torches, the frogs, the insects, the hollering. The villagers awakened too late, too late; a flash of skin a whirl of hair the polished wood of a spear swung all too late. The surge of Jau-Hasthasuna's people giving fruitless chase, falling behind, Pashangali breaking free from the mob and calling for him, yelling his name, positively screaming it. *Runa.* The first time she'd ever said the word.

Twenty-Two

*L*ATELY, RONOAH HAD BEEN DEALING WITH more stressors than he could count. Added to those pressures, a *kidnapping* was altogether too overwhelming to bear, and so—absurdly, with the wisdom only a body understands—he somehow managed to fall asleep, right on the shoulders of his captors.

When he woke, he could tell it was light out through the fabric over his eyes. He tried to move, to scratch some sleepy itch, and his arm went nowhere. He was bound by ropes—instinctively he squirmed, trying to loosen his bindings, but before he could work himself into too great a panic a shadow fell across him, and then hands were reaching to untie the gag from his mouth, the blindfold from his eyes. The cloth came away and morning light poured into his eyes like hot wax.

Abruptly there was spluttering behind him, and then a slew of Shaipurin invective that was no less sour for its incoherence. Nazum was up. "Runa," he said, and Ronoah felt the boy swat at his wrist with the tips of his fingers, "hey, Runa, wake up demon boy you have to—"

"I'm awake," he responded, still squinting at the sudden dazzling sunspots. Was this what daytime looked like? It had been so long under the rainforest's smothering morass of branch and fern and vine that his eyes had forgotten how to work with undiluted light. "Are—are we still on the river?"

"Yeah, kind of." The ends of the boy's loose hair swished against Ronoah's shoulders as he turned his head in scrutiny. "There are bowls where it collects and pools, big lakes and things. This is probably one of them."

Ronoah's sight finally focused, and for the span of a breath he took in the view with something like appreciation. The open water was cut clear and sharp by the palette of dawn; the banks were broad and far away. The sky yawned above them, unencumbered by cloud or canopy.

"So we're fucked," came Nazum's voice a second later, shattering any chance to admire the picturesque surroundings. "Utterly fucked."

Now that Ronoah could see, he had to agree.

They were borne along on a canoe maybe forty feet in length, surrounded by four people on either side—seven warriors paddling the craft while the eighth beat a steady pace on a hand drum. As he inspected each of them, he realized with a jolt in his stomach that the warrior closest to him was staring right back at him, sizing him up like a cat sizes up a cricket.

Perhaps it was the harshness of the sunlight, but she seemed more wan than many of the tribeswomen Ronoah had seen. The green tones in her green-brown skin were more pronounced; they gave her an odd dual-aspect of robust health and disturbing sickness. She had a body seemingly built for activity, precise and peculiarly graceful. She articulated even the mundane motions of rowing in a way that made them mesmerizing. Ronoah looked at her face—squarish and blunt, made even more so by the thick cut of her bangs across her forehead—and she grinned a grin with a gap between her front teeth, and Ronoah knew this was the one who had invaded their cabin, the one so unquestionably confident that she'd waited to see the look on his face before she stole him.

No wonder he'd mistaken her for Chashakva.

Nodding her chin at him, she spoke in a voice like syrup over stones, lazy, languid vowels seeping over gravelly consonants—words that went entirely over Ronoah's head. He'd picked up lots of pleasantries and greetings clandestinely, but not this one.

"Nazum," he called, "I, um, I think she's talking to us."

"What?" Ronoah winced as the boy wriggled around behind him, elbowing him in the ribs in the process. "Who?"

Before Ronoah could say anything, the woman called louder, above the sounds of splashing and drumming—and Nazum's fidgeting froze. After a beat of silence, he called something back. Then something else. A third thing, his lovely voice swooping down and then lilting up uncertainly. The woman made a face at Ronoah like they shared some sort of inside joke, then said something too sweet to be anything but mockery.

He was done being left out of the discussion. "What's going on?"

After a long moment, he got his answer: "Sorry, I misspoke earlier. We're *double-fucked*," Nazum corrected himself, judiciously, "because I can't understand a single word she's saying."

Despite the sunny weather, something cold cut into him. "Nothing at all?"

"I mean I've got a word here and there if I take it apart a bit in my head but that's not the kind of understanding you wanna take bets on." With a dull thud, Nazum dropped his head back to bonk it on Ronoah's. He seemed to intend it as an affectionate gesture, so Ronoah pretended it didn't hurt. "Sorry. I thought if we were together, at least we could try explaining that we're not godfood, see how far it got us."

The memory of last night flashed before him: Nazum, running after the raid, begging to be taken. "I'm glad you came anyway," he said, his throat tight. Nazum made a dismissive sound.

"You think I'd wanna stay with Pashangali after that disaster? No way in shiyalsha." Then, to Ronoah's surprise, Nazum started laughing. It was a laugh that began surprised and ended malicious and mean. "Speaking of—oh brother, our lady's gonna kill every single one of these fools."

Chashakva. She was still on her way back to Jau-Hasthasndr territory, under the impression that an unruly student was Ronoah's biggest problem. She wouldn't know until she arrived that Ronoah was gone.

"Yeeeah, I feel better now," Nazum proclaimed. "It'd be great if she could show up before we get slashed or squished or pushed off a cliff, but even if she doesn't, at least I'll get acceptably avenged."

Personally, Ronoah didn't know who to be more concerned for—himself, or his captors. He alone knew what Chashakva was truly capable of. "Do you know—do you know how they're going to—"

"No clue. I know all eighteen sacrificial traditions, but somehow I'm guessing my rattling off a list en't what you're after right now."

He was right about that. The boat rocked, broadsided by a swell, and Ronoah's stomach rocked with it. He was only just beginning to grasp the severity of the situation. This wasn't some minor obstacle, some challenging ally. This was—this tribe had *raided* Pashangali's, and Ronoah and Nazum were their prize.

This meant sacrifice.

Panic rose in him like a leviathan. They're going to kill you, he thought, they're going to trap you in their village and then they're going to kill you, and it's going to hurt, and you're going to die without ever getting to the Pilgrim State, gods, you're going to die before ever doing anything useful just like you always feared you would.

No. An equally strong voice put its foot down, a voice grown from pure indignant obstinance. Unacceptable, it said. You're going to figure a way out of this just like you've figured a way out of everything else—or you're going to find some way to stall for time until Chashakva shows up and does what she does best.

"So, do we—" Ronoah's mouth had gone dry. He swallowed and tried again. "Is there anything we can do?"

"Do your demon powers include being able to force these eight seasoned warriors into feeling sorry enough for us that they turn back?" Ronoah waited out the requisite seconds that served as an answer. Nazum sighed. "Didn't think so. In that case, sit tight. Nothing to do until we get where we're going. Maybe once I see the village I can tell you what horrible fate awaits us; until then, I'm taking a nap. Gotta be fresh-faced and beautiful for when I show up in hell."

A laugh wheezed out of Ronoah. Even in a situation this terrifying, Nazum managed to retain his sense of humour. It should have been obvious from the start he was born in the heartland.

It suddenly made sense why Nazum had been so furious about being dragged into the heartland, beyond Chashakva buying out his contract. He was being dragged *back*. He'd left his tribe because he didn't agree with its practices, but in accompanying them to the Council of All Tribes, he was going to have to face them again. It would be like forcing Ronoah to return to Acharrio against his will. To walk the streets of Pilanova before he was ready.

It's worse, actually, he thought dryly. Your homeland would just embarrass you socially. Nazum's is literally going to kill him. These are not on the same scale.

Nazum had time for plenty of naps. The journey took three days—instead of travelling while the sun was up and camping when it went down, their captors paused for two or three hours at a time on islands or isolated bays, sleeping in short shifts, which made the voyage feel like one long, continuous voyage, the day feel like one long, continuous day. Ronoah and Nazum were left without blindfold or gag after that first night; after two, they were unbound entirely, allowed to stretch their aching muscles. But there was nowhere smart or safe to escape to, so they did not attempt an escape, and there wasn't much reason to speak, so they said very little. Mostly they waited, gathering their wits for when they arrived.

And then, at noon on the fourth day, they did.

The lake they'd crossed had bottlenecked into a river, which had ballooned into another basin, this one bigger and banked with steep cliffsides, sunbleached and craggy. Their party skirted these stiff slopes until an inlet appeared, a fissure in the rock face; they guided the canoe down the centre, the bluffs on either side soaring up until only a strip of sky was suspended between them, inscribed with wheeling eagles. And then, rounding an outcrop of stone, they came upon a dead end, a blazingly white shingle beach, and a village hacked and thrashed into the limestone.

Nazum hissed in a breath of total disbelief. "No way," he said. "This is Yacchatzul's tribe."

It seemed an odd tone to take. "What does that mean?"

"I don't know what it means, demon boy. The Yacchatzndr—they disappeared years ago, moved their whole village in secret. No one even bothers trying to raid them—I don't think anyone's *seen* them, not since they relocated. Except for their sacrifices, apparently." The boy sat back on his haunches. "I hope you like heights."

"Why?"

"Because we're going to climb up some pretty big ones before they shove us off and we die."

With a jolt, the canoe scraped the rocky shore. The crunch of gravel set Ronoah's teeth on edge.

Eagerly the warriors marshalled Ronoah and Nazum up the beach, over sharp shingles that made even Ronoah's callused feet prickle. Above lay the village, practically glowing in the sun. It was scaffolded high enough on the karst that Ronoah had to crane his neck, high enough that by the time they were reaching level with its foundations, he dreaded looking down.

When they reached the entrance a great racket resounded, villagers leaning from their windows and tossing bales of flower petals down upon what was now a miniature parade, the eight warriors strutting along two-by-two with Ronoah and Nazum in the middle. One of the warriors at the very front broke ranks and leapt forward, nimble as a gazelle, landing on one foot and swirling and springing again, starting a whirling victory dance ahead of their procession to the delighted cries of the crowd. It was the woman who'd kidnapped him, every bit as graceful as he'd guessed.

"Nazum," he asked, edging sideways to keep sight of the woman, "do you think that's ...?"

"Oh you bet it is—" A spluttering sound; Nazum had accidentally got flower petals in his mouth. He spat and wiped his mouth on his forearm. "Say hello to the lady Yacchatzndra herself."

Wisewoman. War captain. Cliff-killer. He watched her dance, kicking up mounds of flower petals with her heels, thick lustrous hair curling and lashing behind her, and felt a shiver shake up his spine.

They were marched through the Yacchatzndr village in a switchback ascent that reminded Ronoah strikingly of ascending the monastery in the caves beneath Chalisto's Belt, the way everything was terraced, set back progressively steeper. A last hedge of sagebrush, and then they came upon a plank bridge arcing upwards. Ronoah and Nazum were sent on alone, with only their leader the wisewoman skipping and striding ahead. The wooden gate framing the threshold was adorned with flowers, with windchimes made of shell and bamboo, with an entire eagle's skeleton—almost entire. It was missing its head.

Burgeoning from the rock like another floral arrangement, a villa clung to the cliff face, nestled in the cleft of an outcrop. Thick thatch roofs waving their frayed edges, walls woven together with something that made them look like bird's nest—and the wisewoman in the shadow of the awning, beckoning them, ushering them in with a coy gleam in her eye.

Being inside the wisewoman's villa still felt, to a degree, like being outside. There wasn't the same sense of separation as in Chabra'i's treehouse, in Pashangali's cabin; instead of solid walls the villa was compartmentalized by shutters and privacy screens, all of which were thrown open to let in the sunlight, the afternoon winds. A macaw preened on a railing as they were guided further into the rooms, a riot of feathers jewel-bright as any shalledra. Up ahead, the wisewoman drew back a folding screen and stepped into the sanctum beyond with a little twirl. Sunshine and vine tumbled from a skylight; linen hammocks were strung up, tasselled and soft. A table, a quartet of cushioned chairs in that same bird's nest weave, a waft of incense roaming the corners of the room.

If he hadn't been there for the days after Pashangali's raid, he would have been surprised. But he knew enough by now to know that the Shaipurin treated their sacrifices well.

The wisewoman flopped down into the cushioned cocoon of a chair, crossing one creamy green knee over the other. From her makeshift throne she opened her mouth and spoke—and Ronoah could have sworn he felt Nazum go cold.

"She—she's speaking Jau-Hasthasndr," the boy said. Even his tone was ashen. "We, she's—*kulim putrash*, give me a second to—" He lapsed into rapidfire Shaipurin, asking questions pointed as darts, to which the wisewoman replied with a shrug of her shoulders and a pretty pout that devolved quickly into that same lip-bite smirk, charming and predatory all in one. Given everything Ronoah had heard about the Shaipurin tendency to openly scorn other tribes and their languages, he could understand Nazum's shock. First they were spirited away to an unfindable village, then spoken to in the language of the one they'd left? Pashangali hadn't spoken to her sacrifices in their home tongue—hadn't spoken to them at all, as far as he knew.

Perhaps she'd been avoiding looking at them, like he had. Looking them in the eye.

"Okay," Nazum said, snapping Ronoah out of his thoughts, "okay, we might be a little less dead than I thought if we can explain to her. You're up, demon boy—let her know it's not worth offing a shiyalshandr."

Easier said than done. If the wisewoman asked for proof of his underworld origins, like Chabra'i had, he would have nothing to show her. And no Chashakva to save face. Swallowing the hard pit in his throat, he croaked out an introduction that was clumsy and uninspired but at least mostly true: "I, my name is—Runa. And this is Nazum. We were—we're in the heartland on a vital mission with our companion, and so you cannot sacrifice us. I'm sorry, I know you already went through all the trouble."

Seriously? he thought. You're *sorry*? Nazum seemed ready to ask the same thing, but before the boy could dig a sarcastic elbow in Ronoah's side the wisewoman laughed and replied and Nazum's eyes widened to the size of guava fruits.

"Oh, gods forbid," she giggled, "I didn't take you to sacrifice you!"

He was lucky he didn't collapse to the ground right there. Not a sacrifice. Not sacrificed, not *dead*. Then— "Then why did you take us?" he asked, relief burning into anger, turning the question into a demand.

The wisewoman tapped her lips with a finger. "I wanted to see if you were real. And there you were, Runazum the Fair, sleeping fast as a human baby."

That she was hidden there long enough to watch him sleep made his skin crawl. "Runazum?" he asked, taking note of the name. "No, I'm just Runa. That's Nazum," he said as he pointed to the boy in question, who was doing a remarkable job of not grimacing as he facilitated two people talking about him. But the wisewoman just laughed again, shaking her head indulgently.

"It's the same thing," she said. "You two are never apart, are you? He follows every word you say—he might as well follow your name as well. That's what everyone's saying. Oh, yes, people are saying things," she added at the confusion apparent on Ronoah's face. She planted a cheek in one hand. "Stories spread fast when you start meddling with little miracles."

Hope and dread clashed in his gut, cold water sizzling around a hot stone. "What—what kind of stories?"

She opened her mouth, then seemed to realize something. "I'm starting this off all wrong," she said, promptly rising and moving to the exit. "Lazy me. Come on, let's do the thing proper."

With little choice left, Ronoah and Nazum went after her.

"How does she know the Jau-Hasthasndr dialect?" Ronoah asked, nearly stumbling over a low stool as he tried to keep up with the wisewoman's brisk, graceful pace. Nazum glared at him with an expression bearing equal bewilderment and suspicion.

"En't just Pashangali's tongue, brother. We're speaking Rugakashndr." He took the lead, allowing a dumbfounded Ronoah to fall in line behind him. "She's got Pai-Zayyindr too. Plus hers, that's one from every quadrant. And everything in the quadrants is similar enough that she could probably use one to understand the rest—if she's not already fluent." The boy cracked his knuckles softly. "A tribal wisewoman speaking foreign tongues. That's something to be scared of, Runa."

"Why?"

"Because it means she doesn't play by the rules."

Ronoah let that sink in as he passed under another garland of flowers and bones and found the wisewoman dressing herself.

She was digging through a chest that reminded Ronoah of Chabra'i's wardrobe, pulling out garments one by one. One of her arms was already wrapped by the time he saw her; as he watched, she took the other wrap, made of beads and dried grasses, and slid it up her wrist. The grass skirt she fastened low on her hips was full and free, belted with bones, claws and fangs and two bird skulls, resting their sharp beaks against one thigh each. But it was when she withdrew a long, whiplike cord that Ronoah truly began to see her as a wisewoman. With fluid motions she wound and threaded it around her torso; she pushed her head through the last loop, shook out her mane of hair, and sighed a sigh like she'd just stepped out of one of Pashangali's steam baths.

"Good to be home," she said with a pleased smile. She lowered her gaze to her audience, her hand poised at her throat. "I am Marghat Yacchatzndra, chief and wisewoman, negotiator extraordinaire, protector of these lands. Welcome, esteemed demon."

Ronoah's first words stuck in his throat. "How, how do you know—"

"Even in a land as divided as this, information still spreads." Marghat Yacchatzndra pointed a finger at Ronoah; to Ronoah's own embarrassment, he took a step back. "First we heard from the Gaamndr, then from the Pai-Zayyindr up north. Word in the wood says that Chashakva is stalking the rainforest again, with a bright little demon familiar in tow, trying to end the War of Heavenly Seeds."

She knew who they were. More accurately, she knew who Chashakva was. Still reeling from the surprise of having a reputation of his own, Ronoah spluttered out his next question: "If you know why we're here and—if you know Chashakva's with us, why would you steal us from her like that?"

"Because I'm hoping she's fond enough of you to come looking." The wisewoman peered at the face Ronoah made in reaction. "Good, so she will. I heard she was visiting all of the tribes and I was getting—" Nazum choked on his words "—getting *insecure* about when my turn would be, so I decided to hasten her arrival. Give her a bit of incentive. And, you know, a beacon to find us by."

"You kidnapped us for *bait*?" Ronoah asked, incredulous. Marghat shrugged and smiled, digging her toe in the floor in mock guilt. "Why would, why the *hell* would you—"

Nazum looked at him, but Ronoah couldn't find the end of his sentence. He just stared at the wisewoman Marghat and opened his hands in a gesture that was more than half plea. As if he could make her take it back; as if he could protect her from her decision.

After observing him for several seconds, Marghat spoke. "Why would I try my luck luring a chthonic being to my home with the use of a beloved hostage?" Mutely, Ronoah nodded. "Because I'm not certain I'll *get* a visit otherwise. We Yacchatzndr have been trying to emancipate ourselves from the War for generations—under my rule, we finally achieved what my great grandmamu dreamed of, removed ourselves from all that nastiness and bloodshed. It's the only solution we had, until you three showed up. Now a Council's being called to decide the fate of the War once and for all, and I want a seat at the table. I'm not going to be passed over just because I got the job done." She tossed her hair, performatively indignant, but Ronoah saw through to the solemn look in her eye. "I have questions for Chashakva, questions that have been waiting for answers for nearly a hundred years. I'm not giving up my opportunity to ask them."

Somewhere amid the mess of emotions coursing through Ronoah, a bud of respect bloomed for Marghat Yacchatzndra.

"Now don't you worry, you'll be treated like the luminary you are." Marghat pulled a box from a shelf, withdrawing a piece of candied fruit. She ate it, hummed in pleasure, and spoke around her chewing. "You even get to stay in my rooms—an honour and a privilege, let me tell you, oh what the young men and women of the Yacchatzndr would do to spend a night with me. It's not like you can talk to anyone else, after all, and I wouldn't want you to get lonely." She licked crumbs of sugar off her fingers. "All I want is for she-with-the-sharp-teeth to bite; I'm ready to lose a couple fingers to those jaws if it means I get to have my say at Sasaupta Falls. I'm sure she of all people will understand.

"So welcome, honoured guests, to the house of Yacchatzul. I hope you enjoy your stay." Preposterously, she winked. She sashayed past them, off to attend to whatever needed her attention; Ronoah watched her go. Darkness flickered at the edges of his vision.

"Runa—?!" Suddenly Nazum was gripping his bicep. He startled, recovered his footing. What was...? "Jeez, I know you're a sensitive flower, but I've never seen you actually *swoon*. You good?"

The boy searched his eyes, that faintly mocking amusement of his tingeing his expression. Ronoah looked back and felt something slosh nauseous in his gut. He nodded anyway, suppressing the sensation, straightening himself.

"It's just..." The altitude. The residual fear of dying. The exhaustion of capture catching up to him. The dizzying purity of all that air and light after so many weeks in the sallow dark. The weird sense of foreboding, beholding Marghat's beautiful villa. Of something coming.

"It's a lot," was all he said. Nazum kicked a tasselled cushion in agreement. It flipped over and landed in the sun, exposing a long stain.

TWENTY-THREE

So BEGAN THEIR WAIT FOR CHASHAKVA. As they settled in, something surprising became apparent to Ronoah—despite the fact that they were captives, their stay in Marghat's villa was going to be a pleasant one. They were allowed to explore any room they wanted while the wisewoman of Yacchatzul tended to her duties.

Ronoah discovered as many treasures in that villa as he had in the caves under Chalisto's Belt: a bower of jasmine, the plants tumbling and tangling over trellis and sill, the heady smell enough to daze anyone into long afternoon naps; landscapes of crystal on tables and shelves, obelisks and pyramids and geode clusters scattering pink and purple stars across the furniture; a whole menagerie of animals, hummingbirds and bright-billed toucans, boas knotted up on artistic driftwood perches, tufted tamarins chasing each other for cubes of fruit, a red-speckled tortoise large enough to set your breakfast tray on. Animals so whimsical, so plentiful, that it was a wonder Marghat ever worried about Ronoah and Nazum feeling lonely.

Every bit as coy as its owner, it took the villa three days to reveal one of its last secrets: it was occupied by someone other than Marghat. Ronoah found out when he heard a great racket heave up from the next room and then saw Nazum come careening into the hall hissing like a cat someone had stepped on. High, bubbling laughter wafted from behind him, and then she appeared: a girl of about six or seven, with chubby limbs and a cropped cloud of wavy hair dark as a crow's wing.

This was Marghat's daughter.

"Oh, you never met Bashti? I could have sworn I introduced you," Marghat said when she came home.

"No, mamu, I was hiding on purpose," the girl corrected. "I wanted to see how long it would take them to notice me."

"That's my little spy," Marghat sang, squishing her cheek into her daughter's fluffy hair. She endured this affection with patient indulgence, peering under her mother's arm at Ronoah and Nazum with an utter lack of self-consciousness.

Bashti—Bashtandala in full—was responsible for taking care of the animals that came to rest and roost in the villa. She was good at making herself scarce, able to carry her childish bulk with a grace she'd inherited from her mother. While she was interested by the guests in her home, she didn't seem particularly interested in *talking* to them—she regarded them much the way she regarded the rest of the menagerie, with the same cool, shining gaze.

"She's a perfect little godsgift," Marghat said one evening over dinner, "she does the cleverest things, you're so lucky you get to spend the day with her."

Ronoah, who had not seen Bashti since the night before, nodded anyway. "Does she have a father?" he asked.

"Goodness, no!" Marghat picked up a mussel from the plate, sliding a finger along its seam. "I didn't either. The wisewomen of Yacchatzul are an unbroken chain of mothers and daughters—we don't sully ourselves with romantic attachments." When she saw Ronoah's confused expression, she raised an eyebrow. "We take lovers, of course we do. But if a boy hands you some flour in the kitchen, would you say he baked the bread—?"

Nazum spluttered. Marghat just smiled her tempting smile, and cracked the mussel clean in half.

Unlike Pashangali's tribe, where the wisdom of a wisewoman was gleaned off the gods alone, the Yacchatzndr trained their wisewomen-to-be from birth. Any time Marghat wasn't tending to the villagers and their needs, she was teaching her daughter. Languages, dances, hunting. It turned out that the vast amounts of intertribal knowledge the Yacchatzndr possessed came from generation after generation going out and spying it, seeking it, each adding her experience and skills to the toolkit that was implanted in her daughter's training. Her child the hoard, the library. It was possible that, at the age of six, Bashti knew more than Ronoah did.

The wisewoman's daughter could be plied into divulging tidbits about her tribe if you found her at the right time. Ronoah caught her delousing one of the tamarins and seized on the opportunity to learn more about the Seed Yacchatzul herself, dragging Nazum over to translate. "Yacchatzul is a god of mountains and of the earth," Bashti recited, plucking a tick and placing it between her sharp teeth. "A god of thunder and high places. She is a god of anchoring and stabilizing but also of shaking things loose.

She gave us architecture and the mason's craft, and she could see most clearly of all the Seeds."

"Does she have any favourite things?" Ronoah asked, thinking of Subin's beehive, Jau-Hasthasuna's snake and lotus. Bashti bit thoughtfully down on a tick.

"She likes birds," she said, turning her head to the open veranda where a toucan sat warming its feathers. "And the thunderstones from deep underground. She likes us most of all, and that's why she told twice-great grandmamu to leave."

Before Ronoah could ask anything more, the girl lost interest. She patted the tamarin's rump, sending it running, and then got up and flowed away, off to some other elusive task.

"What a fucking weirdo," Nazum whistled, appreciatively. "I honestly don't know which of the two is creepier."

Ronoah didn't mind Bashti. It was Marghat that made the back of his neck prickle. Marghat and what she could do.

Every wisewoman seemed to have some sort of knack or talent, whether it was learned like Chabra'i or innate like Pashangali. Marghat's brand of magic was somewhere in between. Put simply, the wisewoman of Yacchatzul was able to talk to things—even the kind of things that didn't usually speak. Pests, diseases, injuries, heartache. She could even speak to the dead, a claim that made Nazum choke on air as he translated.

"It's not *really* them," the wisewoman explained, "it's their memories clogging up the area, usually the nasty stuff, gathers in the corners and sticks under the table. Concentrate enough of them into one object and you get something like a person, for a while. It took me *ages* to get my mamu out of the kitchen."

Some called her an exorcist, banishing demons and plague; others called her a summoner, calling forth wayward spirits and energies in order to quell the disturbances they caused. As far as Marghat was concerned, she had already named her profession: *negotiator extraordinaire*. She was just good at persuading all the things of the world to do what she wanted.

Of course, because nothing ever happened in Shaipuri without a sufficient degree of grotesquerie, she channeled this power through skulls.

"This is Zatul," she said, pointing to the bird skull resting on her left thigh, "and this is Jangyarash. They're good strong vessels, well-tempered, lots of stamina. As I recall, also quite fond of sweetmeats." She showed them a section of the villa where bones lined shelves and crowded tables and hung like plaques on the walls, birds and boars and jungle cats of all ages and sizes—and up there, high on the wall in shadow, a single human skull. An ossuary of a different kind.

The reason for the menagerie became disturbingly clear. From then on, when Ronoah saw Bashti stroking a tamarin, a lump would form in his throat, and he'd look away.

When her busy schedule dwindled, Marghat, who seemed truly concerned about ensuring her guests were not bored, invited Ronoah and Nazum to watch her work. "It's a different show every time," she grinned, palming a lizard skull from the wall and hooking it onto her belt. "No two nasties alike. One of the girls cut her ankle on the rocks and now she's got a raging infection. That should be pretty tame, not hard to talk the blood bugs out of a leg. But the shipwright's son started having nasty night terrors, and those are always tough critics—eerie chorus, body spasms, the whole spectacle. No matter what, I guarantee you'll get a good dance out of it," she said, swishing her hips in a way that made the skulls clack high and hollow on her skirt. "How about it? Come sweep the streets with me?"

And Ronoah was the sort of person whose burning curiosity had led him across a continent, over oceans and under mountains and into graves and ruins and wars—so it surprised him more than anyone when he declined. He watched her flounce out of the room, another pair of skulls nestled in her hands, and wondered at his choice.

Why not? Why not escape the lovely cage for a couple of hours and witness something magical, fascinating, something healing for all its horror?

Privacy, he supposed. That was it. He just didn't want to be voyeuristic when it came to other people's pain.

He wished he *did* want to go; the drama Marghat was describing would have done wonders to distract him from the dizziness that upended him if he sat still too long, the dread that would take him like a flash flood, drowning him from the inside so he had to pace laps around the villa in order to drain it. Nazum seemed to sense his agitation. The boy was more accommodating than usual—he complained less, for one, and he gave Ronoah more space.

Ronoah let that gap widen, let that silence take hold. It wasn't that he wanted to push Nazum away. He just couldn't see anything the boy could do to help quell the chaos inside him.

The problem was simple but impossible: Orchid Ten had come and gone. Ronoah now lived either in a world where Pashangali had sacrificed his salt or one where she'd sacrificed her captives. Either the children were dead or they weren't. But he didn't know which world it was, and it was driving him insane. He'd thought he didn't want to know, but this uncertainty was worse. Should he assume himself guilty of abetting murder? Or should he hold onto hope that he'd worked one more little miracle, as Marghat called it?

But even the salt is a kind of killing, he thought with an airless sort of panic. He'd claimed his little sachet was full of the tears of the undead, that it had power to rival those human lives. It didn't. All the Acharrioni mythology in the world couldn't equate those grains to the literal tears of literal people. Salt was the opposite of fertilizer—it made the ground barren. Suppose Pashangali offered those grains to Jau-Hasthasuna and they starved him, made him sick? Would Ronoah be responsible for killing a *god*, instead?

No good choices. No comforts. The only thing Ronoah had to combat these crushing realities was the grim resolution that they would be *worth* something. They would help end the War.

They had to.

This was the other problem that haunted him, the other knife that cut at his heart as he was trying to enjoy a quiet lunch or fall asleep. With no puzzle to solve for Marghat, no challenge to face like he had with Chabra'i and Pashangali, his mind had space to obsess over a much more terrifying obstacle: the possibility that the Council would come together as planned, and the wisewomen of the heartland would converse, and then decide to just keep killing one another anyway.

Ronoah's nausea redoubled whenever he thought about it. The idea made him shiver, made his veins run cold, made him dizzy and faint. He pushed it away when it bubbled up, cleaving to other thoughts, other unknowns.

Like the Yacchatzndr. Why had they left the War in the first place? Nazum had mentioned individuals who would head for coastal towns as an escape, but this was a whole tribe. A Seed fully transplanted. Wouldn't that upset the balance?

Not necessarily, a voice said in his head. *Not if Yacchatzul is already eaten.*

He hadn't considered the logic of the War in great detail until now. Everyone he had met so far spoke of their Seed with such confidence, such potent present tense, that he'd never questioned their aliveness. But Shaipurin gods were meant to devour each other until only one was left, weren't they?

When Chashakva had explained it to him, she'd been convinced the War would have already wrapped up by the time they arrived, that one Heavenly Seed would have sprouted victorious. Well, following the story, wouldn't that mean at least *some* of the Seeds had been eaten by now? Which ones? How did they tell? Whose sacrifices were feeding other tribes? Who was praying to nothing?

He felt jittery and desperate when his mind circled other issues, but when it floundered upon this one, he couldn't even describe the sensation it left in him. His empathy simply refused to get near it, repelled like the wrong end of a magnet.

None of this could be asked of Marghat, or even Nazum; there was only so much pleading the fourth branch Ronoah could do before one of them got suspicious about his origins, and then it would all be over. His own ignorance infuriated him, shortened his temper as the days wore on. If he could just get *one* answer, one story, give his carnivorous mind one single thing to teethe on, he could find some peace.

Chashakva would have been able to make sense of it all, if only he could talk to her. Chashakva, whose name struck fear and respect into everyone who heard it—even Marghat. Ronoah remembered the day his companion had chosen that name, the way she'd swilled the silence like wine until the bouquet of it blossomed dark on her tongue. Chashakva. *I'll bet they remember her in the heartland.*

What for?

What had she done to earn a name in Shaipuri? What was her part in all this?

Of all his questions, asking about his own companion was probably *most* likely to get him caught. Literally any other line of inquiry would be more forgivable than one involving the creature he should have known better than anyone else.

But for some confounding reason—yearning maybe, or perverse daring, or simply an uncharacteristic rashness—the question pushed its way out of him anyway.

"Marghat, you know a little about everything, right?" he began one morning at breakfast, sipping from his bowl of hibiscus tea. Marghat just twinkled at him from the other side of the table, playful as ever. "Who is Chashakva?"

Everyone stared at him. Bashti had literally paused her bowl of tea mid-lift. "I mean, I mean to *you*," he corrected hastily, appalled at his own lack of caution. *Vespasi wake*, he thought, *are you trying to ruin everything?* "What significance does she have to the overworld? I only know what she's known for down in shiyalsha, but up here—why does everyone make the same face when they hear her name? You said, on the first day you said Chashakva was *back* in the rainforest—why was she here the first time?"

After a few tense heartbeats, Marghat relaxed. "It depends, my Runa. There have been many Chashakvas throughout time, demon and human alike—but there are people saying it's *the* Chashakva. The first. The one everyone else is trying to steal some scrap of glamour from by donning her name, like children wearing their mamu's jewelry." Delicately, she plucked a slice of mango from the platter. "If you're looking for the story of *that* Chashakva, I'm happy to help."

Ronoah thought back to Ithos, to the first time he connected Reilin the fellow stranger with Reilin the Conqueror. He nodded, intent.

"Right. Gather 'round, my little demons," said Marghat, gesturing at the table with a doting smile that was nevertheless a little chilling. "It's time for a bit of history."

And she told them.

When it was over, Nazum took Ronoah's thirty seconds of stunned silence to stuff some fruit into his mouth.

"*The age of Chashakva*," Ronoah echoed faintly. "You're saying she—she became a god?"

"Sure did. She's the creator of the previous cycle. Unclear how long that cycle lasted, most say four hundred and thirteen years, but others push it way back, eight hundred years, twelve hundred and eighteen years. However long it was, eventually it spent her, and the Great Wheel turned and a new age began. More or less." Marghat gestured meaningfully to the table, smiling conspiratorially. "She's the dead body this whole War is built on."

As if in response, Ronoah felt the first bead of a headache press behind his eyes. He massaged his brow, trying to relieve the pressure— but between his fingers he caught Marghat watching him, her smile lingering, and he became hyperaware of the skull beneath his skin, and took his hands away.

"You feeling quite well?" she asked him, swiping Bashti's bowl of tea for herself. "I'd hate to have you feeling down when Chashakva arrives."

"I'm okay," Ronoah replied, reaching for a sliver of mango despite how his stomach clenched. "I just ... she never told me."

"Do you go around telling everyone the origin story of your name, Runa?" Marghat asked laughingly. Ronoah bit his lip. "Besides, it's not like this is *your* Chashakva. Don't go believing the western tribes, they're soft and they spook easy. My guess is she's some higher-level demon intent on leveraging the influence of the name as much as possible— which is pretty clever, actually. But don't mistake her for the original. The thing trying to unite the heartland may be powerful, but there is no incarnated creator walking the wreckage of her own corpse. That's not how gods work."

Perhaps. Perhaps as far as Shaipurin cosmology went, that went against the rules. But as the days rolled into weeks, Ronoah couldn't put it out of his mind. For hadn't Chashakva created a world based on her whim before? Reilin's Lottery attested to that. Five thousand years ago, hadn't she resealed the boundary between life and death for the planet when it was shattering apart? Was it so far-fetched, to imagine a rainforest pouring forth from that neverending starlight inside her?

He found himself hoping for it. Pining for her power—for the way she wielded it with such certainty, such cheery charm. How she could fix everything, the Council, the War, the Jau-Hasthasndr captives if she'd got there in time. All of it. If she was a creator god of this place, then its inhabitants could not refuse her wishes. He found himself craving Chashakva's arrival even more impatiently than Marghat, fretting himself into headaches nearly every day with the want of it. Once she was here, he could straighten everything out without giving away his disguise. Ask her about Orchid Ten, about her plans for the Council. Ask her why she'd never told him about her connection to Shaipuri.

Of course, she must have had her reasons. He would find out when it made sense, he was sure of it. He just had to wait it out.

TWENTY-FOUR

ONE WEEK LATER, Ronoah's patience for waiting had worn perilously thin.

"Marghat."

"Hmm? What is it, I've kind of got my head in something—" She did indeed literally have her head stuck in a cabinet, searching for a skull which had gone missing. Ronoah had cornered her before one of her appointments, first thing in the morning. Having barely slept for all the clamour in his head, it didn't seem particularly early to him. It felt like a continuation of yesterday. Like being on the Yacchatzndr boat again, like one long wobbly hour.

"Those questions you have about the War." He heard her rummaging pause for a beat. "I'd just—I know you want to ask Chashakva, but ask me instead. I want to hear them."

Her voice, muffled by wood and fabric: "Questions about the War, ai?"

"Ahai."

"I doubt you have answers for me, esteemed demon." She retrieved herself from the cabinet, clutching her yellowed prize high. She wiggled it as if to admonish it for hiding, then turned to Ronoah with a smile that was nearly pitying. "Why would I inquire into the finer points of the War of Heavenly Seeds with someone who didn't even know who Chashakva was until I told him?"

"Because I do know Chashakva," he replied, a hot edge to his voice. "Better than any of you." Marghat blinked, and he did his best to clamp down on his impatience before it landed him in trouble. "I just mean—don't underestimate what I can do, or how I can help or, or—"

This was going nowhere. His petition was lacelike, riddled with holes. But even as he cursed himself for it, Marghat was sizing him up. That pity in her gaze seemed to win out, because she sucked her teeth in appeasement. "It is the Yacchatzndr way to exhaust all options," she said, as if convincing herself. "Okay, Runa. I'll use you as my rehearsal partner for when Chashakva shows up." He smiled reflexively, but it disappeared at the wisewoman's next comment: "Why not come with me today? It's quite the stroll out to the fields, we can walk and talk."

"No thanks—" Ronoah shook his head, lifting his hands placatingly at her pout. "I don't want to distract you, I—it can wait. It can wait."

He'd lost count of the number of times she'd invited him to accompany her on her rounds, and it was beginning to needle him. He would have given the wisewoman an excuse to get her to stop pushing him about it, except he didn't have one. It was like every time she asked, he was more repulsed by the idea, more instinctively avoidant. But he couldn't tell why.

Marghat harrumphed good-naturedly as she stepped between him and Nazum. "Suit yourself. Afternoon chat it shall be." He heard her continue to mutter to herself in Shaipurin, clacking around looking for what she needed for the third day of a conference she was having with some pests in the banana crops.

Beside him, Nazum piped up: "En't much you can do to help here if you ask me, brother. Lady Yacchatzndra's got it handled—they're out of the War."

"Except they're *not*," Ronoah said, "they're not out of the War, not really, because if they were Marghat wouldn't want to come to Council, right? Why would she do that if she's happy walking away? Why would she learn all those languages and, and teach her daughter martial arts—"

"I mean that stuff's good to know even if you don't expect another tribe to come in and—"

"*There is something out of place.* I've been thinking about it and it doesn't line up, it doesn't make sense—there's something we're missing, or that she's keeping from us, and I think it might be really important to figuring out where everything went wrong and we shouldn't just *wait* for Chashakva to come and take care of it, we're equals, I should, I should—"

Nazum was looking at him a little funny. "What is it?" Ronoah asked.

A crinkle appeared at the bridge of the boy's nose. He seemed to have some trouble with whatever was about to come out of his mouth. "Are you okay?" he finally asked, much to Ronoah's blinking surprise. "Because I'm gonna be honest, it looks like all that thinking's kicking the shit out of you."

Taken aback, and oddly insulted, Ronoah laughed. "You only just noticed?" he said—and what was meant to be a joke came out hard and embittered. Nazum's eyes widened in a surprise of his own, and Ronoah felt instantly guilty. "I'm fine. Really."

"I believe it." He obviously did not. "Well…"

A beat of silence, more forced and uncomfortable than their silences had been in a long time. Somewhere in the villa they heard Marghat's triumphant laugh.

"Well if it's okay with you I'm gonna go with her," Nazum said hastily as he jerked a thumb in the wisewoman's direction. "That's not the kinda thing you get invited to see every day. You won't need me for the morning, right?"

To Ronoah's disbelief, he realized the boy was worried he wouldn't be allowed to leave. Something about that—the shock of being seen as someone who would force people into things, the revulsion at the assumption he might trap Nazum in servitude, after everything they'd been through—made his answer come out unreasonably snappy. "Sure," he said, "go ahead."

"Okay." It looked like the boy wanted to say something more; silently, Ronoah dared him to do it. But he didn't. He just took a deep breath and repeated himself: "Okay. See you later? Get some shuteye before you go cracking open the mystery of the millennium. I don't want it to finish you off." He gave Ronoah's arm a little swat and ran to catch Marghat before she made the descent to the village.

That left Ronoah alone to gather his wits.

Instead they deserted him, temporarily. Sometime just after noon he woke to find he'd dozed off in the jasmine room, with no memory of turning down the hall or drawing up a seat. Unease wound its tendrils up his spine. It wasn't *out of character*, per se—he'd lost himself in thought before. He'd been known to knock into plenty of doorframes at the academy in Padjenne, and more than once he'd forgotten which direction he was walking in the caves. It was just a little...extreme. There was losing track of time, and there was losing time altogether.

Well, he thought brusquely, in a few hours you'll get some answers and be able to sleep again. As much as usual, anyway.

He brushed a few faded leaves off his leg, turned to make his way to the kitchen for a late breakfast, and that's when he saw Bashtandala watching him from the other side of the jasmine vines.

He nearly yelled; what came out instead was a sharp, hissing inhale. She was standing behind the cascade in the centre of the room, so statuesque he might have walked right out and never known she was there. Her dark eyes nestled in the petals, regarding him as if he were another bird in the menagerie.

They stared each other down. Then Bashti emerged, brushing a butterfly from her hair. She took a slow, pointed step—then stepped back. Experimentally, she rocked to her toes, kicked her foot to the left. A faint smile graced her mouth. As Ronoah watched she advanced on him, crouching a little, her stance like that of someone approaching a wounded animal. Eyes locked on him, feet tapping and sliding and kicking tentatively beneath her.

Footwork, he realized too late. Dancing. She was practicing what her mother had taught her.

All at once he felt lurchingly sick—and Bashti's pudgy face creased in an open-mouthed smile. She called in her high, trilling voice, Shaipurin words simple and common enough that Ronoah recognized them. He whirled on his heel and fled, leaving the bower of flowers and its guardian behind. It was only afterwards, in the sun on the balcony, trying to work through the burn in his chest, that Ronoah's brain parsed the actual meaning of the phrase.

Come on out.

By the time Marghat and Nazum returned, Ronoah had fought his panic back down to manageable extremes. He met them in the sitting room just as Nazum was setting a basket of bananas on the driftwood table, and he and Marghat both turned at the sound Ronoah's feet made on the floorboards. Marghat put her hands on her hips and blew air out in playful exasperation, remarking on something. A couple seconds later, Nazum apparently remembered he had a job to do and translated: "You really meant as *soon* as I got home, didn't you?"

Ronoah couldn't find anything to say, so he nodded. Marghat studied him across the room. Then she called out, "Bashti! Put some tea together, little crab, I'm parched!" She went to kneel at the table, resting her chin in her hands. "And I can't play my part thirsty," she said, looking up at him.

Ronoah realized he was holding his breath. He let it out slow, then sat opposite the wisewoman, Nazum coming to his side.

"All right, my demon, you wanted to know what I have to ask Chashakva?" Marghat twirled a lock of hair around one finger. She'd seemed indulgent when she'd agreed to the conversation, but now that she was actually putting her questions to words, she appeared to be choosing those words carefully. Finally, her eyes flicked up to meet his, decisiveness kindled in their depths. "What—what happens to Seeds when they're devoured, really?"

The hesitation didn't come from her—it came from Nazum. Ronoah threw a look at the boy and saw confusion crinkling his features.

Ronoah had been wondering the same thing lately. It was a shame he knew as little as Marghat did. He searched for a reply, came up empty, and the wisewoman let her hair unspool like a black ribbon from her hand. "Let me be more specific—what happened to Yacchatzul? Did she escape, or did she get eaten, or did she join you people in shiyalsha?"

"Escape?" This time he couldn't even pretend to understand. "What would a Seed need to escape from?"

Marghat gave him a put-upon pout that revealed nothing, sparkles strewn over steel. "So she's not down there?"

"I've—never seen her," Ronoah said, stumbling as he searched through the tight-wound warren of his memory for the shred of underworld geography Chashakva had once explained. "She would be in the fifth branch if she was, and I'm, I'm from the fourth, we wouldn't have crossed paths."

Marghat's pout pushed to one side in mild disappointment, as if she'd expected his uselessness. Ronoah had known from the start that he'd have nothing new to tell her, but he resented that look all the same. "Great grandmamu began planning to remove us from the War after Yacchatzul instructed her to—" hadn't Bashti said something like this, at some point? "—and we did it, because we love Yacchatzul and we honour her memory. But every generation since has wondered *why*—great grandmamu didn't see fit to divulge that part. With a couple of demons walking the overworld I figured it's time to finally find out." The wind poured in through the open screens and tousled Marghat's bangs. She looked very serious indeed. "I care about the rainforest, but I'm not interested in sending my villagers to die if it's not helping. I've got generations of reports, and since great grandmamu's time it's gotten *worse*, not better."

"The deadzones," Ronoah breathed, thinking with another cold lurch of the lagoon, the water.

"What's a deadzone?"

"The—it's a part of the forest that, it's like it all got sick and rotted at once, nothing lives there, no birds, the water burns, the sky goes quiet like it's dead ..."

"Aaah." Marghat tilted her head back. "Now I know what you're talking about. We call them *apghat mayul*, sickwater. One popped up near where the old village used to be. Not terribly close, but enough to worry about it spreading—that's one reason the village finally collectively agreed it was time to relocate."

Ronoah's heart flipped. "It happened that recently? In your lifetime?" When he'd first beheld Chabra'i's deadzone, it had felt static, like it had always been there. He'd wondered whether it wasn't the same putrefaction from hundreds of years ago, a remnant from when the War began. The idea of watching one *unfold* made his skin crawl. He tried to brush it off, eyes on Marghat as she gestured down the hallway that led to the bone room.

"My lineage has been writing the Book of Decay since the War began—annals on the rainforest, tracking its health or disease. The apghat mayul are actually a recent problem. At the least, they didn't show up in such great numbers until a century ago."

Something called for Ronoah's attention then, some echo, some complimentary colour, but it was hard to catch. It was so hot out; even with the breeze, everything felt sticky and oppressive. Finally he pulled it to the front of his mind: the timeline. The mention of Marghat's *great grandmamu.*

Chabra'i had mentioned her great grandmamu too. She was the one that the Heavenly Seed Subin had commanded to start ambushing other tribes in retaliation. The ambushes and the deadzones, then, they lined up?

He thought of Pashangali. Remembered her tight fury as she declared that *nowhere does it say that the gods demanded this.* Insisted it was people, not Seeds, who had chosen this chaos. A tribe who wanted the rest destroyed.

Before he could stop to think it was out of him: "Do you think it's because of the oathbreakers? Are they behind the deadzones, the sickwaters?"

Marghat's eyes widened, and Ronoah pressed further. "Did they—the ones who started the ambushes, did they mess up the balance? Did they ruin the pact by going against tradition—?"

He was cut off by the wisewoman's laughter. A loud laugh, teasing and incredulous. Achingly familiar. "Where did you hear *that* from?" she asked between giggles.

"From Pashangali Jau-Hasthasndra. She told me there was a tribe who, who wants to sabotage the War. She said there were oathbreakers who revolted and want the rainforest all to themselves, that it's not the gods but one tribe's greed that's to blame for the way things have fallen apart."

"Well little miss Jau-Hasthasndra is wrong," simpered Marghat, her eyes glinting under her fluttering lashes. "It *was* the gods—just one, in particular. And it wasn't anything to do with greed. It was for love."

Premonition prickled cold at the back of Ronoah's neck. "How—how are you so certain?"

Marghat gave her answer—and instead of translating Nazum yelled, rising halfway from his seat before he checked himself. Visibly shaken, he lowered himself back to the ground. As Ronoah looked between them, the dread only growing thicker on his skin, he saw the boy lift a face full of horror and awe to Marghat; the wisewomen nodded, as if permitting him to repeat her words.

"Because we *are* the oathbreakers," Nazum said hoarsely, as Marghat spread her arms to the villa, "and it was my great grandmamu who ordered the very first raid."

Verbal vertigo upended Ronoah. Everything he thought he knew about Marghat Yacchatzndra and her village tilted, and the room tilted with it.

The oathbreakers. The ones who turned the old ritual into a bloodbath. It started here—it started in this very villa, maybe even at this table. Vespasi—

"Runa?"

He looked up, realizing he had put his head in his hands as if to block something out. He was absently massaging his browbone, trying to quell the clenching, pulsing pain behind his eyes.

Bashti entered the room with the tea tray, distracting everyone. She placed the tray on the table, settled on her haunches, carefully poured the pale golden liquor into bowls. The fragrance of fresh jasmine floated up. Ronoah hardly felt like drinking anything right now, but Bashti pushed a bowl in front of him, and on reflex he took it up and sipped, even though it was still too hot, even though it scalded. For a surreal, unstoppable moment, they took tea with Marghat Yacchatzndra, great granddaughter of the oathbreaker, like nothing at all was wrong.

Marghat swirled her tea, took a long initial sip. Then she sighed a sigh that was neither relishing nor repentant, gave her bowl a preparatory quarter-turn on the table, and explained.

"My great grandmamu actually met Yacchatzul in her lifetime. That wasn't uncommon, back in the old days, you know—wisewomen would confer with their gods in person instead of straining the silence for omens and signs." She sounded a little contemptuous, a little wistful. Maybe she mourned never getting her own meeting. "In times of great bounty or great danger, they would appear—that's what my mamu Lhatza told me when I was a girl. And the last time great grandmamu ever saw Yacchatzul, danger was approaching.

"She was scared, Yacchatzul. Apparently that was unlike her, she was meant to be very firm and decisive. Not reckless, just steady. But the things she said when she came looking for great grandmamu—she said she was going to die if we didn't do something very drastic for her. The Seeds had started to devour each other and she was probably going to end up eaten, she said.

"Now great grandmamu was sad about this, of course she was, but she thought—well, you know, that is the way of the War, isn't it? The Seeds are eaten until the last one sprouts. If anything she was relieved, because this meant the War was nearly over. All the Seeds would collect in one—no matter which—and reign over the heartland. After centuries of effort, that should have been a celebration, not an emergency.

"But Yacchatzul stopped her rejoicing with one phrase. A plea, really.

None of us were meant to be eaten."

She paused, and Ronoah felt Nazum shiver beside him, and as if it were contagious, the shiver rattled through him too.

"None of us," Marghat repeated quietly, shaking her head almost to herself. "Now, what is a wisewoman to make of that? That's not what it says in all the stories. But when your god—when your friend, because great grandmamu really did consider Yacchatzul a friend—comes to you pleading, you don't say no. You don't harden your heart against that.

"Yacchatzul asked for two things. The first was the ambushes—specifically, she wanted great grandmamu to lead a raid against the Subindr and Naskarahandr tribes. Subin and Naskarahal were the ones eating Seeds, you see, and Yacchatzul wanted to distract them from hunting anyone else down by disturbing their home territory. Her plan was to use that time to gather as many Seeds as she could and escape together; if she was successful, she said, then in a year or two she would return with her cohort and decree an end to the War. I don't know what gave her the power to decide, but whatever she told great grandmamu, it was believable enough.

"Yacchatzul's second request was what you see all around you: she wanted the Yacchatzndr to hide from the War, to distance ourselves from the heartland *just in case*. In case she failed, she wanted us as safe as we could be. She wanted us to live. She bowed her great plumed head in gratitude—my mamu used to say *in contrition*, but I don't know what Yacchatzul had to apologize for—and great grandmamu laid a hand on her in love, and then they each went to do what they must do.

"That was the last time any wisewoman of ours felt the touch of the divine." Marghat gazed out at the vista, the cliffs. The shadows deepened as the sun hid its face. "Great grandmamu waited for Yacchatzul's return— one year, then two, then two more, then to the next double-eclipse, then another five years. Just in case. She never came back. She never arrived to stop the War—and neither did any of the other Seeds, as far as I know, not even Subin or Naskarahal. The raids on those villages opened up a whole new battlefield, a new arena of violence and treachery, and not a single Seed stopped us. They disappeared and the War continued, endless, godless. We've paid the price ever since."

There was a long silence, shimmering taut as an overwound harp string. It threatened to snap in Ronoah's mind, to whiplash and leave him reeling, sickly intoxicated by all this secret history. The raids an act of protection, the Seeds escaping, Subin, *Chabra'i's* Subin, the godless war and the phrase, the plea, *none of us were meant to be eaten.*

He didn't know how to begin sorting it out, how to slot it into place alongside everything the other wisewomen had told him. What was true? What was myth? What was the gods and what was the grudges? It all felt so slippery in his hands, running through his fingers like water. How did, how could he, he didn't—

Like a branch protruding from a fast-flowing river, he grabbed hold of the one fact that centuries of history couldn't obscure, the one thing no one could deny: "But the Vashnarajandr," he said, nearly tripping over the name, "they all—if there are no tribes trying to sabotage the War, if there are no real traitors then, then who..."

Say it, a voice whispered. Say the words—that was no sacrifice, and you know it. "Who murdered them?" he finished. His voice cracked.

Marghat hummed. She readjusted the rope twisted around her torso with a thoughtful look.

"I think they did it to themselves," she offered.

Ronoah's throat seized like it would around a swallow of sour milk.

"What?" he finally managed.

"I've never heard any substantial rumour about one tribe doing it. I don't think any of them did. I don't think it was murdering at all—it was martyring." Marghat leveled him with a look that shook him from deep inside, chillingly matter-of-fact. "*Vashnarajan*. The one who braids the rope." Her fingers lingered on her harness. "He's a circle god, a cycle god. His power came from *self*-sacrifice. When the Vashnarajandr sacrificed people, the sacrifices would hang themselves. The ultimate act of strength; the ultimate offering. Or so they believed—and they believed it strong enough to never take the easy way out."

"What do you mean?" The words were pulled from him, wooden, alien.

"I mean if a ritual battle brought them nothing, if their holy days came around and they had no foreign neck to slip a noose around, what do you think they turned to?" The wisewoman tapped her own collarbone. "The gods had disappeared decades ago, and the Vashnarajandr had never stooped to raiding like the rest of us—they were too loyal to the old ways. They were getting cut down in the jungle, attacked in the night, and their call for a Council went unheard. They must have thought there was never any way they'd emerge victorious from this whole thing."

For just a moment, Marghat's idle nonchalance slipped, replaced by true regret. The table under Ronoah's fingers felt miles away.

"Maybe it was their last-ditch attempt to save Vashnarajan," she said. "Or they wanted to remove themselves from the War, too, only they did it different from us. Maybe they were just weary of this world and wanted to hasten their advance to the next. I don't blame them—this world is cruel. Who knows?" She tipped her head to one side, her stare long and far. "Maybe when Chashakva's cycle ended those boundaries between shiyalsha and the overworld got torn open again, and a bunch of us are walking around up here who don't belong. Maybe that's why the forest won't get better—maybe that's the real fight. Putting things back in their place. Maybe we all need to go down to shiyalsha before the rainforest is set right again."

And then she grinned at Ronoah, leaning forward on her elbows. "How about it? Can I come stay at yours?"

Cold rushed into Ronoah's body, sucked his breath away into the black chasm she imagined him from. He could see it so clearly, a village ending their lives together to escape, to give their land one last chance—gods, there didn't *need* to be saboteurs if there were tribes who thought their own self-destruction would save the heartland, if they were prepared to hold hands and walk into the grave that way. What if other tribes had the same idea? What if Marghat brought her conclusions to Council and some wisewoman took that belief back to her people and more tribes disappeared overnight, more people all going down to shiyalsha—all *dying*—out of centuries of desperation and what if the rainforest kept rotting *anyway*, what if it just ended up a yellow wasteland with tens of thousands of faces in the bog—?

Dizziness overwhelmed him. His head was about to split with its agony. Marghat asked him something—what was it? what did she say?—and he looked up to give an answer he hadn't even formed yet and there was Bashti, sitting quietly in the corner. Watching him with that same seeking quirk of a smile.

Instead of words, bile rose in his throat and he nearly vomited right there, folding in half over the table. The jasmine tea spilled in a lukewarm splash and their voices rose sharp in alarm and then it made sense. It made sense what the little girl had said—*come on out*—and why she said it, who she'd really said it to.

Not to him.

To something *inside* him.

Everything went ringing quiet in his ears as he fought not to pass out, and then it went quiet for real, as that fight was lost.

*F*IRST WAKING. BREEZE. JOSTLING. PAIN. The world a swimming blur, hazy and oversharp. Sliding into feverish focus, Ronoah heard Marghat and Nazum arguing in Shaipurin. Nazum had Ronoah leaned against his chest, his wiry arms supporting Ronoah's limp weight. Whose heartbeat was it, so loud, so sickening? Marghat had her hands out as if expecting something. Nazum spat some caustic, burning word but she only shook her head, her severity a green halo around her. Nazum gestured to Ronoah, then to himself, practically strangling himself with his hand on his throat in desperate demonstration. *I'm his voice.* Marghat crouched down and murmured something that put a stop to his dissent. It drained the fight from the boy, Ronoah could sense it leaving, flowing warmth pressing against his body oddly numb, and he wished the boy had fought harder.

Second waking. Bird trills. Gravity. Milky skin smell. Disjointedly, the realization came to Ronoah that he was being carried, and his first delirious thought was *Chashakva has finally come back* and he tried to call her name but he could not speak. They passed into a corridor of light and through the stabbing sunsparks in his eyes he saw it was Marghat bringing him deeper into the villa. His body light, light like Jesprechel's papered corpse. Nazum was nowhere in sight.

Third waking. Slowly, slowly. Unfurling fern, candle flame growing. Reality opening in a yawn. He couldn't see much at all this time—maybe the lights had all gone, or maybe he just couldn't see properly through the heat behind his eyes. He was lying down, stuck to the sheets for all his sickly sweating and yet so cold he could not cease his shuddering. His limbs at once crowded and estranged, his body launched into its own internal war.

Then Marghat was there, looming from the dim, her face a mask, eyes bright. She swirled around him swift, unknowable—a pinched arm, a pulled eyelid, a forced-open jaw. Her hand, hard and dry, pressing his sternum, his ribs, his belly. The contact made him whimper.

She disappeared, and he didn't know if she was ever really there, and he tried to cry out but something oily and gelatinous was crawling up his throat and he couldn't cough it out of the way. Something all over him and inside him, bloating and rancid, the unceasing march of a hundred thousand biting ants pushing between the very fibres of his muscles. They would chew holes through his skin any moment, any moment, any moment now.

I want Chabra'i, he thought uselessly. I want Nazum. I want Ngeome. I want Chashakva.

But it was Marghat who returned to him. She was holding a human skull in her hand.

*H*e was in the library at the academy in Padjenne. Dry, amber sunlight filtered through the clerestories high in the sandstone walls. The smell of leather and paper permeated the air. Such a familiar smell—every day of the fourteen months he'd spent in this place, his first lungful of air in the library had been a grateful one. The smell of knowledge. The smell of promise. How much he'd missed it. No one else seemed to be occupying this part of the stacks, so he wandered solitary, skimming the honeycomb of the walls, brushing polished wooden scroll handles, stroking calfskin bindings. Their colours shifted faintly under his touch, a muted rainbow. So pleasant. They'd never done that before. He lingered over shelves, perusing the titles on spines and plaques, vaguely aware he was looking for something but not in any hurry to find it. He pulled out a book, checked the cover, returned it with a sound like a dove fluttering from an eave. He paused in front of an atlas encased in glass, tracing a trajectory with his fingers that called to something in him. A journey across the ocean. Across Berena. An adventure dawnwards. Funny. He moved on, his bare feet warmed by the stone floors. They must have renovated the building recently, because there was always noise outside the windows of Padjenne's academy, but now it was silent like one calming breath. He found a book that caught his eye: his own name on the spine, in glowing Acharrioni gold. He opened to a page at random.

He was in Pashangali's cabin, the old wood warmed in the summer mist. The bales of herbs swayed gently in the rafters, lifting accents of sweet hay into the air. Her crystals glinted small smiles in their alcoves. He couldn't hear her—maybe she was upstairs? But he wasn't allowed upstairs. It was all right, though, she would come down when she was ready. And then they could pick up where they'd left off. He scooped a cup of water from the burbling fountain in the corner; it tasted crisper than anything he'd had in his life, like the clouds on top of Chalisto's Belt. He sipped it and watched the light change texture through the cabin. Maybe the sun was out, for once. He went through the front door to see. The village was the way he'd left it, maybe a little cleaner, a little quieter. Maybe all the villagers were celebrating something—they did have so many holidays, the Jau-Hasthasndr, they were always celebrating something. It was a good way to live, in the middle of all this gloom. He traversed the trackways with his cup of water, brushing his way into the woods. The wind stirred the ferns to sighing. He came upon the sinkhole, the doorway to the underworld he'd blessed with lilies on the second day of spring. As he approached, a great head reared from the hole, followed by a sinuous, shining body, looping and coiling its way up to the overworld. Lord Jau-Hasthasuna, a snake as long as a mountain is tall. He settled his black eyes on Ronoah, and a little shiver went up his neck. Tentatively, he lifted his cup to share.

He was on Sweetwood Mountain, the stone gritty with sand under his soles. The sky was billowing white with smoke. He had a bundle of sweet-wood in his arms. The Pilanovani hadn't seen sweetwood in a thousand years—what a gift he was bringing to them. They would accept him with open arms when he showed it to them. They would accept him for who he was. He knew it was a lot to ask—he was troublesome, he started hard conversations, he made that face Sophrastus pointed out—but where better to be troublesome, than Sweetwood Mountain? He navigated paths so worn and familiar to him that it was like floating, his toes just skimming the ground. The sky beyond the smoke was umber honey, ripe and full. He turned a corner and found his family around a lit firepit. They had changed: Lelos had shaved her head, the round of her skull so stately, the point of her chin still so elfin, so fine; she was still wearing their gerbil skull around her neck. Ngeome had creases around his mouth like their father from smiling, but also creases between his brows like their mother from worrying; Elizze was a little less reed-thin, which was good, he always just disappeared food without absorbing any of it, but it seemed he'd found a way to make some of it stick. And Diadenna's arms and face were more dappled, the pale splashes on her skin more numerous, like the slow emergence of islands in low tide. It was amazing, seeing them all so grown up. It made him feel fond, and proud. He stepped into the firelight, and they noticed him with mild surprise, and he smiled and threw the sweetwood onto the fire.

He was on the bluffs of Tyro, sitting with his legs dangling off the preci-pice. The sea unfolded beneath him, an ever-expanding sheet of silver and steel, the surface parting for islets and whales. He was sitting between two people—Bazzenine and Jesprechel were here with him, shoulder-to-shoulder. Velvet red, plum black. Hair shining like stars. He was glad to see them doing well. He didn't know which of them was more beautiful, and he told them so, and they smiled. They gathered what small stones lay nearby and threw them into the sea, trying to see how far they could reach, a contest between cousins while Ronoah cupped his chin in his palms and watched. Bazzenine, with his elegant painter's hands, tossed one so far they heard it bounce off the Shattering, stone kissing glass leagues and leagues away. Ronoah told them everything he knew about the Shattering, how impassable it was, how wide, how once upon a time their great ancestors had fought a war and lost and the only reason why any of them were here today was because of a friend of his. A good friend. The closest he'd ever had. He told them hoping to impress them, and they were impressed, and it made him happy. Bazzenine put lights into the air, drawing delicate voids in the open space before them; Jesprechel waved her arm through their bodies with a feeling like they were running water. The cousins leaned their heads on Ronoah's and told him how to treat them kindly. He promised he wouldn't forget. And Jesprechel brushed the cliff with her hands and together they plunged to the sea.

He was in a land of music and light, a vast plain of pealing illumination swirling far as the eye could see. The realm of the gods. The place he had come from. What a relief, to finally be home. He spent a while appreciating the play of light, the glitter, the glow. He set himself to walking, soaking in the gentle sensations of the divine plane. How much fullness there was here, how much contentment. How whole everything was, replete in itself. Perhaps he had come back to become whole, too. Of course—he was going to see Genoveffa. He called her in his heart and a point of burning light flared in the distance, a galaxy away. He crossed it and came upon her in a wreath of colour and melody, her limbs bright as the sun, her face obscured by flame. First mother. Surest love. She was doing something with her hands, like working a potter's wheel; curious, Ronoah went to her side. Between her magnificent fingers he saw a capsule of light flaring wondrous colours—garnet red, fire lily orange, blazing salt white. Little wishgranter, half-formed, cooing in the cradle of its god. She was spinning it into being. Who was it? Elder sister the exile? Himself? Someone new, someone to join them? It might be nice, to have someone else. He told her so, and she glimmered at him, so playful, so profound. He'd missed her terribly. She chimed, asking if he wanted a closer look, and he nodded eagerly, getting up on his toes like a child while she opened her palms to show him what was inside.

It was incredible.

He gasped awake to rain on his face, to shade under the canopy. Wait—canopy? There was no canopy in Yacchatzndr territory—and even if there was, said a voice in his head, you aren't in any condition to walk around under it. You were sick with something, weren't you? You're supposed to be resting.

And yet here he was. He flexed his fingers and toes, found that they were sound enough to use, so against his better judgement he got to his feet and scouted the area. It didn't look like a part of the rainforest he'd seen before: the foliage was different, darker green, waxier, and the din of the insects hit a different pitch than the ones he'd come to know as Subindr, Jau-Hasthasndr, Yacchatzndr. Where ...?

Where was Marghat? Where was Nazum? And most importantly, most impatiently, where the *kulim putrash* was Chashakva?

He widened his circle of search, regaining his balance. The rain stopped, then started again. And then—

There. Caught in the raindrops like prisms: light, coming from something. Cautiously, Ronoah advanced on it, passing under banana leaves and great exposed tree roots, until finally he got a clear look at what was moving through the rainforest.

It was a person—or at least, it was person-shaped. It flickered too fast for him to make any features out, not so much shapeshifting as overlapping, endless layers superimposed on each other. Whatever it was, Ronoah had the feeling it would take miles to get from the surface of it down to the core. But even as he thought so, the vortex of shape and thought parted and he caught, for a fleeting second, a centre of pure star. Magenta, sapphire, aquamarine.

Chashakva.

He was about to say her name, to yell it across the clearing, but something stopped him. That's not the name you need, it said, that's not the one that'll work. Fine, he countered, Özrek then? Reilin? Which one will make it listen? What do I have to say to make it turn?

He couldn't get his mouth around either of them, so like a massive archive in his mind he scanned every name he knew for an answer, from the greatest idols to the most mundane neighbours. Everyone he had ever heard about, in passing, in myth. Nothing.

Fine. Another way. He turned instead to everything he knew about the creature, all its stories and quips and tenderness, its harsh jokes and secretkeeping, the thousand thousand things it could do, the delight, the deep respect, the way it raged with paradox. A grand and ignoble influence if there ever was one; an enchanting and despicable creature, a creature that was not innocent by any description. Artful, insidious, contradictory, repelling as it attracted and attracting as it repelled—an eon of life unbounded, surging and laughing free.

Ronoah held it all, every detail, compressed it diamond-like under the force of his will and projected it outward. The shadow of a consonant crossed his mind.

The figure in the clearing froze, whipped around—Ronoah saw innumerable pairs of eyes widen in shock—it lunged across the glade, lunged for Ronoah moving faster than anything he'd ever seen, and he took a step and started running too, running on water, certain that some magic word was going to take flight off his tongue any second, and the creature reached for his outstretched hand—

And then Ronoah's foot broke the surface of the water, and it missed. He felt the brush of fingers on fingers before he was sucked down and he let out a sound of fury as he went, fury and triumph, because yes they had missed each other but they had *seen* each other, for just a moment, they had caught each other's scent.

For a good enough hunter, a scent was all you needed. A scent could get you anywhere.

Twenty-Five

$\mathcal{R}$ONOAH STIRRED AWAKE AND DRIFTED OFF so often that it was impossible to tell how much time actually passed. It was a long half-dream of motion and fuzzy Shaipurin voices and firm, careful hands giving him water and broth, waking him to relieve himself, rubbing circulation into his sluggish bloodstream. At times he languished contentedly in the space between wakefulness and sleep, at others he cursed and railed with silent intensity. The deep exhaustion of healing left his mind and body little to work with. He spent a miniature forever coiled in himself, waiting it out.

Until one night, when the heavy fog of his convalescence finally parted enough for him to open his eyes clear-headed and cool. It was probably the sound that drew him up, that cut a clean path for him to follow. Sweet and bright as a paring knife. Steady notes; lengthy pauses for breath. The sound of Nazum singing.

For a while Ronoah just listened, appreciating the boy's voice. So different when it was singing—it barely sounded like him. It was more like the other Nazum, the boy's shadow side. The one whose gaze against a wisewoman was solemn and unflinching, the one whose silences were ripe and electric as he mulled over the paradise of death. He was singing something in a Shaipurin that Ronoah didn't think he'd heard before; it sounded further back in the mouth, the vowels differently shaped, narrower, more oblong. He remembered the last time he had woken to singing in a language he did not know—a final morning on the Chiropolene plains, a priestess and a not-shalledra in harmony—and a keen pain rang in his chest, and Nazum's singing cut short.

"…Ronoah?" the boy said, nearly tentatively. "You awake?"

Ronoah tried to answer, but nothing more than a wheeze came out. By the time he'd pulled himself halfway to sitting, Nazum had fetched some water. He took a long drink, aware that this was the first time he'd held a cup on his own in many days.

"Thank you," he said—in Acharrioni, of course. Grimacing, he repeated himself in Chiropolene. "And—thank you for the singing, too."

"Oh, that." The look Nazum gave was somewhere between indifferent and embarrassed. "It's an old thing."

"It was very—" very melancholy, very mournful, very make-your-heart-yearn-inside-you "—very moving."

"I already sang all the Bhun Jivaktandr work songs days ago, twice each at least. Tried to lurch my way through that super long Jau-Hasthasndr chant too, but I forgot most of it." Nazum shrugged his mismatched shoulders, looking somewhere around Ronoah's foot. Ronoah frowned.

"Have you just been sitting here? Singing to me?"

Nazum scrunched up his nose. "Singing *to you* sounds pretty mushy—I'm here all day keeping an eye on you, gotta do something to keep from dying of boredom—but, yeah. Basically. You got kinda quiet and calm if I did it when you were thrashing around, so I figured it was helpful."

It was pretty unbelievable that crotchety, practical Nazum would willingly spend his time singing Shaipurin lullabies to a Ronoah even more useless and delicate than usual. But here they were. "Thank you," he said again, trying to weight it with the sincerity he felt. "What was it? The song from just now."

Nazum didn't answer. His nonchalance returned, though it seemed thinner, more brittle. Recognizing that he was on the precipice of something important, Ronoah might have pressed the issue—but then another question hit him, cracked into his awareness as solid as one of the skulls on the wall.

"Did…did you just call me Ronoah?" he asked.

The room went a different shade of quiet. Nazum nodded.

Overwhelm washed over Ronoah. "That's, but, it's—um, sorry? Thank you?" He had no idea what to do. It felt like a really momentous gesture, and he felt distinctly like he was flapping at it in response, every bit the bewildered flamingo Chashakva said he would be. "Wh—um, why?"

"It's not like I forgot it's your name," the boy snapped, clearly as awkward as Ronoah. "I was the one who gave you the other one." Ronoah nodded, still wide-eyed, and Nazum hissed out a sigh. "You looked like you were gonna die. Seems only decent to let you hear your own name before you kick it."

Ronoah frowned. "They're both my name," he said, unsure of why he was trying to be reassuring about this.

"Shut up, Runa." Ronoah did as he was told, feeling the astonishment lingering on his own face. Suddenly, Nazum switched tracks. "It's not even that different," he said, his tone still aggravated in that guilty, admitting way, "they probably wouldn't even mess it up that bad, I just—" He scoffed, seemingly at himself. "From the minute I met you it was obvious you were an easy target—look at you, you'd be insta-dead in this place without me or Chashakva. And then I found out we were going to the Subindr and it was so clear you had no idea how scared you should've been so I figured I could, I could start by giving you something to—I don't know, *shield* yourself with. That way when terrible shit happened you could think, well, that happened to Runa, not to me." He rubbed at his nose, unfamiliarly uncomfortable. "You could move on, maybe. I hear that works sometimes. New names, new lives."

This fierce protectiveness was startling—even more so because, apparently, it had been there from the beginning. Ronoah looked closely at Nazum; gently, praying not to push too hard, he asked, "Have you changed your name before, too?"

Nazum gave a laugh that frightened Ronoah with its hollowness, and replied, "Nah, just made it shorter. I'm not the creative type."

His protective veneer dissolving, layer by razor-thin layer. Ronoah could feel it. Abruptly, the boy heaved a sigh and leaned his elbows on his knees. "You know what's really annoying?" he asked.

Ronoah knew it was rhetorical. He waited. "This work en't bad, I've already said. It has its perks. But the part that always makes me want to just *walk*," Nazum said harshly, "is the translating. Not you, you're fine. It's *them*." He lifted his gaze to the door. "Having to say words for people who have no idea what they're talking about. Having to be the voice for everyone proclaiming things like they're so wise and worldly when none of them have a clue what's going on. *That* is the absolute worst."

"What don't they have a clue about?" Ronoah asked. "What sort of things?"

"I don't know—everything." Nazum shook his head. In that moment he reminded Ronoah, of all things, of Sophrastus that morning on the hill. "The reasons the War started, the reasons it changed. The Vashnarajandr. All of it."

"I'm starting to think nobody knows those things," Ronoah pointed out wryly. He was trying to bring some levity into this unnerving intimacy, to find his way back to their regular dynamic.

Nazum shrugged. "I mean, I know what got the Vashnarajandr."

"How?" Ronoah asked—and then it hit him, just what he was asking, and Nazum was looking at him with a look that was almost fond, a look that could break either one of them if they moved wrong.

"Because I was there, demon boy," he said, with his you're-a-real-idiot-aren't-you smile.

Every language Ronoah knew abandoned him. He was rendered completely speechless. And perhaps this was a blessing, because the quiet gave Nazum the space he needed to collect himself, some last thing falling away inside him, falling open.

"Our lady Yacchatzndra got at least one thing right: the Vashnarajandr sacrificed people through self-sacrifice. And when they couldn't claim anyone from neighbouring tribes, the responsibility fell to them." He frowned, shifting as if the story wasn't fitting right. "You could expect a villager to give themselves to the rope once every year or two. The village would draw lots, and whoever pulled the red-tipped lot was Vashnarajan's chosen. My cousin went when I was six. She was twelve, and totally magnificent. When she stepped off the podium, we all held our breath thinking she would just float."

He fell silent, brooding. Ronoah slid the cup of water in his direction, and Nazum took it. "I was training to be a warrior," he continued at length. "You start pretty young in the Vashnarajandr, it's a little like it is here. I'd spend all day out on the rivers, learning the geography of the neighbouring regions, and all night in the combat huts learning how to fight. Any time I had in the middle, I'd eavesdrop on the translators' lessons—we had people whose job it was to learn the dialects, I think all the tribes do, it's one of those crappy jobs where everyone disdains you even though the work's important. But I thought it was interesting, so I'd spy."

Ronoah could see it: a Nazum smaller and knobbier and probably just as obstinate, sneaking under tarps and into crates to listen in on the tutelage of a skill nobody wanted to have. The curiosity of it, the clandestine joy. He felt a prickle hot in the back of his throat.

"I was going to be the best warrior of my generation." Nazum nodded slightly, to himself, as if even now some tiny part of him believed it. "I was sure of it. I put everything into training—you know how kids are, they obsess over stuff, they never shut up about it. But twelve must have been my family's lucky number, because when I was twelve we had another scarce year, and the lots came out of the wisewoman's hut. And guess who drew the winner?" Ronoah's eyes fell helplessly on Nazum's rope-burn scars. "Just like that, my destiny changed," Nazum said, clicking his fingers. "I wasn't going to fight for Vashnarajan's strength. I was going to die for it. Right now.

"They put you in quarantine for fasting before they bring you to the ropes. There's a special hut and everything—" Ronoah remembered the hut in Chabra'i's tree, the rope bridge, Nazum's restless discomfort, oh, gods "—and you stay there for a week, just cleaning everything out and meditating. They don't bar the door, not when it's one of our own. You know you have a special job and you know not to mess it up. So there I was, in the sacrificial hut for five days with no food, just a single crock of consecrated water and my own private thinking about what my life was gonna amount to."

Last time Nazum had divulged something about his past, he'd done it shrouded in irritation, pacing the room and tisking and growling. It couldn't be farther from the way he approached it now, with such matter-of-factness. Beatifically resigned. "Before you say anything about how sorry you are for me, I was fine with it. Honestly I was—well I don't know if *excited* is the right word, but at any rate, I was kinda smug. I thought Vashnarajan must have needed some really powerful help if he was calling on me. Greatest warrior and all that." He made an unreadable gesture selfwards with one hand. Maybe it was the dim lighting, or else Ronoah's own haze of pain flaring up, but he thought he saw the twitch of a smile on the boy's face.

"I was there an awful long time. Longer than usual—I mean it *felt* like a fucking age and a half, of course it does when you're all alone and hungry and kind of bored and maybe a little scared. I felt like a sacrificial hut myself, all empty and windy inside. But I etched lines into the wall to keep time, and finally day five rolled around." Darkness eclipsed his eyes. "And day six. And day seven. And no one came to get me. Didn't come to refill that crock either, and you can make it through a lot in this life but you can't make it through three days waterless, no matter how pro you are at meditating. So my will to live long enough to at least die properly finally outweighed my will to do things by the rules, and I opened the door and left the hut and everything was dead."

The words hit Ronoah a half-beat late. Such was their nature, so lacking in melodrama. His breath hitched; he searched Nazum's face only to find that Nazum was properly in the grips of his story now. His gaze was intense, far away. "You gotta imagine what kind of special treat that is, wandering your village completely delirious with hunger and thirst and that little impending suicide thing nagging at you, just seeing all the people and animals and even the reeds completely stuffed. Parents? Nope. Classmates? Kicked it. Favourite dog? See you in shiyalsha. Even the wisewoman was keeled over and bloated, mouth black, veins all black, and when I saw her there I knew there was really no one left. No one but me.

"So I did what any self-respecting, half-mad kid with a figurative and literal noose around his neck would do," he proclaimed, "and I got the fuck out of there looking for something to eat." Absurdly, Ronoah laughed, a strangled sound amid his tears. Nazum gave him a disparaging look that was also, Ronoah thought, fiercely affectionate. "I grabbed one of the boats I'd trained in and paddled until things looked more alive and then I walked inland until I found water that didn't make my eyes itch to look at. Don't ask me how I knew the river was poisoned, because I don't have an answer. Maybe you get special powers after starving for eight days. Who knows.

"After that I mostly did my best to keep existing. Got me pretty far. Can't survive in a village all alone, ai? Especially not one where even the trees are rotted through. And if I showed up in one of the other tribes I'd probably just end up fertilizer, and not even for the Seed I'd wanted to be, so I avoided them too. I just kept…paddling downriver, hoping something would find me. And then something did." He looked to Ronoah. "And you already know the rest."

Ronoah nodded. Nazum took another swig of water before passing the cup back; after Ronoah had sipped his fill and his tongue felt loosened, he dared to ask, "So where did you get the—what were your scars from?" Had the noose gotten tangled in something? Had someone caught him by it? Setten and Ibisca, had he just worn it that whole way north?

"What?" Nazum squinted, then laughed. "No, no Runa, those literally have nothing to do with it, I told you the truth the first time. I actually did fall out of a tree like an idiot." He snickered again, marvelling at his own antics, but then that humour faded. "But you're right," he said. "It wasn't exactly the subtlest reminder of where I came from."

Ronoah bit his lip. "Reminder?"

"I mean once a lot is drawn, it's drawn, you know?" Nazum's hand had found its way up to cover the scars on his shoulder. "No matter what. Even if there was one person left in the village other than me, that person would insist that I hang, and I would have agreed. So every once in a while my stupid brain toys with the idea that Vashnarajan's still waiting on me—like, not only am I a delicious snack, I'm the *last snack*." Something in the air wobbled. "There's no one else to sacrifice for him, so, so it makes sense he'd want that promise kept. You know?"

Nazum smiled. Then his smile slipped. He took an odd, catching inhale and blinked rapidly and then put his hands over his face and laughed into his fingers. It was a laugh of a different kind. A breathless, breaking laugh. Ronoah could tell; it broke in him at exactly the same time.

"Sorry, wow," Nazum said, full of surprise at his own reaction. He rubbed his face with his hands, giving another shaky laugh. "Wow, I have never told anyone about this before. Whoo."

Ronoah wanted so much to touch his shoulder, to take his hand. But he knew Nazum well enough to know that wasn't a comfort the boy would allow. He hunted for some acceptable show of support—and the ghost of an old friend offered a suggestion, ghost of easygoing smiles and useful, beautiful hands and apples at dawn. "It helps," he said, "talking about it."

"Does it?" Nazum said through a forced grin, eyes still hidden beneath his hand. Ronoah almost smiled hearing his own old doubts echoed back to him. How inevitable.

"It makes it real again," he assured, with a sweet ache. "It makes it yours."

For a long while, Nazum didn't reply; Ronoah had the feeling the boy was trying to pull himself together, to save his dignity. Ronoah let him. He put a hand to his own face, feeling how untidy his scruff had grown. A mark of how much time had passed. He lifted his arm to the light—skin thin from days of not eating, stretched over muscles taut from months of physical labour. On the inside of his elbow, a new scar, a crescent getting dark. The shape of a bitemark.

At last, the silence broke: "Well you've got me there. It *is* mine." Ronoah turned to face a Nazum who was bright-eyed but otherwise composed. "That's it. For real this time—no side-stepping, no tall tales. You're one of the only people left in this world who can say they really know me." His eyes hardened. "I think it's only fair you return the favour."

Ronoah blinked. Nazum sat up straighter, chopping an accusatory hand at him like a guillotine coming down. "Brother," he said, his voice getting louder, "what the *fuck* is an overworlder like you doing in the middle of this mess?"

He knew Ronoah was human. He'd figured it out.

Half-formed lies evaporated off Ronoah's lips. There was no point in trying to save this crumbling artifice, not facing an expression like that, so fierce, so furious. He was made wordless again, stunned into a complex whirl of emotions—anxiety, frustration, relief, shame, joy. "How did you know?"

"Marghat told me while you were under. She said if you didn't come back up, I shouldn't expect you to come back up ever. Here I've been this whole time thinking well, worst case scenario, Runa croaks, ah well, he'll crawl back up after some minor inconveniencing, mostly I gotta worry about exploding beside him or else Chashakva flipping me gut-side out for fucking up—but *no*, apparently all those times you nearly died you would have *permanently died*? How the shit did you get this past me? *Me?*"

"I have no idea," Ronoah said honestly, grimacing as a wash of dizziness overcame him. Might be better to lie down for this one. "Why else do you think Chashakva would be so, so stern about keeping me safe—?"

Nazum crowed a laugh. "Stern, you're cute, more like piss-yourself terrifying—" He cut himself off. "And that's the other thing, because I can get behind you being human, I always wondered why you were such a wimp for a shiyalshandr, but—but Chashakva, she can't be, she's not ...?"

"Oh, no. Chashakva is definitely not human."

"Then what is she?" Seeing Ronoah's face, Nazum waved off any possible answer. "Never mind, I don't wanna know. Better question—what the *kulim putrash* are *you* doing with her? You her servant? Her pet? Some kinda snack she's saving for later?"

"I'm her friend," Ronoah said, with enough firmness to bring Nazum up short.

"However that happened," Nazum said, inspecting Ronoah closely, "is a story I want to hear. I earned it. You owe it to me." Ronoah nodded. "But not now," the boy continued, "because you look like you're one step away from becoming shiyalshandr for real, and that would really mess me up."

Even as a new rain of exhaustion soaked his body, Ronoah couldn't find it in himself to be genuinely worried. "I don't think that's going to happen."

"Well. Good." Nazum snatched up the empty cup and went to refill it. By the time he returned, Ronoah could barely keep his eyes open. With Nazum's help he had another few sips of water and then laid down for his next long bout of rest. He was drifting before his head hit the bolster, but he felt—with enough awkward stiffness to rival Pashangali Jau-Hasthasndra—a hand squeeze his shoulder. "Get better. I'll sing you a thing from home, if it helps."

A faint smile spread across Ronoah's lips. Then he was asleep.

TWENTY-SIX

*T*HE NEXT TIME RONOAH WRENCHED HIMSELF AWAKE, Marghat was waiting for him, leering like a particularly beautiful vulture.

"Rise up, my Runa," she urged, extending her hands to him. Nazum's translation wafted from somewhere near the door. "Time to return to the land of the living. Our tortoise misses you—you don't want to be rude and keep her waiting, do you?"

To his own surprise, he was in fact able to sit up and even to get to his feet. How she knew he was up to it was a mystery—probably the same way she'd known what was wrong with him in the first place, and how to fix him. With the wisewoman on one side and Nazum on the other, he let himself be led away from his sickbed, out into the breezy hallways and spacious rooms of the Yacchatzndr villa. Back into steamy sunlight and bird feathers and the sound of the waves clambering up the rocks below.

It was like coming up out of the caves. He had to brace himself against the onslaught of life—but he embraced it too, with a near-desperate relief at the normalcy of it, the reassuring soundscape of a typical day.

He was still alive.

"I'm pleased as a papaya to see you so mobile," Marghat said while preparing their tea table, arranging platters of nuts and candied fruit alongside a bottom-heavy bowl of broth. "There were a few times this past week I worried you wouldn't make it, or that you'd be half-mad by the time you finally woke up—are you? Half-mad?"

"Past week?" Ronoah asked, ignoring her question.

"Oh yes, I suppose you don't know how long you were out for. Sickness does such strange things to time. It's been just over three weeks since you slammed head-first into my tea table, sweet demon mine."

Three weeks. How many times had he surfaced and sunk through those days? He looked to Nazum for help; just as the boy raised an eyebrow at him, Marghat's words pinched him like static shock. *Sweet demon mine.* Right. She knew he was human. They all did.

"What—happened to me?" He lifted his fingertips to his forehead as if Marghat's mention had summoned the impact, the pain all over again. But asides from the lingering fog of sleep, nothing was there. "Did you—" Sharply he drew his arm away, straightened it so he could see, there, in his elbow, that mark, that crescent— "…what is this from?"

A cleaner, more cutting question: *who?*

Marghat, evidently deciding that two could play at selectively answering questions, plonked her cheek in one hand and said, "You were poisoned. By the stuff in the apghat mayul."

Ronoah frowned. "But I haven't been anywhere near—" Too late he recalled the island, the cloves, the plummet into the water. This time he spoke to Nazum; clearly the boy was the one who had supplied this information. "Really? Chabra'i's? But it was so long ago, wouldn't it, would it not have…?"

"What, shouldn't it have offed you many moons ago?" Nazum's sour tone was cut by the thinnest sprinkle of sweetness; he was even gladder than Marghat to see Ronoah awake. "I dunno, maybe you did real good at holding your breath. Or it gets worse if you let it fester. If I'd known you weren't undead I would have made you talk to Lady Subindra about it but I *didn't know then did I.*"

Chashakva had been concerned, too, the one time he'd alluded to it. *You fell in the deadzone?* So austere, so serious, and he hadn't wanted to ruin the mood, hadn't wanted to sully his stupid victory, so he'd brushed it aside. Maybe if he hadn't, she could have healed him—but maybe, a voice said in his head, then she wouldn't have trusted you to handle yourself in the heartland. Maybe she would have thought twice about seeing you as an equal.

A dizzy spell made him grip the table—thinking too hard about the memory of the water, maybe, or else its lingering effect in his system even now. It was eerie, and a little revolting, to know he'd carried a part of that sludge with him this whole time, riding in his bloodstream, hiding in his tissue, until Marghat Yacchatzndra had called it out.

Which brought him back to his unanswered question. Instead of speaking it aloud, he bared the soft of his arm to Marghat, the scar left by her healing work. This time she didn't bother to sidestep: "As far as teeth go, dear Runa, the only ones sharp enough to cut the heart out of poison like that belong to Mamu Lhatza."

Briefly, like flinching, a memory spasmed through the muscle at his elbow, the sensation of breaking. Being broken into. Oblivious to his silent horror, Marghat rolled a wrist in a demonstration of the villa. "Now you've met all three of us. An honour and a privilege.

"So," she continued as Bashti arrived with tea—jasmine again, Ronoah noticed with a chill—and took her place beside her mother, "before we dig in, I have a little matter to discuss with you. The matter of payment."

"Payment?"

"Payment." Marghat pointed an imperious finger at Ronoah's newly acquired scar. "Not everyone gets my mamu's teeth in their arm, kiddo. She's supposed to last until it's my turn, and you just shortened that timespan considerably. I saved your life," she said, with a meaningful look that added, *your human life*, "and for all intents and purposes, it's still in my hands. I'd like a token of appreciation for keeping it to myself instead of tossing it to the first hungry mouth that comes biting at the Council."

"This is a shakedown," Nazum chipped in archly. "Want me to tell her that her payment is having Chashakva not turn her village into gravel?"

"No—no, it's all right," Ronoah said. He was considering another timeline, another reality: one where Marghat Yacchatzndra had not kidnapped him, and the deadzone's poison had set in while he was still with Pashangali. In that world, he was dead as the tallest warrior. He owed Marghat for this, especially if it had potentially taken literal years off her life. "I don't have much, though. Do you want me to, to do something for you, or …?"

As Nazum translated, Ronoah felt something loosen inside him. Something preparatory, premonitory, something dangerously calm, like a limb going lax to keep from breaking on impact. Even that warning didn't prepare him.

"I like that thunderstone of yours," came Marghat's cheery answer, "the one in your bag. Such a beautiful sparkle! And red like your little demon heart."

She wanted his garnet. Genoveffa's garnet.

A terrible weakness overtook him. For an instant, he didn't know if he was going to crumple or cry or moan as if she had actually wounded him. This couldn't be happening—it wasn't fair—

But that calm spread up his spine, cool and clinical, and like mortar setting it kept him upright. It makes sense, it said to him, reasonably. Of course she'd ask for it. Three wisewomen; three sacrifices. The cloves to Chabra'i, the salt to Pashangali …

"You can have it," he heard himself say.

The garnet to Marghat. It was the last piece of himself that he had, and she'd earned it.

Nazum, who was sensitive to Ronoah's tone by now, gave him a concerned look; Marghat peered at him as if she couldn't quite believe it had been that easy to secure her prize. But she'd earned it, hadn't she, so Ronoah didn't protest, and eventually she gestured an invitation. "In that case, teatime is served. Please be mindful of the solids," she said, already stacking bits of candied mango, "you haven't digested any in a while."

The four of them bent to the meal. The broth, golden and oily on top, was mostly for Ronoah; Marghat capitalized the fruit platter, Nazum helped himself to a bit of everything, and Bashti abstained, reaching only for more tea. Eventually Marghat licked a crumb of sugar off the edge of her pinky and suggested Ronoah go and get the thunderstone. "No point leaving a debt unpaid when you've got the offering ready—who knows, maybe it accumulates interest." She winked. Ronoah met her cajoling with a straight sincerity that seemed to wilt her enthusiasm a little.

"I'll be back in a few minutes," he said to her. He stood up, and Nazum stood with him—but he waved the boy down, insisted on making his way alone. With his back tingling at their curious stares, he left the table and slowly shuffled the familiar path to their room. The journey was both very long and very short. It reminded Ronoah of waiting for the fork in the Chiropolene road, the moment of parting ways. Reminded him of what Nazum had described about waiting in the sacrificial hut. Empty, windy inside.

The garnet was waiting for him, tucked away in his satchel abandoned so casually on a cushion. His hand closed around the smooth of the stone, snuggled so perfectly in his palm, and it was only when he actually held it that something animal and desperate tried to claw at that cool detachment, tried to fight its way out of this horrible debt, to beg Marghat to take anything else—the runa pelt from the tallest warrior, Kharoun's book, even the satchel itself, his own father's handiwork—just not this, it was special, it was sacred, it was his last line to Genoveffa. Chashakva had made it for him back when things were as simple as a treasure hunt and a dose of self-confidence—

Those days were gone, though. It made sense that their relics would follow them. And besides, observed that same reasonable voice, is it not so neat and tidy? Is it not nearly *destined*, how tidy it is? You could argue Genoveffa has saved you three times in this place.

Perhaps it was supposed to comfort him. Reassure. It did neither.

There came a faint slamming noise down the hall, and the sound of the windchimes ringing—alongside an odd high-pitched squeak. It took Ronoah a hazy moment to realize it was Bashti. He'd never heard her like that before, had a tamarin run across the table or something? More noise was coming from the sitting room, birds squawking and Marghat's voice calling rapid Shaipurin and Nazum, too, interrupting her, and then—

And then another voice. A voice that set the planks and the walls to shivering, that electrified the air. A voice so solid, so uncompromising, that Ronoah nearly tripped over it.

But he didn't. He staggered his way back, gripping doorframes and furniture for support, and he turned into the sitting room and saw them all:

Marghat, her grass skirts swirling and snapping in the wind, poised for a fight. Nazum, one arm raised as a shield, still clutching a forgotten handful of nuts. Little Bashtandala, balanced on her very tiptoes, her dark eyes round as the moons, yanked up by one arm, caught in one dusky, impossibly strong hand.

And Chashakva, looking fit to cleave the entire village from the cliffside in her fury.

Chashakva, whose voice spat with ten times the wrath of any creator god, Chashakva whose stance sent even the winds to wailing, the animals to cowering—his glorious Chashakva, whose heartstopping stare softened the moment she saw him, who cut everything short with a gesture, dropping Bashti dropping everything to open her mouth and call—

"Ronoah."

She was at his side before he could breathe. She had him before he even knew he was falling.

"Ronoah," she called again, her hands on him like a whole flock of pigeons' wings, "Ronoah, my little pilgrim, my—" He opened his eyes and there she was, holding his face in her hands and searching every cell of him, looking for the language to express that which no human words could ever hope to contain.

"Ronoah Genoveffa Elizzi-denna Pilanovani," she settled on, her voice sweet figs and warm ochre sands, the sound of his name billowing through him like fire on the plains burning away the fog, the wreckage—"god and gods alike, do you never, *ever* listen to me, I said *no* dying, it was a very clear command if I remember correctly, which I do, and so do you, you're not allowed to *use* that memory of yours selectively, that's *cheating*—" Her reprimands whirled like a flurry of petals, innumerable, inescapable, absolutely splendid, and they tickled a frantic laugh out from deep in his chest and all his steadiness turned to water and they both hit the ground, kneeling clutching each other, her hands cradling his face still checking for the tenth the hundredth the millionth time that he was intact, and he wasn't, but he was, he was. "You will never do this again, you shall swear it on books and Lavolani coffee and on Effie's good name, do you hear me, you—you miracle, you utterly *brilliant* creature, how did you know to find me?" He had no idea what she was talking about, but her amazement and her pride struck a chord in him and he felt himself smiling under her palms, grinning ridiculous and uncontrollable and she did not wait for an answer. She brought his forehead to hers, pressing so hard it nearly hurt, so fierce and full of love it crackled sympathetic on his skin. She held him there until it made him want to cry from relief and then she broke composure first, swept in kissing the corners of his eyes and nuzzling the side of his face with a sharp cheekbone.

"I mean it," she said, drawing away so she could verify his existence one last time. She poked him in the nose, twice. "Never. Again."

And then she rose up, and she pulled him with her, and the world flickered back into existence.

Nazum was visibly struggling with whether he wanted to run to Ronoah's side or stay a healthy distance from Chashakva. Marghat had rushed to Bashti almost as fast as Chashakva had come to him, was holding the girl to her hip and cradling her chubby wrist gone blue with the shape of Chashakva's hand. It had begun to rain outside; the water whipped through the open shutters. Ronoah felt the spatter of droplets like a hundred cool affectionate hands.

"Nazum," came Chashakva's command, and it broke the boy's spell in an instant and he was with them, pale but unwavering at Ronoah's side.

"Told you we'd get avenged," he muttered to Ronoah, a fighting smile tugging at his mouth.

The boy's smile slipped at Chashakva's next words: "Vengeance, indeed. Keep guard a moment, little shark, I'm going to go throw Lady Yacchatzndra's daughter off the cliff."

Ronoah only knew she was serious when she let go.

"Chashakva *wait*—" He grabbed for her, missed, stumbled, and both Chashakva and Nazum caught him, a friend at each arm. "Don't do that," he rushed, trying on some instinct to pulse his sincerity through the conduit of her skin touching his, to convince her, "Bashti hasn't done anything wrong, even, even Marghat—"

"She took you." Her voice wasn't angry. Worse, it was straightforward, sensible. Like she was balancing an account. "She tried to kill you."

"She tried to *save* me," he countered, wresting his left arm out of Nazum's grip so he could show Chashakva the bitemark. Her expression didn't change, but she got very still. "She did save me, I got sick with something—not here, a long time ago, I had something deadly in me and it got worse and Marghat cured me before it killed me. I don't think I'd—still be here, if it weren't for her care."

It only took Chashakva a moment to consider this news, but it felt like an hour, an age. "Well," she said, and every soft thing in Ronoah braced itself— "That does improve my regard for her."

His relief came on so aggressively he slumped again; delicately, Chashakva slid him out of her arms and into Nazum's custody. She turned to Marghat and Bashtandala, addressing them in a Shaipurin so grounded in power that Nazum's translation sounded thin and flimsy overtop: "All the same. You did not steal him to heal him. Tell me, then—what did you want so desperately that you would meddle with demons to get it?"

Marghat was still pressing Bashti into her grass skirt as if she could attach her daughter to her belt like one of her skulls for safekeeping. Her face was shadowed with genuine fright, but she was nonetheless resolute as she replied. "I want the fate of Yacchatzul, little jaguar girl, and I want the secret behind the War of Heavenly Seeds."

Chashakva lifted one hand. Ronoah saw Marghat harden, prepare for battle—but it was only an open palm. An invitation. "What interesting requests." A hint of curiosity in Chashakva's narrowing eyes. "Elaborate for me."

The rain outside slowly dissipated as Marghat recounted her great grandmamu's tale. Ronoah's knees began to tremble—either from the damp chill or the effort—and he sat on the ground, hugging a cushion to his middle. A few minutes later he felt a nudge so gentle he couldn't even be startled. Marghat's tortoise had come to sit at his side. Perhaps she really had missed him.

Chashakva received Marghat's story—Subin and Naskarahal's attacks, Yacchatzul's escape plan, the ambushes, everything—with anodyne silence, sponging it up like gauze staunching blood. Watching her concentrate like that was so soothing Ronoah nearly laid his cheek against the tortoise's shell for a nap. Even these few hours awake had exhausted him. But then it was over—Marghat folded her arms and Nazum muttered "history lesson's done"—and Chashakva was smiling in a way that meant she'd decided she liked Marghat Yacchatzndra more with every word out of the wisewoman's mouth, but also, Ronoah thought, that she wouldn't mind plucking out Marghat's liver and eating it.

Neither of these sentiments made it into her response; nor did any of the things Marghat was seeking, except, ultimately, for one. "I suppose, all that being said, you'll be coming to Council, won't you?"

That was no invitation. It was an order. And cocky, cavalier Marghat actually ducked her head in obeisance of it. Even though it had been her idea from the start—even though it was her desire to attend that had driven her to spirit Ronoah away—here she was, humble where she might once have been triumphant. Such was the chasm of power between them; in front of Chashakva, Lady Yacchatzndra looked every bit as small and squalling as Pashangali on a bad day. How had he ever compared the two?

"Nazum, please fetch your things," Chashakva called in Chiropolene. "I've heard all I need to. We're departing immediately."

"En't no complaints from this quadrant," was the boy's answer as he bolted to gather what few possessions they had—and that was when Ronoah remembered that he still had a debt to pay.

He slid his hand into his pocket, held the garnet clenched in one fist as Chashakva returned her attention to Marghat. They exchanged a few Shaipurin words which Chashakva took it upon herself to translate; without Nazum's familiar brogue, it felt like a different language entirely.

"Lady Yacchatzndra," Chashakva said, "what you did to secure this was incredibly foolish, and I thank you for it. The next time you try to compel me to anything, I will send your legacy into the lake."

"Understood," Marghat replied. And then, having managed to recover some of her flirtatious grace, "You really live up to that namesake of yours, don't you?"

"Don't I." The wind sieved around Chashakva's limbs, ruffling her azure wrapper. Her gaze was wry, and tired.

Ronoah was tired, too—not just in his body, but deep in his spirit. He hauled himself to standing, gave the tortoise a pat of thanks, and then limped his way back to Chashakva. "Where are we going next?" he asked as Nazum returned with Ronoah's satchel slung over his shoulder. "Back to—" his stomach flipped "—Lady Jau-Hasthasndra's? Or a new tribe?"

"To Sasaupta Falls." A macaw flapped across the room, splash of cerulean wing; Chashakva tracked it with her eyes before dropping her gaze to Ronoah. "We're done. All seventeen tribes secured. Now we have to lay the groundwork for them—build the camp, raise the roundhouse, turn over the earth so it's ready for whatever new seeds we sow."

She was the same as ever, not a scratch, not a smudge, not a cell out of place. Even the shave of her head was unchanged, close and fine, glimpsing at the faint plates of her skull. And yet something had shifted, something he could not see with his eyes or touch with his fingers but could nonetheless read in the atmosphere. A vigilance; a weight. Serene and supercharged in one.

He sensed something new inside of himself, too. But it was even less apparent to him what it was.

Marghat called something that broke into their staredown. "Take what's on the table before you go," she'd said; Nazum had just returned and took her up on this offer immediately, bastion of practicality as he was, bundling food even as he resumed translating. "I'd hate to let you leave hungry. And take one of the longboats too, they're the swiftest craft in the whole southeast." Clearly, she was attempting to make up for her behaviour with some graciousness now.

"I don't doubt it," said Chashakva, "but we have no need of a boat—?" Nazum tailed off with a quizzical face identical to Ronoah's. Chashakva only smiled again, mirthless, musing. "Monsoon is coming, sooner than you expect. We go to Sasaupta Falls on foot."

In the four seconds that followed, Ronoah evaluated himself with scathing honesty. "I don't know if I can walk that far," he said.

And Chashakva answered, "You will ride on my back if you have to, little demon."

So it was settled. There was nothing left to do but say goodbye.

When he approached them, he crouched down to Bashtandala first. She had tried to help him before Marghat even knew what was wrong, that morning in the jasmine bower. "Be well," he said in Acharrioni, the language of demons in this land, as sincere as he could get. Then he addressed the bruises staining her arm: "I'm sorry." Bashti, fascinated by the marks on her skin, merely glanced up before looking away again. It was enough.

He straightened to face Marghat. She'd been eyeing him, her smile still faintly lascivious even as her eyes were falconlike in their watchfulness. She who knew his secret, who'd captured him not knowing it would kill her a little bit to keep him. She who was owed an offering, a sacrifice.

Silently, without a fuss, he handed the garnet over to her. Her fingers were calloused and hard upon his.

If he was being honest with himself, he had expected something to happen when that little gem traded hands—maybe Marghat would decline it in the face of Chashakva's presence, or maybe the garnet itself would refuse, would fracture into pieces rather than leave the care of its beloved carrier. Maybe he would feel something, a return of that suppressed outburst, big enough this time to make a difference. To his own dull surprise, he felt nothing. Not wrong; not right. They both just stood there, and the world continued on.

There was no time to interrogate it—Nazum and Chashakva were waiting for him, and for some reason he didn't want Chashakva knowing what he was doing, what he was giving away. He inclined his head to Marghat, said the only thing he could find: "Thank you."

He said it in Shaipurin. He wasn't sure which dialect he'd picked it up from, but it didn't matter. Marghat Yacchatzndra could understand them all.

She smiled a conspiring smile back at him. She waved him out of the villa.

Stiff, ribbed cliffsides, mortared and tufted with green; shallow, narrow bay, luminescent after the rain. Ronoah had not seen it aside from through the picture frame of the balcony; he hadn't set foot outside Marghat's home since he was first ushered in. After so long it felt almost forbidden to step beyond the threshold. He was glad when Chashakva hurried him along, glad that she caught him when he stumbled on all that open air.

"Come along, little demon." Her voice coaxed alien strength into his bones. "For this, at least, you will walk. Hold that head high."

They passed beneath the eagle skeleton marking Marghat's domain; they passed shallow-set, multi-storied buildings painted pale grey and granite pink. Each step a labour, a concerted effort. Chashakva's hand lingered at the small of his back, and Nazum hovered with a springloaded readiness, but Ronoah was on his own two feet and he stayed that way, all the way down the village path. The Yacchatzndr were out in the street again, cheering, chanting, tossing flower petals like a second glittering rain shower; they were applauding the procession just the way they had on the first day, and it struck Ronoah that perhaps they had never been celebrating Marghat's success so much as his *arrival*. Perhaps they had always been worshiping the demon in their midst.

Runazum the Fair. Worker of little miracles. Chashakva's companion—Chashakva's *equal*, in ways none of them could understand. That's right. The reason he wasn't going to let Chashakva know about the garnet was the same reason he wasn't going to complain about how terrifying these weeks had been, wasn't going to cry to her about how difficult it had been with Pashangali: because he could hold his own. He was being *trusted* to hold his own, to be able to handle his side of the adventure. He wasn't going to faint into Chashakva's arms about the rough spots in a journey he himself had asked for. No.

The cheering faded behind them, and Ronoah's legs felt rubbery and untrustworthy but he forced them to cooperate. When at last they reached the shingle beach they turned to face the opposite slope, steep, treacherous, leading into the beckoning hands of the forest.

"All right," Chashakva said, eyeing some mysterious rhythm in the trees, "up you get." True to her word, the woman crouched to let Ronoah clamber onto her back.

He slid his arms about her neck, let her lift him light as a glassblown ornament. No point committing to self-sufficiency if he collapsed halfway up the next slope. But once he was better, once his body flushed itself of the last trace of the deadzone—he burrowed his face into the cool space between Chashakva's neck and shoulder, and swore to himself that he would take care of himself from then on out. No more acting helpless. No more being needy.

They started up the hill. Nazum and Chashakva conversed in quiet Shaipurin; perhaps they thought he was already asleep. He spent the ascent listening—Nazum's voice like crows and cayenne, Chashakva's like the silt and sway of the Sanaat. The sounds of the border between lakeshore and forest, surf conceding to songbird. He gathered strength enough for one question. When they reached the top of the slope, he asked it, whispered in Chashakva's ear:

"Why didn't you tell me you were a Shaipurin god?"

He felt the thrumming of her hundred heartbeats under her ribs. He nestled closer, smelled the smell of her skin, dry as charcoal, sweet as beeswax.

And Chashakva's answer came back to him, lulling and low: "Because I'm not."

Into the forest they went.

"—*h*AD TO WIN A CONTEST before I was even allowed an *audience* with Lady Azm-ka-Habaundra—Ronoah, you remember that play you volunteered for, the one pilfered from the Prophetic Collection, it was exactly that, riddles and trickery, feats of strength—"

"Considering everything, were you the demon or were you Evin?"

"If you think I can't be both at once, you're not thinking big enough."

Ronoah wheezed out a laugh, cheek bouncing on Chashakva's shoulder as she hopped over a fallen branch. Behind them, Nazum demanded, "Who's Evin?"

"Good friend of Ronoah's," Chashakva answered before Ronoah could say anything, "they go way back. Pushed him into a lake for answering a question wrong."

Nazum scoffed. "Ayyeesh, you got a thing for strong personalities, don't you brother," he asked a spluttering Ronoah, his own crackling laugh falling like gravel on the canopy.

This was the shape of their journey to Sasaupta Falls: picking their way through the vociferous jungle, trading stories to sweeten the hard edge of the hike. Come nightfall, they'd hang their hammocks and slumber in the phosphorescent mosslight. Ronoah slept faster and deeper than he could ever remember sleeping—those days were brutal and draining even when he spent the whole time on Chashakva's back.

Recovery was taking longer than he'd hoped. He still couldn't walk for more than a few hours, and only if the terrain was forgiving. After the Ravaging he'd been able to wince around his neighbourhood in just under two weeks—that was the difference, he supposed, between fire and poison. Both could be deadly, but one was honest, was clean. The other lingered, left a ghost.

Neither of his companions begrudged his feebleness. They simply forged on, Chashakva with her arms looped comfortably under Ronoah's legs, Nazum batting ferns and vines out of her way, as the woman preserved them all from monotony by telling tales of the other tribes. "For the Tishpalaazndr, red butterflies are said to be dead souls paying visits," she'd comment as a pair of carmine wings fluttered by, "I covered myself with them before walking in, it's simple, you just make your skin smell of honeysuckle." Or, upon discovering an interesting cluster of stones, "Did I tell you about Umujiyya's Labyrinth? The Umujandr send their sacrifices in there, but sometimes they walk it themselves as a test of faith—they scarify a mark for every successful venturing, usually on their cheekbones, Lady Umujandr's *covered* in them, she walks it the way you'd take a little trip around the garden with your morning coffee—"

It was only when she described the observatories of the Baramsulandr, skywatchers and pyrelighters, that Ronoah's heart squeezed ugly in his chest. "Chashakva," he started, trying not to bite his tongue as she skipped nimble as a goat down an old rockslide, "do you know what became of—when you got to Pashangali's, did the Jau-Hasthasndr, did she…" Those Baramsulandr children, with their clasped hands, their solemn eyes. He took a deep breath. "What happened on Orchid Ten?"

"No idea. Didn't get there in time." Chashakva must have felt the sag of his body against hers, the small collapse that came of either relief or renewed disappointment, because she hiked him up a little higher and added, "Plus I was just a smidge preoccupied by the fact that you'd been thieved. She told me the instant I arrived—the only reason her own eyes are still in her skull is because she seemed so genuinely distraught." Ronoah choked just as Nazum whistled a loud note of appreciation. *Vengeance, indeed.* "Lady Yacchatzndra may have taken you," Chashakva continued as if it were the most logical thing in the world, "but Lady Jau-Hasthasndra allowed you to be taken."

Ronoah held tighter around Chashakva's neck. "She did try," he said. Remembered her sprinting, screaming. "I saw her."

"Sister, hate to say it, but you might've done her a favour if you *did* pop those suckers out," Nazum added, prompting an alarmed look from Ronoah. "If she can't see, she won't want to barf every time she finds a yellow flower or whatever. Only would've made her stronger."

It took longer than usual to realize it was a joke—longer still to realize Nazum was making it because he, too, was glad Pashangali's body was intact. This wasn't a conversation Ronoah wanted to continue. "I'm tired," he murmured before Chashakva could launch into some detailed valuation of Lady Jau-Hasthasndra's eyeballs. "I'm going to—try and rest."

"Dream of lilies, little pilgrim," the woman said, turning her head to nudge her cheek against his. Ronoah went silent, watching the woods rustle by as Chashakva and Nazum chattered in Shaipurin, blissfully unintelligible.

After that, despite the questions chirring cicada-like in his mind, Ronoah held his tongue. If a mere personal anecdote had exhausted him so easily, he didn't trust he had the fortitude to withstand any answers Chashakva might have about the history of the War. Similarly, he glossed over his own version of the last few months when Chashakva probed. He avoided telling her about the fight, the beating, the tallest warrior, even the details of his illness—he just didn't want to relive them right now. After a few significant, secretive glances, Nazum helped him in this omission, talking smoothly around these raw nerves when he spoke. Nazum Vashnarajandr, who knew the value of being able to keep some things to yourself until you were ready.

For certain topics, at least. For others—namely anything to do with Ronoah's life pre-Shaipuri—Nazum's patience had run out.

He had the good grace to wait just long enough that Ronoah could sustain a long conversation without losing breath, and then he cornered Ronoah on his hammock or around the cooking fire, cajoling him into revealing his history a piece at a time. "Explain," the boy would order as he squatted down beside Ronoah. And Ronoah explained it all. He told Nazum about Ithos, about meeting Chashakva in the *Tris Mantarinis*—he had to break for a lengthy lecture on the shalledrim when, amazingly, Nazum admitted he had no idea what they were. He told Nazum about the ripe and flourishing delta of Lavola, like Bhun Jivakta but spiced different, rife with palm groves and studios and the great library of Padjenne as its centrepiece. Fleetingly, he told Nazum of the days before Lavola, made the boy's jaw drop with descriptions of the gold grasslands, the tumbling desert, the world without water. And he told Nazum where they were going. The Pilgrim State, Land of a Thousand Temples, Soul of the Earth.

"You're telling me there's a place where all the gods from all the quadrants of the world go to hang out?" Nazum asked, sceptical but undeniably full of wonder. "So there are people out there who know about—you know …?" He waved at the rainforest in general.

It was far more likely than a shrine to Genoveffa, given how much closer the Shaipurin were to the Pilgrim State. But given their extreme seclusion, Ronoah doubted anyone had ever made the trip to check. "I don't know," was all he had to offer. This didn't seem to deter Nazum, who launched into a cheerful criticism of how bizarre it was that someone would travel all that way to build a shrine for their god in a place nobody even knew them.

"What's the point?" he asked. "Why go through the effort?"

"It's not *for* other people," Ronoah replied. "At least, not to me. It's ..."
A way out; a way in. A way of life, even, a mode of being. He had been
Runa for six months, but he had been *little pilgrim* for two years, and he
loved the way it sat on his skin, the way it chimed in his ear. "It's like
having a conversation with your god," he said, and then, remembering
Nazum's hidden talent for song, "or singing a hymn for them, a really
long one, with your hands and feet instead of your voice. There's a gift
in the effort, a devotion. It's—"

"A sacrifice?" Ronoah looked at Nazum; there was no sarcasm there,
no mockery. He was trying to get it, in the way he knew how.

"I guess so," Ronoah said, quietly. "A sacrifice where no one dies."

Nazum's face softened, scornful and tender. He was quick to regain
himself: "I mean unless you fucking kick it while you're here," he pointed
out, and Ronoah coughed out an offended laugh. "Seriously, what are
you doing taking a detour through *Shaipuri*? No one else frolics through
the heartland on their way to some magic temple ground, demon boy."

"I don't know," he said again—because in truth, he didn't. Back when
he'd agreed to investigate the heartland with Chashakva, he'd been so
focused on prolonging their time together that he'd never stopped to ask
why she cared so much in the first place. Then, he'd gotten invested, and
it had become obvious to him that they should try to help. But it wasn't
actually so obvious, was it? Chashakva had originally taken a casual interest in the results of the War of Heavenly Seeds, the same way you'd stop
by a neighbour's to see if their chickens had hatched—it was only when
they'd discovered it wasn't over that everything had changed. But what
reason did she have to expect the War would be over, anyway? Who was
she to dictate the length of such a battle? "You'd have to ask Chashakva."

"Then I'll live without an answer, thanks." Ronoah couldn't help but
snort; Nazum swatted his shoulder. "Snicker all you like, not all of us are
okay with cozying up to a god in a coffeehouse."

He was glad for these talks, grateful that Nazum asked. It helped
remind him of what he lost sight of sometimes: that there was a world
outside the heartland, and that he had come from it. That he wouldn't
just evaporate into shiyalsha when the Council was over. That this whole
conflict, as intense and all-consuming as it was, was still just a *side trip*.
That he was more Ronoah than Runa.

That perspective was almost embarrassingly precious. He held onto
it during the nights when his worrying about the Council and the War
sent him spiralling, comforted himself—sometimes guiltily—with the
knowledge that no matter what happened, his journey wouldn't end here.

Like a beacon, visions of the Pilgrim State relit the shadowy corners of his heart, showed him his path anew. But a different sacred place was destined to greet him first, as another two weeks elapsed and his feet grew sturdy beneath him again and they passed at last into the valley beneath the Sasaupandr Plateau.

Nothing could have prepared him for Sasaupta Falls. He knew they were close when the faint sound of rushing water filtered through the woods—before long, that rush was a roar, tuneful, voluminous. He caught glimpses of shimmer and white through the trees, felt stray speckles of mist on his face. When they came out from under the canopy, the noise knocked into him like a bird hurtling into his chest—and his own noise joined it, an astonished, terrified shout that fluted midway into a cry of delight.

It wasn't just *a* waterfall. It was *waterfalls*.

They were uncountable, maybe dozens of them, high as hills, as mountains, all splitting and merging as they careened over the sheer drop of the cliffsides, bolting into a frothy emerald bowl larger than Pilanova's whole oasis. Rainbows suspended themselves in the churning mist. Gulls sailed from one side to the other, perching in the shrubs and trees that grew in between the slats of cataracts. Stupendous, absolutely stupendous, the pillars of whitewater, the starbursts and spasms of green, the sprawling silty banks—the drop, gods, the drop. Ronoah only realized he'd gone to his knees when he noticed a twig digging into his shin.

"Welcome," Chashakva said with a nudge, a sly little grin in her voice, "to the home of the gods."

Just like in the monastery, all Ronoah could reply with was manic laughter.

Another laugh joined his, just as loud and almost as hysterical—Nazum's. The boy was standing but staggered, hands covering his face, peeking through the spaces between his fingers. *Place like that en't for human beings.* It was taboo, this valley. Only wisewomen were sanctioned to walk these lands—but right now Nazum was kind of part wisewoman, in his way. Runazum the Fair had every right to be here.

Chashakva had a hand on his bicep. "Come on," she laughed, "I'll want you on my back again for this last bit, no matter how strong you've grown." Ronoah let himself be pulled up, unable to take his eyes off the plummeting water. So much of it, moving so fast. Like the entire ocean heaving off the edge of the world at the speed of a sea per second, unending, unfathomable—

"You *will* be able to see it just fine from the Council site," Chashakva's voice broke in again teasingly. "Even better, from a certain angle, if the trees haven't grown it closed yet. We have work to do before dark—no one's been here in some time. You know how it is."

Images flickered in Ronoah's mind: scrubbing, sweeping, pulling and carrying, building, repairing, preparing. A forgotten place of the world, rekindled by hand.

He nodded, and with a great effort he dragged his eyes away from Sasaupta Falls, and hopped on Chashakva's back for the final climb up the cliffs.

It was no easy feat, to reach the Council site. It was one part hike, one part scramble, one part terrifying rope climb using nothing but the vines that dangled from the damp rock. When they reached the top and Chashakva deposited Ronoah on solid ground, he turned back to the ledge to help Nazum. With a heave and a few tumbling pebbles, the boy rolled into Ronoah and they both lay there in a heap of hard breathing and astonishment. Spitting out a loc and a laugh of relief, Ronoah clambered to his feet and found Chashakva observing the Falls from a lookout that was dizzying in its nakedness, in how simply and abruptly it became sky.

Without looking back, Chashakva extended a hand behind her. Ronoah crept out to the ledge, catching her hand and squeezing it as the divinity of the landscape poured into him. For a minute, maybe two, he was taken out of himself, and all the complexity and heartbreak he was nursing dropped away, and it felt like what he thought it would be when Chashakva first mentioned a visit to Shaipuri: just two friends marvelling together at something extraordinary.

A dramatic cough behind them, loud enough to be heard even over the Falls.

"This is the place where the future of your rainforest will be decided," Chashakva answered, turning to face Nazum, who was standing a good thirty feet away glaring at them with a combination of concern and unfiltered wonder. "Better introduce yourself."

Nazum squinted. "Hi," he said, and though it sounded flat and sarcastic Ronoah felt an empathic leap of emotion from the boy, a frisson, a thrill. "Mind getting back from the edge of the fucking world? We got stuff to do, right?"

With a conspiratorial glance at Ronoah, Chashakva conceded. He wasn't far behind her.

They built their hut that day, waking up celebratory and dry in the morning. The next day, they built another. The next, another. They dug a latrine—"Can't have anyone pissing over the Falls now, can we?" Chashakva simpered as Nazum hooted a laugh and Ronoah yelled, scandalized—and they raised a storehouse, stocked it three shelves deep with smoked meat and whole fruit preserved in honey. They drew up plans for the roundhouse, began its grand and ponderous construction. So the days ran into weeks.

After working up the courage for it, Ronoah came to Chashakva and Nazum asking to be taught Shaipurin. With so much free time before the Council convened it seemed ridiculous not to prepare in every way he could. Obviously learning the language wasn't going to make or break the wisewomen's decision—but it gave his mind a job to do, tricked the frantic part of him into thinking it was doing something helpful.

"A lovely idea," Chashakva agreed. "Which dialect to start?"

Ronoah bit his lip, looked at Nazum—and Nazum saw that glance, so earnest, so determined, and slapped it down like a damselfly. "No, absolutely not, pick something useful." Ronoah scowled, but before he could retort— "Think I wanna hear those words out of your mouth? One last conversation in my mamu's tongue before you leave and I'm holding it solo again? En't such a gift as you think, you romantic moron. Pick something useful."

Stung but humbled, Ronoah chose Jau-Hasthasndr, the language he'd spent the longest in and the one both Pashangali and Marghat spoke alongside Nazum. Now the stories he heard were simpler, fables about fish and coconut trees and how the colours of the rainbow had decided their order, told in a language he had to chew slowly lest its richness overwhelm his palate. He apologized to the memory of Chabra'i, promised he would save time to pick up some Subindr before everything began.

Subindr. Subin. She who began devouring Seeds, alongside Naskarahal, according to Marghat. Ronoah had gained enough distance from the Yacchatzndr village to start thinking again about what the wisewoman had told him. It had stewed in his subconscious, ripening like a cheese sealed under the wax coating of his own convalescence—but somewhere in between building the Gaamndr hut and preparing cuts of boar for smoking, that seal broke, and the aroma of mystery floated tantalizing through the air, begging to be chased.

Where did the deadzones come from? Who had Subin and Naskarahal first devoured, and why? Who was left, if anyone? What did Yacchatzul mean by *none of us were meant to be eaten*?

And what did Chashakva have to do with it all?

One whiteskied morning, he woke up and discovered the need to know was too great to stave off anymore. He found Chashakva seated near the lookout point, a fanfare of palm fronds spread before her as she wove floor mats for the huts. Behind her, from the gorge, the spray rose like smoke.

"The river runs," he called, the Jau-Hasthasndr greeting beading like dew on his tongue.

"Indeed it does," Chashakva said, with an approving chin-tilt at the Falls. They both watched the water galloping over the precipice, and then Ronoah joined the woman in her weaving. It was useful to have something to do with his hands when he had these talks. He used to fidget with the garnet, but—well.

"You know Marghat's story," he began, "about Yacchatzul? I have some questions about that."

Chashakva selected a palm frond, stripped a long leaf and slid it like a ribbon across her palm. "I imagine many of them the same as Lady Yacchatzndra's."

"Yes—I mean, probably?" Chashakva hadn't answered Marghat, but Ronoah wasn't Marghat. He was Chashakva's friend. Her equal. "I just—what does it *mean*? It explains where the ambushes came from at least, the Yacchatzndr started it—but they didn't even do it to sacrifice anyone. It wasn't a raid, it was a decoy." A plot to lure away Subin and Naskarahal to their tribes. To keep them from devouring any more Seeds. "Why would Yacchatzul—why would any Seed ask for that?"

"No seed likes to be pushed from the pot," Chashakva replied, deftly threading her palm leaf into the weft of the mat.

"Is that really all, do you think? She just—didn't want to die?" Ronoah bit his lip. "But it's not really *dying*, is it? You told me the legend in Bhun Jivakta—the Seeds all came from one creator god in the first place, it was always the plan for them to go back together. Like, like taking apart a clock to polish all the gears so it stops getting jammed. They were always part of a whole. They had to know that, right?"

"You'd think so." It was a completely agreeable statement—flippant, even—so Ronoah had no idea why it made him shiver. "But you've hit on something important: they aren't gears. They're Seeds. The machinery of the heavens is not machinery at all, not in Shaipuri; it's organic. And sure, you're organic too, and if I slip your tibia out your leg you're *definitely* going to notice, and you won't grow a new one unless I intervene, just like *it* won't grow a new *you*—but such is not the way of the botanical. What was once a piece can become its very own whole, if you don't pay close attention." A muscle twinged in her jaw; the stillbirth of a smile. "It may very well be that, having split and been granted agency, a few of the Heavenly Seeds decided that reintegration disagreed with them."

Ronoah's fingers clenched reflexively around the palm leaf he'd picked, crumpling the fronds. He released them, trying to smooth them flat again. "You're saying—they *all* decided to be creator gods, by themselves?"

"It is a possibility."

"Then it's no one's fault the War isn't over—no tribe, I mean, no wise-woman—if that's what's happening then maybe that's why the rainforest won't go back together, because the *Seeds* won't go back together. That's—" It stuck in his throat, too big a revelation to slip out easy. He paused, spoke it cautious: "If that's the source of the problem, then more sacri-fices won't fix it."

"Correct." He already knew in his heart that killing more people wouldn't solve anything, but hearing it confirmed still filled him with relief so potent it left him dizzy. "Of course, just because it's correct won't make it easy to achieve. We can't force seventeen autonomous groups to bend to our will, not without some intermediary steps—they have to *want* to stop killing each other, for one, which might take some work in and of itself. Then they have to believe doing it is unnecessary, which means squaring off against the idea that their deities—some, all, who knows?—are no longer their champions."

Setten and Ibisca, that was not an easy ask. After hundreds of years of faith, how could you possibly abandon it?

With testimonial, he supposed. With evidence. "It—it also means making the Seeds cooperate, doesn't it?"

Chashakva flicked a glance at him, a flash of aqua starlight. "It just well might."

Ronoah sensed the path of that glance as a comet tail of tingles—and something fit into place. Chashakva and her terrible timing. She had returned weeks late to Chabra'i, to Pashangali—sure, her sense of time was different from theirs, but hadn't she convinced the other half of the heartland to attend Council in the time Ronoah was with Marghat? That was probably nine tribes in half the time it had taken her to round up two or three before. That was disproportionate. And maybe some tribes were easier to persuade, maybe word had spread and they were ready before she arrived—but he knew Chashakva, and because he knew her as he did, he had to ask. Just in case he was right. "Have you been trying? To round up the gods as well as the wisewomen?"

This time Chashakva did smile—mirthless, ruthless, like a slash. "Trying." Her secret errand revealed, she only seemed put out that she didn't have better news to report from it. "I have issued more than seven-teen invitations to this gathering, yes; we shall see whether any more than seventeen are heeded. I didn't exactly deliver them by hand—none of the Seeds have crossed my path yet. Perhaps they wish to make an entrance. How the young gods cherish their drama."

Young gods. Ronoah's mind watered over that like his mouth would over one of Marghat's candied gingers. "Chashakva," he said, "what does this place mean to you?" Marghat had told another story, after all: the myth of Chashakva, creator god of the last age. When he'd asked about that godhood, Chashakva had denied it, but it couldn't just be that she shared the name. She didn't share it—she'd *chosen* it. "Why are you so determined to see the War end? Why does it matter to you?"

"Because I don't like seeing this place rot." Right. Chashakva had been curious about the War's extension, concerned even, but it wasn't until Chabra'i showed them the deadzone that she'd gotten angry. "A very long time ago, a friend of mine planted these lands with me."

Ronoah blinked—and then it surfaced. The cloves, the story. *The most delightful garden.* "You—you *planted* Shaipuri?"

"Not how you're thinking we did," came her chiding reply. "We didn't remediate a wasteland, the rainforest was here to begin with. We just plumped up the ecosystem, added some interesting new species. Think Reilin's Lottery, with vegetation in place of villagers. To be truthful, we brought the waste with us—or rather, what survived it."

"You said something," Ronoah recalled. "About a land that didn't exist anymore."

"My friend had seeds of her own that needed rehoming, and the Sanaat has always fed this land fat and generous. We took advantage of that hospitality. Now it's been—mm, thousands of years since those first shoots took root, and you know the way of the rainforest, everything getting in everything else's business. A bit like the Pilgrim State, that way." She smirked, beholding the bowl of blue-white that was Sasaupta Falls. "Things mutate, migrate, cross-pollinate—I check in every couple centuries and it's different every time. At this point, there's really no separation between the original growth and what we brought to it—the whole thing is simply one superorganism. Though granted, there are a few who remember being a sprout in my hands."

"Like what?"

"Chabra'i's trees," Chashakva answered, to Ronoah's shock. She craned her neck to peer over the lookout with almost parental fondness. "That moss. The weeds at the bottom of this river."

Ronoah let his gaze drop to the woman's hands, watched her weaving disparate parts into a whole. Weaving a boundary. "But that's not why they named an era for you," he said slowly, "is it? The Age of Chashakva, that had to have happened so much later."

"Indeed. I didn't use the name Chashakva when we sowed this place; that language hadn't even been born yet."

"So the legend—the borders between the overworld and shiyalsha, were they actually broken? The seasons shifting, and the flowers and animals dying and undying—what was that?"

"The stories have been ornamented over the centuries, but the core phenomenon should be simple enough for you to identify, little scholar. Random, isolated pockets of heat, or cold, or darkness, or irrational light?" An idea stabbed Ronoah like a glass shard, lanced him in the back of the neck. "The laws of physics not behaving quite as they should? The elements playing it fast and loose? What does that sound like to you?"

Vespasi wake. It sounded like something he'd seen before. "This far east?" he asked as Chashakva pulled his abandoned mat from his lap and took up his work. "A colony? No—" If a society of shalledrim had lived in the rainforest, they would have tried to rule it, and there was no evidence of that anywhere. The story didn't mention creatures or demons *making* the boundaries weak, only that they had weakened. "A burial ground? Like the caves?"

"Precisely. Goodness even *knows* why, there's no monastery here, no refuge from the Chainbreakers, nothing significant to shalledrim history at all—I never did figure out what made it the fashionable place to go explode at the time, but there it was, and there they were. I arrived for one of my regular checkups and found them. And I erased them."

"You can do that?"

"When it suits me." The hairs on Ronoah's arms stood up. Chashakva slid another palm leaf home. "They asked my name, and I gave one, and they deified me for it. And if it helps them sleep better, so be it, but I have never been a god of this place, Ronoah. Only a gardener. A pest has got into my vegetable patch, and I'd like to flush it out. Simple as that."

Simple, she said, as if millennia could be dismissed so easily. Perhaps they could. Perhaps after the Shattering everything felt manageable in comparison. Quietly, like he sometimes did, Ronoah wondered at the immensity of the creature beside him, the unknowable lives tucked away in the crease of an eye or an elbow, the fact that he got to spend another day with her, and another. When the feeling faded, he picked up another bunch of palm fronds and began preparing a new mat.

"What happens," he ventured, after some time crafting in the roaring silence of the Falls, "if the Seeds don't come? Or don't cooperate?"

A drop of condensation rolled down Chashakva's temple like a pearl. She left it where it lay, thinking, still.

"I will figure something out," was all she said in the end.

Their work continued. Monsoon arrived and the rivers swelled to even grander breadths, the cataracts plunging with even fiercer velocity. The rains came scything across the plateau, stinging like a volley of darts, and lightning blasted steam from the bowl of the Falls. Chashakva told them the names of all the wisewomen, their Seeds, their grievances. The warm wind swung capricious, battering the plateau from new angles. The guava trees bore fruit. Nazum and Ronoah finally held a conversation entirely in Shaipurin. The roundhouse rose above the huts, solid and solemn and brimful of potential. Ronoah's hand burned empty where his garnet should have been. The winds died down. The rains became soft. The Falls thinned and split.

And just like that monsoon was over, and it was time.

Twenty-Eight

*I*T IS ALWAYS A NERVE-WRACKING THING, introducing friends to one another. Risk is inherent in that encounter—perhaps their tastes in literature are irreconcilably different, perhaps one takes the other's chattering nature for rudeness, perhaps that kinetic snap of potential just isn't there. There is always the possibility that the only thing your people have in common is their fondness for you.

If Ronoah were to be hosting, say, the Tellers alongside Hexiphines and Kourrania, this would be about the size of his problem. As it was, the guests coming to this party sort of all wanted to kill each other.

It was one thing to hear Chabra'i make derisive comments about 'the banshees', or to listen to Pashangali's suspicions about a saboteur tribe in the privacy of her own bathhouse; it was going to be another thing altogether to put them in close quarters and watch that mockery turn mean, that suspicion grow serrated. Even Marghat had her prejudices about the other tribes—and given how the Yacchatzndr had abandoned the War, her appearance alone would probably cause a ruckus. Add fourteen more personalities to the mix, each one larger than life in her own way, each one harbouring her own resentments towards any number of the others, and it made sense why Ronoah had started having regular stomach aches. He had no way of predicting their reactions to each other—and even if he did, the possibility of a literal Heavenly Seed or two showing up complicated things beyond hypothesis.

It was hard to say whether it did his nerves good or ill, that the first wisewomen to arrive were strangers.

Three days into pre-winter, when the constellation Jassam Tai had just ascended the ridges of Sasaupta Falls, the Umujandr ascended the plateau in tandem. Lady Umujandra was the oldest wisewoman of them all, according to Chashakva, nearly sixty and going strong. Her slick braid brushed the backs of her knees; her skin was cross-hatched with hundreds of rows of thin hashmarks. Standing at the threshold, she greeted Chashakva with a solemn half-bow and a voice like sparkling chainmail, built of interlocking links of vigour and restraint. She was quick to greet Ronoah as well—Runa, the companion of she who sought to end the War—with an amount of respect that stunned Ronoah, left him struggling for an equally magnanimous reply.

Afterwards, she strode purposefully to the Umujandr hut, accompanied by a young man whose gait and swaying posture reminded Ronoah of bamboo groves. Her translator, Nazum said. They would all have at least one, young men performing the necessary evil of speaking neighbouring languages.

Not a day later came the Baramsulandr, a tribe closer to Pashangali's than anywhere near the Falls. Lady Baramsulandra was lithe as a jaguar herself, and just as dark, with a cunning and a keenness in her gaze that made Ronoah blush. He took note of the wisewoman's chest, toned and breastless, when she bowed to him, with the mental observation that certain aspects of tribal culture seemed to bleed at the provincial borders.

That observation was reinforced as the wisewomen trickled in. The Gaamndr, like Chabra'i's tribe, looked for omens in the physical traits of their people to determine the next wisewoman; the Millikindr held the same ideas about marriage and family that Marghat's people did. The Farhatindr and Hunanundr even deliberately shared some of their culture—they were the closest thing to allies that existed under the War of Heavenly Seeds, and they arrived as one, having spent the journey in a friendly race to the finish. The more Ronoah met and made acquaintance with everyone, the more he saw mirrors between them—mirrors of their jokes, their games, their sorrows. The more certain he was that if the wisewomen looked long enough at each other they would choose to alleviate each other's suffering, if only because it so resembled their own.

And the more distressing it was to see them choose to shatter that glass rather than look, again and again.

"I just don't get it," Ronoah griped to Nazum after they had rushed over to tactfully insert themselves into yet another tense situation between Ladies Millikindra and Baramsulandra. "They're all so poised and level-headed until you put two of them together, and then it's, it's—"

"War?" the boy suggested, mock-sincere. "Yeah. That's gonna happen. There hasn't been a successful Council in a hundred years, Runa—ask any one of these sisters and she'll say she's fighting for traditional reasons, but there's generations of bad timing and misunderstanding and just plain weird shit mixed up in it. My folks knew it, s'why we tried to bring back the battle almanacs—get everyone in tune again, make sure no one was picking on anyone else for personal reasons. Obviously, never got around to it." Nazum smacked him lightly on the arm, his version of a comforting pat. "Kinda neat that it's finally happening. Even if it is going to be a flaming dump of *putrash* to start."

Weird shit. Like an entire village getting poisoned overnight. Like the gods possibly abandoning their own war in favour of their newfound individuality. Ronoah hadn't told Nazum about his conversation with Chashakva; he was, after all, a child of the heartland. What if it was Vashnarajan who had disowned the War? What if *that* was how the boy's village had perished—at the hands of their own Seed? He couldn't get the memory of Marghat saying *self-sacrifice* out of his head, so he'd kept Chashakva's heavenly reconnaissance to himself, and trusted she would figure it out like she said she would.

But even if the Vashnarajandr vision for a Council had not included the Heavenly Seeds, it had to be acknowledged that what they were doing here—what he and Chashakva had achieved in bringing the wisewomen together—was only picking up where Nazum's people had left off. He hoped it was a comfort for Nazum, to see their will being honoured. To be exacting it himself.

Flaming dump of putrash or not, there was at least one wisewomen he could count on not to start a fight. She came two days later, flowers in her hair and fresh skulls on her thighs: Marghat Yacchatzndra, shimmying up the ropes to the plateau with Bashtandala clinging like a tamarin to her back. Despite the unease that had coloured their time together, Ronoah ran to greet them. It was a relief to see some familiar faces.

"My my," Marghat said, shading her eyes as she scanned the plateau, "the whole menagerie's really here. Incredible." Bashti dropped to the ground and wafted her way into the campsite, exploring at her leisurely pace, followed swiftly by a stocky young man intent on keeping the wisewoman-to-be from harm. Wait—

"You brought a translator?" Ronoah asked, feeling foolishly betrayed. "But you—you understand all the dialects!"

"Oh, but that's a secret between us, little demon," Marghat replied, teasing and yet chillingly serious. She took his hand in both of hers in a greeting; subtly, she laid two fingers on his wrist, checking his pulse. He recoiled, and she smiled coy as ever. "This world isn't ready for such grand advances. These people take one look at real innovation and throw it in the river. If they ever get over their pride, I'll be happy to teach them a thing or two. Until then, I keep my foreign mouths shut."

Ronoah opened his own mouth, then closed it, incapable of expressing how deeply he disagreed. Marghat mistook the source of his distress and tweaked his chin. "I know, my Runa, it's ridiculous, isn't it? The squabbles I bet you've seen already! No one's ready to stop picking at their old scabs. But this was always going to be the way it went," she said, somehow managing to echo Nazum's assessment while lacking any of the respect the boy had for it. Her black gaze flicked up at a sound, some shout—someone had recognized her, whether by face or regalia Ronoah could not know—and she withdrew from him with a wink before shimmying into the campsite with all the self-importance of a star, ready to defend her right to an opinion about a fight she had already abandoned.

If anything, Ronoah thought with dull disappointment, Marghat's pride was even more difficult to deal with than the brash arrogance she disparaged in the others. Hers was more discrete, perhaps, but just as conceited and doubly patronizing; the belief that no one else was capable of being open-minded was just another close-mindedness. Suddenly Lady Yacchatzndra's allyship wasn't such a sure thing.

Lady Subindra's arrival was no less dismaying, though at least Ronoah was prepared for that. Chabra'i had been his introduction to the abrasive nature of the heartland; she was probably looking *forward* to those squabbles Marghat disdained so thoroughly. She might not have liked killing, but Chabra'i had always enjoyed a fight. So it was no surprise that the first time he heard her voice at Sasaupta Falls, it was shouting.

"—said you'd do *what* to my bees? Well you'll have a hard time walking there, first you're gonna have to pull my spear out of your—Runa! A sight for sore eyes!"

"Hi," he panted, hands on his knees from sprinting over. "What—what's—?"

"This shrivelled piece of sphagnum's insulting me before I've even put my damn bags down," Chabra'i announced, flinging a hand in the direction of Lady Hunanundra, whose outraged pallor was only matched by the equally bloodless terror blanching her translator's face. Even with the skin on his empathy as thick as he could make it, Ronoah still felt himself about to round on the other wisewoman—but Nazum got there first, firing some low questions at both translators. They floated back confused-sounding responses, and Nazum made a sound halfway between a laugh and an aggravated sigh.

"Gotta train up your tongue better, Subindra," he said to a blinking Chabra'i, "it en't your bees she's insulting, it's your mom."

Every muscle in Ronoah's body tensed—but then Chabra'i let out a guffaw that swept away all her menace, easy as that. "*Oh.* Well that's fair game, all things considered."

Once they had smoothed things out and Lady Hunanundra glided away, stiff-backed but vindicated, Ronoah allowed himself to rub his hands over his face. "Save your posturing for quarterstaff practice, Chabra'i, would you?"

At Nazum's translation, Chabra'i's eyebrows shot up. "Got a little more sour in all that sweet of you these days, ai?" she replied. She was unoffended—impressed even—but it threw Ronoah off like a swipe to the ankles. "Good for you. I'll behave as long as the banshees do, at least until Council's officially in session—then it's score-settling time. We're not here to try each other's food and braid each other's hair, we're here to decide if we're going to stop cutting each other's throats. For the gods' sake, anyway." She tossed her hair over one shoulder; it had been trimmed recently. "I've got a few things to say to Lady Naskarahandra that have nothing to do with Naskarahal."

"She's not here yet," Ronoah replied numbly, too stunned to think of anything else. Chabra'i smiled like he'd shared a joke, and his stomach clenched anew.

"I say these things," she continued, hefting her bag on her shoulder as she tilted her face to catch the mist, "but I really do hope we figure something out, Runa. Subin's will was pretty clear on the whole affair—three of my villagers would be dead if not for that *guguri*, including my blunt tongue here." She gave her own translator an affectionate whap on the back of the head, ruffling his bowl cut. "Talk about a sign. Ai me, and there's Chashakva!" The woman was exiting the roundhouse, striding towards them with a hand lifted in welcome. Chabra'i went to meet her, leaving Ronoah ringing with the dissonance of feeling grateful for and disgusted with his past self all at once.

This was precisely why he needed her to behave—Chabra'i, Marghat, everyone. Why he needed them to cooperate, to choose peace at the Council. A few months building huts had granted him a reprieve from thinking about the terrible things he had done to make it this far, but now those wrongs were coming back to him, literally, face to face.

Except one. Arguably the worst. Pashangali Jau-Hasthasndra had not yet arrived, and the truth about Orchid Ten hung like a scimitar over Ronoah's head every day she failed to appear. He owed at least half of his irritability to waiting for her, and to the unbearable panic that waiting whipped up in his heart—sometimes it got so bad he had to physically shake it out of him, go for a brisk walk in the woods to vent his pent-up anxiety. He remembered so clearly not wanting to know the fate of the children back in the Jau-Hasthasndr village—and then *needing* to know, once he was with Marghat—and now, as that knowledge grew imminent, he found himself swinging back again, wanting to avoid it as long as possible. The incoherence of his own desires was maddening.

The Pai-Zayyindr arrived, and the Dandakhti-Kashndr, and the Tishpalaazndr. The fuller the camp got, the thicker the tension grew. Chiibtandr, Rugakashndr, Azm-ka-Habaundr. It was like being back in Pilanova, in the days leading up to Sweetwood Day. Slowly mounting pressure, insidious, unceasing, obstructive. Ra'ushandr. Naskarahandr. Jau-Hasthasndr.

She came on a clear day, the last wisewoman of all. She arrived when the sun was at its zenith.

Ronoah was sitting across camp and staring at the gate, as if in the act of watching he could will her here faster. That driving white light fell upon a glossy black head, upon shadow-dark body paint, upon sallow sweat-sheened shoulders, and there she was. He had never seen her in full daylight before; he almost didn't recognize her. But he did, eye snagging like a thorn on her outline her posture so awkward but so resolute and in that bundle of discomfort he saw his student, his friend—he leapt from his seat so he nearly tripped as he went to her, half-running, three months of Jau-Hasthasndr language jangling around in his head trying to coalesce into questions he did not want to ask but had to. Pashangali, Pashangali. Finally she would know he had lived, and he would know what version of himself he had to go on living with.

She recognized him too, at a hundred paces—how could she not? They had spent every day together for months. Her eyes widened at his skidding arrival; her rabbit lips parted just slightly, in surprise, in wonder.

"The river runs, wisewoman," she said as he stumbled to a dirt-spraying halt in front of her.

"The, the forest—" He could say it, but he couldn't say it. Not now. "Pashangali—"

She stepped across the camp's threshold, passed between the red-painted posts that marked its boundary and took his hands in hers, and her eyes cut dark and quick around the plateau and whatever she saw there was enough to still her composure, to remind her of her dignity— but Ronoah felt the tremor in her fingers, and when she squeezed, she squeezed with all the force of someone who would shout if they could. A breath—and a small smile bloomed at the edge of her mouth, a crack in her impassive mask, revealing relief.

"Nazum?" she asked.

"I don't need him to—to translate," Ronoah said in Jau-Hasthasndr, prompting another startled hand squeeze from Pashangali, "I can understand you, I learned—"

"Is he alive?" That drew him up short. Pashangali looked over his shoulder, her jaw tight. "Is he well?"

"He's—ahai, he's fine," Ronoah said wonderingly. No other wisewoman had ever shown regard for Nazum except as a necessary condition for Ronoah's presence. Even Marghat, who had seen them apart so many times, called the boy Runazum. Pashangali's concern was completely novel, and it touched him with unforeseen tenderness. "We're both fine now."

"That is a burden lifted. I thought, I feared you had both—disappeared."

Disappeared. Snatched and sacrificed by a rival tribe, launched from a clifftop like the creator god Chashakva from the mountains. Sent back to shiyalsha before she could say thank you, or goodbye. "No," Ronoah said, "never, I was—Marghat, Lady Yacchatzndra, she—"

"*Yacchatzndra?*" Pashangali's face creased in a scowl, and with a sensation like a wasp sting in his throat Ronoah realized he needed to lie about this too. If he wanted Pashangali to forgive Marghat, if he wanted them to agree at Council, he needed to mythologize his capture, needed a version of things she couldn't argue with.

"The spirits told her I was sick, I would die unless she returned to the heartland and restored me. We, we from the fourth branch are very—thin," he said, not knowing the word for *porous*, "soft, we have no protection against the evils of the overworld, they burrow in and—and poison us. Marghat Yacchatzndra was sent for me." This, at least, was no lie. He could say this with perfect sincerity: "She saved me."

And while the distrust didn't entirely fade from Pashangali's face, the worst of the venom left her expression. "You were ill?" she asked. "I couldn't tell when you were with us. What—"

"I'm fine now," Ronoah repeated as he waved her questions away, "it doesn't matter." He hadn't even told the story to Chashakva, it wasn't something he wanted to exhume now that it lay quiet, and besides he had questions of his own, it was time, it was time to find out— "Pashangali. What happened? After I left, did—on Orchid Ten, for Jau-Hasthasuna, did you—did you offer my tears?"

She fixed him with a solemn stare, her waxen face defeated, defiant, her collarbone rising, falling. Even the Falls went mute; all he could hear was her breathing.

She nodded. Ronoah's legs nearly gave out then and there.

"We are hosting the Baramsulandr children until after the Council of All Tribes concludes," she continued. "In case I need to try again." Her lips quirked unhappily—a reprimand, restrained. "I couldn't do it, Runa. I'm sorry."

"Don't be," Ronoah managed, his voice pitched oddly high. "Don't be, don't apologize. I don't know if you'll need to. Try again, I mean, I don't think you'll—" His words were falling like beads from a snapped necklace, chaos and clatter all over the ground. He didn't know how to act, especially when they were at such odds, when the same thing that filled Pashangali with shame had swelled like a tumour of elation in his chest, hard and scary and thrumming with life. But there was no time to figure it out, because Pashangali's translator came up the ridge of the plateau then, hauling their sleeping rolls and a skin knapsack—and then Nazum called something meant for Ronoah, Chiropolene tugging on his ear like pinched fingers, and he turned toward the boy's voice—and there was Chashakva, standing in the middle of the path that led to the roundhouse. The air around her practically shimmered, a heat-shine of purpose that drew the eye of every other wisewoman and translator in the camp.

"Lady Jau-Hasthasndra," she called, and such was its gravity that it felt like an entire conversation had just passed between them. She invoked that epithet as greeting and discipline and blessing and threat, and Ronoah was close enough to Pashangali to feel her receive it all. "Welcome.

"Assorted Holinesses," she continued, widening her address to the whole coterie, "the last of you has arrived. May it fall upon me, then, to call you to the fourth Council of All Tribes in the Cycle of Unknown." Something opened upon them all, some great maw of beginning, and Ronoah shivered. "Take the rest of the day to prepare. Partake of our banquet, send your prayers down the Falls, brief your translators as needed. We commence at dawn."

She repeated herself a few times in different dialects, but that seemed more for propriety than anything. Multilingual or not, everyone knew what had been decreed.

Council was in session. When the sun came up next, it would paint its pinkish light on a gathering that hadn't happened properly in a hundred years.

Ronoah reached for his garnet—remembered again that it was gone. Let out a slow exhale. Gave Pashangali one last glance, fleeting, reeling, before hurrying to join Nazum and Chashakva in laying out their months of storehouse goods for the banquet. Hoping the prayers he'd whispered fervently over all those honeyed jars would be enough to sweeten the wisewomen's minds, to sway their hearts. To make a difference.

The afternoon passed in a heartbeat; the evening flew by in a blink. Midnight descended, the stars an audience of crystalline eyes, and Ronoah was up and pacing the plateau beneath their expectant gaze, hard-pressed to remember any of the hours he had just lived and helpless to control any of the ones that were coming. The same feeling about Orchid Ten haunted his heels about the Council, the same disjointed ambivalence. He was ready. He wasn't ready. He was impatient. He was unprepared. He spooked himself with the half-hope that a Heavenly Seed would arrive now, intercept him alone in the black of night. Nothing came.

The lightening sky finally frightened him to bed. He caught a single fistful of sleep, waded through dreams like bogs full of all his friends dead and half-sunken—and then that yolk of morning light seeped through the slats in the hut, as much a curse as a mercy.

Ready or not, dawn had come.

TWENTY-NINE

CHASHAKVA WAS ALREADY IN THE ROUNDHOUSE when Ronoah entered, seated leonine at the opposite end of the room. He went to her side, stifling a yawn that shook him from the sternum out. "Hard night, I see," she remarked as he reached her. Ronoah shrugged, and she squeezed his elbow. "Soon we will be on our way."

As soon as the next couple of days, if all went well. Ronoah couldn't begin to fathom it right now, so he let the promise lie between them as he watched wisewomen prowl into the roundhouse, adjusting their plaits or their ropes, their paints freshly applied, their translators like fretful hunting dogs beside them. The room slowly filled with the cocktail of their perfumes, ginger and amber and frangipani. There were nineteen chairs erected in the roundhouse, ringing the empty space crouched like a living creature in the middle of the room: seventeen for the wisewomen, one for Chashakva, and one, to Chashakva's left, which was fated to remain empty.

None for any divine guests, Ronoah noted. "Are we, should we be expecting—anyone else?"

Chashakva leaned forward, lips brushing the steepled tips of her fingers. "It remains to be seen," she said. No Seeds yet, then. "Granted, some of our hypothetical guests are too big to fit in the roundhouse, let alone get through the door. But if my hunches are correct, that won't be a problem."

Ronoah was about to ask what those hunches were, but then Nazum shoved his way through the tent flap and started towards them, and he was forced to stow his curiosity. Even if he and Chashakva had the secret language of Acharrioni between them, it would feel too strange to discuss this right under Nazum's nose. The boy took up position beside Ronoah, wedged between him and the empty seat; out of the corner of his eye he caught Nazum looking at it, an unfathomable expression on his face. In another gathering, in another life, maybe he would have

246

been translating on behalf of a wisewoman in that chair, instead of for the strange softhearted not-demon he called *Runa*.

But translate for Runa he did. As the last wisewoman took her seat—Marghat, with Bashti sitting on the floor leaning her head on her mother's knee—Chashakva began at last to speak, and the interpretation flowed to Ronoah in the same measured, unobtrusive tones Nazum had always used:

"Wisewomen, good morrow. The jaguar's pelt goes golden. The river runs. The blade of day unsheathed. Health and humour to you."

Traditional greetings for each territory, acknowledging the presence of each tribe. Ronoah lost count somewhere around ten. Then Chashakva said something else and a ripple went through the wisewomen, mutters of surprise and doubt and disdain. "What is it?" Ronoah asked, leaning closer to Nazum.

"Our lady wants a traditional calling-in," the boy replied in hushed tones. "Apparently, we're gonna sing the old Council hymn."

The scepticism was not lost on Ronoah. "Apparently?"

"Yeah." Nazum set his eyes on the ring of gathered wisewomen, something like a challenge glinting within. "I kinda think I know why. Watch close, demon boy—you'll find out real quick which of these people are gonna be the troublemakers."

Chashakva stood, and as if compelled by some atmospheric pressure everyone stood with her. She swept the roundhouse with a look like the Falls, ancient and unceasing and containing all the life of Shaipuri inside, connecting with every wisewoman present and touching on whatever grand and intimate gestures had persuaded them to come here. Then she began to sing.

Marghat was the first to join in. Marghat the leader, the innovator. Then Lady Umujandra, whose own predecessor had possibly attended the last of the regular Councils. Then Lady Millikindra, whose culture held singing so precious, who wouldn't have misremembered this hymn even if it had been a thousand years quiet instead. Pashangali wasn't far behind—Lady Jau-Hasthasndra, stuffy and overly-formal and so deeply devoted to tradition. Lady Pai-Zayyindra came in two verses late, but she came in committed. To Ronoah's surprise, Nazum himself joined in a line later, quiet but steady, that same dare in his eyes.

The boy was right—this opening ritual immediately established who was in what corner. Some of the wisewomen sang in staticky bursts, muddling through the verses they remembered; others were silent and stricken, their shame scrawled across their faces that they did not know these binding words; others still kept their silence like a prize, speaking their stance plainly without a word. Seventeen histories, woven into one song—and Chashakva, and Ronoah by way of Nazum, doing the weaving by sheer force of will. A portrait; a portent. A promise.

Under the last lingering notes, as everyone was shuffling to retake their seats, Ronoah turned to Nazum. "How do you know that song?" he asked. "Doesn't it—isn't it for wisewomen only?"

"Chashakva taught it to me when we built the Chiibtandr hut. You were off knifing snakes or something." He glanced behind Ronoah at Chashakva, who was still standing. "Guess we'd look pretty unprepared if you didn't even join in on her carolling, ai?"

That was right. Nazum wasn't just Ronoah's translator; he was his voice. At least for a little while longer. Soon they would split and individualize—something Ronoah discovered he was also completely unprepared for. He hadn't even thought about it yet.

There was no time to ruminate. Until the Council was over, they were one. "Venerated ones," Chashakva was saying, "we are gathered, and now we are grounded. Bound together until we reach consensus—until, dare I say, we restore strength to the heartland. Let us begin."

And they began.

Looking forward, Ronoah hadn't had any clear idea of what the Council's order of business would be. He didn't get a vote, after all—he was not a wisewoman, no matter what Pashangali said—and so he'd trusted Chashakva to lead, to mediate. *An arbiter, if you will.* Looking back, he wished desperately that he'd asked. It might have helped him arm himself for the brutal hours that followed.

Quite simply, his empathy agonized under everyone's combined enmity. The energy their opening hymn had raised was intense—Ronoah thought he'd gotten used to the constant hum of tension arcing between wisewomen, but that hum had just changed pitch, felt like it was resonating in the chamber of the roundhouse in a way that made his sinuses hurt. He wasn't the only one who sensed it—indeed, it became apparent very quickly that nothing was going to be decided about the War until everyone had sufficient time to unload the suffering and injustice her tribe had endured. ("You took *my daughter*, Gaamndra, my pregnant daughter and my grandchild inside her—") So the Council became a sort of deranged Sweetwood Day after all—even more deranged because several more fights broke out over poor translations of already-sensitive material ("—how *dare* you insinuate we had anything to do with the Vashnarajandr, you unworthy piece of—") to the point where Nazum lost patience with the patchwork interpretations and began cutting across the stumbling of the other translators to save them from mistakes before they made them, just like he had with Chabra'i ("—for the love of the Great fucking Wheel, no, they didn't *hang* the bodies, they *heaped* them, under a burial mound like you're supposed to do with any Farhatindr sacrifices—") and suddenly the boy had no time to be Runa's voice because he was busy being everybody else's, which was just as well, because somewhere past the second hour Ronoah simply couldn't take any more visceral accounts of maiming and murder and he started to actively tune them out. He blurred the words in his mind and redirected his focus inward, attempting to soothe the sensation that every pore was clogged with emotional detritus, with some slime of indignation or resentment or radiant rage, none of it his, all of it his to bear. It was all he could do to stand up straight for that interminable morning, to not double over and retch or sob or cry out in genuine pain, the excruciating opposite of insensate. He thought, *I haven't felt this bad since Bazzenine and Jesprechel.* He thought, *This is worse. This is too much.* He heard another snippet of grief ("—you people could have taken our warriors, fine, but *why did you have to burn our medicine hall*—") and he stopped thinking, redoubled his efforts to simply survive the onslaught.

It felt nothing less than lifesaving to hear Chashakva speak in those hours. To catch and cradle her familiar rumble—not even the words, just her timbre, the constancy, the reassurance. Sometimes she sounded like she was being reassuring; others she sounded like the jaguar she was named for, growling a warning that would temporarily level the fury in the room. But no matter what, she never lost her patience. She bore witness to pain and exhaustion the likes of which had blown Ronoah completely out of himself, out of reason and time—Chashakva took it in stride, acknowledged every litany of grief, held it with grace even as she held equal and opposing griefs in her other hand. In that room so charged with volcanic feeling, she glowed like an oasis, cooling, gentle even. In her gentleness, her power was absolute.

Slowly, slowly, her efforts paid off. The sun reached the top of the sky, slamming its white light through the roundhouse smokehole in imitation of the Falls, and they were still going but it seemed as if a certain rhythm had been achieved, a conduit opening up between them all, seventeen estuaries flowing into the great channel that was Chashakva, powerful as the Sanaat. At some point, the first true apology arose. Later, the first true thank you.

Ronoah would have wept to hear it, but there were no tears in him by then, just a tinny buzzing all throughout his body like he was one of Chabra'i's beehives. He didn't feel the energy shift from combative to collaborative, although it must have occurred; he didn't feel the change in focus from past to present. He didn't feel the creeping approach of their consensus, the alignment of their opinions like planets, didn't even really feel Nazum's fingers digging into his arm when hands around the circle went up and some motion was passed.

But he heard what the motion was.

"Very well," said Chashakva, surveying the gathering with unfathomable calm, "may it be known that on this day the Ladies of the Heavenly Seeds agreed to reinstate the battle almanacs, the yearly Council of All Tribes, and henceforth to carry out the War in line with original tradition."

They were going to continue it. Eight hours, a hundred years of pain poured out on the ground, and they were agreeing to continue the War.

What? asked the part of him that was still listening, and then it fell out of his mouth, shaky plaintive Acharrioni: "What?"

Tentative conversations had murmured up between the wisewomen, so the only one who heard him was Chashakva. She laid a hand on his arm that felt both too hot and too cold, said with a matter-of-factness that struck him blunt between the eyes, "This was always a possibility. Frankly, it is a tremendous first step." Some remote, analytical piece of Ronoah noted how she sounded as if she were nearly talking to herself, as if she were distracted. "We cannot force their future upon them at a pace they are not ready for."

And maybe it was because he'd just had an entire past forced into him before he was ready, maybe it was because he was feeling unreasonable, but he laughed one hard, hollow laugh of contempt. He hated that answer. He hated how impotent it was, how cowardly. He hated how okay Chashakva was with it—how okay they all were, going on butchering each other's kin after everything.

He hated it so much that, when Marghat Yacchatzndra raised her hand for attention, he was coldly glad for the announcement she made. "I just want it on the ledger," the wisewoman said, letting her hand drop to caress the vulture skull at one thigh, "that the possibility to end the War altogether was here, and you all chose not to. That there were other options, and the Yacchatzndr were ready to explore them, but the rest of you refused. I want it written for future generations to remember."

Translators shuttled this proclamation around the room—and then several wisewoman abruptly stood from their seats, Pashangali among them—but it was Chabra'i who was quickest to answer. "Yacchatzndra, don't get hysterical over it," she drawled, managing to sound genuinely amused as she pushed her hair back from her face. "You and the rest of your coward tribe en't losing anything either way—unless of course we hold you down and pry those new coordinates out of you. Or your kid. Same difference."

Even across the room Ronoah saw Marghat's eyes flatten. Her smile sweetened from patronizing to poisonous and Chabra'i set her feet like a boar preparing to charge and a crackle of real violence superheated the atmosphere—and then Chashakva rose from her own chair, and the severity of the movement nullified that electric charge, cut its hamstrings then and there. "I would not deem it a refusal," she said, pointing her mild and dangerous gaze at Marghat, "so much as a request for a snack break. We're not finished yet, remember."

Not finished. Was the Council not over? Had he missed that part? When Chashakva said *first step* did she mean— "We shall revisit the matter of the War tomorrow, and then we may address how best to dress the wounds of the rainforest. Perhaps we shall explore some of the *other options* Lady Yacchatzndra is so eager to describe." She tilted her head; Ronoah saw one cheek round in a smile. "But there is only so much you living creatures can take at once."

Ronoah certainly couldn't take any more. He could barely take in that the Council's decision today wasn't final, that it was only the first future they could all agree on—*no matter what else happens, let us end the raids.* That was good, that *was* progress, but—but oh, tomorrow. Tomorrow, this again. And maybe the day after that—who knew how many days it would take, to discuss a hundred years' worth of difficulty? They hadn't even opened the matter of the Vashnarajandr to his knowledge, and they were going to have to discuss the deadzones and sometimes just hearing them named made him nauseous—

"Going for a walk," he heard himself say. He was already halfway around the circumference of the roundhouse, his body moving itself. He heard someone call that name—*Runa*—maybe Pashangali, he thought he saw her step towards him but he quickened his pace and pushed out onto the plateau and it was like pulling a pot from a firing kiln too quickly. The air and the cool spray contracted the overheated clay of him and something cracked, fractured, began to spill and he was pretty sure that wasn't mist on his face those were tears and he didn't even know what they were for but he knew he couldn't cry them here, not with the swish of grass skirts just behind him, not with that name in their mouths, no—he found himself running, making fast for the forest, and maybe Nazum hollered something but he ran faster because even Nazum could not hold this, would not indulge this, it wouldn't be right, it wouldn't be fair, it wasn't his *place* to be so upset—

But he was. He was sick with it, suddenly, sick and sobbing like a child. He wanted to leave Shaipuri behind; he wanted to escape its cruelty, its carnage, its horrible sorrow. He wanted to be back in Bhun Jivakta, just passing through—he wanted to be in the Tellers' caravan, wanted made-up stories to be the worst thing he'd ever heard again, he—*sketas naska*, he wanted to go *home.*

But home was a world away. So he took the woods as second best.

THIRTY

$\mathcal{R}$ONOAH KNEW THE SLOPES around the Sasaupandr Plateau nearly from memory. Three months of searching for food and materials had taught him where the ground was reliable, where the thickest foliage lay, where the termites piled their mounds and the birds wove their nests and the nocturnal animals lay sleeping in their dens. And so even though maybe there were people following him, he got shy of them good and quick; even though he kicked up a racket as he tripped his way into the thicket, gasping and crying, he remained unfound.

Good. He didn't want anybody seeing him like this. He'd worked so hard to keep a brave face through the Council session, what use would it be if they watched him fall apart now? It wasn't for him to shed tears the wisewomen could see; they were the ones who had suffered so much, who deserved to be held through their mourning. He was just stealing it, soaking it up like the spirit sponge he was.

By the time he finally slowed he was deep in the foliage. He stumbled between wild fig trees until picking one to lean against, trying to find a sense of safety in the press of smooth bark to his back. The iron-red emotions of the Council were still shaking him up, so he slid to the ground and sunk his hands into the mulch, bracing, breathing.

It wasn't really his *fault* that this was happening. His reaction made sense: he was an empath, and trying to control what that meant was new to him. He might have been assigned to train Pashangali, but ultimately he was still a novice in the art of shaping and moving this emotional receptor he possessed. He found, to his surprise, that he didn't feel bad about feeling bad. There was a time when he would have chastised himself for something like this, for getting worked up, causing a problem—but that admonishing voice was absent.

Grief crested in his chest all the same. His fingers were trembling in the soil. Sitting and grounding was good, but moving was probably better—it might help to burn off this vicarious agitation, to work it out of him like a cramp. Wiping his eyes with the backs of his wrists, he hauled himself upright and set off walking down the slope. He would head to the base of the Falls and chart his course back to the plateau. Hopefully he would feel steady by then; hopefully no one would probe too closely at his sudden departure. Underworld business, he could always tell them. Shiyalshandr things.

Would the real shiyalshandr care so much about ending the War? Would they rejoice to know that, at the very least, no one was going to be stolen away from their beds again?

Now that he was out of the roundhouse, he had to admit that Chashakva was right. It *was* a lot to ask, to bid the wisewomen end the War in a day. The debts these people were settling were on a completely different scale from the little squabbles and insults the Acharrioni tallied up and saved for Sweetwood Day—of course they needed time to weigh it all. The Council was always going to have more than one session.

He just didn't know if he could attend the next one.

To begin with, the mere thought of re-entering a space that emotionally charged made his throat seize up. He could argue that he would be more prepared the second time, but he could counter-argue that he would also be more worn down, weakened by today's exposure. What if he wasn't able to hold it together? What if something they discussed—the deadzones, the Vashnarajandr, even the Heavenly Seeds—prompted a wave of feeling that knocked him flat?

What if they talked through it all, and their decision to continue the War stayed the same?

No, he thought firmly, before his own panic could claw up the ramparts and infiltrate the raw spaces where everybody else's panic was finally seeping out. "No," he murmured, to cement it. Chashakva wouldn't let that happen. She had a plan. The Heavenly Seeds still hadn't arrived, and once they did there was no telling how that might change everyone's mind. And if they didn't arrive, the woman said she'd prepared for that, too. If he trusted anything, it was Chashakva.

If you trust her, pointed out a voice in his head, you should tell her how difficult today was. You should tell her you can't do another day like it. Tell her why. *Be honest* might not be a rule anymore, but you're not honest because someone told you to be. And besides, *keep up* isn't a rule anymore, either. Just because Chashakva can stand in that room without flinching doesn't mean you have to.

That was—probably what he was doing. He didn't think he was *trying* to keep up with Chashakva, but maybe some of that old mindset had slipped in. Maybe he'd pushed himself a little far, trying to be like her. Maybe it was wise to respect his limit, to let her know so she could help devise an excuse for his absence. Maybe—maybe it was time to tell her about the other things, too. About being sick. About fighting Pashangali. About the tallest warrior. Maybe—after the Council was over and done, after they were released from their duty—he could afford to come to her as one last wisewoman, Runazum Chashakvandra, and lay his own burden into her hands, and have her listen.

The uncanny tingle had faded from his hands; his heartbeat was nearly down to normal. Look at that, he thought with a scrap of a smile, you *can* handle yourself. But it might be nice to ask for help anyway.

He returned his attention outward, and that was when he realized he didn't know the slopes of the Sasaupandr Plateau quite as well as he thought.

This was a part of the foothills he didn't recognize. The foliage was different: dark green, waxy. It triggered some dim spark of familiarity, so he must have come across it at some point. He just had no idea how it connected to the rest of the terrain. The argentine thread of a stream caught his eye and he started in the opposite direction; it was probably runoff from the bowl of the Falls. If he traced it back, he would arrive at a landmark he could use.

Before long the foliage thinned out—and he stepped into a glade, sheltered by the canopy save for a few amber shafts of afternoon sun. By the colour of the light, he still had time to make it back before dark. He skirted the perimeter, trying not to get his feet too wet.

But then he slowed down soon. It was something about this place. The clearing; the water. He was absolutely sure he'd been here before, only he couldn't remember when. Sometime searching for long grasses? For mushrooms? Sometime in the beginning of monsoon, for sure, when the days were longer—he remembered the clearing bluer, brighter.

Curiosity tugged him to the banks. Then, hesitantly, into the shallows. The feeling of his foot breaking the surface made him shiver.

Sunlight filtered through the humid gloom. The water lapped at his ankles, his calves. The poignancy of it, the weird warmth—had something important happened here? How could he have forgotten? Him, of all people? He dug in his mind for answers but discovered nothing for certain. Only a feeling, like the ones he'd had in the monastery, the same kind of feeling that would creep up on him when he was alone in a cavern with a shalledrim portrait. The sense of being together with something. The sense of being watched.

Wait.

What was—?

He tore his eyes from the spot they had been lingering, forced his gaze in the direction his intuition was bridling, the vector his instinct was drawn to. He looked down, into the undulating current.

Something looked back.

He knew before he knew and it made his blood run cold—and then the thing in the water broke the surface with a splash that drowned Ronoah's scream in white noise. Coils the width of Chabra'i's tree trunk; scales the span of the shutters across Marghat's villa. Two eyes, dark and fathomless as Pashangali's sinkholes.

The Heavenly Seed Jau-Hasthasuna had arrived.

Any plan Ronoah had—to run, or to kneel, or to anything—dissolved in his mind as the snake fixed him in its gaze. After an eternal moment of staring at each other it slid forward in the water, lowering its head to Ronoah's height—up close it was so much that his eyes unfocused, afflicted, powerless under the magnitude of what they saw. He felt like he was falling, only he hadn't so much as twitched. He was breathless, thoughtless.

But just as he felt he was going to pass out, Jau-Hasthasuna spoke, in a Shaipurin Ronoah's mouth would have bled to repeat, in a voice that upended his inner ear, a Jau-Hasthasndr sentence like the rustling flight of a hundred million leaves.

I know you, it said.

It was curious, pondering, hypnotic. Its tongue lashed the air, so near to his body he felt the urge to recoil like a slap. *You smell like she does. Are you a new god?*

Ronoah would have laughed, but he couldn't. It foundered in his throat, mewling, hysterical. A few moments later it was hard to remember why he'd wanted to laugh in the first place. His consciousness was slippery; his brain couldn't work right with those rustling words disrupting it. Jau-Hasthasuna didn't seem to notice.

You're a little small, it noted, almost kindly, *but there were small gods once, and they were quite powerful. Chiibta, Subin, Naskarahal. None so powerful as me, though.*

It retreated from Ronoah, sinking comfortably into the glade. Widening the space between them was like creating a vacuum, like all of Ronoah's soft bits were going to be dragged out of his body into the void—but the power of the god's presence lessened just enough that he could hear himself think, and his mind sputtered to life again like a fire on wet wood and painstakingly he strung together the words he was being given until they made sentences, until they had meaning, and then—

Did she send you to meet me? Jau-Hasthasuna asked. It seemed genuinely interested by this possibility. *Have you been hiding all along? You are so small, it would have made sense to miss you, only you would be number nineteen, and she said there were only to be eighteen of us.*

She. It stuck in Ronoah's head, dug in amidst the maelstrom of contact, a handhold, a thorn. She. He clung to it even though it hurt.

Jau-Hasthasuna's massive head strayed slightly to one side. It flicked its tongue again, great gout of silky flesh. *Did she bring you here to feed on me?* it inquired. Ronoah wanted to shake his head but movement was still beyond him. *If so, I'm afraid that won't be possible. I will be feeding on you instead, little god.*

Feed on. Him? Eaten? He blinked, slowly at first, then harder. Wait, hold on, he wasn't, he wasn't—

I have been waiting a long time, prompted the snake, as if it genuinely hoped for a bit of conversation before it devoured him. *I did not want to eat the others, because they were my friends. But it is the way of the War. They live on inside me.*

A sound escaped Ronoah—a sibilance, an attempt at a word. He pushed at the suffocating presence around him, the noxious crawling of his skin, and wheezed it out: "J-Jau-Hasthasuna."

A noise not unlike the Falls rumbled from deep within the glade; the Seed was pleased. *I am Jau-Hasthasuna, yes,* it said. *I am the Heavenly Seed that sprouted. I am the last god left. Except, perhaps, for you?*

"No, no, I—I'm not, I'm not a god."

No? A gust of choking wind as Jau-Hasthasuna exhaled through the slits of its nostrils. *But not human, surely. I have heard whispers of you. Runazum the Fair? You swam in my lake and survived. You have been calling an end to the sacrifices.* An idea seemed to come to the snake. *Are you a catalyst? A fertilizer for a Seed?*

"I don't know," Ronoah said, his words slurring together. "I don't think so."

Another noise. Disappointment. *A mystery then,* it said, and Ronoah's entire body numbed with primal terror at some shift in the conversation. *How pitiful it must be, to not know your purpose. It must be very lonely.*

"It is," Ronoah agreed, feeling himself shaking, feeling tears overcome him without his permission, without his understanding. Jau-Hasthasuna did not nod, but a sense of acknowledgment swept Ronoah like a gale.

I suppose I shall feed on you anyway, of course, the snake said matter-of-factly. *Just in case. You do not have to be lonely if you are part of me. Perhaps it will help—your soul will fly down to shiyalsha and your strength will serve the creator god of this age, and you will become greatness, no matter what you were before. How does that sound, little thing?*

The presence of the Heavenly Seed closed in, erasing everything, wiping the world from his grasp. His entire horizon filled, his inner space colonized. He almost agreed.

"Unfortunately, I will have to object."

The world refocused with a snap.

Air exploded in Ronoah like a punch in the lungs as he sucked in a breath, released from his paralysis only to stumble sideways—into a hand like a tree trunk, like a cairn, into a grip with all the sureness of nature behind it. Into Chashakva, appeared like a bolt in the clouds, appraising the god before them while everything inside her flickered and flared with effusive sapphire light.

"It's you," she said, a murmur too quiet to be for anyone but herself. She sounded almost revelatory in her surprise. "Really. Of everyone."

And then she stepped into herself, and by her side Ronoah felt the sternum-shuddering gong of power that resonated from her body. "Jau-Hasthasuna," she said as her skin flared with a rash of luminescent jaguar spots, eyewatering bright, "my, how you've grown."

Chashakva, Jau-Hasthasuna said in recognition, and Ronoah feared that the snake was going to lunge but instead it writhed, enormous coils wriggling in the water in a way that reminded him absurdly of an excited pup. The glade sprayed droplets up to the branches. *It is you. I am so happy you've come home. Something is very wrong.*

"Yes." The woman lifted a glittering hand, turned it palm-up at the god. An indication. "Yes, I'd say so."

I knew it, exclaimed Jau-Hasthasuna with another whip-splash of its grandiose tail. *I knew there was a missing step, or a trick I had not learned. I have eaten all the others like you said to, and yet I remain—was there a special way to do it? An order I did not know?*

Such an indomitable force was Jau-Hasthasuna's voice that it forced Ronoah to hear its questions, even though his mind had already stopped dead on one phrase.

Did my tribe not sacrifice enough? I always wondered if perhaps mine was a more difficult sacrifice to make. How few the numbers they fed me! But then, the power of the other Seeds was imparted to me when I ate them, so surely it matters little? When it received no answer, the snake pressed: *Why have I not ascended? Why have I not shed this lesser form?*

Chashakva watched Jau-Hasthasuna with a raptness that pulled like gravity, hands loose at her sides. "Why," she said, as if she were pondering the god's question. Some sprint of light climbed the ladder of her body, flashing out like sheet lightning beneath her skull. When next she spoke she gave no answer, only posed a question of her own, the terminus of a long sigh: "Why have you done this?"

Because you told it to, Ronoah thought. You told them all.

Chashakva wasn't just the body the War was built on. She was the one who'd started it.

Jau-Hasthasuna swayed back and forth in hesitation. *I'm afraid I don't understand. I did everything you asked me to.*

"Except leave." It punctured the glade like a needle. "You were supposed to leave after it was over—all of you were. Intact; unsullied. None of you—" feverish memory swept up Ronoah's spine, jasmine petals and high places "—god and gods alike, none of you were meant to be eaten."

Of course we were to be eaten, said Jau-Hasthasuna, flicking its bruise-blue tongue once, twice. *That was our duty, god and gods, to sacrifice ourselves to the strongest.*

"It was a curse, not an address." Chashakva's mouth pressed into a line; all the rampant starlight in her body compressed to pinpoints. Vertigo set in as the glade was shrouded in shadow, aching from the loss of her illumination. "You were never gods to begin with, none of you. No mountain of sacrifices could lift you from that *lesser form*, no number of swallowed friends. You knew this—I know you knew it, when we all began." She closed her eyes, and the centuries unfolded around her. "It was a story. It was a game. Don't you remember?"

A sound like the steam blasting up from the Falls: Jau-Hasthasuna hissing. It shook Ronoah's bones practically to splinters and he grabbed Chashakva's arm to steady himself—and came into contact with something so utterly shocking it cauterized everything together, re-fused his shattered framework and alloyed it, marbled it with something that shivered and sang like a blade. In the midst of this confrontation, Chashakva was neglecting to veil herself from his powers. His empathy dashed against her like the waves against the bluffs of Tyro, and her emotions blistered his soul where they touched. Alien, amaranth things that bent time in a fisheye, that caught every edge in starfire, that made him tender for everything and hateful for everything and hungry for *everything*—

"—walked these lands for nearly a year," she was saying, her voice purple and smelling of cinnamon, "I paid more than one visit to the tally, I summoned whoever was left of you months ago—why are you only coming to me about this now? Why have you waited—no." The smell changed, suddenly ammoniac. "Why did you *hide?*"

It might have been a trick, I thought, Jau-Hasthasuna insisted, *or a new creator god come to replace me before I could ever do my job—I could not know it was you for certain, you look so different than you once did—*

None of that was it. Ronoah saw it clearly as he struggled to suck himself back into himself, to relinquish Chashakva's emotional landscape. He glanced Jau-Hasthasuna on the rebound, and he saw, and it put a fresh crack in his heart. The truth, the deeper reason—it was the same reason he had run away from Pilanova when Diadenna had said *we need to talk*: because he'd felt the unshakeable sense of having done something wrong, and he'd been afraid to find out what.

Now you come bearing Chashakva's smell, and her marks, yet you are telling me such—things! Jau-Hasthasuna's body lashed indignantly. *It is not a game, not a fantasy, it is real, you told us we were to be gods—*

"I said you were to be gods in the eyes of your tribes."

Jau-Hasthasuna reared its colossal head. *Is there a difference?!*

Chashakva did not answer. She just fixed her gaze on the snake, and even sidelong Ronoah staggered under the weight of it. The judgement of all seventeen devoured Seeds peering from her eye sockets, the reproach of old ghosts that did not live on anywhere after all, nowhere but in their shared memory.

"Why did you poison the river," Chashakva asked, her voice a flint-edge stained with sorrow, with fury.

It was the only thing I could think to do. I ate Yacchatzul, the last Seed beside me, and waited to feel myself sprout and nothing happened. Nothing for years. I kept waiting to become the river, the soil, the sky like you were before me, but I just stayed me. And I worried the people would stop their sacrifices if they mistook the forest for saved and so I wounded it, just a little, just the places they would notice, so they would not forget to feed me.

"And then?"

And then Vashnarajan's people gave up their fighting and it seemed like such a sign—the tribe of self-sacrifice just sitting and waiting like ripening fruit. It was the logical next step. Jau-Hasthasuna's voice climbed in pitch, the high whine of every insect in Shaipuri in concert. *There was no other way! You never told us what to do once the last of us was alone! I had no guidance!*

Like a parent scolding a child, Chashakva shook her head. "You aren't listening. I told you all what to do once the game was played—leave this place." She smiled a wry, agonized smile. "Leave it like I left it: in search of some other way to entertain yourselves."

The temperature dropped in the glade, chilling the water at Ronoah's feet.

"I should have stayed. I see that. I should have come to you sooner. When you set something in motion, you don't let it alone unsupervised; you don't leave the house when the kettle is on the boil. You think I would know that by now." The sound of her tisking, whipcrack in the glade. So raw, so disillusioned. Then she drew herself up, determined in spite of her disappointment. "You have a chance to redeem yourself. You know the Council is on the plateau; if you come with me, we can make it right together."

Make what right? Jau-Hasthasuna asked. *How?*

"We reveal you as the last Seed standing. They believe their War is finally over, and they cease their sacrificing once and for all."

But then how am I to ascend? If there are no more sacrifices, this is as powerful as I will ever become.

"There is nothing to be done about that, Jau-Hasthasuna."

No! Jau-Hasthasuna's glistening coils sent the water churning in its distress. *I am the creator god of this age!*

"To them you will be," Chashakva said, and it seemed an attempt at true consolation. "Your name will be affixed to the Great Wheel of Ages, and you will enter their lore as the Heavenly Seed who sprouted victorious. It will be but a story—but oftentimes, a story is the best you can hope for. A story is enough."

What happened to glory? demanded Jau-Hasthasuna, the howl of a dust storm scoring Ronoah's mind. *What happened to power? To protecting the boundary between the overworld and shiyalsha? I cannot sustain the rainforest like this! I cannot be reduced to a story, to a lie, it's not possible, you said, you said together we would be GOD.*

Chashakva smoothed her hands over her face. In that moment, she looked so old.

"Really holding onto that one, aren't you?" she muttered.

Her fists curled, the stars rekindling inside her. "It is not in my power to give you what you want," she said, and now the air tasted different, nearly acidic with omen— "Whatever enlightenment you envisioned is beyond our limits; you must content yourself with the life that is yours. Please."

Ronoah's heart constricted. Oh, no. "Ch—Chash-shakva—"

Never, cried Jau-Hasthasuna, its jaw unhinging like an eclipse. Fangs long as stripped saplings frothed with venom. *There is more. There must be! This cannot be all that there is! Impossible, impossible—*

A sound emanated from Chashakva, a hiss like a long, slow breath. Despite the quake that ripped through him, Ronoah reached for her arm again, trying to distract, to dissuade, to say anything. Chashakva, he thought, stop. Chashakva, don't. Give it some patience, please, it's only just found out. It's just reacting, give it some time to, like you would for me, Chashakva, please—

But nothing came out of his mouth. And Chashakva was not in a mind-reading mood. He clung to her, helpless, as she faced Jau-Hasthasuna still spitting with denial. "All you really want is to ... how did you put it?" A pause. "Sustain the rainforest? That is your wish, no?"

It is my duty, said Jau-Hasthasuna, sinkhole eyes flashing with pride. *My duty as a god.*

Chashakva nodded. "Very well," she said, and there was nothing but respect in her voice. "So you shall."

She brought her free arm up above her head, palm flat. Her hand a nebula; her hand a miniature of the entire night sky. She made a slashing motion across her body, diagonal and down. There was a whistle, a crunch like the forest being felled. And Jau-Hasthasuna's eyes, so great and godlike in their inscrutability, registered a mote of surprise as the creature's head split from its body and dropped, hurtling to earth like a meteor.

Ronoah went down before it hit, throwing his arms over his head; water sliced icy through his nerves, carving him awake. The boulder of weight on his consciousness was suddenly lessening, lightening, blowing away. In his surprise he nearly tried holding on to it.

He peeked between his arms. Chashakva was wading into the water, up to her knees, her waist, laying a hand on Jau-Hasthasuna's severed head. Behind them the glade was alive with the death throes of the body, its rippling twitching spasms, but the head was still, stunned, mute with the shock of being proved wrong.

Ronoah watched Chashakva stroke the creature's nose. Watched her bend to put herself level with its half-submerged eye. "You know, in a way this is a gift," she said. Her words were like crooning mothers, like cooing doves. Sympathetic, crushingly fond. "Your girl Pashangali, she worries so constantly about her sacrifices. Now hers is the biggest sacrifice of all. Talk about improvement, ai?"

The last scattered pebbles rolled away in Ronoah's mind, and he knew the creature Jau-Hasthasuna was dead.

Chashakva remained in the water for an interminable moment, staring into the great snake's eye. Then, letting her hand slide off Jau-Hasthasuna's head, she turned to face Ronoah. Her expression was as close to self-conscious as he had ever seen it.

"I was really hoping we could avoid this, you and I," she said.

"You...you killed it." His body felt hollow as a gourd; his words rattled inside him. But they made it out. "You killed it. You, you murdered a Heavenly Seed, you cut its *head* off..."

With one last anticlimactic splash, the body of Jau-Hasthasuna fell still in the water. Chashakva turned her head slightly at the return of silence. Not even an insect chirred.

"You killed it." He was like Jesprechel's Echo Chamber in reverse, repeating himself in a louder voice every time. Then the pattern broke: "You *made* it. You made it all. Eighteen gods, eighteen Seeds, you—you set them loose and then walked away and *forgot* about them and when you come back the last one alive asks for your help and you *murder* it—"

"It wasn't going to be convinced, Ronoah, it was going to keep poisoning the forest."

Jau-Hasthasuna's head was seeping blood into the water. In its resting pose, half-submerged, Ronoah saw again the bog burial of the tallest warrior.

That death was Chashakva's fault as much as anyone's. "Only because you *told* it to, because of—because of your *game*—" Chashakva's mouth twisted up, and his breath hitched, sparked. "Don't smile like it's *funny*—"

"I'm not—"

"When you said you would figure something out I—I didn't mean this, I never thought this—Vespasi wake, you started the War of Heavenly Seeds. You *designed* it, you let them slaughter all these people—" for one instant, just one, all the feeling came burning back into his body and he felt the dreadfully perfect awareness of his own presence, *here*, his own involvement in the heartland "—and then you brought me here."

Chashakva was looking at him with more patience than she had ever afforded Jau-Hasthasuna. "To end it, yes."

"Why," Ronoah said, like molten metal bubbling up from his throat, "didn't you tell me?"

Slowly, that smile returned, full of guilt or pity or perverse irony; slowly, she shrugged one bony shoulder.

"Would you really have wanted to know?" she replied.

It hit like a slap. Like that diagonal slash. It forced one cracked-glass laugh out of Ronoah, and that exhale carried all his sensation with it, blew him out like a candle so he stood there feeling bodiless, decapitated from his fury, his anguish. His voice came out shaking but clinical: "So you were *never* going to tell me—you were going to pretend forever like this had nothing to do with you, like everything that's happened here, everything I—like it's not your fault. I was supposed to be tricked like everyone else, tricked into helping without knowing what I was helping you for." Jau-Hasthasuna's blood had reached his legs, creeping around him in rusty tendrils. He looked up. "If I died, I was supposed to not know you'd killed me. So much for rule number five."

Chashakva's irises were perfect circles. "Ronoah," she said. That had hurt. Good. It was meant to. He'd learned how to hurt people because of all this, and that was her fault, too.

"That's fine though," he said, "because we *threw the rules out the window*, didn't we, so it doesn't matter. We *make our choices together* now, right? We're *equals*." He was getting quite loud, wasn't he? "Good to know we're only equals when it *doesn't fucking matter*, that's great—no, I'm *glad* to know that gets abandoned the second something important happens, that's—!"

"For the love of Evin's bones," Chashakva interrupted, "twice in one day?"

It was such an—*inappropriate* reply that it made Ronoah pause. It didn't make sense. And then—

"I never said we were equals." Her hand strayed back to Jau-Hasthasuna's head, and then Ronoah knew what she meant by *twice*. No, but he—he hadn't *misunderstood*, she'd said— "I would never say that, not even as a joke, because it is impossible. We will never be equals; we will never see eye to eye." She levelled him with a look like the winter moons, cold and clear and unbelievably far away—and then she turned her back to him, doing something with Jau-Hasthasuna's head he couldn't see. "There will always be things that I keep from you, because they are private, because they are dangerous, because I am *not in the mood* to share. You are welcome to keep your own secrets—in that respect, we are equal. In our shared destination, we are equal. Perhaps even in our love of the journey. That is my hope."

Ronoah's mind flooded with images, Iphigene islands and the docks of Bhun Jivakta, all the choices he had made for the love of the journey, everything he'd agreed to for the sake of a little more time. His teeth were clenched so hard his jaw creaked.

"But make no mistake," Chashakva said as she turned and started hauling Jau-Hasthasuna's head to shore, "there are certain chasms between us which cannot be crossed. That is the nature of the game." She glanced up, her eyes two comet trails. "Are we still willing to play?"

More memories: crowded tables, acrid coffee, a debate, a conversation, a proposition. Ronoah felt stabbed in some deep, soft place. He didn't know whether he wanted to scream or cry.

He did neither. He just stood there, quaking, until she had already passed him, and then he said the only thing he could think to say: "How does it feel, knowing you destroyed your friend's garden?"

Chashakva froze, and Ronoah knew with bitter triumph that he'd overstepped. He braced himself to be struck down just like Jau-Hasthasuna before him. Released from the pain of knowing, of seeing.

But it never came. The creature before him just bowed her head, readjusting her grip on Jau-Hasthasuna's fang. The snake's venom was sizzling against her fingers, trying and failing to chew through. To make contact.

"Thank you for coming on my side trip with me," she said.

Then she gathered herself and started up the slope, dragging her burden behind her.

THIRTY-ONE

*I*T WAS A STROKE OF FORTUNE that nobody had started another fight in Ronoah and Chashakva's absence. Granted, they seemed pretty close. In one corner a squabble was happening in front of the Chiibtandr hut; in another, Marghat was speaking in hushed tones to Bashti and their interpreter, a fierce frown on her face; further down, a cluster of translators had Nazum cornered, asking him questions while he tried to beg off.

Ronoah didn't take in the details. What he took in was the way all the air on the plateau disappeared, vanishing the wisewomen's irritations, when they saw what emerged from the woods: Chashakva, demon or deity, stalking out of the shadows with a massive *something* in tow—and Runa, her companion, her familiar, eyeing the thing in Chashakva's fist with a hope and a horror that couldn't be missed.

Lord Jau-Hasthasuna is coming to Council one way or another, Chashakva had said on their way up the plateau. *We are ending this tonight.* Now, with a flick of her wrist, she tossed the severed head of Jau-Hasthasuna into the clearing. For an instant the scales caught the glossy light in one liquid rivulet, a last fitful flash of life. Then it landed, and all the dusk birds were shaken from their roosts at the quake.

Even the Falls seemed to go quiet.

Someone was going to have to say something eventually. Ronoah certainly didn't have anything to contribute. He stood apart from Chashakva, awaiting a reaction, a response, the uproar— "*Chuta ka saag,*" came a hiss at his shoulder, and Nazum grabbed hold of Ronoah's arm while ogling the megalith in their midst. "That—that's—"

He knew who it was. Ronoah wanted to name the god anyway, but he couldn't. He swallowed. "Yeah."

"What." The boy's question was a breath, a wisp. He dug into Ronoah's arm, but Ronoah didn't feel the pain. Just the trembling fingers. "What the fuck is going on."

Nothing important, Ronoah thought. Just a game. Before he could think of something to actually answer with, Chashakva was laying the ground work. "Behold," she said. "The source of all your problems." She tilted her head. "Well. Not all. I wouldn't discredit any of you in your ability to make each other miserable. But it certainly didn't help. I present the head of the fallen god Jau-Hasthasuna, and in so doing I call a for second session of the Council of All Tribes, to begin immediately."

She waited there, loose and lethal and covered in steaming godsblood. She waited just long enough to let the sight sink in, and then, conversationally, she added, "My apologies if I've disrupted your evening plans."

And what else could they do? With the menace of the divine in her voice, with her prey already beginning to attract the insects, real as real could be, what could they do but obey her? One by one the wisewomen tore their eyes from the glorious monstrosity before them, turning and dragging their translators behind them into the roundhouse—everyone but Pashangali. Pashangali stood rigid in their midst, a battered stick of driftwood in a flowing current. Hands covering her mouth, dark eyes wide and awash with tears.

"Can't even imagine how that's fucking with her third mind," muttered Nazum beneath the commotion. "On top of everything else. Shit." Solemnly, he spat on the ground. There was sympathy there, concern, maybe even protectiveness—all things that made sense to feel. Ronoah felt none of them. He wondered if that made him terrible. He nodded anyway, leading the way to the roundhouse, avoiding Pashangali's eye as he went.

They skirted the inner circumference of the room, took their assigned places beside Chashakva. The woman's full attention was on the Council— Ronoah could tell because the air between them had stopped threatening to smother him. The journey back had taken over an hour, and all the way up the only thing he could feel was fractured trust, distance blistering up between them where nothing of the sort had been before, pushing them further apart with every step together they took. A few short hours ago he'd been ready to tell Chashakva everything, to lay his heart in her hands; by the time they returned to the plateau, he felt like nothing more than one more severed limb she was pulling behind her.

It was a relief to watch her step back into her performance. It deadened him to whatever complex and delicate things were breaking in him.

After far longer than was comfortable, Pashangali finally entered the roundhouse, her face twisted with grief. As she shakily took her seat, Chashakva began to speak, and only then did Ronoah realize that no amount of emotional distancing could spare him from the pain of this.

The awful, awful last laugh of it.

"The Lord Jau-Hasthasuna came today to kill you all."

Because Chashakva couldn't tell them the truth. No. She was going to feed them one last lie.

"He intended to sever your people's connection with the gods so that you would continue to war forever. But as you saw outside," the woman said with a slight lift of her fingers, "Runa and I took care of it."

"What do you mean you *took care* of it?" Of all people, it was Marghat. She was holding Bashti in her lap, her face drawn tight. "Why would a Heavenly Seed want the War to continue forever?"

"Because this Seed was infected." There was a collective intake of breath. That was an insult the likes of which had never been uttered. The wise-women would rile each other for days, but never would they discredit each other's gods. After all, in the end all the gods were really just one. "The Heavenly Seeds derived their essence, their power, from the sacrifices your ancestors made. They were fed by your actions—and the intentions behind them." Chashakva looked upon them all sternly, and Ronoah had a crackling presentiment of what she was about to do and nearly yelled aloud— "Your ambushes. Your raids. Your thievery. The other Seeds refused to touch those who were sacrificed in this manner, but Jau-Hasthasuna hungered, and he fed, and so he was transfigured into something sacrilegious. A spiteful god. A mutated Seed, full of malice and bloodlust."

She was turning it on them. On the wisewomen, on the tribes. She was passing the blame.

"In truth, your War ended ages ago—you have a creator god, a sprouted Seed. Only Jau-Hasthasuna was left here, in the overworld, confined to a mortal form for his transgressions, condemned to never become part of the creator god he was separated from. The creator refused to eat him— if you eat rotten fruit, you get sick." A sob, dampened by fingers, from Pashangali's side of the room. Chashakva continued regardless. She was delivering all of this in Jau-Hasthasndr; whether it was a gesture of mercy or ruthlessness, Ronoah could not know. "Made malicious by your dishonourable behaviour, Jau-Hasthasuna has sought vengeance for this slight ever since. Instead of repenting he has poisoned the land, striking it blow after blow, trying to drag the creator god back down and take their place." The woman narrowed her eyes. "*That's* what your deadzones are. The petty, destructive impulses of a deity that felt entitled to more than it was owed."

The silence rang like death. Nobody knew what to do. It was clear in their posture, their expressions—this was unknown territory, fragile as newly-smoothed beach after high tide. None of them knew how to tread lightly enough to leave it intact.

Except for Bashtandala. "So we have a creator god after all," she stated, clearly enough for the whole room to hear her—little Bashti, picking at her nails, speaking with the cool certainty of one who is doubtless about her priorities. "Who is it?"

Chashakva nodded, her eyes intent. "That should be obvious, little one."

Ronoah looked at Bashtandala—and then the canyon-echo voice of Jau-Hasthasuna rebounded in his head, the confession, the admission, *I ate Yacchatzul, the last Seed beside me,* and he knew. Of course. Yacchatzul, the god who tried to tell her wisewoman that the War was a lie; Yacchatzul, the god who had tried to stop Jau-Hasthasuna's rampage. Marghat Yacchatzndra, who knew so much about their common history, who had untold insight into the heartland and the tribes and how they could all work together—and Bashti, who would inherit it all and then some, Bashti who hadn't been born until after the village was relocated, who was part of no War, who harboured no resentments. The Yacchatzndr, so ready to take this great step forward. It made sense. It was even almost true.

"It's Vashnarajan, of course."

The room exploded. Wisewomen gasped and shouted, translators jumped to their feet or fell to their knees, the air shuddered with grief or hope or righteous fury, and Ronoah felt his own cry pushed from his lungs, adding to the tumult, the tempest. Only Chashakva was silent, eyes glimmering with some endgame unknown.

And Nazum, who had gone stiff beside him.

"Of course," Chashakva repeated, with heavy emphasis. "What do I keep saying? In a ritual war, intention is everything. The Vashnarajandr never succumbed to greed or resentment; they never sacrificed anything but a good, wholesome meal. And so Vashnarajan succeeded as the Heavenly Seed who sprouted. He abandoned Jau-Hasthasuna to the mortal world—and out of spite, Jau-Hasthasuna killed Vashnarajan's beloved tribe. Perhaps if he had not, you would have known your War was at an end." The woman made a banishing gesture. "Fear no longer. You are in good hands, now. If you've anything to say about how long it took, I would take the issue up with our guest outside."

That reminder was cruel, was crucial. What could you say against the proof of a Seed's severed head lying on the doorstep? It was irrefutable.

The War of Heavenly Seeds was at an end. It had happened in their lifetime. The heartland was free from its obligation at last.

Chashakva had *figured something out.*

And Ronoah was struck by the blinding brilliance of this final lie, struck and crumpled, though he stood tall all the same. It couldn't have been the Yacchatzndr. Learned though Marghat was, she had her faults, her pride. From the beginning she had been convinced she was better than the other wisewomen—awarding her the name of the creator god would only have puffed that pride to intolerable levels. So too for Chabra'i, even for pious Pashangali. For anyone at this Council. The only way to make sure a new power struggle didn't erupt was to negate the whole thing, to nullify the notion of divine favour by giving it to the one tribe that didn't exist anymore.

Except for one boy. To Ronoah's left, Nazum was standing carefully still, his famously sharp tongue kept firmly behind his teeth, his face fixed determinedly in a mask of impassivity. Useless efforts, all of them. He was absolutely glowing. He caught Ronoah's eye, and his composure broke and he smiled—not a sly smirk, not his sharkish grin, but a bright arc of joy and relief and release like nothing Ronoah had seen before. Right then and there, he watched the boy shuck off his burden, watched him grow an inch taller for it, watched years of faith and fear collide and react and dissolve down into one insoluble truth: everything had been worth it, in the end.

And Ronoah knew he could not tell Nazum the truth. It had been wedged between them. He was alone.

A voice uncoiled from somewhere deep in his spine, sinuous, rustling— and does it matter, it asked, if he knows? If any of them do? No one here will learn the truth, and Jau-Hasthasuna will forever be remembered as a rancid thing harbouring malice and hate when all it really wanted was help—and none of that matters, does it? What really happened doesn't matter nearly as much as what *needs* to have happened in order for these people to feel comfort. To make amends. They will live this lie forever, and be glad for it.

So why champion truth at all? Why go in pursuit of the real story when there are lovely and useful fables everywhere? Why bother holding to a creed of honesty if all it does is wipe the smile off Nazum's face?

Why didn't you tell me?

Would you really have wanted to know?

Something cut through the cold flow of his thinking, hard as a harpoon: "The only question left is, how to punish you?"

Ronoah blinked. The roundhouse came back into focus. And he saw Lady Naskarahandra standing up, pointing at Pashangali.

Suddenly that fighting heat was back. Lady Dandakhti-Kashndra stood as well with a scoff and a "You can't be serious", but Lady Gaamndra was up just as fast and just as passionate— "It's your Seed that tried to kill us, your Seed that would see the War continue for all time!" Sides magnetized with dizzying speed as one wisewoman after another weighed in on Pashangali's guilt, on the culpability of her tribe, it happened so fast that Ronoah could hardly react, he was only catching every other sentence as everyone's translation dissolved into chaos—no, he wanted to say, *stop,* the point is to stop punishing each other, you can't—

But they could. With their reality shattered, the wisewomen were scrabbling for a decision to make, *any* decision, any next step, and this step was familiar. This step was hundreds of years old. Ronoah searched for words but all his words had deserted him, three months of Shaipurin gone to ashes as he listened to the discord of sixteen people arguing about how badly his friend deserved to hurt for what her god had done. The Jau-Hasthasndr, tribe of the Seed who would spite the flow of life; Pashangali Jau-Hasthasndra, the wisewoman who had brought her lord to slaughter them all—

"We should sacrifice her," said a wisewoman. "Throw her off the Falls in repayment."

"We should sacrifice them all," said another. "Just to be safe. Just to appease Vashnarajan."

"No way in shiyalsha," said a third, "didn't you idiots hear a word the lady said, the sacrifices are *done,* that's the whole point—"

It was Nazum, loud and unimpressed. Ronoah hadn't said anything; neither had Chashakva. The boy was just finally fed up. He was speaking for himself, advocating for Pashangali as loud as he could.

No one took notice. Why would they? As far as they knew, Nazum was Ronoah's translator, the host to Runa's chthonic parasite. He was still only Runazum, half of a whole. He made his vain attempts, and smooth as a shiver of smoke Chashakva slipped in where the boy left off, translating Nazum's words alongside everyone else's for Ronoah's disoriented benefit.

"The Vashnarajandr understood balance better than any of us—would want the Jau-Hasthasndr sacrificed—maintain balance in the heartland—"

"Shut up Millikindra, no they didn't—extremists, they only wanted sacrifices done the traditional way—"

"So build a gallows and bring the Jau-Hasthasndr and make them—"

"But it has nothing to DO with them!" Nazum's retort was like the roar of the Falls: deafening and yet entirely unnoticed. Background noise. No matter how loud he yelled, everybody else was yelling, too, and his was simply not a voice that warranted listening.

"Vashnarajan was denied his people! His tribe! There needs to be penance for that—"

"Vashnarajan cares about self-sacrifice beyond anything else, his people were selfless and brave—obviously when Jau-Hasthasuna came for them they gave themselves willingly, if they thought it meant going back to their god—"

"Absolutely not, my warriors invaded the Vashnarajandr once and I saw the truth of them, they would want this injustice to—"

Abruptly, Nazum stopped trying. The boy sucked in an inhale; his very frame was vibrating. He made a small prevaricating movement—a rocking on his heels, up and down, like the very first night Ronoah had ever spent with him. He sighed long and low, said something in Chiropolene that Ronoah didn't catch, something about being sorry—

"I met Lady Vashnarajandra at the Tishpalaazndr border and she was a generous woman, she would tell us to let Vashnarajan sort it out in time—"

"Lady Vashnarajandra is dead, devoured by a sick corrupted Seed, and you would defend her devourer?"

"Do you have a better idea, Subindra? There's no more Lady Vashnarajandra so we have to decide for her—!"

The rebuttal cut off with a squeak, and then Chabra'i gasped, and Lady Chiibtandra put a hand to her mouth and stared in shock at Ronoah—everyone, everyone was staring at Ronoah, their hands midway through furious gesticulations, even Chashakva had turned to him and—no.

Not to him.

"All right, that any better? You bunch of egotistical *putrash* hear me now, ai?"

Ronoah turned his head.

Nazum was standing atop the Vashnarajandr chair.

"First of all, none of you knows the first thing about Vashnarajandr principles," the boy said, full of scathing derision. "This is like watching people trying to decide what the armadillo in the bush wants, how are you supposed to know? You en't an armadillo and chances are you never will be." Someone tried to say something, possibly to tell Nazum to get off the chair, but he stomped his foot and amazingly she fell silent. "SECOND of all, you're stupid as logs. Vashnarajan *became the creator*, there's literally no reason why he would *need* sacrifices anymore—apparently he's been the creator for years while all of you keep *supplying snacks to his nemesis*, so now that our lady's chopped the thing I think he's *more* than fine for food. Third of all, Pashangali, lady—when was the last time you talked to Jau-Hasthasuna? When was the last time you sat in your cabin muahahaing over how that oversized snake was gonna wipe out a tribe?" The boy's face creased in a consoling sort of grimace. "Never, that's when. You en't never spoken to the real thing, and if you had, I'm sure you'd've pitched yourself into another cenote for the shame of it. Whatever messed up way it grew en't just your fault—it's everyone else's too. Jau-Hasthasuna ate *all* the nasty sacrifices, which means every one of you banshees is responsible for making the thing that killed my tribe." His eyes flashed. "If you're gonna pitch blame, at least have the decency to pitch it fair."

"R—Nazum, enough." Marghat stepped forward, hands up placatingly. "Runa's always given you lots of freedom, and I know you're in Chashakva's favour, but this—you don't have the right to speak like this."

Nazum cocked an eyebrow at the wisewoman. "I heard that slip-up," he said. "You're not anywhere as smooth as you think you are. Runazum, right? Not worth my own name, so I get tacked onto his instead?" With a jolt, Ronoah realized Nazum was talking about him. "Lady, you don't know my name. You never bothered to ask. None of you did. The only ones what ever asked is them, sitting right there." He pointed, and Chashakva glinted quietly, pleased as a cat. "Sister, what's my name?"

Chashakva's lips curled into a winning smile.

"Nazum Vashnarajandr," she said.

"Too fucking right it is." Nazum's voice trembled—not out of fear but significance. Out of might. He took up all the space in the roundhouse, chased every shadow out the door. "Nazum Vashnarajandr. I am the last survivor of Vashnarajan's tribe. I lost my aunt Ziwa to a Pai-Zayyindr raid eight years ago, the twins Bar and Jukapta were taken by Hunanundra's brother at the Battle of the Chasauga River, we won four sacrifices outta your tribe when your mom was still in charge, Millikindra, and I've got the rest of the tally right here in case anyone wants to settle up. I am the greatest warrior of my generation. I am the best sacrifice Vashnarajan was ever given. It was only because of my selflessness that Runa and Chashakva could make it here to end the War. So now if you'll excuse me, I am going to take this seat seeing as no one in this rainforest is more qualified to sit in it than me."

And without another word, he plonked his scarred, snarky, impossibly important little body down on the chair, crossed one leg over the other, and waited for someone to try him.

Silence for about five seconds. Then Lady Rugakashndra burst out laughing.

"What are we doing, indulging this?" she guffawed, flapping a hand at Nazum. "This pageant has gone far enough—boy, even if you are Vashnarajan's kin, you cannot just claim wisewomanhood like so. There are traditions to uphold, lest you wish to dash the last fragments of your culture on the rocks."

"Last I checked," Nazum snapped, eyes afire, "culture's just a bunch of things that everyone's agreed to, stupid or no. Tradition serves the needs of the people, and I'm the only person what's left, so I'll uphold what I please."

"There are rituals to be observed," Lady Rugakashndra persisted, "rites of passage that prove you are worthy of—"

"Lady, if you want to throw me in the fasting hut, go for it. I've done it once already."

This statement threw Lady Rugakashndra just long enough for someone else to jump in—Lady Azm-ka-Habaundra, looking down her nose in distaste. "You can't," she said. "You're a host. You're a servant."

"I'm a servant to *Chashakva, god of the last age*," Nazum corrected, wagging a finger. He tilted his head in Chashakva's direction. "Hey. War's over. Free me."

Chashakva's smile split into her own grin, dazzling white against her dark face. "With pleasure."

"There," the boy said, waving Lady Azm-ka-Habaundra's complaint away, "issue resolved." Ronoah smiled despite himself—Nazum's abrasive personality actually fit him better when it had room to breathe. Perhaps the boy didn't remember, but Ronoah did: the words Chashakva had said when they first met Nazum, the promise she'd made if he was true to their cause. *The favour of the gods themselves may just descend upon you.* For a gleaming, oracular moment he could see it—a possible future, a beautiful victory. Nazum Vashnarajandr, most beloved of the heartland. Peacebringer of Shaipuri.

Lady Azm-ka-Habaundra wore a face like she was sucking on a lime. Lady Millikindra, on the other hand, didn't seem to think it needed to be so complicated. "You can't be a wisewoman," she said, hiding her smile behind her hand. "You have to be a *woman* to start." Ronoah flicked his gaze to Marghat, two seats down—she wasn't nodding along, but she was obviously uncomfortable with Nazum sitting where he was.

"Is that so?" The response didn't come from Nazum—it came from Lady Baramsulandra, folding her arms across her flat chest and glaring pointedly at Millikindra. "And here I thought the Millikindr were known for their high philosophy. What a disappointment, to hear something so backward."

Marghat did open her mouth at that, and so did Millikindra, and it might have become another all-out clash right there and then if Pashangali had not finally pushed her chair back and stood.

Ronoah knew Pashangali as an exceptionally brave woman. Brave where Chabra'i was fearless, where Marghat was daring; Pashangali had fears, and stood against them. She had done it daily for the three months Ronoah had spent in her company, and she did it now, shaking herself from her mourning and crossing the distance to Nazum. She stood before him, tall and taut and glaring—and then she got down on one knee, bowing her head in supplication. "Lady Vashnarajandra," she said, and the wisewomen stirred like disturbed reeds at her address. "My Seed has committed unforgiveable crimes against your people, and yet you spare me and mine. I am overwhelmed by your mercy." She looked up and met his gaze, and from Ronoah's vantage point he saw the fervour of her face, the ghost of the night where Nazum had knocked her flat with two decisive strikes. Her respect for him went back a long way.

With an exasperated crankiness that was utterly predictable, Nazum wrinkled his nose at her sincerity. "Yeah, yeah," he said as he pushed at her leg with his foot, trying to get her to stand. "I've got some friends in that swamp you call home, I'd rather not just off them all. I don't make friends easy." He jerked his chin at her. "But you owe me like a thousand jugs of that bogberry wine. Upon request."

A hint of a smile crossed Pashangali's still-stricken face. "I swear it," she said, and Nazum sighed and pushed harder with his foot and at last she relented and rose, twisting to face the Council. "As the wisewoman of the Vashnarajandr, and the connection to the creator of this age, Nazum has the sole and final right to decide the fate of the Jau-Hasthasndr people." She lifted her chin. "I will honour whatever she asks of me."

She. It was official now.

A murmur, a trickle of unrest—and then Chabra'i clapped her hands once, loudly enough to make a few translators flinch. "You know what, toss it, count me in." She grinned her feline grin, flicking her hair over her shoulder. "You're a cheeky bitch, Nazum, but you're a lucky one. You and Runa delved the underworld for the sake of my tribe—I'll take my chances on you."

"So will I." Ronoah's heart leapt. Marghat had stepped forward, Bashti holding her hand. Her smile was coy and playful, but Ronoah saw through to the uncertainty beneath, and it made him all the more grateful. "Nothing I appreciate more than someone willing to toss a stupid rule off the cliff, after all."

"Not that there has ever been a vote on this sort of thing," came Chashakva's voice behind Ronoah, "but if there were, you should know she has my support."

If he could say one thing of value, let it be now. Ronoah cleared his throat. "And mine," he said.

"And mine." Lady Umujandra rose from her seat and bowed to Nazum. "Lady Vashnarajandra, welcome to the Council of All Tribes."

Lady Naskarahandra was the next to accept Nazum; then it was Lady Baramsulandra. One by one, the wisewomen of Shaipuri acknowledged one more to their number. A few did not openly welcome Lady Vashnarajandra into the position—but they did not openly disdain her, either. After all, Chashakva was right. It was not actually the business of the Council to determine who could and could not be wisewoman. That privilege lay with the tribes themselves. They could find whatever fault they wanted with the situation, but it would not change the fact that Nazum had unassailable claim to that seat—if for no other reason than by default.

And so Vashnarajan's will was done, and Pashangali and the Jau-Hasthasndr were spared.

"Your new era is upon you," Chashakva said once all the exchanges had died down. Night was mellowing the sky out the smokehole. "From the Age of Chashakva into the Age of Vashnarajan. The Great Wheel has turned another cycle—and it seems it shall be a merciful one. You are fortunate. Not every cycle is." She inclined her head at Nazum, and for all the weeks and months she had spent bossing him around, she showed him nothing but deference now. "Would you care to mark the occasion?"

Nazum reclined in the seat that, possibly, had been destined for him the moment he drew that red-tipped lot when he was twelve. He took his time pondering; finally, he sucked his teeth. "Why not," he replied. He stood up, and as he went he reached and undid the ties binding his topknot and it fell loose around his face. He looked at the room of waiting faces—seemed to hesitate, shy for the first time in his life, and then he spotted Ronoah and one side of his mouth twisted up in a smirk as he regained himself. He took a deep breath, and began to sing.

The world lay lighter when he was done. A new age had been ushered in.

"Well." Chashakva's voice, rich as the timber of the roundhouse, smooth as the last splash of lavender light, brought them each gently back to themselves. "Even for warriors like yourselves, I would guess this day has been rather trying. It seems fitting to pause the proceedings with that cosmic kiss goodnight." She rose from her seat, outstretching an arm towards the exit. "There is much work yet to be done—starting with the matter of Jau-Hasthasuna's head. I doubt any of us will sleep well with *that* lurking just outside the door flap. If those responsible for the issue will follow me, we shall see what can be done to purify him before we send him at last to shiyalsha. Come."

'Those responsible' was literally everyone except for Ronoah and Nazum, and so very quickly they found themselves alone in the roundhouse. When the last person had left, Nazum waited about three seconds before letting out a loud *ayyeesh* that nearly sent Ronoah crashing into the nearest chair. "Sorry, brother," he said in Chiropolene, flopping back into his seat, "a whole lotta stuff just went down. So basically, when—"

"I know." Nazum looked up, surprised. Ronoah smiled at him—the brightest light in all of Shaipuri, the one person who could make things somehow feel normal. Even now. "I—I know. Chashakva was translating for me."

274

"Wow, she tells me to do the job for a year and doesn't even let me tell my own legend? My words not good enough for you anymore?" the boy demanded, brushing his hair back with an arrogance that made Ronoah burst out laughing, and then Nazum was laughing too, and for one last moment they were the same person, laughing identical laughs that swallowtailed through the rafters, laughs that said *can you believe we survived all of this? Isn't that amazing?*

Then it ended, their fits dying down, sound settling in the thatch, and they straightened and looked to one another and Ronoah knew they were severed. They were each only themselves again.

"You were a little busy," he managed. "I think—I think other people need your words now more than I do."

"Holy shit Runa are you going to cry about losing your babysitter because—"

"I am," he declared thickly, swatting at Nazum, "and your first real chore as wisewoman is to deal with it, Lady Vashnarajandra."

Lady Vashnarajandra cackled the same nasty crow's laugh she always had, and together they staggered into a nighttime flecked cool by the Falls, the ground rich and tender beneath their feet, the clouds patterned like one great night leopard's pelt stretching from sky to sky. They circumvented the oily stain that was all that remained of Jau-Hasthasuna's head, pilfered the storehouse for late-night snacks, and then they stole back to their hut and ate and talked about everything. Nazum divulged secrets about his time on the Chiropolene merchant ship, Ronoah revealed how he'd pulled off his trick with Chabra'i's cloves, they argued over which tribe had the best food—everything, everything. Far away in some queer, thoughtful part of Ronoah's mind, their unending conversation was likened to Bazzenine's paintings: wondrous, uncompromising, released from inhibition. Full of the desperate poignancy that all last chances are. Only one topic remained sealed; only one truth was off-limits. Ronoah pretended he didn't know it, permitted himself to live in Nazum's shining reality for just one night. They celebrated for hours, refilling their lamp once, then twice, their heads close together, their voices raucously loud and then furtively quiet, Chiropolene and Shaipurin and even Acharrioni mingling together under their roof.

And if, at some point in the darkest hours of morning, after even Ronoah and Nazum had bid each other goodnight, Chashakva slipped into their hut and made herself silent in a corner, Ronoah pretended he didn't know her, either.

THIRTY-TWO

*L*ASTING CHANGE TAKES A LONG TIME TO ROOT. Even the seemingly instant simmers secretly for years before it heaves up and happens—the slow build of pressure before the volcano erupts, the petty squabbles of shalledrim sects before the battle that causes the Shattering. It happens with good things, too: reparations, healings, changes you want with all your heart to witness. Sometimes despite all your efforts and your labours and your wanting, you do not get to see the final result before you go. You must learn to detach, to move on, once your part in the Great Wheel's turning is over.

Such was the case with the Council of All Tribes. Although the most dramatic issue was settled in a day, the most *important* issue had yet to be decided upon: what was going to happen next. The following morning was packed with discussions—what the wisewomen would tell their people, how the tribes could demonstrate their repentance and their forgiveness, what it meant to have a wisewoman with no tribe of her own but the entire people of Shaipuri under her god's protection. Evidently it was going to take several days to come to any solid decisions, possibly even another week. But upon breaking for lunch, Chashakva informed everyone that the shiyalshandr would not be sticking around for it.

"Our time in the overworld has run its course," she said. "We have completed our task, and Runa has relinquished Lady Vashnarajandra as his vessel, so we must hasten to shiyalsha. After all, you don't need us to teach you how to live." Her mouth curled up in a smile. "That's not our business."

Ronoah had sensed this coming, but it stung nonetheless that his *relinquishing* of Nazum was being used as the reason for their departure. That he was being used as an excuse. As one more piece in the game Chashakva was wrapping up.

When the time came for goodbyes, something happened that did surprise him: they came to him as a group, Chabra'i and Pashangali and Marghat and their translators, separate from the long line of blessings and platitudes that the rest of the wisewomen formed. They came to him together.

"Who would've thought that snarky little punk was actually Queen of the Heartland?" said Chabra'i by way of greeting, jerking her head in Nazum's direction. The boy was off talking to Chashakva. "Just goes to show how funny Vashnarajan is. I always thought there was some dark humour hiding behind that stiff traditionalism."

"It's going to take me a while to stop calling him Runazum," admitted Marghat. She pursed her lips. "Then again, I did it this morning by accident, and he told me he didn't actually mind so much."

"Trying to leverage your memory," laughed Chabra'i as she reached out and smacked Ronoah, "to keep us from overthrowing her. Oh, sorry, was that—?"

Chabra'i looked to Pashangali, who sighed. "Am I such a dewdrop to you?" she snapped, although Ronoah noted none of her real aggression in her tone. "You can tap her on the shoulder, Chabrai, I'm not going to keel over."

First, Ronoah thought *her?*—it had been so long since he'd been referred to in the feminine—and then he thought, *Chabrai?* "You'll never believe this, shiyalshandr," Chabra'i continued excitedly, her translator doubling her in slightly uneasy Jau-Hasthasndr, "but the Desecrated One over here and I got talking about how you helped her out with her third mind, and it turns out I just might have something in my apothecary that can take the edge off all that nausea."

"You've been—you're helping each other?" Ronoah said, squinting a little.

"A bold new dawn is upon us," intoned Marghat, giving every impression she would roll her eyes if she could.

"Here meaning Ma'aat's totally useless for it," Chabra'i chipped in, waving her hand flippantly at Marghat. "All those fancy skulls and she can't figure out what's going on inside this one." She tried to poke Pashangali in the head, but the woman dodged, glaring sharply.

Here, at last, were the distinctions of the Shaipurin languages revealed. Subtle, elegant. Marghat became Ma'aat, Marahat; Chabra'i became Chabrai, Chabrayyi. Even Pashangali's name, while not outright changed, sounded different from different mouths, the emphasis on syllables slightly altered. The only name they could all agree on, it seemed, was Runa's own.

"It's a shame you have to go so soon," Marghat said. "I'd've liked to petition Chashakva about—a few more things." Her biggest question, after all, hadn't been answered even by Chashakva's grand lie—*none of us meant to be eaten.* Ronoah didn't know whether he wanted Marghat to hold onto that uneasiness or to let it go, whether he could bear to direct her to Chashakva who would undoubtedly find a way to manipulate even this last shred of evidence to her will. He wound up saying nothing. "And I was planning on showing *you* a dance before you left, bit of a goodbye present." She ignored Pashangali's horrified snort and Chabra'i's rude cackle, rubbing a fleck of dirt off the ridge of one of her bird skulls. "I suppose it'll have to wait."

"Please, o Lord Vashnarajan, let Ma'aat die long before I do so I never have to see that, in this life or any other," Chabra'i said, prompting a swat from the Yacchatzndr wisewoman. As the two of them bickered back and forth, Pashangali ducked between them and drew close to Ronoah, staring into him with her serious eyes.

"I didn't know," was all she said, after a long, searching moment.

Didn't know what? About Jau-Hasthasuna? About Nazum? About Ronoah himself, about who he was, what he'd done? There were so many things she didn't know, that she would never know.

Ronoah nodded. "It's okay," he added, a little ineptly. "I don't know if—if you were supposed to."

There. The closest to truth he could get. She met his gaze, and he thought he saw some thin flake of grief lift up and away, and it would have to be enough.

"Will—I guess, I suppose—" She cast about for the words, uncharacteristically flustered. "Lady Vashnarajandra has omitted me and my people from guilt, but even so, I hope—if there's anything I must do to earn entry to shiyalsha..."

Oh.

That's what it was. That's why they weren't saying goodbye, why they were acting like they would see him again. Because from their perspective, they would. One day, after everything else was done, there would be shiyalsha, and Runa within it. An old friend in a new land.

"You're fine," he managed, hiding the tremble in his voice behind a laugh. "Everything's fine, now. Trust me."

Horrendously, she did. She lifted a hand to his cheek, her fingers barely brushing, and then withdrew; Chabra'i and Marghat broke up their fight in time to notice, and then it was an all-out contest of who was most in Runa's favour, and they pinched and poked and kissed and bit him until he yelped for them to stop and they also drew back, laughing. They shooed him off, waggling their eyebrows in suggestive manners, while Pashangali walked away, looked back, walked a little further, looked again. None of them actually said the words, not a one, and so he said them himself, under his breath, watching them traipse off to their Council and their lives: "Goodbye."

There was only one person left to see, then.

"Hey, demon boy." Without looking up from his lunch, Nazum patted the seat beside him. He did always have a sense for Ronoah's presence. It had been his job to. "Get over here, I gotta ask you something."

Ronoah sat, folding his hands in his lap. The boy made him wait until he had swallowed his mouthful of catfish; he took his time, now that he was entitled to it. At last he set the bones down. "You're off to that place you mentioned, ai? The Pilgrim Place or whatever it's called?"

"The Pilgrim State," Ronoah corrected reflexively.

"Yeah, that thing." Nazum picked a bit of flesh from the catfish bones, popped it into his mouth. "Once you get there, can you do me a favour and check for Vashnarajan?"

Ronoah blinked. A sense of unease crept upon him, slow as rising tide. "You said every god's got a home there," the boy continued, "so he's gotta be there somewhere, right? And if you don't find him can you like—I dunno, put some rope up for him?" Ronoah balked, and Nazum whacked him in the arm. "Not a *noose*, calm down, just—a nice braid of red rope hung up somewhere. A sacrifice where no one dies, right?" A little of the teasing drained from his expression. "I'll put in a good word for you with the ruler of the Age if you say yes. Fuck knows you need the good luck."

Yes, absolutely, of course I'll do that for you—these were the words Ronoah wanted to say. But for some reason he hesitated. He held his tongue, and he felt tears sting behind his eyes, and didn't know why.

Then Nazum squinted at him and he backpedalled and blurted out "Of course!" and the boy took his odd reaction for surprise because he shrugged and said, "You people taught me how little is actually out of reach. I'm taking it and running with it. If I have my way, there's gonna be a few changes coming to the heartland soon. Maybe to Bhun Jivakta, too."

"Maybe I'll come back," Ronoah said, half-joking, half-so-sincere, "and see how those changes are getting along."

Nazum burst out laughing, throwing his catfish bones at Ronoah. "Holy fuck no, never, get out of here and don't come back," he said, wiping imaginary tears from his eyes. "You're lucky you survived it the first time. You're exiled."

Something in Ronoah drew itself up. "I've dealt with exile before—"

"Shut up. You're banned from the rainforest and if I ever see you here again I will *let* Marghat dance for you." Nazum grinned his sharkish grin. He had the entire world at his fingers, and here he was, playing Ronoah's shield one last time. "People'd cause a ruckus if they saw you again anyway. Go back to your soft underworld, demon boy. Leave my queendom to me."

But he couldn't. They both knew it, looking at each other. Ronoah couldn't go back to his soft underworld, his tender heart, his trusting, honest ways. He had changed. Shaipuri had changed him. Shaipuri, and Nazum, and the wisewomen. Jau-Hasthasuna. Chashakva.

"Nazum," he said.

"Shut up," Nazum repeated, full of fondness and easy confidence and loss. "Go to your lady and leave, already. Tell her to make it flashy—I don't want anyone forgetting you for a long time."

And when Lady Vashnarajandra told you to do something, with that final look in her eye, you didn't object. He rose from his seat and turned to go, and he expected a last snarky remark or a caught wrist or something, he wanted that last fit of farewell even though he knew it would hurt, but Nazum let him go. Nazum released him with the grace that only a wisewoman could hold. He wasn't being cold. He was just in tune with the cycle, with all cycles, with the way this cycle ended.

It is the way of things.

Chashakva needed no telling how to make an exit. "Would you like to give them one last show?" she asked once he arrived at her side. She smiled her dangerous smile and gestured with a tilt of her head at the vista, the best spot to see the Falls, the edge of the plateau. He nodded.

In full view of the Council of All Tribes, Chashakva and Runa advanced to the precipice of shiyalsha. The god of the last age turned back, casting her gaze upon the wisewomen with the detached amusement that all gods had. "Live well," she called, a blessing, a challenge. She put her hand into Runa's, and they turned to the abyss, and together they stepped off.

It occurred to Ronoah that it should have been louder, brighter, possibly with more screaming on his part, but it was none of those things. He remembered when falling into a piddly bay in Chiropole had rattled him; now, leaping into one of the largest waterfalls on the planet, he felt no fear, no lurching panic. He was calm, quiet in his own mind. The world swung up around him and it was like plunging into the underworld for real, like hurtling towards the gates where he might meet the severed head of the god Jau-Hasthasuna, clear-eyed and speaking, and say sorry for all they had done.

Except it wasn't. Because shiyalsha didn't exist—not how he'd imagined it, not how Nazum imagined it, possibly not at all. Jau-Hasthasuna wasn't a god, or Subin, or Yacchatzul or even Vashnarajan.

And maybe they weren't alone in that. Maybe this was the closest you got to gods—misguided intentions, like the Shaipurin Seeds, or misplaced reverence, like the shalledrim gods of Tyro, or Chiropolene bedtime stories gone a little too far, believed a little too hard. Figments of imagination. Tools of manipulation. Pieces pushed in a game being played by something bigger and crueler than any of it.

Maybe real gods didn't exist.

The world a flurry of rainbows and white and the possibility suffusing everything, every fleck of spray, every mote of clattering light:

Maybe real gods don't exist.

On the shore downriver, Ronoah and Chashakva sorted through what supplies they had, goods undamaged by impact or water thanks to Chashakva's powers. Ronoah brushed his fingers over his satchel—leather, glass, Acharrioni, still whole after all this time. Still his. Inside, wrapped safely in waxcloth, was the book Kharoun had given to him when they'd parted ways, the book written by Maril Bi-Jelsihad over two hundred years ago. Wedged beside it, a piece of crystalroot, chipped carefully from the caves beneath Chalisto's Belt, the last left after their bartering on the Iphigene. And tucked between both, the *runa* pelt, golden and glossy and soft.

For an instant he felt the urge to pitch the whole bundle into the water. The sick impulse to throw the satchel as hard as he could and smash through the skin of the river like stabbing the body of a betraying Universe, to reverse the flow of his empathy and wound the world by wounding himself.

But the instant passed, and he dismissed it as melodramatic. That's stupid, he thought. Nothing will happen except you'll lose a good bag and some keepsakes. No point throwing it away when it's all you've got.

So he tucked the flap closed, tied it long so he could sling it over his shoulder. And then, pushing away the squirming dread as yet another bout of useless hysterics, he turned to Chashakva and asked the same thing he'd asked long ago, in the age before this one, an age of innocence and doubtless destiny: "So now that that's over with, how do we get to the Pilgrim State from here?"

Chashakva peered at him intently. He felt her probing, stealing in, felt her reaching to lay a finger on the broken detritus inside him and he shut her out, without knowing where he'd found the strength or the method, he expunged her to a safe perimeter and held her there, arm's length from his heart.

"I'm guessing Ay Hang's a little out of the way by now," he added, and the deadpan in his voice would have been perfectly funny if only it had been intentional.

Chashakva's face creased in a smile, a token appreciation of his token joke. "Just a smidgen," she replied. There was a mutedness to it, a lack of flamboyance, that whispered to Ronoah that the woman was working her way towards an apology.

"So what's our course?" He didn't want an apology. Not this time, not ever again. "Paddle back up the Sanaat and hope nobody notices? Burrow underground due north? Head to the East Ocean and get swimming?"

To Chashakva's credit, she did not press him. Whatever unforgiveable softness she held receded; her smile exaggerated, the smirk of an adventure's beginning plastered to her face, perfunctory, performative. "That last one's pretty close," she said. "Seeing as we've ended up this far southeast, I figure we might as well pay a visit to one last corner of the earth before we make our way to our destination."

Ronoah knew enough about Bereni geography to know there was only one nation further east than Shaipuri. "Ol-Penh," he said. Chashakva beamed.

"Haven't been to a proper library in a while, have you, little scholar?" she asked, her teasing overbright, overdone. "Perhaps we'll check out a volume or two for our walk up the Holy Corridor—that's the tract of land Ol-Penh retains that leads directly to the Pilgrim State. How about it?"

Libraries. Not just any libraries, but *the* library, the oldest of the Trans-Bereni system, the one that had started an exchange of knowledge lasting thousands of years. It was waiting out there, a jeweled egg in a nest of wonder and learning and innovation. One big bookish revelry and one straight, easy line to the end.

Ronoah nodded. "Sounds like fun," he agreed, hefting his bag on his shoulder where it was digging in. Again, something in Chashakva's sharp face softened, and he pressed, "Which way to start?"

And she relented. She even almost sighed. "This one," she said, twisting away and beginning down a path. She moved with her typical wealth of speed and certainty, and Ronoah followed her at his typical only-slightly-behind-her pace, and it was all typical and normal and fine. It was just like it had always been, and nothing was out of the ordinary, and it was fine. The sunlight came in golden green. The two-striped tarsiers scattered through trees. The pitcher plants lured their prey and trapped it and dissolved their wings their legs their bodies their tiny vibrating insectoid hearts. They swung gently from their vines, their nectar sweet as the wind.

Part Five

THE AGNOSTHESIAC

*O*F ALL THE MEMBERS *of the Wishgranter's sacred company, the Heretic Saint is perhaps the most controversial.*

This may be as a result of her recent addition to the canon (this was written thirty years ago, but even now her appointment's still under a century old) or else her birth overseas, her life and love and loyalty owed to those calamitous conquerors, the Qiao Sidhur. Certainly, the most salient factor is embedded in the name chosen for her by Ol-Penher theologians: in all the years of her life, even after three decades dwelling on Ol-Penher soil, the Heretic Saint never accepted Our Lady the Wishgranter as sovereign force in the Universe. Indeed, from what firsthand accounts survive it seems quite the opposite: like every great force the Heretic Saint clashed with in life, she chose to view the Wishgranter as an opponent *(emphasis mine, sorry), as a will capable of being tested, and bested, instead of simply served.*

It is unclear when she adopted this view; perhaps during her campaign against Ol-Penh, in the course of commanding her warriors against the Wishgranter's faithful, or else sometime after the stalemate wore her forces out, when she sailed overseas herself, to confront the Beloved and Borrowed Generals in the war tents of Trengkar An. Certain historians see the Flower Edicts as her first true move against Ol-Penh, the battle and bloodshed a mere prelude. Others question her very legitimacy as a saint, given no other saint in the company actively denied the Wish as truth absolute.

But (this part gave me chills when I first read it) as the most faithful understand, antagonism is another form of love. To challenge something is to deepen your bond with it. In other words, it is precisely the Heretic Saint's devoted opposition to Ol-Penh's Wishgranter that, when taken together with the deeply considered ways she altered the course of Ol-Penh's future, bolsters her credibility as a sacred model.

Like all saints, the Heretic Saint has accrued several monikers: the Silver

Saint, for her heritage, and the less-prevalent Dawn Hierophany, no doubt chosen for her east-laying cradle and for the new era one could say she 'dawned' upon Ol-Penh. She is, of course, known also by her mortal name, Saint Hanéong, and historians of a non-theological bent insist on referring to her by the title in her soldiers' mouths: Hanéong Qøngemtøn, or simply, in Ol-Penher, General Hanéong.

To speak of hierophanies, it is also worth noting the many miraculous aspects of the Heretic Saint's arrival to Ol-Penh. Oral traditions in the villages along her route each add new layers of mystery: Poh Nuir legend says a new fjord cracked for her when no port would allow her safe harbour. One village in Trengkar An's lowlands reported she made her way inland 'on a six-legged dragon, slick as a fish and fierce as a tiger'. Her weapon was generally known to be unwieldable except in her hands, an unusual sword with a blade like needlepoint, so thin as to be nearly invisible and so strong as to pierce a sternum. (It doesn't say so in here but you should know, objects that only one person can use or operate are commonly thought of as having celestial properties, or even sometimes as angels manifesting in solid form. So, big deal.)

Of course, the Flower Edicts remain the most important part of the Heretic Saint's story. When she arrived at the plum-coloured war pavilions of Trengkar An, the Beloved and Borrowed (—that's Phou-Rantrang and Makhab, who was ka-Khastan. Ol-Penh sent for aid after trying to fight the Qiao Sidhur alone for the first eight years; everyone here knows who they are, most of the time their names aren't written down; anyway, so, the Beloved and Borrowed—) were already strategizing about how to prune the remaining invaders from sovereign soil. The Beloved and her guerilla force of archers and acrobats sought to evict the Qiao Sidhur settlers through diplomacy, while the Borrowed's ten-thousand-strong army was prepared to handle the warriors' departure by force. The question was one of methodology; it was a forgone conclusion that the invading force had to be expunged. It was only when the Heretic Saint intruded on their congress and proposed her treaty that this conclusion was set on its side.

Who can say what she argued to convince them? The debate was unrecorded, the details lost to the changing vagaries of memory. The only document emergent from that wished encounter was the Edicts, that list of graces granted to nonmilitary-affiliated Qiao Sidhur settlers. The Elderflower Allowance, for their tradespeople; the Geranium Allowance, for their lovers, their Ol-Penh-born infants; the Aster Allowance, for their dead. Nine in all, a number chosen especially for its importance in both cultures, a vine entwining their fates. So ended the Silver Invasion; so arose the most drastic change to Ol-Penh's social landscape in recorded history. So began General Hanéong's legacy as the most unconventional saint the Wish has ever set into motion, a woman of innovative mind and industrious method, a strategist able to turn every loss into a gain, a champion for longshots and lost causes, for carving new truth out of old convention by whatever means necessary. For those who honour her, she is a symbol of just how fickle the fortunes of the Wish can be.

(It goes on like that, but most of the rest is mystics arguing semantics. Basically, Saint Hanéong was such an insurrectionist that she challenged the rules of engagement themselves, and then talked her way into those rules refashioning for her—honestly, kind of like the Wishgranter, opposing our very own two Dragons with an ask so big it shook the Universe into new shape. You need friction to get a spark, and her challenging the Wish as a Universal principle set exactly the transformative fire the Wishgranter needed. Make sense?)

THIRTY-THREE

*T*HE BAY OF YANYEL WAS A BRUSHSTROKE OF COBALT laid into the surrounding mountains, curlicue clear and mirror-bright. Towns clustered like bunches of oranges on its sandy coastline, fortified villages with buildings of white plaster and burnished terracotta; onion-capped spires sprouted from the bright froth of masonry, and lines of drystone wall spun in lacy filaments up the mountainsides to farms and old battlements. Apparently, the Bay of Yanyel had been formed by asteroid strike, the backsplash debris of the larger meteor that created the indent of ocean between Shaipuri and the Ol-Penher Peninsula tens or hundreds of thousands of years ago. The remnants of that cosmic visitor still lay somewhere on the seafloor, beyond noise, beyond light, quiet in its cradle the crater.

"These policy changes are *ridiculous*, I thought I had another *three years* before I had to renew this—"

Two hours into the wait in Yanyel's branch of the Ol-Penher Consulate, Ronoah was wishing for some quiet of his own.

Ol-Penh was unlike any place he had been before in many ways. One of those ways was that, unlike Tyro or Chiropole or Shaipuri, the bureaucrats of Ol-Penh actually kept track of the people that crossed its borders. As it turned out, not every nation in the world would just let you in with nothing more than a bit of side-eye; their very first task after disembarking was to apply for travel documentation at the Consulate, lest they be disallowed from entry into Ol-Penh proper. Ronoah supposed he should have seen it coming—Ol-Penh was the birthplace of libraries, of archives. It only made sense that they'd be a little obsessive with their recordkeeping.

Sensemaking though it was, that knowledge was cold comfort while sitting in a crowded room stacked to the rafters with babies wailing and

288

civil servants hollering ticket numbers and gaggles of people complaining directly into his ear.

He'd noticed a rack of books in a corner, seemingly placed there as talismans to ward off boredom, and he'd picked one up and was now hunched over it, flipping pages and scanning the unfamiliar, unreadable glyphs. The language Chashakva had given him didn't include the written word, but he wanted something to look at. Something to be busy with.

"They're called bureau rags," Chashakva commented, back from some excursion outside the waiting room. "And their history is utterly hilarious in its pragmatism, its cutthroat capitalism of your wasted time—you think we've been here long, oh no, Yanyel's a sweet port but it's on the skimpy side, we'll be through here in half the regular wait time of an Ol-Penher Consulate—you'd think after centuries of honing their civil sensibilities they'd've quickened the pace a bit, but here we are."

Ronoah turned a page.

"So, bureau rags. Somewhere after the six or seven hundredth brawl broke out in a Consulate waiting room, some genius in public relations thought to give these people something to *do* with all that fidget time, and they commissioned a slew of short stories and popped them on stands for people to peruse. Cheap, easy to produce—and nobody likes to read like the Ol-Penher. Caught on like wildfire." In his peripheral vision, Ronoah saw Chashakva point out a sheltered bench near the exit. "They even built designated reading areas in case you want to finish off the last couple chapters once your fishing license or your provincial tax papers are sorted. Epilogue Benches, they're called."

"Sounds creative," Ronoah said, eyes flicking to the bench before he fixed them firmly back on the book.

"But the truly fascinating thing about the bureau rags is they've transcended sheer functionality—in recent decades they've become a *genre*. They have their own tropes, their own flavour profiles, you can't just slap a lollipop cover on any old novella anymore, now there's *convention* to follow—there are even authors who specialize in rag writing, can you imagine, a whole class of artists profiting solely off the inefficiency of their public service sector, wouldn't the Chiropes appreciate that—"

Ronoah's fingers turned the page loudly enough for the sound to shear between them, the sharp rasp of paper abrading paper. The snap of it cut Chashakva short; he felt her gaze lingering on him. He glanced up, nodded some affirmative, hummed some sort of conciliatory indulgence, and returned his eyes to the words. After another moment, the elastic tension of her attention relented. She left him alone until their ticket was called, and when it was, she only rose and made a small gesture toward the kiosk, saying nothing. Ronoah got up and followed, one finger inserted between pages on ridiculous reflex, eyes trained at last on the back of his companion, now when she couldn't see him looking.

Chashakva was no longer Chashakva. She had taken care of that sometime on the ship between Auyyid Gar—"the Bhun Jivakta of the South"—and Yanyel, in the moonless space between sleeping and waking, shucked her body overnight and emerged stretching and fresh into next morning's sunrise. Gone was the planed, shaven Acharrioni with the hard hands and the supple bones; in its place was something unassuming, easygoing, something with rounded shoulders and tender limbs and underwhelming stature. Plump cheeks, grey eyes, a mouth made for smiling, all under a shock of silver hair coaxed into a short, neat sidesweep. She was nearly exactly Ronoah's height, maybe half an inch shorter, and a few months shy of his age as well, and Ronoah didn't actually know if she was still a woman or not; he couldn't tell by looking, and he wasn't about to ask.

It wasn't that he didn't like the new body. It was just—a little abrupt, for him. A little sudden. How quickly Chashakva could toss that dark, disquiet skin into the deep, banish it back to shiyalsha and pull on something more palatable. Discard battle armor for casual wear. How quickly she moved on.

He wasn't the only one made uneasy by his companion's latest mode of dress. People were looking at Chashakva funny—he'd noticed from the moment they walked in. *Specifically* Chashakva; unique though Ronoah was among the throngs of Yanyel, their eyes slid past him with mild interest and nothing more, but he sensed the stilted pause in the air when they saw her. He knew those stares, the concern mingling with distaste under the veneer of politesse. Years in Pilanova had taught him how to triangulate a troublemaker by the vector of those looks. In the heartland, Chashakva had chosen her body to facilitate their journey. Not this time. He didn't know what it was, but whatever she had done to herself made her stick out at an angle from everyone else. She had made herself the target of something—

But that was her business. It didn't matter to him what games she was playing with the locals; he had other things to think about.

"Good morning, and welcome to Ol-Penh! If you'll take your seats we can begin registration—"

Like navigating the Ol-Penher legal system with only one third of the language to work with. Not only did he lack the written script, he also lacked *handhalf*, the gestural lexicon that intertwined with spoken words to make up Classical Ol-Penher. He could still get by, Chashakva had assured him; plenty of tourists and visitors made do with what he had, which was essentially an aggressively-truncated version of Simplified Ol-Penher. He'd asked why she wouldn't give him the language in full, and she'd replied with something about how training the hands was different from training the tongue. *It's more invasive*, she'd said. Growing the spoken language in his mind, forcing those pathways, that muscle memory—*a cheap trick* she called it—was going to hurt enough already.

Well, that courtesy wasn't helping him now, sitting on a bolster in front of a civil servant he could only half-understand. The Ol-Penher man's left hand dipped and fluttered in rhythm with his speech even as he picked up a pen with his right. At least Ronoah wasn't in charge of his own paperwork.

"Now, even though you're traveling together you do need separate visas." Their attendant turned to him and asked, "Family name?"

"I—Elizzi-denna," he answered, hyper-aware of his hands folded still on the table.

"Given name?"

Runa, he thought. Cold tingled in his stomach. "Ronoah," he said. The attendant noted this, then asked his age, and what nation he was born in, and then his purpose in visiting Ol-Penh, and Ronoah was struck by the weird realization that he wasn't going to double back to ask if there were any other names to write down.

"The library," he said, an odd catch in his voice. "The—I'm here to see the library."

"No business," Chashakva intercepted smoothly, her fingers framing her words. "Just a leisurely trip to Khepsuong Phae before we head up the Holy Corridor."

"It's the off season," the attendant said, sounding oddly proud of them, like they'd done something clever in showing up when they had. He looped a sentence onto the paper. "You'll get to see the students in their natural environment. Gender?"

There followed an awkward moment where Ronoah opened his mouth and nothing came out. "Um—sorry, I don't, I'm not sure what—?"

"Term of address?" said the attendant. "Colour?" He plucked at the collar of his purple robes. "What you wish to be known for?"

"Your direction," murmured Chashakva in Acharrioni, and a hot flash of irritation leapt through Ronoah at the sound. You wouldn't have to translate, he thought, if you'd just done the job properly. That's why I asked you to do it. He would've taken another night of moaning pain into his pillow while his brain grew spikes inside his skull if it meant he could control his own conversations.

He didn't even know his options. He thought of his roles in Shaipuri, young man and wisewoman both, thought of himself on the Chiropolene plains, shawlless but covered just the same, thought of that sprinting dance that all Pilanova's wishgranters made from Pao to Innos or the other way around—and a dull ache bloomed in his chest, and he stopped thinking.

"I don't know," he said. "Is that an option?"

"Certainly." The attendant made a mark in a box, then asked after a detailed physical description and medical overview which Ronoah gratefully moved along to.

It very quickly became clear, just why it took three hours to be seen at the Ol-Penher Consulate. The list of questions was neverending in length and utterly bizarre in specificity. Lots of them were about things he didn't have the first clue how to answer, even with Chashakva's help, and left him feeling weirdly out of touch with himself. The attendant didn't seem to mind that he had to leave so many spaces blank; he just moved on to the next in an eternity of questions. Most of them slipped Ronoah's mind the moment after they were asked. But there was one, right near the end, that stuck.

"And just for our census data, do you accept and believe in Our Lady the Wishgranter?"

The breath lodged in Ronoah's throat. Wishgranter. *Wishgranter.* Like him, like his—? "I, I'm sorry, do I—?" The word echoed, *wishgranter,* tugging sympathetic on everything it connected to: a vast expanse of salt, glowing cold in the moonlight; a fire underground, burning steady by his hand. A waterfall, the largest in the world, and all the grief that lay beyond and beneath it. "...No." Something flickered in Chashakva's presence beside him. It made him set his jaw. "No, I don't."

Watching the attendant write this down, he felt a stab of regret— paradoxically, that was what prevented him from changing his answer, as he doubled down in retaliation to his own sense of guilt. It was just some regional lore, some local religion. It wasn't hurting anyone that he didn't believe in it. He shouldn't be offering his faith to every deity that popped out of a bush anyway, that kind of innocence was dangerous, it—

Not *dangerous*, something scoffed in his head, just unnecessary. Don't be so dramatic.

The attendant ticked some final boxes, penned some final signature, and the ink sank into the paper and set there, and it was done.

"All right." Ronoah would have interpreted it as clipped if he hadn't caught the accompanying gesture, one of the few handhalf signs he knew: the ring around the heart formed with thumb and first two fingers, the one that meant *thank you.* The attendant shuffled his papers, refilled his pen, and looked up at Chashakva. "Family name?"

"Kvanzhir."

"Given name?"

"Han Yang," she said, or seemed to say, and some small recognition flexed in the air above the attendant's hand. "Shall I spell it for you?"

Hvanzhir Hanéong. That was it, then; it was official. A new name for a new face, smooth and youthful and full of potential. A fresh start unmarred by worry, untarnished by guilt. Untroubled by all they had done.

For the first time ever, it seemed fake to him. Flimsy, like this new skin was prone to slip any minute. When Ronoah looked at his companion's magic, those wondrous transformations, he couldn't find anything to surprise him except for how worn out he felt in comparison.

Another hour and they had their visas signed and finalized—"valid for three months, after that you have to get them renewed"—and were officially allowed to pass through the Consulate into Yanyel, and with it, Ol-Penh. They passed the Epilogue Bench as they went; Ronoah laid the bureau rag facedown in the space beside two people sitting and reading. He gave it a small parting thanks, internally. It wasn't the first book he couldn't read that he'd nonetheless taken comfort in.

Hanéong took the lead once they came out onto Yanyel's uneven cobblestones, walking the sloping streets with jaunty strides. He—the paperwork had confirmed it—made lots of noises about the sun-bright architecture and the freesia-filled planter boxes and the gutters smoothed by centuries of runoff, about the famously funny nicknames the locals gave the unnamed streets, about how their numerical system worked in intervals and not absolutes and how that had enabled them to achieve great technological advances. He talked a lot, but, it felt, said very little. He certainly didn't say anything about how they were getting to Khepsuong Phae, and when Ronoah overcame his own silence to ask, he received only a wink and a smirk and a "wait and see".

Which was only fair, he supposed. He'd demanded normal, so normal was what he was going to get.

They emerged through a narrow alley into a market awash with colour, circling a central fountain that jetted water from the mouths of two entangled stone dragons. Groups of visitors examined their purchases on ironwork benches; locals haggled down the price on dyes and fabrics, exchanging strings of shell beads as currency; an artist had set up an easel under a carob tree and was sketching the fountain statuary, chewing absentmindedly on a pod. It looked to Ronoah like a party—petals scattered everywhere, everyone wearing these festive hues of lavender and lime and egg yolk yellow, the air alive with easy, careless optimism.

In their midst, he felt more like a demon than ever. Shiyalshandr walking where it didn't belong—

Stop it. He clenched his jaw, cut his melancholy short. *You're human, aren't you? Shaipuri is far behind you; leave it there. Enjoy the sights.*

Hanéong elbowed them through it all, homing in on one of the many garment stalls and selecting a long sleeveless vest cut from that same lavender fabric. After some scrutiny, the man also slid a long scarf of pink cotton from a peg. In easy, mellifluous Ol-Penher, he bargained for the garments with the stallkeeper; Ronoah noticed that their price never dropped much, but Hanéong didn't seem to mind. He withdrew a long strand of shell beads, cut a length of about six inches, and handed it over with a smile. Ronoah watched him re-knot the loose end afterward, shell slipping through his bronzed fingers like chips of coral and carmine.

The scarf, Ronoah was surprised to find out, was for him. "What do I do with it?" he asked, lifting it from Hanéong's outstretched arm.

The man shot him a playfully scornful look. "You wear it," he said, as he shrugged his vest on over his dark long-sleeved shirt. "On your waist, over your shoulders, on your head—doesn't matter. It's less for looks than convenience, though the Ol-Penher do appreciate a curated appearance." As if to underscore his point, he found a loose thread on the tail of the long garment; with a tisk, he pinched it out of existence.

"Convenience?" Ronoah asked, watching his companion twist to check the cut of the fabric from behind.

"Do you expect people to *guess* what to call you?" Satisfied with his inspection, Hanéong straightened back up. "That's how people know your colour—your direction, your social role. It's basically a big sign saying *think of me as such.*" His hands flashed through gestures—habitually it seemed, since Ronoah couldn't read them. "This lovely shade tells anyone within eyeshot that I consider myself a man. And you, you chose *none of the above* as your role, which makes you a *ngoh*, a step outside the classic Ol-Penher gender trine. It's a good thing pink flatters your complexion—you're going to be wearing a lot of it."

The word fluttered against Ronoah's mind, alit like a jay from a branch in the forest of new language Hanéong had planted there. So that's what it meant. He felt the context resolve and settle within him as he tied the scarf around his head. "What are the other colours?" he asked, pulling the trailing ends over his shoulder.

"Purple for men, pink for ngohk, as I said." Hanéong set off again through the market, pointing out people as they went. "Green's for women, and that lovely deep gold is for *taik*, the amphibians of the trine. Willing and able to be called upon for the responsibilities of both men and women, plus one or two extra." Like the artist in the square: Ronoah noted as he passed the cheery daffodil of their pants, the fluid flash of gold polish on their nails. Their rendering of the fountain now included a third figure. Looking up at the real thing, Ronoah caught the sculpture of a woman peering from behind the spiralling dragons. Or maybe a man, or another role—the stone was secret-keeping grey. It had no place in the paradigm he'd just learned, only a depth to its gaze that made him jolt, as if he was the one being watched and had only just realized.

The spray of the fountain hit his cheek, and he flinched and turned away, tripping over the gutter as he hurried to Hanéong's side.

The building Hanéong led them to was wide and shiny, with the sharp corners and unblemished bricks that suggested it had only been built a few years ago. They passed through tall brass double doors into an atrium echoing with the sounds of people passing to and fro, dragging children or luggage. Hanéong bought them passage to Khepsuong Phae; Ronoah didn't hear the details, distracted as he was by the sight of the same two dragons represented in mosaic on the ceiling. Before he could capture the full length of the creatures with his eye he was being tugged away down a corridor, and he was just thinking that maybe he would ask Hanéong about the dragons when the corridor opened up into a vaulting glass-domed hall and he saw the machines.

They were stationed in parallel, two of them, hulking and long, split into segmented carts. Pistons sat like coiled muscles, connected to tall chimney-like structures wafting steam. Whimsical scrollwork decorated the central cylinders, the guardrails; Ol-Penher names were painted in gold on their sides. They were *vehicles*, Ronoah realized. Connected like the camel trains of Acharrio, but with no load-pulling animals in sight, no energy source he could find, only beds of metal wheels as tall as he was.

"These," said Hanéong, in response to Ronoah's gasp, "are the water trains."

A laugh escaped him—so they *were* inspired by camel trains, or something like them, the homage was in the name. "How—how?" He knew from his time as a scholar that technology was making all sorts of leaps in other parts of the world, especially in the areas tied to the Trans-Bereni libraries, where the tradition of invention ran sap-strong in the blood of their residents. Centuries ago, Ka-Khasta's library city of Aç Sulsum had been the first to come up with a way to write without writing, carving letters onto blocks and arranging them into a cast that could stamp an infinite number of pages; his own Padjenne had built beautifully intricate astronomical clocks using gears and bells and flowing water, clocks so precise and farseeing they could even predict eclipses. The newfangled art of photography had come out of the library system, too—through its grainy, miraculous lens he'd been able to study snapshots of Old Chiropolene murals standing hundreds of miles away. But he'd never heard of anything like *this*—mechanical transportation on such a large scale? Covering the distance between cities?

"That's *incredible*," he said aloud, shoulders gone slack in his astonishment. Beside him, the sunny hum of Hanéong's pleasure.

"I've heard rumour of the railway system, but it wasn't here last I visited—the Ol-Penher are obsessively progressive, they revere their mad geniuses like they do their saints, always tinkering with their way of life. They must be only a few years into production." Hanéong touched his wrist to his mouth as if he was thinking, but his feigned nonchalance was belied by the hungry spark in his eye. "We have a few minutes before we need to board, if you'd like to tour the exterior ...?"

Ronoah didn't need asking twice. He was already making a beeline for the cluster of pistons and wheels at the front of a train, puzzling all the disparate pieces into a mental whole. Hanéong hurried after him and for a whirlwind five minutes they skirted the water train and pried into its secrets, skimming fingers along wheelspokes, crouching and jumping to glimpse inner workings, exclaiming at every new little understanding of the mechanics. They must have looked ridiculous, childish in their excitement, but Ronoah found he didn't care. Hanéong found some new detail and reached for Ronoah's hand, grabbing him to see, and Ronoah went eagerly and trustingly and with nothing but wonder on his mind.

It was like a veil had been lifted from Ol-Penh. As if the steam gushing from the water trains' chimneys had scoured away some grime coating Ronoah's own internal lens. His senses felt clear, keen, eager to drink up everything they could. The sleek iron lines of the trains, their glittering fittings of brass—and beyond that, to the skipping echo in the vaulted hall and the bend and flex of Ol-Penher sounds and hands and the swirls shaved into a man's hair and the billow of a tai's honey-coloured dress as they stepped through the narrow draft whistling between the cars.

See, he thought, deliciously overwhelmed, *this* is why you need to be present here and now. All this luster and shine, all this novelty—and just you wait. Soon you'll step into the oldest surviving library in the world.

A pang of anticipation chimed in his sternum, lit up the lines of his nerves. For the first time since he'd heard it was where they were going, Ronoah felt truly excited to go.

The conductor signalled a last-call warning and they quit their antics to board the train, grabbing cushioned seats facing one another across a table. Hanéong spread out the snacks he'd procured: hard-boiled eggs, shelled pistachios, basil flatbread sandwiches with goat cheese and pear. "After all," the man said, with a judicious crack of an egg against the table, "even the express route will take something like thirty hours."

Thirty hours. Just over a day to get halfway across the peninsula. What the traders of Acharrio would give for that kind of speed. Even Diadenna, lover as she was of the stark and solitary journey across the desert, would have been impressed.

They jolted in their seats as the train gave an initial shudder, and then they were rolling along the tracks leading out of the station, out of Yanyel, into the Ol-Penher countryside. The windows—they had beautifully clear glass here, where in the world did they get the sands for it?—were mobile and they wasted no time in throwing the latch so that the breeze sieved in from the hills and landed in their laps. Ronoah reached an arm through the window; the air parted around the wing of his hand, cool as water. He glued himself to the view, taking in the patchwork of fields and farms and olive groves, the scarlet cones of sumac, the shadows running riverlike in the dells.

Most strikingly, Ol-Penh's landscape was dotted with quartz crystals huge as tree trunks, raw chunks and spikes pushing up from the dirt like they themselves were growing. Sunlight prismed off their milky sides, threw rainbows into Ronoah's dazzled eyes. They were more than simple stone, according to Hanéong—there was something about the electric charge the crystals conducted that kept the earth rich and fertile, seeping nutrients into the soil at a seemingly inexhaustible rate. They were Ol-Penh's natural wonders, its most precious and protected feature, the source of the region's endless good harvest.

It should have gone well from there, a leisurely, lighthearted tour of the Southern Ol-Penher countryside. It should have stayed that easy—it *should* have. But Hanéong made a remark, just a passing comment, and Ronoah's fluttering enjoyment was pinned midair.

"Some say they're the old bones of the Wishgranter," the man said, lifting his chin to a block of quartz in the center of a melon patch. "A hotly-contested opinion among the sects, but in any case, people agree they're not to be trifled with ..."

The rest faded out, eclipsed by that word. That name. *Wishgranter.* Ronoah remembered it from the Consulate; he remembered the twisty emotion that had come with it, the dread, the dragging heaviness. *Do you believe...?* And then the rest that came, too: a garnet sparkling as it passed from one hand to another, a pair of sinkhole-black eyes going cloudy with death. A friend no longer trustworthy, no longer safe.

He hugged his middle, trying to defend against the same curling, clenching feeling. It was so stupid that a word was making him feel like this. It was unreasonable, melodramatic. It certainly shouldn't be able to ruin such a nice time. But it was, and it was too late to shove it down and pretend otherwise—Hanéong had noticed him disengaging, Ronoah could tell by the way the man had trailed off, by the awkward ring of his silence. In a blink, the lively thing between them fizzled out, leaving them as nothing more than what they already were: a boy, and a god, and a game too cruel to stand.

It hurt worse, after a moment of peace. After forgetting, even for an instant. Sensing that softness, that opening, the unnameable things in Ronoah brought their claws out resharpened, accusations and confessions all trying to tear through the protective barrier he'd put around them, conflicting, confusing—exhausting. Silencing them was exhausting. But he did it. The alternative was unthinkable.

"Any idea what you'll look for first in the library?" Apparently trying to breach the tension, Hanéong switched subjects, voice carefully light. "They might still have that replica crystal cave in the geology section. Like in Amimna's story."

The scene painted itself anew in Ronoah's mind. He thought of tiger-faced androgynes, and snow gardens and plains of black glass. He thought of a journey made in vain.

"I don't know," he said. He faced the window. "I'm still considering."

The power in Hanéong's lingering gaze—the, the *pity*?—made him want to scrunch his eyes shut, but he forced his face neutral. He fixed his gaze on the blue distance, letting the scenery roll over him as if it could form another layer between him and all the things he couldn't bear to touch.

"No need to be too choosy," Hanéong said softly. "We have all the time you like."

The train turned a curve; a shaft of sunlight fell across Ronoah's arm. He pulled away, into the shade.

It was going to be a long ride.

THIRTY-FOUR

$\mathcal{K}$HEPSUONG PHAE CAME UPON THEM like wavebreak on the surf. The sandy stretch of hours aboard the train was met by the tumble and froth of the city, seeping and sprawling up around them in what seemed the very final minutes of their journey. With a last screech of halting wheels, they disembarked in a station that made Yanyel's seem like a toolshed in comparison. They descended the wide stairs, discarded yesterday's snack wrappings, and ventured out into the city's core, navigating alamedas and steep alleyways toward Khepsuong Phae's greatest and most infamous attraction.

Precisely which trees swayed above the promenade, or what shops lined the paved streets—that was all lost to Ronoah. He gave his surroundings a cursory sweep, enough to note that Khepsuong Phae looked like a bigger, more exuberant Yanyel, and then he turned his attention to his destination, refusing to be distracted. The city's particulars blurred, background noise drowned out by the great peal of the library calling. All he could think about was how impossibly large it would be, how easy it would be to lose himself, blissfully inconsequential, in that largesse. It sounded cowardly when he thought about it that way but that's what it was: a desire to disappear inside something too grand and implacable to notice.

The need to get some distance from Hanéong was grating on him, hard. The man hadn't done anything *wrong* on their way here, or said anything to frustrate Ronoah. Hanéong just had this terrible knack for making Ronoah aware of himself, just by being there. It didn't seem likely that Ronoah would be able to properly sink into the library with that presence forcing self-consciousness upon him; he just wouldn't be able to enjoy the experience the same way. And he needed to enjoy this. After everything that had happened, everything he'd done to get here, he—he needed to enjoy this.

So when Khepsuong Phae's library, the first and oldest in all the world, finally arced up around them, Ronoah was quick to shake loose.

"They have some new acquisitions from Shaipuri," Hanéong noted; a sick jolt went through Ronoah before he realized the man had actually said *Jalipuri*, the soft consonants muddled in the foyer's echo of activity. "The Completed Works of Maqqat Zadhya, one of Jalipuri's foremost poets—she's doing incredible things for that language, airing out all the musty old meters—and look at *this*, they've got a traveling collection from Aç Sulsum on Evnism, I might as well drag you to see that, seeing as—"

"How about we take some time to look at things separately first?" It came like a river stone out of his mouth, smooth but hard. Hanéong paused reading the welcome sign to look at Ronoah; immediately he felt like he'd been caught at something, and his gesture down the hall was a little more jerky than he'd wanted. "I'm heading this way. Meet back here in—" how long? his eyes hooked into the clock above the circulation desk "—two hours?"

He had no idea if that was right to ask for. It felt both like a stressfully short allowance and like far too long than was polite. But Hanéong acquiesced all the same, waving Ronoah off with an airy dismissiveness that nicked Ronoah's heart as it glanced off him. Instinctively he tried to go looking in the man's face for something deeper, some air-clearing honesty— but he caught himself. With the strange, elated guilt of getting what you probably don't deserve, he turned on his heel and retreated into the stacks.

So, he thought, you're here now. Might as well make the most of it.

Ol-Penh's legendary library unfurled around him like a gold-gilt chrysanthemum, revealing polished halls and echoing vestibules and sheltered, shelf-lined nooks one after another. He did his best to give it the appreciation that it warranted. It was a different kind of reveling from the water trains: it lacked that glorious spontaneity, that inspiring sense of surprise. It wasn't his typical bibliophilia either, all held breath and heart-in-throat as he scurried gawking from one curiosity to another. Instead it was a carefully focused enjoyment, channelled, fuelled by the sheer determination to have this be remembered later as an uncomplicatedly nice experience. The fact that it couldn't just come naturally was a disappointment—but disappointment was a dark smudge on the moment, so he marshalled that, too, playing gatekeeper to his emotions with a swiftness and a strength that astonished the part of him primed to notice its own changing shape. *When did you get good at this?* it wanted to know. Haven't you always been terrible at this sort of self-management? How did you suddenly find such solid command of yourself?

Even these questions, mostly admiring in nature, were confined to the back of his mind. Considering them meant considering something other than the library. And the library was what he was here for.

The good news was the library of Khepsuong Phae was every bit as alluring as he'd hoped, every bit as capable of drawing him out of himself. It was the ideal place to wander, to linger, to be lost. The architecture, smooth strong lines of force and intention, old wood, older stone, columns and crosswalks and the great illuminated ceiling; the endless multitude of books, books in all shapes and makes, the thought of this much knowledge housed under one roof, the tactile reality of tooled leather and toothed paper and printed velveteen; the old thrill of *seeking*, of roving fields of books gleaning for one he could actually read. Many were in Ol-Penher, but this was Khepsuong Phae, the largest collection of texts on the planet—there were whole wings of books written in other languages, and all it took was a quick inquiry at a lending desk to locate them. He arrived in the Chiropolene section with an hour to spare.

He found the ladder and brought it to rest against the shelf, climbing up and reaching for the seventh row. His fingers landed on the first in a quintet of burgundy tomes. *A Chronicle of The Chiro-ka-Khastan Invasions, Vol. One.* He didn't even come down to the ground; he just cracked it open, right there, and the familiar Chiropolene script caught his eye like an embrace from an old friend, and the whiff of dust and ink whisked away the last of his ambivalence, and finally his quest to immerse himself in the library succeeded, as effort itself dissolved.

He might've stayed there until closing time, if someone hadn't poked him in the shoulder.

Alarm blazed in his body as he was ripped from some clifftop ka-Khastan military tent and he nearly pitched off the ladder, barking his knuckles on a rung as he threw a hand out to steady himself. He glared down, already drawing breath to tell Hanéong that startling him had gotten old a year ago—and a distinctly not-Hanéong face peered back at him.

One wild moment scrambling to switch from admonishment to civility: "What are you—what are you looking for?" That made it sound like he was a librarian, and a rude one at that. He tried not to grimace.

"Something up top." His interrupter knocked on the ladder pointedly with one hand, signing Ol-Penher handhalf with the other—hands laced at the wrist with chiffon sleeves the light yellow of lemon meringue. A tai. "There's only one ladder for this section, you know."

Trust him to accidentally hog the high ground. "Sorry," he said, ears burning. He hopped off the ladder and got out of the tai's way as they grabbed it and maneuvered it two shelves down. He probably should have made a quick getaway while they were distracted picking and pulling at books, only he was still clutching *Chiro-ka-Khastan Invasions* and he wasn't planning on checking it out of the library and he couldn't put it back without the currently-occupied ladder and it scandalized him to think of just putting it anywhere and leaving, and so he was forced to stew there in his embarrassment while the tai fetched their tome, wondering if he should say something so he didn't just look weirdly possessive of the ladder—

Apparently some things never changed.

A frustrated sound brought Ronoah back. The tai was reshelving another book with a huff. "Can I help you find something?" he asked, struck by the sudden want to improve their first impression of him.

They turned their head in his direction. "What?"

"I—what are you looking for?" Yet again, he cursed his inability to communicate in full Classical Ol-Penher. Having it wedged in his head the way it was made it hard to know if he was actually saying the right things.

The tai dragged one hand across the titles on the shelf. "Raphmales' *Meditations on Biodiversity*. Had a hold on it and everything, only I had a thing when I was supposed to pick it up, so they reshelved it and I had to pay half a thumb of shell—"

"That's the *P* section," Ronoah interrupted carefully, pointing. The tai scowled in surprise at the lettering on the spines; as they scanned the titles, Ronoah came and examined the shelf at eye-height, two below where they were searching, and found the name *Raphmales* on half a dozen books of varying sizes. He squinted. "Smallish, blue cover?"

"Should be?"

He slipped it out and handed it up to the tai on the ladder. They skimmed the cover, their eyes flicking disbelievingly back to the shelf.

"Dragon's tits, those letters look *exactly the same*."

"There's a swash off the right of the P," said Ronoah, as if he hadn't made this mistake on and off for fourteen months in Padjenne before Amimna corrected him for good.

"My Chiropolene's not great," they admitted as they wrapped a hand around the side of the ladder and swung down. Ronoah stifled a gasp—they were five feet in the air and the hall was narrow—but they landed light as a dancer, the dark mustard fabric of their culottes fluttering. They tucked the book under one arm to free up their handhalf: "You do know there's a reading room back there, right? You'll strain your neck hovering over books like that."

And despite Ronoah's plan to replace *Chiro-ka-Khastan Invasions* and retreat to the foyer, he found himself allowing the tai to steer him out of the aisle and back to the main quadrangle of the Chiropolene section, a modest but well-appointed space with rows of dark reading desks interspersed with the odd globe. Startled to be having this interaction at all, a blunt question stumbled out of him: "Why take out a Chiropolene book if you can't read Chiropolene?"

The tai spun him around by the shoulders so they were facing each other. "Okay, first of all, I can *read Chiropolene*," they said, hands flashing, "I'm just not good at fancy script, and second of all, the Ol-Penher translation of Raphmales' work has this weird pompous undertone to it that seriously distracts me, it's hard enough finding good unbiased shalledrology references as it is—"

Something struck Ronoah below his sternum, sharp as the coldest underground river.

"Sorry—did you say shalledrim?" he asked. The tai gave a little head wobble, the Ol-Penher affirmative, and internal vertigo passed over him like a shadow.

People knew what shalledrim were in Ol-Penh. That's right—they had a whole museum of shalledrim artifacts attached to the library, if he remembered right. They were common knowledge here, a cornerstone as ubiquitous as anywhere else on North Berena. It was a stark reminder that he was out of the shady insulation of Shaipuri, where no one knew the creatures had ever existed, and back into—what? The normal world? Reality? Neither of those felt right to say. He bit the inside of his cheek, hearing Nazum's voice asking what the *kulim putrash* a shalledra was—

Don't think about that, he told himself. Just—don't.

"What makes Raphmales a good source?" he asked the tai as they found two empty desks. "There's endless misconception surrounding the shalledrim."

"True. But he was around during the Great Decline, when the hunts were really gearing up. He was a famous naturalist—don't know if he originally came from ka-Khasta or not. According to his biography, he was summoned to Tyro when they caught Shannonai in 4232 to perform a full analysis on the body, and then he published the results, including this—see, what did I tell you about straining your muscles?"

Ronoah's hand was on the back of his neck. He hadn't noticed. Quelling the eerie pressure that flickered there, he clasped his hands in his lap.

So followed the first truly intellectual conversation Ronoah had had about the shalledrim since Kharoun. His partner was no superficial scholar, either. Ean-Bei—that was their name—was a student of at least half a dozen disciplines, from shalledrology to agriculture to political theory to Tyrene mythology, and gifted with the acuity to network ideas from these disparate fields together in order to make their points. Ronoah had never seen a mind so quick to ricochet between thoughts, apart from his own; it was astoundingly refreshing. They had to sit very close together to talk, nearly head-to-head, because Ronoah didn't know handhalf and Ean-Bei was hard of hearing. It was a common thing in Ol-Penh, he learned. His hands twitched with guilt, ineffectual on his lap, but Ean-Bei said they could hear well enough in a quiet space like the library. "Then again, indoor voices," they joked, flashing a smile that revealed a chipped canine. At Ronoah's request, they coached him on a couple basic gestures, yes and no and the fairly ironic *sorry, I don't use handhalf,* traces of gold glitter gleaming on the backs of their hands. They had skin like almond butter, smooth and speckled everywhere with tiny dark freckles, and ears that stuck out comically, and a bouncy crop of brown hair that fluffed whenever they wobbled their head, which was often. They were an altogether disarming personality; of all things, they reminded Ronoah a little of Hexiphines, what he might become in another five years' time.

"I haven't seen you at any of the shalledrology lectures this term," Ean-Bei eventually said, pinky curling into a handhalf question mark. "Did you just enroll? How long have you been studying?"

"Oh, I'm not—" Ronoah rapped on his sternum with his knuckles, the gesture for *sorry.* "I'm not studying anything. I mean I was, I did, a long time ago in Padjenne—"

"Oh wow, so *that's* what you are," Ean-Bei exclaimed, leaning forward with their chin in their hand like they'd been trying to figure him out since they sat down together. "A visiting scholar from the South. You're Lavolani?"

"Acharrioni, actually," Ronoah said, and to his surprise, for the first time since he could remember, the words filled him with satisfaction instead of shame. "From Pilanova."

"That's the place with the salt flats, right?"

Ronoah's eyes went wide. "Um, *yes,* actually." Of all the people he'd met since crossing the ocean, no one had ever heard of Pilanova. Ol-Penh really was the hub of all knowledge, if even that quiet, irrelevant city was known to them. He flipped a questioning pinky finger at Ean-Bei, who shrugged with a nonchalance that did nothing to dispel how clearly self-satisfied they were.

"I know a bit about everything," they said. "Keeps me from getting bored. That's a long way, Acharrio to here—there's a six-hour dawn delay? Seven?" Ronoah had never considered that before, but it was true; back home, a new day was probably just beginning. He thought of his family rising to their morning chores, and a creamy dollop of yearning warmed his chest. He wouldn't have minded sweeping the yard today, or sand-rinsing the dishes, before heading to the temple—

The feeling curdled just as Ean-Bei asked, "So what brings you all the way out here?"

"I—" The answer hovered, waiting, the answer he'd always given, the shining bit of destiny that had guided him all this way. That place on the other end of the Holy Corridor, that place his godling had called him to. "I'm—here to see the library, like you said. I've always wanted to see the other Trans-Bereni libraries."

Ean-Bei made an admiring noise. "That's ambition right there. Saving Aç Sulsum for last?" Ronoah nodded. "Are you gonna hit the Pilgrim State on the way up?"

Under the table, he clenched his fists.

"Maybe," he said.

"You might as well, it's the easiest route between here and ka-Khasta anyway. Hey, so you're fluent in Chiropolene, right?" Ronoah blinked, the fog of the moment passing. "Like, you could read this no problem?" They tapped *Meditations on Biodiversity* on the edge of the desk.

In a reversal that would have shocked a younger Ronoah, he was actually much more comfortable speaking Chiropolene than reading it—but there was a sudden impulse to impress, to see where the conversation would go, to taste the electric fizz of another little lie. "Probably."

Ean-Bei's freckled face split into a grin. "This is so wished, running into you like this, because I have this friend I think you'd get along really well with, and she's working on a thesis that includes some Chiropolene references, only her Chiropolene's shit. I'm seeing her for dinner tonight with another friend—do you want to come? You could talk to her about it and see if you're interested."

This was quite possibly the first time Ronoah had been invited to dinner in his life, family gatherings notwithstanding. After an initial second of complete bewilderment, he nodded, changing it midway into an Ol-Penher head wobble. "Sure."

"Great, I'll let her know to—oh, and. And!" Ean-Bei's hands fluttered exuberant patterns, their gestures getting ahead of their words. "There's another thing before that, an acro show, you might really enjoy it, there's going to be wheel and pole and I think Yengh-Sier's bringing out the dragon poi—you know what, just trust me," they said, interrupting themself laughing at the blank look on Ronoah's face, "just come see. You're new to Ol-Penh, you can't *not* see an acro show."

Well, he had already agreed to dinner. Why not one more thing? "I'll trust you," he said, prompting Ean-Bei to give him a triumphant little slap on the back of the hand.

"Great, here's the address—" They whipped a piece of paper out from a cubby in the desk, tore off a strip and scribbled something down. Before Ronoah could think to tell them he couldn't read Ol-Penher, he saw them write what looked like directions in careful Chiropolene. His shoulders softened, caught off-guard by the tai's thoughtfulness. "It's at seven, so you've got a couple hours to do whatever—"

And that's when Ronoah remembered Hanéong.

He knocked his chair back as he jumped up, snatching the paper from Ean-Bei. "I might, I might bring someone, if that's okay?" he asked, and he just barely saw them gesture a yes before he was leaving, knocking a sorry on his sternum as he called "I'll see you there!" and then turning to zigzag back through the library, tripping over his own haste.

He drew up short just before the main quadrangle, breathing hard, nearly an hour late. He hung back at the corner, scouting the room for Hanéong; he couldn't find the man, not anywhere, and old memories of sitting alone on a fence in Ithos spiked his apprehension, unmade all his stubborn independence, for a fleeting instant made him regret sending the man away—but then he looked again and found him easily, a silver head in a room of chestnut-brown and honey-red, tucked on a bench and engrossed in a book.

He'd been looking for the wrong thing again. For dark limbs and shaved head and looming hunter's presence, for a smile not yet strained by impassable distance. For Chashakva. Seeing Hanéong as he was now, newskinned and apparently content, strangled Ronoah's guilt with resentment. For a moment he watched the man reading, and considered not inviting him, not going to him at all, considered just walking out of the library alone.

Why would you do that? a voice asked, appalled, and his anger was squashed by more guilt in turn. That doesn't make any sense; that's your companion, your friend. You've walked a continent together. What's wrong with you, that you would think to just run away without so much as an explanation?

He didn't know. He really didn't. So he hurried over and made his apologies, unsure whether he was relieved or not when Hanéong shooed them away with a familiar, forgiving hand. The man asked whether he'd found something interesting in his wanderings, and Ronoah filled him in on meeting Ean-Bei, and on their new evening plans.

"Well look at you, little pilgrim," Hanéong said. His grey eyes were full of pride, a pair of clouds veiling a sparkling starry sky. "Come a long way from huddling quiet in a coffeeshop now, haven't you?"

Ronoah's belly clenched. He covered it with a shrug. "Life is transformation," he said, the old Pilanovani aphorism, the saying that simultaneously smoothed and disturbed the unquiet mire of his heart. Long way, indeed. For the first time since they'd met, he was the one lighting their path, leading their way. He was deciding their future, and Hanéong was falling in line. In another life, he would have called them equals for it.

THIRTY-FIVE

*T*HEY ARRIVED AT THE AMPHITHEATRE just as the sun was setting behind the mountains, the reaching fingers of afternoon light withdrawing into evening. Lamps were already being lit along the promenades, swaying with the cool gusts of wind. Ronoah watched the lamplighters at work through the open layers of the amphitheatre's architecture as he stood in line with Hanéong to purchase tickets.

He wasn't exactly sure how much they cost; everyone seemed to be handing over different lengths of shell bead, and there was no haggling that he could hear. Perhaps it had to do with social status. If so, the arm's length of pink shell Hanéong handed over should have put them in pretty high regard. The woman at the ticket booth regarded them with cool civility anyway—regarded Hanéong, that is. Again, Ronoah wondered what it was that was casting such a shadow on the man. He was mulling it over, following Hanéong's lead in the hunt for good seats, when Ean-Bei intercepted them.

"Hey, Elizzi-denna, over here!"

Ronoah looked up, mostly out of the sharp shock of hearing those names, and there the tai was, ferreting between milling showgoers until they popped up in front of Ronoah. They wore a swishy jumpsuit patterned with the black and marigold detail of a butterfly, and their forearms and face were done up in swirls of glitter and gleaming paint; it was by this costume that Ronoah realized Ean-Bei had invited him to a show they were part of.

Something warm ached inside him. It had been a long time since he'd watched friends perform onstage.

"I'm so glad you showed up!" they were saying, hands framing their face in what Ronoah took to be the gesture for happiness. "I know it was short notice, I can never make it to same-day things, my schedule's just too packed, so thanks, it's totally gonna be worth it—" Their hands paused mid-movement even as their words trailed on; they'd been distracted by something. It only took a shifting of their eyes to figure out what it was: "And this is …?" they said after recovering themself, gesturing to Hanéong.

That didn't sound particularly enthusiastic. Ronoah swallowed. "This is—my friend, Hvanzhir Hanéong," he said.

"What?"

"He's—" It was a lot harder to talk to Ean-Bei in the amphitheatre, crowded and noisy. He leaned in, tried to raise his voice. The tai seemed to understand this time—but again, Ronoah caught the telltale shift of their eyes to the right, and saw a flicker of pale handhalf out of the corner of his own vision, and knew it was because Hanéong was making his own introduction. He clenched his fists at his sides, trying to ball up the frustration tingling in his palms. Yet again, Hanéong's refusal to implant handhalf in him was getting in the way.

Ean-Bei was wobbling their head along to whatever Hanéong was saying, but it seemed a little restrained. "Neat, welcome to Ol-Penh, glad you could come tonight. Ronoah, actually I've got something to show you—" Before Ronoah could protest, Ean-Bei had grabbed his arm and pulled him away to a quieter corner of the amphitheatre, in the shadow near one of the exits.

"No offense, friend," they said, with a glance behind them, "but what's got you hanging out with, ah, someone like him?"

For a surreal second all Ronoah could think was *someone like him? A something-worse-than-a-shalledra?* with a twin surge of bitterness and alarm. Ean-Bei brought their hands up as if stalling for time, then continued in a voice whose unease poked through like sharp rocks in the river of their amiability. "Look, you just got here so I don't know if you know this, but …okay, so Khepsuong Phae is a super progressive city, people from all over the world come to learn or live here. I mean, Ol-Penh in general—we've got all kinds, trust me. There are just …some people who don't fit in as well as the rest. Like the Sithies—the people from Qiao Sidh?"

It was like a lamp had been lit in the promenade of Ronoah's own mind, illuminating his companion's new form, revealing the details of everyone's distaste. So it wasn't Hanéong himself, it was …his birthplace? "What makes them stick out?"

But Ean-Bei only shook their head, their bouncy brown hair swishing. "It's a long story, this is the wrong place for it. I'm already cutting it close—the show's about to start. Is he coming to dinner, too?"

And it was not unkind, but Ronoah felt the stilted pause before the question, tasted the sandy taste of buried significance, of politeness mask-ing honesty, and maybe it was the familiarity of that flavour that woke the old Pilanovani instinct to keep peace, maybe that's why he found himself blurting, "No, he's just here for the show. He's got—plans, after."

His sense of decency uncurled from his gut, chilly with reproach; he countered it with fierce objectivity. Didn't Hanéong always have some-thing to do? *Trouble to get into and out of again?* Ronoah didn't have to visit that trouble upon his new friend if he could help it. Hanéong would probably be glad of some time away from Ronoah anyway.

The way Ean-Bei relaxed further quashed the rumblings of his conscience. "Okay then!" they replied. "I'll see you at the south entrance once things are over—sorry to dump this on you and run, I was just surprised. I'll explain later. Enjoy the show!" They squeezed Ronoah on the shoulder as they passed him, shimmying away to disappear around the curve of the amphitheatre's risers.

Which left Ronoah to find his way back to Hanéong, to sit down and lean over and ask, in irritated Chiropolene, "Why didn't you tell me you were a Sithie?"

Hanéong raised silvery eyebrows over his pale grey eyes. "I didn't know it would be important to you," was his answer.

Ronoah balked. "It's important to me if you're dressed up as a, a *social pariah*—why do they dislike you so much? The Sithies, I mean."

"Only the Ol-Penher call them that. The correct term is Qiao Sidhur." Hanéong leaned his cheek into his hand. When he spoke, Ronoah was surprised to detect none of the ensnaring pleasure the man usually took in his storytelling; it was delivered plain, unwhimsical. "Not too long ago, the Qiao Sidhur made an ill-advised attempt at conquest, sailing west from their Empire to the shores of Ol-Penh. It ended quickly enough: one incursion too many and Ol-Penh called in their allies from ka-Khasta, and the Qiao Sidhur put their hands up and feigned innocence. Some of them stuck around, though—the Qiao Sidhur are loathe to call anything a complete loss, so they erased the words *failed conquest* from their history books and replaced them with *successful cultural exchange*. The joviality is decidedly one-sided."

Ronoah frowned. "So they're a bunch of invaders."

That earned him a sharp look from Hanéong. "I would think you, of all people, would know better than to write off a whole society like that."

He was right. Of course Ronoah knew better. Carelessly condemning an entire culture—why had he said that? It roiled in him alongside what he'd told Ean-Bei, two little cruelties in as many minutes, and in his haste to distance himself from that discomfort he turned to something he could be angry at without complication. "You put on a face everyone here hates, and you didn't think to explain *why* to me?"

Hanéong was looking at the stage; he tossed a glance overshoulder at Ronoah. "When should I have told you?"

"I don't know, Hanéong, we had thirty hours of sitting and doing nothing on a train, you might have fit it into your schedule then—"

"You were busy taking in the view," Hanéong said mildly, and Ronoah's retort went sour in his mouth. This, too, was true. He'd more or less ignored the man for the entire ride—and before that, with the bureau rag at the Consulate. Really, he'd found reasons to avoid talking to Hanéong at pretty much every significant moment they'd had between them since leaving Sasaupta Falls.

There was a nastiness in there he didn't want to face, an ugly unfairness. His irritation simmered, made all the more uncomfortable for the fact that it had no clear target. He let the issue drop. They settled into fragile silence, the six inches between them squirming with the unsaid, and as the amphitheatre filled up with showgoers saving seats and buying paper cones of sugared nuts Ronoah was permitted a moment to review the kind of person he was becoming.

Two days in Ol-Penh: so far, he had rejected attempts at connection with unprecedented coldness, excluded someone from a social situation—the very sort of shunning he'd experienced when he was young in Pilanova, the sort that had hurt so private, so sharp—and told a litany of little lies. *I can read Chiropolene well enough to help your friend with her academic project. Hanéong is busy after the acro show. I'm on a tour of the Trans-Bereni libraries. I may or may not visit the Pilgrim State.*

Why, of everything, did that last one feel the most true?

All told, it was a relief when the lights dimmed and the show began.

An Ol-Penher acro show was one big unraveling gymnastics routine, comprised of different acts: performers whirling across the ground on massive hoops, twisting and flipping airborne on bright strips of silk, leaping between ribbed poles twenty feet tall. Ean-Bei appeared as one of a half dozen acrobats who rolled and dove through hoops and each other's legs in tightly-coordinated synchronicity, their butterfly costumes all flaring as they flew. Ronoah had seen bits of circus before, but Ol-Penh's show didn't quite seem like a performance for the sheer sake of entertainment. There was a continuity between the acts, as if each was guiding the audience to the next. He saw enough handhalf decorating the dances to confirm his suspicions. A story was being told here, one he didn't understand.

It was absorbing to watch, the acrobats and their tricks and talents, the otherworldly feats they performed in twos and threes to the sternum-vibrating drums beating in a semi-circle along the back of the stage. But it was when the lights were doused to near darkness and a lone figure took centre stage that Ronoah was properly transfixed.

One acrobat, tall and lean and lavender-clad, twin balls of fire burning at the ends of the ropes in his hands.

For a second Ronoah swore he could hear the crackle of the flames, close as a whisper—and then the drums started, and the dancer's frame lit up in deep streaks of colour as he got the fire swinging in loops, hypnotically slow at first, then building to evermore intricate patterns, twisting reels and flowering spirals, quick enough in the dark to transform into brilliant ribbons of flame, powerful and dangerous, and the dancer so calm, so steady. The grace of his motion, the utter focus—at one point he struck the ends of his tethers against the ground like matches, mid-swing, and an explosion of sparks sprayed up and Ronoah couldn't help the noise he made, gasp of apprehensive wonder, gripping his seat hard enough to feel the aftershock in his fingerbones.

This was Yengh-Sier.

Ronoah found out after the show, when the audience was filing out and he was waiting with Hanéong at the south entrance—Ean-Bei came jogging toward him with the fire dancer in tow, both clad now in civilian clothes but with their streaks of bright makeup still intact. Ronoah saw them coming and a wisp of Ean-Bei's voice echoed, *I think Yengh-Sier's bringing out the dragon poi,* and he knew.

"That was—I don't know what to say," he began, breathless, as the two acrobats joined them. "That was unbelievable."

"Isn't it?" Ean-Bei's cheeks were flushed like milky rose tea, warm from exertion. Residual adrenaline left their hands a little shaky in their gestures. "I told you you couldn't miss it, am I ever glad you saw *this* one, I didn't know this guy was going to pull a double-act!" They nudged Yengh-Sier in the ribs; seeing the man in steady light, Ronoah realized he'd also been part of the pole-climbing routine. But the memory was faint, eclipsed by the gravity of his solo act. Even now Ronoah felt he could see the afterglow of the fire flickering on the man's skin, and it tugged something in him hard and soft all at once.

"That was unbelievable," he said again to Yengh-Sier—or tried to. The man raised his eyebrows, touched his forearm and then his lip, and Ronoah had to suppress yet another stab of frustration as he dredged up the gestures he'd learned only that afternoon: "Sorry, I don't use handhalf."

Yengh-Sier's brow furrowed even as he smiled; evidently he saw the same humour in the phrase that Ean-Bei did. He signed something, and Ean-Bei opened their mouth to translate.

"He thinks you said you were impressed, in which case he is grateful." That wasn't Ean-Bei. It was Hanéong. Abruptly everyone in the circle was reminded of the young man's presence as he read Yengh-Sier's words out to Ronoah. "It's the first time he's given a public dragon poi performance; it's good to know practice has amounted to something worthy of sharing. This is Ronoah Elizzi-denna," he continued, switching to speaking for himself in response to some unseen inquiry from Yengh-Sier; Ronoah saw his own name traced in the air, ephemeral, indecipherable. "And I am Hvanzhir Hanéong. Pleased to make your acquaintance."

They traded a few more words exclusively in handhalf. Presumably Ean-Bei followed along, but Ronoah was left stranded, struggling with this infuriating isolation, with the newfound knowledge of what it meant to bring a Qiao Sidhur into a group of Ol-Penher and the strange embarrassment it provoked. At the least, Yengh-Sier seemed to take it graciously. When they finished, Hanéong turned to Ronoah, and he must have caught the mote of accusation in Ronoah's eye, because the smile he offered was so wry.

"Sorry," he said. "Force of habit."

Ronoah was saved from the disarming pang in his chest by Ean-Bei's interruption. "Sooo," the tai said, "we should get going, Ngodi's probably holding our table and the longer we wait the higher the chance that she'll eat all the tapenade before I get a chance at it. Let's move. Sorry you couldn't come, Hanéong!"

Chuta ka saag, Hanéong still didn't know he had been disinvited. Ronoah swung back to the man, grasping for some way to explain—and met a gaze that held utterly no bewilderment, no hurt surprise, a gaze that already knew perfectly well it had been dismissed. That wry smile was still there. It made Ronoah's mouth go dry.

"Likewise," the man replied, "but a commitment is a commitment." The words had secondary meaning, secret meaning, Ronoah was sure of it—but access to that meaning was unexpectedly barred to him. Somehow, Hanéong had become as impossible to decipher as the day they met. "Ronoah, I'll see you at the boarding house," he said with a wave goodbye, and then he left, and no matter how long Ronoah stared at his retreating back, suddenly desperate to throw his empathy hard enough to reach, the space between them remained inert and ungiving.

He bit his lip so hard it hurt, and then he turned and followed Ean-Bei and Yengh-Sier out of the amphitheatre, determined to put it out of his mind.

The two acrobats managed to distract Ronoah with their whirlwind tour of the city's nightlife as they made their mad dash for dinner. He hadn't taken in the shape of anything that morning, hurrying as he'd been to get somewhere, to get away from something. His first true glimpse of Khepsuong Phae was its nocturnal side, buskers and drunkards and dancers gathered in wells of light thrown by windows, by streetlamps, going about their business under the cobalt cloak of the dark. He saw bistro after bistro spilling their patrons onto patios, their floor-to-ceiling shutters pulled up so there was hardly any distinction between outdoors and in; they passed through pockets of aroma as they went, blue cheese and roasted eggplant and tender spiced goat, sweet polenta and balsamic, basil and sage and nose-tingling chili pepper. Ronoah's stomach was nearly cramping around its emptiness by the time they arrived at their destination.

It must have been a popular restaurant—despite its two floors it was crowded elbow-close. Ean-Bei led the way up a set of stairs at the back, out onto a rooftop garden set about with globulous glass lanterns and flower baskets and ironwork tables. A red-haired woman was perching on one of the few larger tables—not at a seat, on the table itself—and waved with both arms when she saw them.

"Ngodi!" Ean-Bei called cheerfully, and immediately went and whacked her on the small of the back. "Don't hunch like that in public, bad posture's for ugly people, you can be a gargoyle all you like in the privacy of your cave. Where's the olives?"

"Haven't ordered yet," was her flippant answer, "but all the bread-sticks are finished."

"Dragon's tits, what's wrong with you."

"I haven't eaten all day, and you two were running late! Later than usual."

Yengh-Sier signed something at the same time as Ean-Bei wrapped a hand around Ronoah's shoulder and said, "Ah, I see how it is. If I'm not appreciated, then I'll go and take the answer to all your thesis problems—" they shook Ronoah playfully "—away with me."

With a victorious shriek the woman launched herself off the table and seized Ronoah out of Ean-Bei's hands; he stumbled into her grip, blinked up into her hungry brown eyes. "It's you?" she asked, and for an instant all he heard was the Ol-Penher itself, reduced from word to sound: *nhai?*

"Ahai," he replied without thinking. It pinched his throat, and he wrestled out a correction— "Yes, yes it's me. I, ah, heard you need help with reading something?"

"*Yes,* so I'm doing a dual-discipline thesis, comparative literature with a theological focus—"

Yengh-Sier swatted the woman on the shoulder, signed something which Ean-Bei jumped in to translate: "Ngodi, please. Food now, business later."

Mealtimes, Ronoah discovered, were a ritualized ordeal in Ol-Penh. The Khepsuong Phaer, at least, did nearly all of their eating socially— likely due to the fact that they otherwise held such industrious lives and needed scheduled time to relax with friends and family before returning to the library or the laboratory or the law firm. As such, their cuisine was built around shareability: dozens of little baskets and plates to suit everyone's tastes, and the food itself neatly wrapped in steamed dough or thin-sliced meat or pickled leaves, packed into rounds, cut into squares, food fit for plucking from. They had a staunch smalltalk-only rule while the meal was being served, too—as Yengh-Sier had said, no business allowed at the table. It was oddly soothing, to have nothing to do but try bite after bite of unfamiliar fingerfood, watching the idle catchup between what soon proved to be three longstanding friends.

Ngodi—Ngoluydinh to her parents and research supervisors—was the oldest of the three, followed by Ean-Bei, with Yengh-Sier bringing up the rear as 'the baby'. Ngodi and Yengh-Sier were both Khepsuong Phae-area natives, with their fairer skin and auburn hair, but Ean-Bei had come down from the mountain towns further north. The tai had met Ngodi in a lecture on Shatterlands mythology, and later had joined the local acro centre and hit it off with Yengh-Sier, and then dragged the two major parts of their life together. Yengh-Sier read nothing except for the odd bureau rag, and Ngodi thought exercise was for masochists, and yet they all got along with the affectionate teasing of people who, in the end, had great respect for each other's passions.

When the last plates had been cleared away and they were all serving each other silver demitasses of chocolatey coffee, Ngodi rounded on Ronoah once again. "So," she said, slapping the edge of the table with the flats of her fingers, "thesis." Ronoah, halfway to a sip of coffee, looked up at her over the rim of his cup. "Like I said, it's multidisciplinary—theology but also literature, and world history too, once I get to stage two. I'm building a sainthood test for the Wishgranter's company."

The coffee, so smooth and rich in Ronoah's mouth, went bitter. Of course.

Ngodi explained in further detail: she was a student of the apocry-phal, the gnostic texts of the Wishgranter's faith. What other theologians dismissed as imitation or misdirection, she pored over with fevered inter-est. For phase one of her dissertation, she was compiling a review of the literature on the company of Ol-Penher saints, humans who had been granted pseudo-divine status by virtue of their deeds in life or in death, with the aim of creating a litmus test for sainthood itself. Once the test was satisfactorily complete, phase two applied it to historical figures outside of Ol-Penh, to see if any ka-Khastan princesses or Jalipurin healers or Chiropolene merchants could be canonized as saints in their own right.

Weirdly it reminded Ronoah of his own studies in Padjenne, only mirrored. He'd come to the academy to browse global systems of faith and had zeroed in on the shalledrim as a focus point; Ngodi was reversing that trajectory, starting with a portrait and then backing up to see the landscape. Her proposal sounded like a book Ronoah would have read back in those days—would have missed dinner for, busy devouring pages instead of prawn fry.

He almost refused her. There were plenty of reasons to say no: the sources she wanted translated were complicated enough that he'd need to dedicate significant time to brushing up on his Chiropolene, and phase one of the project alone was the work of several weeks, maybe more if it got out of hand, which Ean-Bei said it was likely to, and also—also if he was being frank with himself, the topic was—disquieting. There was nothing *wrong* with it, nothing bad. He'd just—had his fill of mythologies for now. Of gods.

All right, said that rustling voice in his head, the new one—all right, so you'll be going back to the boarding house and spending tonight with the god already waiting there, will you?

"…I might need extra time with your sources," he said, and Ngodi squealed in delight. "My Chiropolene—I don't want to mess up your research with bad translations."

It was something to do. It was something *interesting*, weren't they always hunting for things that were interesting? He wouldn't get another chance any time soon to delve so deep with his Chiropolene, and if it took a few weeks—Hanéong had said *take all the time you like*, hadn't he? A few weeks was nothing compared to the side trip the man had put them through. And the topic—

Well. It was a matter of academic interest. It was a logic puzzle. It didn't mean he had to believe any of it.

"Take a week on each citation if you have to," Ean-Bei butted in, grinning their chip-toothed grin. "Shit, take two, it's still faster than the turnaround at the translation desk. Their waitlist is longer than the Khepsuong Phae Consulate's."

"I—" Ronoah's breath hitched; reprimanding himself silently, he tried again. "I don't know anything about the saints, or the, the Wishgranter. You'll have to explain what I'm looking for."

"Easy," countered Ngodi with a checkmark chop of her hand. "I can prep you a primer for tomorrow—"

Yengh-Sier pursed his hand, the gesture for *no*. "If they learn it from you, they'll only end up more confused than they start," Ean-Bei translated, snickering. "True. Ngodi, let the acrolytes take care of the basics. Give us 'till the next show and we'll hand Elizzi-denna back to you at least semi-equipped to handle the utter madness that is your hold stack."

Ngodi pouted, but conceded in the end. And Ronoah finally had his opening, his chance to try saying what he'd wanted to say to Yengh-Sier: "Your dance, the—dragon poi?" he tried, with Ean-Bei nodding encouragingly and signing along, "they were—I think they were the most beautiful thing I've ever seen on a stage. You looked so—" A welter of feelings assaulted him, half-formed and inexpressible. The memory of the Ravaging licked at his scars; under the folds of his pink scarf, he flinched. "So at home."

"I find home in motion," Yengh-Sier signed back. "I hope that doesn't seem pretentious. Not everybody feels it, but there's a certain security I feel when I'm constantly moving like that."

"It's not pretentious at all," Ronoah replied; it came out a little more intense than he'd meant for. "I get it, I—I get it."

"Why not try it yourself?" That was Ean-Bei breaking in with their opinion. Both Ronoah and Yengh-Sier blinked at the tai as they shrugged a lively shrug Ronoah's way. "Yengh-Sier's a great teacher, he taught me on hoop diving and whipped my handstands into shape. Why not take a lesson or two? You're gonna be here for a while anyway," they goaded, at Ronoah's hesitation, "and trust me, you're going to need the excuse to leave Ngodi's den of paperwork."

Again, it would be easy to say no, to deny himself this complicated desire. Easier even than before, because unlike Ngodi, Yengh-Sier didn't seem overly enthused about teaching him. They met eyes over the table, and Ronoah saw a reflection of his own reluctance—distorted, differently reasoned, but it was certain they both had their doubts.

But even as he was finding a way to politely back down, something resolved in the man's eyes, and he lifted his hands. "All right," he signed, to Ean-Bei's whoop of glee, "if it really calls to you, we can try."

Ronoah's heart pinged with unknown pressure. He gestured a thank you, and Ngodi quipped that it would be a little hard to teach someone who only spoke half the language, and the rest of the evening became an impromptu handhalf lesson as the three Ol-Penher at the table drilled Ronoah on the syllabary, refusing to let him leave until he'd got it right all the way through. Ean-Bei tried to insist on testing him through it backwards too, but Yengh-Sier said that was cruel, and so finally they released him, laughing and hand-sore, from their company. Ean-Bei took it upon themself to walk Ronoah back, bidding him goodnight at the boarding house, and with his head still full of patterns and planes of gesture he went to his room—

And there was Hanéong, sitting at the desk pushed under the window, cheek in-hand like some daydreaming youth, stroking the flowers in the vase at the windowsill and watching them change colour. His skin was limned in moonlight; he glimmered sapphire and aqua beneath the bones. He turned at the sound of the door, and the two of them looked at each other from opposite sides of the room, and for a disoriented instant Ronoah wanted to run to him—and then Hanéong opened his mouth and Ronoah blurted, "I'm helping this girl with her research."

He explained it quickly, wilfully, how they needed him to translate, how they'd offered the poi lessons; he explained it like a defense. *Nothing's wrong. Everything's fine. I just have things to do here for a while.*

Hanéong took the news with no complaint, no impatient tisk—like with everything else, every other stupid petty riling thing Ronoah had said or done since the Council of All Tribes, the man let it be. His only challenge wasn't even a challenge—it was just a look, he gave Ronoah a *look*, soft and a little smiling, totally out of sync with the conversation, and Ronoah had to physically stop himself from asking what it was about, had to kill that naïve reflex, because he didn't want to know. He didn't.

"So is that all right?" he asked at length, hearing and hating the frayed edge of his voice.

Hanéong's gaze lingered in a way that made Ronoah want to flee back out the door. "Reasonable amounts of dawdling," the man said eventually, and turned back to his flowers.

It was impossible to tell whether he meant it as concurrence or admonishment. Even if Ronoah could sense the man's many layers like usual, he was suddenly too weary to try. He dressed for bed and all but collapsed onto the mattress, curling up facing the wall, facing his own shadow softly cast by the glow of Hanéong's body. He shut his eyes. On the backdrop of that blue dark, Yengh-Sier's hands sketched themselves in his mind's eye.

If it really calls to you, we can try.

Nothing was calling to him. The last time he'd felt Genoveffa's presence was before he'd arrived at Sasaupta Falls. Not a wisp of her flickering warmth since then.

A younger Ronoah would have worried himself sick thinking perhaps he'd angered the godling, displeased her somehow, certain she'd withdrawn from him in punishment or disappointment. But he had left that innocent anxiety behind. The Great Wheel had turned; there was no anxiety now, only dull, dreadful resignation. It might not be that he'd disappointed her. It might be that she just wasn't there to be disappointed. Wasn't there at all. Didn't exist.

If it could happen to the Shaipurin, it could happen to anyone. To Acharrio. To him.

He could think no further about it. So his mind shut it down, shut him off, plunged him into sleep like a rock down a well, like the meteor of Yanyel, buried safe under fathoms and fathoms of unfeeling sea.

# Thirty-Six

*T*HE NEXT WEEK PASSED IN A STREAK, in a smear. It wasn't for another five days that Ean-Bei and Yengh-Sier could make time to bring Ronoah to an acro show, but Ronoah didn't mind. Hardly noticed. There were, after all, plenty of ways to kill time.

His Chiropolene, for instance. His tenure as Ngoluydinh's research assistant would run short indeed if he couldn't read the manuscripts she was pushing to him. In an echo of Padjenne, he spent hours each day holed up in the Chiropolene section of Khepsuong Phae's library, formalizing his now-instinctive understanding of the language, shoring up his sense of context and convention and field-specific jargon. He busied his mind with the rolls and reams of grammars and dictionaries he'd stacked in hillocks around him. Once, as he flipped a page, an image leapt out at him: Old Chiropolene art, words tamed into silhouettes, into figures. An arch. A half-moon. A hand extended. He lingered, looked away.

When he wasn't honing his Chiropolene, he was practicing Ol-Penher handhalf with his new friends, trying to marry word and gesture, to fuse them in-mind so that it would be awkward not to produce them in tandem. No one was a particularly proficient language teacher, so Ean-Bei had the idea to enroll Ronoah in an intensive class meant for long-term visitors and new citizens; though the three-hour lessons were exhaustive and demanding, Ronoah relished the idea that he was transcending the role of mere tourist. Soon enough, he would fit in here better than the average foreigner. He chased that belonging like a prize.

And whenever his brain felt too pressed flat for any more verb conjugation, whenever his leg started bouncing without respite, there was the acro centre. Ean-Bei was all too happy to escort Ronoah to the gymnasium where most of the city's acrobats trained, and just as happy to stay for the duration of Ronoah's lessons with Yengh-Sier—the tai would lounge in their marigold jumpsuit and translate the handhalf that Yengh-Sier slipped and snaked through the gaps in his whirling instruments. He was an exacting teacher, strict and disciplined. The practice poi he bequeathed to Ronoah were little more than children's toys, satchels of sand slung from a forearm's length of cord. This made sense given the obvious safety issues with letting a total beginner play with a pair of unpredictable firebrands, but still Ronoah was disappointed. Like so much else, he buried that disappointment under hard work, throwing himself out of his mind and into his body so he could learn to move it in this new way.

It was surprisingly difficult—he was used to sponging up information with relatively little work, but his perfect memory didn't apply to muscle and sinew, to articulations of wrist and waist and sole. His brain was quick, but his body learned at the same sore pace as any. Admittedly, it was another stumbling block when he found out that dragon poi—that all Ol-Penher gymnastic arts—were worship practices, liquid prayer. That he was essentially learning to perform the scripture of the Wishgranter.

You're not going to back out just because of *that*, are you? he thought archly. Don't be absurd. You learned to whistle the Chiropolene arches alive; doesn't mean you believed their gods would poke their heads through the gate to see who was knocking.

Or maybe he had. It didn't matter. It was a long time ago.

Even with all these pursuits asking so much of him, it was a challenge to truly fill the days from sunup to past sundown: there were scheduling conflicts or moments of solitude on the walk between the acro centre and the boarding house at the end of the night, hiccoughs of loose time like threads waiting to snag and unravel. But Ronoah found a way to pull them all tight. He dovetailed his commitments evermore finely, pressed every minute into service, leaving no gaps, no moment alone, no dark blister of time where reflection could fester. No time in solitude meant no time in contemplation, which meant no ground gained by the inde-scribable feeling that was tracking him, day by day, since the jump from Sasaupta Falls. By the possibility—the *probability*—that he was every bit as godless as the heartland. The probability that he'd been praying to nothing all this time.

Like a coward, he dodged that reality as long as he could. He hid under stacks of books to avoid it; he distracted himself with the ache in his forearms to bypass it. He encased himself in the smooth resin of busyness, suspending his heart so the sight of a garden snake or an open flame or a boy with his hair in a topknot wouldn't undo him, render him inconsolable.

Because who was there to console him about all that had happened? No one. In all of Ol-Penh there was no one who knew anything about what he'd gone through, no one who could understand, no one but—

"Hanéong, I'd like the Ol-Penher orthography, please."

Day seven in Ol-Penh. It was a rainy afternoon, the streetlamps lit early out the window of the boarding house. The damp air made their room feel closer, more intimate. It chafed at Ronoah like bad fabric. He stayed near the door.

Hanéong looked up from the book he was reading on his bed, tucked against a plush of pillows. Ronoah couldn't tell whether the smile was from the story or for him. "Oh?"

"I can't write anything down for anyone," Ronoah said, laboriously adding his new-learned handhalf to his speech. "Academically, I'm barely functional. What am I going to do, just orate everything to Ngodi?"

"I believe the library employs scribes-in-training for exactly this sort of issue, you could—"

"No. No more scribes, no more—translators." The word ached deep in his chest. He set his shoulders against it. "I just want to do it myself. Can't you make that possible?"

A crease appeared between Hanéong's silvery brows. "I'd say it's ill-advised; we already tampered with your neurons once at your request, it wouldn't—"

"But you *can* do it, can't you?" Rain-chilled air spilled in from the open window. "So do it for me."

At those words Hanéong ceased his dissuading—at those words Ronoah hated to say, those words he knew would work. The man closed his book, contemplated its backing. His pale toes nosed into the warmth of the blankets, apparently absently, exactly like a human's would.

"Come here," he eventually said, his soft voice a concession, and he set his book down on his lap.

It hurt. It hurt worse than the first time: burning like magma poured between the lobes of Ronoah's brain, ringing pain in the hollows of his elbows, the feeling that all the fluids in him were evaporating, a dry itch in his wrists so great it made him want to claw the tendons right out. He endured it with his fists tucked safe to his chest, pressing his forehead to the edge of Hanéong's bed where he'd come to his knees, whimpering through the twist of bedsheet he was biting on. He endured it without complaint.

When he could breathe without his head catching fire, he spat out the fabric and stood, dry-mouthed and migrained, and turned for the door.

"Stars," came the low oath behind him, "come now, little—Ronoah.

Would it not be wise to wait out any aftershocks in the privacy of your own space?"

The concern was palpable, brushed against him like the chill. He flinched away from it. "I'm fine." His teeth rang metallic in his mouth when he spoke. He suppressed the base urge to yank them out.

Silence; the space where a human would sigh. Then, with measured lightness: "I could go out instead. If you wanted."

"I'm *fine*." The insistence rattled his brain. "Thanks. I'll be back later."

And he left, trying not to think about how he would let Hanéong hurt him but not let the man help him. Left with his hands shaking and his feet stumbling but stubborn, resolute. He really didn't have time to rest anyway.

After all, the show was tonight.

There was no need to buy tickets this time—Ean-Bei explained Ronoah's status as a student of Yengh-Sier's and the man at the kiosk waved him in without paying. "Usually these things are free to prac-titioners," Ean-Bei explained to Ronoah's confusion. "Ordinary people make donations to support the centres, but your donation is your time, your devotion to the art. Nifty, huh?"

Ronoah bit his lip to hide a grimace. Five days testing out a practice didn't mean he had any kind of *devotion*—but Ean-Bei had already pulled him through the lobby, and his head was still hurting too bad to protest very loudly.

The third row from the front was the sweet spot for viewing, accord-ing to Ean-Bei; they shooed Ronoah in and then plunked down beside him, blowing their brown hair out of their eyes. When Ronoah asked if they were in tonight's show, they only laughed. "Nah," they said, paus-ing to pick a stray flake of glitter from their eyelashes, "this one's way above my level—seasoned professionals only. I mostly do acro for fun, but Yengh-Sier's kind of made a career for himself out of it. He's really dedicated. This program's made up of Khepsuong Phae's best and a few out-of-towners, people who live performing on the circuit."

Like the Tellers. *Funnier priests.* Or in this case, ones that could fly. The amphitheatre was, in a way, one of the largest churches in the city. That was why they had come, to introduce Ronoah to these holy stories in a way that went beyond ink and paper. To immerse him in the experience, the full sensory journey—to make him *feel* it.

He might have liked to just read them first. Especially because— "How am I going to tell the acts apart if I don't already know them? It's—it would be rude for you to talk to me during the show, right?"

"Oh, this is a formal recital, they'll have a surtitle—there!" Above the stage at the far left and right corners, large Ol-Penher words glowed against a black cloth backdrop. Twisting around for the source, Ronoah saw two taik adjusting metal plates with the same words punched out in front of a pair of spotlights.

Well there you go, rustled a voice in his head; you get what you want. Aren't you glad you learned to read today?

His eyes watered at the memory of that evaporating pain. He grit his teeth against it, turned again to the stage, looked upon the very first Ol-Penher glyphs he could understand:

THE MARVELOUS LIFE AND PASSIONATE DEATH
OF OUR LADY THE WISHGRANTER

The title seemed to grow brighter even as he read it—a side-effect, another aftershock? No, the house lights were just dimming. The show—the recital—was about to begin.

"They'll screen the story up there while everyone performs it down here," Ean-Bei said, leaning their head close to Ronoah's, hands moving fluid and borderless in the lowered light. "Good thing you've already seen Yengh-Sier do his thing, or it'd probably be a lot to take in—but we're going for dinner after, so save any questions you've got and we'll answer them without Ngodi pulling out quotes from some weird forty-seventh century mystic—oh, here we go!" A twitch of the curtains, a slice of light; Ean-Bei squeezed Ronoah's shoulder, a silent enjoy!, and settled into rapt silence.

Yengh-Sier took to the stage. The suggestion of a man interposed between two waiting flames, the deep plum inhale between quotation marks of light. The drum ensemble struck its first bone-deep note, and Yengh-Sier dawned his upswing exactly the same as last week—except now the glaring, glowing text was changing, the title replaced with a new slide, new lines of scripture. Now Ronoah could follow along.

So it was, eyes flicking between star-white words and flame-licked limbs, that Ronoah watched a creation myth possess his friend.

*I*N THE BEGINNING THERE WERE THE DRAGONS. *Then, in the great Before, all was without form; no earth or ochre or gem yet present, no buoyant water nor the salt wind, no dayflame, no aether, no element however slight. Not a single grain of matter in the whole of infinity—and infinity itself could even be said not to exist, as it was boundless and thus disembodied. All was but Heaven, vast and sable swirl, braided bands of empty darkness and empty light, airless, songless, replete in absence and in scintillant void. And the Dragons resided in the Heavens, and moreover were the Heavens themselves.*

Within the holy frictions of the Heavens lay the spirit realm, where manifested the celestial beings. Multitude and sundry they were, endlessly coming into being, undying and everlasting, at once infinitesimal and horizon-wide, and wider still, and yet again small enough all to fit together on the point of an eyelash, for proportion meant nothing in the great Before, in the non-world of the Heavens. The host of celestial beings spent perpetuity in exaltation of the Dragons, and innumerable benedictions and prayers were fashioned to them in brightnesses and frequencies we cannot know. Eternity was flat with satisfaction.

But there arose the celestials of the host who were dissatisfied, who wished for more than the colourless sparks and streams of the spirit realm, who sought to distend the dimension of creation. And the Dragons heard the displeasure of the restive host, and thusly they decreed: Let all you who kindle wishes in your brightest and darkest of hearts come forward and dictate them; we shall grant unto you that which you desire.

One by one, the members of the restive host approached the Dragons with their wishes. And so many wishes there were. For peace and for pastime, for substance and for soul, for all things cruel and compassionate and careless, for the valence of emotion and the power of ideation; for virtue and for violence, the wound of curse and the salve of wealth, for shame and acquittal, for the ripening of hunger and the differentiation of danger; for misery and miracle, for gravity and grace, for beauty, for body, for boundary. A great and ceaseless cavalcade of wishes did the host bring to the Dragons, and the Dragons heard out each. But the Dragons, made as they are of the luck and chaos of the Heavens, granted each wish as a twist of itself, the outcome as seen through the eye of the loophole in the wisher's dictation. No spirit could outsmart the Dragons' shrewdness; no wish, however wily or wise, was match for their Heavenly prescience. It became known among the spirit realm that to approach the Dragons with a wish was to take a great risk, to contest the Heavens themselves.

So passed an interminable eon wherein the restive host sought among them for one who could best the Dragons' wit, and found none.

And then she arrived. From nowhere, it seemed, did she come, an even greater nothing than that which the spirit realm languished in, for the other celestials had hardly noticed her before—she had either only just come into being a twinkling trice ago, or else had spent an eternity in quiet contemplation, at remove from the rest, observing the thick sinuous dance of the Dragons for time untold. She came before the Dragons, and the Dragons pronounced: Thou who holdst a wish in your brightest and darkest of hearts, come forth and speak thee freely. And this quiet, watchful spirit replied: O Heavenly Dragons, I will do as you command me—only I beg of you your patience, for it may take some time.

And the Dragons were intrigued. What need to warn of time, in the endless forever of creation? The watchful spirit—who might have been a little softer than the restive celestials, a little less bright and a little less dark—began to speak her wish. And as she spoke, the strangest thing occurred: from her words a steady tempo flowed, a presence of time that could not be stretched to infinity or collapsed to an instant, that refused all sublimation, a stubborn sense of state as majestically immutable as she was mild. She spoke, and the Dragons were intent on her speaking, enough to slow their great undulation of creation, to pause the Heavens in thought. In the stillness of their cosmic coils, the first particles of matter emerged, and were drawn magnetic to the spirit as she spoke her wish, entering her and becoming one with her, such that she was become something that had never before existed: a body. In the wishing she was born to solid form, and within the walls of that form she gave birth to many wonders—texture and pressure, pattern and proportion, warmth and odour and the colour pink, which is so precious. All of infinity was rapt about her as she uttered her heart's desire.

When she at last came to an end, she sat palpable and plain in a way that choked the host for joy. And the Dragons considered all she had said, this severe little miracle who had wished herself alive, and they could find not one fault in her speech, not one loophole for their shrewdness to slip through. Be glad, the Dragons thus proclaimed, for thou hast dared the Heavens and won.

The spirit smiled. I am glad, she replied. And then, being the first to be truly born, she became also the first to die.

From her inert body the Dragons fashioned the earthly sphere, soil for the seed of her great ineffable wish, and set the sun and moons about it, and called down the restive host to become the waters and the sky and the rosebud and the olive grove, and they called down still more to create the sheep and the fox and the sparrowhawk, and all the other flora and fauna of this world, and last of all the humans, pulled from the navel of the Wishgranter and set down to forward her glorious end. May all who hear it remember: the great Wish is you, and you are the Wish. Blessed are you who accept the dominion of Our Lady; beloved are you who attend to her divine designs; righteous are you who dedicate your actions in her name. Feel no fear, nor shame, for there are none in this life who can judge you.

*Y*ENGH-SIER FLICKERED AND SPARKED IN THE DARK, encircled by the comet trails of two Heavenly Dragons. The duality of the set was mesmerizing, the way it seemed simultaneously that the acrobat was controlling the fire and the fire controlling him; at points it was impossible to discern who was the one truly tethered. It was an odd thing, odd and fascinating, how the Ol-Penher represented scripture with their own bodies this way, because if the poi were the Dragons and the dark amphitheatre was the murky non-world of the Heavens, just *positionally*-speaking that meant Yengh-Sier was assuming the place of the Wishgranter. His body the body of their god, of the entire world struggling to come into existence—no wonder he'd wanted to practice so hard before giving a public performance.

If you took that metaphorical staging even further, that meant Ronoah—meant every one of the audience members—was one of the *restive host.* A celestial being thwarted, deprived of a wish. A creature whose dreams had been used against it.

Ronoah didn't know if that would be blasphemous to say, so he didn't say it. But it rang in him all the same.

Many acts followed, bright bombastic tales of the first Ol-Penher saints: Saint Nam-Chai who saved the north from plague, and Saint Sakangpenh who united the mountains and the valleys, and Saint Yu who had demanded the Holy Corridor be built, had cleared the jungle with their own hands, and fearsome Saint Oupha who had committed terrible crimes but who had endured the suffering endowed by those crimes in the Wishgranter's name. Saints, Ronoah learned, were not necessarily charitable or kind. There was a Thief Saint, a Mad Saint, an Assassin Saint; the sanctity of these individuals came not from their goodness, but from their resolve to further the Wishgranter's designs no matter the cost.

He asked Ean-Bei and Yengh-Sier about this at dinner, over plates of lamb pastries and a carafe of raspberry wine: "How do you tell saints apart from regular people if goodness isn't how you measure their deeds? They make the Wishgranter's will manifest, but—but doesn't *everything*, wasn't that the point of the opening act?" If absolutely everything was pushing toward that divine design, why did Oupha or Nam-Chai get special distinction?

"And *this* is why you'll make a great assistant for Ngodi," quipped Ean-Bei with a grin, lifting their glass in salute.

Yengh-Sier chose a more informative approach. "I didn't understand either when I was younger," he said. "My parents explained to me like this: everyone has the potential to fulfill multiple parts of the Wish, some smaller, some bigger and more essential. The big parts are usually harder, or more thankless. People who choose to walk those paths give up a lot of personal comfort, even safety sometimes, in pursuit of that grander plan."

"It's the long-term impact that distinguishes them," Ean-Bei put in. "It's the *scale* that matters. Local doctors change a lot of people's lives, but inventing a treatment for plague's what got Nam-Chai sainted. Any common vandal can tip a monument or throw a Consulate's archives in the sea, but Oupha—well! You saw."

"Not always good," Ronoah observed, "just big?" Ean-Bei head-wobbled emphatically, and neither they nor Yengh-Sier could understand why Ronoah laughed, or why the sound of it was so harsh.

Yengh-Sier excused himself after the first course on account of being an early sleeper, but Ean-Bei's energy only grew more vibrant the later it got, and Ronoah fell into that chaotic brilliance gladly. They ordered more lamb, and more wine, and later tiny almond cakes and candied spices and several shots of a lowland specialty liqueur nicknamed *changohk* for its rosy tint. By then Ronoah was already inebriated; the slippery pink liquid only spread that confidence to the tips of his fingers, chased down the last shreds of headache so that he hardly remembered what had caused him such agony that afternoon. It freed him up to ask the kind of probing, sceptical questions he might otherwise have kept to himself.

"Explain," he said, "why is she called the Wishgranter if the Dragons granted *her* wish? That doesn't make any sense."

Ean-Bei laughed, pinching the air with both hands, a double *no.* "You've got it the wrong way 'round, oh acolyte—it's because she was able to grant the wishes of all the *other* spirits by besting the Dragons. All those things they wanted—*for peace and for pastime*, that litany, you know?—we have those here! The Dragons had no choice but to follow through on her words, because the words were so perfect." They drained their shotglass, set it down, tinked a brilliant note off the rim with a golden fingernail. "In a way, she granted it herself, by making it so perfect."

"Perfect," Ronoah echoed, the Ol-Penher round and whole in his mouth. Even the cynical things he had to say tasted sweet. "But what about when tragedy happens? When—I don't know, when a relative gets sick, do you still think that's part of the Wish?"

"Duh—the Wish isn't in any individual's best interest, it's *bigger*."

"Okay, bigger—the Qiao Sidhur. Part of the Wish?"

Ean-Bei pulled a face. "*Yes*, nitpicker, and don't ask me how they fit in because I haven't got the slightest. None of us can know the ultimate design of the Wish, it's beyond our grasp. But everything happens in service of it, even if it's just a little."

It certainly was a tidy story. Pretty. Convenient. It sounded like Ean-Bei—like everyone here—believed in it at least a little. It sounded like empty appeasement to Ronoah, even more contrived than the War of Heavenly Seeds or a made-up neverwhere called Thesopole or a magic cloud of sweet smoke appearing over a mountain once a year—

Something in him contracted. The words he'd been trying to stuff away for a week slid up a slick throat and out before he could catch them:

"So it's just her? Just the Wishgranter, no other gods?"

"Well there's the saints, all the stuff Ngodi's got you working on, and the angels—they're like saints but they didn't start human, they're celestials who guide people on the Wishgranter's path, and the Dragons are there, obviously, aaand...the Wishgranter. Yeah!"

"But other *gods*," Ronoah pressed, leaning heavy on the emphasis. Ean-Bei looked at him strangely, perhaps a tad embarrassed—and then he realized, with a cold uncanny jolt, that the word had come out in Chiropolene. They didn't even have a name for what he was trying to get across.

That semantic void answered his question more firmly and finally than anything Ean-Bei could say, but they answered none the wiser. "Listen," the tai said carefully, "people all over the world need something to believe in, and not everyone knows about the grace of Our Lady. Stories get passed around—for comfort, you know? And that's fine! Whatever gets you through the day, right? But..."

They paused, looking at Ronoah with the same agreeable unease they'd worn while talking to Hanéong, and Ronoah knew they were remembering now that he was from elsewhere, from far away, from Pilanova. All of a sudden he wondered what, exactly, the educated Khepsuong Phaer thought of his people. He hadn't asked.

"Well speaking as a friend of yours," Ean-Bei continued, "those stories are just a society's *interpretation* of the Wishgranter. Like—mm, like looking at the world through pitted glass. Once they can see clearly, they see Her. Or else, sorry, but maybe those stories are actually shalledrim. You know the stats."

Something resolved in Ronoah then. Some fitful creature, finally subdued. There it was, all laid out at last—he'd just needed someone to say it out loud for him to finally stop running from it. From the truth of the matter.

"Yeah," he replied too quickly, "of course, that makes sense." Ean-Bei shot him a furtive look, apparently worried they'd offended him. But they hadn't. They'd only released him. "It does make sense," he repeated, insistent, belligerent even. "The, the shalledrim didn't get that far south, I don't think, but I see your point. Stories."

"Maybe your ones are angels," Ean-Bei offered up hopefully. "If believing in them brought you here."

"Could be," Ronoah said, and poured another shot of changohk, watching the world distort through its rosy lens.

Sometime past midnight, when even the heat sloshing in their bellies couldn't keep them comfortable on the chilly patio, they parted ways. Ronoah walked with the tai as far as the Lap Chai monument, then waved them home and wandered his own way down the Boulevard of Sumac, fingers trailing in the bushes that lined the walk, head full of slow-swimming thoughts. He thought: so that's it. He thought: so what if. What if she's a fiction. A fake.

Then she's a fake, and that's that.

How else could he react? He'd already heard it, that crushing idea—*maybe real gods don't exist*—and there was no unthinking that, no unseeing what inspired it, no matter how he tried to stuff his head in the sand. Ignoring what he knew, pretending it didn't matter—he was too smart for that kind of behaviour, for denying evidence like—

The wind hissed through the sumac. He pulled his hand away, guilty even now.

He wasn't stupid, and he wasn't deluded enough to believe he was the exception, that the Acharrioni gods were somehow different. *Maybe those stories are actually shalledrim*—didn't the old Tyrene, the a-Meheyu, didn't they worship shalledrim as gods? Hadn't he once visited those temples and thought of their masons, their long-gone supplicants, with just the tiniest bit of pity? If he went on stubbornly insisting that his gods were real despite all proof to the contrary, who would be pitying *him*, decades or centuries from now, for his helplessly confused beliefs?

No one, that's who. He wasn't going to give them the chance, he—he was going to take the lie of her in stride. Genoveffa. He would put her myth down before anyone could rip it from him. Renounce her first. Get ahead of history.

It wasn't even difficult to do. You should have known, he told himself as he stumbled up street after street, you should have known from the start that Genoveffa was fake. She's from Pilanova. You rejected every other piece of that place, the holy days, the saying-without-saying, the forced conformity, the suffocating civility, you called it wrong and threw it all away so how come you held on to her? If everything else was so false and so failing, why was Genoveffa special?

Because she made *me* special, Ronoah confessed blurrily. When he was alone with his honesty, or ignored for his truth, or left by his lonesome on the Salt Flats, there had always been Genoveffa. He'd clung to her as the one person who was always proud of him—and in times of tumultuous emotion, he'd wielded her as justification. *You can't tell me to be quiet, I'm Genoveffa's child!* Without her, he wouldn't have had the guts to plunge into the Ravaging; without her, he wouldn't have left Pilanova at all. She'd shielded him for that, too—given him something to focus on that wasn't the pain of his family. She was his excuse, his escape. He would have been too weak to do it alone.

But he didn't need that excuse anymore. He was so much bolder, so much stronger since the day he'd fled across the desert to Padjenne. He didn't cower now, didn't bite his tongue, didn't apologize for existing. But more than that—he'd gone on wild adventures, uncovered ancient secrets, survived deadly foes. Wars had ended because of him; the bones of shalledrim had brushed his fingers. The Chiropes told legends about him—about *him!*—he was literally the stuff of myth.

A younger you would *admire* you now, he told himself. He'd see you and think you were one of *those people*, the ones he was always chasing, trying so desperately to become. He made it; you made it. You got what you wanted. You should be happy.

He grinned into the dark, trying to appease himself.

And if Genoveffa's not real, he reasoned tenderly, thoughts tumbling over each other as he climbed up the boarding house steps, if she's not real then you did all that yourself, nobody's guided you or watched over you so, so that means you had it in you all along, you made it here under your own power and you can do whatever you want now because there's no one to please anymore. If you have no destiny then you don't have to do anything for anyone.

You don't even have to go to the Pilgrim State. It's nice in Khepsuong Phae—the food's great and the library's here and people want to be your friends, why would you want to leave?

Because you said you'd go with Reilin, a voice said. No, wait, Chashakva? No, Hanéong—that's right, with that thing whose name he didn't know, the one who'd been so patient with him, so patient and so awful, the thing that saved the world from the Shattering just to slay it in Shaipuri and Torrene and other places, the one who gave Ronoah whatever he asked for, shell and language and time, who had found him in Marghat Yacchatzndra's village and found him in the icy-black grotto of the monastery and found him in the *Tris Mantarinis*, found him and found him worthwhile. That unspeakably old not-shalledra who turned mangoes blue for boredom, who couldn't tell time worth a damn, who murdered and thought it a game, who looked at Ronoah with such bright open pride, the one he was being so cold to, so unkind, the one he couldn't face, couldn't stop being angry with, the one he loved so unbearably much, the closest thing to a god there was left. He was going with that.

A laugh was gutted from him as he fumbled for the keys to the room. Right. Sure. As if it meant anything now.

After the fragrant noise of nocturnal Khepsuong Phae, the blaring lights and overbright smells, the room was a quiet and a shadow so sudden it made his stomach sour. He felt his way to the bed he'd pushed up against the corner of the room, collapsing face-first onto the mattress. A loc of his hair wound up in his mouth. He spat it out, thinking how it had gotten longer again, untidy at the roots, how he needed to retwist it but it was hard to do alone. Özrek had done it for him once, in the caves.

"Özrek?" he called out the side of his mouth not squished into the bed. No answer. He probably deserved that—deserved this, this silence, this loneliness lurching in after all that company. Deserved to deal with this new empty world on his own. This new empty heart. This.

He didn't realize he'd fallen asleep until something nudged him awake. Özrek's hands, sliding the shoes off Ronoah's feet. It struck him as funny that he hadn't even been able to remove them before dozing off, funny and sad, and he hiccoughed another half-laugh and let the man tuck him in with those new hands he liked because they were friendly and hated because they were cruel. Those hands rolled him on his side and turned the sheets down at his chin and, after a pause, pulled his hair out of his face. He thought a glint of Özrek's starlight hummed at him from beneath the man's skin, and he hummed back, a soft sound, a stupid little mewl he was too unselfconscious to quash. His yearning, so absurd. So meaningless. So stubborn-willed. *Maybe we'll still go*, it said. Not for any reason. Just because. Maybe you'll drag me there anyway. Maybe.

"Night, 'zrek," he mumbled into the pillow as the hands retreated.

The sound of a bicycle bell down the street. The sound of a bed creaking under weight. The sound of his own blood, beach of red in his temples.

"Sweet dreams, little pilgrim."

THIRTY-SEVEN

*I*T'S A SURPRISINGLY LABORIOUS THING, to reinvent yourself godless. What Ronoah thought would be one agonizingly simple severance turned out to be a seemingly neverending series of surgeries, delving each soft and faithful place in him and excoriating them one by one. Finding all the little fires inside him, and putting them out. He'd never realized how much he prayed in his head to his gods until he consciously tried to stop; he'd never seen clearly all the habits he had, thanking his food before eating it and closing doors extra-softly and staring at the moons with a grandchild's filial fondness, never known with such squirming contempt how they all stemmed from this defunct worldview. Even after a month of reorganizing all the rooms in his mind, he'd still catch himself basing certain thoughts or opinions on foregone conclusions which were no longer foregone, and have to endure the dull embarrassed pain of smothering yet another mental shortcut and starting again.

This, he supposed, was what happened when you made something the basis for your entire life. In hindsight, it had been a stupid thing to do. It had left him so deeply vulnerable. But he hadn't known any better until now.

Not that *now* was any easier, or felt any better. As if the internal work needed to rip out a belief system wasn't difficult enough, he was doing it in Ol-Penh, land of the flamboyantly faithful. The Wishgranter, the Dragons, the Saints—they were in everything if you knew how to look, and thanks to Ronoah's work with Ngodi, it literally became his job to look. Nothing was spared from the Wishgranter's touch: dancing, dream interpretation, physical intimacy, street art, the meditative swirls drawn in sand and embroidered on silk and shaved into hairstyles—even the teas at the library café had names like Dragonscale and Nam-Chai's Blend. They'd go down his throat and burn, just below his heart.

The other problem—possibly an even larger problem than Ol-Penher culture—was Hanéong. After a few weeks making himself available at the proverbial snap of Ronoah's fingers, the man presumably realized Ronoah didn't intend on warming up to him and left. Walking into the room at the boarding house and finding it empty was a glassy shock that took Ronoah full by surprise, cold sweep of giddy devastation that muffled all his racing thoughts under the ringing of *he's gone, he's gone, he's gone without me*. He sat hard on the edge of the bed, insensate, trying to coalesce a plan and coming up with nothing—and he was still there four hours later, when Hanéong came back with a shopping bag looped on each elbow.

Ronoah almost screamed. He almost threw himself into Hanéong's paper-laden arms. Instead he picked himself up, quickly, and excused himself to the library for a late night of translating.

It wasn't that Hanéong was leaving—it was just that the man was *living*. Living his life. He disappeared some days, or didn't come back some nights, and never bothered to explain what he was doing, and Ronoah didn't ask, and so he never knew which disappearance—if any—would be the last. Hanéong wasn't doing anything *wrong*. But Ronoah bristled when the man wasn't in the room, because at any point he might arrive or he might never arrive again—and he bristled when Hanéong *was* in the room because being near Hanéong was a stronger tug toward whimsy and wonder than all the Ol-Penher worship arts combined. Listening to Hanéong talk—looking Hanéong in the eye—doing anything alone with the creature made Ronoah remember a version of himself that *was* warm, tender, awestruck, entranced, a version of himself that was dead now, and it wasn't fair, it was horrible, Hanéong had no *right* to inspire that horrific openness when it was the one who had, who had—

"You're getting ahead of yourself, slow down. Find control."

Ronoah was practicing dragon poi with Yengh-Sier one late spring afternoon. These days they were able to work largely without Ean-Bei's translations, given Ronoah's progress with handhalf and that so little of poi was actually explained with words. Today it was just the two of them, Yengh-Sier working Ronoah sternly and patiently through new skills.

If he'd thought the poi difficult to handle at first, now they were truly like two obstinate dragons—Yengh-Sier had decided it was time to introduce weaving into their practice, and what little confidence Ronoah had in his coordination was upended by the way his tethers kept tangling. He kept at it doggedly, relentless in a way that Yengh-Sier approved of. He wasn't hitting himself in the face anymore, that was something to celebrate, and Yengh-Sier said he was particularly good at allowing his arms to swing out fully, something many beginners struggled with.

"It's probably because I throw knives," Ronoah mentioned during a break. He mimicked the long smooth motion, eyeing his imaginary target in the center of the coal pit being set up across the hall. "If you keep your arm shy to your side, your blade doesn't get far."

"Where did you learn to do that?" Yengh-Sier asked, and Ronoah told the man of childhood throwing contests in Pilanova, of whetting the skill anew in Chiropole, of hunting for food in the mountains. The story was a little stilted—there was a lot to leave out, to obscure, to lie about—but he got the facts in order. The man listened intently, one lock of reddish hair fallen loosely into his eyes; he pushed it back when Ronoah finished, straightening from his keen lean forward. "I'd be interested in trying, if you don't mind sharing your expertise."

"I'll find a set to practice with for next time," Ronoah promised, and the two fell to watching the other acrobats as they sipped their citrus water.

An upkick of sparks from the other side of the hall caught Ronoah's attention. There—a fluttering blur of bright fabric. The dancer who'd spread the coal pit was practicing, prancing on it light and pointed as a stag in a meadow of fire-bright flowers. There were two main versions of the Ol-Penher coal dance: a slow, austere sort of waltz, whose main point was an uprightness in the torso and a pride in the lift of the chin, and a quicker, more airborne variety. It was clear at a glance which version the dancer preferred—they were as flashy as their dance steps, with skin pearls encrusting their cheeks and twists of green and purple silk wrapping their arms and legs. With the high leaps, the reliance on legwork and momentum, it reminded Ronoah forcefully of the kinds of dance Lelos always favoured.

Yengh-Sier nudged Ronoah's thigh for attention; he'd noticed Ronoah staring. "That's Eng-Vaunh," he said, spelling the name out in a quick flash of fingers. The man's eyes darted sidelong to the dancer and back; Ronoah thought he detected a frisson of awe hidden under the cool professionalism. "One of the best acrobats there is, or at least the most unforgettable."

Looking at the bed of embers Eng-Vaunh gavotted upon, Ronoah had to agree. "I've never seen a coal pit like that in the centre before."

"None of the Khepsuong Phae regulars can do it—even in a city this big, isn't that incredible? Eng-Vaunh's here temporarily, on the acro circuit from … up north, from Ay Hang, I think." That name—that name like a needle, injecting pain. Ronoah breathed through its dull bloom, blinked it away. "Probably here to sharpen up before the next round of shows."

"So you'll be on the same program as him—her?" Ronoah looked again. A relatively still moment, a delicate hand drawing back a curl the colour of flax, a taffy-like twist of green and purple fabric. "What, what colour should I use?"

Yengh-Sier made a face. "That's debatable. Popular culture calls Eng-Vaunh a tai, but they've explained in interviews how that isn't accurate. They're assuming both the spirits of a man and a woman—but separate, not blended the way the taik do it. It's complicated, they explain it much better—but don't go asking," the man warned suddenly, putting a hand to Ronoah's arm as if Ronoah was already standing, which he wasn't. "It's not the right place to ask questions like that."

"I promise I'll be respectful," Ronoah answered, biting his lip to hide a smile. Yengh-Sier wobbled his head in accord, seemingly oblivious to how obvious his celebrity infatuation was. Ronoah was still nursing that private amusement when the man caught him off-guard:

"Have you given any thought to your own colour?"

Ronoah blinked, then hooked a pinky. Yengh-Sier clarified: "Just seeing as we're talking about it. Ol-Penher children begin as ngohk and confirm as something else once they grow up. When people transition colours, too, they reclaim ngohdom while the paperwork goes through. *Ngoh* is a phase, for most." Watching the man speak, some chemical reaction of knowledge in Ronoah's brain welded the connection he'd never noticed before between the sign for *ngoh* and the one for *cocoon*. A class of the transforming, the emergent. The unknown. "There are some adult ngohk, philosophers or social leaders—Ean-Bei has a ngoh professor who said it was a *statement of latent potential*. But it's only library people that do that kind of thing."

"I am library people," Ronoah reminded the man jokingly, but the question unnerved him nonetheless. All this time, he'd been walking around in the rose-coloured trappings of the undecided? His reinvention process—with all its failures and false starts, its detours, its derisions, its chronic avoidance of the neighbourhood next to the Holy Corridor—that was all on display, draped on his skin for everyone to see. They just didn't know they were seeing it.

What a ruthless little coincidence. In another age, he would have called the Universe out on this joke, this poke in the foot, this nudge of *Perseverance* half-worn into his sole.

But the Universe didn't make jokes, just like it didn't make wishes.

"What luck, to catch you mid-break."

Ronoah twisted around fast enough to tweak a muscle in his side. Behind him, waving a greeting, silver hair brilliant against his lavender silks, was Hanéong.

Newly-instilled etiquette had Ronoah's hands forming a greeting back;

his mouth was far more inclined to rudeness. "What are you doing here?"

"Oh, I was in the area and thought I would pop in to chance a look at your practice." Hanéong's eyes shifted. "Yengh-Sier, wasn't it? Lovely to see you again—tell me, is he living up to your expectations?"

In response, Yengh-Sier signed something Ronoah didn't have time to turn and see. All he got was the rustle of the man's sleeves, and Hanéong's answering smile, bright and peach-cheeked. "He's like that with everything," the man replied. Not wanting to be left out of a conversation he was literally in the middle of, Ronoah moved so he could see both Yengh-Sier and Hanéong—and Hanéong took this as an invitation to stay, engaging Yengh-Sier in conversation about the man's own practice, asking about the multiple disciplines he maintained, the unique routines for each. He probed, he teased, he asked for unnecessary detail, unnecessary depth—and it was all Ronoah could do to wrestle this criticism, this stinginess that spread in him like a rash whenever Hanéong inserted himself into group events. It was bad when they were alone, but in public it was almost worse—like the squirming embarrassment of watching a parent try to ingratiate themself with your childhood friends, the jokes that landed wrong, the mortifyingly earnest attempts to relate. The insurmountable sense of otherness.

He was sorry on Yengh-Sier's behalf. Not only was Hanéong impossible to dismiss or ignore, he was also currently wearing the skin of an intruder. Ean-Bei's hesitation about the Qiao Sidhur had stuck with Ronoah ever since that first acro show. Now, he was carefully aware of when and how Hanéong interacted with his friends. He didn't want to make them uncomfortable.

Of course, Yengh-Sier was unflinchingly polite. He sat and listened to Hanéong's story—something about dragons on a different continent, or a different part of this one—and asked questions and laughed along and seemed for all intents and purposes entirely at ease. It only made Ronoah's sense of indignation flare brighter, that the acrobat's goodwill was being exploited so.

"That one over there, on the coals? I've heard the name before. Let's introduce ourselves, shall we?" Ronoah's attention was yanked back by a noise he almost never heard—a hoarse vocalization from Yengh-Sier, knocked out of him by the force of his alarm. The acrobat was frantically signing "no, that's all right, we shouldn't—" but Hanéong had risen from his crouch, mind already made up. "No sense in loving from afar. Aren't you people all about taking risks for the sake of it—for the glitter, the thrill?" He extended a hand down to each of them; despite himself, Ronoah reached up and took it.

Nothing special happened when their skin met. No sparkle, no spasm of arrogance, nothing but cool impassive fingers. With a strange sense of impotence that he quickly restrained, Ronoah allowed himself to be dragged over with Yengh-Sier to meet one of the greatest acrobats Ol-Penh had ever seen.

It went fine. Eng-Vaunh, fresh off the coals and glowing with sweat and effort, was very gracious with them despite being interrupted during private practice. The dancer asked their names and complimented the state of the acro centre with airy hands and a tinkling laugh—and then somewhere into the fold of their small talk Hanéong slipped some secret offhand saying, and the celebrity tilted their head, their long-painted eyes narrowing slight, and their smile lost its congeniality and gained something greater, something raw and wry and real, and that was how their brief introduction became a conversation lasting nearly an hour. Yengh-Sier had the pole-stiff posture of someone who was doing all he could not to fly straight through the roof; his face might've been composed, but his hands couldn't go fast enough for everything he wanted to say. Ronoah nearly laughed. He would have—would have joined in, engaged, had a nice time—if only this wasn't just another instance of Hanéong doing what it did best. Ensnaring people with its charm and attentiveness, mindreading the best ways to get everyone on its side. Manipulating the whole world to its will.

Ignore it, Ronoah told himself as his irritation mounted. Who cares what Hanéong is up to with this? Let Yengh-Sier enjoy himself. In the old days he would have lost this battle against his emotions, but the flustered Ronoah of clenching hands and gritting teeth was long gone. He just cut the feeling from himself and dropped it out of sight, detached from his discomfort, and the choppiness in his heart smoothed to the faintest of abrasions.

Eventually someone noticed the time, and Eng-Vaunh begged off on account of having dinner plans. The group said their farewells and traipsed back ensemble to their own equipment, the sizzling smell of doused coals at their backs. Yengh-Sier was angled Ronoah's way, talking as they walked. "It's a little late to pick up where we left off—do you mind?" This was coming from someone who was known to practice so late he'd been given keys to lock the centre up at night, but Ronoah wobbled his head in acquiescence anyway. Probably hard to get back in the right mindset after meeting a hero. Yengh-Sier wasn't to blame for his hijacked lesson.

"Ah, if I had known you were already engaged—" Hanéong began, but Ronoah cut him off with a pinch of the air.

"It's fine. I need to hit the markets before they close anyway," he gestured nonchalantly, "if I'm going to get a set of throwing knives." He glanced at Hanéong—at the amethyst silk of his shoulder. "You know if there's a good bladesmith?"

"I'll ask around," was the man's obliging reply. They both knew there would be no asking; Hanéong would just go home and make a set himself, spin it out of the infinity inside him and leave it on Ronoah's pillow.

Ronoah's hand flashed the heart-level circle of a thank you, quick enough to miss entirely.

Once Hanéong had departed, Ronoah rounded on Yengh-Sier with exasperated apology tingling in his fingertips. "Sorry, Hanéong's always dropping into things uninvited and, and forcing people to do things even when they're uncomfortable, I'll tell him to stay out during practice time—"

"No, don't. It's okay." Yengh-Sier's gestures were unexpectedly sharp, down-chop of admonishment. Had Ronoah's sulking been obvious after all? He was about to ask, and then the man continued, face tight. "He's probably banned from enough places already just for being him. Don't make it worse."

Being him. Being Qiao Sidhur, that meant. Ronoah was halfway to a handhalf defense—he didn't have any issue with the Qiao Sidhur, that wasn't even close to the reason he was holding Hanéong at arm's length—but how would he explain the truth? *It's not that Hanéong's got silver hair, it's that a few centuries ago he decided to murder thousands of people for a game? It's not that he doesn't belong here, it's that he belongs everywhere, that I can't even breathe without inhaling the same air someone probably used to talk about him, hundreds or thousands of years ago? It's that he took me on this adventure and then destroyed me without even trying?*

What was the point? How could anyone understand the situation he was in? What even *was* the situation anymore—because if Hanéong was so unforgiveable, well, Ronoah could just *leave*, couldn't he? Call an end to their journey, crash at Ean-Bei's or Ngodi's place until he figured out a new life for himself. The opportunity was always there. Day after day, week after week, he didn't take it, and he didn't know why.

He'd been silent too long. "You know," Yengh-Sier gestured, startling Ronoah back into himself, "Eng-Vaunh's got some Qiao Sidhur blood in them, too. The most adored acrobat of our time, on track for sainthood even, and they're a quarter of this thing we disdain and ostracize." He picked up his bag and slung it over his shoulder. "Funny how we can ignore it when it suits us. Hanéong's a human being. Don't forget that just because most of the Ol-Penher do."

Ronoah's palms registered pain; he was digging his nails in enough to cut. "Sure," he said, and left it at that.

He was too busy simmering with pent-up indignation to pick up on the curious thing Yengh-Sier had said until later that week, when he was alphabetizing Ngodi's research portfolio. It had been a few hours holed up in the reading room she had rented for the trimester, a tiny, windowless, book-barricaded vestibule. Usually they talked more, Ngodi lecturing him in her deep voice about the history of Ol-Penher religion, hunched over heaps of notes in a way that would make posture-conscious Ean-Bei screech. Today they were collating references in preparation for Ngodi to actually write the first part of her thesis, and so their hands were kept busy flipping pages. Ronoah was absentmindedly skimming excerpts when it came back to him: "Ngodi," he called, giving the resonant floorboards a firm little stomp to make sure he'd got her attention, "are there living saints?" Yengh-Sier had deemed Eng-Vaunh *on track for sainthood*—but was that even possible?

"There aren't any living *right now*, but it's theoretically possible," was Ngodi's answer. She pushed her tangles of long auburn hair out of her face, mouth pulled taut in thought. "Sakangpenh was sainted before she died. But it's rare, because it's generally hard to tell what anyone's impact on the world is until at least a few decades after they die. Why?"

Ronoah told her about his conversation with Yengh-Sier and she flat-out laughed, slapping her palm against the stack of new library holds they'd fetched from circulation earlier. "Dragon's tits, Yengh-Sier is so dramatic—and he thinks he's not, which makes it even funnier." She recovered herself, still smirking. "I don't know enough about Eng-Vaunh's life to say whether that's an accurate assessment, but even if it is and they end up a saint, it's not going to revolutionize the way the more conservative Ol-Penher think about Qiao Sidh's place in our canon. We've already got a fullblooded Qiao Sidhur saint and nothing much changed; one quarter's not going to budge the train very far down the tracks. If anything, it's the little things that are going to build up over time and change us: some of the newer liturgies are composed in Qiao Sidhur scales, and the common household incense everyone uses these days is a direct import. Yengh-Sier's own festival has drinks that we flavour with pine syrup from Qiao Sidh."

For a surreal moment, Ronoah had no idea what Ngodi meant. Then it clicked. "Yengh-Sier's named after a saint?"

"Sure is—Saint Yengh-Sier of Mercy, or the Mountaintop Saint. He revolutionized our justice system around the forty-fifth century. We used to do a lot of executions, death for a death, lots of punishment-based stuff. Saint Yengh-Sier felt that if destruction was truly as much as part of the Wish as creation, then the agents of that destruction shouldn't be handled so cruelly. He had a vision, went on a big pilgrimage into the mountains, came back with plans for a system that was less about hurting the criminals and more about helping them recover from their part in the Wish. He's the founder of the Penitent Houses—ah, it's where criminals and victims go to negotiate atonement attempts with the restoration councils." She scratched at her stubble. "Basically he's the reason we don't kill people anymore."

Ronoah thought of Yengh-Sier—his Yengh-Sier, pensive and stern and more disciplined than anyone Ronoah had met before. Suddenly that integrity made a lot more sense.

He found himself gritting his teeth. For all Yengh-Sier's namesake had abhorred cruelty, the acrobat's parents had apparently felt fine about burdening their child with a mountain's worth of responsibility from birth. What a weight to put on a person.

Ngodi was entertaining less distressing lines of thought. "Honestly," she mused, "from a syncretic perspective, the most interesting change the Qiao Sidhur have brought to Ol-Penh's religious practices is also the reason why they're still here at all." Ronoah hooked his pinky and she elaborated: "They have this theory, the *bilateral realm*, the philosophy that there are two worlds, two realities stacked on top of each other—when you die in one, you go to the other, back and forth across spacetime. The original Qiao Sidhur settlers claimed that all the warriors who had died here were reborn *also here*, but like invisibly, on the other side. So if all of their kinsmen retreated, they'd be leaving their own people stuck here with us."

So the Aster Allowance was written into being, named for the aster flower which was traditionally planted over Ol-Penher graves. So the Qiao Sidhur were given leave, for religious reasons, to stay indefinitely in Ol-Penh, tending to their revenant ancestors. According to Ngodi, now there were even certain Ol-Penher gnostic congregations—"you can't exactly call them *churches*"—where devotees practiced Qiao Sidhur spirit communication, trying to talk to the dead.

"It's the furthest from Ol-Penher traditional worship you can get," Ngodi declared with a shrug. "But that's eclectic practice for you."

Ronoah was thinking, perhaps ungenerously, of the Ol-Penher belief in angels and saints in the first place when he asked, "Why is it such a strange thing to do?"

And Ngodi scoffed. "Because you *can't* talk to the dead, Ronoah, come on. There aren't spirits or ghosts or whatever the Qiao Sidhur call them— there *is* no bilateral realm. There's no living after life, period."

"Oh?" Ronoah prompted.

And then he actually heard what she'd said. It caught up to his blasé mouth and smacked him in it, twice as hard for his inattention.

"They—people rejoin the Wishgranter when they die, don't they?" he asked. Ngodi looked at him funny, shook her head. "Then where—" oh, he'd made a mistake, he was making a mistake, he could feel the collision coming and couldn't stop it now "—where do they go?"

"Nowhere." Ronoah blinked at the gesture Ngodi made, her left hand pulling at the air, like a *no* only grander, more final. "There is no world 'after' this one—there's only one Creation. When you're done, you're done."

It flexed like a sour fist around his stomach. "Even the saints?" he asked, hiding the suckerpunch of his surprise behind scepticism. This was—he hadn't thought about this.

"Even them, wished though their lives may be. That's one reason why we venerate them—that's the only reward they get, to be remembered as part of the great Wish's innermost workings. That's why this work is so *important*." She patted the hold stack again, affectionately, like whacking the rump of a steed. "The only thing we leave behind is our part in the Wish—our legacy, you know? So if there are saints out there whose work *hasn't* been recognized, they're just turning to worms without anyone praising them. Why should it only be Ol-Penher natives who get that posthumous recognition—everyone should have a chance at that, right? Wouldn't you want credit for your work after you're in the ground?"

She was actually asking him, he realized belatedly. He didn't know. He didn't know how to respond. All his trying to go around godless, and he hadn't stopped to consider what it meant for him if there were no gods to go back to.

He heard himself laugh, faintly. "I'm no saint-to-be," he heard himself say. "I don't think anyone's going to be looking for my legacy."

"Well with an attitude like *that*," Ngodi shot back jokingly, and it was meant to be a joke, he knew that, in another time it would have provoked a scandalized laugh or even a retort out of him, but all it found was a hollow in his chest. He smiled tight, resignation bitter on the back of his tongue, and Ngodi must have noticed the greying of the mood because she changed topics abruptly. "Hey. You ever been to church? A real one, not the gym."

Ronoah shook his head, too slow to see where this was going. Ngodi smiled and curled her hands into each other, the gesture for *together*. "You should come with me for tonight's mass. Ean-Bei's right, I work you too hard—we should go have some fun!"

Ronoah's mouth went dry. "I—you don't work me too hard."

"No? Good to hear, I'll work you harder." The wickedness in her eyes dimmed as she resettled her gaze on him. "But really, come tonight. Like we said, there's only one Creation, and it's right now and not forever. As far as we know, the world itself might disappear once the Wish is granted, so it's our holy responsibility to partake in as much of it as we can while we're here."

Ronoah hesitated. Something about the idea of being that intensely public—that *communal*—made his head swim. But—but why say no? Did he really have anything better to do? If Ngodi was right and there was only one lifetime, was he going to waste it all brooding?

So he swallowed the dread pressing on his throat. "Where do I meet you?" he asked.

That evening, to Freesia Street. To Saint Sakangpenh's Cathedral, lit like a split plum in the dark, stained-glass windows illuminated from the inside with an almost eerie blue-violet light. To church. Ronoah circled the perimeter twice, indecisive to the last, before finally being drawn as if by gravity through the arches and into the bath of light and sound and seething dancers. Loud, boisterous, colourful, chaotic; air hot from bodies, a hundred or two, damp and sinuous and exalted; drums and drones sending spangles of reverb up medial arches, possessing frame with sway, willing, involuntary; smoke-hazy ceiling, carnal corners, floor a forgiveness of believers. Ngodi found him, her hair wild and her smile wide and her bare arms glowing with painted swirls; she took his hands and pulled, and he was pulled in.

She told him after that he was a storming good dancer. She told him people were going to come to her asking where she snagged the good-looking ngoh with the skin like a map and the abandon like a priest-ess. She told him she hadn't expected him to fit in so well but sweet Saint Yu, there he was, pulling lungfuls of *nuam* leaf like an expert, not afraid to get up close to everyone. A natural-born worshipper.

It was news to Ronoah. He hadn't been keeping track of how he was moving, what he was doing. He'd done his best to get intoxicated as fast as possible and then step away from himself entirely, evaluating the world inside the cathedral through the fisheye lens of the faraway.

Honestly, it surprised him that he was even capable of doing that. Detaching. His empathy should have been spiralling out of control in a place like this, splattered messily all over his insides, but it wasn't. The quiet, the dissonance of his heart so tame in this riot, this luminescent rave—like Sasaupta Falls, like the jump. He just rocked and swayed through the throngs, light as a cargoless vessel, taking it all in eerie stride: the confectionary colours, the sumptuous food, the moaning in the alcoves, the lavish blue spirals fingerpainted on his arms—all so aggressively *much*, all so determinedly maximalistic. All at the edge of oblivion. This was the Ol-Penher way: have fun or else, because soon comes the long dark, and nobody to remember you but the Dragons in the end, but don't stress out about it because once you're gone you won't be around to be upset about it.

No wonder they needed to drown themselves in all this. He would too— he *did*, all of a sudden, needed to lose his bearings completely, to forget his name, his year, forget everything that led him here, because otherwise he was in very real danger of spoiling their party with the poison of his contempt. Contempt for them, the Ol-Penher, thrashing and splashing all over the atrium and believing there was a *reason* for it, a pattern, a design. Contempt for their Wishgranter, who didn't exist. Contempt for the word *wished*, for how annoying it sounded in someone's mouth. Contempt for his own contempt, for having the gall to feel superior when everyone in this building had more happiness in their little toe than he did in his entire body. It ate him up invisibly right on the churchfloor, the contempt and the despair and the hatred—cold, dull hatred, for Hanéong, for Chashakva, for the thing that had made him this way, and hatred for himself for letting her do it. For not noticing sooner. For saying *equal* when it had never been said.

Ayyeesh, if I'd known you were gonna lose your head like this I would've given you some pointers for dealing with the end of the world less pathetically, demon boy.

Shut up, he thought, swatting away the wretched comfort of that voice, the way it made him feel so overwhelmed to hear, so crazed with pity and fury. You don't get a say.

Because his contempt and his hatred were empty, too. He was feeling them out of habit, out of perverse obligation, but they had no substance, no staying power. There was no real *point* to letting any of it torment him, was there. He should just let it be. Let other people do what they want. Do whatever he wanted, too, and not think too hard about it because all that overthinking and agonizing would come to the same annihilation in the end. The Wishgranter may have been a lie, but her proponents had at least one thing right: *There are none in this life who can judge you.*

This was what it meant to go godless. This was the shape of the rest of his life. Better get used to it now.

He stumbled home just before dawn, immune, inured, untouchable. A couple of nights later, he went back.

THIRTY-EIGHT

*T*HE NEXT STRETCH OF LIFE IN KHEPSUONG PHAE was measured in Ronoah's mistakes.

The first was the swirls. It happened on one of the rare days when Ean-Bei, Yengh-Sier, and Ngodi's schedules all lined up for more than a couple hours of free time together. They were all sunning on one of the city's many green terraces, snacking on polenta cakes and berry wine. Ean-Bei had just showed off their newly-neatened haircut, lifting their bouncy crop of brown hair to reveal the lazy spirals underneath, and casually Ngodi asked Ronoah if he'd ever thought of getting his own hair done.

"Sure would look nice," she said to his blank expression. "Your hair's so dark and dense."

"Oh wow, wouldn't it though?" Ean-Bei leaned forward, examining Ronoah's head with a keenness that made his scalp prickle. They smoothed their hands along their own hair. "Like on the sides, yeah, I can totally see that. You should do it!"

"I—is it expensive?" Ronoah asked, not knowing why of all things that was his first question. Money wasn't an issue for him in Khepsuong Phae.

Ean-Bei shrugged, flip-flopping their palms. "It depends. I'm sure my place would do it at a discount, I've been going there since I came to the city. They're still open now."

Now? As in today, as in *right* now—exactly the kind of joyously impulsive decisions the Ol-Penher were so fond of making. The kind made just for the sake of shaking things up. Ronoah looked to Yengh-Sier—the man was usually the one who roped in Ngodi and Ean-Bei's recklessness. Yengh-Sier looked back at him with casual curiosity, like he had no strong opinion either way. The choice was Ronoah's alone.

A frisson of something trembled through his ribs; his pulse quickened, thickened.

"Sure," he heard himself say, "why not?"

Ean-Bei whooped and the four of them collected themselves and left the terrace en route to the stylists. Ronoah took the wooden steps with more force than necessary, trying to mask the jangle of his heart under the jostle of his bones.

He hadn't cut his hair since he'd met Hanéong. Hadn't cut it since he left *Pilanova*. That was the way of his people, leaving locks unshorn until a birth or a death or a marriage or some other ritual moment. Until now, the idea had never even entered his mind to do it for aesthetic reasons. An old part of him was appalled, aghast—but he rushed past it, pushing it out of mind as he ran down the streets with his friends.

It'll be fine, he thought. It's just off the sides, like they said. Ngeome's been doing that since he was sixteen, and nothing bad's ever happened to him. Look at it like this: you're following in your brother's footsteps at last. Wouldn't everyone be happy about that.

The stylists were initially surprised to see Ean-Bei twice in a day, but their confusion quickly warmed to cheer as the tai explained their vision for Ronoah. "I'm thinking not too clustered, two or three per side. Not symmetrical, but definitely continuous. Maybe start a little low, it's their first time—midbrow?" Ronoah had no idea what most of this meant, and no opinion of his own to counter with, so he let his friend dictate to the stylists, and then he let them sit him down in a chair beside a table bedecked with all manner of clippers and combs, forcing himself not to laugh nervously, not to grip the arms too tight.

Everybody was there in the mirror facing the chair, ranged around him like a host of the Wishgranter's angels: Ean-Bei checking their own new cut, Yengh-Sier watching the stylists prepare their implements, Ngodi watching Ronoah watching everybody else. He startled when she caught his eye in the glass; she grinned and signed a word, and even though it was reversed he knew what it meant.

"Yeah," he signed back, just before they draped a sheet over his arms. "Ready."

He wasn't ready. He felt overstretched, elatedly panicked, like he knew he was doing something bad but couldn't bring himself to stop. The stylist untied his rose-coloured headscarf and let his locs down; they fell nearly to his shoulder blades, the longest they'd been since the Ravaging. With a deft, greensleeved hand, the stylist sifted through the rows of twists, presumably searching for a clean line to cut from. The ghosting tingle of her fingers so close to his skull was bizarre in a way that made him a little queasy. He suppressed a shiver, tore his eyes away from her hands in the mirror and fixed them squarely on his own image.

Funny, how rarely he checked his reflection. After all this time he was still expecting the chubby cheeks and worried brow of Padjenne's Ronoah, the untidy scruff and the skittish eyes. What looked steadily back at him was something else entirely: something straight-spined and square-shouldered, something with a sharpness in the jaw, with a look that was level and dark as the sky just past sundown. He looked like his brother—no, he looked like his *mother*. Like Diadenna, Indigo Queen, hard and proud as polished terracotta.

He stared, fascinated. His mouth set a little crooked, a little wry; his posture, lean and keen and hungry; his eyes, deep blue and burning. He didn't know he looked at everything like that, with that glass-thin sliver of a glare buried in his gaze.

A chewy snip from the scissors. The first loc fell.

He closed his eyes, breathing in evenly through his nose. It's all right, he thought; it's good. Just like Ngeome. He always looked so fetching, so fair, but you're a fine sight yourself now, Ngodi said so, and wouldn't he be so irritated if his little brother came back sporting his signature look? Wouldn't it be just the thing, to exasperate him like you used to? Your father, he'd take one look at the two of you and make some kind of joke, and it would make you both cringe and he'd laugh because that's exactly what he wants. And Lelos—he inhaled again, a little more sharply, as the cold steel of the scissors slid past his ear—Lelos would yell at you for getting so nervous about something so ridiculous, she'd tell you to get it over with if you're going to do it at all, she'd say make a damn choice, Ronono, and once you make it defend it no matter what anybody says. That's how you earn respect. That's how you live regretless.

Someone tapped him on the shoulder. He opened his eyes to meet the stylist's in the mirror. "Want to see how it's going so far?" she asked, holding his locs back.

He turned his head to the side. A clean line carved, half a harvested field, a fine fuzz of black and a peekthrough of brown, scrolling his skull in two loosely-wound spirals. It looked eyecatching, handsome even.

He was going to throw up.

"I can't do this—I can't—" This rush of strangled Acharrioni; nobody knew what he was saying, knew the twisted lurch of his stomach or the sick flush of warmth blossoming across his body, nobody knew he was thisclose to full-on hyperventilating so if you could just *calm down Ronoah*, chuta ka saag, can you imagine how they'll react if you flip out over a *haircut*, stop deathgripping the chair and back out with poise.

He shook a hand out from under the sheet, lifted it to his bare scalp. Pressed hard with his fingers so nobody could see them trembling. "It looks great," he said, forcing levity into his tone, not able to look at anyone but himself, at his own eyes, those distant eyes that were so good at masking his horror. "I think—" use your hands, you need to speak properly "—I think I like it just like this, actually."

"Really?"

The stylist seemed a little put-out; Ronoah felt the cold sweat of inevitability break over him at the thought that he might let her finish out of *politeness*, of all things—but then Ngodi interrupted. "I agree," she said. "You like the symmetry thing too much Ean-Bei, one-sided is fashionable."

Ean-Bei huffed, but they didn't seem truly offended. "It's not just style, it's symbolism. Does it feel right for you, Ronoah?" Ronoah made himself freshly dizzy with his head-wobbling. "Then it's wished and perfect as is. And half the price, too!"

So he was spared. He cut a string of red shell to pay the stylist for her work. It took him three tries to tie the loose end, his fingers were so numb. On the tiles around the chair, his locs were strewn like black snakes. His gut clenched so hard he nearly doubled over. Maybe, maybe he could ask to keep them—?

And do what, he thought scornfully, glue them to your head? Hide them in your satchel with the other things you can't bear to look at but can't stand to lose? Pathetic. It's done. You made your choice.

But he hadn't. That was the problem, viscerally evident every time he turned his head in a shop window thereafter. He'd last shaved his head when he was initiated into the temple of Pilanova for training; his hair marked his status as a priest, as a *pilgrim*, marked his commitment to his journey. The body was the soul—godless or not, that was a belief older than dogma, an association too root-deep to weed. To cut his hair was to permanently release that stage of his life, to banish it and begin anew—to *half*-cut it was like leaving a plate of food half-eaten, leaving a body half-buried. Unfinished business. That wasn't a decision, that was a *tantrum*, fruitless little fit against the tightening bindings of his life.

Well, drawled a voice in his head, was it worth it? Was the thrill good enough to pay with the shame?

He didn't know. On the one hand, it was the most alive he'd felt in weeks, that stab of fearful feeling through the dead flesh of his everyday. On the other hand, it was haunting him, costing him. Now he couldn't look at his own face without being reminded of what he'd given up on—without wondering if all of him had truly given up.

He'd been evading all mention of the Pilgrim State lately, especially when Hanéong was nearby. Hanéong practiced a similar avoidance. Ronoah could only guess why the man wasn't pestering him about their departure. He had technically finished his work for Ngodi a few weeks ago, but he'd found one reason after another to stay. Petty reasons. Stupid little things. And yet Hanéong indulged him. He did not pressure Ronoah; he did not even ask.

Hanéong didn't need to ask. The question asked itself every time a breeze chilled the sensitive skin of Ronoah's scalp: *Is our time together over? Are we going, or aren't we?*

The second mistake was the dragon poi.

Yengh-Sier and Eng-Vaunh performed together at the amphitheatre in mid-spring. They had separate acts, but they crossed each other at the edge of the platform as Eng-Vaunh's act ended and Yengh-Sier's began, which technically meant they had been onstage together—a point Ean-Bei made loudly enough for Yengh-Sier to clap the tai's hands between his own, silencing them, a flush of mortified delight on his face.

As always, Ronoah had fallen headfirst into the performance, following the hypnotic trails of the dragon poi in Yengh-Sier's hands, feeling the warmth pour into his pores, feeling an easing of the constant constriction of his chest—feeling *something*. He didn't feel much these days. He didn't know how it happened, but somewhere in the twisting boulevards of Khepsuong Phae he'd lost his sensitivity, dropped it piece by piece like running with an open bag of honeyed nuts. The anguishing grief of his early days in the city had blunted and faded, the heartbreak diffused, defused, too nebulous now to catch and examine even if he wanted to.

Sometimes he wanted to. In the breath before he opened a book, or the dark minute before he tumbled into exhausting sleep. Sometimes he wanted to pry his floorboards up just to see if there was anything living underneath. But they were varnished shut, and his fingers couldn't remember how to scratch through. He walked through his days with eyes permanently affixed to the middle distance, pressing at the barrier between looking and seeing and finding it insurmountable. Everything was hazy lately; everything was unreal. He supposed he hated it, a little.

But the four and a half minutes watching Yengh-Sier spiral fire weren't flat, or grey, or indistinct. They were gripping minutes, wrenching, nearly painful, but Ronoah wasn't fussed about a bit of pain in exchange for a sense of time moving *forward*. Hadn't everything felt, once, like it was moving forward together—sometimes so fast he couldn't catch up, couldn't catch his breath? Hadn't it been that the intensity of everything could sweep him along like the crest of a wave, onward to some end, some glorious—?

It had been. It must have been. He couldn't quite remember how it felt, but—but nothing like fire in your hands to jog your memory, right?

When Yengh-Sier performed, he seemed like the most solid thing in the whole world. Ronoah wanted to stop feeling blurred around the edges.

So the day after the performance, he asked.

"When do you think I can stop using the practice poi?"

Yengh-Sier seemed surprised at the question. "When you can perform the whole dance flawlessly with them," he answered, and then, to Ronoah's frown, "At your pace, probably another two or three months."

A dull pang of dismay echoed in Ronoah's chest. That may as well have been two or three years. "There's no way I can get there faster?" he pressed. Yengh-Sier raised an eyebrow. He wasn't used to Ronoah acting impudent; Ronoah was a good student. Ronoah was hardworking, diligent, methodical, mechanical.

"They're dangerous without proper care," he said eventually. "You have to prove you can perform safely."

Maybe that's what did it. The implication that he might be careless, or else the reminder that his body was a thing that could be harmed. The idea that one more person was doing something to keep him safe. *Something* had to have done it, to have lit the long fuse leading to irrational insurgency. It can't have been nothing that drove Ronoah to wedge a second-floor window open with a stone, that pulled him back to the acro centre in the dead of night, scaling the façade of the building with the muscle memory built up from an underground long ago. It can't have been nothing that led him to stealing through the equipment room, to pilfering a candle and a can of fuel, to standing in the middle of a moonlit gymnasium with a pair of dragon poi clenched in his hands.

Fuck safety. Fuck two or three months. He was the Firewalker.

How did Yengh-Sier prepare the weights? He'd seen the acrobat do it before, he just had to remember. The fuel, the can, the evenly-soaked wick. It was tricky in the dim of the night, but he couldn't risk someone noticing light in the windows and coming to investigate. The light of the poi themselves was already going to make his heart pound like a thief's.

The candle, lit and flooding a flickering arena of dark gold. The light up—no, wait, shouldn't he have a towel? Yengh-Sier always had a wet towel around for extinguishing the wicks. He put the poi down, their chains clattering obscenely in the gymnasium, and fetched one to lie in a shallow bucket of water. See? Not so careless after all.

Now. Now, the light. Now the quick hot *fwish* of ignition, and the other one, and now the dry pressure of the flames so close to his body, ready to do what he told them, or to do something else entirely, to burn capricious and unpredictable like fire always did.

He gave them a tentative swing, saw his shadow ripple and distort as these little suns changed position, skipping ceilingward, sweeping to ground—a strike, a spark, a startled gasp and a step back before he grit his teeth and planted his feet. Don't be so jumpy, he chided. Fire's never hurt you before. Why would it start now?

He found he was scaring himself. That was more a reason to continue than a reason to stop.

He swung them again, careful this time not to let too much chain out. The poi circled lonely as two meteors in space, graceful, unstoppable—but he did stop them, he stalled them and switched direction like Yengh-Sier taught him to, and for a thrilling moment he thought his technique was wrong and gravity would just veer them into his hands but they obeyed his command, streaking heat across his body. His bare arms illuminated in the furnace glow, his hands mottled at the knuckles, darkscarred with evidence of a rash past. You have been punished for this recklessness before.

Then punish me, he thought, bringing the poi down in a slashing X and out again, changing their timing, their rhythm, challenging his abilities. I am giving you every opportunity. I shouldn't be here. I shouldn't be anywhere near here, so are you going to say something about it or not?

The poi haloed him, dazzling and dangerous, tearing at the air with their flaming claws. Around his head, winding his sides, behind his back—his scarred shoulder twinged and he exhaled one hard punch of a laugh but no, that wasn't proof, that was just muscle stiffness, just lack of warmup, that could be anything. Not good enough. Around and again, livid arcs of light slicing the world into cross-sections of abyss and afterimage—the constant changing brightness was an assault on his eyes, left him blinking hard to scrape phantom shapes off his retinas. To scry them into something meaningful.

This is *nothing*, he thought, this is two piddling bits of fire on *leashes*. I jumped into the heart of the Ravaging and survived—I was in a *world* of burning, and even then you could barely nudge me, so you *can't* find me through this, can you? Can you?

"Try anyway," he snarled aloud, eyes on the poi winging overhead. The bridge of his nose prickled horribly. "*Try.*"

"Um, hello?"

Ronoah jerked around and the poi ricocheted off the concrete, swerving into a sparking tangle that he dropped on yelping instinct. It spat in a glowing pile, throwing a ring of illumination on the person who had snuck up on him.

Pale curls. Green and purple sleeves. It was Eng-Vaunh.

"I—I—" He scrambled for words, for an explanation, for anything. His mouth, his hands, nothing would work for him. He felt like a freshly snapped twig, whiplashed out of his misery, chest heaving, ears ringing from the impact. Adrenaline stabbed in his veins. "What, why are you—"

"I like to practice alone sometimes," was the not-tai's silky answer. They spun something on a pinky finger, something straight and glinting—a key to the centre. "You too, hmm?"

He was too paralyzed to reply. Eng-Vaunh checked over his shoulder at the abandoned tangle of burning poi, then flicked their long-lashed gaze back to him, searching him over, sizing him up. Their eyes were like crystal, the colour indeterminable in the low bobbing light.

"...you're Yengh-Sier's student, aren't you?" they asked at length. Mutely, Ronoah nodded, and something he couldn't interpret resolved in Eng-Vaunh's face.

He had no idea which way this was going to go. He felt the urge to plead Eng-Vaunh's silence, to beg them not to tell Yengh-Sier what he'd done—but there was another urge, equally fierce, to dare them to tattle, to get on their bad side, to get himself banned from ever picking up the poi again. He was caught like a bee in amber, waiting airless for which way they would choose to crack his immediate future open.

Eng-Vaunh stepped forward. Ignoring Ronoah's flinch, they took his hands in their own, lifting them up to examine. Their skin was startlingly uncalloused. "I'm sure Yengh-Sier has told you," they said, letting his hands drop, "but there's a dress code for practicing that stuff."

Ronoah blinked. Eng-Vaunh's mouth curved up.

"I'm happy to be your spotter, if you like. But if you're going to do it, you should go get changed." They signalled with a languid roll of their head. "The gear's in the costume room, two doors down from equipment."

At first he just stood there, too bewildered at being allowed to get away with this. Then somehow he backed up a step, and another, and then he turned and staggered into the costume room.

He fumbled through the faint blue light, looking for the flame-resistant gear. His hands skimmed hangers of cotton and beaded silk and reinforced rubber. Slowly, after combing through the first aisle, he came to a stop.

Dragon's tits, what was he *doing*?

Common sense slammed into him like an ocean wave, cold and stinging with salt. What on earth was he trying to prove to himself? Breaking and entering, stealing, lying to his teacher—what was *wrong* with him? He marveled, for an abstract moment, at his own foolishness.

Then he shook himself out of it and fled. As he slipped up the stairs he thought he saw, out of the corner of his eye, Eng-Vaunh hefting his untangled poi in their hands.

Only later, when he wasn't addled with fear and adrenaline and vindictive passion, did he recognize the acrobat's play for what it was: a distinctly Ol-Penher helping hand, a way to give Ronoah some breathing room, to silently help him reassess. Instead of open chastisement they'd gone for discretely removing him from danger, so he could realize for himself that the danger was in fact present. It was the kind of quasi-intervention the Wishgranter would approve of—it was the kind Pilanova would approve of, too. Ronoah nursed a clandestine gratitude for the celebrity thereafter, especially when he realized Yengh-Sier wasn't going to be hearing about his student's midnight practice session after all. Lessons carried on as usual, with no trust or love lost between them.

Ronoah tried to find Eng-Vaunh again later, to catch that crystalline eye and communicate some silent thanks, but he couldn't find them. According to Yengh-Sier they'd moved on, south down the circuit. They never appeared again.

Eng-Vaunh was not the only one to whom he owed a clean getaway.

He was halfway home that night before he noticed it—a stinging on his left forearm. He moved to rub it and recoiled as pain flared under his fingers. At the next streetlamp, he paused his guilty speedwalking to examine his elbow under the light.

A burn mark. A shiny stroke about two inches long, like chipped paint on his arm. As he laid eyes on it, the pain swelled up over whatever barrier of shock had suppressed it. It didn't look like the kind of mark he'd have gotten from the poi; it looked like the kind you'd get from not being careful with your fuel, from leaving a smear on your skin. A scalding; a scolding.

Careless, careless.

His eyes watered. He cursed himself, and then he made it the rest of the way to the boarding house, to Hanéong.

"I need you to fix this," he said as he walked through the door. Hanéong glanced up from whatever bit of magic he was toying with at the writing desk; he surveyed Ronoah's out-stuck arm, lingered on the angry little burn. "Yengh-Sier can't see it."

A corner of Hanéong's mouth quirked, ruefully, and Ronoah knew in that moment that the man knew exactly where he'd been, what he'd done. He didn't reply, just locked Ronoah's injury in his sights with an expression Ronoah would have been able to parse, once upon a time.

"I know you can do it," he added bluntly, as the seconds ticked by and the pressure built in his chest. "You did it with my hand in Chiropole."

Either Hanéong could do it or he could just *refuse* already, and Ronoah would find some other way to hide the mark and the wincing when he bent his elbow. Whatever was pent up in this choking silence was worse.

Hanéong ran a hand through his hair. It was such a human gesture—so weirdly humble—it made Ronoah flinch. "So I did," the man finally conceded, and he reached for Ronoah's arm.

It had been a long time since Hanéong touched him. Since Ronoah had allowed himself to be touched. He still expected something to happen every time, some crashing melding mesh. A rebound of the indescribable sensations that had overwhelmed him when he'd connected to Hanéong—to Chashakva—the day they killed Jau-Hasthasuna. He was still waiting to be yanked into that vast and howling landscape, to feel the leap of lightning between them. He craved it, hatefully, ached for it.

The silence he received instead was oppressive, inflexible, nearly judge-mental—and what did Hvanzhir Hanéong get to judge him for? To begrudge him for? When it was the one that had slaughtered so many, when it had lied and murdered and ruined so much, what right did it have to veil itself from him? To hide behind caution and care? What right did it have to look at him like that, with that unfiltered concern like *he* was the problem here?

Hanéong's cool fingertips traced the burn. Ronoah clenched his fist. When the magic seeped in, he almost tore his arm away.

Smoky sapphire light curled up from the wound as Hanéong had his private conversations with the things that bound Ronoah together. A lark called outside the cracked-open window. "That's two now," Hanéong murmured; Ronoah only realized the man was talking to him when he elaborated, glancing up to Ronoah's face, to the spiralled side of his head. "Two decisions you've made in haste." Ronoah's eyes widened; Hanéong's narrowed in a smile. "You know what we say—"

"It doesn't matter." It burned his throat on the way out, more caustic than any lighter fuel. *They* didn't say anything anymore. "I don't—I don't want to hear your catchphrases right now, Hanéong."

Whatever smile that was creeping in flattened out. "No," the man agreed, bending again over his work. "No, of course. You're here to be fixed." Even numb as he was, Ronoah felt that statement like a slap, sudden and incomprehensible. What was Hanéong trying to say? Was he making fun of him? Why wouldn't he just be clear—why did Ronoah have to work so hard to figure him out? It wasn't always like this, it—why, why did there have to be such irredeemable distance between them?

After a moment, in those same mild tones: "The last time I fixed you was the first time I used it. My *catchphrase*, I mean. Under the mountain, remember?" *Remember?* Of course Ronoah remembered, he remembered abruptly, violently, the memory invaded him like a parasite, flooded all the places where the caves had cleaved a piece from him, all the places that had cried out for comfort then, his ribs his elbow his cheek where Özrek had laid his fingers so gently—

"All this time and here you are, still too distracted by surface wounds to get at what needs healing most." Ronoah froze. Hanéong smiled with its mouth this time. "You remain an exemplar of your kind."

If the first comment was a slap, this one was a stab, a stiletto through the soft of this vulnerable instant. How, how—how *dare* Hanéong taunt him about this. How dare it. Ronoah stared hard at the window over Hanéong's shoulder, forcing himself not to yank away or leave the room or snap back with something he'd regret. His resolve lasted. He kept his silence long after his burn had vanished, long after he'd bid Hanéong a curt goodnight and curled himself fetal under sheets. Teeth clenched so hard his jaw ached. Heart clenched so hard his spirit choked, begged for mercy.

Remember?

He remembered so much, when it was the two of them alone in a room. The banter, the teasing, the catchphrases. The jokes no one else understood, the words that meant more than themselves. His usual habit of throwing a heavy blanket over these thoughts failed him tonight, left him imagining over and over a different end to the conversation, an end where he hadn't stonewalled, where Hanéong had pressed for more, where they could lie back-to-back again, spine to starlit spine, instead of on opposite ends of a room a galaxy wide. Gods, even an end where Hanéong finally got fed up of Ronoah's atrocious behaviour and *said* something about it, where the creature took the situation into its own hands—he wanted it, he realized, wanted it so bad, for Hanéong to just decide their fate for him, to say *we're going next month and that's final* or *I'm leaving in two weeks whether you're with me or not* or *I'm leaving tomorrow, and I'm leaving you behind.* Why wouldn't it just leave Ronoah behind? It baffled him, enraged him, left him wretched. Left him susceptible to *making decisions in haste.*

Two mistakes so far, Ronoah; where's the third?

It was such a stupid saying, this thing about threes and fives, such a puerile superstition, it didn't make sense and it shouldn't matter—and yet. And yet in the vacuum of their shared aloneness, it hounded him.

Where is the third, Ronoah? Where is the third?

It's right here, he thought savagely, fist curling into the sheets over his heart. Come get it whenever you like. Come get me.

Come get me.

THIRTY-NINE

"**Y**OU KNOW, THERE'S ACTUALLY A LEGEND about the library that says there's a second, hidden library underground, buried beneath the first."

"Have you ever gone looking?"

"What? Oh, nope, tunnels freak me out. You couldn't ask me to climb into a sewer, never mind a thousands-of-years old catacomb or whatever. But I believe every word of it."

"Why do you believe it, if you haven't seen it?"

"Because," said Ean-Bei, gesturing at the overstuffed, understaffed waiting room, "they've gotta stash all the paperwork *somewhere*."

They were an hour into their wait at the Khepsuong Phaer Consulate. All the good bureau rags were gone. Ean-Bei had brought a clutch of green grapes to share in order to stave off the snackish irritability that might set in before someone finally saw Ronoah to process his visa. More specifically, to renew it.

Had three months really passed since he'd first set foot on Yanyel's crumbly, cobbled streets? It seemed impossible, and yet the date stamped on the papers proved it so. It was actually a little over that—adding on the week it took Ronoah to notice, and the additional week it took to muster up the motivation to do something about it. According to Ngodi, the act of overstaying didn't land Ronoah in any trouble, but the paperwork did have to be turned in. She was the one who'd finally put her foot down on his reticence, throwing him out of her study until he could return with a freshly-minted visa.

Of course, she had sympathy for him—no one *enjoyed* a trip to the Khepsuong Phaer Consulate. But she couldn't make the time to come sit with him in solidarity. Neither could Yengh-Sier. Shockingly, it was the perpetually-busy Ean-Bei who'd cleared their socialite's schedule to wait the requisite four hours with Ronoah, equipped with rations and stories to pass the time.

"So I learned something totally zany at the guest lecture today," the tai gestured, pausing to pop a grape into their gold-gilt mouth. A benefit of handhalf: being able to talk while chewing. "You know the shalledrim."

"I do," answered Ronoah, not without an edge of wryness.

"You know how they did the whole human subjugation thing during the Empire, yeah? Even after the Shattering, the ones that survived just rebuilt and kept at it?" Ronoah head-wobbled an affirmative. "Well guess what, there was this expedition in the 48th Century to an old colony in ka-Khasta where they interviewed a bunch of village elders and confirmed that for like, two hundred years, they'd lived with a shalledra *peacefully*, as—well, I don't think as equals, but close as it gets." Ean-Bei looked expectantly at Ronoah; obligingly, Ronoah feigned surprise. "Mindblowing, right? It's not the only case either, professor Pheng said there are like a half-dozen reports of human-shalledrim cohabitation across the continent. It's called *alternate coupling theory*, it's a super fringe subset of shalledrology, Pheng's one of like four people who are studying it. There isn't even a proper compendium of the accounts."

"We don't like our shalledrim reasonable," Ronoah quipped. "Too complicated, no thank you. We like our magic tyrants clean-cut and easy to skin."

Ean-Bei laughed. "Apparently alternate coupling theory gets flak from the other sub-disciplines because so many of the accounts could fall under the category of shalledrim worship—it's like a one shalledra per village thing. That's not having a neighbour so much as it is having a local saint. Hard to tell what the power dynamic was, right? But Pheng said there were exceptions to that model, like this huge colony in Chiropole up in the mountains—"

Ronoah, who had been somewhere slightly away from himself, was slapped back into the conversation.

"—was a whopping three to one ratio of shalledrim to humans, and evidence they lived in the same houses even—"

"What evidence?" A flutter of velvet red and plum black against his plummeting heart. The curl of mountainous clouds in pearlescent paint. *We were the last in all the land to see the sun rise, the first to see it sink.* Ean-Bei blinked, and Ronoah pressed, "What, was—was anyone still up there?"

"Still up there?" Ean-Bei's smirk parted to reveal their chipped canine. "What, when they launched the expedition? Dragon's tits, no, it was abandoned hundreds of years ago. They just found artifacts, basketry and stuff, weathered-down houses, a couple gravespots—you know, those imprints shalledrim made when they passed naturally?—that kind of thing."

Ronoah's heart bounced painfully off the hard surface of this assurance; he tried not to let Ean-Bei see the relieved sag of his shoulders.

"But just think about it," the tai continued, gesturing widely enough to nearly thwack a passing family on their way to the check-in desk. "Imagine living foot-to-face with something that much more powerful than you. How would that relationship even work? How would you handle that kind of irreconcilable difference under one roof?"

Ronoah did not have to imagine. Ronoah tried very hard not to think about it at all. He picked a grape off the bunch and chewed, watching a young ngoh rise from the bench in a flurry of rose-coloured silks, papers clutched eagerly to their chest. "Filing income tax must have been a nightmare."

"*Taxes,*" Ean-Bei spluttered, "are not even part of the equation, think bigger Ronoah, what if the shalledrim taught the humans magic, or raised them from birth like that prophet from ka-Khasta, or, sweet Saint Yu, *what if they banged.*"

Ronoah gave the tai such a look of withering disinterest that they broke out laughing again. "I know, I know, not your thing," they relented, "but just …it's like when I read field reports for my Ol-Penher Ecology class and hear about how some tiger in the northern cloudforests adopted a baby macaque after eating its mother. Don't you want to know where the gentleness came from, after so much violence?"

Despite himself, Ronoah snorted—a bitter, careworn sound—and Ean-Bei looked curiously at him and for a moment the tide rose cold and churning in his body, the pressure pent like a scream, the centuries of Shaipurin bodies in the bogs and Chashakva's killing slice and the scornful laugh of a freshly-crowned queen saying *You're lucky you survived it the first time* and he felt perilously close to telling Ean-Bei everything, everything he'd suppressed so thoroughly, he felt like laying it all out and then upending a few chairs for good measure.

Only it just wouldn't come.

"Are you ever going to pick a discipline and stick to it?" he found himself asking instead.

Ean-Bei's face darkened a shade, and too late Ronoah realized he'd accidentally made it sound like a mockery. Cursing himself, he hurried to smooth it over: "I mean, sorry, I mean it must be an advantage to be able to pull laterally from so many areas of study, I just—why did you come to Khepsuong Phae? I discovered shalledrology in Padjenne by accident, when I was researching—something else. Is it like that for you, too?" To his abstracted relief, he realized he wasn't just asking for the sake of having something to do with his hands. He actually wanted to know. "Was it a change of plans, or did you always want to learn a little bit of everything?"

Apparently the sincerity he'd wedged into his expression was enough to convince Ean-Bei to open back up. "*Want* is a funny word," they said, with a wistful crimp at the corner of their mouth that might have been a smile. They sighed, looking across the Consulate's waiting room, and Ronoah realized two things. First, that he had once again unwittingly stumbled into a revealing of someone's tender insides; second, that he had never asked Ean-Bei this astoundingly basic question before. He had a few detached moments to evaluate how self-absorbed that made him before the tai began.

"The library *was* the change of plans. It was never in the plan at all, per se. I guess..." They paused, stilled, hands dropping fractionally as they measured the weight of what they had to say and found it heavier than they'd anticipated. Ronoah waited, and they rallied themself: "It's the nicest punishment I've ever been sentenced to."

What did *that* mean? "A punishment," Ronoah repeated, frowning lightly, only vaguely aware that he'd leaned in. Ean-Bei plucked the last grape, ate it, and explained.

"My hometown, Ruppanteak, up in the Ol-Penher Massif? You should visit sometime, it's gorgeous at the end of summer, all blue-greens and burnt gold and pink outcrops. Like a painting out of the pastoral collection." Their hazel eyes gleamed with the relish of it, this dewy watercolour world where they'd been born. "It's quaint and idle and lovely, and I was basically the terror of it."

Ronoah sized Ean-Bei up, all five feet five inches of them, and found it hard to imagine their sunny countenance terrorizing anyone. As if sensing this, the tai lifted a finger to tap at their temple. "It's this thing that happens to me, where I get bored so easily with what's happening around me, and when I get bored I get restless and I start causing trouble. I'm not *trying* to cause trouble," they added, with the decisive gestures of someone who'd had to explain this many times, "not exactly, I just—need movement. Constant movement. I need *change.*"

Like Yengh-Sier. Like Ronoah. The hairs on his arms lifted, despite the stuffiness of the waiting room. Some long-sleeping creature inside of him roused its head, shifted in the dune it was half-buried under, sand slipping rivulets down its side. *Change or die*, it whispered.

He couldn't remember the last time he'd thought of that phrase, that mantra—and now here it was, reborn in the sheepishly eager face across from him, all freckles and gold and enthusiasm that he swore used to sing from his own blood, once.

"I caused problems for my family, for my town," Ean-Bei said, "small ones mostly—but then a big one."

"What did you do?"

"Something stupid. I—" They glanced around. Angled themself closer to Ronoah, cradling their hands to their torso where only he could see them, where their wrongs could remain discrete. "I messed with one of the wishbones."

"*What?*" Ean-Bei snapped forward and clasped Ronoah's incredulous hands in their own, shushing him, but Ronoah was too taken, too taken in, and he repeated himself in stage-whispered Chiropolene: "You what?"

The wishbones were those massive chunks of quartz crystal whose presence kept the fields rich and fertile. Ol-Penh's most precious natural wonders. How did someone *mess* with one of those?

After hard-staring Ronoah into complacency, they released his hands so they could tell the tale. "Unless you're with one of the ministries or it's literally on your farm, you're not allowed within twelve feet of the wishbones. It's a public safety protocol; sometimes if you disturb them badly enough, they stop working so well. But I was … bored. And my brother had this azalea shrub that got stunted in the late frost and he was all bent out of shape about it and I just—wondered." Again, the wistfulness on their face, like the wondering itself was the crime. "I wanted to see if the soil had the same sort of nutrient-rich charge even when it was removed from the site. I wanted to help. I passed the farm every day on my way to the mill, and on the way back it was usually deserted, so I brought a sack and a spade one evening to dig up a bit of the dirt—just the dirt!—but once I got there I didn't know which dirt to try first. How does the charge work? Do I take from where the radishes are growing, or closer to where the crystal meets the ground? Should I take samples from different ranges and run some trials? Why don't farmers plant right up to the edge of the wishbones anyway?

"That's how they found me," the tai said, and reached out and flicked Ronoah on the knee, and Ronoah startled, just like Ean-Bei probably had. "The farmer and the magistrate she'd gone to fetch. They found me kneeling in the dirt with a trowel in one hand and my runaway brain in the other, and—" they broke off laughing, a strained, stifled sound through the nose "—well, I *hope* nobody thought I was stupid enough to try dislodging the wishbone with a tool that puny, but people thought a lot of things about me that weren't very generous."

So Ean-Bei was hauled off to the province's penitent house, set to testify before the Council of Elders and the Council of Juniors, and ultimately charged with trespassing, attempted vandalism, and breach of the peace. Ordinarily these charges wouldn't have carried such gravity, but they were exaggerated by the vandalised object in question being a sacred object of Ol-Penh, and compounded by Ean-Bei's trailing record of past misdemeanours. The sentence devised by the Council of Juniors was both whimsical and extremely serious, as was the way with children's logic: they committed Ean-Bei to the library of Khepsuong Phae, sending the tai away for three years to shake the restlessness out of their bones, or else to put it to good use.

Another exile. Trust them to fling into each other like magnets on Ronoah's first day.

Cloudshadow seeped through the windows, muting the light in the Consulate. A pair of taik were called to the front and jumped from their seats, fingers intertwined. The clock above the check-in desk chimed a pretty note. "Has it worked?" Ronoah asked eventually.

Ean-Bei relaxed back into their seat, making an indecisive clicking noise with their tongue; evidently the classified part of the story was over. "I've definitely learned a bunch of things, found good outlets—honestly, the acro centre's helped with the mind wandering more than the library ever has. It's a lot easier to focus when you're twenty feet off the ground." They grinned, but it faded quickly. "I'm having fun, but I don't think I've done what the Council wanted me to. We're into year three and I must have taken a class on literally every subject Khepsuong Phae offers, but I haven't found anything that I stick to. I don't know if…if I *have* a thing, Ronoah, you know? I don't know if anything can make me happy—make me *behave*—forever. I'm kind of dreamless. Like a miswish."

"A what?"

"Something obstructing the flow of the Wish, like a branch in a creek. Something that's already fulfilled its purpose and now's just in the way— or something that's only purpose is to *be* in the way. An obstacle for someone else to push through."

This kind of self-dismissal, coming from the perpetually-boisterous Ean-Bei, was enough to render Ronoah speechless. Calling Ean-Bei a burden was like calling rainbows too gaudy, like wanting to lampshade the sun. It was foolishness bordering on flat-out slander. If the Wishgranter were real—if the Wish existed, and its logic were sound—the miswish would be Ronoah, not Ean-Bei. It would be him.

"I miss Ruppanteak," the tai was saying, their casual tone belied by the agitation in their fingers, "but I worry when I finally get to go home I'll just mess it up again. I really like Khepsuong Phae—but the library masters can only justify a scholar's stipend when the scholar, you know, *contributes*, so soon enough I'll have to find work, and I'm even worse at that. It's a big cosmic dead end and sometimes it makes me want to jump off the top of Saint Sakangpenh's, but—can I say something?"

Ronoah nodded, too engrossed even to remember his cultural norms. Ean-Bei's little crimped smile was back.

"It's easier when I get to help people find *their* thing. Like living vicariously, right? It's such a rush, seeing someone I like find their place in the Wish, even if—even if I don't have mine, I figure maybe it's good to help everyone else click into place. Right?" They looked at Ronoah with prelusive shyness. "That's why I invited you to dinner, the day we met. You were a puzzle piece that Ngodi was missing, but also—also you had this *look* on your face, this thousand-yard stare like you were adrift, and like you kinda hated it, and I wanted to see if I could…get you back on track."

Ronoah went very still.

A long time ago, in the middle of a sad story very much like this one, another friend had pointed out Ronoah's expression—*intense*, he'd called it. *Curious. Considerate.* The kind of words Ronoah was initially embarrassed about, but ultimately proud to embody. The kind of traits he longed to identify with. In the end he'd felt complimented, seen for what he was in a good way.

Not this time. This felt like an intervention, like being confronted out of the blue, like his mother's *we need to talk* six weeks before Sweetwood Day—the very notion that his nameless desperation could be so easily visible to another party sickened him, shamed him raw. As if he hadn't tried with all his might to be mellow and easygoing instead. As if the weeks and months of rigorous self-monitoring and contrived bravado and faking fun at church came to nothing. As if it were so easy, to see what was wrong with him and to fix it.

"Has it worked?" Ean-Bei asked lightly, a joking echo of Ronoah's own question masking a much dearer, more self-conscious hope.

It wasn't like there was any point to telling the truth, was there? What was he going to do, tell well-meaning Ean-Bei that their efforts were a waste? Hate to break it to you, hardworking, ever-optimistic friend, but I only ever used your concern as a weapon to lance myself with? Of course not. You couldn't just say you were suspended in one long bleakness, that some mornings the futility of everything paralyzed you in your bed, that your capacity for wonder had atrophied from willful neglect, from emotional impotence, that you'd forgotten how to bridge the gap, how to love or hate or even to cry—you couldn't *say* all that to someone as considerate as Ean-Bei and expect them not to try harder. He didn't want anyone trying harder on him. It wasn't worth it.

So, then. "You're getting there," he lied.

"That's good to hear," said considerate, too-trusting Ean-Bei. And then: "Maybe it might work better if you broke up with your boyfriend."

"It's—" Ronoah groaned. The only reason he had even the faintest idea what Ean-Bei meant was because they'd had this conversation before. "I don't know how many times I need to explain he's not my boyfriend."

"What is he then?" As per usual, Ronoah was silent. As per usual, Ean-Bei took that silence for concession. "Doesn't he need to get his papers renewed too, if you came in together? Why aren't you here with him?"

"Because," said Ronoah, thinking he would improvise an end to that sentence—but then he was thinking of Hanéong, and he fumbled whatever lie he'd been about to utter. After all this time, he still couldn't be dishonest under the creature's watch, imaginary or not; every time he tried, he tripped over the silvery ghost of *rule number three, be honest with me.* It was profoundly annoying.

Ean-Bei observed his brief struggle with the bland dispassion of someone who was already assured of their version of the truth. "All I know is that every time I see you with him—which is only like, five times in three months, don't you literally live together?—you seem *this close* to some massive fight."

"Hanéong's not angry with me," Ronoah objected, and it was true. No matter how Ronoah had ignored or provoked or treated him like an endless repository of household items and services, Hanéong hadn't lost his temper with Ronoah.

"I know. It's very one-sided." Ronoah shot a glare at Ean-Bei's cavalier tone; the tai shrugged it off undeterred. "If you're not happy, you should walk. No one would blame you, it's really hard to date a Sithie, they're really demanding."

Ronoah grimaced. "That's not—"

"You don't have to defend him! It's part of their culture; they expect perfection all the time. I tried dating one once," they admitted, a sour wrinkle at the bridge of their nose, "and she straight-up told me I'd never make anything of myself. It's that wartime zeal their grandparents passed down: everything's a competition, or a test, and they have to be the best at everything or they get pissy but at the same time they look at you like you're not trying hard enough. Sound familiar?"

It didn't. It was worlds apart. Ronoah knew what a test from Hanéong felt like; he'd survived plenty of those. Hanéong was not testing. Instead he was—he just *was.* He existed like gravity, invisible and omnipresent and assiduously heavy, impervious to all of Ronoah's attempts to break free from, to break down. Untouchable. Incomprehensible. Inhuman, inhuman in a way that made Ronoah want to rake his nails down his own arms, mad with the pressure of its endless patience. Hanéong was *waiting*—what for, Ronoah had no idea. It was as opaque and alien as everything else about him.

No. No, that wasn't true. Deep down, there was a part of Ronoah that knew, that had always known what Hanéong was sitting sentinel for.

We have all the time you like.

Hanéong was waiting for Ronoah to be ready to talk about Shaipuri. About the War. About Jau-Hasthasuna. Hanéong was waiting for an opportunity to apologize.

But Ronoah wasn't going to give it to him. Ronoah would never be ready. It was too late. It was too late to talk about it, the moment had passed. All the moments, each one that had laid itself at his feet, he'd brushed past them all. It was too *late*, and yet—oh, you coward, you *coward*—he couldn't bring himself to actually tell Hanéong to leave, because this impasse, this stalemate of theirs, it felt like the last important thing in his life, grotesquely precious, and once it broke that would be that for him. Hanéong was going to have to give up first, was going to have to be the one to leave, because Ronoah—he could wait it out. He could waste his whole life on this standstill if that's what it took. He didn't have anywhere else to be.

"Ronoah Elizzi-denna?"

He jerked his head up at the touch on his arm, a quarter-way to raising his fists. The attendant raised her eyebrows, smiling the routine smile of the public servant. "Right this way, if you please," she said.

Ean-Bei sprang to their feet, giving a long vivacious stretch and clapping Ronoah on the shoulder. "I'll catch you back at the library," they said. "Have fun!" Ronoah watched them walk out the door, their duty as a friend fulfilled. Then he turned to the attendant, followed her to the desk where the promise of another three months lay crisp and awaiting his hand.

And after that? a voice asked softly in his head. Will you return to this room again, when those three months are up? How many times will you restart this cycle?

For a tantalizing moment he could see it: a life in Khepsuong Phae, a Ronoah forcibly reborn. He would take up a proper post at the library, or else do bookkeeping for any one of the shops; he would master the dragon poi with Yengh-Sier, maybe even be part of an acro show, a smaller one like Ean-Bei did. He would go with the tai to Ruppanteak once their exile was over, to witness the mountain's idle loveliness firsthand. He would spend bright mornings drinking chocolatey coffee with Ngodi and discussing the latest in Ol-Penh's scientific discoveries, and long nights tunneling through the labyrinth of the library, reading anything that took his fancy. They would be sun-drenched, carefree years, full of pleasures and distractions and easy company.

Except.

Except the Pilgrim State would always be there.

The vision crumpled on itself, curled like burning paper. He couldn't do it. Even if Hanéong left, Ronoah could never put down roots here because the Pilgrim State would always be there, just over the horizon, just a week's walk away, and everyone *everyone* he spoke to would eventually ask if he'd been, would always eagerly suggest that he go. He would spend his days tensed for the next mention of it, that destination he'd once almost reached and then abandoned forever; he would endure the endless discomfort of always declining the opportunity and never explaining why. He would never escape the reminder, the reprimand, never be allowed to forget Hanéong, forget Genov—

But if he just *said* he'd been already—another story slithered through his mind, compulsive, involuntary. An image of himself packing for an expedition, announcing that he was journeying to see the Pilgrim State at last, trekking halfway up the Holy Corridor before swerving into the mountains to camp out—to hide out—for three weeks, living like he had on Chalisto's Belt, coming back claiming he'd seen marvels and wonders so everyone would get off his back about it—

Chuta ka saag.

How repulsive, that he could imagine reducing himself to this. How despicable. The person he'd become didn't deserve the Pilgrim State even if he wanted to go. Didn't deserve friends. Didn't deserve gods.

"—lucky your copied forms came in from Yanyel, we can use the information on file to fill out your new records, if there are no updates to be made." Ronoah blinked, looked up. The attendant was smiling again. She spread his papers on the desk, picked up a pen and gestured onehandedly: "Is there anything you'd like to change?"

Ronoah looked down: the tidy Ol-Penher script, the underlines and scratch-outs, the circle around an answer, the checkbox on the last page. He looked until the dry ache behind his eyes felt like it would never, ever leave him, and then he opened his mouth.

"No," he said. "No, thank you. Everything here is fine."

FORTY

ONCE UPON A TIME, a creature made wise through tragedy wrote: *Living things need to be touched. If that is impossible, then there is no point to anything.* He wrote this and other missives, other pleas, lessons learned at the bottom of the world, brushed loving and fearful onto the walls of his and his cousin's tomb. He wrote this and then died, unable to do anything with his hard-earned truths except preserve them, and nine hundred years later, when a boy uncovered this counsel, that boy swore to himself he would heed it.

But good advice is difficult to heed when you're translucent.

In the weeks after his visit to the Khepsuong Phaer Consulate, Ronoah's sense of solidity began to peel away, one skin-thin layer at a time. Details went first: complex flavours, depth of colour, wordplay, warmth. The world shallowed up; things greyed into sameness, flattened into limbo. Became fragile. Time had long since severed from any meaningful meter, but now it displaced itself entirely, and he lost any feel for how long life was taking to run out around him. He displaced himself in turn, abandoned his mind to sit quietly with the calm certainty that he would simply crumble into dust any day now, with the mildly embarrassing fact that he was, he supposed, waiting around to die.

The world was a bog, murky and cold, and he was slipping inexorably into it. No one was even going to sing him down as he went.

Soon enough, he started isolating himself from his friends. Yengh-Sier, Ngoluydinh, Ean-Bei—they were all noticing the change in him, and nothing he tried could conceal it. It wasn't like he couldn't see them trading looks across the bistro table, or like he didn't know they were privately discussing how to help him. He loved them, in a brittle and tender way, for wanting to make the effort to rescue him, but he felt he might do something drastic if they ever actually breached the subject.

He couldn't bear the idea of anyone acknowledging what he'd become, so he retreated into himself, which only made them worry more, which only made him hide harder. Become more distant, more remote. Corner himself in tighter and tighter spaces.

If Jesprechel were alive, Ronoah would ask her to make him completely insubstantial. If Bazzenine yet drew breath, Ronoah would beg for a void to vanish inside. If it could happen faster, the sinking, if it could be over with all in one go, maybe he wouldn't be so afraid.

But Bazzenine and Jesprechel were dead, and the only help they were able to give had already been given. When he reached for their words—for anyone's, for anything, anything at all—he only heard white noise. Rushing water. Hissing.

He saw to his commitments, too emotionally exhausted to do much past bare minimum. He stopped trying to force himself to Saint Sakangpenh's in the evenings. Spent days alone reading books that he couldn't remember by morning. Slept in longer and longer, dreaming of a small room and a sputtering candle and a paintbrush in his hand. Didn't see a sunrise for weeks.

And Hanéong watched his long and graceless decline into the dark, and did nothing. Perhaps the creature saw the finale coming. Perhaps it felt it was inappropriate to intervene.

Or perhaps it simply wagered Ronoah had more Jesprechel in him than Bazzenine. Perhaps it was biding its time for the moment that lanced gift finally returned.

It happened the same day Ronoah's life ended.

Comparatively, there was nothing more daunting about that day than any other. If anything it felt lighter, easier to breathe—one of those days where he found a branch floating in the bog and held on for a little longer. Today's branch was the fact that this morning Yengh-Sier had finally announced his satisfaction with Ronoah's foundational work. Tomorrow, he would officially be trading in his practice tethers for a pair of dragon poi. And Yengh-Sier's knifethrowing lessons were also going well, enough so that several curious onlookers had approached him wondering if they could learn; there were rumblings of Ronoah potentially teaching an actual class. His head didn't feel so separate from his body today, which meant he'd be able to concentrate, to be useful to Ngodi instead of blankly flipping through her papers pretending to be cross-checking something or looking up a reference—no, today he didn't feel like just a mediocre imitation of himself. He could be useful. Functional. He could maybe even enjoy it.

All things considered, he was in relatively good spirits when he arrived to find Ngodi tearing up her research.

"Um," he said, articulately, as the woman neatly ripped a page of yesterday's work into strips. "Um, Ngodi—?" Delayed, he jerked into motion, reaching for the pile of crumpled shreds on the table like he could reverse their destruction: "Ngodi, what, wait, why are you—?"

"It's all *wrong*," the woman growled, punctuated by another teeth-gritting tear of paper. She let the pieces fall, signing in irritated slashes and snaps. "I'm approaching this with completely the wrong set of parameters, the reasoning doesn't lead anywhere, and if it doesn't work for Princess *Gamzhey* then we need to rethink the whole ka-Khastan section—"

They were a month into phase two of Ngoluydinh's research. Her sainthood litmus test had passed muster, first under her own scrutiny and then, more dauntingly, that of her supervisors. Her model had been granted value, if only in theory, if only temporarily: in order to maintain that value, it had to be successfully applied. Ngodi and Ronoah had spent the last four weeks combing through Ngodi's list of likely candidates for extra-Ol-Penher sainthood, holding them up to the candle of her criteria to see if they caught the light. They were making progress—or so Ronoah had thought.

"Maybe—maybe don't destroy it all just yet, though," he said as he skirted a stack of books to the writing desk. He planted a palm on the sheaf of papers awaiting execution, frowning at Ngodi. She made another irate noise in her throat, but she didn't try to steal the work out from under his hand, which was a step forward from her usual bullheadedness. "Can't we use them to point us in a new direction? Take out what doesn't fit and, I don't know, use the shape of the hole left behind to guide us?"

"Backforming logic like that doesn't work," Ngodi huffed, seemingly irritated not by his suggestion but by the fact that it couldn't be so easy. "Once you start wedging in things patchwork like that, the integrity of the methodology starts breaking down. Even a junior scholar will see the seams. We can't olive-pick from history, Ronoah."

Ronoah, who privately thought that was exactly what they were doing with this entire exercise, head-wobbled just the same, trying to keep his body language appeasing. "Okay. So what's actually wrong with the logic you have? What tripped you up?"

"There's just—there's so little precedent!" Ngodi sat down, right on the ground amidst the piles of her research, a grumpy green-robed princess in her castle of books. It was slowly dawning on Ronoah that this was less an issue with any practical aspect of the work and more an existential crisis about the work as a whole. "It's just *hard*, Ronoah, it's hard to do something no one's ever done before. Cross-disciplinary work is peerless enough, and all these fields are so intangible—theology's not like engineering, you *can't* give anyone irrefutable proof of your theories. I have no milestones, no map, nothing to tell me that this isn't a complete waste of time."

Ronoah's gut clenched. "Hey," he said. "You have me."

Ngodi looked up at him from her pouffe of mint-tinted crepe, brushing her long hair out of her face. She wasn't crying, but her eyes had a dangerous shine and the chestnut in her throat bobbed up and down with a hard swallow. He offered her a hand; she stared at it for a moment, and then laughed, and took it and bonked her forehead against it. At times physical touch was like rubber, or else like nothing at all, but today he felt the warmth of her body, the light slip of oil on her brow, and it made him smile.

"It's not like I'm giving up and burning the room down or anything," Ngodi said after a long, relenting sigh. "I'm still going to do this. There are just days where it feels impossible to move forward."

"I get it," Ronoah said.

Ngodi hummed in acknowledgement, closing her eyes to the world for a moment, retreating into herself like Ronoah had done so many times before. Assessing the way ahead, the path to her desires, and finding it hostile and lonely.

And then she did what Ronoah never could, and opened her eyes again, and forged on. "Get a blank page and a pen," she said, settling with a susurrus of pages into her seat on the floor. "There's *little* precedent, but there's not *none*. I'm going to run through the apocryphal saints that are already accepted and see if we can get some inspiration going here."

Obediently Ronoah fetched his materials. Thinker aloud as she was, Ngodi had already started listing before he was ready; he had to race to catch up, standing in the middle of the room with his tablet balanced on his forearm, pen sprinting across the page. "There's Saint Maryaçe, they're the most obvious, the Winged Saint from the Pilgrim State … Saint Evin from ka-Khasta, that's low-hanging fruit though, being a prophet is almost cheating … Saint Baheed from up in Jalipuri, she's the one who brought *nuam* to Ol-Penh, patroness of gifts … oh, of course there's Saint Hanéong, but she's a little more—"

The pen clattered to the ground.

Ngodi squawked to a halt, pulling the hem of her dress away from the ink splatter pooling on the floorboards. She looked up at Ronoah, whose hand was still raised, frozen.

"*Saint* Hanéong?" he asked softly. "As in my Hanéong?"

His ears were so full of buzzing he almost didn't hear Ngodi's reply: "—more like the other way around, he's named after her, isn't he? Hanéong the Heretic Saint."

Tingling in his fingers, in his arms. "You never told me about, about—"

"I absolutely told you about the Heretic Saint, there's no way I didn't, she's the Qiao Sidhur one we talked—"

"But you never said her *name*." His voice came out tight. Tinny. Wrong. He inhaled, forcing himself absolutely level despite the way the buzzing had climbed in pitch to a whine. "Tell me the story. I think—I think I forgot, or confused her with someone else in the Wishgranter's company." He glanced over the edge of his tablet to see Ngodi staring at him sceptically. He took another deep breath; it welled weirdly in his chest cavity. "For—to help you with the candidate list? Please?"

The suspicion remained in her eyes, but she shrugged an allowance. Perhaps she figured it was faster than fighting him on this, a more efficient use of time; perhaps she had sensed a fissure, an opening into the dim despondent mystery of him, the one that she and the others were always trying to crack.

"You really should know it," Ngodi said, rifling through the stacks until she retrieved a leatherbound book and flipped it open, "she's up there with Saint Oupha in my top five; as our only overseas saint, she's a main inspiration for this research." She found her page, cleared her throat: "Of all the members of the Wishgranter's sacred company, the Heretic Saint is perhaps the most controversial."

And she told him.

Ronoah didn't know when it was during her reading that he ended up on the ground. He just found himself there, when it was over, legs folded under him like a dazed fawn, tablet discarded beside him. His pulse thumped, flashing hot—thumped *everywhere*, his arms his throat his skull, his entire body thrumming with sickening festering heat.

"Yeah," he said, his voice coming from some other body entirely. "That makes sense."

Ngodi's voice was muffled too, her gestures weirdly fisheyed, distorted. "There's not much in the literature about her, this is probably the most comprehensive resource. Surprisingly enough, the people who accept her are all farmers in little rural towns—it's the cities and the coast that dismiss her." She smiled an ironic smile. "Turns out there are a lot of world-shakers in the boondocks, huh?"

World-shakers.

Ronoah exhaled.

"Yeah," he said, and then, "I need to go."

Somehow, he got to his feet.

Somehow, he strayed over to the desk and picked up his bag.

Ngodi asked him something, probably *go where* or *why now* or *Dragon's tits Ronoah, are you okay?* The shape of the words bounced meaninglessly off of him. Somehow he gave her an answer; somehow he told her he'd come back tomorrow to pick up where they'd left off. And then he was in motion, out the door of her study, pulled through the halls down the stairs out of the library into the streets—

World-shakers
wishgranters

His lungs felt like they were collapsing. His heart felt peeled like an onion. His hands had clammed up, were shaking, wouldn't *stop* shaking no matter what he did with them, stuffed in his pockets or tucked in his armpits or squeezed into fists. They wouldn't stop. A force so powerful it nearly had him retching yanked him through the city, stumbling harder than any drunk walk home from church, nearly lurching into bicycle traffic as it compelled him mercilessly onward.

Where? Where was it taking him? This sick thing seething up from every inch of him was pulling in so many directions, wrenching like a dozen ravenous wolves in different directions, each howling louder over the last. He was going to walk to the train station, get on a train, and leave. He was going to walk to the train station, get on the tracks, and wait. He was going to beat Ean-Bei to the punch and climb Saint Sakangpenh's spire. He was going to the nearest high bridge he could find. Anywhere— anywhere he could snuff himself out, silence this cyclone taking form inside him, frothing up out of his marrow and jerking on his nervous system like a meat hook. Because if he didn't—

World-shakers
wishgranters
every loss again
friction spark fire

He gasped breath in hot dry stabs. If he didn't, if he didn't end himself then he was going to end Khepsuong Phae, Ol-Penh, the entire world. All of it, Wish or no Wish, gods or fucking *no gods*, something was coming up in him bigger than any Shattering and it demanded blood demanded sacrifice demanded now now *now*—

Antagonism is another form of love.

He reeled to a stop so hard it was like something punched his sternum, rebounded off of it. The quaking. Righteous. Screaming. The fury. In his heart, in his white-hot heart. In his mind a hand, a red hand, a red cheek.

A thing that is alive will do anything to remain alive.

"Fuck this." A whisper; a threat. A body taking itself back.

He wasn't the one who had to answer for this.

He turned around, and the thing inside him sprang to his heels. The boardwalk could have cracked as he set off running. He could hardly breathe and he didn't need to breathe because something else was sustaining him, fuelling him, feeding him full of its black bile until he felt it would pour out his eye sockets, until he made it, made it where he had to—made it to the boarding house, to retribution, to the center, to the source.

"YOU," he snarled, bewildered and bereft and understanding exactly why.

Hanéong stood by the mirror, running a comb through his hair, a perfect tableau of a young man preparing for a jovial evening out. He raised his head at the door slamming open, met Ronoah's burning eyes through the glass.

"Me," he answered. He had the gall to sound surprised.

"*You*," Ronoah said again, strangled hiss, "you just have to *be* in *everything*, don't you?" He kicked the door closed behind him, tasting iron and bile, looking at this *thing*, this thing that was— "Nothing is *safe* from you, is it? You just play us all like a game and don't give one *putrash* what happens to us because of it—"

Hanéong put the comb down. "Would you mind telling me what, precisely, I am on trial for tonight?"

He was still surveying Ronoah through the mirror. Ronoah was going to break it. "*Saint Hanéong*," he spat, and there she was, the glinting shadow of her cradled in the shell of Hanéong present, clever and brazen and brave, brave like— "The Genoveffa of Ol-Penh."

Any shred of hope he'd had of backing down disappeared when the rusted blade of her name split his lips.

Hanéong stood poised for a moment, considering this like he had been posed a mathematical equation. At last he turned from the dresser and faced Ronoah. "I suppose there are a few similarities, come to think of it," he mused, like it was just that, just a passing conjecture, instead of, instead of— "But I am not she."

"*I know that.*" His nails cut bloody crescents into his hands. His joints were crying from the pressure. "She's not you because *she's not real*, none of them are, not Pao or Innos or Eje or the Wishgranter or Roryx or the Maelstrom or—" so many, so many of them rushing to mind to mouth the fabrications of five thousand years and all the people who'd loved them and lived for them and died for them and he was yelling now, voice rattling and hoarse with the horrible truth "—NONE of them, except you. You're the only thing there is—so you made them all up. *Admit* it, you *made them up*, you had five thousand years to do it, you told stories after the Shattering and you spread them so it would feel like there were others, so you wouldn't be so *alone*, so people would praise you wherever you walked because you have to be *the best at everything*, you're so desperate to have a place, to be *loved*—"

"No, I'm not." Ronoah would have continued right on going if the response hadn't caught like a cold hand around his throat. He choked on his next breath, looking at Hanéong—Hanéong whose presence was charging their suffocating space with the low sternum-shake of sub-audial thunder. "I do not need love from you people. I do not crave praise. I do not even need respect—although it never hurts to sprinkle some in when talking to a friend."

It flared its nostrils, the lights guttered—and then it turned its head sharply to the side, stopping itself. Its words came smooth, deliberate. "Literally *any* other night, I would be delighted to have this out with you—but as it happens I actually have somewhere to be. And believe it or not I will just as delightedly pick up where we left off when I return—"

"No," Ronoah cut across, his whole body trembling. "You don't get to turn your back on me."

"For one night? After months of your side-eyes and hostile silences?" Hanéong's bones flickered radioactive blue beneath its flesh. It took the three strides necessary to come nose-to-nose with Ronoah, looking up slightly to account for their height difference. "Yes," it answered, quiet assurance, eye of a bruise-black storm, "I do."

And Hanéong pushed past him, gently, light as toeing a withered leaf aside, and opened the door and left.

It took about a minute for the furious shock to galvanize into action, for Ronoah to wrench the door nearly off its hinges as he gave chase.

How surreal, that dash through the boulevards of decadent Khepsuong Phae. How intoxicating. Night had fallen at some point between the library and here; the moons were magnified to absurd proportions, swollen fit to crush the stars. He was crushed too, pulverized under an all-consuming purpose, a ghastly keening yearn that rode him, animated him past all conscious effort. His chest a void. His brain a bruise. Gasping, euphoric, he ripped through the heart of the city, hounded the sizzling signature of Hanéong's lifeforce through the streets with a madman's absolute luminous certainty that whatever it took—*whatever it took*—he would catch what he was hunting.

He toppled through crowds until the crowds disappeared and only the wind was left to scour his cheeks, only the bricks to scrape his arms as he barrelled down and down into the tight twisting warren of the Old Quarter. He saw a wisp of lilac around a lefthand corner and lunged for it—he felt a flicker of magnitude past the next wall and scaled it, hit the ground wrong and kept running anyway. He skidded to a halt, assaulted by the electric smell of ancient power, followed its giddying sweep through his spine around a bend and—

There. Hvanzhir Hanéong, monstrous and irresistible, on the other end of a long alleyway.

Ronoah had no idea what came next. No clue what he was going to do now that they were both here—the feeling hadn't got that far, hadn't given him a plan. The thing sizzling his brain like meat wasn't clear on where to go from here, what, was he going to *fight* Hanéong? Translocate this pain onto him, visit this misery on that unassuming frame with his fists, or was he just going to yell, to yell and yell until his smoke-ruined throat gave out for good, gods, he—

Hadn't realized that there was someone else in the alley. With Hanéong. Who? Who was what? Why were they standing so close together? They were right up against the wall, and—

The image resolved, registered, and something flooded icy cold through Ronoah's seizing synapses. His shoulders dropped, shocked slack.

Menacing stance. Predatory posture. A forearm pushed against a collarbone, against a milky windpipe. A slim body pinned to the bricks.

Someone was *attacking* Hanéong.

No way. No fucking way. By Jau-Hasthasuna's severed head, there was *no way*—but there it was. He saw Hanéong—small, slight Hanéong, littler than Ronoah was now—lifted a few inches off the ground; he heard the scrape-*thud* of toes kicking and scrabbling for purchase, and this was impossible, there was no sane or logical or even indifferent Universe where Hanéong could ever be caught off-guard by something as crass as random street violence, no world where it could be taken away by something so utterly meaningless, there's *no way this is happening* his mind told him—but he saw slim hands pulling futile and heard a strangled wheeze and—and instinct kicked in.

It was so simple, in the end. He just plunged his hand in his bag—

—snatched the first knife to split his fingers—

—planted his feet sucked in breath like a spark and whipped his arm back

and he threw.

The first knife struck Hanéong's attacker at the soft joint of arm to torso. The second, when they flinched back, lodged in the juncture between shoulder and neck.

The third was already in Ronoah's hand and he was ready to lash out with another, another, as many as it took until he ran out and then he'd think of something, he would—a sound cleaved through the surge of elation, a clear note ringing over the roar in his ears:

"Ronoah."

His throw stuttered to a halt. The world pulsed, bloomed open from its tight dark tunnel, and he realized his quarry was on the ground now, moving oddly, and—and Hanéong was there too, Hanéong crouched over the writhing figure with its hands pressing down on something spurting oily black in the moonlight, Hanéong with its clothes rumpled and its hair in disarray and its throat unblemished unharmed and its look like, for the first time ever, Ronoah had truly and fully surprised it.

There was an awful noise coming from somewhere, a gurgling, foamy wheeze, like a wet sponge being squeezed.

He heard himself hyperventilating, the panicked staccato of air scalding his throat. His fingers ached the festering ache of new wounds. Hanéong, he wanted to say, Hanéong, Hanéong Reilin Özrek *Chashakva*—and as if it could understand his gasping, abortive sounds, the creature's skin thinned translucent, eddies of stars emerging like a second twilight. The alleyway plunged into light, pooled into eyewatering sapphire and violet. The world tilted on its axis. Suddenly they were in the glade again, haloed and hallucinatory, under the secret-keeping canopies of Shaipuri. Ronoah stood at the banks and Chashakva knelt waist-deep in the water, the both of them witnessing the passing of a once-great creature. Ronoah felt the tug, the sweeping sucking pull-away of a life from its vessel—and this time, the answering ecstatic tingle in his own hand that told him to whom the killing blow belonged.

His fellow stranger locked eyes with him across the alley, the waves—a soft bronze saint and a hard dark god and a swarm of other faces, other lives all looking out the same eyes at once, with the same inevitable expression—and opened its mouth.

"Now you've done it," it murmured, breathing sympathy and starlit scorn. "Brace yourself."

Ronoah took a step forward, chest still heaving. "Brace—"

It hit like the meteor of Yanyel.

Brick barked his shoulder as he listed into the wall, racked and shaking. A thing worse than pain was engulfing him, a beast that had eyes only for him, eyes like bottomless sinkholes full to the brim with malice. He was drowning in them. He was drowning standing up, doubled over airless, everything convulsing, everything corroding. Glass shards in his gut. Wasps in his lungs. Acid wailing in his veins, through his heart, ripping great steaming blisters across the surface of that organ he'd thought was so calloused but wasn't. It wasn't anymore.

His empathy.

That's what this was.

Empathy resurrected, revenant, returned with a vengeance.

He'd—what, what had he done. What have you done, he asked blankly, then frantically, insistently, *what did you do Ronoah what did you do,* and he hauled himself upright enough to look and through the bars of that beast's teeth, he saw.

Blood pooling. Body cooling. A human, a human dying, a person punctured cut open stuck through. His knives like friends smiling guiltily from the body's neck.

You just, came a voice in his head—a clear voice, gentle, it was his, it was his own voice—you just killed someone.

He took a step back. Another. His eyes gravitated helplessly to Hanéong's like the creature could tell him this was fake, was hallucination—but Hanéong wasn't looking at him, was focused on the body. The body, the body Ronoah put there. It was real. It was realer than anything.

So he fled. He ran like he was being chased, blundered through a welter of backstreets and hedges and crash-landed against the door to the boarding house. He threw himself inside their room, threw the bolt home like it could protect him, like he could stay sane so long as that door stayed locked.

It didn't work. The last wracking shreds of another person's death throes gave way to something entirely Ronoah's own: the spine-freezing panic of fear-beyond-fear, back from its own grave to haunt him. His own heart was choking him in his throat. His limbs shook so badly he couldn't stay upright, collapsed to all fours. A swarm of torments like millipedes was invading his body, so strong he felt them swelling under his ribcage, chewing through everything keeping him together—you're no better, they said, you're no better than Chashakva, you killed someone and now you can never go home, you did the unthinkable you murderer you can *never go home,* and the stench of it surrounded him like the corpse itself was mortared into the walls.

He crawled into the tightest space he could find, weeping an endless stream of apologies into his knees, and his soft heart bled out before him.

DAY ONE. Daylight felt sinister. The air on his skin made him flinch. A silverfish found its way into the room, slithered around the ceiling corner for hours before slipping out of sight. He couldn't leave the safety of his corner, or something scarier than death would find him. Daylight faded, replaced by worse. He was still a murderer.

$\mathcal{D}$AY TWO. Sleepless. He vomited every morsel of food he tried to keep down. It all tasted bloody. He was nine years old again, huddled between the sleeping mats and the wall, tortured by the invisible menace of everything, how it all felt sentient and malicious, how it all felt like it wanted to hurt him. He cried until he was sick. He wanted his father to draw for him while he watched. He wanted to press his clammy forehead to the man's knee. He was never going to see him again.

DAY THREE. Nazum Vashnarajandra had once spent seven days alone in a room waiting to die. Ronoah shamed himself in comparison. He was a useless sacrifice, he wouldn't have made it, he couldn't bear it. Breathing felt obscene, nauseating, but he couldn't stop. He wanted to throw his body off but couldn't. Wanted to undo it all but couldn't. Wanted to stop thinking, to obliterate thought. Such great pain in waiting. He begged to be released. He knew it was punishment but he begged right on anyway. He pleaded with every god he knew.

Nothing answered until late that night, when he heard the deadbolt scrape in its cylinder.

A corridor of light opened on the floorboards, disappeared again as the door was softly shut. A pair of feet appeared in his bleary vision, padding quiet as a jaguar, and stopped in front of him. Slowly, a body crouched before him. A pair of hands—warm, square, pale hands—reached and took his own, stroking the cut-up, nailbitten fingers with a thumb. "Okay," said a pleasant, silvery voice, a voice he hadn't heard in— "Now it's your turn."

Ronoah looked up. Short hair the colour of nutmeg; broad, smooth, sly features. Beauty spot under the left eye. "Reilin?" he whispered, not daring to believe.

A smile more heartbreakingly familiar than all the dunes in the desert, than all the stars in the sky.

"For a moment, little pilgrim," said Reilin, rumbling comforts as Ronoah launched himself into the man's arms. "For a night."

FORTY-ONE

*T*HERE WAS A LOT OF MELODRAMA in the next half hour.

Ronoah, who'd thought he had cried himself into a husk, discovered an underground cistern of tears reserved especially for this, and a fresh deluge spilled down his cheeks as he alternated between burying his face in Reilin's shoulder and hitting the man with weak, shaking fists. He soaked them both with tears and snot and reopened the deepest knife wounds on his fingers with his fitful clutching; whatever breath he could choke in was spent on cursing in every language he knew, Ol-Penher and Shaipurin and Chiropolene and even Acharrioni, that language which was so difficult to be harsh in. He found a way. And Reilin bore it with that old familiar calm, brushing Ronoah's hair away from his face and resting the point of his chin upon Ronoah's head and making low, consoling hums at all of Ronoah's piteous gestures, weathering the firestorm in his arms until it burned down to exhausted embers.

Then he picked Ronoah up, just as he'd done long ago on the other side of the sea, and propped him on the edge of the bed. After three days of the unforgiving stiffness of bare floorboards, the soft give of the mattress nearly hurt. Through puffy, swollen eyes, Ronoah watched as Reilin poured a cup of water from the ewer. The man turned and wrapped Ronoah's blood-grubby fingers around the ceramic, then settled himself on the ground in front of him, hands laid paperweight steady on Ronoah's still-trembling knees. His level gaze was suddenly so obvious, so easy to interpret. *When you're ready*, it said.

Ronoah gulped down water, trying to slip the scored edges of the shattered vessel of his throat. When it felt smoothed, he let the first tentative words trickle out: "Ngodi's probably really—really worried."

He said he'd be back the next day. Now he couldn't ever return.

"Naturally. Ean-Bei and Yengh-Sier, too. I handled it for you." Ronoah looked blankly at Reilin; after a moment, the man caught on and laughed. "Not with this face, of course. I found them and let them know you were unwell and that I was taking care of you. I don't think they're *convinced* that I've cut you into pieces and packed you into a cargo train, but the suspicion is definitely there." He looked up at Ronoah, a gleam of old mischief in his narrowing eyes. "You have good friends. I'd hate to be set upon by them."

Ronoah swallowed painfully. "But you weren't."

"No, I wasn't, although it wouldn't surprise me if Ean-Bei attempted a rescue mission—"

"You weren't taking care of me," he amended, finding it within himself to scowl at the man. Reilin lifted his long fingers fractionally off Ronoah's knee, splaying them as if to indicate Ronoah to himself: *well, obviously not.* "So where, what were, where did you—"

"Dealing with Kauryingh." And then, helpfully, at Ronoah's uncomprehending stare, "The mess you left on the floor."

Trust you to put it like that, Ronoah wanted to say, but he couldn't because he was doubled over again, cup clanking to the ground, hugging his aching middle while images swarmed up behind his eyelids and pressed his temples with the aura of another episode, the blood, the cold, the dread—

"Shh," came Reilin's voice, like a warm wind on Ronoah's clammy brow. He found his hands clasped between the man's own again. "Breathe."

The man inhaled smoothly, like he was showing Ronoah how to do it. Lessons from a pair of impostor lungs. Ronoah needed the reminding though, so he took it. His own breath was choppy, coughing; it took a while to stabilize. When he got the hang of it again, the first thing that rose to the surface, trembling with terrible wonder, was: "How have you done this so many times?"

Whether he meant it as an accusation or a bid for advice, he didn't know. His soul was reeling with the kinetic shock of one death to his name—he couldn't make the leap to two, never mind a hundred, a thousand. It was too horrific to conjure, even for his grisly imagination. "How are you still—still you?"

Reilin raised his eyebrows, mild and affable as any other day, and Ronoah's heart broke.

"I did say, didn't I," the man commented, ducking to retrieve the cup, "how we'd save this talk for when it was more relevant?"

The flicker of a fire between them; the stone sky above. "More engaging," Ronoah corrected, miraculously still capable of reproach. "You said for when it was more engaging."

"My mistake. Forgive me." Reilin was still for a moment. Sitting vigil, maybe, for a more innocent time, a time when conversations like these were still unnecessary. He rose to fetch a refill from the ewer; the twinkling in his wrists reflected off the glazed edge of the porcelain. "We're different," the man said, as the water ribboned silently into its cup. As if it were all the explanation required.

Maybe it was. Maybe it was that simple. Ronoah felt a grim kinship with Reilin that had never been there before, felt more alike than ever—and yet he saw their difference with a sort of full-spectrum clarity that was also totally new, a lucidity ripped open by dire circumstance. Understanding was nesting in his head like a mourning dove: hesitant, musical, a little melancholy. He heard *we're different*, and beneath it he heard *we are not equal*, and for the first time it didn't hurt that that was true. For the first time, he was glad of it.

He let himself sink a little more into the give of the mattress. As his mind relaxed around this comprehending, a new question wiggled its way in: "Kar—Kauryin?" he asked. "You knew their name?"

"Kauryingh, yes." Reilin drank a long sip of water. "We're friends."

Ronoah's attempt at an answer resembled nothing like speech, but Reilin got the gist. "I suppose not *friends*, not explicitly," the man continued, returning to press the cup once more into Ronoah's hands. "Work in progress. Kauryingh's inherited certain prejudices toward the Qiao Sidhur from their family; I was prodding at those prejudices to see where they'd suppurate. The long game *is* to end up friendly with each other—some gambits just look uglier than others. Kauryingh was a ..." Reilin's eyes softened. A smile tugged at a corner of his mouth. "A side trip," he said finally.

Ronoah couldn't help himself. "Do all of your side trips end in games where people are killed?"

"Certainly not. Kauryingh's still alive."

The cup fell from Ronoah's hand again. Reilin swiped it out of the air before it crashed.

"Where did you think I'd gone all this time?" the man asked over Ronoah's jagged gasp, rubbing circles into his crumpled quaking shoulders with a perfectly disdainful sigh. "Would I abandon you to this unless I had good reason?"

It was rhetorical; there wasn't any need to answer. Thank the gods there wasn't, because Ronoah didn't think he could make himself speak—his voice was a wheeze, a heave, a physical embodiment of the relief tearing through his body, the relief and the terror. Any second, Reilin was going to tell him the other half, the terrible thing that was true in place of death, maybe *worse* than death. Any second. It couldn't just be that Kauryingh survived. It couldn't be that the Universe had dealt Ronoah such mercy. The Universe was not merciful.

But the caveat didn't come, and after maybe a minute bracing for it Ronoah was forced to accept that it would never come, that the voices screaming *murderer exile murderer* for the last three days were—remarkably, miraculously—wrong.

He . . . *hadn't* actually killed anyone.

Like water sucked down into sand, all the bleak non-futures he'd surrounded himself with sank out of sight. He wasn't an exile. Didn't have to be banished. He could face his friends again. He could go home.

"W-w-why—" His teeth were chattering so much he bit the inside of his cheek. His heart was jackrabbiting around his ribcage, so hard it pulsed in his palms. "Why didn't you t-*tell* me—?"

"When?"

"Before, earlier, the s-second you walked *in*—"

"Because I wanted you to live with it, a moment longer." It stilled something in Ronoah, reduced his hysterics to indelicate hiccoughing. It thrummed in his inner ear, set him off-balance again. He raised his head and Reilin—his old Reilin, jackal-laughing hackle-raising troublemaking Reilin—was staring out the window, considering the rain Ronoah hadn't even realized was falling. "Because it's never been my job, to make the bad thing go away. Only to show you all how to live with it."

He turned his head and Ronoah met a gaze that pared him right to the pit, a gaze every bit as searching and scalpelous as the day they'd first met, scattershot with stars and strange emotions that, he realized, he could taste again. They scalded his palette, the honeyed approval, the plummy nostalgia, the crystalline, camphorous sympathy.

"Just because they're not dead," Ronoah said slowly, "doesn't mean I didn't try."

That was a consequence even a five-thousand-year-old not-god couldn't erase.

Reilin's eyes were solemn, but at this they narrowed in a smile. Proud, even now, in the windblown, bittersweet way of the old watching the growing pains of the young. He uncoiled from his crouch and placed a kiss square between Ronoah's brows.

"Which leads me to my only true question," he said as he withdrew— and all the gentleness evaporated with a snap palpable enough to leave Ronoah's mouth dry. "Ronoah, for the love of every book in Khepsuong Phae, why on *earth* did you do that?"

Ronoah smushed his face in his hands. "I, I don't—"

"Were you aiming for me? Because—"

"*No*, gods, no I would never, I just couldn't—"

"Surely you knew I was in no actual danger—"

"I did, I did know, of course I knew, but you were so—"

"I don't *breathe* Ronoah, that should have been your first clue—"

"I *know*," Ronoah barked, and then, absurdly, he started laughing. It was a digging, razor-edged thing, not pleasant and not benevolent but necessary, unstoppable. "Sorry for confusing you for human for one fucking second, all right?" Silence; no pithy response slid between the staves of his laughter, and he discovered in that void a challenge, and a gut-deep need to meet it. "I was just—I *am* so angry at you, I am so angry, it's like you tore something *out* of me in Shai—" His throat closed, trapped the words and squeezed the life out of them. He couldn't say it. It still wasn't safe. "I'm furious, I'm *disgusted*. At you. At me, at—everything. Everything that happened. Everything we did. But it doesn't mean I want to watch you *suffocate*," he said, peeking through his fingers at Reilin. His own voice a plea. He didn't know what for, and then he did. "It's not—there's nothing to—I can't *fix* anything if you're dead."

So. There was a part of him that still considered something salvageable here. That hoped for another chance. He didn't know how to feel about that, whether it was mortifyingly degrading or else indecipherably resilient. He didn't know.

Reilin did. "Likewise," was the man's reply, after a delicate moment of deliberation. Ronoah had a flashing insight into how he must look from the outside: grimy, haggard, gaunt-eyed and half-starved. Reilin must have seen the death wish coming off him like toxic smog for weeks now. It must have been so obvious, so pathetically obvious how he'd given up, it must have been—

"Does it feel good?"

Air hissed in between Ronoah's teeth; he'd been holding his breath. His hands were clasped together, pressed hard to his brow, and Reilin was working his pale fingers into that tangle, gently releasing Ronoah from his own bruising hold. Addressing his question to that snarl of pain, plainly. "To hate everything so?"

Did it? Maybe once, at the beginning, when they first arrived. Maybe it felt like refuge then, to reject everything. Maybe hating had saved him, or maybe it hadn't. But now?

"No," Ronoah whispered, wetting his cracked lips. "I'm tired."

"Then you're allowed to stop," the man murmured. It was like a steadying hand on the flank of the thrashing, screaming thing inside him—he wanted to buck it loose as much as he wanted to be soothed by the comfort, the contact. "You have a choice; you always do. You can turn back, if you want."

"I don't—I don't know *how*." His reply, high and pining. His fingers spasming helplessly in Reilin's, grasping at shadows.

"I shall give you a hint." Reilin was observing him with such gently amused fondness that it hurt. "Not on three days of sleep deprivation. This grudge has been lodged in your conscience for months—lovely as it would be, I don't expect a single night to magically wash it all away." That inside-joke smile found its way to his lips. "Even I can only perform that miracle so many times."

Ronoah felt the cool damp of deep underground flit across his skin, and shivered. Eyes closing, Reilin hummed in response like the memory itself was a statement he wished to affirm.

Outside, the pebbling of raindrops on casements. Through the wall, furtive creaking—someone pouring a glass of water before retreating once more to the warmth of their bed, or else an early riser up before the purple pale of dawn. For a moment they both just sat and listened to the way the world continued on around them.

When it fell back into the ambient, Reilin got to his feet. "Let's clean you up, then," the man said, and promptly went fussing about in their chest of drawers. He withdrew a lavender handkerchief, wet it at the washbasin, spat into the cloth. Whatever he'd added was invisible, but it made Ronoah gasp when it touched the cuts in his fingers, stinging like lemon, soothing like aloe, tingling like blood flushing a sleeping limb. His digits were stiff, curled like claws; Reilin plied them back carefully but a panicked whimper slipped Ronoah's teeth nonetheless. He counted six, seven lacerations like long wicked gills on a diagonal across his palms, his fingers, the delicate webbed skin between. The two first fingers on his left hand were especially messy, the skin around the wounds puffy, shiny, hard. Infected. He thought of Marghat Yacchatzndra arguing the bugs out of a wound, made another pained sound, one that had nothing to do with how Reilin peeled back the slits to see inside. The creature tisked in response, tender and scornful in one, and swabbed the injuries until their itchy overtight sensation drained like poison.

Not all of the cuts would scar, but these would. Two more jagged black lines, almost but not quite intersecting the old cut across his palm, the place where another blade had split his skin, where Reilin's steadfast hand had pressed it closed.

After his hands, his face. The damp cloth on his swollen eyelids was cool and toothache-sweet. Reilin gave him the handkerchief to blow his nose with, plucked it back and draped it aside, waited out the coughing fit that Ronoah's newly-cleared airways demanded. The man pulled Ronoah's old, sweat-fettered clothing off his back, sought out a clean nightshirt from his own neat lilac stack of garments, draped it over Ronoah's head and threaded his arms through the sleeves. Then he bundled Ronoah into bed—not Ronoah's own, which he'd spent so many dreadful nights in and honestly wished to avoid, but into Reilin's, unrumpled and blank as the first page of a journal. A new chance.

"Sleep at least a few hours," he rumbled as he set Ronoah down. "We'll sort everything else out in the morning."

But Ronoah wasn't done. More accurately, he feared being done—feared the spell breaking on this liminal moment, greased with shellshock, where they could be friends once again. Some distant part of him knew that in the morning things would be more difficult. That same stilted awkwardness would creep back in, rime the edges of the same chronic lakes of anger. And the shame, the utter *embarrassment* that the anger had only ever been one-sided, that no amount of needling or insolence or flat-out antagonism had ever pushed Reilin to hate him back.

"Why are you doing this?" he asked in a small voice as the sheets were drawn up snug around his chin.

Reilin raised his eyebrows, seeking clarification, and a jumble of phrases stuffed Ronoah's mouth like bitter rind, puckered it like vinegar—why have you let me hold you back so long, why didn't you leave me behind, gods, why are you being so *kind*, so consoling like I haven't hurt you, like I haven't tried *everything* I can to hurt you, why haven't you given up on me and found someone who can handle the whole of what you are, *chuta ka saag*, I tried so hard to waste away, *why are you making me grow.*

They foundered in his mouth, rancid and unspeakable. He didn't have the courage to share any of them.

But his shield was cracked, his armour pockmarked and crumbling, and when Reilin's hazel blue eyes did their hunting track across Ronoah's body he had no doubt, for the first time since Sasaupta Falls, that the man could see everything. So he heard it all anyway.

Tsk. That clicking, impatient sound. And the accompanying flare of light beneath Reilin's cheekbone, strike of metallic magenta, as he looked down at his swaddled charge, looked like he remembered something Ronoah couldn't, something almost dangerously precious.

"Because you are preposterously brilliant," said the creature who'd mauled and mended the world, "and I would hate to lose you now."

His fingertips trailed patterns on the exposed side of Ronoah's head, mapped tender, effervescent geographies along his scalp. They said the rest, spiralled it in code along his skin: Because you deserve to make it

388

to the end of this. Because there are so many people who would never forgive me if you didn't. Because there is magic and wonder and joy in you yet. Because all of our rules are dust now, all but the last, and you promised me this one you would not disregard. Because you clatter with light, little Firewalker, and I am selfish by nature, and I want to see what you do next.

An unseen tension dropped from Ronoah, let him slump finally into his three-day fatigue. He watched Reilin through drooping eyelids, trying to drink in one last sight of him, easy in this body, before it vanished again come morning. He watched his friend and fellow stranger cross to the other side of the room, retrieve a dark rectangle from Ronoah's satchel slung over the bedpost—he felt a nudge and opened his eyes again to find Reilin had wedged himself onto the bed, curled around him like a great cat, a book propped open in one hand. Pine green cover; ka-Khastan lettering on the spine. The man turned a page, skimmed the lines, smiled to himself, and Ronoah knew no more.

FORTY-TWO

$\mathcal{R}$EILIN WOKE HIM JUST BEFORE NOON—or rather, Hanéong did. Hvanzhir Hanéong, slight and silvered and round-cheeked again. Ronoah tried not to begrudge him for it. It wasn't fair that one body bore the brunt of his rancour. It was all the same creature underneath.

"I have a proposition," the young man said as he slid a plate of raspberry pastries under Ronoah's nose. Ronoah raised a sardonic eyebrow at Hanéong, rightfully suspicious of sudden propositions following emotionally-fraught encounters. His sceptical silence had nothing on his empty stomach, though—it growled almost comedically long, loud enough that he felt it in his spine. So be it. He tucked into the first meal he'd been able to keep down in days, and Hanéong took his breakfasting for what it was: *go on, hurry up, while I'm eating and can't shoot you down.* "I hear it's lovely on the east coast this time of year, and we've done so little sightseeing. What would you say to a field trip? No grand mysteries," he added promptly, raising placating hands at Ronoah's pointed glare, "no ancient ulterior motives, swear on whichever saint you like—just a few days out of the city to talk. You need the fresh air, and perhaps the space to yell at me without all of our neighbours hearing."

"Space would be good," Ronoah quipped between bites. The jab had no structure, no certainty; it was putting him off, hearing Hanéong speak so acceptingly of his own impending censure. It put him off even more to realize the adjacent patrons of the boarding house had probably heard his muffled breakdown through the walls for the last half-week. Even more reason to want to get away for a few days.

"In which case, I shall away to fetch us tickets—should be able to nab something for this afternoon, pack for a week on the beach would you, and perhaps spruce yourself up before you appear in public—"

Hanéong's waving hand slipped out the door with the rest of him, leaving Ronoah glaring at an empty room, trying not to acknowledge the old, weakly fluttering feeling of adventure in his gut.

Breakfast was an intricate affair. His digestive system needed to be reminded how to do its job after its temporary relief of duty. That, and sitting still in the noontide light filled him with a skittery sort of restlessness that edged into panic if he looked it dead-on. After all this time forcibly apart from himself, he didn't really know how to sit with his own company. He wound up resorting to his old busyness, taking the odd bite of jammy pastry in between tasks, chewing slowly while washing his hands or his face or changing into clean clothes of his own. It was a familiar process—even in Pilanova, whenever his fear-beyond-fear got the best of him, he'd always tried to act normal as soon as possible. The normalcy helped scrub away the sour aftertaste. Buffered against the possibility of a relapse. Of course, *normal* was nonexistent on a day like this one, but the motions served their purpose; paradoxically, before too long, he was distracted enough to be able to sit back down and enjoy the last pastry whole, savouring the flake and crackle of the crust with tastebuds who felt grown overnight.

That is, until a pounding at the door startled him into scattering crumbs everywhere.

"Ronoah? You in? We heard you were sick and things, buuut we were in the neighbourhood and we saw Hanéong leaving and the average recovery period for stomach flu is like two days so we figured we'd check up on you to make sure your *boyfriend's not a lying*—"

Ronoah cracked the door open on one very keen face. "Hello, Ean-Bei." Opening the door wider revealed two more. "Ngodi, Yengh-Sier."

"Hey," said Ngodi with a salutatory gesture, which she promptly turned into a cheerful swat at Ean-Bei's head. "I told you this was totally unnecessary—"

"Can't a tai visit their friend to make sure they haven't been stuffed in a mattress—"

Yengh-Sier slipped sideways between the two bickering scholars, regarding Ronoah with the critical eye of someone with intimate knowledge of the body's mechanisms. Under the man's gaze Ronoah felt all the places he was hunched or shrunken. He was suddenly grateful for Hanéong's excuses—he certainly looked like he'd been ill.

"It's good that you got it all out of you," Yengh-Sier gestured. "You look a little brighter."

"I—" He raised his hands, trying to ignore how Yengh-Sier's eyes widened slightly at his sliced-up fingers. "Thank you."

Ngodi broke off from whatever she was preaching at Ean-Bei to peer at Ronoah. "You looked like you'd been run through a mangle the last time I saw you. We've been worried."

"Thank you," Ronoah repeated, unsure of what else to say. It had been a long time since he'd been the recipient of this kind of community concern. Burn scars and heroics kind of long time. It had been ages since people had come to his door just for the sake of seeing if he was all right—since he'd *let* them, since he'd let anyone say they were worried for him.

"Why are we making them stand?" Ean-Bei said, elbowing their way into the room. "Sit down Elizzi-denna, you *still* look like something the Dragons chewed up and spat out."

"Would that I were so lucky," Ronoah answered, feeling the first sputtering revival of his humour.

He sat in bed while the others crowded around him and reported the goings-on of the past few days: the controversial lecture that a hundred students protested against, the packing up of the Evnism exhibit from ka-Khasta's sibling library of Aç Sulsum, the fellow tumbler in Ean-Bei's amateur acro troupe who sprained an ankle after their combination somersault went wonky. They chattered at him with the eager indiscrimination of people who expected you to want every detail, no matter how insignificant, because you were an insider, and the details mattered to you.

It was by the light of this carefree warmth—just four friends discussing the minutiae of their lives, leaning on desks and bedposts, cracking a window to let in the balmy summer breeze—that Ronoah saw just how distorted the past weeks had been. Past *months*. Despite his fatigue and his soreness, he was participating, asking them questions not for courtesy's sake but for the curiosity nibbling timid at his heels. That nibble was alarming—because it used to be a gnaw, a hunger keen as a blade.

Somewhere along the line, he'd forgotten curiosity. Only by gaining it back was he noticing its absence inside him.

"You okay?" Ean-Bei asked as Ronoah scrubbed at his eyes with a forearm, clearing the watery wobble from his vision.

"Yeah," he said thickly, "I think—no, actually, no, not really, not really at all. Everything feels awful, but I think it's *supposed* to, I think that's a good thing? It hurts, it hurts a *lot*, but I think the hurting means it's, it's—"

"Mending," signed Yengh-Sier. Ronoah blinked at him, semi-surprised that his rambling hands were intelligible at all, and the man continued. "Like re-slotting a dislocated shoulder."

"Or going out barefoot in the frost on the mountains," added Ean-Bei with an encouraging head-wobble. "You don't feel the cold much until you come back indoors and the woodstove's going and all the little tingles in your toes turn into ten thousand needles of revenge."

"Or when Ean-Bei decides to play physiotherapist on your poor, harassed spine."

"Ngoluydinh, without me you wouldn't *have* a spine anymore—"

They were prevented from further accusations by a shaky sound: Ronoah's bubbling, grateful laughter. "Thank you," he said to the three gathered at his bedside. "For understanding." Ngodi offered him a smile that hinted at an understanding deeper than her words suggested. She'd been there the day he broke down; perhaps she knew this was about more than a stomach bug. Perhaps they all did. Perhaps, like Eng-Vaunh before them, they were giving their care at the pace he could receive it, skating lightly across the surface of a very deep wound so he wouldn't shake them loose.

If for no other reason, he owed it to these people—their unconditional camaraderie, their wide-open hearts—to try to put an end to all of this.

"Listen," he said, two fingers touching chin and then ear, "I'm getting out of Khepsuong Phae for a couple of days. To go...see the ocean." Another little thrill, feeble but struggling up: he'd never seen the East Ocean before. "With Hanéong."

Ean-Bei squinted. So did Ngodi, though hers was more of a mischievous, *two people going to 'see the ocean' wonder what that could mean* teasing than anything genuinely suspicious. Yengh-Sier, as per usual, was the one who took it in stride; he simply rifled through his duffel bag until he retrieved a pair of poi and coiled them in a snug heap on the desk. They were unlike any Ronoah had seen him use, with silky tangerine ribbons streaming from the weights. "The beach is a good place to practice," he said with a slight shrug at Ronoah's quirked brow; "Open space, hard to hit anything. Pensive. I'd send you with the dragon poi, only we haven't gone over safety precautions."

Ronoah caught the acrobat's eye—tawny brown tree-ringed with red cedar, how had he never noted that lovely colour?—and saw the gift for what it was. A support, a bit of solace for the uncertain days ahead. *Security*, like Yengh-Sier had called it once. Home in motion.

"Sorry for scaring you," Ronoah said, hand rapping softly at his sternum. "All of you. Can we—we'll pick back up when I come home?"

Head-wobbles all around. They wished him a good trip—Ean-Bei strong-armed him into promising souvenirs—and collected themselves and exited, leaving Ronoah to sit in stunned gratitude at just how right Hanéong actually was. These were good friends. He had no idea what he'd done to earn them.

The man reappeared not long after, sidling in with two tickets in one hand and a wide-brimmed felt hat shading his spry eyes. "Visiting hours over?" he asked when he saw the poi on the desk—as if he hadn't been lounging politely in some café across the street waiting for the crowd to clear out.

Ronoah couldn't quite find it in him to smile back, but he didn't scowl, either. "How much time do I have to pack?" he replied.

Khepsuong Phae's central station sat like one big wave goodbye made of scrolling wood and glass. They boarded the Number Four train, found a compartment, and strapped their luggage in overhead. With that same rumbling shudder Ronoah remembered from months ago, the train pulled out of the glass-domed concourse and into a syrupy summer afternoon. It lulled Ronoah almost immediately; the Ol-Penher trio's unexpected drop-in had drained what little energy he'd gathered from his short rest. He wound up dozing, head against the warming window, through nearly all of the trip.

Time went stretchy and benevolent, obligingly slipping hours into minutes. Sensations filtered through his drowsy awareness, leaving soft imprints: a porter in green uniform asking to see his ticket; cool blackness behind his eyelids as the train rolled through a tunnel in a mountain; Hanéong's voice, speaking melodious unknowns to a pair of young silver-haired passengers in the hall. The way the rhythmic vibrations lulled his limbs limp. The rocking of the carriage, the gentle gravity as they wound a bend, the slipping of the sun like warm honey over his skin.

By the time they arrived and Hanéong's shoulder squeeze roused him awake, it was an hour to dusk. Ronoah disembarked with the man and followed him through the mosaiced halls of the station into a world glazed in the buttery terracotta of a seaside sunset. They followed the downward slope of the boulevards, twisting tightly around hedges of rock rose and boxwood and dappled, domed post offices and a small but lovingly-appointed church, its windows filled with the crushed candy of stained glass, until the street opened up and—there it was.

The East Ocean. It hemmed in the lace trim of Ol-Penh's fjordic coast-line, spreading placid and majestic to the end of forever, glittering like molten bronze under the burning drop of the sun rolling down the vault of the sky behind them.

The other end of Berena. He'd made it. He'd made it across the continent.

Awestruck silence overtook him, swept in on the tide of this staggering realization. No Acharrioni had ever stood here; he was the first of his land to lay eyes on these timeless waters. A childhood hungering for knowl-edge, for adventure, and now here he was, come against the precipice of all his knowing, the sheer dropoff into fathomless mystery—because the worlds beyond these shores answered to none of the laws he knew, none of the legends. They had their own, powered by history Ronoah couldn't begin to imagine. Not even the shalledrim had ventured out there.

He brought his hands to his mouth, instinctually trying to stifle his laughter even as it gushed up in a flabbergasted spurt. Hanéong let him have it, standing slightly apart, angled toward the shimmering cauldron of the bay, where the white dabs of sailboats circled below as the black-backed gulls wheeled above, from where the bracing smell of brine whisked up into the hills.

"Come on," urged the creature when it was time, hair lifted and teased beneath the brim of his hat, "don't you want to say hello to the edge of the world?"

It took them until nightfall to make the descent, threading through cypress trees and orange groves, feet crunching on gravel paths, kicking up the scent of crushed juniper berries. The town clung to the slopes in plastered blocks of peach and sienna, like the mountain itself was shingled. Lanterns had been lit in the patios and plazas, illuminating evening coffees or after-dinner games of *duchang*, Ol-Penher garden bowling. A duet sounded beyond some corner, two lutes in counterpoint; the sound faded, and the light, as they crept toward the edge of town and into the fragrant scrubland winding down to the cove. Hanéong compensated for the loss of visibility, emitting a dappled aqua phosphorescence that poured over the few feet ahead of them—until those few feet ended, abruptly, in liquid shadow. Ronoah looked up.

They were on the point of a promontory reaching like a swimmer's arm into the depths. The full belly of Innos was rising over the ocean like a jellyfish, with the slim red snapper of Pao just behind. They were so close it seemed you could walk to them, could just tiptoe their lightfloes like stepping stones until you could press your palm to their luminous swells.

"There's an old lighthouse nestled up here, abandoned after the Qiao Sidhur used it as an outpost during the invasion," said Hanéong. "Salt air, space from the townsfolk, and we do have a habit of rekindling old ruins. I'll sweep the floors and hang the hammocks. Come when you're done."

And he turned up the path and left. Ronoah barely heard him, too hypnotized by the view.

To think, murmured a voice in his head, you nearly missed this. The expanse, the moons, the spray on your face, this gorgeous eerie wind borne from other lands. You nearly never had any of it. But you found your way.

He sat down on the edge of the rocks, knees drawn up to his chest, and stared out at the other side of the world for a long, long time. "Hello," he whispered, and the wind billowed his tunic like a sail.

It took until the moons were high and quiet for him to gather the courage he needed. Bracing himself on the rocks like he could slip any moment, heart somersaulting in his chest, he hiked up his pant leg and stretched his foot over the side. Nothing, nothing—and then the shock of first contact, the stinging foam and the chill submersion, as the abyss introduced itself back to him.

He snatched his foot back, head full of lightning, body singing with the primal fear of a holy encounter. Then he pulled himself from the seafront, picked his way up the slabs of saltbush-crusted karst to the lighthouse glowing furnacelike in the night, and slipped through the driftwood door.

Hanéong had outfitted the single circular room in rustic but comfortable fashion. The pebble mosaic of the floor washed clean, the thorny weeds uprooted, their bags hung on iron hooks driven into one wall and their hammocks slung on the other. On the table, a candle and a cloth laid out with sliced sausage and wax-wrapped cheese. The sconces had all been lit. And Hanéong sat in the bubble of their radiant embrace, legs crossed demure at the ankle, in one of the two chairs beneath the unglazed window. He was toying with one of the knives he'd made for Ronoah—one of the two he'd retrieved, no doubt, from their night in the alley. He caught Ronoah's eye, and the long-absent prickling of the man's attention came alive on Ronoah's skin, slow, attentive, like a hunter checking his trapline. When he got to Ronoah's face, he smiled.

"All right," Ronoah said to the creature who'd contrived this seaside sanctuary, "answers."

If a smirk could turn solemn, then that's what happened.

"The time has come," Hanéong replied, "to speak of many things."

Ronoah opened his mouth—and made a frustrating discovery. He didn't know how to say anything. Language just—wasn't available. He'd spent the better part of three months being as cagey as possible with Hanéong, burying all his indictments and his accusations and his pleas like turtle eggs under the sand. Now he'd come to excavate them, but the landscape had shifted, and he had no idea where to dig.

Hanéong splayed a hand at the table, and with no better ideas, Ronoah took a seat. They ate together in silence, knees nearly bumping. Hanéong took turns considering Ronoah's face and the black waves out the window, expression smoothed as if, even by this slim token of tolerance, he was contented. Ronoah peeled the rind from his meal as if the motion in his fingers could remind him how to break the seal on his words, too.

Eventually, he happened on a topic so recently discovered it hadn't had time to bury itself yet. "So," he said, casting a pointed glance around the lighthouse, the former Qiao Sidhur base. It was a start. "*Saint* Hanéong. Are the stories true?"

The accused looked up from cutting the rest of the sausage, grey eyes gone the same colour as the lighthouse. "The thing about stories," he said, returning to his slicing, "is there are so many of them. There are as many versions as there are tellers."

"Those are all different slices," Ronoah pointed out, lifting his chin at the array of sausage rounds Hanéong had cut, "but they come from the same meat."

"And you don't even want that." Hanéong's tone was oddly approving. "You want the breathing animal it came from." Ronoah let his silence speak for him. After a moment of deliberation, Hanéong rolled a shaving of cheese into a sausage round and popped it whole into his mouth. "The decision to anoint Hvanzhir Hanéong Qøngemtøn with sainthood had little to do with me. As no doubt you already know, most Ol-Penher saints are named posthumously." Ronoah could see it now: an old battle-bronzed Qiao Sidhur woman bedecked in funereal silks, cracking her eyes open and absconding from the tomb she'd been laid in. "There was a ruling to evict the Qiao Sidhur, though, and I did turn it around. It was a delightfully hard sell, and in three languages, what with the ka-Khastan contingent at the table—"

"The Flower Edicts, I know," Ronoah said. Hanéong inclined his head in assent. "Why, though. Why did you argue for them to stay?"

"To answer that, we'll need to brush up on our Cygmian history." Hanéong spread the sausage slices in a rough circle, picked a piece of cheese off the wheel and placed it in the aperture where the circle broke. "The ethnic Qiao Sidhur we see today—Imperial standard, silver hair, that whole aesthetic—were originally the inhabitants of a smallish island. Through a combination of careful infiltration and outright warfare, they captured the much more sizeable island south of them. They repeated this pattern over the next century until they'd successfully taken over a truly astonishing land mass and claimed it under Imperial rule. That was two hundred—hold on, what year is it?"

"Forty-nine eleven," said Ronoah, with a long-suffering note to his voice.

Hanéong impaled the piece of cheese with a knife and waved it around triumphantly. "*Exactly* two hundred years ago, well, *that* explains why everyone's so twitchy about Penh-Sidhur relationships right now, even the most carefully-assimilated settlers are putting portraits of the royal family in the windows. Anyway. Eventually they tried to repeat the whole thing further south, but they met some…resistance." A twist of a smile. With delicate precision, Hanéong ate the cheese off the point of the knife.

"Not to mention a civil war broke out," he said through his chewing, "so their efforts were doubly dashed. They folded into themselves for a while—but once they'd shaken out all the problems at home, they got restless again. This time, they set their sights west. Endeavoured to cross the carousel of the ocean, to see what new jewels they could set into their crown of Conquest."

"Pause," said Ronoah, who heard the capital C like a gong strike. "Why was it so important to them, to take what didn't belong to them?" No one in Acharrio would dream of seizing something this way—each of the city states had responsibility for their own lands, and it made no sense to try and assume responsibility over more than you could handle. The ka-Khastan Unification was the closest example he could reach for, and from what he knew of the politics involved, it had had as much to do with securing continued protection under the Chainbreakers as anything else. A bargain had been struck, even if some of the bargaining chips were bloodied.

Hanéong put the knife down, resting his chin in his palm. "To be honest, this is one thing you Bereni Supercontinent folk have managed to avoid at large," he mused. "The subjugation of your nationly neighbours. I believe the comparison to shalledrim puts you all off. You subjugate each other in the microcosm instead, it's far more insidious." Another image: the thatched arcades of Bhun Jivakta, the throngs of bodies for sale, the confident jaw and knobbly knees of a boy approaching them with a deal—

His ears rang. No, not that. Put that away.

"—for the Qiao Sidhur, Conquest is one of the nine core values of their society. They don't see it as a disruption; they genuinely believe they're doing a service to the world with their military and cultural campaigns. That industrious stereotype has more than a few grains of truth to it," Hanéong said in response to Ronoah's sceptical look. "They have typhoon-proof architecture, incontestable dental hygiene, they practically invented jazz—it is not a lie, to say they have much to offer. But these cultural sophistications have them so fundamentally convinced of their own superiority that they try foisting it on everyone else, even when the other party is patently disinterested.

"So. Why negotiate to keep the Qiao Sidhur in Ol-Penh? Because then they chalk it up to a victory—different from the one they'd anticipated, but a victory nonetheless—and don't go trying it again in thirty or fifty years." Hanéong spread his hands at the half-eaten array before them, the haphazard map of an island and its conquered surrounds. "Shalledrim or none, the world finds a way to destabilize itself. But sometimes it's nice to put out a war before it really gets going."

There it was. Offered so smoothly he nearly missed it: an invitation. Come, it said, I've left myself wide open for you. Make your move.

But Ronoah couldn't do it. Shaipuri, Jau-Hasthasuna, the War of Heavenly Seeds and what it had done to him—it was too volatile, too uncontrollable. So eager to consume him, drag him right down into the bog with the tallest warrior. So precious, so terrifying. He couldn't just dive in like that. His breath went short just considering it.

So he sidestepped. "Where did you get the idea for the Flower Edicts?"

Hanéong caught his eye, tilted his head with a nearly animal curiosity. Wondering, maybe, why his bait hadn't been taken. Wondering why he was being spared another night. Ronoah shied away from that prying gaze with perhaps more force than necessary: "Just—just talk to me about it, okay? I'm," he said, and felt stomach-warming honesty pool like liquid wax inside him— "I'm curious."

He was curious. Not necessarily about the Flower Edicts: Hanéong obligingly launched into an explanation of the document, the secret codes that sanctified it, Ol-Penher flower language and the significance of the number nine and something about Qiao Sidhur professions or paths— Ronoah heard half of it, retained less. It was something far simpler, more elemental, that had caught the eye of his heart.

What would it look like, it asked, *to have this again?*

To let Hanéong spin his tales, to allow himself to be caught up in them—to be two travelers discussing the marvels of the world, entertaining each other, exploring together? To share interests, musings, secrets even? To let trust creep ivy-like up his walls, digging into the mortar, dislodging his deepest hatreds? To lower his defenses? To feel safe in Hanéong's presence? What would it look like, a quiet voice wondered, to be less afraid?

He had absolutely no idea. The notion was a total unknown. Might even be impossible. But he was curious.

He picked at the cheese, discussed Qiao Sidh with its one and only saint. Watched Hanéong speak—the creature's voice so buoyant, its gestures so grand, so unassuming—with a feeling that couldn't pretend to be anything other than the wistfulness it was. Wished, harder than he'd wished anything in forever, for something he couldn't name.

Moonlight poured milk-blue through the windows; outside, the ocean undressed itself against the shore.

# FORTY-THREE

$\mathcal{T}$HE NEXT DAY WAS a very bizarre imitation of a vacation.

Ronoah woke to the proud cry of gulls pirouetting a blazing blue sky. He picked up Yengh-Sier's ribbon poi and took them outside, practicing warmup routines while the water bore witness. The wind stinging his ears, the sand stippling his soles. Hanéong found him and invited him to brunch, and they hiked up to town to spend a few hours on shaded patios with plates of artichoke dip and tomato basil prawns, sampling fluted glasses of juniper wine. They toured the town, which was named Poh Nui, in the old unearthing way they used to, with Hanéong extracting trivia from pediments and pergolas until all the town's cracks seemed saturated with character.

"See the words stamped on that brick there? That's the street name," Hanéong said, drawing a finger along the ragged corner of the church. "Notice anything unusual?"

Ronoah took in the scene. "It's—it's technically on the wrong street. Myrtle runs that way."

"Now why would they make a mistake like that?"

"They…didn't?" Ronoah crouched, skimmed the join of building to ground with his fingers. He stood and took two steps back, shading his eyes as he looked at the stained glass in the façade, imagined it catching the light like it was meant to. "This was originally an east-facing building."

Hanéong's eyes sparkled as if they'd eaten all the light the church had missed out on. "Spot on. This was the only building that survived the destruction of Poh Nui's old quarter during the Silver Invasion. Rather than tear it down and rebuild, they lifted the whole thing as a single unit and relocated it to more stable ground—but some inattentive urban planner failed to notice the ninety-degree rotation that occurred in transition. Even when things stay intact, they change, hm?"

Over and over again, this old routine. Wandering, wondering, tasting, trying—all intensified by Ronoah's reawakened empathy, this awkward organelle that arrested him at crossroads and shop windows and chalk drawings on the flagstones, that seized him by the gossamer flicker beneath the visible. He had to pause and squint for it, every time, trying to parse it. Trying to relearn how to see that way.

He was relearning a lot of things. Like how to walk beside Hanéong. How to exchange casual conversation about a town neither of them had any personal investment in, a topic that wasn't emotionally charged. How to choose listening instead of dismissal; how to be civil. Be friendly. Be friends.

Hanéong, for his part, sailed on with the same easygoing verve as ever, the same sort of co-conspiratorial delight. In another time, Ronoah would have found this endearing, enthralling. Now it felt profoundly unsettling. It wasn't just that it jarred him to be in close proximity again—it was how easily they were pretending at camaraderie in public. Because it wasn't pretending, right? But it *felt* like it, like a performance, a front. A lie. He had no one but himself to blame for this distrust; it was his own fault for insisting on normalcy in the days after Sasaupta Falls, for demanding they carry on as if nothing had happened. Now, with the precedent lodged paranoid in his mind and his emotional weathervane knocked off its axis, he couldn't tell if these spice tastings and *duchang* games and bilingual puns were sincere. Didn't know how to *be* sincere with Hanéong anymore.

Or maybe he just didn't know how to do it while so much yet remained unsaid.

At the very least, that seemed to be what Hanéong thought. Ronoah could tell because the man kept dropping *hints*, more and more obviously as the hours wore on.

"—plenty of seafound delicacies here, Poh Nui's got quite the reputation as a fishing town, I've heard their grilled shark is especially something to write home about."

"—up for a hike we can go poking around the fjords, splendid scenery down there, lagoons and beaches and Saint Chunh-Hay's Skirts—it's a big block waterfall, very pretty, although we certainly have seen a bigger one before."

"—watch your step off the garden path, they've got milk snakes slithering about in here."

All these little openings; all these little opportunities. They were parrying invisible blades and Hanéong kept flashing weak spots, waiting for Ronoah to strike. He had even less idea what to do with this bid for candour than he did with the pastoral posturing of their allegedly nice day—and that was all the opening his self-contempt needed, and it was a much more decisive striker. Four months of avoiding this conversation, it said, not to mention you nearly killed yourself and someone else over it, and you *still* won't open your mouth? You have no right to criticize Pilanova's chronic avoidance ever again; you're just as bad as everyone else. If you were more dignified or more responsible or even just more *decent*, just a decent person Ronoah, if you were any of this you would take Hanéong by the elbow and drag him to some private corner and discuss—things.

Things. Stuff. Shaipuri? Even his self-contempt shied away from the specifics. He didn't *have* specifics, he had no idea where to even start. Maybe at the base of Sasaupta Falls, when Chashakva had first tried to broach the subject, he could have untangled his traumas and tragedies, ordered them by colour and shape of their pain, but so much time had passed and so much pressure applied that those separate issues had compounded, merged and melted and mutated into one cancerous mass. There was no way it was leaving his mouth without breaking his jaw in the process.

Enough of his self-preservation had returned for him to fear that exorcism of emotion. The notion of it, the ghost, the blood and broken teeth, the wet snap. It overwhelmed him; he flinched from the mere possibility. But Hanéong kept *asking*, in his subtle-yet-unignorable way, and that meant Ronoah effectively had to keep saying *no*, had to shut the man down time after time, and every time made him wince worse at his own spinelessness. Shame rose in layers—for not being able to discuss this now, for not being able to discuss anything for months, for how he'd treated Hanéong since their arrival in Ol-Penh. The ignoring, the spurning, the using. So much misery could have been avoided if he'd just been an adult about it and addressed the problem instead of hiding. And being nasty. Ungenerous. Unkind.

"Sweet Saint Yu, but Poh Nui's upped its culinary game since I rode through here, just look at the confections in the window. This is three separate bakeries we've run into now, it's not that big a town, they don't *need* three, but any place with a penchant for pastries is a friend of mine. I would eat that cake whole, what a piece of architecture, and all those little fondant garnishes—those are modelled after frangipani, wouldn't you say?"

"Would you *stop*?" was Ronoah's answer. Hanéong lifted his eyebrows, running a hand through his hair—and Ronoah heard himself, his tone so clipped and acidic, and heaved a sigh to hide the frustrated sting behind his eyes. That rancour hadn't been meant for Hanéong. "Sorry, I'm—I'm sorry I keep doing this. I've been so—so *rude* to you."

Hanéong's amiable expression didn't budge, but something in his demeanour shifted. "As far as I can tell, you haven't been especially rude today."

"Yesterday then. This week. This month—since we got here, since we got to Ol-Penh I've been such a pile of *putrash* about everything and I'm just trying to apologize about it now, okay?" It wasn't the first time he'd considered how foul his resentment had made him. It was just the first time he was refusing to let his mind plaster it over with excuses. Hanéong hadn't tried hard enough; Hanéong had tried *too hard*; Hanéong couldn't be hurt. All this rash justification leaping from the rafters of reason—all of it wrongheaded, sickhearted. No matter what cruelty Hanéong—Chashakva—had exacted, the logic didn't follow that Ronoah could be cruel in return. How petty of him. How— "Callous, I was callous and contemptuous and *mean*, I've been mean to you since we set foot in Yanyel and I'm sorry."

It wasn't easy to apologize, to admit he'd done wrong like this. He'd invested so much into this deplorable behaviour that to turn back on it felt like losing something. But there was no moving forward until he took responsibility for himself, no enjoying each other's company until this miasmic shame had been cleared from the air. "I'm sorry," he said again, and found that he meant it.

And Hanéong said, "I don't need an apology."

Ronoah's next sentence died on his lips. Before he could swallow this surprise, Hanéong chased it with another: "And I don't mean your apology's worthless, I can take it off your shoulders if it's important to you to shrug it free. I mean you're fixating on the wrong point." He tilted his head, looked up through his fringe. Locked eyes with Ronoah. "Why are we focusing on how you've been unkind to me when you are so clearly the one that is suffering?"

Ronoah's throat tightened. Tingles of dread bled up his fingers, his arms. He—this wasn't how this was supposed to go. He was supposed to apologize, and then Hanéong was supposed to accept it, poke a bit of fun at him, and together they would move on. But Hanéong was still looking at him, awaiting an answer to a question that was not rhetorical at all but alive and real and genuine, and something quickened in Ronoah and he shied away from it instinctively before it could emerge from the deep place he'd shoved it. "I'm not *suffering*, I'm just—" Hanéong flat-out snorted and he hurried to talk faster, louder, to drown out whatever the man was seeing, to fix it before they lingered too long "—I just don't understand *why*."

That got Hanéong's attention. Good. "I don't understand why, Hanéong, you never—" *You never explained it to me*, he wanted to say, but he remembered with another heat rash of shame that he was the one who'd rebuffed all the man's attempts at explanation, so he swerved into a more neutral statement: "—there was never a good time to explain it. The War of Heavenly Seeds. And why you designed it. Why that game had to be played. I still don't even know why any of it had to happen, so if you could just ... explain to me. *Justify* it to me, like the Torrene Empire, if you can—I mean, maybe I won't like it, it might probably upset me or ..." Lilies falling into the sinkhole; Marghat's mother's skull biting jawless into his flesh. Jau-Hasthasuna's headless body deliquescing into the glade.

Too close. It was too close again, so he switchbacked, cleaved even harder to the safemaking distance of the intellectual. "It doesn't matter. You—you know me. If I can just understand why, I'll be fine. I'll figure it out."

Hanéong gave one slow blink, every bit the jaguar he once was. "You think explaining it will make it better?" he asked. A presence gathered at the edge of his voice, thick like a stormfront. It made Ronoah flinch.

"It's the only way to stomach a lot of what you do, you know." That came out harsher than he meant for. He regretted it instantly, but there was no taking it back now. Hanéong lifted his chin nonetheless, as if in agreement. That almost made it worse.

"Very well," he said before Ronoah could muster up another mangled apology, "where to? The lighthouse or the lutes? They're still playing back on Beryl Street."

Ronoah was pretty sure that whatever he was about to hear wasn't going to be softened or soothed by musical ambiance, they made the trek back to the lighthouse.

"Okay," Ronoah said after he'd closed the door behind them, wiping sweat off his brow. Today the hike downhill had been just as effortful as the one up. Or maybe he was just nervous. "I—ready?"

Hanéong was already halfway up the spiral staircase, disappearing into the crumbling lightroom. His voice flittered down, neat as a finch: "Ask away, little scholar."

Clearly it was meant to be lighthearted—affectionate, even—but it made Ronoah recoil. He wasn't asking to be *scholarly*. He didn't want to know out of some academic curiosity, he wanted, he *needed* to know because, because—

"Okay," he said again, and again under his breath, a meaningless little mantra to get him up the steps, an empty little encouragement to ask what he had to ask. He shoved the frenetic feeling down, pressed it into a squirming block somewhere under his floating ribs. Faced Hanéong through the occluded glass of the lighthouse lantern. "You started—no, you *created* the War of Heavenly Seeds. You set eighteen monsters on a land of vulnerable people, and on each other. You let them wreck the land for centuries. Why?"

Hanéong crossed to the crumble-down edge of the lightroom, where the bricks had caved and the afternoon poured through, and perched on the bed of broken stone beneath the breach. He looked out over the water like he could see across the world, all the way back around to Shaipuri behind them, a Shaipuri younger in time. He started straight in—no thought-gathering pause, no tension-building beat. He'd been ready to tell this story for a long time. "The world is so full of hungry things," he began. "Sometimes the most interesting thing to do is to place them all at the same banquet.

"Once upon a time, there were eighteen creatures. Each one unique, born of accident or confluence—creatures of power, of longevity, of unfortunate reputation. A few were born in the heartland; most had wandered to it, escaped into its rustling hideaways. Some, I brought myself. They were all there for the same reason: the myths of their homelands had deemed them abominations. Berena does that—scores tight borders around what's to be revered and what's to be reviled." He picked up a stone from the rubble, cascaded it through spidery fingers. "Not much gets to walk the line."

Hanéong palmed the stone, flourished a wrist, and opened his hand to reveal a newly-sparkling jewel. Red like a ruby, or—a garnet. "Eighteen little orphans, and a bit of pathos, and a lot of spare time. The question was simple: under what conditions could these creatures thrive? Through what mythology could they exist free of persecution? What happened when you fed them love instead of hatred? From the questions, the game.

"I gave each of them new names—nobody remembers this, but you know, the tribe names actually came first—told them to leave their old behind, in the mouldering pile of bitterness from which they'd come. I gave them teams, villages of humans that would not be so quick to the cudgel or the crossbow, communities that would heap glory upon them. I gave them a target, a scoreboard, a playing field. And I gave them a story. A story they'd never heard before, one of dignity and dependability, a story where they starred not as antagonists but protectors. What do you do, when for the first time in your life you are given something fragile and trusted to take good care of it?" Hanéong's voice was a musing murmur, asking the ocean, the wind. "You get ready to count to a thousand."

Count to a thousand. First to the finish line wins. Ronoah had been a bookkeeper once; his mind calculated the sum before he even asked for it. At absolute worst, it said, in the most drawn-out scenario possible, that was seventeen thousand, nine hundred and eighty-three sacrifices. That was less than the Torrene Empire's body count by far; it was less even than the death toll from the unification of ka-Khasta, an entirely human-led endeavour. Putting it into perspective like that should have helped, but it just made him queasy. Maybe because it was still three Pilanovas' worth of people.

"I made some estimates," Hanéong continued, as if he could hear the numbers shuffling in Ronoah's mind. "Given the population of tribal Shaipuri, the rate at which ritual battles were pitched, reaching a thousand for any one side would take most of these creatures to the end of their lives. Whoever was left could sort it out amongst themselves, who was to be god of the new age—it wouldn't matter by then."

"Wouldn't *matter*?" It certainly seemed to have mattered. At least to Jau-Hasthasuna.

"If they hadn't cheated, if the code of honour was respected, then no matter whose offerings heaped highest everyone would come out victorious. Each Seed was permitted to sprout, in a way—to bloom into something beyond a countryside menace, something with purpose. Regardless of who took the title, they could all ease back into the land they had guarded so long, having accomplished what very few monsters do: a long life, and a beloved one."

A contest where the winner was irrelevant was no contest at all—except by Hanéong's estimations. Ronoah knew because he'd been put to the same test, in the caves. Given an arbitrary task to mask the slow growing that task would encourage. Given his own time to sprout. "The point of the game wasn't to win," Ronoah said slowly. He looked over at Hanéong. "It was to play."

Hanéong beamed, and Ronoah's stomach squeezed.

"But," he started, vaulting his voice over the hurdle of that revulsion, "but you played by *killing* people. Who came up with that as the mechanism, who built that into the rules? Aren't there more—more *imaginative* ways to win a game?"

"Everything has to eat," came Hanéong's answer, made brutal by its plainness. "Some of these creatures did in fact feast on humans, or else warmbloods of comparable size. Their sacrifices of choice were obvious. And you've got to make it fair and equally difficult for everyone, or else it's not a very exciting game."

Shouldn't that have helped, too? If it was literally a matter of diet, of nourishment, a matter of feeding oneself, shouldn't that have made him feel better about it? Then why wasn't it working?

"We did give alternatives," Hanéong added, tilting the red gem in his fingers this way and that. The walls danced with bloodred sparks. "I told you from the start, in the legend: birds of prey, apes and caimans, even the jaguar herself. Shaipuri was no stranger to sacrificial offerings—it already governed itself by the cycle of rot and rebirth, already cleaved to the creed of pouring life back into the land when the moment demanded it. Sacrifice was in their vocabulary of worship long before us; it was one of the reasons I gathered our players there in the first place. But the rules allowed for a whole menagerie of offerings." Hanéong watched the bricks flittering with innumerable tiny lights. Despite himself, Ronoah was drawn too into their pattern, their prettiness. A constellation of lights, of lives, a thousand little red souls.

The lights snuffed out like a punch. A gasp startled from the roost of Ronoah's mouth. "It didn't matter," said Hanéong, fist closed around his jewel. He pulsed, then flung a handful of gleaming red sand out the breach. "Nearly all of the tribes sacrificed exclusively human offerings anyway. I do wonder why they did that, given the options. Didn't stick around long enough to find out—perhaps they saw themselves as worth more, you people often do—but no," the man said, musing now, smoothing a hand along his jaw, "no, more likely they just couldn't bear to hunt down the animals inhabiting a dying rainforest. So much was already lost; it would be antithetical to their goal. Go against the point, such as it was." An appreciative hum rumbled up from his throat. "The heartlanders never fail to amaze with their pragmatism."

"But if it was a matter of food," Ronoah pressed, "then why did it have to be so gruesome? You can't tell me that makes for a better meal. Pushing off cliffs and suffocating and, and—"

And making people step off platforms, ropes around their necks. Nausea seared the underside of his tongue. He forced it back, forced aside everything but the purely logical. "Even if you decided people had to die, they didn't have to die painfully. They didn't have to die afraid."

"Most of them didn't, when I was in charge of things—die in pain or afraid. There are herbs to dull sensations, to make the world go soft, to transport sacrifices to a place of ecstasy that goes beyond a care for their mortal vessel—not everyone believes the body and soul are akin, you know," Hanéong said, to what was probably Ronoah's unconscious frowning. "Most of the ritual battles weren't even *fighting*, yes there was spear throwing but also there was spear *making*, crafting, drumming and handstands and comedy routines. Contests in contests, enrichment for all." Now it was Hanéong's turn to look perturbed, petulant. "Another nuance that was smeared out of existence sometime after I left, I presume."

Ronoah took a deep breath. "This version of things does sound objectively better," he intoned. "The details, the modifications—the version where you were around." He hugged himself, gripped his elbows hard. Looked somewhere around Hanéong's shoulder. "So why did you *leave?*"

Hanéong said nothing. Ronoah gripped tighter, trying to ignore the plaintive hissing in his mind. "Why did you just cut loose without giving them any—any guidance? Why did you leave them to figure it out on their own? They're not like you, Hanéong, they don't share your vision, they can get confused by things, or surprised, or lost or stuck or *hurt* or ..."

A prickling sensation carved a swath up his side, up to his cheek, his face. Hanéong was staring at him very intently. Ronoah stiffened under that gaze, frightened without knowing why.

"We are still," said the creature opposite him, "talking about eighteen fully self-sufficient monsters here, yes?"

Oh. That was why. Because Hanéong had marked what Ronoah had only just come to realize, sickeningly, embarrassingly—that he wasn't talking about the monsters at all. He was talking about himself. About how Chashakva had abandoned him, left him to the menace of the heartland all alone.

Alone? And what am I then, a pile of snake shit you stepped in?

His vision flickered, twisted. Hearing that voice meant he was unbearably close to something soft and squishy and excruciatingly vulnerable. He rebounded, swapped topic fast: "What about the rainforest?" he asked, pressing his shaking down until it ached, until it lay flat and level and still. "The heartland, the garden you and your friend grew, you were okay just letting it rot and die for your experiment? Unobserved? That seems so, so *disrespectful*. Wouldn't she be angry with you for using her labour of love that way?"

"Oh, furious." Hanéong picked up another pebble and flipped it—it returned to the crucible of the creature's palm bearing the honey lustre of gold. He gazed into its glimmer, fondly. "Positively furious. And also she would have placed her bets, immediately and with vigour. And bet wrong, in hindsight. Jau-Hasthasuna—none of us would have expected that. Not bloody-minded at all, that one, nor egomaniacal by nature. Only regrettably impressionable." That curious blue tongue, those shining scales, that eagerness. Ronoah knew, and the knowing made him heartsore. "I'm absolutely certain it got the idea to devour its friends from someone else; it just happened to implement that idea better than its originator."

"From who? From—" A memory, buried deep with all of Shaipuri's memories, bloomed to the surface in a sickening whiff of jasmine: "Subin or Naskarahal? Marghat told us they were the ones who started eating Seeds, Yacchatzul warned her tribe about them."

When Ronoah looked, Hanéong's gaze at the nugget of gold had gone forlorn. "That sure was an interesting story, wasn't it," he murmured. Some premonitory presence passed whalelike over Ronoah's head, and he fought back a shiver. "I had my guesses about who had gone astray, but I also have my prejudices, so those guesses were effectively useless until Lady Yacchatzndra confirmed them for me."

"You guessed it was one of them?"

"Of course." Intent on his handiwork, Hanéong pinched and twisted the nugget easy as beeswax, rolling it out into a wire between his palms. "Subin and Naskarahal were the two shalledrim."

Gracious to the last, he let a moment of silence hang while he worked. Left it there for Ronoah to dwell in while he digested this gamechanging fact. Then, "This much, I am at fault for. I should have known better than to put two of them in competition with each other. If there had been only one, who knows what our endgame could have been? But two—historically, two shalledrim on opposite sides of something hasn't done the planet any favours." Another pause, suspended in the sweep of the waves below, as the creature came to silent terms with this. He wound the golden wire around his finger, a ring newly fashioned. Ronoah looked at Hanéong's face and saw the Shattered Sea in his grey eyes. Dangerous; secretive. Turbulent. "It would not surprise me if they grew to take the attainment of godhood literally. If they began treating the War of Heavenly Seeds as a contest between two and not eighteen; a proxy war, just like their ancestors. Rallying forces, splitting sides. Re-enacting the same old feud, the same old story. Imagine their surprise when something showed up to their pageant that was stronger than either of them." Shadow flashed in his expression—a strangely weary menace, tired leviathan beneath the surface of the water. "How I would have liked to see that."

And just like that, the darkness cleared from Hanéong's face, cloud sliding over to reveal a sunny sky. "You know," he said, "of all the Seeds who could have festered in existential crisis, I'm glad it was Jau-Hasthasuna. Misguided perhaps, and stubborn precisely when it oughtn't be, but eternally, eternally sweet. Tried to keep everything safe, Vashnarajandr aside; some of the others would have caused significantly more trouble had they been so inclined. Those deadzones will clear up in a decade or two without their maker reinforcing the poison. It was a beastly mess to untangle, the sociopolitical repercussions will echo for generations—but given how the board was set when we arrived? This was the best possible outcome."

That hit harder than anything else, than the rest of this whole conversation combined. It seared Ronoah, branded him with its brightness, its blitheness. Its truth.

The best possible outcome.

Laughter squeezed itself out of him—a dry, desperate little chuckle. It made something twist ugly and out of place in his gut, like a fist had taken hold of his insides and yanked. Hanéong tipped his head to one side; *let me in on the joke*, said the narrowing of his eyes. Ronoah tried, but every word he found was too raw, too dramatic. He rejected them all, cast them back into the deep.

"So that's it," he finally managed. "That's the story. I have the facts now." He shrugged—a reflexive gesture, defensive, like his body was trying to divest of some burden but couldn't. "Thank you for explaining. I feel better now."

Hanéong's eyes glittered. He smiled with all of his teeth. "No you don't."

"Yes I *do*," Ronoah retorted, overstrong, overloud, trying to persuade them both, push it like a fingerprint into the wax of the world, trying to force it true— "yes I do feel better, I feel fine, there is no other way to feel because, because—because it's the best possible outcome, like you said, everything turned out *fine* in the end. No one did anything wrong—even *you*, you were trying to give these creatures a place to belong that made sense to them—everyone was just doing their best and everything turned out okay in the end, so *why* would I feel bad? Why would I be upset?"

Hanéong looked at him with the kind of pitying wonder reserved for a bee bereft of its stinger. "Why would you?" he asked, disturbingly gentle.

"Right? It's ridiculous!" Ridiculous, how ridiculous he was. He forced another laugh, short and sharp and hard, like a stab in the heart of his ridiculousness. Like he could vanquish it so easy. "Nothing even really happened! Nothing even—take Pashangali for instance!" He hadn't said her name in months; now like a fishing net it dragged up all sorts of dark, slimy things in its wake. "I was so upset when I realized I was helping her sacrifice people, I was in pieces about it, Hanéong, I was so torn—but it turns out she didn't actually kill anyone! So it's okay, it should be fine! And when she attacked me—" Hanéong cocked his head like a bird on alert, gods, right, Ronoah had never told him about their fight "—yeah, she beat me up a little bit, but she was so stressed and it was only a few kicks and she made amends so it's fine—" Hanéong's aura compressed, stern, concerned, maybe Pashangali was a bad example, maybe Hanéong was wondering why nobody stepped in to intervene, but that wasn't the point, "It's nothing to be upset over is the point. It's nothing—it was *way* scarier getting kidnapped by Marghat, we really thought she was going to sacrifice us, I thought, I thought I was going to die—and then I thought I was going to die from the poison, from the apghat mayul, Chabra'i's deadzone, it infected me when I fell in and it nearly killed me, Marghat had to use her own mother to fix me and sure it was terrifying but I lived and I'm fine now so, so it's fine." It's *fine*, believe me, believe me, it's true, it— "It was nothing compared to—I felt like I *wanted* to die in the roundhouse, the day of the Council, when everyone was fighting, remember? They decided to continue the War and I just—all that work, everything we did just to have it not matter, I was horrified, I was choking on despair but later they agreed to end the War after all. The War of Heavenly Seeds is over! So that despair is pointless, it has no point—and the fear of Jau-Hasthasuna, the, it looked at me and it *did* something to me and I couldn't move or think and I would have let it eat me if you hadn't shown up, I would have, I would have, my heart was going to explode but it didn't because Jau-Hasthasuna's dead, because you cut its head off so it can't hurt me and you *cut its head off* and I'm furious about that but—but I *shouldn't be*, because I'm safe and the rainforest is safe, the—the *best possible outcome*, we did it, we won, so I should feel fine, I should be *grateful*, even though I had to watch you do it, even though I nearly came apart feeling it I should—everyone's happy now, everyone's at peace, you and the rainforest and the Seeds and the tribes and, and—the whole world is *fine* so why, why would I, why do I—?"

He was crying. He realized it after the fact. Crying and breathing hard, gasping, like his lungs couldn't grab enough air to keep them going. Hanéong simply looked on, unjudging, and the man's words rose up between them: *Why are we focusing on how you've been unkind to me when you are so clearly the one that is—*

"Suffering." Before, that word had felt padded, dampened somehow. Now it rang like a bell, resonated painful in all his hollow spaces, curled him around its keening vibration.

It hurt so much, to acknowledge he was hurt. To face his own wounds. Give that pain any space at all, and look: how it rose up and took everything.

"I'm suffering. I'm suffering so much for something everyone else is happy with, and I don't—I don't know—I don't know what to do?" No matter how harshly he scrubbed at his eyes with his hands, the tears overflowed. He hid his face, agonized and mortified in his agony. "I don't know how to stop being so selfish, so bad, I don't know how to be happy that it turned out okay when all I am is scared, *still*, even with a whole sea between us I don't know how to just *move on*, it's stuck in me, it's stuck and I don't know how to get it out, nobody ever taught me how, there—there was no other way." Jau-Hasthasuna's plea, reanimated in Ronoah's helpless, all-too-mortal mouth: "There was no other way, I had no guidance, you—you never told me what to do once I was alone."

Hanéong's smile softened. Grew rueful. "You were never alone," he said. "You had Nazum."

A noise pierced the lightroom, a keening sob so despairing it should have cracked the lantern glass. Another followed, and another, an ugly, desolate melody. A sound like an attack, like a violence, a wail that wanted to rend the sparkling seaside air apart. It hurt Ronoah's ears to listen to.

Then Hanéong called for him: "Ronoah," the creature said, and its voice was so steady, so kind, and there were only two of them in the lighthouse, and by that process of deduction Ronoah knew the sound was his own.

He gave in. Let gravity claim him, let himself collapse, knees driven harsh into the stones of the lightroom floor. He barely registered the pain under the tidal wave submersing him. It came serrated, corroded like acid engulfing his chest, spat like a splash of the black Sanaat—he was full of it, always had been, from the moment he'd plunged into that dead lagoon, it had invaded him and killed his wonder and his joy and now it was rushing up from its hiding place to claim the rest. He curled in a defenceless heap, inconsolable tangle of fever-flushed limbs, and sobbed the only word he had, the last one left at the bottom of his heart:

"*Chashakva.*"

And just like that, she was there.

He didn't even sense her change—there was no crackle of energy, no flash of sapphire starlight, just the new sudden smell pervading the air, that resinous smell of Chashakva's skin that touched some raw, damaged place deep in the back of his brain, and he heaved with new tears even as she came to his side. She pulled him onto her lap, let him butt his forehead hard into her thigh and pine like a starveling newborn. She let him cry the infinite wound of his loss into the infinite void of her body while she brushed her fingers over his back, scratched between his shoulder blades, cradled his shuddering side in her broad, steady palm. She held him, and in the dark harbour of that holding Ronoah grieved for Nazum Vashnarajandra.

"His entire family died," he gasped. "His entire village. He sang to me when I was sick, he sang to make me better. He saved me from Pashangali. He gave me a name."

Gods, the longing in him. The love. He'd never known it was love until now, never understood the fierce sweet protectiveness he carried by that name. Together they had been Runazum; they had been like siblings. No one had ever been so candid with Ronoah, so close. No one had ever been harder to let go.

"He protected me and he was my friend and he almost killed himself for a god you *made up*."

"I know." Chashakva smoothed the fabric of his shirt. "I'm glad he didn't."

Her voice, so caring, so warm. It only made his anguish sharper. "I miss him," Ronoah whimpered into Chashakva's leg. "I miss him and I miss him and we're never going to meet again. I never got to thank him for everything he did, I—he was always so annoyed when I said sorry but I *meant* thank you, every time, I just didn't know, I didn't know how grateful I was until too late and now that thank you sits in me and *burns* because it has nowhere to go."

Chashakva received this with all the grace of the sea: in confidence, in quiet solidarity. The gravitational temptation of her listening was too much, the pull of her patience unbearable; it was too good, it was just too good to feel heard after so long shut up in the echo chamber of his head. He cracked at last, his first confession spilling into more, admissions emptying themselves one after another out the breach of his salt-stained lips:

"Chabra'i stopped speaking to her bees. She talked to them every morning, it was part of her routine, but she stopped because she thought they didn't want her, because I—because I lied to her, about Subin." He'd been so triumphant at the time. Nearly smug. "I lied to her about the most precious thing in her world because it was the only way I could stop her from killing people, and it worked, they're alive, no one died but—but do you think the bees missed her? Do you think they missed her voice?"

Chashakva's thumb traced the nape of his neck. "Undoubtedly," she murmured, and it felt like sting and balm at once. How strange the relief, the comfort of confirmation.

"I can't look at my arm without flinching anymore—the mark there, Marghat used her mother's skull to heal me and her teeth left a scar and Marghat told me *she's supposed to last until it's my turn*. I don't know how many years I took away. I don't want to be the reason Marghat has to die earlier. I don't—I don't want—what if Bashti's still a child when her grandmamu's skull stops working? What if she has to, what if—who will take care of her then?"

Tingling from those fingers, cool then warm. "The Ladies Yacchatzndra know how to do their jobs. I'm sure you only took a little. Two years, three at most."

"That's too much! That's too much, I should have been more careful, I should have—all I wanted was not to hurt anyone but I failed, I hurt so many people, I literally killed someone—"

"Remember, Kauryingh is alive—"

"In Shaipuri," Ronoah cried, gripping the linen of Chashakva's trousers, the cold stone of her knee beneath. "In Shaipuri. In the—he died in my arms, the tallest warrior of the Jau-Hasthasndr, Pashangali tried to help him and she couldn't so they turned to me and I *couldn't*, I tried so hard, I tried *so hard*, I did everything I could think of, I was streaked to the elbow in his blood and it was so hot and then it got so cold, he got so cold and waxy and still and I knew I couldn't do anything anymore. We sang him down to the bog, we sent him with waterlilies, they gave me his runa pelt and they *shouldn't have* because I failed, I failed him, I let him die."

For this, Chashakva had no salve. Her only offering was her silence. She did not even try to assuage his guilt. Absurdly, that made him feel more understood than anything she could have said.

"I failed him," he said again, the knot in his chest loosening ever so slightly— "And I don't have a right to be destroyed by it, because he's the one who's dead."

A pulse above him. A switch; a shift. "You do, though. You do."

"No, *no*, if anyone does it's him and his family, his loved ones, I can't be sad about this if it's my fault, I don't, I can't—"

"You can." More softly: "You must."

"It *hurts*." He dug his nails into Chashakva's knee. Pushed himself up to face her—her body a tear-smeared blur, her dark limbs stark against the pale stone floor. Her hundred heartbeats so close he could feel them—feel them knocking, mocking the raw space in his chest. "It hurts, Chashakva, I can't even, even *describe*—I feel so unraveled, I feel un*real*, all of this happened and then it was just *done* but it's still in me and no one knows. No one knows." Another sob swelled up in his mouth; he grabbed her shoulders to catch himself, arms trembling. "I didn't mean to come out of that year bitter, and cynical, and coldhearted and a liar and, and *godless*. I didn't mean to, I didn't mean to." His words, his words in fragments. His words in tatters and scraps. "But I had no choice. It was the only way. To stay together, to hide it away, to *live*, because part of me died in that rainforest too, and—and nobody *knows*."

Chashakva curled her hands over his wrists, locking the two of them together. Let her gaze rove over the ache of him, the full-body crave of him, the yearning so purple it bled. Settled, at last, on his face. "*I* know."

Chashakva knew. How it filled the carved-out hole in him, how it quelled the fit in his soul. How it ended his world over and over and over to have to croak out, face creased with an awful, sorry smile: "But it's your fault."

"It is." Chashakva looked at him like he was an eclipse. Like he was something precious, inevitable. Like he was something she'd waited to witness forever. "I'm sorry."

And the very last atom of his self-control shook free.

The world thundered up. The world ignited. Feeling flowed through Ronoah like he was nothing but a hollow reed, and he was, he was. He wanted to hurl himself out of the lighthouse—and he wanted to be caught and saved—and he wanted to turn his knives on Chashakva even though she would only reabsorb them. He wanted to be absorbed. He wanted to be like Hanéong's garnet, to be crushed to crystalline powder and scattered, restrung among the fine nebulae of Chashakva's core, where there would be no more suffering or at least never the need to suffer it alone. He wanted to stop suffering alone. To accept her apology. To allow himself to love her again. How it made him wretched. How it made him ravenous. How it made him light.

Chashakva held him as it poured into him, held him heart to thousand hearts, both on their knees in crass parody of a day long ago in a windswept villa when all of this had still been too buried for them to be anything but happy to see one another. She braced him in her arms—the arms of death and regeneration and the eternal cycle that tied them. She put her cheek to his, and she squeezed him, and the sun blazed behind her, and Nazum's ghost crowed a laugh like a triumph, and he squeezed Chashakva back, gripping her with shuddering fingers, never sure whether he was trying to wound her or weld her to him, to push her away or cling her close or just to break through. To make contact.

He made it. He landed. He landed in her embrace, in the arms of the world's unbearable sorrows, the arms of grace in the face of atrocity. Grace in the face of resentment. In the face of a godless world. These arms the arms of the Great Wheel turning. These arms the arms of a monster. This monster who cared back. This monster who swayed him in its embrace, in silent recognition of his pain, this ancient thing he could not understand and could not be equal to and loved anyway, who kissed his scratchy eyelids and pretended to breathe for his benefit and spoke long-forbidden solaces into the seashell of his ear:

"I'm sorry, little one. I know. I'm sorry."

FORTY-FOUR

*L*IFE IS TRANSFORMATION. Its relentlessness is its most accursed quality, and also its most redeeming: not good, not bad, just big. Just more. Another darkness, another delight, another surprise just over the hill. Life demands your attention, your participation. Life demands to be lived. Rise to that challenge—*change or die*—and it will bear you through even the deepest abyss.

The body wants to rise. It is built that way, loyal first to the world it was born into. While the mind festers, perseverates, the body will hunger, will squirm, will set its restless sights on new pursuits. While the mind will languish, believing its misery infinite, the body knows the truth: that everything has an end, even sadness. You move through it—you let it move through you—and then, rinsed clean, you move on.

Ronoah thought he would cry forever. He thought he would never run out of grief, that once he let it go it would just gout out of him like blood until he withered up and died. He felt bound to a few more short hours in this life, bawling and heaving until he heaved free, abandoning the world and disappearing into the long dark. But the body had other ideas. It interrupted the purity of his desolation with practical demands: he couldn't breathe for all the snot clogging his sinuses, so he had to pause to blow his nose into one of Chashakva's lavender handkerchiefs; he started coughing at one point, nearly choking really, almost comically extreme, and couldn't stop until he'd soothed his swollen throat with water; his stomach clenched and clawed and whined for, of all things, a snack. It was hard to convince yourself of your imminent demise with a cluster of fat pink grapes in your hands, with the crystalline crunch of them between your teeth.

Ronoah didn't cry forever; he cried for an afternoon. A good solid wedge of an afternoon, stark blue sunny sky soaking up his tears.

416

He blubbered on about all the things that had hurt or scared him in Shaipuri, and Chashakva listened like picking out thorns, a listening deep enough to hold all those sharp bloody bits. He accused her, and he accused himself, and he forgave her, and he forgave himself, and the nausea fell and the nausea rose and when it rose too high he stumbled outside, down the stairs and out into the stripping seaside wind. Chashakva rubbed his back as he gagged and retched over the edge of the rocks, as he apologized through bile to the beach peas, and braided and unbraided his locs, changing the pattern of the plait each time. Changing; transforming.

"You know, it's remarkable how many times I've heard you throw up in our time together," she observed, watching him wipe his mouth. "That stomach lining of yours knows how to take a thrashing."

Ronoah held his burning ribcage, fingers tracing the raised edges of his darkscars through the thin linen of his tunic. "This is nothing," he replied, almost sheepishly. "It used to happen way more when I was a kid. Gengi tried to eat it once, it was awful."

"Speaking of kids. Food-motivated to a fault, that goat?"

Ronoah snorted. "If Gengi was a people-eater," he said without thinking, "he'd be the new god of Shaipuri—none of the Seeds would've stood a chance. Watch out, Vashnarajan."

A moment like a startled flock of starlings as they both realized simultaneously that Ronoah was making a joke. And then Ronoah's stomach was churning all over again and he groaned from the sour punch of it but Chashakva was laughing a full-throated guffaw, and his own shoulders were shaking with mirth as much as with vomiting.

"You wicked little thing," Chashakva said, with abject satisfaction. In spite of how rotten he felt, a small smile tugged itself free from Ronoah's lips.

That was what the evening brought them: stilted attempts to amuse each other, to bridge the chasm they both knew they couldn't fully bridge. Hiccoughs of humour, reflexive in nature, appearing like unexpected flower fields in the roiling topology of Ronoah's turmoil. They were exhausted, beleaguered little things, sodden with sarcasm and pain, but their blooms were bright nonetheless.

The moons slid up from the cup of the sea; they beheld their stately ascent until Ronoah started dozing off, and then they carried themselves indoors. Of course, the second he laid down in his hammock to sleep he was wide awake, stalked by the scourge of his old nighttime dread. He tumbled out of his hammock and went to Chashakva's, fingers twisting a petition into the tassels, hesitantly, wordlessly. She opened her eye, and then her arm, and he climbed in and curled up like a prawn at her side. They slept like they were back on the Iphigene: the ropes rocking like the boat, Chashakva humming mysterious nothings in the language of the tides, Ronoah tucked in the crook of her neck, rubbing the nub of her collarbone like a worry stone until the repetition swept him away.

And then, equally hesitantly, in the morning: "Chashakva—er, Hanéong?"

"Mm?"

"Would…do you want to see what Yengh-Sier's taught me so far?"

"Thought you'd *never* ask. Grab those Dragons and let's away to the beach, I love a creation story for breakfast."

Life demanded participation, and so they participated.

The next days were one big concerted effort to get back on familiar footing. It was shy work, but rewarding. They went roving the headland for wildflowers they could arrange in jugs for the windowsills, sprigs of sea lavender and myrtle branch. They hiked back up to Poh Nui for more of those delicious prawns, for a grueling game of duchang which Ronoah, to both of their surprise, won. "Suppose it's just that marksman's aim of yours," Hanéong sighed, with just enough wistful disappointment to tell he hadn't actually lost on purpose.

Ol-Penher garden bowling wasn't the only sport they competed in. At the end of the week, during their noontime hike, Hanéong brought Ronoah off the trail and into the evergreens. Twenty minutes of pushing through cypress and parasol pine delivered them to a clearing with a carpet of creeping thyme underfoot—and a target painted to a trunk ahead.

"No," Ronoah said, dread washing over him as Hanéong flicked out a fan of knives to choose from, "no, no I, I don't think I can—"

"You must. Or you never will again." Ronoah tore his nervous gaze from the knives to frown at Hanéong. The man ticked his chin at Ronoah, his expression unyielding. "You can skirt around a lot of what we've done, little pilgrim, but you must be firm on this. If you want that alley to be the last time you pick up a knife, walk away. But if you ever want to hold a blade again without spiralling into the panic of the past, I would suggest you start making new memories to outstack that one's disproportionate weight."

So they played. Hanéong was right; the memory made itself heavy, made itself known. Ronoah's arm kept locking in the wind-up. His throws landed low, or bounced at the handle—the first time he did gouge the target he panicked enough to need to sit down for a minute and manage his shaking, glancing up at the tree every minute or so to make sure no blood leaked from the bole. Hanéong calmly went about collecting all the fallen knives, digging them out of the creepers and pulling them from the trunk. He returned Ronoah's to his hands, damascened steel flaked with bark and glazed in sap, and then sat sunning himself, giving Ronoah time to clean them and let the turpentine smell clear out the phantom iron tang in his nostrils. Once the blades were steady in his hands, Hanéong cracked his eyes open, slid his gaze in Ronoah's direction.

"Again?" the creature asked.

Again. It went more smoothly this time, with less breath-holding and heartshock. Hanéong's throws were as deadly precise as they'd been on the Chiropolene plains, despite his doing increasingly ridiculous things to even the odds. ("Hanéong, closing your eyes isn't a disadvantage if you don't need eyes to see.") It made Ronoah feel insultingly like an amateur—but it occurred to him that perhaps he shouldn't be comparing his skills to a five-thousand-year-old supernatural being. And it made him laugh, which, judging by the grin on Hanéong's face, was most of the point.

Over the course of a couple rounds, Ronoah began to recapture the smooth movement that he remembered from teaching Yengh-Sier in the acro centre—and better than that, to recover some of the satisfaction he remembered from sun-dusted days with Lelos and Ngeome, whiling away an afternoon together post-chores with a competition in the corner of their yard. He'd always had the best aim of the three siblings, even when they made him use his right hand. It was just such an instinctive thing to imagine a pathway, to will a bridge between object and target and then to build it midair—the geometry was simple, and the body so confidently obeyed it, and then it was just a long-learned blur of sequence and velocity and the muted thud of a blade sinking center ring on a sandbag—

Or a body.

Ronoah's next throw landed high. He sucked in a breath through his teeth, let it out slow, and then went to sit cross-legged on the ground again to ride out another wave of wooziness.

After completing his scavenger hunt and depositing the knives in a pile, Hanéong crouched by his side and joined him in staring at the pine they had pierced full of holes. Slowly, the sound of birds trilling and cooing to one another filtered back in above the pounding of Ronoah's heart.

"Flips everything on its head, doesn't it," Hanéong said, "when you cross a line you never thought you would."

Ronoah curled his toes into the creeping thyme. He couldn't find anything to say.

"Especially for someone like you, who already knows there is no jumping back the other way and scrubbing the footprints out of the dust. What you did to Kauryingh is a part of you now; denying it will only fragment you further, will only make you feel more dislocated from life than you already do." Hanéong tilted his head Ronoah's way. "Am I getting it right so far?" At Ronoah's nod, the man leaned back on his hands, surveying the clearing with his characteristic aplomb. "I appreciate you may not want to hear this from me, but I understand."

At this, Ronoah did reply—with a scrapingly sceptical look that brought a smile to Hanéong's face.

"How long have I been alive, Ronoah? How many of my own poor decisions do you think I've had to face consequences for over the millennia?" It was not actually something Ronoah had considered, that Hanéong could be wrong—or rather, that he could *admit* wrong, that he was capable of regretting his choices. He'd thought that kind of self-disappointment was reserved for humanity alone. "Learning to imitate you people took centuries of fine-tuning—the constant posture adjustments, the nesting habits, blinking, bowel movements—"

Ronoah's exasperated groan expressed exactly how much he wanted to hear about Hanéong's simulated digestive system. Hanéong only spread his hands and continued, undiscouraged. "Trying to interact with you all was an entirely different exercise in error. Nowadays I can read the colour of the lightning storm in your brain—but to begin, it was one mistake after another. There are mistakes I have made regarding you people that have torn the world apart. I will surely make another." He rested his cheek against one knee. "Yet here we are."

"You're still meddling with us," Ronoah agreed, another half-jab half-joke.

"And I try to meddle more cleverly. There is no 'us' and 'you' in this equation. I live in the same world as you do; I have as much right to shape it as anyone else."

Ronoah looked for the coy sparkle, the conspiratorial curve of a smirk, and found none.

"If I pretended I *wasn't* in a situation where I could destroy this entire peninsula with a little concentration and a long after-nap—I don't mean playacting as human in the *Tris Mantarinis*, I mean true self-delusion—disaster would find us far more frequently. The same goes for you, little would-be assassin." The word made something flinch in Ronoah—and Hanéong caught hold of that something in his grip, pinned it for both of them to examine. "You have to accept responsibility for the power you have without running and trying to carve it out of you. You can no longer pretend at being that soft young scholar, innocent of cruelty or violence. Nor can you go giving your power away to make yourself safer to be around. There are things even in these gentle hills that would take you up on the offer, after all, and you would not find their terms disagreeable until too late."

The wind dropped a few pinecones to the ground. Above their springy impacts, a different sound, a different brown moving in a different direction. A falcon, landing like a long comma on the scribbled line of the pine branch, scouting prey.

Ronoah shivered. Dug his hands into the creepers, into the cool earth. The question, when it came, came out helpless: "How do I accept being— being *dangerous?*"

The possibility of being dangerous—however dubious, however improbable—was partly what had moved him to leave Pilanova in the first place. It was what had motivated that foolishly idealistic declaration of his, watching the Maelstrom, his vow to run the gauntlet of Truth no matter what it took:

I want to learn about as much as possible, about everything, so that I know how not to hurt anyone.

Deep down he'd always been frightened of it. Of hurting people, of *being someone* who hurt people. Frightened of following in his elder sister the exile's footsteps, straight into unforgiveable territory. Frightened of making Gen—

Well. He'd done it now, was the point. And it went so vehemently against everything he stood for that he didn't even know how to begin digesting it.

Luckily, Hanéong had plenty of experience. "You absorb the shock instead of bracing against it. You embrace that you *can* without jumping to the conclusion that you *will*, or should. You have to wield your shadow wisely, which sometimes can mean simply knowing it's there and doing nothing at all with it. Knowing it's there—and letting it know you know— is the surest way to getting it on your side."

It seemed sensible. Self-knowledge was always valuable. All the same: "I was never taught to know my shadow," Ronoah said quietly. "I don't think I could find it if I tried."

"According to your people," Hanéong countered, matching his tone, "the desert sun burned it small enough to never need to. Montane squabbles aside. For seven months under Chalisto's Belt you *were* your shadow, and it did you enormous good."

The memory rose—dark passageways, watchful portraits, his own fears and gifts lifted out of him into the atmosphere—and with it, a perverse sort of fondness. "Are you telling me I'm overdue for another impromptu Sweetwood Day?"

Hanéong grinned. "You did say it was your favourite day of the year. How does it go? *From language, life?*" He cupped his palms, lifted them to Ronoah. "Speak me a shadow into being."

It had been a long time since they'd talked like this: not so much in words as in references, in networks of context and meaning. Phonal shorthand, ratified by each of their forever-long memories, vivified by the wealth of shared experience between them. The ease of it startled Ronoah, flintsparked a flamelet of nostalgia. Softened him enough to talk.

"Everything I know about myself has changed," he began. "I mean, it changed suddenly. In that minute, in—in the span between throw and touchdown." He'd known, of course, that he was changing over time. But it had taken until that breathless instant to appear clearly, just how much his self-image was compromised. How outdated it was. "It reminds me of the day I did this," he said, lifting a hand to brush self-consciously at the side of his head. His hair had grown enough to blur the spiralling swirls. "When I sat down and looked in the mirror and had no clue who was looking out at me. I saw …I saw such tightly-banked fury. I saw someone I'd be intimidated by. Someone I might—be scared of."

Hanéong flicked his gaze down to his cupped hands and smiled a secretive smile, as if he approved of what pooled there. Ronoah fidgeted with a piece of creeping thyme, and pressed on.

"In the alley, that bank broke. That fury took form, and the form, the form was—" He twitched back from it, but the soundless thrum of Hanéong's presence egged him on. He cursed under his breath. "I'm the kind of person who can end lives now, Hanéong. What am I supposed to *do* with myself, knowing I'm capable of that? That's one of the greatest crimes a Pilanovani can commit. If anyone back home ever heard of this, I would be banished for good, for real, *forever*, no questions asked. So I have to *lie* to them if I want to go back, and—and I'll do it. There is no doubt in my mind that I will keep this from everyone, from even my own family, and the simplicity of that choice frightens me too. How easy it is to make." He shrugged, staring up into the boughs, into the chiaroscuro of the falcon's vantage point. "Feris was right—everyone lies. *Everyone* hurts people. It's only a matter of what will push you to it."

"You really believed you could hold to that standard of virtue forever, didn't you," Hanéong mused, half to himself it seemed.

"I did." The falcon spread its wings. Ronoah watched it take off. "And I was wrong."

The two of them sat silent for a time, as if in honour of the innocence-eroding nature of this fact. The scent of crushed thyme wafted up from Ronoah's fingers. Eventually, Hanéong took a breath. "Do you think," he said, and Ronoah's neck tingled with premonition, "your elder sister the exile faced the same devastation, when she was wrong?"

And there she was. Of course. A hard ambush of laughter punched up from his diaphragm. "Probably," he said. "It probably took her completely by surprise that she could do whatever she did. It probably broke her heart. I bet she didn't even try to seek shelter in another city, or the nomad camps out in the bush, no, I bet she walked right to the Salt Flats and found a dry patch to lie down on and cried it wet again. I bet she begged to be remade." He licked his lips, tasting the ghost of the salt. "It's what I would have done, if I were there."

"But you're here." Ronoah glanced at Hanéong, who was looking into his hands again as if *here* was more than a place. As if it was a standpoint, a crossroads. A choice. "So what will you do instead? Now harmlessness isn't an option."

Ronoah let his gaze drop to the upturned soles of his feet, watched a couple of ants explore the faded missives of *Perseverance* and *Solidarity*. Thought about Sweetwood Day, about speaking of things to no one. About how you couldn't even tell someone they were fickle or inconstant in Pilanova without needing a whole ritual container to do it in, permanent ink and all. About how his people tried so hard to prevent harm—and how they wounded him anyway.

"Harmlessness was never an option, was it?" he asked, to his tattoos, to Hanéong, to anything that might answer him. "No matter how much I learn or how many precautions I take, I might still mess something up. That's what you're telling me—that avoiding causing problems is impossible. That it's not even the point." Hanéong had sluiced open that listening presence again, like a current for Ronoah's school of glimmering thoughts to swim in. "The point is to try and repair what you break. To own your mistakes. To take an active part in fixing them, however you can. Like you did with Shaipuri."

"Like I do with most things."

"I should have stayed." A chill ran up his arms—now it was Chashakva's words to Jau-Hasthasuna coming out of his mouth. How uncanny, that he could slide so easily into both roles. "I shouldn't have gone for the knives, I should have—called out, or run to you both, or hit Kauryingh with my *hands* if I had to hit them at all. I don't know why I didn't. My head was just—on wrong." He hugged his arms, anchored himself. "But most of all I should have stayed and helped you to save them. I should have seen the consequences through instead of running and hiding. If—" Oh, this was hard to say. This was like sandpaper against his throat, because saying it would be admitting that it might be necessary to say. But—that was the point, wasn't it? To be okay with admitting it. To hold it with grace. "…If something like it ever happens again, that's what I'll do," he finished, and felt some young limb inside him harden, strengthen, mature. "I'll do everything I can to make amends."

"And if I hadn't been there?" Hanéong suggested, lightly but deadly keen. "If Kauryingh had well and truly perished? If there is, ultimately, no way to atone?"

"I don't know, Hanéong," Ronoah sighed, "I'm still figuring it out. Try better next time? Learn to carry that failure on my shoulders? If I'm not trying to walk in the world as *someone who never hurts anyone* but instead as—as someone who tries my best not to, then it's different, right? It feels different." He sat on it for a moment, dissatisfied nonetheless. "Worst comes to worst, I can always compare myself to you," he added, the ironic tang of the words twisting his mouth into a grim smile. "My shadow is bigger than I thought, but yours turns the sun dark."

That earned a cackle from Hanéong. "Behold, an introduction," the man proclaimed, and mimed tossing all of Ronoah's confessions into his lap. Ronoah was so busy trying to figure out whether the man had actually dumped anything there that he almost missed Hanéong's subtle turn to the sky, to the sun, his second murmured invocation: "Behold, an improved model."

That ached in a way he couldn't think about. He clutched his shadow close, glad all of a sudden for the strength of its terrible resilience.

"The entry wounds were perfect, by the way." Hanéong lifted a knife from the pile and tossed it casually forward; it hit the target dead centre, as always. "Clean and lethal. Would absolutely have died if I weren't there."

With an even more indignant sigh, Ronoah resisted the urge to protest that if Hanéong hadn't been there, Kauryingh's wellbeing would have been spared altogether. Everyone could have made choices to prevent those two killing blows, even Kauryingh themself. It was a fruitless argument. It wasn't the point.

So instead he leaned into the strange compliment of the strange creature beside him, assumed its alien ethnolect—just for a moment—and said, "Thank you."

He picked up a knife, spent a moment fidgeting and fine-tuning his angle, and let fly. And perhaps he was that good, or perhaps he was that lucky, or perhaps Hanéong was feeling like a symbolic moment was in order, but the knife struck center ring as well, nestling up to Hanéong's with a rasping ring.

Ronoah took in the sight: two sharp objects buried in the same soft wood together. Then he nestled up a bit, too, leaning sideways until his shoulder bumped Hanéong's. "I never thought about you as someone who lived in this world. I always thought..."

Hanéong's voice rumbled with wry humour. "I dwelled above it?"

"I don't know." Ronoah bit his lip. "But I'm sorry." With a deep, steeling breath, he pressed his shoulder into Hanéong's. Hvanzhir Hanéong, the Heretic Saint—the face who'd put up with Ronoah's hatred. It was one thing to throw himself into the arms of Reilin, one thing to snuggle into the familiar breastbone of Chashakva, but Hanéong's sweet countenance was the one who'd borne the brunt of Ronoah's malice, who'd patiently taken his abuses. However much it was all the same creature underneath, this particular aspect deserved for him to try and make amends with it. This, too, was shadow-knowing, and this too was taking responsibility. "I know you said before that you didn't need the apology, and I was probably saying it then to avoid everything else, but I'm telling you now, really. I'm sorry. I held you to the standards of a human and a god at the same time, whichever role you were failing more. I can't imagine how that kind of double-standard must feel."

"Oh, it's grotesquely unfair, of course," Hanéong said breezily, ignoring how Ronoah's press turned into a shove. His ears were burning, but he forced himself to listen. "But it's no surprise. Sometimes you people see me as one, sometimes the other, but very few recognize that what I am is something apart from both, and that I pledge my allegiance fully to neither. Or to anything else, for that matter—Chiropolene demons, Ol-Penher angels, Thalthashan elementals, the dead-and-risen revenants of Svarok. Even to the shalledrim, though that would perhaps be the conscientious thing to do. It makes sense that none of you would know what to expect from me; you have a very small sample size. You have a sample size of exactly one." He touched a fingertip to his cheek, lightly. "So I do not blame you."

If what happened next hadn't happened, Ronoah might never have noticed what he was actually being told. He very well might have sailed on oblivious, to his apology and their discussion and their day, their lives. But it did happen.

What happened is Hanéong faltered.

It was such a minute gesture. One finger still to his cheek, his eyes flicked down; the finest crease appeared between his brows. He looked displeased—no. No. He looked *disconcerted*. Like he'd only fully realized what he was saying after it was out.

That hesitancy was enough of a surprise for Ronoah to turn back and retread the man's answer. Enough for him to turn over every line, seeking the source, the offending phrase, the culprit. And then he found it, it dawned on him, he found it.

Exactly one.

God and gods alike.

"There's no one else like you," he breathed, and the forest creaked under the revelation.

"Ah. What sweet compliments you give." Hanéong was smiling now. It was never more obvious than at that moment, that his smiles were not human smiles, did not express human feelings. It was never more apparent that between the bright and boisterous stars of Hanéong's galaxies lay endless forlorn void. "There used to be, once."

A queer wind blew through Ronoah. "Once?"

Hanéong closed his eyes. "Once."

He was still a long while after that. Perhaps he was savouring the irony.

Ronoah had no idea what to say, what to do. What did you do with something like that? What did you do when you found out your friend's species was one body—the body in front of you—away from extinction? His own body was alive with heat and tingling, like he was back in the Lightning Room, absolutely fizzing with energy, presence, with tension. It felt like every cell in his body had undergone a spontaneous chemical reaction, changed irreversibly by this secret the way a drop of dye colours water. No one else. No one else like him.

But wait—hadn't Hanéong said once, a long time ago, that he had children? Unless—Vespasi wake, it barely bore thinking about—unless those had gone, too. How? Were they hunted like the shalledrim? Did they diminish each other in the same sort of war that ultimately caused the Shattering? Or was it the Shattering that had claimed them all? How did Hanéong make it out alive? Why was it still here?

Underneath the churning of his intellect, his heart. His heart aching one long sorrowful note. A loss on that scale—even the sea couldn't swallow a feeling so wide. He could scarcely touch it.

"I'm not in the mood to get into it today." Ronoah startled to hear Hanéong's voice, so light, so breezy. The man rested his crossed arms atop his knees and tucked his chin into his arms, looking out over the clearing. "The weather's too fine."

He was so still, all the micromotions of false humanity laid aside, that a pair of small cream butterflies mistook him for warm stone and landed on his head. So poised; so inscrutable. Ronoah thought of the Maelstrom, thought of the Shattering, thought about how it did no good to confuse librarians with their libraries, how all stories had real feeling people at their cores. He made a soft noise in his throat, a reassurance. *I won't ask if you don't want me to.*

But he reeled from it. From the imprint of that hesitation, burned

426

forever now into his memory. He had only ever caught Hanéong off-guard like this once, when Hanéong was still Özrek, in the monastery. They'd been talking about learning from losing, about changing from challenge; in a word, about growing. *I take it you've been the same for a while then, haven't you?* That's what Ronoah had said. And Özrek had replied: *Indeed I have.*

Something shifted in him—a whole constellation of impressions and observations was trying to coalesce, nearly incomprehensible in its magnitude, its complexity. He felt a huge pressure inside his head, like it was being stretched twice as wide to accommodate whatever was forming and still it hardly fit. He felt like he had to get up and pace around, like he did before finding Bazzenine and Jesprechel, only he was rooted to the spot by the force of the construct trying to put itself together. It ached in his temples just trying to hold it long enough to think it at all, to pull it all down from the sky: Özrek's little melancholies, and Reilin's, and even Chashakva's sometimes, the creature's insistence on the point that it *did not know everything,* its hunger for the thrilling, its endless questing nature, its agreement that the lifelong sprint for Truth was *one of the only things that matters at all*—and its reticence to share of itself, its habit of redirecting conversation away from itself, honed over centuries, over millennia maybe, not out of slyness or obstinacy but *uncertainty,* the very uncertainty Ronoah nursed in his own heart.

Where were you born? Where did you start?

You know, I don't quite remember anymore.

Hanéong was a spirit adrift. Hanéong was a vacuum trying to fill itself with itself. For all its power, all its knowledge, it had no elders, no mentors, no peers, no guides. No guidance.

Chuta ka saag. Hanéong was the same as Jau-Hasthasuna—the last thing left, just trying to sort out what to do next. To find meaning.

There was wonder in his voice when he spoke. Reverence, and pity, and awe. "There's no one to teach you how—how to *be*, is there?" He'd never been surer of anything in his life. "There isn't. I have an older brother, and parents, and priests and research professors and friends and books, thousands of years of books, I have an endless well of advice and encouragement and when it all fails me I have *you.* You've studied us so much you could teach me to be human if I really needed it. But—but for you, to learn to be what you are—you have ..."

No one. That's what he expected Hanéong to say. But Hanéong had a different answer.

"I have the world," it said. Ronoah was taken aback by the firmness of this, the sureness. The trust. It lifted a hand to its head, coaxed the butterflies onto its gently crooked fingers, held them aloft. Up close, fine grey veins creased the delicate linen of their wings. "The world, and the mistakes I make in it. That's how I've learned—well. Everything, really."

"*Everything?*" Ronoah couldn't accept that. That was hyperbole, it had to be. "But you said there *used* to be—surely they passed down *something*—"

And he heard himself, and came to a guilty halt. Hanéong glanced over and smiled, and there was something so close to vulnerability there, something so cousin to gratitude, that Ronoah nearly forgot to breathe.

"I'm glad," was what he said instead, bumbling, blunt-edged, true to the bone. He looked Hanéong right in its starry eyes. "I'm so glad you're still here."

A wave of something knocked into him, made the whole world go rosy and opaline, made him dizzy, drunk as a bee in a berry patch. It was Hanéong's affection—for him, for the world he was a part of, for the whole Universe. "Me too," it replied.

With infinite care, Hanéong enticed the butterflies onto Ronoah's knee. Then the creature rose and made its way to the tree. It gathered up the pile of knives as it went; Ronoah saw it slipping them into its arms as if its skin were just a sleeve, under and away. Hanéong freed the final two blades from the target, vanished them with the rest. And then it brushed a palm over the sap-crusted wounds, and placed a kiss on the bark, and like the waves washing the sand smooth a drift of magic bathed the trunk and purled the holes closed.

FORTY-FIVE

ONE FINAL DAY IN POH NUI: the coast a cerulean scroll, the gulls a rowdy ballet. They explored the fjords, thanked the lute players with shell and bouquets of fresh-plucked mountain flowers, sucked up a platter of pan-seared sea scallops from a tiny shack on the bay. Ronoah spent the majority of the afternoon perusing boutiques and sidestreet stalls in order to pick out gifts for everyone: a pewter bookmark engraved with Poh Nui's local saint for Ngodi; a pot of lemon myrtle sea salt scrub for Ean-Bei. Yengh-Sier wasn't the type to want gifts, so Ronoah had planned to forego him and just be sure to return the ribbon poi in good condition—but when he passed the town's modest acro centre, he noticed a poster in the window. The sun had already leeched the colour from the red-hot coals, but there was no mistaking the green and purple sleeves. Eng-Vaunh had passed through here on their tour. Ronoah asked for the print, and made a note to present it to his teacher when Ean-Bei wasn't around to heckle.

One final night, moongazing, watching the clouds as they polished the black opal of the night sky. And then it came time to leave the mellow leisure of Poh Nui behind, to turn back toward the hectic bright of Khepsuong Phae. They purchased tickets for the morning train westward, slipped aboard the railcar, and sought themselves a compartment with two upholstered red bench seats facing one another. When the train steamed out of Poh Nui, they were the only passengers aboard. The sense of peace as they trundled past the first valley was immeasurable. It felt timeless.

Three stops later the carriage had picked up another dozen travelers, and Ronoah's sense of peace was eroding fast.

This ride was *not* timeless. Quite the opposite: it had a strict schedule, an estimated time of arrival. By the end of the day, they would roll back into Khepsuong Phae—into the city and all he had left there. Every moment, every mile, they were drawing closer. With every stop the train made, another jolt of nervousness seared the insides of his wrists, the hollow of his throat.

What were they going to do, when they returned?

It wasn't a subject he had broached with Hanéong yet. For all their making up and renewing their friendship and confiding in one another, they—hadn't actually talked about what should happen now. Now that Ronoah wasn't hiding behind the bluster and busywork of the city. Now that he wasn't trying to drown himself in it. Now that Khepsuong Phae no longer functioned as a distraction—now what? Pack up and go? To the Pilgrim State? Just like that?

Another anxious jolt, potent enough to make his bones cringe in their sockets. No matter how much better and safer he felt with Hanéong, the idea of heading up the Holy Corridor still filled him with dread. It had—he discovered, to his own irritated amusement, his own self-deprecating surprise—nothing to do with Hanéong. It basically never had.

No, his aversion to the Pilgrim State came from the fact that he no longer had a reason to go.

Come on, protested a voice in his head, there are plenty of reasons. Kharoun's book is a reason—the one by Maril Bi-Jelsihad, the one she gave you to read in the Pilgrim State. Delighting Ean-Bei and everyone is a reason, too, they've been asking you about the Pilgrim State since the day you met, they would be ecstatic to hear you've got a trip planned. Nazum's promise is a reason (he thought, and his heart squeezed). You said you would hang a rope up for Vashnarajan; you can't back out on the last request of your best friend. Hanéong's going one way or another, and Hanéong's company alone would be reason enough, wouldn't it?

It might be. But also it might not. He'd never intended to go to the Pilgrim State for the sake of other people; their hopes and expectations followed him like goats over the grazing lands, but his own heart was the goatherd, always had been. He wasn't going so he could make his friends happy. He was going—he'd *thought* he was going—for the spark in his soul, for the fire of destiny that had since blown out.

So. Was there a *real* point in going to a land of gods, if gods didn't exist?

Sound broke the murky bubble of his thoughts—Hanéong, laughing that loud, crystalline laugh of his. When Ronoah turned to look, he saw the man had slid the compartment door open and struck up a conversation with a young girl and her mother in musical Qiao Sidhur. They didn't look much like Hanéong: for one, they both had dark brown hair, except for a tuft of silver at the mother's right temple. Their eyes were similarly dark, not the mirror grey Ronoah had gotten used to in Hanéong. But there was something—maybe in the small foreheads, or the fingers—that suggested they did indeed all come from one place.

The girl's fingers flashed, and Ronoah looked again. Hanéong was playing some sort of game with her while he talked, a game with a bright blue string woven and crossed between their hands. She pinched and pulled the string from Hanéong's hands, and a new shape emerged between her own palms. Suddenly, viscerally, Ronoah remembered a similar game he used to play when he was a child too young for throwing knife competitions: Obagli's Web. The same long piece of yarn or leather, the same intricate flexing and twisting of the fingers, the same beautiful shapes. The only difference was that Obagli's Web was a solo game. You could hold contests to see who could go faster—and Ronoah nearly always won, given his predilection for geometry—but you couldn't play collaboratively, like Hanéong and the girl were playing now.

Somewhere deep down, the child in Ronoah felt an envious pang. He offered a shy smile to the girl's mother, watched the two players at work, and as he watched his thoughts returned once more to the creature known as Hvanzhir Hanéong.

He was thinking about everything Hanéong had said in the forest, in the pines: living in the world, and shaping it. Meddling, and mistakes, and a solitude so immense it eclipsed Ronoah's every attempt to grasp it. It had used to fill Ronoah with wonder that Hanéong figured in so many legends, had woven so many shining threads of history; he'd been left awestruck at every turn. Then it had filled him with irritation, with contempt for the creature's perceived ego. But now—now it felt fair. Fitting. He was realizing that Hanéong's constant involvement was never about trying to take advantage of poor, unsuspecting humanity. Neither was it about nursing them, about accepting responsibility for human growth and wellbeing. It wasn't about humans at all. It was about wanting to engage in the world-at-large, to play in it with the same exploratory spirit as—

Well, as Ronoah himself.

You knew this to begin with, said a voice his head. Before you knew anything else about Hanéong, you knew its vicious appetite for the world. You felt it like an orbit you were pulled into.

He'd lost sight of that. It had been pushed from his mind by other, more important-seeming truths: the shalledrim, and the shapeshifting, and Reilin's Lottery, and Chashakva god of the last age. But it shouldn't have. It should have stayed front and center, the first impression the creature had made, that young, excited declaration about stepping into the glorious unknown. It was unknown to *both* of them; it always had been.

It was for that realization, that remembrance, that Ronoah found himself seriously considering asking Hanéong whether the Pilgrim State was worth it.

It came as a surprise. Until now, he wouldn't have so much as hinted at it with Hanéong. First, because for the longest time Ronoah had associated Hanéong with false gods—with *artificial* gods, created for Hanéong's amusement—and he'd been too achingly furious with Hanéong for inciting this existential crisis to ask him much of anything. He could see now that it wasn't actually Hanéong's fault; the creature could be rightly blamed for a lot of things, but it would ultimately be wrong to say that it *made* Ronoah stop believing.

The second reason was more recent, more furtive. It was simple: he didn't want to mark himself as unworthy. Unworthy of the journey, of Hanéong's companionship. Unworthy of all those hopes and promises his friends had placed on him. Deep down, he worried that confiding this most fragile of fears to Hanéong would disappoint the man—would, in a way, make Hanéong lose faith in *Ronoah*. He couldn't bear that. He wanted Hanéong to keep seeing him as someone with *incorruptible whimsy*, even after that whimsy had long since spoiled. He wanted Hanéong to keep expecting him to find lemons in lychees, wanted to be seen as someone who was in tune with the world, in *love* with the world. He wanted his own sincerity to be unquestionable. He wanted to maintain that image, uphold that old ideal of two seekers on an adventure for the transcendent. He wanted to still be worth the name *little pilgrim*.

Even in Poh Nui, Ronoah had worried that confessing this scepticism to Hanéong would spell the end of their time together. But that talk in the forest—about making mistakes, and knowing your shadow, and learning to live even when atonement was impossible—that heart-to-hearts, and the gut instinct Ronoah had about Hanéong's own lack of absolute certainty, made him wonder now whether it might not be a death sentence after all, to ask about this. Maybe the shadow side of curiosity was critique. Maybe doubt was part of the adventure, too.

So, quietly, while Hanéong played with the world in the shape of a girl with some string, Ronoah came to a resolution.

"Hey," he called softly, once the Qiao Sidhur pair had wandered back to their own compartment. Hanéong twisted around, eyebrows raised. "Teach me to play?"

Hanéong reached for his own wrist, just up his lavender sleeve, and withdrew a long whip of quicksilver like pulling out a vein. He looped the gleaming, glowing cord, soldered it shut with a pinch. "Gladly. Hold out your hands."

The game was similar enough to the one Ronoah remembered that he caught on without too much explanation. The cord was made of something utterly alien, not wool or leather or chain but something cool and fluid and silky, something that seemed to chime when he picked it up. He watched his own fingers transforming one shape into another, kept one eye on Hanéong doing the same, used the breath held in the game to steel himself.

You've already established that you want to live, he told himself. That much is certain. Now it's just a matter of trying to figure out what you're living *for*. Well, there are two options: either gods are real—she's real—and you have a destiny you're bound to, and you can get back to living that out with twice the gusto. Or they're not. And then you have to start getting serious about taking care of yourself, because there's no divine hand who's going to do it for you. You have to decide what's important to you for yourself, without guidance—just like Hanéong. Even if gods don't exist, that doesn't mean this world is without beauty. Far from it—there's the East Ocean, and libraries, and Eng-Vaunh's coal-dancing and Nazum singing Vashnarajandr hymns, there's Bazzenine's paintings and Sophrastus carving roses from apples and Kourrania's lightning-blue eyes. There's the shalledrim. There's *Hanéong*. Isn't it—he thought, with a queer sort of thrill—isn't it *more* astounding, if all those things exist just because? For their own sake, their own beingness? Isn't it almost more incredible if everything is random chaos but out of that chaos came such splendour? Can you not love a world like that precisely *for* its precarity?

He pulled his hands taut. The pattern between his fingers fractalized yet again, spidersilk as canny as it was beautiful.

He was calmer about this than he'd expected. Maybe he had a skewed view of himself, but he'd assumed he wouldn't be able to so much as think the question without dissolving into incoherent panic. Maybe he was veiling his feelings again, smothering them in methodical thinking.

Or maybe it just wasn't the first time he was thinking it. Maybe he had always been thinking it—in the background, in the basement, while dancing parables with Yengh-Sier and studying permutations of faith with Ngodi and exploring the marvels of Khepsuong Phae with Ean-Bei, while wandering Poh Nui with Hanéong, while throwing knives, while touching toes with the ocean, while heaving and sobbing about Shaipuri—maybe under all that fuss, all that busyness, his subconscious had been working on it clandestinely. Just like back in the monastery. Maybe something deep inside him had been whittling away at it this whole time, patiently, attentively, and now instead of the splintery thing he'd expected it came to him smoothed and honed and steadier than he could ever anticipate.

Steady or not, it took him another four rounds of the Qiao Sidhur string game to muster up the courage. It took until they rolled into another train station, and the next three were named: *Chuyneng, Khar-em-Mai, Khepsuong Phae*. The city couldn't be more than a couple hours away.

If he was going to have this conversation, it had to happen now—on this train, in the midst of this passage from seaside to cityscape, from private to public, from shadow to light, this liminal space where everything moved while staying still. There was psychological power in a moment like this. He wasn't going to get another. His opportunity was dwindling.

So he sucked in a breath, and he took it.

"This looks a lot like a game I used to play in Pilanova," he started. Hanéong smiled, none the wiser.

"Ah, there's things like it all over the world," he replied. "The Qiao Sidhur version is called *Winter Palace*. Each shape is a different room in the Emperor's famous palace in Hvallánzhou. You try and puzzle your way through all the chambers, one after another, and if you make it to the innermost chamber you get a marvelous congratulatory feast with the royal family. In the imagination, of course." A smirk streaked across the man's features. "Telling, isn't it, that it's not really a game the actual royal children played much. I only taught it to one son of the Emperor, and he was long past childhood by then."

"Why teach it to him as an adult?"

"You're asking now as an adult, aren't you?" Hanéong teased. Ronoah's ears went warm. "Dexterity, mainly. Limbering up the fingers. He was a musician in training."

Obagli's Web was to build hand-eye coordination in children, too, but the story that came with it was different. "My version calls the shapes webs. The eight webs the spider Obagli wove to catch the eight different types of knowledge—or, no, more like ways of knowing, eight separate kinds of intelligence she needed to become divine."

Obagli's children were the ones who grew up to become oracles in Pilanova, the ones to identify the godlings of all the city's infants. One of them had been studying in the temple when Ronoah came to begin his own ill-fated training; he'd known another as a next-door neighbour, married to a child of Nataglio, of all things. A witch and a weatherman, and their kids always getting bullied into games like this one by Lelos when neither Ronoah nor Ngeome would budge. He smiled—a little wistful; a little tense—looped his thumbs through the silvery string, pulled a new web from the tangle. "She's the only godling who has a sort-of mortal origin story. Who—started on the material plane, and transformed."

In that halt, a hissing. Perhaps just in Ronoah's mind; perhaps in Hanéong's too. Either way, it was there, and it demanded one last sacrifice.

"Hanéong," Ronoah said, "I want to ask you about gods."

"Which ones?"

"All of them, kind of." He bit his lip, held out his hands for Hanéong to take his turn with their game. "It's just—so many of the things people think are gods, aren't. They're creatures like Jau-Hasthasuna, or shalledrim like in the a-Meheyu temples. Or you. A lot of the time they're you." The train rounded a curve. Ronoah swayed with it, leaning left; Hanéong stayed perfectly still. It struck him as almost funny, the pointedness of it, the acknowledgement. "I know you can't help that, a lot of the time, people just see you and think—you said yourself most of us don't know what to make of you, so—what I'm trying to say is so much of, of *theology* can be traced back to ..."

To falsehoods. To misunderstandings. To you. There were a lot of ways to end that sentence, so he just shrugged, and let the curve of his shoulder hold them all.

Hanéong splayed his fingers, displayed the geometric loveliness between them. "Ah. You did say something about this, before everything with Kauryingh."

That got a wince out of Ronoah. "I did, yeah." It didn't feel great to remember. He broke eye contact, sought refuge in the view outside. The sumac, the hills, the river. "You ... you threw salt on my fire once. You sat down and spoke to my godling when I asked if you wanted to. You called her *patron of the wise* and *daughter of the red moon*, and you proposed a deal, and it looked like you really heard an answer. Was that just—indulging me? Was it just pretend?"

"I didn't make her up, if that's what you're asking. She's—what was the phrase?—she's *safe from me*."

Ronoah turned back and saw Hanéong smiling—a smile like a surrender, like a sinking feeling, a smile like the creature knew Ronoah had every right to double-check but was still a little bitter anyway. Ronoah flipped through what he'd said, saw all the places he'd punctured something soft without knowing: *you're the only thing there is; you made them up so it would feel like there were others, so you wouldn't be so alone.* Way to hit a target with your eyes closed, Ronoah.

He felt ashamed, but not that ashamed. He had to give himself at least a little compassion for that day. And Hanéong, though it may have been stung, did not seem at all interested in hearing an apology. So he just nudged Hanéong's knee with his own and said, "I know that now, but thanks for saying so." He took a deep breath. "It's not exactly what I'm asking, though."

"What are you asking, then?"

"Is she—is Genoveffa—" Oh, saying the name made it harder. But he had to know. He could live with a yes, and he was pretty sure he could even live with a no, but before he could get back to living at all he needed to know— "Is she *real*?"

"That depends on your definition." This was just so spectacularly *not* a yes or no answer that Ronoah's mouth dropped open. He had no idea what was going to come out of it—a whine, a reproach, a curse, a yell of frustration—but before anything at all could happen, Hanéong clapped its hands together so sharply Ronoah squeaked in alarm. "Hang on. *Hang* on. Surely you don't mean—"

Hanéong cut itself off, eyes snapped to focus, tracking something in that discreet layer of Ronoah that Hanéong alone could interpret. What it found there made its eyes go wide.

"Surely not," it said.

"You dropped your pattern," Ronoah replied. It was the only thing he could think to say.

Hanéong hardly spared a glance for the gossamer string looped limp between its palms. "That game is over," the creature said, half to itself, still examining Ronoah with what seemed suspiciously like wonder. "We start a new one now—and both of us with the same set of rules this time, *heavens*, I thought this was all still to do with the War, swear on Saint Hanéong's sword, but it's grown beyond that, hasn't it? This isn't just to do with a lack of faith in me, it's a lack of faith in—but how did you come to this? How did this spread so far as to choke your trust in your own godling?"

How? Ronoah could not adequately explain how. He thought he could, at first; he made a grab for something logical and clear, something like *the moment you told me none of the Seeds were gods*, but it went before that, didn't it? He hadn't made a ritual fire for months before the Council of All Tribes even started, not since—before he got sick. And paid the garnet to Marghat. And accepted the cost like it was nothing, like it *meant* nothing, so he must have had doubts then or he would have fought to keep it, so it had to have been before that, too, maybe before he'd even arrived at Marghat's, maybe the internal vertigo had started when the Yacchatzndr stole him away, maybe faith had been cut out of him slice by slice as he worked with Pashangali toward her unbearable ends, maybe when he failed to save the tallest warrior's life it sank with him into the bog, maybe, *maybe*—

There was no good answer, in the end. And it was more painful that he'd expected, to try and find one. This was the hard part—the embarrassing part, the one that felt like a betrayal or a shaming or a disappointment.

Like trying to justify his own fall from grace. He tried to stay principled about it even though he felt like a kid explaining why he'd pushed his sister into the dirt, defensive and sort of panicky and like he was bound to be disbelieved. If there was a point in this discussion where Ronoah's fears were going to come true, and Hanéong become disillusioned about Ronoah's worth as a companion, as a friend, it was now.

But it didn't happen. Hanéong listened to Ronoah's babbling as he tried to piece together the shape of his last known moments of faith. He listened without interruption, without disturbance, and when Ronoah finally fumbled the thread of his guesswork for good, when he gave up his diving for the shards of something already swept out to sea, Hanéong vanished the quicksilver cord and reached across to squeeze his hand.

"I did wonder," he said at last, "about all the churchgoing."

Ronoah snorted a laugh. "What was it we used to say," he asked ruefully, "about building new bricks to replace the old?"

Hanéong smiled back. Thoughtfully, he turned Ronoah's hand over and began to trace lines up his fingers. Each one felt like he'd dipped it in warm water. "Alas for you, little apostate," the man said, with a consoling squint at one of Ronoah's hangnails, "for you have wandered into the mists of cynicism, where even the toughest of bricks disintegrate to ash. Didn't you go to Padjenne's academy to study other belief systems? That's what you told me back on the plains—did you not find anything to be concerned about then? Nothing that threatened you? Nothing that contradicted what you knew to be true?"

"I—did do that." Ronoah blinked. Frowned. "I guess. I mean, I got side-tracked by the shalledrology stuff pretty quickly, so I guess I just didn't give it enough time." Maybe, given his initial subject of interest, this would have happened anyway—this crisis, this disintegration. Maybe he would have had this breakdown of faith in Padjenne. Without a friend to talk to about it. The idea made him shiver.

Hanéong hummed in consideration. Laid Ronoah's hand on his knee and took up the other one, drawing Ronoah's shoulder down from its unconscious hitch. "If you *had* given it time," he mused, "you'd have come across the delightful secret all spiritual seekers eventually find: that things can be in contradiction of each other and still all be true. That Truth herself is not only elusive, she's *non-absolute*. She's mutable—she's multiple."

A memory swam like an eel up into Ronoah's awareness: that amber afternoon in the *Tris Mantarinis*, the very day he and Hanéong had met, the first mention of Truth and her gauntlet—and the arguing with Hexiphines about what did and did not deserve the designation of divinity. The shalledrim, the ocean, something more. *I can think of at least one place of worship that makes your idea of 'weird' seem downright unimaginative.* They had begun this conversation long ago. It had, in a way, been their first. It had, in a way, been the conversation that made their journey to the Pilgrim State possible. Made it manifest.

Which was almost too ironic to stand.

"Let me exemplify." Hanéong let go of Ronoah's hand so he could gesture freely; they were speaking in some patchwork pidgin together, swerving in and out of Ol-Penher, Shaipurin, Chiropolene, even Acharrioni. Such was the complexity of the topic, that they needed every framework to hand. "Chiropolene classics. Remember Amimna's tale, the poison boy and the birdhouse girl? In one version they reunite and die together; in another they turn into birds; in another, they manage to live and love on as human beings. In another, she never even makes it to the mountaintop. Each version directly contradicts the others, and all of them are true."

"But those are *stories*," Ronoah protested. "They're fictitious, of course they can all be equally true if that truth isn't grounded in—I don't know, the real world."

"Fine. Something realer for you: the Heavenly Seeds were mortal animals, playing a game of my devising. They also were gods." Ronoah began to form another protest, but Hanéong intercepted him. "Of course they were. They were gods in every way that counts—they commanded the love and respect of an entire rainforest, they shaped its future almost unilaterally, they were the recipients of worship and prayer and offering, they could grant blessing and curse, they had magnificent powers to heal and to harm, as you experienced firsthand. Is there something missing here?" Before Ronoah could respond, Hanéong switched tracks: "What qualifies as *real* to you, anyway? What does that mean?"

Now Ronoah was truly taken aback. What was real? How did he even begin to answer that?

Hanéong gave him precisely two seconds to flounder before listing off possibilities. "Does it have to be physical, tangible to the senses? I'd assume not, you're an empath—the emotions you drink up aren't solid, and yet you know them to exist just the same. So. Does it have to 'work'? What work, and to what end, and how measurable or replicable the results? Does something have to be demonstrably independent of your own belief? Must it exist *whether or not* you believe in it—?"

"Yes!" Maybe he felt pressed into a corner, snatching at something to anchor himself. Or maybe it really was what he believed. Either way, Ronoah grasped the idea tight: "Yes, it should—it's got to exist objectively, without me, not just because I believe it's there."

Hanéong flat-out laughed, his voice like a wind chime flung high. "And what point has a god if no one believes in it? Your thinking presupposes two ridiculous things: one, that you are inherently disconnected from everything beyond yourself, that your own heart and mind are not legitimate bits of the Universe for something to exist in; and following that, two, that whatever you produce from your own power is insignificant or untrustworthy somehow, that belief itself is not a truthmaking spell. That is an absurd disservice to yourself—you are denying the power you have to shape reality as you move with it. Which is unsurprising. Most of you people are afraid of your own magic."

"Belief can't be its own *proof*, Hanéong—" Ronoah was spluttering a little. It was just so, so— "Things can't be true just because you *want* them to be."

"What a kind world that would be," Hanéong agreed. "I am not saying it is a kind world we live in. I'm saying it is a mysterious one. The furnaces that power it are fed by strange fuels indeed—and belief is one of them." And then, without warning, "You don't think Tycho insane for hearing her gods, do you?"

"What? I—no?"

"You don't tisk in dismissal of Marghat Yacchatzndra, who cut out her own mother's skull for a god she already knew was gone? You don't condemn your family's faith in their godlings, do you? Your sister, your brother, your father, your mother the Indigo Queen? Their beliefs are not similarly flimsy?"

"No, *no*—" Ronoah's hands were balled into indignant fists. He was, he discovered, deeply offended on all their behalf. "Of course not!"

"Well why not? Is there any more *proof* of their gods than yours?" Hanéong locked eyes with Ronoah. "There isn't. You are simply—never-endingly—excepting yourself to your own internal rule system, and as a scholar, you should know better." A smile, glowing with fondness and mischief. "Instead of assuming nothing exists, I'd be much more inclined to assume that *everything* does. If I were you."

Everything exists. It was so deeply and desperately what he wanted—and had been revealed as so devastatingly false in the midst of his depression—that hearing it turned him cold. "So would I," he said, his voice disgruntled, complaining, despairing, "if I could feel literally any of it."

"Ah, now see, we're getting into the realm of perception here." Hanéong relaxed back into his seat, regarding Ronoah with an infuriating cheekiness given the situation. "This has a lot less to do with what's out there, and a lot more to do with whether you personally feel tapped into it. Whether or not you're picking up signs has nothing to do with whether the signs are there."

A bitter pustule of laughter erupted from Ronoah. "*What* signs?" he asked. He felt stung. Like he was being taunted with something he couldn't have. "I haven't, I told you, it's not just been Ol-Penh, I haven't heard anything since ..." He didn't know. A dream here, a warmth there—who was to say these were anything but the desperate phantasms of a mind determined not to get too lonely?

"Since the Ravaging?" Hanéong had clearly decided to go for the throat. "You chose to see that as a sign," he continued over Ronoah's sharp inhale, "and the choice has propelled you all the way to here."

Ronoah backpedalled, bizarrely scandalized. "I mean I said I chose it but it didn't, it didn't feel like *choosing* at the time, Hanéong—"

"Of course it didn't. It just felt like listening. So *listen*." On that word Hanéong's blasé attitude evaporated, sharp as hot steel hitting the quenching oil. "You've spent the last half year blocking out positively *everything*—memories, fondnesses, rages. You poured so much wax over your heart you couldn't even feel your own pain, and it caterwauls fit to shatter the glassware. Do you think you'd really notice something quieter trying to make contact?"

All of a sudden the *whump-whump* of the train wheels went muffled. Hanéong had covered Ronoah's ears, too fast for him even to flinch. He heard the man's voice as if from underwater, curbed and belled: "There are signs for you everywhere. The world is positively saturated with signs, everything communicating in a tongue beyond tongues, everything seething with knowledge and gossip and intent. When you learn that language, even a piece of it, even a single miserly dialect, the world unfolds delights and divinities galore. All day long, I see you people brushing off chances to learn. It is not a secret language. It wants to invite you in on the game. But you have to listen for your invitation."

In the echo chamber of Hanéong's hands, Ronoah heard the rushing river of his blood. The tympanic tattoo of his heart. The barest swish of something else.

"So take your hands off your ears," Hanéong said, and then he did just that, and Ronoah's ears crackled like they'd passed through a spike of atmospheric pressure. He rubbed at one, at the tender space behind his jaw.

"And if I listen, and she doesn't call for me?" he said, almost to himself.

Now it was Hanéong's turn to snort derisively. "You spurned her for six months or more and as far as I've seen it, your Genoveffa's hot-tempered and high-maintenance. I wouldn't be surprised if she straight-out ignored you for a while, out of teasing, out of spite. Out of challenge." He leaned even closer, enough to press his cheek roughly to Ronoah's— Ronoah felt the infinitely fine fuzz on the man's skin, worried absurdly for a second that his scruff would scratch it. "*Persevere*, little pilgrim. Persevere and prove yourself worthy of the great inferno you came from, and she'll come for you in the end." And then, drawing back and regarding him with narrowed eyes, "Tell you what, do you *want* Genoveffa to be real?"

"Setten and Ibisca, because falling apart in public about it wasn't enough of an answer?" Ronoah blurted before he could stop himself.

Hanéong's mouth curved in a smirk. "I re-emphasize: do you want *Genoveffa* to be real. Not just any god. Her." He investigated Ronoah's bewildered face, sweeping it with critical, genuinely curious eyes. "You have spent most of this journey trying to reach her, yes, but you have spent an equal amount of time trying to rid yourself of Pilanova's influence. You have rejected—quite happily—many of the values and attitudes that no longer serve you, in favour of things you have found on the way. Is this a piece of home that you wish to keep? Have you outgrown your godling's patronage, or does she still hold a place of honour in the great Trans-Bereni bricolage that is your sense of self?"

Ronoah opened his mouth—and paused, frowning. This had crossed his mind before. Pilanova had upended him, pushed him to seek refuge in the rest of the world; it had suppressed his curiosity and fettered his gifts and asked him to follow a creed that was contradictory at best and downright neglectful at worst. Genoveffa was a part of Pilanova, and Pilanova had wronged him.

But also—had it really?

Was Pilanova really the cloister of passive-aggression and forced conformity he always told it as? Or had he just not had the insight, the wisdom, the *coping skills* to manage living there? Maybe it was the sweetening blur of distance talking—he hadn't so much as turned in the direction of Pilanova in over three years, now—or else the firsthand experience of other cultures and their unique blend of triumphs and challenges. Chiropole's prolific art against their rigid limitations on love; Shaipuri's celebratory spirit against their casual violence. Ol-Penh's technological brilliance against their religious small-mindedness. When he'd left the desert, it had been with the aim of finding somewhere better, but did *better* actually exist?

Maybe it did. He hadn't seen everywhere yet, after all, and that ocean had sure seemed wide enough to hold perfection on its far shore. But he had a hunch that was only wistful thinking.

So maybe there was no Ronoah-shaped paradise for him to find and plant his roots in. Maybe nowhere on the planet was perfectly matched to his temperament, his whims. Maybe the only way to be satisfied, to be happy, was to average out all the goods and bads of all the places, to sample it all, to roam and taste and cut and paste and appreciate that, in the end—

Home is not a place. It is a state of mind.

Who did he want warming the hearth of that home?

"I want Genoveffa," he said at last, and to his frustration and relief his words came out hoarse with tears. He'd done so well at facing this conversation with grace, he'd handled even the possibility of oblivion with dignity—but now, as he voiced this innermost desire, his vision blurred and swam with the power of how badly and badly he wanted. "I want her every second of every day. I want her warmth and her goading and her terrible sense of humour and her high expectations. Her urgency, her *impatience*, her big wide hyena laugh—I want it all. I want it, and I want to be it, to embody her wishes, to fulfill them. I want to carry that for both of us. I'm all she has," he said, and felt, fragile miracle, his own stalwart devotion stirring under his breastbone. "I want that to be enough."

"Then tend to your wanting, Ronoah Genoveffa Elizzi-denna Pilanovani." Hanéong's eyes glittered with approval, with rambunctious pride. "Nurture it, respect it like the planet-turning power it is, and *something* will happen."

The two names, godling and place, slipped with perfect heartsore relief into the empty spaces they'd been banished from so many months ago. Ronoah felt them reassert themselves with an almost sentient determination. Like they were reclaiming their home.

"Smart choice, if you ask me," Hanéong added, slyly confiding, tapping a finger to his chin. "Seeing as you've already put so much effort in. Be a bit silly to start from scratch, wouldn't it? I am sure she appreciates the diligence." The sparkle in his expression softened, turned inward. "It's a lot of pressure, to be the only one of anything. But it can be very rewarding."

Ronoah nodded. On this, at the very least, they understood each other.

The rest was more complicated, more difficult to wrap his head around. The way forward as Hanéong told it was simple, in its way, but it required an exhausting mindset shift, gruelling and unglamorous and the opposite of instant gratification. It required him to allow himself this last, deepest vulnerability: to believe that what he wanted mattered to the Universe. That he both had a destiny *and* got to choose what it was. That Truth—like everything else—could be more than one thing at once.

That kind of growth wasn't going to happen in a snap. It wasn't going to come clear and revelatory like he wished it would. It was probably going to feel a lot more like his time in the caves—like cleansing his caustic self-talk one phrase at a time, like dislodging the obstacles and carving a new path for his heart to follow. Drudgery, discouragement, uncertainty. It was tiring just to conceive of the kind of effort this was going to take.

But god and gods alike, did he want it. After all, a long time ago one of Obagli's children had consulted her webs, put her hand on Ronoah's three-year-old head, and decreed him a world-shaker. Like Hanéong said, it wouldn't do to let that go to waste.

He wiped his eyes on his sleeves, and then, as his body caught up to the fact that they'd just had this conversation and it *hadn't* ended in total disgrace, a belated wave of enervation swept in strong as a headache. Limbs suddenly heavy, he slumped against his seat. Hanéong scooted over to sit beside him, to snake a slender arm behind his back; Ronoah let his spine curve into the man's chest, sank into his fatigue. Hanéong's heart was oscillating somewhere between four and eight beats.

"Give me some time to try it," Ronoah murmured, watching the orchards sweep by outside through leaden lids. "And then we'll go. When—when something happens. I can't now, not yet, not like this—but when something changes, we'll go." He closed his eyes. "I promise."

"I know." With a feline stretch, Hanéong resettled Ronoah against him, placed the point of his chin on Ronoah's shoulder. That heartbeat fractalized into sixteen, thirty-two, beyond. "To be honest, I never doubted you."

Ronoah's face twitched in a frown-smile, equal parts appreciation and apology. The world beyond his closed eyes went dark as the train entered a tunnel. "I'm sorry if your friend gets mad. I'm sorry I made you wait so long."

"Oh, Firewalker mine." Hanéong shook his head, cheek brushing absently against Ronoah's. Ronoah leaned in, felt gently through the layers of emotional landscape beneath the creature's words: the vast satisfaction of grassy plains ruffled by gusts of amusement; the alien magnitude of the seafloor shimmering the whalesong of ruth; the cosmic perspective of the mountain's zenith, seeing pin-clear through eons to the end. "It wasn't so very long at all."

The train emerged from the tunnel back into the light. A city flared in filamented gold on the backs of Ronoah's eyelids, beckoning.

FORTY-SIX

"*B*REATHE. SLOW DOWN BY A HALF-BEAT. Let's try again."

Ronoah readjusted his grip on the tethers, taking a stabilizing breath. Yengh-Sier stepped out of range, and he started spinning the poi in split-time, forcing his nervously impatient rhythm down a notch. They had to be equidistant, in concert, before—okay, right hand came up under left armpit and the dragon weave fountained up and over his body, and then—feeling for just the right transition point, the downsweep toward the feet, the moment the righthand poi passed beneath and he rolled his wrist and released it and it flew up over his arm and *don't lunge for it*—he caught it out of the air with a shout.

Yengh-Sier fanned handhalf applause, a wide smile on his face. Ronoah huffed out a surprised laugh, grinning back through the orange-yellow streaks he quickly stalled to a halt at arm's length. Even from that distance, the flames painted his body in prickling warmth.

The inspin toss: a feat of daring and trust even without the poi on fire, given it was so easy to send them rocketing off in all directions. He'd been drilling the transition with Yengh-Sier for the better part of three days. It was one of his trouble spots—his heart always stopped for the fraction of a second the poi was free in the air. For all he was good at throwing things away, he was, it seemed, reluctant to reel them back in.

"That was great," Yengh-Sier said, "but don't stop there. Use the momentum to get back into your starting spin. I want you to loop the weave and toss—" he mimed it, flicking his wrist under and then catching an imaginary tether above "—into something you can repeat endlessly. If you can build to that seamless flow, you'll achieve real freedom of motion. Go ahead."

Wiping the sweat off his brow with an awkwardly-raised elbow, Ronoah head-wobbled an affirmative and got the dragon poi moving again.

It had been two weeks since he and Hanéong had returned to

Khepsuong Phae, and the first thing Yengh-Sier had done when Ronoah showed up at his door with his pair of ribbon poi and a creased poster of Eng-Vaunh was to make good on his promise and trade the ribbons out for flames. Ronoah accepted his own promotion with a strange combination of zeal and hesitation; he couldn't forget that this wasn't the first time he'd swung a kindled wick. It still chafed at him, that he was hiding his first reckless foray into firedancing from Yengh-Sier, but he couldn't find the reason or the courage to come clean. That night only felt half-real, a fever dream of thievery, a taking hostage of himself. More than Yengh-Sier's disappointment, it was the fire itself Ronoah was cautious of. As if it might still decide to mete out a punishment for his transgression.

He gave himself to it anyway, willing to accept whatever came for him. He leaned into the wariness, the discomfort, the slow and unspectacular work of mending things. Of changing his mind one more time.

Arriving in Khepsuong Phae with his empathy intact had been like arriving for the first time ever, like opening a free-flowing channel between the city and his heart. He'd tumbled head over heels into loving the place, shocked with delight at the thousand things he'd never noticed, never had the will to investigate—like the brightly-painted public pianos at certain parks and street corners, or the peerless patience with which Khepsuong Phaer citizens communicated, putting down books or coffee cups to talk with their whole bodies, to listen in kind.

Likewise, he was realizing with sheepish shame that his friends had far more depth than he realized. He'd never given his full attention to Yengh-Sier or Ean-Bei or Ngoluydinh, never taken in the whole of their personalities before. Now, he marvelled at all their small hitches and habits: Ngodi's wont to leave tea steeping too long, doomed to perpetually be nursing a cold and bitter cup; Yengh-Sier's nervous nailbiting, especially his thumbs; Ean-Bei's way of holding a book loose in one hand, so that when they walked it smacked rhythmically against their thigh. They were like completely new people. He loved them all the more for it.

Just as his arms were beginning to tremble from effort, Yengh-Sier called an end to the day's practice. "Great work today. It's really beginning to smooth into one sequence." The man waited for Ronoah to douse the dragon poi before continuing. "I wanted to talk to you about picking a performance date."

Ronoah nearly dropped the poi in his haste to hook a pinky in question; Yengh-Sier's shoulders twitched in silent laughter. "It's good to have a tangible goal," he said. "Encourages steady progress. You wouldn't be the only one performing, we would slot you in somewhere with other beginners. Not open to the public—a small show, acro company only, plus friends."

Ronoah considered this as he removed the safety gloves, tugging one finger at a time. That kind of semi-private show meant most of the audience members would have already seen him practicing at some point in the acro centre, so logically he shouldn't have been so nervous. But he was. There had always been something about performing in public that made even his most perfected talents seize up in self-consciousness.

When his hands were free, he looked up. "How long do you think until I'd be ready?"

"If you book a few extra hours per week with the equipment, I would be comfortable sending you onstage in a month."

Ronoah's eyes went wide. Yengh-Sier's hand flowed through the familiar fingerspell of Ngodi's name. "Nearly done her thesis, right? Does that free up some of your time?"

"It—it does." He'd had no idea Yengh-Sier thought so highly of him; the man wasn't exactly a harsh teacher, but neither was he effusive with his praise. Perhaps this confidence in his abilities was nothing new, but it sure *felt* new. He thought of Yengh-Sier's own ability, his grace, the quiet diligence with which he practiced his arts, the certainty in his hand as he gripped the poi or the silk or the cyr wheel. He thought of trying to take the man's place onstage, to dance the same dance half as well. How could he live up to someone who could so sweetly and gently reject the very concept of gravity, who moved in air like it was water? This acrobat named for a saint, who lived his offering in his entire body every day—how could he compare?

That was when the idea came to him. It filtered into his awareness like sunlight through silvery clouds, bathing a problem in warm possibility.

" ...Okay," he found himself signing, his hands strangely buoyant. "Let's try for one month."

It wasn't just a performance Yengh-Sier was asking of him. It was an offering. A ritual. A demonstration of faith.

That was something Ronoah was trying to get better at, these days. Something he was trying to relearn. It wouldn't do to brush off an opportunity so freely given—to ignore a sign, if that's what it actually was.

"Good." Yengh-Sier took the poi from Ronoah and slung them over his shoulder. His light brown eyes took on something of a guarded expression. "Would Hanéong be interested in coming, if we settle on a date far enough in the future?"

Ronoah frowned in confusion—Hanéong would sit in the rafters and shout commentary during their *practice* sessions if he were allowed—and then he realized the uncertainty in Yengh-Sier's face for what it was, and a laugh escaped him. Unlike Ean-Bei, who had stuck to their lovers' quarrel theory right to the end, Yengh-Sier had simply assumed that the reason Hanéong never showed up to group outings was because he was very, very busy. Ronoah had done nothing to correct this assumption.

"Yes," he said, waving away Yengh-Sier's quizzical blink, "definitely, Hanéong will definitely be there."

Beyond mending his own daily relationship with Hanéong, Ronoah was trying to take responsibility for the bad first impression—and second, and third—he'd imposed on his friends about the man. Hanéong did still have his own loose ends to tie up, predominantly checking in on Kauryingh's health ("amazing what saving somebody's life can do for their opinion of your people, I ought to thank you, Ronoah—") but never did Ronoah offer an outing that Hanéong refused. More and more, Hanéong tagged along to their library guest lectures, their long lunches on the terraces; he got on like wildfire with Ngodi, and Yengh-Sier, who was already on good terms with him, took pains to loop the man into their inside jokes as they cropped up. Even Ean-Bei had warmed up when Hanéong got the tai talking about their current syllabus: a melange of civil engineering and environmental biology, with a weekly Ol-Penher calligraphy lesson for a change of pace. As it turned out, it was hard to stay prickly with someone who exclaimed with a parent's perfectly unironic enthusiasm over your slightly crumpled but very precise poem in the shape of a leaf.

"I'm glad," was what Yengh-Sier ended up saying. He shifted the tethers on his shoulder. "It's my responsibility to coordinate these events with the other teachers. You don't have to do anything except prepare your routine. I'll draw up a timetable to give you some milestones—look it over tomorrow?"

Tomorrow. A day, and then a month, and then a test. A trial by fire, as it were. "I'll be there," Ronoah promised, and then he packed up and went home. To the boarding house, to their room, to the small collection of candles bolstering the corner of the desk in beeswax and powdered clove. He sprinkled the pillars with a pinch of spice, set a different sort of wick alight.

"Hey," he prayed, fixing his eyes to the growing flames. "So I'm going to try something."

Since the train ride back to the city, he'd been trying to take Hanéong's words to heart. About tending to his wanting; about nurturing his belief in belief itself. Over two weeks it had developed into a daily routine, making time to sit and absorb the amber glow of this makeshift little fire, to peer into the flames and deepen his breathing and call out for his godling. *Pinion of flame, cistern of change,* he would murmur, little sand-soft Acharrioni poetics, or else *Genoveffa, unbelievably patient guardian of incredibly insensitive wishgranters,* or sometimes, very simply, very quietly, *I'm listening. I'm here.* Each day he spent anywhere between ten minutes and an hour in the possibility of her presence, watching shiny welts of wax swell and drop from their melting points. Sometimes he felt weirdly self-conscious about it, and other times defeatingly silly—but there were moments folded in where, fleetingly, he thought he felt something else, something precious enough to endure the other embarrassing feelings all over again, something too fragile even to name.

Today he was in the mood to speak more casually, so that's what he did. "Yengh-Sier says I'm nearly ready to perform in front of everyone," he explained, watching the circles of melted wax slowly grow under the hunger of the candleflames. "I don't know about that—you know me, I'd probably never do anything in front of anyone if I could manage it. But he is my teacher. I want to thank him somehow for all the time he's put into training me. And I…" He bit his lip. Inhaled the tingle of clove powder burning. "I wouldn't mind a performance, if it was for you. I know it's, it's not how the priests taught me to honour you, but it *feels* right, it did from the moment I first saw Yengh-Sier dancing, and…"

His own honesty drew him up short. He'd never acknowledged just what it was that had driven him to learn Ol-Penher acrobatics, but that's probably what it was, wasn't it? He'd sublimated a desire for Genoveffa's closeness into a desire to learn this art. Traded one dance with fire for another. Even in those grey months stuffed with grief and godless contempt, when Genoveffa's very name was forbidden in the halls of his heart, he'd been unable to part with her entirely.

A smile twitched at the corner of his mouth. "And I want to honour you somehow," he finished. "So I'm going to do it for you. I'm going to—be bold. Be brave, like you always wanted me to be. I'm training as hard as I can, and I'm dedicating the outcome in your name, and I hope—I hope you come and see when it's time."

Nothing answered—at least, nothing definitive. No gust of clove-scented smoke up his spine, no laughing crackle in the back of his mind. The flames wavered; one or two grew slightly taller, stretching ceiling-ward. Did it mean something? Was it a response? When he reached inward he *did* find a sense of satisfaction, but that could just as easily be his own pride in devoting himself this way.

Maybe, maybe not. He grabbed the wick dipper up from the desk and busied himself with adjusting some of the candlewicks, silently reciting

Hanéong's promise about perseverance. *Prove yourself worthy of that great inferno, and she'll come for you in the end.*

He had to trust that. Trust Genoveffa. Trust his own love for her, his regrowing ability to feel her presence. He had to take responsibility for his end of their relationship, the end he'd let drop for half a year or more. Like Hanéong had said, Genoveffa had every right to be cross with him after that abandonment. If he truly wanted her back in his life, he had a duty to make amends, to pour himself out to her without expecting immediate returns. To give for the pleasure of giving, for the love of making her proud.

He never thought he'd be looking to his younger self for guidance, but that's what he found himself doing these days. Pilanova's Ronoah could do this without thinking; it came to him simple as song. Who knew, he thought as he set the dipper back down, that you would come to appreciate someone you couldn't wait to leave behind?

"It smells delightful in here, you should know."

Ronoah jumped, jostling the candles as his knees bumped the desk. He turned and there was Hanéong, a paper cone of raspberry ice in each hand. Tactful to the last, the man took his time elbowing the door closed, which gave Ronoah the ten seconds he needed to take a deep breath and release the ritual—determined though he was to lean into his faith, he still couldn't do it when anyone else was around, even if that someone was Hanéong. He thanked Genoveffa for listening, kissed his fingertips and skimmed them over the glittering tips of the flames, and got to work dousing the candles.

"Is that second ice for me?" he asked as he straightened a few stray wicks. Behind him, he heard Hanéong snort.

"It certainly is not. Come to the shop with me and get your own, they have new flavours today, I saw a sugared violet one your tongue would cartwheel for."

"And after?"

"After?" The timbre of Hanéong's voice changed, went rich with mischief. "Providing you don't happen to already have plans, there's a papermaking workshop at the library for which I might happen to have reserved seats."

All Ronoah could do was laugh. "I don't have plans," he said, rising from his seat. "Take me out."

Such was their way these days, making up for lost adventuring time. There were plenty of sights in Khepsuong Phae that Ronoah had never seen, and with Hanéong's oh-so familiar grin and tugging hand to lead the way, he was stumbling wonderstruck into bushels of them: the resplendent medicine gardens of Saint Nam-Chai's Cathedral, up on a hill in the North

End with its truly gargantuan wishbone, quartz block tall as a house; the Quarter of Stone, where vacationers wandered and statue-spotted their mornings away, where Ronoah found a near-exact replica to the granite Wishgranter's fountain in Yanyel; the Qiao Sidhur district, where everyone packed into jazz cafés before nightfall to drink imported elderflower wine and hear lush arrangements of flute and mahogany harp. After some time wrestling down his embarrassment, Ronoah shyly requested a redo of their first visit to the library itself, too—arm-in-arm, he and Hanéong traipsed the many ells of Khepsuong Phae's collections, exploring exhibits on the water trains' engineering and the biodiversity of the Ol-Penher fjords, Hanéong providing verbal marginalia all the way. Ronoah allowed himself to chatter back, asking questions, probing for stories, telling Hanéong about whatever was lingering on his mind. Rebuilding trust here, too, one delicate musing vulnerability at a time.

There was one place Hanéong did not offer to take Ronoah, and for this he was grateful. It would have felt too much like being pressured. But he woke one day with an urge to lay eyes on it—to know it was there, to see it was possible—and so he asked Ngodi to come with him to visit Saint Yu's Arch, the entrance to the Holy Corridor. The way to the Pilgrim State.

The Arch sprawled cinquefoil-topped and petal-strewn at the northwest edge of Khepsuong Phae. Like a wishbone, it cloaked itself in chirruping gardens, eschewing the company of buildings in favour of cypress and bullfinch and box hedge parterre. They settled in those gardens, selecting a hill with a good view of the structure, and propped open a picnic basket to snack from, watching other visitors mill around the sun-struck marble. Looped through the keystone, the drupes of Ol-Penher script: *If it is wished.* Saint Yu's eternal edict.

"They're actually buried beneath it," Ngodi commented, picking a fig from the clutch in the basket. "Saint Yu, I mean. Legend goes they died before the Corridor was all the way finished, so we buried them in some other grave garden until the work was done. We dug them up and replanted them under their opus so they could become part of it."

It seemed, of all things, like a very Shaipurin thing to do. The image of the tallest warrior in the bog surfaced, like it did every so often—but this time Ronoah didn't push it away. He shivered in the sunlight, and let it pass through him until it sank out of sight again.

"Have you ever been?" he asked after a while. "To the Pilgrim State."

"Oh yeah, three times," Ngodi replied, surprising him. Her tone reminded him of a conversation long ago, over a board game in a Chiropolene parkette—Kharoun, descendent of shalledrim hunters, speaking of the Trans-Bereni Highway with the irreverence of the overfamiliar. Ngodi, for her part, held a little more admiration for her local world wonder: "You've never seen anything like it. I wept for pure joy the first time, it was like a blessing straight from the Wishgranter's mouth. So much worship all mosaiced together like that, it does something to you. Lifts your spirits." She laid a hand to her stomach, the emotional center according to Ol-Penher thinking. Shook her head. "I don't even know how to describe it without feeling like I'm getting it wrong. I went back twice to try and pin that sensation down, get a record, you know? But every time I arrived, the idea suddenly seemed silly, because it felt like I'd never forget this feeling. It's tricky that way. I still have dreams about it, the church I stayed in, the light through the windows in the morning. All gold and blue."

He'd never heard her so wistful. When he looked, he saw her staring at the Arch, gaze gone soft in remembrance. As if even now, beholding the entrance to that mystical place, she was once again considering a journey.

Maybe it was the general ambiance—the gardens, the archway, the Holy Corridor just beyond—or maybe it was Ngodi's longing stealing into him through some empathic channel. Maybe it was his very own wanderlust, rearing its head after a long sleep. But hearing her talk about it, so specific and yet so frustratingly vague, kindled an urge deep inside him, an itch that pined for scratching. Some little chip of irritation grating at his stasis, goading him to move.

He'd promised Hanéong—promised himself—that they would head to the Pilgrim State once something happened between him and Genoveffa, but for an instant, watching as a green-clad traveller took her first steps through the Arch and disappeared, Ronoah wanted to break that promise. Wanted to go. To begin.

He didn't. He was trying to prove himself reliable, after all. He had his picnic with Ngodi and then he walked away from the Holy Corridor, back to his duties and merriments—tuning his ear for Qiao Sidhur jazz, playing audience for Ngodi as she rehearsed her thesis defense, fabric shopping with Ean-Bei and Yengh-Sier so they could custom-fit his costume. But the Holy Corridor stuck in him, a chord struck and unsilenceable. He drilled his dragon poi until his soreness turned sweet. He helped Ean-Bei study for exams. He plucked up his courage and invited Saint Hanéong to sit with him at the becandled desk, to be in communion with Genoveffa, one patron of change to another. The gold-blue light of Ngodi's dreams pervaded it all, tinting, taunting, tempting. Waiting.

And the month flew by as if caught in a great gale of wind, and suddenly the night of Ronoah's performance was upon him.

FORTY-SEVEN

$\mathcal{B}$ACKSTAGE, LEANING ON A STRUT, Ronoah stared down the metal bucket in front of him and dithered about whether or not he was going to hurl into it.

It was probably a bad idea. He'd never recovered from getting sick quickly—it could take him up to half an hour to stop shaking—and he might smudge the pink and gold paint Ean-Bei had brushed his face with preshow, and there was no time now to find them and ask for a touch-up. He was just going to have to stand here and bounce his leg nervously and hope that was enough of a siphon for the thunderhead of energy in his body.

Through the thick curtains, the drums resounded. Not the full company of a typical acro show, but still enough to make the ground jump under his feet. Who was on right now? Was it Ar-Panyeung with their silk-climbing routine, or Vai doing her trapeze? Definitely something airborne, or else he'd be feeling the decisive thump of a surefooted body landing marks on the stage. He didn't dare twitch the curtain back to check, but Yengh-Sier had scheduled him for after Vai, so if it was Vai that meant he was up next—

The bucket glowed with promise. He turned away from it, willing his stomach ironclad, wringing his poi in his hands.

It was kind of funny, in a totally absurd way. He'd survived a wildfire and a war and a god had once nearly eaten him but the thing that truly got to him was *amateur dramatics*. Courage or none, he hadn't grown an inch more comfortable with it since sitting awkward in the Tellers' caravan.

It goes to show, said a voice in his head, that no matter how much you change, some things you just don't shake loose.

For a private moment he reveled in the cosmic humour of it, laughing at his own incorrigible humanness. Feeling oddly overwhelmed with affection for it.

Then Yengh-Sier appeared between the struts, a shallow pan in one hand and a bucket of fuel in the other, and Ronoah's stomach flipped and flattened. So it was Vai, then.

"Everyone's really warm out there," Yengh-Sier said after soaking Ronoah's poi with fuel. He looked up at Ronoah from his kneeling point on the ground; Ronoah was proud, and further terrified, to see the glint of anticipation in his teacher's eye. "They've seen you practicing hard—they're all rooting for you. Watch your shoulder extensions. Keep pace. And catch what you throw."

Swallowing what felt like a third poi, Ronoah head-wobbled an affirmative. Yengh-Sier spared him one half-smile in solidarity, and then struck the match and tossed it to light.

The dragon poi unfurled twin flares of virulent orange, licking Ronoah's wrists with heat. Over the growling of the flames, he heard applause break out. Time to go.

Yengh-Sier parted the thick cotton of the curtain with an outstretched arm, enough to let Vai skip on through, to let Ronoah out. With both his hands occupied, Ronoah couldn't say any last thing to the man; he just took a deep breath and passed through the gap, feeling Yengh-Sier's hand clap like a boost on his back on the way.

The lights were already dimmed when he set foot on stage, doused to the barest flicker. All the better to see him by. From his perspective, the seats were filled with shuffling shadows—a couple dozen, the more seasoned acrobats and the performers' friends and families, faces obscured by the dark. He could just make out the front row in detail: somehow Yengh-Sier had managed to spirit himself back to front and center in the time it had taken Ronoah to get into position. Ean-Bei was positively wiggling beside him, and Ngodi curled up on her seat beside them.

And to Yengh-Sier's left, Hvanzhir Hanéong sat with a box of treats on one knee. As Ronoah watched, the man ate one and passed the box down the line—and then he changed, uncrossing his ankles and resting his elbows on his knees in that lean hunter's posture that turned him from just another casual spectator into something with the attentive force of a planet.

That force swept Ronoah up and held him—not just from Hanéong but from all of them, this complement of friends that had seen him through the bleakest time of his life. Their patience, their compassion, their eagerness to see him succeed. Their faith in him. Tonight he was going to show himself worthy of their care.

And yours, too, he thought with a glance at the fire. If you'll let me.

The drums struck his opening note.

There was a lot to be said for the power of muscle memory. For how it let so much fall away in the moment, for how easily, how unconsciously his body sank into well-trained motion. How much space it allowed to open up in his mind. The slow loops to loosen up, the first spiral wrap, the weave and reel, all of it came to him as if in a dream, as if those tethers were telepathic, responding to his barest suggestion with swooping arcs of crackling light. They burned away his nerves, his overthinking, until he all but forgot there was anyone there at all. He'd thought he would feel exposed, but what he found instead was a cocoon. An altar; an altered state. An unlimited instant in time to free-float, to flow.

A lot came and went in that instant. Snippets of the call-and-response chorus for the Pilanovani fable of Ezrah and the Twelve Gazelles; the afternoon spent feeding cubes of fruit to the old beaked tortoise in Marghat Yacchatzndra's villa; the memory of the deckhand's roughened fingers on his arms as he presented Ronoah to his Tyrene contact family. The shalledrim temple, frieze defaced but still emanating power. His father's loving jokes about his mother's blanched spots, claiming she'd hidden bits of herself in the desert so she would never be fully still. Tycho's face, sober and kind, her bark-brown hand on his proclaiming *Your gods are old, and their stories will be around for many years to come, but your stories are as good as theirs and you won't be around forever to tell them.*

It was good advice. But this story was for him and his godling both.

The ground hissed at the strike of the poi, tossing twin wheels of sparks skyward. They coiled past his feet, up his shoulders, above his head, comets trailing a mesmerising double helix; down and around, shifting planes, snaking through the slim gaps between limbs. Tossed and caught, just like Yengh-Sier said. Caught and whipped through another spiral wrap, the fire's high rush like a god's ferocious laugh, like an adventuress' challenge, and he kicked off and slungshot and bled all his wanting for her into this invocation, this offering—

This is for Genoveffa, daughter of Pao. This is for my first mother. This is from her wishgranter.

He gave everything he had, and in the giving he dissolved. In the giving he became, for a passing preposterous moment, absolutely perfect.

When he came to the end he came with regret, and with relish. He landed the last flaming roundhouse in his arsenal, led the dragon poi through a cooldown combination loop, and with a slow quarter-turn to face front of house, allowed the weights to stall. He ended with arms wide open, ribs aching with new breath, eyes on the splashes of afterimage he saw in the rafters. He barely registered the rockslide of applause.

He didn't know if she'd heard. He couldn't tell if she'd responded.

And yet.

"That was *impossibly* good," Ean-Bei gushed later, when the rest of the show had tumbled over into the chattering after-crush of the foyer. "Like I know Yengh-Sier trained you and he's the best, but still, *wow*."

"It was very cool," agreed Ngodi judiciously. "I guess I can sort of see why you people do this to yourselves."

Ronoah's hands were occupied trying to undo the tight coil he'd wound his hair into so it wouldn't singe. "Thanks," he said when he could get one free; his locs tumbled in a twist down his shoulder. "Mostly I'm—glad I didn't throw up."

"No way. You get stage fright, too?" Ronoah wobbled his head. Ean-Bei's smirk split into a disbelieving grin. "Didn't look like it from where I was sitting. You move *fast*, Elizzi-denna; you threw together moves I don't even know names for!"

"Some of them don't have names," Yengh-Sier said, and it was perhaps Ronoah only who saw the undertow of confusion on the acrobat's placid face. The conversation continued until one of Ean-Bei's fellow troupers came up to say hello and Yengh-Sier surreptitiously steered Ronoah away from the group, talking from a slightly more private angle.

"That was truly lovely," he said, every bit the dedicated instructor, "but you put the moves all out of sequence."

"I—" Ronoah flushed, rubbed at a bit of paint glimmering on his nose. "Did I?"

"You made it look like a completely different story."

"I suppose I...rebelled," he said, with a sheepish smile. "In the heat of the moment. It was just—probably nerves?" Yengh-Sier waved away his apology, but Ronoah kept up the bashful act anyway, until the puzzled crease smoothed from the man's brow, until they turned back to join the main discussion, where Ronoah's glow of secret, dogged happiness could go unnoticed.

Because he'd begun the dance in earnest. He'd meant to follow the sequence, the story he'd so meticulously practiced for so long—but midway through the story had changed. Morphed into something closer to home. A story about a different sort of wishgranter, lowercase and humble, and the great laughing wildfire it could try to serve.

Yengh-Sier was well-versed enough in the first story to know a different one was being told, but not precisely what. The others were too unfamiliar with the material to notice there had been a revision at all.

But Hanéong had seen it for what it was.

Ronoah knew it like he knew the buzz of adrenaline in his own limbs. The way the man had perched so perfectly still in the midst of all that clapping, incongruous and uncaring of it, satisfaction radiating thick as the lowest note on a harp—the electric thrill that ran through Ronoah now, when their eyes met across the exuberant gestures of their company. Oh, no. Not a chance in shiyalsha Hanéong hadn't seen.

Ronoah didn't know if this offering had made it to Genoveffa—and he couldn't let that stop him. That was the epiphany that'd lifted him off the ground, the ecstatic knowing he had embraced mid-dance. It was devastatingly simple in the end: somewhere in those scant minutes, he'd realized he was giving Genoveffa the culmination of his entire stay in Ol-Penh. The learning, the work, the despair, the salvation—all of it. An offering like that bore no revision, no second go. It was as whole as it was going to get. Whether she accepted it or not, it was all he could give her from this place. Anything more, he was going to have to gather from the journey forward.

He had done all he could here. It was time to go.

He felt it all through the boisterous afterparty, and the smarting headache of the day after. The thought enlivened something in him, quickened his wits. Made him restless. He stretched the soreness out of his triceps, gulped down the cups of headache-healing coffee Hanéong brewed for him, climbed to the rooftop at moonrise to sit and dangle his legs over the edge, to look out over the city and feel his bones lightening as their binding load spilled out of him, to catch the scent of exodus rising in the air. Looked down to find the bitemark scar in his arm smiling, coy and conspiratorial. Closed his eyes to feel the ghost of a shoulder, ridged and ready, squaring against his own.

Looks like your own personal Great Wheel's finally turning. Enough dawdling, demon boy. Get a move on.

With the moons as his witnesses, he started planning his goodbyes.

Ean-Bei was first and easiest. After all, they had suggested it themself. Ronoah accompanied the tai to get their hair restyled, strolling arm-in-arm down the bright boulevards of the South End to the salon; he picked an unobtrusive moment halfway through the appointment, while the stylist was preparing her tools for detail work, and set free the words: "You know how you asked me about the Pilgrim State?" Through the mirror, Ean-Bei wobbled their head. "I think I'm going after all."

The thin sheet draped over Ean-Bei's torso bunched up with a surge of crinkling as they shoved their hands out to reply: "Double-checking I got that right, my reverse-reading's shit. You? Pilgrim State?" When Ronoah gestured a yes, they punched their fists in the air, startling a yelp out of the stylist— "YES. Amazing! When are you going? Is Hanéong coming with you? Are you gonna stay for Ngodi's thesis defense is the real question, because I've really appreciated the work you're putting into making her less crazy and if you could just keep that up until after her thing's ushered into the hallowed halls of respected theological discourse we would—"

On it went, a scintillating stream of rejoicing splashed by the flying fish of quick-fingered questions. Even after the appointment was over Ean-Bei pressed on, needling for details Ronoah didn't even have yet, dancing a couple steps in front of him with their back turned to the oncoming street so they could keep talking. This nearly killed them when they tripped over a loose cobble—but being Ean-Bei, they turned it into a backflip and sprung back up to continue, heedless of Ronoah's hollering objections. They were just too pleased to let it be—and after the tenth question, the fourth street corner, Ronoah remembered why.

It's such a rush, seeing someone I like find their place in the Wish.

Nosey, overbearing, indefatigably considerate Ean-Bei. In a way, this was a victory for them, too. A validation of their efforts, their piecemeal purpose. A sign that their friend Ronoah was no longer adrift, that he was finally, finally getting back on track. Like a dislocated wishbone, set back in place to flourish, and the tai looking on with dirt on their knees and a trowel in-hand.

"Maybe I'll come catch up to you," they considered aloud, "in a few months, once my sentence is up. Might be a nice way to clear my head before Ruppanteak."

Something softened in Ronoah: a pre-emptive wistfulness. "I'll keep on the lookout," he said, and egged the tai off the high wall they were tiptoeing on so they could walk side by side up the flowering street.

Telling Ngodi was considerably more jarring—though not for the reasons Ronoah thought it might be. He came to her two days after she'd defended her thesis in front of the committee, asking if she wanted help cleaning the last of the papers from her reading room. She seemed happy to see him, but for the next hour of filing and organizing he couldn't get rid of the tang of tension hitting the back of his tongue. Couldn't source it, either. The words "Pilgrim State" were hardly out of his mouth before Ngodi descended on him like an auburn hawk:

"I know," she fluttered, "Ean-Bei told me."

It struck Ronoah that by confiding in Ean-Bei first, he had essentially taken a personal ad out in the local paper. "That gossipy—"

"I have a confession to make," the woman blurted, and Ronoah blinked. "I—sweet Saint Yu, it's—I need to make a choice, I need to make a *decision*, only it's, I'm—"

"What's going on?" Ronoah prompted, the edges of his confusion curling into worry. A nervous jolt in his stomach: "Did something happen with the dissertation—?"

"Good Holy Lady," Ngodi sailed on, hands nearly tangling in her long hair as she talked, "by the bloody blade of Oupha, the paper—*Dragon's tits*, Ronoah, it's—"

"Ngodi," Ronoah said, "I'm really bad with suspense. Explain, please."

Ngodi dropped into a chair hard enough Ronoah worried she would ricochet right out of it again. "Okay. Okay. Holy—so you know the committee called me in a day after the defense." Ronoah head-wobbled. "And you know how that doesn't usually happen?" Ronoah head-wobbled again. "And you know how we were just a little worried about the two to three to five percent chance that they would expel me from academia or excommunicate me from the Wish or *both* but I told you it went fine—"

"Ngoluydinh," Ronoah forced through gritted teeth. "Suspense."

Ngodi's hands flew like birds released from their cages: "They asked if I wanted to *teach*."

Of all the things Ronoah had prepared for, this wasn't on the list. His shoulders dropped slack, and the woman laughed a breathless laugh and explained. "My supervisor's a real actual angel, apparently, they've been in contact with some of the more unorthodox churches in the country and they found one or two places who'd like to partner, they want me to go teach—I guess *preach*?—these modern saints to their clergy. To see if it catches on. The library's willing to offer me a fellowship for expenses." The stone in her throat bobbed as she swallowed, eyes overbright. "They didn't just accept the theory. They want me to put it into practice."

Somewhere in the midst of this news, Ronoah had sunk into the chair opposite Ngodi, as giddy relief yanked his balance out from under him. He was so surprised by their fortune that it took him a good minute to absorb the ambivalence in Ngodi's wringing hands, to make sense of the strain and the fretting. "You don't know whether you're going to accept?" he asked.

"Both of the churches they named are in really remote towns, I don't know how long I'd be gone for or if I'd be going to both or just one, and what if I'm en route and they rescind their interest, what if I get there and I don't do it right, or nobody *cares*, I'm no good at explaining this stuff off paper—!"

Ngodi squawked as Ronoah did something he'd never done before—reached forward and clapped her hands shushed in his.

"*Chuta ka saag*, Ngodi, go!" He spoke it without handhalf, forgetting even his most basic etiquette in his ballooning excitement. The rest came signed: "Figure out the rest on the way! They're taking your madcap apocrypha *seriously*—you don't throw that away over a long train ride and some stress about public speaking."

Ngodi blinked. "You really think so?" she asked, and it panged in Ronoah to hear all her usual bluster removed, replaced by raw apprehensive hope.

"I know so," he said, and he did. "Trust me, Ngodi, I—I've been where you are. It's so scary when you ask for something already hearing *no* in your head, and then they tell you *yes*. A whole world suddenly opens up and it's too wide to quantify, to predict, and there is so much room for new failure, but also—also you suddenly open up too, and you become more than the sum of yourself." It was the only way to explain it, that flowering feeling of purpose. "Someone said yes to me when I expected no; I wouldn't be here with you if I'd refused." Ngodi met his eyes, and he said what he had to say: "Take the opportunity."

"You make it sound so easy," Ngodi protested, but she'd started to smile.

Ronoah laughed. "It's really, really not," he assured her, "but it's worth it."

They finished tidying, bundling files in twine and stacking them into Ngodi's rolling suitcase. Ronoah could practically taste her thinking it over, could hear the splash as she cast her net of conjecture into the wide waters of possibility. It made him inexplicably happy.

This was probably how Kourrania felt, he thought, when she convinced you out the door. What a privilege, to pass that encouragement on.

When the last clumps of dust and crumpled notes had been swept from the now-vacant reading room, they trundled down the long halls of the library, reveling in its echo, its relative emptiness. Everyone had packed up and left, away to their own adventures until the new trimester began. The leftover trace of their eagerness crackled, tugged at his sternum, made him want to break into a run.

"You know," Ngodi said after hefting the suitcase down the last step of the wide staircase, sweeping her hair back from the breeze, "for a minute there I really thought I was done for, with the committee." She shook her head, puffing out a breath. "They were so stone-faced about it. I nearly went and packed up before the meeting, just in case."

And something struck Ronoah then, out of the bright blue sky.

"I know the feeling," he said, softer than he'd expected.

He attended to Ngodi's one-handed thinking aloud about train schedules and neo-worship and turning a syllabus into a sermon, and he waved her off down the boulevard, and turned to stroll his own way home with his eyes full of a different library, his ears full of a different committee's request.

He'd been so sure of it. All this time it was the life he'd lived, the story he'd told himself: Padjenne had expelled him. He'd flubbed his examination and they'd summoned him to throw him out. The academy didn't think he was worthy, didn't want him.

But maybe they did.

Maybe they hadn't sought to dismiss him but to offer help—or even praise. In hindsight, it was possible as anything else. He'd had such a bad impression of himself then, of his efforts, his worth—maybe he hadn't made such a mess after all. Maybe they'd looked at him and seen a young scholar in need of guidance, not a disaster who happened to be able to read. Maybe it wasn't Elio Padjenni that had expelled Ronoah, but his own insecurities projected.

Maybe.

It was guesswork at best. It didn't change anything. But he let it nest in the warren of his mind, let the possibility of it grow comfortable, espied it furtively from time to time from behind the foliage of other, more immediate concerns.

After all, there was one more goodbye to go.

It happened on one of the rare nights where Ronoah was hanging out with Yengh-Sier in the man's apartment. For all that the Ol-Penher were ultra-social people, you were hard-pressed to receive an invitation to their homes; there were enough community centres and public gardens to occupy that it wasn't really necessary, and even the most open Ol-Penher needed to pull the privacy curtain somewhere. Nevertheless, once in a while after a particularly grueling practice, Yengh-Sier would offer to make Ronoah dinner at his place. Cooking was something Yengh-Sier enjoyed doing, and Ronoah had learned very quickly to accept every time, because it turned out it was also something the man was immensely good at.

Tonight's fare was Penh-Sidhur fusion, combining the thick noodles and ground lamb of traditional Ol-Penher comfort food with the rich spicy sauce of overseas. Ronoah was scraping up every last smudge of it, stalling while he worked up the courage to tell Yengh-Sier about leaving.

It wasn't like he didn't expect Yengh-Sier to already know—again, there was the Ean-Bei factor to consider—he just worried about facing his teacher's potential disappointment. It was impossible to overstate how training with Yengh-Sier had kept him going through the grey months. It might actually have saved his life. He didn't want to disrespect the work they had both put in.

But Yengh-Sier, efficient even when he didn't mean to be, soon removed the need for such dawdling. "Hey." The two-fingered tap on

Ronoah's forearm had him looking up from his empty plate into Yengh-Sier's unassuming face. "I've got some news," the man gestured. Ronoah lifted his eyebrows.

And Yengh-Sier told him, and Ronoah dropped his fork with an unheard clatter to the porcelain.

"You're *leaving*?" he repeated, forgetting all hope of breaching the subject gently. "When? Why?"

Gods, and he was worried about *Yengh-Sier* sounding accusatory. Quickly he backtracked, hands grasping for decorum, but Yengh-Sier only laughed at his surprise and explained. In the fall, he was leaving Khepsuong Phae to headline his first acro show on the circuit. After years of polite refusals, he had finally accepted an invitation into a professional touring company.

At first Ronoah could think of no reply except to leap around the table and squeeze Yengh-Sier in a long, tight hug. By the time he drew back, he was already biting his lip against his own joke: "It was the poster that changed your mind, wasn't it?"

"A little," Yengh-Sier admitted, stopping Ronoah's teasing in its tracks. "I've been content teaching the Khepsuong Phaer acrolytes, but ...I think centre stage wants me more than the wings, right now. And I want it, too—to meet legendary acts like Eng-Vaunh's on equal standing. You and Ean-Bei got to me," he said with a tenor stroke of vocalized laughter; "I've grown an ego at last."

"You wear it better than we do," Ronoah shot back with a lopsided smile. "Definitely wished."

Yengh-Sier's expression went soft, as if he hadn't expected this affirmation. Ronoah's heart throbbed in response, charmed by the familiar flicker of restlessness in someone else's eyes, the breathless anticipation of a chase about to begin.

"I commissioned a new pair of poi this week—trying to commemorate the moment, I think—but I'm realizing I don't actually want to part with mine. They've gotten me through a lot." Yengh-Sier gestured another sentence—and surprised Ronoah again, so much that, even after nearly six months of handhalf practice, he had to double-check he'd understood.

"Are you sure?" he asked when the man head-wobbled an affirmative. "How—how can I repay you?"

"By using them." Yengh-Sier met Ronoah's eye, steady as his namesake. "Our Lady gave you this gift—like She gave it to me, I suppose. We both have a duty to honour that."

And despite the fact that Ronoah still was not a devotee of the Wishgranter like his Ol-Penher friends, he had to agree. If he was going to lean into the idea of everything existing—even when it contradicted itself—then he had a lot to thank this Lady for. He stood taller, wondering if Yengh-Sier, devoted as he was to the art of motion, could read his acceptance in the set of his shoulders, his gratitude in the plant of his feet. "Say hello to Eng-Vaunh for Hanéong and me," was all he said in the end.

"And you greet the Pilgrim State for me in return," Yengh-Sier replied, eyes twinkling with that precious hidden mischief of his, and they spent the rest of the evening picking through Qiao Sidhur chrysanthemum biscuits and marveling together at just how heinously good Ean-Bei was at spreading other people's secrets.

Yengh-Sier sent Ronoah home with a few treats folded into a waxcloth. Ronoah took the long way back, running his fingers along the staves of ironwork garden fences, inhaling the aromatic steam of late-night dumpling stands, feeling all around him the thousand small farewells he was bidding. To the shop window displays, to the freesia planters, to the understanding granite creases around the eyes of Lap Chai's monument. He floated home, awash with the preciousness of ordinary things.

By the time he turned the handle to their room at the boarding house, the feeling had accumulated to an almost painful excitement. Heart in his throat, he stepped across the threshold and waded, it seemed, through the galvanic fizz in the air to the desk where Hanéong was sitting.

Of course, Hanéong knew. The man must have scented it from three blocks away. But he played the game anyway, because it mattered. Because it was their way. He twisted in his seat, looking up at Ronoah like a silver wolfdog eyeing the bone it had coveted for months. He tilted his head softly: a question too big for words. In answer, Ronoah held out the bundle of biscuits.

"I think," he said softly, "I'm ready if you are."

Hanéong grinned like it was dawn in Ithos all over again.

Forty-Eight

A FORMAL DATE WAS SET: four days hence, on the morning of the midsummer double full moon. Like their passage through Phys two years before, into the heart of Chalisto's Belt. The way north lit by the blessings of Pao and Innos both. A promise kept in order; the chaos of new adventure. It was a good time, Hanéong mused, for moving.

Once it was decided, the long-tensed elastic of the world finally snapped, releasing a torrent of activity. Ronoah spent the next days combing his favourite markets, crossing items off a list: bedrolls, waterskins, copper pot, tea; geranium soap, cured sausage, cheese sealed in blue wax. Cloves, salt, flint and firesteel. He came back from his last excursion to find a garnet shining succulent and saporous on his pillow, as if a god had pricked her skin and squeezed her thumb to the cotton. A warm shiver grazed his skin as he rolled the stone in his palm.

Somewhere in the middle of all the packing and preparing, everyone made time for one last brunch. They assembled on the same rooftop restaurant where Ronoah had been introduced to Ngodi after that first fateful acro show, all five of them, and ordered the entire menu while taking turns reminiscing on old mishaps and predicting each other's successes.

"One of your churches is only a daytrip away from Trengkar An, isn't it Ngodi?" Yengh-Sier pointed out. "If you're still there by the beginning of winter, you could come see the show."

"I wouldn't mind it," Ngodi said thoughtfully, before a wide smile cracked through her reserve. "But I'd be *really* incentivized if you choreographed a routine for one of the saints I'm preaching. Then I'd bring the whole congregation with me. Like a field trip."

Hanéong raised an eyebrow. "Daresay there are a few gaps in the canon I'd like to see filled," he said with a teasingly meaningful look at Yengh-Sier.

"Hey, no, that's not fair," Ean-Bei interrupted overtop Yengh-Sier's baffled expression. "If Yengh-Sier's gonna premier a whole new dance onstage he's not gonna do it where I can't watch."

"Better buy a ticket to Trengkar An for next trimester's break then, huh?"

"That is so far from *anything* I care about—"

Ngodi thwacked Ean-Bei on their gold-glittering shoulder. "*We'll* be there, don't tell me you won't want to see your friends after four months—"

"I have *other friends*, Ngoluydinh—"

"It's amazing," Hanéong commented sideline as the two continued bickering, "that they don't get thrown out of more lectures."

"Isn't it?" Ronoah said, watching them with unrepentant fondness.

When the last crumbs had been licked from the dishes, Hanéong flagged a waiter to foot the bill while Ronoah said his goodbyes. He hugged everyone at least twice, just to savour the flaring palettes of their auras, to embed their emotional topography deep in memory. He showered blessings on each of them in as many languages as he could spare. Of all things, he got teary-eyed when Ean-Bei did the math and realized aloud that Ronoah's visa had expired a couple of weeks ago again.

"You know, it's always been so freaking obvious you're not from here," the tai laughed, surprising him. They shook their head, smiling at him with a smile that he thought he remembered getting from other faces, other friends. "No respect for bureaucracy. You look at all our officious paperwork like it's just so much kindling."

"What a bonfire it would be," Ronoah said, scarcely believing the sacrilege coming out of his mouth. Ean-Bei cackled again and rose on tiptoes to kiss his cheek.

"If you can't be bothered to visit the Consulate, you can at least visit the post office." The tai flourished a piece of paper at Ronoah's quirked brow. "Write me when you're settled in the Pilgrim State."

It was an address—the address for their home in Ruppanteak, to be specific. Whether or not they arrived before Ronoah's letter did, they explained, their parents would hold it or forward it to wherever Ean-Bei was at the time. Overhearing this, Yengh-Sier and Ngodi swooped in to cram their own ancestral haunts onto the page, places where correspondence would land in caring hands and be sent along to wayward children. Ways they could keep in touch instead of vanishing from each other's lives forever.

The yearning to give a stable address of his own struck Ronoah unexpectedly strong. Never before had he wanted the security of a permanent home quite like this. Careful, a voice chided playfully in his head, now you're *really* coming across like your brother. Your adventure will stall out before it begins.

As if. All the comfort and calm in the world couldn't match the thrill of running Truth's gauntlet. He didn't want stable earth—he wanted to shake the world. Always had.

And now, finally, in his own way, he was going to do just that.

Wakefulness found him early on the morning of their departure. The sky was still dark, bunching at the horizon for the breakthrough of dawn. He crept up to the roof and waited for it, tumbling his garnet in his fingers, waited with bated breath for this inevitable moment, the commencement of this final stride. Waited, like a child on the eve of his birthday, for the bowl of the city to swell with champagne light.

When it came, no trumpets sounded. No clarion bells called. Not even a flock of pigeons to mark the occasion. The sun just reared her magnificent head, reached with wordless encouragement across the leagues of space and time between them, reached to cradle his face with her golden hands.

Ronoah cherished the moment, head tilted back, until the breeze could no longer pick out the tear trails on his skin. He scrubbed the salt off his cheeks—one more offering, he thought—and then, with a deep breath, he descended to begin his pilgrimage anew.

Saint Yu's Arch was even more regal in the early hours of the morning. The whites of the marble went blue in the light, gave the structure an air of almost ethereal translucence; up close, the Arch was five times Ronoah's height, about as wide as three of him lying down, and deep enough for a well of liquid shade to pool in the voussoirs.

"A kindred spirit, that one," murmured Hanéong as they stood staring at the entryway. Ronoah caught the gleam in the man's eye, that unassailable regard he held for all great forces past and present. "Worth sainthood five times over. Be sure to say thank you when you pass over them."

Curling his toes, Ronoah nodded. The empty space between the pillars beckoned him, pulled on him like one of Bazzenine's voids; the road beyond was calling, longing for his feet on the grass and the gravel. The only thing between them was this, the threshold of destiny, like the frame of a painting you could walk into, like a portal between worlds.

There was only one thing to do. He took Hanéong's hand—felt a pulse of pleased surprise—and advanced, leaving the last of the hedges, entering the cool of the frescoes, craning his neck to see the engravings up above while his wonderment sank through his toes to Saint Yu buried deep below.

Wherever you are, he thought, I hope you are content. You and all the rest. Thank you.

He emerged with his empathy buzzing, stirred by the muttering, giggling echoes of all the pilgrims, euphoric and jittery and seeking, that had walked this way before. He took their blessing willingly. Hefting his pack on his shoulders, he felt through the jumble of joys in his body until they magnetized, aligned in a stripe arcing northward. An arrow. A straight shot.

"Nearly there," whispered Hanéong, so close and quiet it might have only been in his mind. So intent, so intimate. So full of arithmetic Ronoah did not understand.

He grinned at the not-knowing of it, and squeezed the creature's hand, and started walking.

Those days were some of the best in his life. The trek on foot up the Corridor, the parting of the ancient hills making way. The wishbones studding the scenery like prismatic milestones, like Chiropolene arches seen from the side of the gods. The glow in his chest growing stronger, the tang of destiny gilding every breath. The intoxicating thicket of energy lifting like an updraft, like a thermal, and he a butterfly borne bobbing along in the current, migrating the same route as so many before him—generations of them, all the way back to when the Shattering was young and the shalledrim yet roamed the world. More than ever, when he turned his thoughts to the immensity of this human ritual, Ronoah felt an ecstasy permeate him, an instinct that pulled him along with the same inexorable undertow that had pulled all the rest. Perseverance to the end of the world. Solidarity on the cosmic scale.

He was going to need new tattoos when he got there. He was going to need to shave his head properly. He was going to need a lot of things.

It fizzed inside him with terrified excitement. He offered that feeling in turn to Genoveffa, lay his elation at her feet, bade her sip from the nectar of his nerves. The way he worshipped her felt different now; he spent a lot of their walking time trying to figure out how. What was this new texture to their relationship, the new savoury note in his love? He still prayed to her every day, building campfires and casting his cloves to their coals. He still didn't know for certain whether she was with him again. But he worried less and less with every mile.

He wasn't the only one reflecting on his relationship to what was coming next. One night, as they were setting up the firepit and the bedrolls, Hanéong offered to trek over the next hill to refill their waterskins. He'd been unusually quiet all day, and he was gone for far longer than necessary, but Ronoah wasn't worried about this, either. It could have been his imagination, but he thought he felt a frisson of energy ruffle the grass in the direction opposite to the wind. The aftertaste manifested bright and floral in his mouth.

A couple of hours later, when the fire was crackling steady and the scent of cloves wafted the campsite, a rust-brown child in a marigold shift scrambled over the hillside and hop-skipped their way down, a pair of waterskins slung crossways on their back.

"Still Hanéong?" was what came out of Ronoah's mouth, after a long look at the newcomer. They handed him their waterskins, checking their own arms in the firelight as they did so. Knobbly like Nazum; pudgy like Bashtandala.

"I think so," said Hanéong, scrunching their nose up at a beauty mark on the inside of their elbow. "For a little longer, anyway."

"Dressing up for the occasion?"

"It would be the height of insolence for me not to," Hanéong replied. "The Hanéong of yesterday was beachwear, entirely bereft of panache, but this is—what?"

Ronoah raised a hand to stifle his laughter. "I never thought how it would be to hear your voice out of a child's mouth," he teased. "It's, it's a bit—well, it's incongruous. It's not bad!" he hurried to add at Hanéong's raised eyebrow. "Just, I've never seen you look so, so ..."

"Young?" the child supplied, a hint of irony in their voice. Ronoah nodded.

"But it kind of makes sense to me, too," he continued, shy despite himself. Hanéong plopped down on the other side of the fire and stared at him, waiting. "On a layer underneath. I can't change like you, but if I could—I feel younger inside right now, too. Is that strange?"

"Such is the nature of ancient places, to make us feel comfortingly small."

It was obvious from the tenderness in Hanéong's black eyes that this place did not make them feel small—it made them proud, proud and protective and gleeful and sad, sad in that stately, glacial way of theirs. It was obvious that they had been here long before the Pilgrim State's first humble brick was laid. And yet Ronoah heard their sincerity ring true.

Looking at the child in front of him, watching them coax some fluff into their springy coils of charcoal-coloured hair, it struck Ronoah the same way it always did after long periods of forgetfulness or self-absorption that this was Hanéong's journey too, that they had their own motives for this pilgrimage. They had been on their way before Ronoah ever walked into their life. "Are you going to tell me who you're meeting at the Pilgrim State yet, or is this a secret you're taking right to the end?" he asked, half-joking.

Hanéong smiled along, wide and benign. "It's a family visit."

Stunned by the unexpectedness of a real answer, scrambling to make sense of it—there was only one of Hanéong, they'd said so themself—Ronoah was, once and always, too slow to respond. Hanéong laughed and waved away any follow-up they might have had. "A few more weeks of mystery, then. No harm in one last puzzle now." Drumming their heels on the ground, they asked, "What about you? What are you expecting when you arrive at last to the Soul of the Earth?"

What did he expect—what did he want? Genoveffa's return? Hanéong's continued companionship? For both his godling and his friend to choose him? But the Pilgrim State couldn't offer either of those things, not explicitly; simply arriving there couldn't *make* either of these people love him and keep loving him. That was something they needed to decide for themselves.

So maybe it was better to expect his own self-satisfaction—except the Pilgrim State couldn't give that to him either. He had to give it to himself, and he was finding, with every day on the road, that it was easier and easier to do. He didn't need the Pilgrim State to be happy with himself.

What was going to happen there that couldn't happen anywhere else? What was finding or building that shrine to Genoveffa going to change? He thought it through—really thought, squinting into the rippling flames and sifting through all his scenarios, his hypotheses, his daydreams and catastrophes—and when an answer finally found him, he smiled with a sudden éclat of pride.

"I don't know," he said.

"Couldn't be more glad to hear it," beamed Hanéong. "Pass the cheese, please."

On they went. The grassy path of the Corridor was soft beneath their feet. In the daytime, Hanéong's hair revealed tufts of sunburnt blond tucked in with the black. They insisted Ronoah let them continue to carry half the supplies, and Ronoah insisted equally stubbornly that, shapeshifter or no, it was just too hard on his conscience to let a child heft a pack that heavy. He won the argument, and an extra dose of lumbar soreness. It didn't matter. He could have carried Hanéong themself and still not complained of the weight—for even then it wouldn't contend with the lessening of burden from his mind, the lifting of his spirits, the increasingly persistent sense of being more than one thing at once.

More than more than one thing. As they neared the Land of a Thousand Temples, Ronoah felt a nearly giddy expansion of his capacity for thought, for feeling, like he was reaching roots out into the ether and drinking what strange intoxicating nourishment lay there, until his head was swimming with its own limitlessness. Everything he laid eyes on he felt a sudden tenderness toward like he knew its innermost secrets, the stonecrop and the swallows and the other pilgrims they passed. Even his dreams seemed charged, electrified with insight, limpid and lucid and afloat with motes of gold.

This was the enigma, the sensation Ngodi had tried and failed to capture in something as stymied as words. *This* was the thing that made the Pilgrim State so unique, so enduring. It got into positively everything: the shells of the beetles, bloomed with patina worth scrying over; the cast of the opalescent clouds, spelling out pasts and futures in cirrus glyphs; the invisibly fine particulate Ronoah was breathing, lining his lungs with secret knowledge he was always on the verge of exhaling. Even Hanéong seemed affected by it—sharpened, somehow, as if they'd brought the infinite scope of their attention to a single point, shed their many distractions in favour of one irresistible call. Ronoah had plenty of sympathy for that—he had sympathy for everything now, and in spades.

"I understand now," he kept on saying, gabbling like one of the swallows, "Hanéong, I get it, I get why this place is legendary, I understand why we've come here for thousands of years, I know—"

"Oh, my little empath." Hanéong laughed a high, raspy laugh that was confoundingly, delightfully similar to Ronoah's own. "Never quite stopped getting ahead of things, did you? Hush. You don't know anything yet. The front lawn's nice—but the house is something else entirely." Their eyes glittered with starshine, bright even in the day, all of the adoration with none of the reverence. They took his hand and tugged it, tugged him up a step—and where had the steps come from? When had they started up this hill? "Come and see."

Come and see. Come and see, Ronoah, the thing you have been striving for, yearning for, the place that plucked at your bones from the other side of the world, the dream of every starry-eyed devotee like you—come and see, little Firewalker, the outcome of all your prayer, the reward for every candle lit, every clove sown, every fear-beyond-fear endured, every callus on your feet and every darkscar on your skin. The answer to every question granted. The debt to every friend repaid. The end of the world as you know it, sweet one, the brink of the glorious unknown. Come see.

He stumbled up the steps hand-in-hand with Hanéong, and it seemed like falling upward, like another two years climbing the slope, like he passed a whole other lifetime in grassy windblown limbo but then the land leveled and—

There it was.

Oh.

Hanéong was right. He didn't know anything yet.

Part Six

TO BRAID THE THREAD OF ÉNOUEMENT

OH, IT'S A STORY YOU WANT, IS IT?

Some sweeping epic, some wonder-filled fairy tale about that thing and its capering—like the jaguar-faced creator god, or the warrior of Torrene, or whatever else you've heard, you want more, ah? I'm insulted you didn't ask sooner. A myth from the mouth of a myth, no?

Very well. Let me tell you the thousand ways I tried to kill the thing that saved the world.

Saved the planet is more accurate, seeing as the world was in shambles then. More holes than a pumice stone. The Empire was over, thank mercy, but shalledrim still flicked out fans of territory beyond the Shattering, and were twice as jealous for it. I couldn't so much as go gleaning for leeks in the glen without some laser-shooting whelp coming and pissing on all of the trees to assert dominance. Stupid, pointless, and it fouled the onions besides. I took them anyway, just to spite. It really didn't do to challenge me.

When it wasn't the stale leftovers of the Empire causing a ruckus, it was volcanoes erupting or sinkholes swallowing new-built bridges or poison gas seeping up from lakes to stifle a town. Your kind are so short-lived, so malleable, you'd already adapted to the harsh conditions, but you have to understand for someone of my stature, having the world go off like a tantrum every year or ten was a lot to handle. Our mutual friend slept those first few centuries away, but I was there, and I saw it all. I watched the ruined cities oxidize and settle, watched the moss begin to grow. I nursed this colicky world through its new infancy, massaging its limbs and combing its hair and, once in a while, blessing the naïve little parasites who stumbled deep enough into the woods to find my cabin, giving them a medicine or a recipe they could use to do their own nursing work.

It was endlessly frustrating. It made me yearn for the attunement of my home, for how easy it all would have been with just a little of that old power at my *fingertips. It made me work, which is something I should never have to do. It made me listen so hard, I heard it like a gunshot when that creature finally woke up.*

Even I don't know where it hid itself all those years. Could have been anywhere. The Mel-melu told legend of Uwha Nur, The Perfect Guest, a creature who'd come from the stars to devour all the evil in the world and digest it somewhere deep in their sacred forest; the rebel state of Djantaab passed the torch-tale of Qalinka, Infinity Woman, a lady-shaped shadow of light who slumbered under the great cairn at the center of their stronghold. Every shalledrim warlord left claimed direct descendance from the thing that had cooled the seas and calmed the skies, and they were all right, and they were all wrong, all of them. Sin-eater, sentinel, whatever spin fit the moment, everyone took what they'd heard, what their great-grandparents had passed down in whispers, and exploited it for their own. I never understood how it was fine being claimed like that, misrepresented the world over. I understand better now.

Ah, but you don't mind a side tangent, do you? I see why it likes you.

To the point: it woke, and I felt that tight-furled bud of power flood into bloom and it knocked my entire childhood back in place, my youth in those humming magnetic fields, it called me home with all the unstoppable might of a mother, and I went. I went, summoned by the source of the exquisite energy whose absence I had felt like an ulcer since the day my homeland Shattered along with the rest. By the time I found it, I was besotted, bumblebee-drunk on the wafts of synergetic nectar it seeped.

Tch—you nod, but you don't know. No matter how uniquely sensitive your spirit is, mine was a hundred times more by its very nature. That thing collided into me miles before we were even within eyeshot; with a hundred meters to go, it felt like dying. Dying and being reborn fresh and fulfilled after generations of bone-deep weariness, soul-withering dissatisfaction—home after home had stifled and betrayed and disintegrated into dust. I needed it. I needed it near me and I needed it inside me and I needed it gone, all at once—so I went to harvest the thing that stood watching me, waiting. It smiled like it didn't know what was coming. What a swindler; what an absolute crook.

I tried simple first—a snapped neck, a crushed windpipe. I couldn't even get close enough to brush it with my fingers. We danced around each other for a day and a night, I all claws and snarling gold and it all bubbling fizzling beckoning life, dodging me with a hairs-breadth finesse that the old flashy generals would have bowed and scraped for, and when it finally let me—let me—get a hand around its throat, it was only to show how completely and utterly futile it was to try and squeeze. "What will you try next?" it asked—the first words ever passed between us.

To weapons, then. I took the finest blades from the blacksmiths, then came back to demand finer yet when they all broke or bent around my target's grinning forearms. I brought gleaming heaps of alloy for the steel, chromium cobalt boron

474

and more, things dug from meteors, from the magmic fissures in the earth. Even the shalledrim warlords didn't know how I'd obtained such quantities; they let me into their forges in exchange for flipping a cube of some legendary metal or other their way. I came back with a scythe that could reap the stars from the heavens, and it couldn't so much as touch a twinkle in that thing's nose.

Poison powders made it sneeze like it had a bit of pollen in one nostril. It caught projectiles out of the air like dandelion seeds. I tried explosives, once, and received the only retaliation it ever cared to give. Not because it was in any danger, no, it's because the blast burned a dead streak into the forest. That creature didn't set the world back on-axis just to have someone wreak careless havoc, and it told me so—it knifed into my periphery and told me, right to my face, before it slapped me like a lightning strike, left me reeling and furious and howling with laughter. Fine, I thought, no more playing with my food. I admitted to myself I'd been holding back, and stepped into my true power.

Ah, if only you could see. If only you could feel—the things I could do in those days, the ways I could bend and twist matter to my whimsy. The pliable Universe, in all its alchemical splendour. I didn't need explosives; I could destabilize the air in your very lungs, strike it against itself and set it aflame. I could cross-pollinate fungi to raise soporific spores, throw a whole town into stupor with a puff of the north wind. I could alloy anything, forge or none. I was the kind of powerful it had taken a whole city to suppress, a whole culture to restrain, and I suppose they won in the end, because I used my gifts so scarcely, so scaredly. But in that moment, with that thing's taunting invitation, I dropped my restraints and threw a tempest of magic at it like nothing anyone had seen since the heyday of the Empire.

And none of it worked. Only then did I begin to understand what it was I was facing.

I should have known I didn't stand a chance. You never do, against home. Do I regret spending the first chapter of our epic trying to obliterate it? Don't be absurd. For a cycle of seasons I yanked godliness down to me and forced it to play my game, and it was too intrigued to refuse. The traps I set, the ambushes I sprang, every tactic in my mother's mouldering military treatise, and I never came close—but the thrill of setting and springing, the bright of the battle, the release. It was cathartic in a way that defies description, to be allowed to feel through violence, to hurl every last passion into destruction, to finally, finally let loose. Let go. Let go of all that had happened since that plate-shaking catastrophe, of all I had already lost.

The need was still there, even after all that. But the need was alloyed, too, by the time I finally collapsed at its feet, spent of my wealth and my rage for the first time in centuries. That scoundrel combed my hair and massaged my calves and very politely pretended to be surprised when I tried to kill it again, *after a few days of living quietly in each other's company. I failed, sulked for a week, tried again, failed again, sulked for two. We had made camp by then. I started telling it I would strike again, to not underestimate me; it happily waited out the intervals, two months, six months, eight. The respect it had for me, for my futility, was like nothing I'd ever experienced before. That much, I can see, you do understand.*

I don't know when it was I finally stopped, but I know why. It was a stunningly simple reversal—one day, while we were playing cards or jumping off waterfalls or dancing at someone else's wedding, I realized that what I'd yearned for had become a shadow, a habit, and that my new true desire had been met some time ago. The need was not to devour the thing that smelled and walked and smirked like home. It was to dwell near it, to embrace it, and thus to embrace the fact of my own homecoming, something I thought I would never ever achieve.

It knew our relationship had shifted long before I did. Ever the smug one, ever the patient, it let me figure things out on my own. I never said as much; I just looked at it with certainty one day, and it perked up in that way it does, the way that flips your heart on its head. It gave me rules, and I laughed in its face. It gave me the spiel about the glorious unknown, and I fell a little bit in love. It promised wonders, wonders and mischief, and it followed through—we put your world together, one prank at a time, one pursuit of knowledge and joy after another. This here was our last, and second best, and certainly the most enduring—after all, you're here, aren't you? The story's not over. It continues with you.

...Beg pardon?
You want a name?
Tch. What for? Don't you already know the one that's worth the most?

476

FORTY-NINE

WHEN RONOAH WAS TWELVE, the temple of Pilanova seemed the most beautiful building in the entire world.

At first he'd only seen it from the outside, skirting its perimeter while on the way to join the fig harvest or help his mother carry goods to the trading post, tugged along by the hand so he wouldn't drag his heels to look at it. The way it sat stacked and dazzling like a puzzle, or a beehive, every tiered terrace and façade exuding the sweet syrup of hidden knowledge. When he was inducted as a priest-in-training, when he took that first step into the smoky shade of the inner cloister, he'd nearly fainted with excitement. When they taught him to write Genoveffa's name, he knocked the slate tablet to the ground and shattered it, his hand shook so hard.

He made it up to her. He learned to write with both. He spent untellable hours in that place, soaking it in until his clothes smelled of their incense, until he gave himself headaches reading. The first darkscar he could remember sustaining—he stabbed himself with his stylus by accident. A scholar marked forever; a blood offering no one asked for, ground into the dust and the clay of the building that helped him breathe easier than his own home. Even when his training soured, it was never the stones he felt trapped by. *Speak of this to no one* didn't apply when you were whispering your secrets to the columns, the walls. He loved that temple like he'd never loved any human being. It was why, so many years later, one of the first books he'd cracked open in Padjenne was a monograph on religious architecture. It was why he always longed to touch every a-Meheyu shrine and Chiropolene arch and Ol-Penher church he came across, reaching for the indescribable thing they all shared.

It was why, descending into the Land of a Thousand Temples, he could not for the life of him stop crying.

"Take a look behind you, on either side, those are the Penitent Men, took decades for the sculptresses to finish carving the cliffsides, right giants even kneeling down, aren't they? Their heads would brush the Highway if they shook the mantle of that mountain off their shoulders— and see that, you may recognize it, it's a miniature of the Moon Tomb, you know, down in Faurelle? The real thing's built in the exact shadow of a double lunar eclipse, but given the awkward wedging of this one into its surrounds, a similar event may have taken place—ah, and this hadn't even been *built* last I was here, you people can move so *quickly* when you've got the lantern of something bigger than yourself to tug the way—"

Hanéong's little brown hand tugged in Ronoah's, tingling like they clasped a whole field of fireflies. The creature talked like a gale, lifting the dew from the grass and swaying the silkworms on their threads with buoyant excitement, launching into each new sighting with the joy of a dolphin breaching the sea, and it was all Ronoah could do to scrub at his eyes to get them clear enough to see all the wonderful things being described to him. There was a sense of something that flushed his cheeks and swelled his heart drum-tight behind his breastbone; every fresh sob was like tripping over it.

This place—with its mossy flagstones and cicada hum and its all-pervasive amber mist like whiskey in a tumbler—it positively *sang* exaltation. Mystery dwelled in every pore of wood, every bloom of lichen—mystery, but not secrecy. Not silence.

Speak of this to everyone, the Pilgrim State called. Revel in it all together.

Fear and reverence trembled equally strong inside him—Setten and Ibisca, it was just, it was so *much*. It was like walking into endless laundry lines of silk scarves billowing in the wind. It buffeted him, disoriented him, but he hesitated to brush it away lest its preciousness tear in his hands. He let Hanéong guide him between upturned stones and under boughs of ruby maple as he wrestled with the conflict of motion in his body, the double urge to break into a sprint and to sink to the ground. He was struck by the frantic panic that he was going to miss something in this unrepeatable first experience, that he was going to fail to take it in with the degree of understanding it deserved—and struck deeper by the serene surety that that was okay. Inevitable, in fact.

You're an empath, not a god, he thought, tilting his head to follow the path of a pair of cranes in the orange sky. How could you possibly think to process everything at once, when the Pilgrim State's roots are so many thousands of years long, when it sprawls as sparkling wide as Khepsuong Phae? How could you ever hope to know it all at a glance, silly one?

Ronoah blinked, frowned. He rubbed at a bright spot in his eye—a fleck of dust, a gold mote caught in his lashes—but before he could get his head on straight, Hanéong was pulling him forward, skipping toward a gracefully-columned gazebo crowned in fronds of blue wisteria. A fountain, a well, with a short line of pilgrims waiting to draw their first cup of holy water. They joined the queue, and then, when he'd finally stopped moving, Ronoah began to feel himself absorbing the monumental shock of being here at all.

The Land of a Thousand Temples, under his feet. The Soul of the Earth, in his lungs. The Pilgrim State, here. Ronoah—Ronoah Genoveffa Elizzidenna Pilanovani, also here. God and gods alike.

Something else differentiated the Pilgrim State from the sacred sites he'd visited on his journey, set it viscerally apart from the monastery or the plateau at Sasaupta Falls. It was obvious from the valley floor in a way it hadn't been from up high: the Pilgrim State was *full* of people. Even just in the queue, Ronoah could spot three Ol-Penher ngohk, a lean Faizene supplicant, and what looked like a Chirope woman, to tell it by the cut of the embroidered shawl around her shoulders. Nowhere else had he ever seen such a melange of nations, each in their own garb looking like they'd walked out of their taverns or temples just a moment ago. *The great equalizer*, Hanéong had called this place once. It felt like it—like seeing all these pilgrims, his hundreds of fellow strangers, was symbolic of what it took to get here, of all the highs and lows gone level into one light-limned horizon.

For a moment he wished more than anything that the shawled woman in front of him was Kharoun. That Pashangali was the one lifting her nose to the flowers. That Hexiphines waited, boisterous and impatient, on the well's far side. He yearned for his friends, every one of them, that they might know they shared in his victory.

Already it was their turn at the fountain. Ronoah stumbled up the low threshold, Hanéong close at hand; together they chose tin cups hanging from the rim of the well, dipped, and drank. The water tasted of all the precious sediment of the river delta, rich with mineral, like you could subsist on cups of that cool liquid alone. Ronoah drank another one down, and another—it hit fast, just how parched he was between sweating all the way up the last hill and crying all the way down. Hoping it was not too irreverent a move, he scooped a palmful and splashed his face clean.

The fountain's attendant caught his eye as he raised his head. At the look on his face, they scrunched up their nose in a smile, drawing attention to the faint pink scar marking its left side. They said something—and it took Ronoah a full three seconds after the fact to realize they'd said it in laughing, lilted, slightly-stilted Lavolani:

As you believe it.

Ronoah stood there like a fool, mouth open as he tried to figure out which language made most sense to reply with. Hanéong got there first. "As you believe it," they echoed in their high voice. In Ol-Penher—no, ka-Khastan?

"Why can't I tell my languages apart here?" Ronoah asked as they bowed out of the wisteria bowers. Hanéong made a soft noise, wavering in the warm tones of scorn and approval.

"Because they're closer family than you think. All human language is." The child waved a hand at the majesty around them. "Things blend here; useless barriers dissolve. That is why you come."

That *you* filtered through the prism of the buttery air: you, all of humanity gone and yet to be, and you, Ronoah Genoveffa Elizzi-denna Pilanovani, and you, Hvanzhir Hanéong, you, too. You more than anyone. Ronoah watched the creature ahead of him, its dimpled little elbows, its unassailable stride, and sensed indeed the delicate fizzling away of a layer between them.

Suddenly new shade slid cool over his head—he looked up and beheld a massive tree, big as the willow that guarded the Jau-Hasthasndr bay. Pairs of rope sandals were strung from the trunk, countless pairs, so many the tree looked shingled with them.

"Go on," Hanéong urged him with a gentle pinch on the arm, "pick your pair."

Ronoah floated his fingers over the tough, twisted grass bindings until they curled unbidden around a cord. In the minute it took him to untangle the sandals from the other pairs without knocking anything to the ground, Hanéong explained: "The sandal trees are stationed at all the entrances to the State. Like I said—shoes must be left at the door. This place represents an otherwise unheard-of balance between the built and the organic. No other site on earth gets as much foot traffic, so you must ensure you tread lightly."

The creature wiggled their toes, scrunching them into the leaf litter. Clearly they intended to go barefoot—the best way to go, if Ronoah remembered anything from the monastery. He took a moment to consider the option before taking a seat on a flat stone, sandals hung over his arm. Right now, it was sort of nice to do the thing everyone else was doing. After a whole life spent serving a god solo, he wanted to partake in the communal ritual. He wanted every step to remind him where he was.

The soles of his feet revealed themselves as he removed his shoes. Barely a scrap of tattoo in sight. Sanding down the calluses would likely take the last bits away. He wondered, as he tied the sandals to his feet, what new traits would get inked in, what new lessons he had to learn. For once in his life the thought held no tinge of insecurity—he was actually eager to find out. Perseverance and solidarity were ground in, grounded in him; what new growing would his feet carry him towards?

Today, the path was simple. He stood up and stretched, flexed his toes and felt the soft hug of sunwarmed grass.

"On we go?" he asked Hanéong, tying his shoes to his pack.

For a moment, it seemed that Hanéong hadn't heard him. Ronoah lifted a hand to tap the child on the shoulder, then dropped it as something occurred to him. On instinct, he tried instead to push on Hanéong's energy field, to stir the clouds in that weather system of theirs. He didn't know quite what he was doing, but it made sense on an intuitive level in a way it never had before.

And it worked. "Mm?" Hanéong said, turning from their distraction. A moment for them to sweep their eyes over him, to—astonishingly—catch up. "Ah, yes. On we go."

"Do you…need a minute?" Ronoah asked, looking at Hanéong closely. Something was different, but he couldn't tell what. The creature shook its head, smiling a blithe smile.

"It won't change anything, it's like this every time. Ai me, but look at you," they sailed on, ignoring the curious eyebrow Ronoah raised, "all decked out in Pilgrim State threads, it's like you were made to be here."

Ronoah's ears went warm. "It's only a pair of sandals," he muttered through an embarrassed laugh.

"It is not." Hanéong's left eye glimmered mauve with stars. "Not in the slightest."

They weren't just talking about the footwear. Ronoah ducked his head, tingling with pride, feeling more like a child than the one standing in front of him. He offered a hand to Hanéong; the creature reached back, linked their pinky with his. Together, they turned. Together, they went.

The Soul of the Earth was more fanciful than even Ronoah's well-fed imagination could have believed. It was like walking into a Chirope Teller's Thesopolene dream, like all the Shaipurin wisewomen's huts he'd never seen, like breathing in the luscious air of ancient Acharrio, before the Shattering, when it was green. Delightfully shambolic, just like Hanéong had said. Here a forest of steeples, spired or domed, their lanterns wafting chamomile smoke or burning flames like a peacock's eyespot, their belfries alive with the warbling coos and sandstone pink plumage of a thousand laughing doves. The ground beneath their feet went from flagstone to wildflower to packed dirt to flagstone again as they advanced through the districts. They paused to refresh themselves at one of the water temples, a cracked granite building on a small island surrounded by lotus and koi; Ronoah stood at the lip of a reflecting pool, surrounded by curtains of water and the grainy smell of wet stone, and prayed his thanks to the elephantine effigy from whose trunk the fountain sprayed. They passed an Evnist shrine shrouded in ka-Khastan aspen and pine—and Hanéong scandalized Ronoah by swooping in and stealing a snack off the altar, returning victorious with an armload of plums. "Oh, he won't mind," they said to Ronoah's horrified look, swiping at the rivulet of dark juice running down their chin. "He didn't even like plums."

"...As you believe it," Ronoah tried cautiously, and Hanéong grinned with a mouth stained purple and held out a fruit to share.

They wandered until Ronoah could barely remember where they'd come from, until it was all one long streak of gold-dusted wonder in his mind—and kept going. And going, and going. They were nowhere near the other side yet. Eventually even Ronoah's reverent astonishment was usurped by practicality: it's going to take a very long time to find one little shrine, it observed, if all you do is amble about aimlessly. If the shrine even exists.

Did it? Was there a brazier hiding in all this palatial prayer that already burned with clove smoke? Did a garden of pink and orange lilies lie tucked away between the ka-Khastan chanting hall and the Jalipurin labyrinth? Was there, somewhere, in the shadow of this continent's gods, a quiet altar with a bowl of sand and a bowl of salt and a garnet big as a heart?

"Maybe we should start looking for something broadly Acharrioni," Ronoah suggested at another rest stop. "Pao and Innos, or even Eje— someone all the city states worship, someone more easily recognizable. Do you know if there's anything like that?"

"There's a reconstructionist Lavolani quarter to the north," Hanéong offered. "If such a thing exists, perhaps one of the attendants can guide us from there."

One meadow and one meditation garden later, the first cupolas and keyhole windows could be seen further down the valley. Sandstone, smooth plaster—Ronoah's heart squeezed so painfully at the sight of that familiar architecture that he had to steady himself against a tree.

Hanéong touched two cool fingers to his elbow. "It's a dizzying thing, to see visions of home after so long away, isn't it?"

"Home is not a place," Ronoah countered, but even as the words left his mouth he found himself searching for somewhere else to look, to steady his eyes upon. The tufts of red maple and almond blossom, the procession of white-robed devotees carrying a glittering litter up steep temple steps, the—

"Is that what I think it is?" he asked, straightening up.

"First one we've seen all day," answered Hanéong.

A Chiropolene arch rose gracefully from a patch of clear land, near a couple of smaller conical temples that did not look even remotely Chiropolene. A smile tugged Ronoah's face; a softer feeling pervaded his chest, a gentler wistfulness, one he could better withstand.

"Shall we go?" came Hanéong's rumbling rustle of a voice, somehow low for all its high. "Pay our respects, say our hellos?"

Ronoah nodded. Something there beckoned him—the symbolism, the circularity. Chiropole was where he'd stopped running from and started running to. How good it would feel, to rest his forehead against that great displaced stage one more time, to whistle a shimmering victory tune through to the Audience. How neat.

They made their way down the wide, winding steps, curving away from the Lavolani district and facing instead this wind-whipped piece of less complicated history. Not so wind-whipped, actually—perhaps the Pilgrim State had fewer torrential rains, or else the State's attendants had more skill in preserving buildings, but the arch before them was in better shape than any Ronoah had seen in the Chiropolene countryside. It even had carvings, something none of the plains' gates had sported. A small cluster of priestesses were examining the bas-relief with interest; perhaps it wasn't a Chiropolene convention at all, but the eclectic influence of the other religions in the area. Ronoah saw the painted silk of the priestesses' shawls, the elaborate braids and ornaments of their hair, and bit his lip as the greatest pain so far bloomed under his sternum.

Carefully, so as not to impede on their privacy, he skirted the group and chose a spot at the other end of the arch to contemplate. Creatures from someone else's legends peeked out at him from the stone foliage of the carvings, flying boar and lions with snakes for tails—but there, half-hidden by a blossoming branch, was unmistakeably a Chiropolene steed. He stroked its haunch with a finger, leaned his head against it and closed his eyes and thought of Effie, her spiralling horns and her antelope stripes and her unending patience with the anxious boy on her back, and hoped she was eating her fill of sweet hay now.

"Thank you," he whispered in Chiropolene, to that animal and her rider going so uncertainly into the tragedies and triumphs that awaited beyond. "Thank you for never giving up."

In his mind, that young, soft-hearted wishgranter turned and caught his eye, blue on cobalt blue.

"It's you."

That was—not his voice, younger or otherwise. Ronoah scrunched his brow against the stone, then lifted his head and turned around.

Hanéong was there, holding hands with a priestess in a blue and gold shawl. She stood a couple inches taller than Hanéong, even without the plaits and piles of her hair to help. Gods, it must have grown fantastically long to tease into that shape—but then again, they must have had plenty of almond oil to help it along in Aeonna, and two years was plenty of time.

"Recognize me?" said Tycho.

FIFTY

*I*F SWEARING WAS SACRILEGIOUS TO THE PILGRIM STATE, it must have been quite offended by the time Ronoah was done.

There was just no other way to express the pure sunshine shock of seeing an old friend in this new place—he swore like it was prayer, hearty and laughing, and he picked Tycho up by the waist and swung her in a circle, chattering questions and exclamations quick as Chiropolene rain—"It's you! You're here! Here? Why—why are you here?"

"Why are *you* here?" Tycho responded when he set her down, rearranging the long thick braids running over her shoulders. "I thought you would be long gone by now."

"Got held up," Ronoah answered, rubbing the back of his neck. For a moment it felt, embarrassingly, like he had to answer for his tardiness, but Tycho only smiled. *Tycho*, his friend Tycho, she was here in front of him, gods, but this was—"You made it! To, to Aeonna I mean, you clearly—" Wordlessly he waved his hands at the cluster of priestesses at the other end of the arch, some of them now watching the spectacle taking place. "How has your training been? Am I allowed to ask that? Are you happy in the temple, in the city? Was it—have the others come to visit you?" His heart squeezed. "Feris and Kharoun and Amimna and Sophrastus, have they—are they—!"

Tycho caught him by surprise when she swatted his arm with the back of her hand. "That's a lot of questions to ask a girl in under a minute," she scolded. "Even an oracle can only talk so fast!"

Ronoah scanned her face, nervous for a fleeting instant that he'd actually misstepped—but then he saw her smirk. He ducked his head and grinned sheepishly. "Apologies, priestess. Please, at your pace."

She put her hands on her hips as she thought about it. *Sketas naska*, she'd gotten so *big*. "I saw them once after they dropped me off. They came back to attend the Green Gate Festival, you know, all the famous Teller families doing the classics—they told Birdhouse Girl with a happy ending, that was nice." She cocked her head, every bit the brightly-feathered bird herself. "But I left for pilgrimage a few months after that, so it's been a while. Probably over a year."

"How long have you and your entourage been here?" Hanéong asked, butting back into the circle. They seemed every bit as surprised by the priestess' appearance, and every bit as delighted. "Which route did you take?"

After seeing the Maelstrom, the mere thought of Tycho crossing the Iphigene Sea was enough to make Ronoah hold her by the shoulders for safeguarding even though she was standing perfectly healthy in front of him. Seemingly on instinct, she reached up and patted his hand; his knuckles tingled at the ghost of her tracing their scars. "We took the mountain trail through southern ka-Khasta. The northeast passage is an old tradition for Chiropolene priestesses—so there's lots of temples and rest stops," she added, pointedly, to Ronoah's concerned frown. "Honestly, you arrive *years* late and you're worried about me? What happened to you? You look like—" she squinted at him with a scrutiny that was so familiar he nearly spun her around again "—like you grew into it."

Ronoah's frown changed. "Into what?"

"What I saw back then," was the girl's reply. Even Hanéong stared at her with puzzled interest, but she only shrugged her shoulders, redirecting the rivers of lustre on the cerulean silk of her shawl. "Maybe not yet. Maybe you have to build it first."

"Build?" Ronoah asked, but then it clicked into place. He hadn't expected her to know, was the thing; he hadn't even decided on this path until long after they'd parted ways. Trust this little augur to dream it before he did: "The shrine?"

Tycho nodded. "We arrived two weeks ago—we'd planned our journey so we would be here in time for Phandalos, the Month of Feathers, that's our holiest month. We're ahead of schedule, so after we got settled I asked the attendants about Genoveffa's shrine—I wanted to say hello!" she huffed at his astonished look. "Wouldn't it be nice if you came back and saw a note from me? But no one could tell me where it was. I got sent all over these different quadrants and didn't find anything, so—"

"So it's mine to make," Ronoah finished, a lopsided smile tugging at a corner of his mouth. Tycho nodded again, and his fingers twitched at his sides, already searching for the sandstone, the clay. "If I, would you—" He took a deep breath, clasping his hands in front of him. "I would be honoured if you would help me. If that doesn't interfere with your plans for Phandalos."

486

"This is the kind of serendipity the Month of Feathers was made for," Tycho answered, with a gleam of her old mystique. She had blossomed in the company of the Aeonnene priestesses and their kinship, quicker to jibe, to smile, but she still had her secrets. "I just need to tell my sisters first. Want to come meet them?"

They spent the afternoon among Tycho's float of priestesses, introducing themselves, asking about Phandalos the Month of Feathers and what rites were to be performed these coming weeks, learning the different gods each girl was called to and blessed by. The youngest was a year younger than Tycho, the oldest one eighteen, but it was a sixteen-and-a-half-year-old oak of a girl named Magdalo who had command of the group. She was the one Tycho pulled aside and conferred with in hushed flutters of Chiropolene on the path back to their lodgings, and it was her nod Tycho needed before she could spin back around and offer them a place to stay the night.

"Just not in the cloister," she added, rolling her eyes at the giggles of the others. "You remember how it is." All of a sudden Ronoah was reminded of his own masculinity, from a Chiropolene standpoint. As if she could feel his surprise, she gave a slight wince of apology. "One of the inner courtyards has a verandah you could sleep under? It smells really beautiful, I think they brought the almond trees all the way from home."

"We have made our beds on your floor before," Hanéong acknowledged, ever gracious, and it was at this point that Ronoah realized Tycho had taken it completely in stride that Hanéong wasn't—well, wasn't *Reilin* anymore.

He fell into step with her, speaking under his breath: "Did you always know that, that Han—Reilin—that it could ...?"

"Change?" Tycho's eyes were on the small creature in front of them, holding hands with two older priestesses and pleading to be swung between them. "I didn't. But it made perfect sense when I saw him. The magnet inside him doesn't change, you know?" She pressed a gentle fist to her chest, then let it fall to grab Ronoah's hand. "And anyway, who else looks that proud when they look at you?"

Any reply Ronoah might have had disappeared as his throat went tight. He squeezed Tycho's hand, remembering that last hour they'd spent together on the plains, remembering how much could pass between them on the gossamer line of silence. He sensed her contentment in turn, peach and pastel pink—and maybe something bigger behind it, the grand laughing flashflood of augury that swirled along in her wake.

"Hey," the girl said before he could try to get a closer look, "did I tell you Amimna cut her hair?"

That evening, they ate at the long table in the temple's kitchen, grilled pepper and spiced rice and eggplant dip like Ronoah hadn't tasted since the plains. Hanéong entertained the priestesses with stories of their own gods, half-made-up things with just enough scandal salted in to keep them squealing and clutching their shawls. Ronoah escaped for a quiet minute beyond the glow of the party into the prayer hall, to bow his head to the statuettes of the Chiropolene pantheon and send them his gratitude. He had a lot to thank these deities for. Their land was the land this journey had begun in; he wouldn't have gotten anywhere without their blessing.

When evening dyed the Pilgrim State indigo, Ronoah and Hanéong took the proffered bedding to the courtyard and nested on the verandah floor, listening to far-off bells tolling the twilight hour. Ronoah could tell before he even laid his head down that Hanéong would be awake all night, vibrating with that magnetic might Tycho had described—that, quite possibly, it *couldn't* sleep, not here, not in this place.

So, even though it made his chest tight, he curled his fingers into the sheets and whispered: "You can go, you know."

Hanéong's silhouette shifted. "Mm?"

"You don't need to—I don't know, stay here all night pretending to rest. With me." He bit his lip. He probably should have brought this up earlier today. But there had been so much to see, and then the surprise of Tycho, and Hanéong had seemed so at ease, so eager to keep exploring with him, to continue at his side—and selfishly, Ronoah still didn't want to ask about it. Because it might make Hanéong go, and there was no telling when it might come back again. He didn't want them to part ways on their very first day. A gain flipped instantly into a loss.

But this was Hanéong's journey as much as Ronoah's, and he needed to honour that. It needed to be acknowledged: "Don't you have someone waiting for you?"

She. That mysterious being who had, apparently, been waiting on Hanéong for years now. Hanéong's family.

"No need for waiting anymore," Hanéong chuckled, and Ronoah's stomach hollowed with guilt.

That was it, then. They had taken too long. Whoever Hanéong had come to see had given up and left.

"I'm so sorry," he began, but the creature hushed him with a nudge of their foot that sent the nerves tingling all up his calf, the back of his knee.

"You have no reason to be. I have exactly what I came for." Ronoah frowned, uncomprehending. Hanéong was being honest—he could tell by the pitch of those tingles, the texture, how buoyant, how bright. There was no disappointment to be found. "You think I'd drag you to a party on the other side of the world just to leave you in the mudroom? It's a big house, little pilgrim. I worry I'd lose you in it."

Some excruciatingly soft place in Ronoah contracted hard around those words, trying to fix them in place so they wouldn't morph or escape, so they would remain true. Hanéong didn't want to walk away from Ronoah just yet. Hanéong wanted to stay.

"How could you lose me now?" his mouth said, to the giddy horror of his heart. What are you doing, it groaned, why are you arguing this, why are you pushing for exactly what you don't want? Didn't we leave that self-sabotage behind? But he wasn't trying to undermine himself—he was trying to understand Hanéong. After all, "The entire Shaipurin rainforest couldn't stop you tracking me down. You found me in a lightless subterranean cave once. You said you could smell me from the other side of a town."

"Well, I can't here."

That made Ronoah pause. "Why not?" he asked, curiosity overcreeping his personal concerns.

Hanéong's shadow lifted one pudgy arm and waved it at the black lapis sky of the Pilgrim State. "You try picking out one person's thread in this age-old tapestry of emotion, empath."

As a matter of fact, it actually felt easier for Ronoah now. It had honed itself in him with every step further into this amber land—a leap in discernment, or palette, or *something*. Once, between Shaipurin tribes, Ronoah had confided how his empathy had begun to feel less like a calamity and more like a current, a river he could ford; back then Chashakva had pondered whether he would gain enough mastery over this sense to ride it intentionally, to listen in at will. Somehow, just being in the Pilgrim State had accelerated that mastery. He felt more permeable—and yet also more protected—than ever before in his life.

He told Hanéong as much, and Hanéong made such a petulant scoff that Ronoah was surprised into laughing. The creature huffed their own laugh, defeated and delighted in one. "Lucky you, then. Tell you what— once we please your Genoveffa, I'll happily give you two some alone time."

Even then, Ronoah wanted to say, don't go. Stick around. You said you need me more than she does.

But it was too much to ask for, especially after Hanéong had just essentially agreed to help Ronoah build Genoveffa's shrine. It was too much to hoard. He had wrestled with asking Hanéong for more time since the Iphigene, since Hanéong was Özrek—first he'd thought it was his low self-esteem blocking him, then his fear of rejection, then the dreaded inertia of habitual silence. But it wasn't really any of those things. He'd thought he would work his way up to asking, would grow confident enough to just say, one day—*hey, when this is over, do you want to keep doing this together?* But his hypothesis was wrong, inverted; it hadn't become easier to imagine keeping Hanéong by his side, it had become harder. Because it wasn't a matter of confidence. It was a matter of what was fair.

The world was huge and marvellous and clever and beautiful, and Hanéong was even more in love with it than Ronoah. He couldn't hamper its free exploration for much longer. He couldn't strip other lands, other sights, other—other fellow strangers from the privilege of knowing this creature. Child of wildfire or not, he couldn't bring himself to be that greedy.

So he just nudged Hanéong back, the last faint lines of *Solidarity* pressing against his friend's fluted ankle, and the both of them got down to pretending to sleep.

Halfway through his fretting that he was too electrified to find rest, rest found Ronoah instead. He only noticed he was dreaming when he saw the rivers of history running through the polished maple floorboards, the doors hanging carmine red in the abyss of the night. A lady made of sunbeams sat curled on one of their stoops, one leg dangling languid into oblivion, watching him with feline amusement. *I made it,* he called to her, *I'm almost there, I'll build you a home in this magnificent place, I promise.* The lady laughed like a million chimes laughing and flicked him on the nose with a fingertip like a star.

That stalwart determination faltered in the morning, when Ronoah realized building something meant...building it. Of all the things to get held up by, it was *logistics* that had him fussing all through breakfast.

"Does the Pilgrim State have, have *zoning laws*?" he asked Hanéong, picking up and putting down his empty teacup for the third time in a minute. "Can I just build anywhere, or are certain sites off-limits—and how much *space* needs to be between them? It looks different everywhere—"

"It is different everywhere," came Hanéong's helpful reply.

"What am I allowed to build with?" Ronoah protested, fidgeting with his cup until Hanéong snatched it away to pour him a refill. "And where do I get it from? Do I need to draft blueprints first? Do they need to be approved? Are there attendants who—"

"Thinking like an Ol-Penher after all, aren't you," Hanéong teased, sliding the cup across the scarred surface of the table. "If only Ean-Bei could see you now."

"Who's Ean-Bei?" Tycho entered the kitchen with a yawn, patting an almond blossom hairpiece into place.

"Hanéong," Ronoah groaned. "*Please.*"

The creature took its time pouring Tycho a cup of tea; when it had finished, it stood up and walked around the table to plant itself in front of Ronoah with a tisk and a sigh that seemed almost comical coming from so young a throat. "Listen here, little architect," it said as it took Ronoah's hands. "There is an authority here much higher than the attendants—they don't control the Pilgrim State, they *care* for it. They're really more like long-term residents than anything. Community organizers, if you like." It scanned Ronoah, eyes creased at the corners with amusement. "One day you might even become one yourself."

A series of reactions all clashed and fought for dominance—confusion, dismay, delight—and succeeded only in getting Hanéong to snicker at the melee on Ronoah's face. "Figure out what you *want*," they said, turning Ronoah's left hand palm-up, the old Acharrioni symbol of receiving. "What you need for it will follow. Trust me."

So began the search for an Acharrioni temple. Tycho said farewell to her sisters, and together the three of them picked their way through the Pilgrim State's dawn delights on their way to the South Bereni Quarter. Ronoah's heart began to race when he saw the sanded curves of Lavolani buildings on the rise—but it wasn't the full arresting sensation of yesterday. Perhaps the second sighting was bound to be less intense than the first; perhaps, with one more friend at his side, what would have felt daunting was suddenly more possible. Perhaps he'd just breathed enough of the Pilgrim State's air to no longer be nervous about anything he encountered inside.

They wandered through checkered courtyards and corbelled archways striped bright as wasps, light on their sandaled toes as they crossed a group of honest-to-goodness Lavolani devotees clapping and singing morning hymns—Ronoah found himself tapping their syncopated rhythm on his thigh long after they'd moved on. Each of them took the lead in turns, Hanéong suggesting directions based on the area's architecture and Tycho crossing off paths she'd already walked and Ronoah, tugged by instinct, by destiny, taking out his garnet and cradling it in his hand like a lodestone.

Eventually, their collective wayfinding paid off.

"Well hello there," Hanéong echoed from the other end of a half-collapsed tunnel. "We may have a prize."

Ronoah nearly tripped on the stonecrop pushing through the cracked earth as he rushed to find out—he came clattering out into the warm morning light and a note pinged sharp as crystal in his heart when he saw what he saw.

Unmistakeable.

A brush at his side and he startled; Tycho had plucked at his sleeve, staring with him at the quartz-flecked façade. "Is that Acharrioni?" she asked, sweeping her fingers at the vertical lines of script flanking the gaping entryway. "It has the same shape as my lily charm."

For an instant Ronoah's mind was blank, and then—oh gods, that scrap of parchment he'd doodled for her? She had kept it all this time? "It is," he said, his voice raspy with gratitude, soft as the grass tickling the tops of his feet.

He approached the entrance, hands poised to catch, like the words were butterflies ready to take off at the next sudden movement. His outstretched fingertips swooped the divots of the symbols, and an entirely new softness overcame him, an uncertainty. It had been so long since he'd seen Acharrioni written by a hand other than his own. He'd half begun to wonder whether he had shifted the glyphs over time, whether years without reference material had caused him to accidentally evolve his script into something idiosyncratic, something only he could actually read. But one taste of the weathered abjad under his hands and he knew he was safe. He could read this. He could read this if it was a hundred years old—and it was, if not older. Acharrioni wasn't like Chiropolene; there were no New and Old periods, no ka-Khastan sound adoptions, no quirky century-long orthographic fads. Acharrioni script never changed.

"*From Nkefe's mouth to your ears, be whole again,*" he read aloud. He stepped back, peered into the shadowy apse. "It's a sound bath."

"You told us about those in the caravan," came Tycho's voice behind him. "It's like musical medicine, right?"

Ronoah nodded, swallowed. "But—but I don't know who Nkefe is. In Pilanova, Nataglio brings music on the winds ..."

"Then it is safe to say," Hanéong piped up, advancing to lay a finger on the façade, "that it is not from Pilanova."

Indeed it wasn't. It took another ten minutes of combing the abandoned sound bath for clues before Ronoah figured it out, but eventually he saw it: the name of the builder, too proud of their accomplishment to omit themself from their work. Four names, given and godling and parentage and—

"Mbazalzni." Place. The air caught in Ronoah's chest, clung tight like a child to the skirts of the word. "My mother's city."

Someone had been here before. Not Pilanovani, but some intrepid wishgranter, two or three hundred years ago—*someone* had been called across the desert, across the world, to lay these bricks down in imitation of Mbazalza. In honour of some incarnation of godling that Diadenna would have recognized, had she been here. But Diadenna wasn't here. Instead it was her son, beholding the tumbledown sound bath with the same trepidatious reverence he'd held for the shalledrim temple in the Shatterlands, discovering for the first time in his life a sense of allegiance to the culture this marvel had come from.

If home was a state of mind, this wasn't a bad neighbourhood to start in.

"We're close," he called. He turned from the sound bath, promising the tug in his heart that he would return soon, and faced the treeline behind it. He surveyed the froth of fern and bleeding-heart until something like a path revealed itself to him—a suggestion of passage, a quickening corridor of air—and set forth, ears pricked like one of Pilanova's spotted dogs, picking up the scent of destiny and tracking it back to its den. The jungle squeezed in, fluted out—and he walked into a vault of open air, a broad lawn and a bronze pond and the sky like yellow sapphire above him, sprinkling its mist into the meadows until they sparkled like dunes, and a tingling shiver raised all the hairs on his body because—because this was it.

This was it.

He stared, nerveless, speechless, and the vista rustled like it had roused itself to look at him in turn, glowed like it found him worthy of its gaze. Worthy of this land, of the monument he would build upon it, worthy of everything.

Hello there, sweet one.

When Hanéong and Tycho pushed through the underbrush, they found Ronoah with his arms flung out wide enough to hold the whole horizon, a cry of joy on his lips. The cranes on the pond honked back, and he yelled again, a great wordless greeting that dissolved midway into exhausted, elated laughter. Hanéong was right—you didn't need language to be understood here, and there were no words big enough anyways.

He spun to his friends, face aglow. "Grab me a branch," he said.

Soon he was sketching lines in the dirt, skipping and skating the circumference of the structure he saw in his mind's eye, tracing it life-size on the ground. Here the cloister, and there the courtyard, and oh, wow, but he was going to have plenty of space for firedancing in front of this pond, wasn't he? He leapt over his blueprints, landing light as Yengh-Sier ever did, and paused to catch his breath and stare out across the water. Secluded, but not completely isolated—the far side played host to a pair of stout pagodas and what looked like another Evnist church. Neighbours, he thought with a grin and a strange eager pang. Good. Picky though she was, Genoveffa was anything but a recluse.

"East is that way." A hand closing over his own, adjusting the branch. Hanéong pointed their chin down the long edge of the pond. "If you're aiming to align with the sunrise, you're a little off-course."

Tycho made a noise of assent, crouching on the sandy shore. "And do you want to set it back further from the pond in case it floods?"

Ronoah sighed out another laugh and surrendered the branch to Hanéong. "This is why I'm glad you're here," he said. "Trust me to ruin it at the last possible moment."

It was just a flicker, but Tycho and Hanéong both glanced at Ronoah— and he knew, in that weathervane way of his, that they were checking to make sure he was joking, because they remembered a time when he wouldn't have been. Gratitude twined like grapevine around his heart. Yet another blessing, to have such protective friends.

As he stepped back to let the priestess and the pseudo-god mull over his design, his smile snagged on the thorn of a realization. He *was* joking, but—come to think of it. This really was the last moment, these precious liminal minutes. An age of himself was coming to close as he fulfilled this great and burdensome promise; on the other side of it, someone new. This shrine would be a capstone, a final flourish on a years-long quest. But it would also be an opening act. It was the start of a new relationship to Genoveffa, founded not on fear of her disapproval but instead on excitement for her guidance, her verve. A building like a birth, with all the promise of dawn at the doorstep. To do it justice, he was going to—oh. Right.

"Hanéong? Tycho?" They turned from their work; at their gaze his scalp tingled, anticipatory. He swallowed, took a breath. Reached up and set his hair loose from its bun. "I have another favour to ask you."

He was going to have to be reborn in turn.

Ronoah took issue with a lot of the core cultural practices of Pilanovani life, but the ritual shearing wasn't one of them. He explained it while he led them to a stretch of shore away from the shrine site: it was more than just cutting hair, more even than cleansing the body. It wasn't nearly so insular as that—on the contrary, it was a family event, a community-led course correction. Much the way your friends and extended family came together to decide upon your tattoos, they also gathered to relieve you of your past follies, one snip at a time, and to deliver benediction to the bare, tender skin beneath. Unlike tattooing, you could decide for yourself when the time had come to shear down and start fresh, but the hands that held the knife could not be yours.

"That would be like—like declaring you were self-made, in the worst way," Ronoah said as he unwound his pink scarf from his waist and laid it down as a blanket. He took a seat at the centre, cross-legged like he was about to pray. "Like rejecting the help of everyone around you. The more people are involved, the stronger your luck for what comes." Even Ngeome, with his rebellious aesthetic, had wheedled his siblings into maintaining the close crop on the sides of his head, Ronoah on the left, Lelos on the right. Distantly, he wondered whether Ngeome felt any less lucky now that only one pair of hands did the clipping.

"Did you meet someone whose blessing you wanted really badly?" Tycho asked. Ronoah's brow creased; in explanation, she gestured at the section where his locs had already been shorn away, swirled down in Khepsuong Phae.

His stomach flipped. It was such a pretty sentiment when she said it like that, so devoid of shame; he could rationalize his way into it being true if he wanted, and he wanted so badly for it to be true.

But he wanted even more to be honest with her. She was, after all, moments away from being his judge. "No. I did something—irresponsible." He tried for a smile. "You already know how I disappoint my people. I'm reckless, sometimes."

Tycho looked at him closely. "But sometimes," she countered after a moment, "you do a reckless thing that makes your people proud, Firewalker."

Ronoah huffed out a relieved laugh. "Practically half the city came to cut my locs off after *that*. The line was out the door."

"As well it should have been." Ronoah glanced up in time to catch Hanéong mid-making, striking their finger off the flint of their forearm and igniting a blade into being. It was unlike any knife Ronoah had ever seen, a vorpal slice of carbon that ate even the multilayered light of the Pilgrim State right out of the sky. That was a knife that could cut away every mistake you'd ever made. "Are you ready?"

Ronoah caught Hanéong's eye and saw their impatience shimmering like mirage around them. He smiled wide at the deeper emotion throwing off all that heat: the unfettered glee of someone unspeakably old trying something new. Learning from the world one more time. Running his hands over the coils of his locs one last time, he straightened his back and nodded.

"Then allow me." When Hanéong padded onto the pink square, Ronoah's ears crackled at the pulse of power they brought with them. They stood behind him, close enough for their knee to bump into his back. A moment of selective scrutiny, enough time for Ronoah to properly come to terms with what was about to happen. Then, Hanéong's hand caught a loc. "Ronoah Genoveffa Elizzi-denna Pilanovani. I shear from you any last shred of worry that you will follow your elder sister into exile, that you will bring shame upon your family or your self. In its place, I wish you the indestructible knowledge of your own intrinsic value—the certainty that you are, after all else, deserving of this bewildering privilege of life."

The loc dropped softly to Ronoah's side. He hadn't even felt it sever. Maybe Hanéong was just that gentle, the knife that sharp—or maybe Ronoah was too busy flooding with tears to notice. Dragon's tits, he thought with helplessly affectionate exasperation, there's no warmup here, is there?

"My turn." The blanket tugged as Tycho stepped onto it. She took the knife from Hanéong—"careful, it's sharp"—and ran a finger down a line of his scalp like script, stopping at a point near the back of his head. He shivered as her hand closed over the hair. "Ronoah Genoveffa Elizzidenna Pilanovani, I shear from you the need to prove yourself to your gods." She paused and the world paused with her, thinking. "In its place I wish you the simple happiness of their company."

In the vastness of the sky, made pale by the light of day, a pastel Pao and Innos perched above the treeline, come to bear witness to his renewal. Nataglio's wind blew across his brow, stirring his hair as if to let him savour the sensation one last time. Tycho cut the loc through.

"I shear from you the years of biting your tongue—"

"The fear that no one likes you—"

"The guilt about the one you tried to save—"

"The hard night in the rain—"

"In its place, I wish you—"

"I wish you—"

How strange it was, to listen to them going back and forth, to sit still and be the object of their playful heartfelt one-upmanship. To receive blessing after blessing, relieve burden after burden, in loud proclamations and secretive murmurs and four or five or one hundred languages. One hundred voices—Hanéong's changed, refracted, resounded deep in Ronoah's being as one cosmic choir of the mind. How strange it was, to hear that great riot and still to know how many voices were missing. How many invisible lives directed his own. He lassoed their empty spaces in his mind, reached across space and time and pulled them in close enough to glimpse what would have been:

I cut from you apathy. Loneliness. Fear-beyond-fear. That sabotaging helplessness of yours. The pain of my purple anger in your gut. The doubt when you first looked back. In its place, passion. Peace of mind. The end of melancholy. The might to call the mountain down. A soft underworld all to your own.

"I wish you lemons in lychees, little one, for as long as you care to find them." Hanéong passed the knife whisper-close over his head, caressing the coarse black hedge of what remained. To the roots, to the smooth of his skull. "I wish you all the glorious unknowns in the world."

Smooth as honeyed water, a hum of approval flared the air gold.

Ronoah lifted a hand, stalled, then passed his palm over his shaven scalp, feeling the infinitesimal prickle of a fresh start. "That's it," he murmured, to himself or to the others, he wasn't sure—a smile was fighting its way onto his face, a silly lopsided thing that had no place being there for such a thoughtful, solemn moment. He couldn't help himself. Something was quickening in him, burning the tiredness out of his bones and turning all the blood in his veins to glitter. He couldn't wait to get *started*.

"I thought you would look more different without it," Tycho commented as he stood. "How does it feel?"

"Lighter." He stretched his arms above his head, flexing his fingers heavenwards. The sun was already making the top of his head tingle. "And sensitive, like a newborn. You're going to see me wearing headscarves for a while."

"Speaking of," said Hanéong, lifting a corner of the scarf where Ronoah's hair lay in a tidy pile. "What do we do with this? Burial? Bird's nest material?"

Ronoah laughed. "What do you think, Hanéong?" At the creature's raised eyebrow, he stooped to gather the edges of the scarf, hoisting it into a bundle and holding it tight in both hands. With a thrill, he nodded over his shoulder, to the imaginary shrine awaiting its very first offering. "We build a fire."

FIFTY-ONE

*I*T TOOK ALMOST A WEEK to prepare the first round of cob. They dug a pit of sand and subsoil, filled it with water from the pond and sweet yellow grasses from the hills. Ronoah sat at the edge of the wallow and fitted together wooden frames, watching while Tycho and Hanéong jumped around stamping it into consistency. The method was simple, known even to Pilanovani children, but the recipe was a gift from his mother. *Your house was built of Mbazalzni puddle clay, mave lai—one day those walls will weather, and it will be up to you to fix them.* Familiar, the pungent scent of the mudheap, and familiar the sweat running down his back as he shoveled it, and the meditative smoothing of the bricktops, the thin film of clay that coated his palms so that, when it was done and he closed and opened his fists, it cracked and displayed the thousand lines of his palms clear as any summer salt flat. So the place he had come from mingled with the place he had come to.

Tycho was proving herself invaluable. She returned to her Chiropolene cohort come nightfall, but she was back every morning bearing a basket of fruit or flatbread to snack on during the day's labour. She managed to persuade some of the Aeonnene priestesses into extending some pre-Phandalos generosity, and so a few more hands and feet were added to the mix; the girls wrapped their heads and shoulders in homespun and dug in. Ronoah was surprised at how strong they were, how swift with the spade or the hoe—until Tycho informed him that, like her, they had all come from rural towns where even divine favour did not exempt you from the housework. You didn't forget the motions, she explained, even if your newly-softened muscles quivered to repeat them. On breaks, she dipped her hands clean in the pond and then brought out the small, sturdy lacewood lyre she had chosen for herself in Aeonna, plucking absent arpeggios as background music to their conversations.

498

"Tellers and priestesses used to be the same thing, a long time ago," she said one day, in response to Ronoah asking about the history of the Chiropolene gates. "I learned in Aeonna. That's why we love theatre so much, why our actors can bend so many rules."

An apple-crisp voice caught Ronoah's ear: *we're like funnier priests.* "What was it like, before the divergence?"

"They had one specific guardian god—think like you and Genoveffa—and they would learn how to playact that god for … well, for possession I guess, but not in a bad way, not like we talk about demons possessing people today. A girl would be linked to Cataphis and so she would practice talking like Cataphis and standing like her and acting like her, so that when you needed to call Cataphis down, she could just slip in." Tycho drew a hand up the lyre like a flight of starlings. "Divine impersonation, they called it."

According to Tycho, this ancient practice had mostly dwindled and split into two groups: the Tellers, actors without the mystical core, and the priestesses, vessels without the theatrical flair. But deep in the cloisters of Aeonna, certain priestesses were still trained in these arcane rehearsals. Magdalo, the leader of their pilgrimage, was herself a divine impersonatrix, and studied the quirks and habits of her guardian god Hyla as closely as she would those of a lover.

"The thing is," Tycho said, with a resonant chord clinging like pollen to her fingers, "it's only ever one. Even if you're not a divine impersonator, it's always one god for one priestess. But I have lots." Easygoing, weather-spelling favourite as he was, Roryx was not the only god in Tycho's ear—she had half the pantheon whispering portents to her as they saw fit. Even among the fellow blessed, she stuck out.

There were so many reasons why Ronoah understood that combination of camaraderie and alienation. It was why he was here, building his own temple, and not back in the heavily-incensed shade of Pilanova's. "No wonder you're quiet so often," was all he said. "Even when no one is speaking, it's loud for you."

Tycho smiled. "Kind of like how you're always reading people and ponds and things like they're storybooks, right?"

She offered her hand, fingertips crooked. Ronoah touched his index finger to her own and caught, for an instant, a flash of that pressing effervescence surrounding her, mantle of the divine. "Yeah," he said, as a fountain of Chiropolene voices filtered in and back out of his inner ear, "it can get pretty busy. Especially here."

"But not lonely," Tycho said, squishing her toes into the undergrowth, the mallow and long grass. Ronoah watched her, felt a gratitude well up that was every bit as exuberant as it was tender.

"Not lonely at all," he said, and shyly asked if she might show him how to play something simple on her harp.

Hanéong was helpful in a different way. Their presence was like the walnut oil you slide across a packed earth floor to seal it whole and shining; they knew the best place for soil, for straw, for bamboo to bend into framing. When the first sample of puddle clay came out too sandy, bricks crumbling at the edges, Hanéong pursed their lips, went and splashed around in the mudheap, and then asked Ronoah to try again. The consistency was perfect, pliable and smooth and strong as any hearthstone Diadenna would have laid. Whatever secret alchemy had transpired between the cob and the creature's soles remained secret—when Ronoah asked, Hanéong only smiled, and when Ronoah pried, his companion rolled their little dappled shoulders and told Ronoah to come away from the construction site for the evening, to sit down for a chapter.

Because the time had come to fulfil a promise, one of the first promises Ronoah made on his trek across Berena. *For when you get to where you're going*, Kharoun had said. *Have him read it to you.* It had taken considerably more time than anyone expected, but they *were* in the Pilgrim State—and her book had traveled with him all that way, safeguarded, sanctified. Now, at last, in the brandy light of the temple site, as motivation and reward for a hard day's work, Hanéong marked each dawn and dusk by splitting open the pine-green tome and setting Maril Bi-Jelsihad's words awaft on the wind for Ronoah's enjoyment.

The novel's title was *The Prophesier*, and from the first page it became obvious why Kharoun would think to pass it on to someone like Ronoah. It was a fictionalized account of the life of Evin, that ancient ka-Khastan prophet and revolutionary, following him on his travels and detailing the events around the prophecies he gave. While it pulled from the same Prophetic Texts as the Aspenheart Chronicles, the novel was considered an adaptation rather than a compilation, given the amount of liberty the author had taken to fill gaps in the official narrative. *The Prophesier* was considered a modern classic in that it both successfully emulated the stylings of its source material, and brought fresh life and emotion to this ubiquitous folk hero.

Bi-Jelsihad's Evin was sweet, wry, raw-hearted, not at all the stoic stone-jawed figure one would expect from ka-Khastan tradition. The author had written him with disarming humanity; Ronoah felt almost as if he were meeting a new friend, dipping his toes into the edge of the pond and letting his eyes wander the Evnist church across the water while Hanéong told tales of a young man's misadventures trying to walk the line between the mundane and the mythic.

Always the chapters were self-contained, never a cheap trick or a last-minute twist, and yet always Ronoah found himself clamoring for another despite the fact that Hanéong never obliged, only closed the book and clutched it to their chest with mischievous, secretive glee. On anyone else, Ronoah would assume it was the fatigue of translating ka-Khastan to Chiropolene at the speed of a speaking voice; on Hanéong, he knew it for the appetite-whetting limitation it was. *Dream another day of this tale*, they said through the closing of green covers, the insistence on lingering over one chapter at a time. *Do not rush so eagerly toward the end.* Dream Ronoah did, of a young man with bare feet and a red-brown braid and all the wonder and sorrow he beheld wrapped around him like a shawl of glittering gold.

While the book began with Evin already grown to sharp-edged adolescence, some of the chapters delved back into memories of the prophet's childhood. Chapter Three was one of those, involving an encounter with a deepwood denizen, a frog so dazzlingly enormous and so keen on eating the young Evin that Ronoah shivered with kindred reminiscence.

So was Chapter Eight.

Ronoah heard it on the fourth night of their labour. He was sat cross-legged on the wide flat stone near the pondside, triceps aching from the additional load of firedancing practice after a day of hauling rubble and riverstone for the shrine's foundation drain. Tycho curled on the shore beside him, having been invited to listen in that morning and wanting to recreate, perhaps, that sense of cozy camaraderie they all remembered from their nighttime stories in the Tellers' caravans. She'd brought a sheaf of clipped bleeding-heart and was busily bending and twisting the fronds into a flower crown, sating the hunger of her nimble fingers while her imagination waited on different sustenance.

Hanéong emerged from their campsite with *The Prophesier* in tow—did they know, Ronoah wondered, that this chapter was going to be different from the others? Did they know Kharoun had divulged this secret, that Hanéong had met the author, guided his hand in the telling? Could they taste the difference in Ronoah's anticipation, the potency of his curiosity, pickled in the brine of two years' time?

If Hanéong did know, they gave no sign of it, not even in that ethereal, energetic undercurrent Ronoah could drop into nowadays. Hanéong just sat back on their haunches, toes squidging happily into the silt of the shore, and rifled for their place in the pages. They flipped the book so Ronoah and Tycho could see—the woodblock illustration of an empty boat on a lily-padded pond, the unfamiliar glyphs that practically glowed, *Chapter Eight*—and then turned the page, cleared their throat, and dove in.

*T*HE FIRST TIME THE YOUNG PROPHET *met the dreamwalker, he'd fallen asleep on a lily pond.*

He'd rowed his boat out to talk to the carp and find the fullest water lily for his mother, but the rocking of the boat was soothing and the forest had assured him before that this pond held no murky denizen waiting to devour him, so he curled up like a kitten in the cattails and stole a short nap in the cradle of his dinghy.

When he raised his head, a child was walking towards him. They were perhaps three or four years older than Evin's tender nine—an age gap which to children makes the elder companion almost godlike in their self-assurance and their seemingly mystical knowledge of the world. Even Evin, who was more self-assured and knowledgeable than most nine-year-olds, was susceptible to this shy breed of awe. Perhaps it even held him in deeper, stronger thrall, because he had encountered so few human children before and to him they seemed mythical creatures, special and precious.

The last time Evin had tried to make friends with a human, he had broken her. They had been climbing the oaks in the woods and she'd fallen and landed with her neck at the sort of uncanny angle that makes the body clench low in the gut, full of instinctive horror. Despite his parents' comforts, Evin knew it was his fault—he had convinced the girl to climb that tree, had assumed it would be easy for her because it was so easy for him, because that tree was a friend of his and had always held him close and safe—so he had made a very serious vow to himself not to play with any more human children in case he got them in trouble. This had left him very lonely.

But the child who now approached him was walking over the water, gold-sandalled feet padding quiet as a fawn over the surface, so the young Prophet felt that perhaps this one would be safe to talk to, because even he couldn't do magic like that.

"You shouldn't be here," was the first thing the child said as they reached Evin's boat. "There's a storm coming over the forest and your little rowboat is going to tip and drown you." Evin looked around at the water, so placid and pearlescent, the banks nearly erased in silken mist; the water lilies grown the size of boulders and striped with shocks of soft colour, pinks and blues and burnt-sugar browns like a flock of colossal lazuli bunting and rose finch were perched on the pads, impersonating petals.

"It seems fine to me," he replied, and then frowned. "Is this my pond?"

The child shook their head. "This is a lake in the land of dreams. It's my lake—I live here."

The young Prophet commented, "It's very beautiful," and the dreamwalker smiled a wry twist of a smile.

"Thank you," they said. "Come back and visit any time, but for now, you should really wake up."

"How do I find you?" Evin asked, and the dreamwalker shrugged.

"Just fall asleep. If you look for me, I'll be there."

The child flicked Evin in the forehead and he jolted upright in his rowboat, gripping the gunwales for the pond was, in fact, whipping into a fine churn from the stormwind skirling over the clearing. Already rainwater puddled in the bottom of his boat. He scooped it out and rowed back to shore, taking shelter in the shade of the oak and aspen, tentatively calling his thanks to the vision who had helped him. A friend.

That night, after his parents had tucked him into bed, he dreamt his way back to the dreamwalker. The child seemed startled that he had made it. "Not many people actually find me," they said.

"Well, you told me how to do it," Evin said. The child narrowed their eyes, appraising the young Prophet.

"…you're a bit special, aren't you?" they eventually asked, and Evin shrugged but could not help preening a little because he was very special, his mother told him so all the time. Slowly a smile blossomed on the older child's face. "Let me show you around," they said, and all night they frolicked and played hide and seek among the colossal bird-lilies and Evin was not afraid of either of them climbing anything, no matter how high, because there was water beneath them to catch them if they fell.

O, the delight of having a friend his age and species to play with! The excitement and mystery of exploring a world that could disappear with a snore or a sunrise or a flick of the dreamwalker's fingers on his forehead. They flew in the dreams of owls, feasted in the dreams of foxes, walked among the fluted towers of elfin saddles in the dreams of mushrooms. The young Prophet slept more and more, stealing afternoon naps and waking up so late in the morning his mother scolded him for lollygagging. Eventually, his parents demanded to know what had made him—a buoyant, bouncing, overeager child—so slumberful.

When he confided his secret friend to them, their brows clouded over, and Evin felt immediately that he had done something wrong. His father drew him aside and warned him that there were dangerous things in the dreamland, especially the ones that speak like humans can. He told Evin to send the creature away before it got too attached. But the young Prophet didn't listen. He dutifully agreed and then continued his nocturnal sojourns anyway, frustrated that his parents would so easily overlook his only human friend. He knew he didn't deserve another one after he broke his first, but he was lonely, and it felt good to be with someone other than the bears and the beetles and the trees. Thus, he continued.

His stealth necessitated fewer visits, though, and one night the dreamwalker confronted him about it. "You come less often than you did before," they observed, blinking slowly. "Did I do something wrong?"

"No!" Evin gasped, affronted that his friend would blame themself so readily. "My parents just said...that I shouldn't be here. They don't think I should have people friends."

This said in haste, in anger, because even if it wasn't true it felt true, and feeling is a kind of truth all to its own.

The dreamwalker listened in grave silence to the young Prophet's dilemma; when he finished, they tilted their head, thinking. "I wasn't going to show you this," they eventually said, "maybe not ever, because it is very secret and very special, but it makes me sad to think you are so lonely—I've been lonely before, too." They explained they knew of a place where Evin could find people who would suit him, not fragile as human children so often were but also not monsters who would try to eat him once his back was turned. Strong friends. Equal matches. "It's a tricky journey down through the dreamland. There will be tests, because only the worthy can descend. But I know the way, and I can guide us there. What say you?" They looked at him with curious eyes. "Shall we go to the dream at the bottom of the world?"

The place and the promise it held excited Evin very much, and so he agreed. The dreamwalker nodded and took Evin's hand, and they sank below the surface of the lake, the first time the water had ever broken for their bodies. Evin worried he wouldn't be able to breathe, but found his lungs could take the waters of the lake like inhaling the cloud of steam over a fresh cup of juniper tea. When they touched the bottom, he saw the lakebed was layered in beautiful pearls of all shades and hues: quartz pink, dove grey, cream white, the lustrous black of molasses. No wonder the surface shone so bright!

The dreamwalker swept a hand at the lakebed and said, "Go on, pick one for the journey." Eagerly, Evin scanned the sliding heaps and hoards of pearldrops, and came across a very beautiful blue one. It reminded him of the whales his father had once told him about—but it also reminded him of the eyes of his first friend, the girl fallen from the oak, and then he remembered the stories his mother had told him.

Evin shook his head and refused. The dreamwalker tilted their head and asked, "Why not?"

"Because," the young Prophet recited, "these are not pearls, they are the spirits of the dead resting before they continue their journey to the great City. Taking one would be like kidnapping someone off the soul-road, and that is unforgiveable."

The dreamwalker grinned. "You pass," they said. "A first rule: You can do whatever you want with the living, but the dead must be left to their own affairs. Don't worry," they added as they reached for Evin's hand, "I wouldn't have let you leave with one. We just wouldn't have been able to go any further is all."

And Evin wanted very badly to go further, because this was a magical place, and because he liked being clever and solving riddles, and because the dreamwalker seemed pleased with him. So he took his friend's hand and they waded through mountains of soul-pearls until they found a trench and swam down into the depths.

After a long time diving, they approached a winking light at the bottom of the trench, growing closer, closer—just before they reached it Evin realized by the ripple of the water that this was the surface, or rather another surface, that they were going up even as they dove down. With a final flipper-fin kick, they splashed their way out of the water and dropped into a shallow pool on the ground. Above them was the sea they had swum through, the deep globe of water suspended in the dreamland like the ceiling of a storm. It looked to Evin's eyes like it might crash down on them at any moment, but he knew it wouldn't.

The cavern they found themselves in was full of lapidary light. It looked like the inside of a cut diamond, all refracted rainbows and prismatic glassy angles. The planes were so polished they worked just like mirrors—Evin saw himself reflected back a thousand thousand times. The dreamwalker managed somehow to be always just out of frame: half a calf here, a lock of silver hair there. "Each of these facets have tunnels behind them," they said. "Only one hides the way down, and you have but one chance. Pick the facet that contains the real you, and we will be able to move onward."

The young Prophet peered at the clear mirror shards, scrutinizing. One of them showed him riding the back of an enormous black wolf, pups running playfully at his side; one showed him at the base of his oak, helping the girl up as if she were merely scratched and not dead; one showed him snuggled between his parents, fed on warm bread and wondertales until the whole world scintillated with possibility. One showed him asleep in a boat on a lily pond, one showed him struggling in the mouth of a leviathan toad, one showed him swimming with a friend to the dream at the bottom of the world. Some showed him exactly as he was, standing in this luminescent cavern, hands clutching at his elbows in indecision, red-brown braid still soaked from the descent—and even they didn't feel right, or true, or real. For a long while he stood there, stuck. And then an idea came to him.

Evin shook his head and refused. The dreamwalker tilted their head again and asked, "Why not?"

The young Prophet hugged himself and said, "Because the real me is right here, and not contained in any diamond mirror." And then, with a stroke of brazen cleverness, he closed his eyes and, pressing his fingers into his arms to make sure he stayed solid, he backed up into the glossy cold of one wall. He sank straight through to the tunnel on the other side; when he opened his eyes again, the dreamwalker was beside him, smiling.

"Did I pick the right one?" Evin asked, anxiously.

The dreamwalker replied, "You made the right one. A second rule: any law of the world can be bent and reorganized with sufficient understanding of that law and a forceful enough will."

Evin asked, "Would we have been stuck here if I couldn't figure it out?"

His friend replied, "Oh no, I just would have had to take you back is all."

And Evin wanted very badly not to go back, not now, when this adventure was so thrilling and when he was being so brave and smart and when the dream-walker seemed so proud of him. So they descended the wide sloping steps of the crystalline cave, spelunking ever-further downward.

They passed through the layers of the deep dreamland: the layer of light sleepers, made of shiftings and lightning and sudden creaking noises; the layer of those who don't know they're dreaming, full of more people than Evin had ever seen, eating around campfires or building impossible monuments or running without moving, running from something frightful enough even he didn't dare turn to see what it was. The layer of dogs dreaming, grey and yet somehow vibrant, buzzing with vitality and rigour and the hot salt of blood; the layer of trees dreaming, a vast cavern of sunlight though there was no sun, where they walked across bridges made of roots entwined like held hands and fought not to let the breeze tip them over the edge. Even Evin would not survive that fall. They passed through one of the deepest layers, the layer of those who know they are dreaming, and this was the most challenging for the young Prophet to cross, for he felt suddenly very weak and hungry, and thought he heard his parents' voices calling for him. But his friend slung Evin's arm over his shoulders and they slowly made their way through, and once they passed beneath it he felt better again.

The very last layer—the dream at the bottom of the world—resembled the woods of his childhood. It was a very close space; it had the sense of being small and cozy, like the inside of an egg. Velveteen moss covered everything, the ground and the boulders and the trunks of the trees, so that it seemed like one gold-green tapestry they wandered through. At one moss-threaded stone the dreamwalker stopped, and stood aside, and gestured for Evin to place his hands on the plush surface and push. "Roll the rock away," his friend said, "and we will step into *a place where you can play and explore and exist exactly as you are, and never hurt anyone again."*

Evin frowned. "Is there a trick to this one?" he asked, and the dreamwalker shook their head.

"Only a third and final rule: once you make a choice, the choice is made. The course is set. You cannot take it back."

And the young Prophet already knew all about this rule—if he could take back what he'd done to his first friend, he would have done so in an instant—so he nodded and pushed on the rock, and although it was easily three times his size it moved smooth as a bead on a string. The hole behind it looked sheltered and inviting, warm as a rabbit's warren; a faint purplish light teased him from somewhere just around a bend. The dreamwalker held out his hand, and Evin reached to take it.

Then came a sound that tugged on all his bones, a word as sharp as basil and as sweet as white honey: his own name, in his father's voice. He half-turned and there was his father, looking afeared and aggrieved and a-fury, and his mother not far behind, tied to one another at the wrist with a skein of silver like spidersilk. (Remember: his mother was a witch, and knew the ways of the dreamland as well as any walker.)

"You have been asleep for weeks," called his mother, "and nothing I do will revive you. We warned you, we warned you—you are already taut and thin as a drumskin, and if you do not come back at once you will die."

At his mother's chastising, Evin nearly wanted to step into the warren to spite her—but the look on her face made him pause, because it was also afeared, and he had never known his mother to spook at anything.

His father held out a hand for Evin, but the man's eyes were on the creature behind him, the one with one foot still in the tunnel. "It isn't worth it," he said, to Evin or the creature or to both. He sounded nearly pleading, and Evin had never known his father to plead for anything.

The young Prophet swallowed. Turned to the dreamwalker. Shook his head and refused.

And the dreamwalker sighed and tilted their head, examining Evin with that same wistful twist of their mouth. "Remember that third rule," they said, and as Evin grasped his father's hand the creature leaned forward and flicked Evin in the forehead again. He returned with a rasping gasp to a body like a parched and twisted little root, grey-skinned and crying for nourishment, aflame with fever and bedsores, and his parents descended upon him in an instant, petted and pampered and kissed and cossetted their child until some weeks later he regained his health and could walk once more through the woods. For some time he was half-afraid to sleep, to dream, but the dreamwalker did not visit him again, and he learned to accept that most things which speak like humans *but aren't were too dangerous even for him to befriend.*

Throughout the years to follow, the Prophet Evin had thought often about the rules the dreamwalker had imparted. A rule for the living and the dead; a rule for a will and a way; a rule for first and last chances. Almost in spite of himself, he followed those rules as he grew up, and it has to be said, they led him to great triumphs and joys.

But they had exceptions, those rules. For example, the dreamwalker had told him, by way of rule number three, that they would never meet again. Fancy Evin's suspicious, wide-eyed surprise when, ten years later to the day, he fell asleep and encountered a familiar face.

"*N*o," RONOAH ALL BUT WAILED as Hanéong closed the book, "that is *not* where it ends."

Hanéong flipped the pages open again just long enough to waggle the woodblock print of *Chapter Nine* at him. Ronoah stuffed his face in his hands, pent-up tension escaping through another impatient groan. So much for self-contained chapters and no last-minute twists.

"That's how it goes sometimes," Tycho said soothingly from her perch, twisting a few final bleeding-hearts into place on her crown. Hers was a culture where oral storytellers cannily paused at the best bits to get paying audiences back in their seats the next night; in Ronoah's, they told it in one go, no matter how long it took. "Which was your favourite dream layer?"

If he was honest, he'd felt that dangerous tug toward the soft silent green of the very bottom, the held breath of the moss, the great mystery just behind that boulder. If he'd been that close, he didn't know if he would have been able to turn back. But it seemed like too easy an answer, so he said, "The layer of those who know they're dreaming. It was barely described, but imagine—what must it be like to have all the lucid dreamers in the world convene in one place? It sounds like you could talk to anyone anywhere, so long as the two of you were dreaming of one another."

Gentle blue melancholy settled somewhere in his gut. There were a lot of people he'd like to talk to again. Nazum; the Tellers; Hexiphines and Kourrania. His family.

"Mine's the one with the dogs. I like that something can be grey and colourful at the same time." Tycho rose and coronated Hanéong with her craft, a return gift for the tale. "What about you?"

Hanéong put the book between their knees. They reached up to fuss with the crown, tucking the springs of their curls between petals. "Each has its merits," they eventually said. "And its perils."

Now *that* was an easy answer. "Cheat," Tycho said playfully, and Hanéong reached up and flicked her on the forehead and she swatted their wrist with a giggle—and like the moment you realize the mountain on the horizon is actually a sandstorm, Ronoah's perspective shifted, and he saw plainly the creature in front of him and its part in the story it had just told. Of course.

"Do you think the dreamwalker was trying to kill Evin?" Tycho asked as she resumed her seat, dipping her toes into the pond. "There's all sorts of stories that warn about following strange things into the woods. Demons are always trying to get people lost so they can eat them or enslave them or something like that." She furrowed her brow. "But they seemed so sincere with Evin. At least, the storyteller wrote them that way."

"*Trying* to kill him, I don't—think so." Ronoah paused. "I mean, I don't know enough about ka-Khastan metaphysics to get the implications, so I can't be sure."

"What do you mean?"

Ronoah gave a self-effacing laugh at the puzzlement on Tycho's face. Talking like *library people* again. "There's context missing," he clarified, smoothing a hand along the shaven back of his head. "Like what the ka-Khastans think *dying* even is, what happens to someone. It seems like a soul can exist without its body, the pearls show us that, but they're not human in shape when we see them."

"Oh, I get it," Tycho replied. "There's an idea—maybe the dreamwalker was trying to make another pearl for the lakebed. They did say they lived there."

"Maybe." Ronoah turned his eyes to the sunset, the way it glimmered gilt on the pond. "Hard to play with a pearl like a person, though. And didn't they have a rule about leaving the dead alone? So if they killed Evin, by their own code, it's not like they could force his spirit to do anything." A frog hopped from the cattails, plunked into the water like a skipped stone. "Seems against the point."

Tycho hummed in thought, swishing her legs a little. The croaks and twangs and chirrups of an evening ecosystem filled the silence; then, "I wonder what the dreamwalker meant when they said they were lonely. Lonely how? If they knew a place where they could both make some friends, well, wouldn't that mean they already had friends?"

"I think they said they'd been lonely *before*," Ronoah mused, "so maybe they did have someone down there."

But even if they did, that might not have rescued the dreamwalker from feeling alone. It was one thing to have company, another to have kinship. No matter how many kindly faces surrounded you, it was still possible to feel isolated if you were the only *you* in existence.

The dreamwalker was Hanéong. The riddling, the rules, the thirst for deep unknowns—it was so clear to Ronoah that it almost felt brazen, the way this creature had shared its story with a besotted author, with no fear of getting caught out. Maril Bi-Jelsihad probably went to his grave not knowing. Perhaps he only found out when he was himself a pearl in a lakebed, on his journey to the City of the Dead.

Or perhaps not. It was impossible to tell how much of this myth had been embellished or modified to suit ka-Khastan tastes, to fit an existing gap in the Prophetic Texts. Kharoun, believing as she did that Reilin was a shalledra, had probably assumed this was a family tale passed down generations, the ancient mischief of Reilin's shalledrim great-great-grandparent. Ronoah knew Hanéong well enough to safely dismiss that theory, but the rest was wide open for interpretation. It wasn't even necessarily true that Hanéong had actually met Evin—the hapless protagonist of the real event could have been any witch's woodland child. Perhaps Maril Bi-Jelsihad had simply been in the mood to borrow inspiration when he heard it.

A simple "how much of this is true?" could have revealed the answers, but Ronoah didn't seek to clarify. He wasn't going to ask in front of Tycho, after all. He—might not even ask alone. On the one hand, it would be a mystery unsolved, but on the other, he felt a potency inherent in that mystery, in the fact that Ronoah had a secret bit of insight that Hanéong didn't know he knew. That had never happened before. He toyed with keeping it to himself, the hoard of it, the private high.

For now, he put it away to concentrate on this long-loved Chiropolene tradition of tearing a story to shreds. It struck him halfway through that this was actually the first time he'd ever done this with a Chirope; back then, with the Tellers, he'd been too shy and insecure to join in on their conjecture. It felt like finally setting something right. They theorized on the dreamwalker's intentions some more, had a rousing debate about the rules and whether or not they were total nonsense, and then Tycho hopped up and took the path back to her priestesses, leaving Ronoah to notice belatedly that Hanéong had barely spoken.

"Tire yourself out reading?" he asked, not without a hint of teasing.

Hanéong looked up, one hand still fiddling with the bleeding-heart. "Mm?"

Distracted again. And what was more, there was a look about them, a *wistful twist of their mouth*, that twitched Ronoah's own lips up in a knowing half-smile. To reread this story was probably to regret a lost opportunity, to rue the missed connection—or else to rue the trickery, or the miscommunication if that's what it had been. The terrible ease with which you could accidentally kill a boy, even a magical one.

"Just listening," was all Hanéong had to offer in the end. Ronoah let the creature get away with it.

This daydreaming softness had been Hanéong's mien for the last week. Something odd was going on with the creature, had been ever since they arrived in the Pilgrim State. For every moment Hanéong had spent cheerfully stamping clay with Tycho or leading the hunt into the jungle for materials, they'd spent as long digging out the shrine's foundations in contemplative solitude. It wasn't the humming quiet Ronoah remembered from the monastery, springloaded and ready to snap into joyous lecturing the moment the right question was posed. It was almost…absentminded. Ronoah wouldn't dare try to startle Hanéong, but if ever there was a place to see if he could, it was here.

After eating and washing up, Ronoah's only remaining priority was tossing himself into bed—after all, *Chapter Nine* awaited in the morning, and then they were going to be stacking the stem wall, arguably the most laborious step in construction. He and Tycho had taken the hour-long walk around the pond to beg a wheelbarrow from the neighbours' flourishing garden—and to introduce themselves to the pagoda-dwellers, a trio of pink-cheeked, flat-nosed monks from Fufori across the ocean—and had used it to ferry facestones and hearting from anywhere they could scavenge it, including the ruin of the Mbazalzni sound bath. Tomorrow would see them lifting all that stone and fitting it to course. The potential for squashed fingers and toes was significant even accounting for good night's sleep.

But as he turned for the hammocks, Hanéong called out, with a deference that was almost startling: "Might I continue the work overnight?"

Ronoah hesitated. Turned to the shrine site, appraising it. Turned inward, searching for a spark of approval. Is it okay, he prayed—do you mind?

He hadn't really expected an answer. He was just retraining the reflex of reverence, establishing the habit of communion with his gods. But a bud of warmth surprised him, right beneath his sternum, tiny and vibrant as a single clove blossom. Notions coalesced in his mind: a monastery wall rebuilding under Özrek's conductor touch; a small sleepless form sitting sentinel amid the stars; a will to participate, to play with the world as the only mentor there was. He held these ideas, so gingerly he scarcely breathed, and the bud unfurled, encouraged. Go on.

"Go ahead," he answered, just a bit hoarse, and Hanéong smiled and a giddy wind swept Ronoah's spine, tingling anticipation at what wonders he might open his eyes to in the morrow.

So the basso notes of boulders scraping like knife to whetstone lulled Ronoah to sleep. So he dreamt of Genoveffa watching, gold-and-garnet eyes fixed to the little stonemason, as her tribute rose from the ground. So he woke in the conch shell of dawn to Hanéong sanding a hand along the low unbroken undulation of a black basalt drystone wall.

"It's—it's beautiful," were the first words out of Ronoah's mouth, still smoky with sleep. Hanéong turned and fixed him with such a radiant look his heart skipped.

"It's yours," the creature said, wiping a stray constellation from their cheek like a mud smudge.

FIFTY-TWO

*R*ONOAH HAD LEARNED THE FUNDAMENTALS of many crafts in his youth, but he wasn't especially good at any of them. He could throw a decent clay pot if he concentrated, and his beadwork was consistent, if not beautiful like his father's. But in his estimation he was particularly bad with textile arts—to the shame of his Pilanovani heritage. Most of the wool he'd spun from Gengi's coat wound up uneven and lumpy, and all the winning games of Obagli's Web in the world couldn't teach his fingers how to weave for real. He and his family's loom were not friends.

So when the time came to honour another promise, he sought out a little expertise.

"Tycho?" The girl waved at him as he approached her and the other priestesses, on break from slathering clay onto the shrine walls. With everyone's help, the building was rising fast; it had gained another foot of height, the first curving windowsills appearing between bamboo staves. "Do you know much rope craft?"

"Sure do. I learned macrame when I was a kid—and, you know." She gestured at her sisters, their heads a meadow of brown braids and twists and fanciful knots. "I've had lots of practice. Why?"

Watching her weave the crown of bleeding-heart was what had given him the idea. That, and— "You made me this, a long time ago," he said, offering her the little braided cord charm she'd given him in Chiropole. She took it into her hands and turned it gently over, examining it with a fondly critical eye, while some of the others crowded her shoulders to see. He took a deep breath. "Would you be up for making something bigger with me?"

And so they let Hanéong and the priestesses shape the shrine for a bit while they embarked on this new project. Tycho quizzed him on what sort of craft he wanted—*a tapestry, or a shelf, or a hanger for some flowers?*—but

514

Ronoah had no clear answer for her. Nazum hadn't been very specific. 'A braid of red rope' could have been thin as a bracelet or wide as a wall hanging.

At this indecision, Tycho huffed. "Well make some choices, because I can make anything." She paused, reconsidering her boast. "Not *anything*. There are big swinging chairs in the temple at Aeonna, with canopies and everything. I don't know if I could make one of those."

After agonizing over the infinity of choice before him a little longer, his rational side kicked in the door and reminded him that Nazum probably would never see this monument anyway. The fact that Ronoah was bothering to honour Vashnarajan at all was what mattered. "Wall hanging it is," he answered, thinking of the braided herbs decorating Chabra'i's treehouse and Pashangali's hut, the drapes all aflutter in Marghat's villa. Tycho nodded, but she wasn't done. She demanded specificity around the hanging's dimensions, prodding until Ronoah pulled open his wingspan like a startled goose, demonstrating a length of about five and a half feet. It was definitely going to take longer than the afternoon he'd envisioned to make something that large, but Tycho seemed undaunted; she just dragged him into the woods to look for a shapely branch to use as a dowel.

"Are you putting it in the shrine?" she asked, and Ronoah had another miniature crisis.

"Yes!" he yelped at her castigating look. A decision made on impulse. Genoveffa wouldn't mind the company; he only hoped Vashnarajan wouldn't, either.

Tycho traipsed back to the priestesses and pulled Magdalo aside from leaping in the mud to ask about art supplies. The older girl had been sprucing up their lodgings with macrame shelving earlier that week; apparently there was a monastery not too far from the Chiropolene temple where the monks plied and dyed cordage as part of their contemplative practice and were happy to give spools away to pilgrims looking for materials. They paid a visit and Tycho deftly selected her palette. Ronoah mentioned that the hanging should be red, but Tycho also picked out a soft soil ochre and a phthalo blue that, when asked about it, matched Ronoah's eyes. The girl topped it off with a few spools of undyed jute and tossed them all into Ronoah's arms for carrying. They prickled where they rubbed up against his inner arms, bulky yet almost alarmingly light; he cradled them like a bale of coloured clouds, gripped by a will to protect them.

Pondside again, and the light going from white gold to pale amber as the afternoon thickened upon them. Tycho was setting up her workstation, fitting the branch between two leftover pieces of bamboo, draping cords overtop, crossing and uncrossing lengths of velvet red and sandy brown while she tested out how they wanted to comingle. "I'm guessing," she said while she worked, with a dry humour she'd definitely lifted from Feris, "you haven't decided how you want it to look?"

Ronoah had been fretting about this the whole walk back, sketching and scrapping designs in his mind while the bundles of cordage jostled in his hold. It made his heart hurt that she was ultimately right. That for all the time he'd spent with Nazum—a whole year shoulder-to-shoulder—he didn't know any of Vashnarajan's symbols or signs, had no clue how to definitively mark this tribute as a tribute to the god of Shaipuri's new age. That he could not, in the end, do what he was asked to do. That his friend's culture could be wiped so easily clean.

And yet.

Culture's just a bunch of things everyone's agreed to. The old declaration echoed in his head, sonorant with sudden insight. *Tradition serves the needs of the people, and I'm the only person what's left, so I'll uphold what I please.*

Chuta ka saag, trust him to miss the point until now. Trust him to be so in his own head that he failed to listen properly. Ronoah wasn't really making a monument to *Vashnarajan*, was he? That was never actually what the ask was about.

Softly, he said, "How about this: I tell you the story of the person this is dedicated to, and you pull inspiration from there."

That effervescent aura of Tycho's seemed to brighten, a pink flash at the edge of the eye, as she smiled. "Not shy about telling stories anymore?" she asked, felicity warm in her voice. "That should make this a lot more fun. Who's it for?"

"For Nazum." And easy as that, the tears came back. He wiped them away, clearing his eyes as the name rose up from the dark, flapped free of his mouth like a haughty, huge-hearted crow: "Nazum Vashnarajandra, Queen Wisewoman of Shaipuri."

This request wasn't about preserving an endangered culture, memorializing a dead god. This wasn't Bazzenine and Jesprechel. It was Shaipuri—alive and sly and capable, Shaipuri with a whole new future spread out before it. It was Nazum, making his friend Runa promise he wouldn't forget him after their time together was done.

What a ridiculously roundabout way to show you care, Ronoah thought as his chest throbbed with fondness. What an unnecessarily sneaky thing to do. As if they both didn't know his memory was perfect.

Slowly, reverently, Ronoah told Tycho the story of the War of Heavenly Seeds. He tried to keep it trim, pretty, to give it the mythical quality of the Chiropolene traditional stories she was used to, or else a chapter from Maril Bi-Jelsihad's book. At first it worked; he told her about cosmic calendars and creator gods and a rainforest halfway rotted, named eighteen tribes and saw them drop into her mind, substantial as pebbles into a cool well. She started arranging colours with purpose after that, looping larks-heads of off-white and ochre and deep blue onto her dowel. He described the Council, and what it was for, and why it stopped meeting. Skipped forward a hundred years to a knobby-kneed, button-nosed, fox-eyed boy, the last of his ruined tribe, seeking peace for himself and finding peace for all the heartland instead.

But the myth fell apart there. It was, Ronoah discovered, simply too close to heart. The longer he talked, the more he tumbled into something untidy and meandering and real. And no wonder—he'd never told anyone that wasn't Hanéong, which meant he'd never told anyone who wasn't involved. In a way, he hadn't told anyone at all. And Tycho was the kind of listener that made you ache to pour yourself out to her. He supposed that was part of her job, being an oracle. Perhaps her gods were also gathered around to listen; they did love a good spectacle.

The story overcame him. It flooded his mouth with bittersweet complexity like the darkest cocoa the jungle had to offer. He told Tycho about his own trials, how the wonder and suffering of Shaipuri had made a home in him alongside Nazum. He fetched the *runa* pelt to show her; he cried a little when he noticed those distinctive stripes and spots in her knotwork. He cried again when he showed her the scar on his forearm, the souvenir Marghat's mamu had left in exchange for his life spared, and Tycho ran one brown finger light as a willow twig forgivingly along its curve. He cried so much, on and off through the telling, that he was sure the spirit of Lady Vashnarajandra herself would arise from the macrame and take him to task for his weepiness. He could hear it now, full of affectionate scorn: *Ayyeesh, let the lady work for five minutes without having to wipe your snot away for you, demon boy.*

He wouldn't have listened. This whole craft was, after all, becoming an exercise in realizing just how sentimental Nazum Vashnarajandra could be.

And Tycho wasn't bothered by his gentle sensibility. She simply wove that tenderness into her tapestry, entangled with patterns of helixing leaves, long fronds of cord left loose like waterfalls. Like the Tellers before her, she organized his scattered anecdotes into a cohesive whole, adding sections and layers and lines as his story progressed, guiding his fingers to find and tie the simpler knots himself, until they were done three days later and a piece of art lay before them that was coloured like the desert at sundown but *felt* like it belonged in a wisewoman's hut, leaf motif and all. A fusion of origins; an embrace between opposites. A soft underworld, there to honour any time he liked.

"I do not know," Ronoah said, gazing at the finished piece as it swayed in the teasing breeze, "how I will ever thank you enough. I am indebted to you forever."

"That's not a bad thing," Tycho replied, taking his hand and squeezing it. He felt the pulse of her pride radiating from her palm. "You're in debt to Hanéong, too. And your parents, and Nazum, and that inferno the Ravaging. Just like I owe my life to my family, and the priestesses, and Amimna and Feris and everyone. Even to you, a little bit." He glanced down, surprised, but she only reached for the tapestry and gave it a gentle tug, settling the threads more firmly. "The gods give us a life and a role to play in it, but that role doesn't mean much without other people to see it and know it's real. We're all held up by each other."

Nothing could be truer at that moment. It resonated in Ronoah like a fundamental law of the Universe, suffusing him with the same limitless mutuality he'd felt on the foothills of the Pilgrim State. He felt like one more delicate bleeding heart in Tycho's hand, twisted and twined into shape by the kindnesses of others.

"But also I will accept sweets as payment," said the priestess, who was after all a twelve-year-old girl, and the moment broke on the clatter of Ronoah's laughter. "I like candied almonds."

Those treats were going to have to be delivered on Ronoah's own time; after two weeks, Phandalos had arrived, and Tycho and her sisters were needed for their own holy ceremonies. They pinched Hanéong's cheeks and let Ronoah kiss their wrists and departed, a flock of starlings migrating to their Month of Feathers. The work was left to Ronoah and Hanéong—and to the increasingly persistent glimmer in the corner of Ronoah's eye.

He had been reluctant to name it in the opening days, trying as he was to respect her autonomy, to not reel her back to him so presumptuously, but it was inescapable now: Genoveffa had returned to him.

If he was being honest, he never could have predicted just *how* close she would get to him in the Pilgrim State, never would have imagined all the little gifts and synchronicities she would put in his path to reveal herself. At most he had hoped for a return to normalcy, to the security they'd had with one another pre-Shaipuri, but this was—she was almost audaciously present, goading and laughing and fey. The higher the shrine rose, the stronger her signs came through, gleaming godling in the stubbornness of the bamboo and the fiery red of the clay. Ronoah's dragontail practice felt like an embrace, like a return to the Ravaging, dancing for the love of Pilanova's great chaotic firestarter; when he said something particularly thoughtful or clever to Hanéong, he felt the tingling of cloves on his lips; he mistook at least three different flowers for desert lilies, his nose and eye leading him astray, fooled by Genoveffa's divine sleight of hand. She toyed with him, meddling in his daily tasks, sending wordless nudges of approval or admonishment that had him scraping his fingers on the stone in surprise—usually such a careful architect, he sustained not one but two splinters as a result of her winding like a cat around his ankles.

"Stop startling me," he chided her in the twilit mist of his dreams, where her spirit would sometimes coalesce into something almost resembling a woman. The hills glowed with her laughter; the pond churned with it. "You're—I can't concentrate on doing a good job for you when you're underfoot like that!"

It came like it always did in those dreams, in a gust of gold and a language he felt just on the cusp of knowing: *So learn to step livelier.*

It was interesting to him, that golden sheen. It was interesting because it wasn't classically considered Genoveffa's colour palette—yellows and golds meant much more to her brother Nataglio. It gave him something to meditate on while he knitted fresh loaves of clay onto the shrine walls, contemplating these theological oddities.

Was Genoveffa growing alongside him? Was she developing new preferences, new tastes, as they sampled the world outside the desert together? Or had she always been like this, and it was tradition that got it wrong? Tycho had mentioned one afternoon how the Chiropolene deity Hyla was widely believed to hate offerings of fish, but according to divine impersonatrix Magdalo, Hyla loved a trout as much as the next god. Maybe it was the same with Genoveffa, and Ronoah's understanding of her was being undercut by Pilanova's limited religious canon.

Whatever the reasons behind it, the fact stood unopposable: Genoveffa was making contact, in new ways as well as the ones he recognized, held dear. Any lingering spiritual doubt was put to rest by just how brazenly her messages came through—perhaps she was putting in the effort to assuage her wishgranter's worries, or else just making up for lost time. Especially after so long in deadened isolation in Khepsuong Phae, this playful pestering was almost embarrassing, like an overbearing parent. When Ronoah toured the tumbledown Mbazalzni sound bath, he heard her humming in his mind, teaching him the pitch he'd need to make the stone sing if it were whole; when Hanéong read from *The Prophesier*, Ronoah felt his godling's presence perched on him like an off-balance falcon, peering over his shoulder at the story, at the ageless child telling it. Apparently she was just as intrigued as he was—which, really, he couldn't blame her for, because the story had only grown more compelling.

As Maril Bi-Jelsihad told it, the Prophet Evin's second encounter with the dreamwalker was just as perilous as the first: the creature roused Evin's rebellious streak, and also his adolescent pride, and persuaded him he was clever and strong enough to free a human workcamp from their shalledra warlord. That didn't go as planned. Evin spent a year as a slave to the shalledrim until his parents risked themselves to rescue him, and still he nearly died. He probably would, if he met the creature again, Ronoah mused. Rule of threes and all.

The silver in this slurry was that during his year of imprisonment, Evin met the woman who would—one day, several years later—become his wife. She had a no-nonsense attitude to rival his mother's, and a birthmark like an oak leaf across the left side of her face, and where Evin failed she later succeeded, organizing her fellows and leading their liberation effort. She lost an arm to the fight, but, as she explained to Evin when they crossed paths again, *Compared to the freedom of doing as I please with the one left to me? Worth it all.*

"I'm really glad Bi-Jelsihad brought her back like that," Ronoah said when the chapter was done. "Or—that it happened that way?" Sometimes it was still tricky to figure out what was original myth and what was the author's embellishments. The dreamwalker themself was apparently an unusual focus in Bi-Jelsihad's version of Evin's life; they weren't mentioned in any of the historical Prophetic Texts. Ronoah could only assume—for obvious reasons—that this character's appearance was due to Hanéong's contribution.

"It happened that way," confirmed Hanéong, privately amused as they closed the book.

"I just—it was such a *bad* year for Evin, it was brutalizing, it—" It made sense, said a voice in his head, why hunters did what they did to Bazzenine and Jesprechel, however many thousands of years later. The memory of that cruelty was inlaid in the marrow of humanity. He shivered, pushed back to his point: "It could so easily have just been a plan gone horribly wrong and that's the lesson, you know? ka-Khastans love a tragedy as much as the Chiropes do. I appreciate that he gets *something* in return for what he endured, it feels—fair." He leaned his chin in his hands. "Almost makes up for how awful it was."

Hanéong's little dappled cheek dimpled with a smirk. "Finding a wife is like that sometimes," they said—and Ronoah felt the urge to physically duck as Genoveffa tisked like a branch snapping, charmed and affronted in one. Hanéong raised an eyebrow at Ronoah's twitch, his exasperated hiss. Setten and Ibisca, he was starting to hear Genoveffa the way Tycho heard her gods—literally in his ear. That was another novelty. It unbalanced him every time it happened.

Did every wayward pilgrim in the State knock flat into their faith like this? Did everyone feel it this strongly? Was it because he was an empath—was he attuned to this sacred space in a different way than the rest?

One night, when he dreamt her arrival on the back of a great jasper stag, he asked. "We never talked like this before, not even when I would fall asleep in the temple back home," he said, hands open to her in question. "Not even on the Salt Flats, it never—it's *different*. Isn't it?"

Genoveffa observed him from between the antlers, a ladypool of light draped languid up the neck of her steed, sunray fingers flirting with the pearling of the bone. She shrugged a shoulder, sunrise and set. *When you figure it out, be sure to let me know.*

It took until he woke before he finally noticed.

He nearly missed it, shaking free from the last fuzzy strands of sleep—but he caught the edge of it, pulled it back into focus, and once he realized what it meant he was out of his hammock almost before he could think. "Hanéong?" he called, crossing the threshold to find his companion sculpting desert lilies onto the shrine's inner wall. "Hanéong, what's going on?"

Genoveffa's mount of choice was not the deer. It was the hyena.

When Hanéong's eyes found his, Ronoah felt a stormfront of preparatory prickles sweep the plains of his arms. "Going on where?" the creature asked, but their liquid black gaze roved his features like they were a step ahead of their question already.

Ronoah did not give them time to guess. "I've been having these dreams, these amazing vivid dreams ever since we got here, ever since the first night, dreams of Gen—of this golden lady, watching over us and talking to me, and it happens when I'm awake too sometimes, she, she jokes around, she trips me up—" Coy and mischievous and *not quite right*, not the Genoveffa he knew and loved. He ran his hands over his head, clasped them behind his neck, turned to Hanéong. "The thing is I don't actually think it's—!"

Hanéong's hands were on his waist. Gods, he hadn't even seen it move. "You mean to tell me," the child began, and its voice was low and even but nebulae flickered and bloomed under its skin like sheet lightning in the heart of the Maelstrom—"You mean to tell me she's been with you all this time?"

The last time Ronoah felt that incredulous squeeze of Hanéong's fingers, the creature had been seven feet tall, and had promptly tossed Ronoah into the air for sheer glee. The fact that currently Hanéong barely cleared four foot nine did not seem an adequate barrier to repeating that feat. Ronoah was bracing for it when something else clicked. "When you say *she*—"

"HONESTLY." Ronoah jumped but Hanéong had already spun away from him, facing the world at large with arms flung wide in reproach. "I go through all the trouble to give you my undivided attention," it called, its voice bubbling prismic and multilayered, bouncing off the walls and sweeping loose bits of straw into the air, "I dress for your memory, I bring you a breakfast from the other side of the *world* and you don't even bother to thank me for it before taking a bite?"

Another stronger wind blew, tossing Hanéong's curls into disarray and rattling the bamboo vaults above them. Of all things, Ronoah thought of Kourrania and Hexiphines joking about feeding him to the demon locked in Kourrania's alligator limbs. "Dragon's tits, Hanéong, who *is* that?"

"That," tisked Hanéong, swiping its hand at another giggling gust and nearly getting knocked off-balance for it, "is none other than the Soul of the Most Obstinate Earth." It recovered itself, sweeping its hair back from its face and meeting Ronoah's wide-eyed shock with a look like a garden of hyacinth, bursting with soul-lifting merriment. "It's the Pilgrim State, Ronoah."

Out on the pond, the cranes honked a chorus of ascent. Ronoah heard the splash as they took off, turned his head at the shadows of their wings in the honeyed sky.

Whoops. Secret's out.

Ronoah surprised himself by laughing—a loud, gut-level laugh, bright with the lime-rind of hysteria. He surprised Hanéong, too, who watched him like a cat watches a sandfly, tail twitching, unsure if it wants to pounce or scramble away. Like a friend watches a friend in danger of fainting. Was he going to faint? "Okay," he managed through his chuckling, hiding his face in his hands. He sucked a deep breath through his fingers. "Okay—sure!"

A pulse of power plucked at him, gentle but insistent. Even with his eyes closed, his amplified empathy made it so he could practically see the scrunch of Hanéong's brow. *Sure?*

"What, did you expect me to—what was it—" he pressed his hands to his brow "—to, to dissolve into a puddle of enthusiasm? Completely lose my cool? To yell myself *hoarse* at you for keeping such a good secret so long?"

Deep down, something winked at him. A tiny flame, peeking out true from the ostentation of mirrored gold around it. Not one deity, but two. Genoveffa, waving under the arm of the impostor—the *Pilgrim State*, poking and prodding and messing with, with *him*?

"I am *working up to it*," he said, and as he surfaced from his hands he felt himself grinning so hard his cheeks ached. "Give me two minutes of silent wonder before you go digging for dramatics, you insufferable, *incomparable*—"

He was interrupted by a sound like an earthquake of harps, like a typhoon of violins, a sound like the unfathomable friction at the point where the land met the sky. He yearned toward that sound, seized on it as instinctively as a babe latching to its mother's milk. It was only when he saw Hanéong's slim little shoulders shaking that he realized that was the uncovered sound of its laughing.

"That didn't seem like two minutes," the pseudo-god said, holding its ribcage and hiccupping out another rockslide of mirth. "But you know me and timing."

Ronoah spluttered another laugh of his own, still trying to wrap his mind around this news. Really, it was the same problem as when he first tried to process the enormity of Hanéong itself, long ago: it wasn't that the creature existed, it was that—"She's visiting me day and night. Does she do that with everyone?" Hanéong's snort was answer enough. "Why, then? What's so interesting about me that it's caught the whole Pilgrim State's attention?"

It was one thing to be admired when you were on the road, when you were the sole roving wake in otherwise stagnant water—he could almost understand someone's interest in him as a stalwart pilgrim on a journey. But *everyone* here had been a stalwart pilgrim on a journey at some point. Among the thousand valleys of the Pilgrim State's starry-eyed devotees, there was nothing to set him apart.

Except. "You're forgetting who brought you here." Hanéong drew a hand across its collarbone like a comet, trailing self-satisfaction and something more—genuine pride. Ronoah could not help but hear a voice he tried not to hear often, a waterfall hiss wise as the centuries: *you smell like she does.* Had Hanéong actually rubbed off on Ronoah so much? Was that possible? More importantly, why did it matter here?

"So who is she to *you*? How do you know each other, how—why does she show up how she does in my dreams?" Hanéong raised an eyebrow; Ronoah felt profoundly bizarre asking this question aloud, given its subject was literally in the air he was breathing to ask it. "Why does a landscape bother to take the shape of a woman?"

"Because once upon a time, that's what she was."

Ah, *now* the time for dramatics had arrived. Ronoah felt a heat rise in his scalp even under the shelter of the shrine walls—but Hanéong lifted a hand for silence. No; for patience. "I will answer all your pressing questions, little pilgrim, I swear on Yengh-Sier's favourite pair of dragontails. But I will answer them in an order that makes sense. You must understand—this is not a story I often get to tell."

Ronoah blinked at the shift in atmosphere, the pressure drop, the warmth. He looked at Hanéong, looked with heart as much as eyes, and saw something burgeoning there. A lavender blush young as the dawn, some fathoms-deep fondness twined at the root with pain so gentle he barely felt it slide under his skin.

This was more important than he could understand.

Feeling like everything around them was suddenly blown thin as Pilanovani glass, one careless move from cracking, Ronoah nodded his assent. His friend and fellow stranger offered a smile, the one he'd only ever caught in glimpses, that achingly intimate curve of memory whose appearance in plain sight told Ronoah more than anything else that, at last, he was getting let in on the joke.

"Walk with me," Hanéong said, extending one small dappled hand. In that moment it possessed everything—all of Chashakva's poise, all of Özrek's tender surety, every last fraction of Reilin's unappeased appetite. "Walk with me and I will tell you everything."

So Ronoah took Hanéong's hand, and they walked.

FIFTY-THREE

*T*HE SUN ROSE, THREW TOPAZ LIGHT into the scattering mists of the State. They moved in silence, a thick, electric sort that magnetized them to each other. Vaguely, almost intentionally beyond his notice, Ronoah noted the landscape changing much quicker underfoot than it had in all his wandering so far; the treeline ceded to a carved karst canyon, to a terrace of rainbow eucalyptus, to a stone concourse glistening with petrichor, to another treeline yet. The quarter of doves, the quarter of clover, the great turquoise cenote with its skylights and divinatory divers—they were taking much greater strides, he grasped, than human legs could achieve. Hanéong had a destination in mind, and it seemed even cartography had no say in how quickly the creature got there.

So this was what it was like to move like Hanéong, unencumbered by mortal companions—Ronoah might have recognized this dreamy current from a moment carried half-conscious from a grotto long ago, might have known the taste of its undertow when Chashakva appeared from nowhere to save him from the glade at Sasaupta Falls. He felt on the constant verge of falling. It was wondrous.

The lake where their winged pace slowed to normal was blue like the claws of the lobsters in Ithos, rich and iridescent. Groves of flowering crabapple and dogwood reflected in its surface, strewing the blue with fragrant clouds of pink petals. Ronoah could see the far side, but couldn't judge the distance; islands dotted the intermediary, scrapes and sweeps of grassy gold velour and raised rock faces. He counted no fewer than five water temples scaffolded to the banks, plus a flotilla of ceremonial barges moored a hundred feet offshore. All in all, it was a part of the Pilgrim State like any other—brightly decorated and busily devout, one more facet in the jeweled circlet of worship upon this land's brow.

But he felt the knee-weakening pulse of something deep beneath them that told him this was a lie.

"The first thing you should know," came Hanéong's voice, with the agonizing care of the first incision into an overripe fruit, "is that she had a name. Before she was the Land of a Thousand Temples, she was Raphyanachel."

A flurry of dogwood blossoms overtook them, rushing past like pink minnows in the stream of the sky. Ronoah thought he heard the syllables whispered between the petals. *Raphyanachel.*

"My Yanah," murmured Hanéong, eyes on the glow of the lake. There was a pride to the creature's tone that Ronoah could understand, and a tightness he could not.

"In order to know Yanah—to understand the circumstances under which we met—you must have context. You need a scene set. You need to know," Hanéong said, "about Chamya Bor." A ping against the inside of his skull; Ronoah was sure he'd heard that name before, from Hanéong's mouth no less. For once in his life, he couldn't drag the memory to the surface. "It's a country, a great green tract of land upon which sits the walled city of Soth Tel. In another age, you would have been neighbours." Hanéong picked a rock from their path and tossed it into the lake, watching it skip one two three. "But that age is past, and all the green has vanished from Acharrio, and Soth Tel is in the sea."

Ronoah's heart stopped. The stone dipped into the lake and was gone.

"Soth Tel—Chamya Bor in general—was largely responsible for the shalledrim's failure to take their skirmish further south. The humans who lived there were…different. The borders of Chamya Bor demarcated a particularly powerful energetic field, and they'd spent hundreds of years figuring out how to tap into it for themselves." Ronoah thought of the wishbones in Ol-Penh, those massive crystals and all the providence they exuded. Hanéong must have seen them in Ronoah's mind because they cut him a look like he was being unimaginative. "Far less common than that—and far more difficult to harness. But they studied patiently, and as the generations unfolded, they were rewarded. The citizens of Chamya Bor lived to a hundred and twenty. They relayed messages instantly from one city to another. Their healers could talk an illness out of you as quick as Marghat Yacchatzndra, and they didn't even need their mothers' skulls to do it. They were the only human civilization ever to make the shalledrim think twice. Into this land of secrets and miracles, Raphyanachel was born."

Ronoah could see it, the thick gouache of Hanéong's description covering the canvas of his mind: the girl and the succulent country she grew in, the citadel that stood tall long before Pilanova was so much as a brick in the sand. Before there was sand at all. He stumbled on the path; Hanéong steadied him with a hand squeeze.

"Even among such unique individuals, Yanah was exceptional. Gifted in a way they were not. Her time in Soth Tel belongs to her alone, and so I will not tell you of it—but to say one thing." Creases appeared in the corners of Hanéong's narrowed eyes, fault lines in the slipstrike of amusement and condolence. "Much like you, she felt the double-edged blade of her people's demands. She suffocated under the restrictions placed upon her. Much like you, she chose one day to shuck the shackles and be off, somewhat impulsively, to trace a route north and find her fortunes and return, one day, when she had sufficiently proven herself." A beat of silence, vibrating in the earth below. "She took too long."

"The Shattering," Ronoah breathed. Hanéong squeezed his hand again.

"In a final ironic act of defense, Soth Tel was the southernmost casualty of the great chain reaction that began the Shattering. Perhaps it absorbed the shockwave; perhaps it was just on the outer range. Just unlucky. In any case, the citadel vanished on contact, and the rest of Chamya Bor crumbled into the boiling ocean in the days and weeks thereafter." Hanéong ducked under a low-hanging crabapple branch, petals clinging to their black-and-sunburnt-blond hair. Ronoah looked at the soft arm guiding him along, brown like a long-ago ancestor of Acharrio might have been. *I dress for your memory.* The ghost of Chamya Bor led him on, to a world where its people no longer existed save one.

"Our Raphyanachel was ensconced in the jungle that would one day be known as Shaipuri, planting seeds from her satchel, when it hit. In an instant, the seeds in her hands were all that remained of the country she loved and was caged by. But she had no time to grieve, because the noon sky was already darkening, and the wind already rising to a scream. The world was about to crack in half." Beneath the thin veneer of Hanéong's skin, thunder. "So Chamya Bor's part in her life ends, and mine begins."

Ronoah trembled—unconsciously, instinctively, in awe. Hanéong interlaced its fingers in Ronoah's for one last affectionate pulse before it pulled away, skipping ahead to a promontory facing the lake. As Ronoah caught up he saw Hanéong lift its arms, fingers splayed like a dancer, like a sculptress, like something small about to placate something very, very big. For a second, reality skewed, and he thought he could see the whipping, churning chaos, feel the acid burn of ash in his lungs, the seismic vertigo as the planet threatened to tip into oblivion. When he reached Hanéong, he clung to it—and yelped when a spark surged through him, a magenta-blue dendrite of—of what?

Of panic. Of five-thousand-year-old fear.

"I wasn't sure I could do it, you know," Hanéong said in answer to Ronoah's wordlessness. "Contain the Shattering. As I said, I am a part of this world exactly as you are—I did not know if I had the necessary perspective, the override power, to countermand the end of all things. Maybe if—" The creature stopped itself, shook its head. "I was unprepared," it said, in strangely final tones, and Ronoah knew that some sensitive thing had risen and been repressed in the span of a blink.

"But you did it," Ronoah supplied softly, tearing his eyes away from Hanéong and looking instead at the lake, tranquil and blue and unharmed. "You—you took the rent fabric of this world and you sewed it shut so perfectly."

A subliminal rumble, like the purr of a mountain. "Poet," Hanéong said, nudging Ronoah with a gratitude that made Ronoah lightheaded. "I did what I could. And everything that was still alive to feel me doing it, felt it. The molewhales cowering on the abyssal plains sent songbubbles of encouragement to the surface; the scarabs and stag beetles swarmed in a neverending wave, sacrificing themselves to shield me with their hardened shells. And somewhere in what had only just become North Berena, Raphyanachel felt a tug, and decided that, if she survived, she would hunt it to its source.

"It took a while—namely because you need a very long nap after achieving the impossible. I was asleep for the first, oh, two hundred years while the planet scabbed over its wounds? Roused myself once or twice to check in, didn't want to miss anything important, but all in all I did not make myself easy to find."

Ronoah could see it now: Hanéong curled like an old guard dog in some primeval forest, some ancient cave, sparing a baleful one-eyed glare and a warning growl for only the most serious mischief-makers and otherwise letting it be. For two hundred years.

Sometimes small numbers hit harder than large ones, being as they are just inside the cusp of comprehension. Where *five thousand years* had never quite percolated through Ronoah's intellectual filter into gut-level understanding, he could grasp *two hundred* just fine—and it chilled him in a way all the other more grandiose perspective shifts never had. He got nervous when Hanéong slept for a week, but it was possible for Ronoah to live a full life three times over and still not be alive for when this creature tumbled out of bed.

"What happened when she finally found you?" He sounded a bit scrambling even to his own ears, but he couldn't help it. It had finally bloomed, the full understanding of just how lucky he and Hanéong were to have met at all. How stupendously high the odds were against it. How little time, in the grand scheme of things, they had left. His throat went tight at the thought of that cosmic countdown, but still he forced out, "What did she—how did she react?"

He didn't quite get the story he expected.

"Oh, she tried to kill me for a year or two."

Ronoah squawked, bewildered right out of his angst; Hanéong laughed and turned back to the lakeside trail, motioning for Ronoah to follow. "Perhaps that's too simplistic a term. Have you ever felt so intensely about something that your instinct is to tear it to pieces? Such a forceful pull that you want to crush it right into you?"

Hanéong glanced overshoulder at Ronoah, who felt his ears go warm. Of course he had. They both remembered that day in Poh Nui's lighthouse.

"Imagine: you come from a land with a special *something* permeating every pore of soil. It glitters in your water, it crystallizes in your hills, it's spread thin and even across hundreds and hundreds of square miles. For you, that something says *home*. It disappears from the earth for two centuries—and then you come across that same energy, a whole country's worth of it and more, compressed into a space the size of an average human being. You'd throw yourself at it without a second thought. You'd try to eat it alive to keep it from slipping away again." Another chuckle escaped Hanéong, trailing the sounds of ocean surf behind it. "Of course, she was about as dangerous to me as a fox pup to its mother, but I played the game. I don't think anyone before or after has so persistently tried to annihilate me; you cannot understand how completely delightful it was."

Indeed, Ronoah could not. But he could try. When you were five thousand—*more* than five thousand years old, gods, who knew how old it really was—and powerful enough to put the apocalypse on hold, strange things would tickle your fancy.

It was in the midst of this musing about age that his calculus kicked in.

"Hold on," he breathed, and then—"Hold on, you were asleep for two hundred years and *then* Raphyanachel found you?"

"You can call her Yanah," was Hanéong's reply. "She much prefers it."

But he couldn't, not right now, because even her name was a clue, was a giveaway, a function in the equation heating up his brain. One hundred and twenty, that was the lifespan of people from Chamya Bor, and Raphyanachel—Yanah—had lived at least part of a life before the Shattering even happened, which put her at least a hundred years over-estimate, which—

Something else clicked then. Fit into place with the electric snap of a lightning room, the hundred approving hums of an echo chamber.

Ronoah stopped walking. Sank his awareness into the air around him, felt that fizzling transference of energy, that giddy creativity he had come to associate with the Pilgrim State—and imagined minimizing it. Down to, say, the size of a room. The size of a cavern. Stupid, stupid—he'd been thrown off by the sheer size of it, misled by its mythos, but the tingle on his tongue was too familiar to ignore. This place—Yanah, *Raphyanachel*—

"She's a shalledra," Ronoah said, and the surface of the lake positively shivered. "The Pilgrim State is a shalledra."

Absurdly, Hanéong actually sighed.

"She was," it replied without turning around. "But don't let that stop you from enjoying the view."

It had nearly disappeared into the thicket before Ronoah's feet unlocked from the earth and he tripped forward. He laid his hands on the scales of the dogwood trunks to steady himself, stepping into the waving bleeding-heart of Hanéong's wake and emerging on the lawn of a temple. He hop-skipped the stones of the water garden, watching fish the length of his forearm flash by, and joined Hanéong on the far side.

"You must understand," Hanéong began before Ronoah could open his mouth, "Yanah is from a time before the Shattering—before the hunts, before human interbreeding, before all of it. In comparison to the shalledrim you know, she is a completely different species." It pursed its lips, eyes on the pair of waxwings braiding their way through the eaves. "The ancient shalledrim weren't even a species at all; rather, each one comprised a species unto itself, each beholden to a unique set of esoteric senses, each bequeathed a unique understanding of the Universe."

"Sort of like you?" Ronoah ventured. Hanéong grimaced in distaste.

"Not even remotely. If only they were." The creature shook its head at Ronoah's probing frown. "The point is that calling her a shalledra means only as much in those days as calling her a person would. Less, perhaps, in her case, given she was raised among human civilization. She may have been born from a former brigadier general of the great war—" Ronoah's heart jumped "—but she lived in Soth Tel, a society whose ideology surrounded something other than her own existence, and it seeped in and changed her. Thank goodness it did," Hanéong snickered, "or I'd've found her dreadfully uninteresting."

A splash and a volley of droplets made Ronoah yelp; one of the bigger fish in the garden had leapt up to flick water at Hanéong. The child looked disparagingly back at the pond, where the culprit blew bubbles from beneath the surface. A corner of Hanéong's mouth turned up.

"The time to tell you of Yanah as a shalledra will come," it said, turning to the flagstone walkway winding down the temple to a lakeside promenade. "For now, let me tell you of Yanah as a reckless, impetuous, imperiously stubborn woman."

Hanéong unfurled their sprawling dalliance for Ronoah while walking the promenade, the inhale and exhale of water audible under the boardwalk, the lungs of the lake working just beneath their feet. One myth after another, as grandiose as Hanéong ever told them, and yet all of them achingly intimate, beautifully light. Tales of building and burning North Berena, tales of inventing potion and poison, tales of fifty years alone together in the deepwood, doing nothing but listening to the trees. Hanéong's old penchant for competitions, for bets, back in a day when there was one who stood a chance as an opponent; Yanah's shalledrim power to fuse and synthesize substances into strange new alloys, whetted and directed by a force with more experience, more control. They raised armies and fed each other pomegranates and sought the secret portals of the world together, they bled monsters for coin and taught chemistry to ka-Khasta and danced and danced and danced. Ronoah let the stories wash over him like he was walking into the water, like the long streak of cerulean was closing over his head and depositing him in another world.

He was so entranced by it all that he nearly ran into Hanéong when the creature stopped.

"We're here." It caught Ronoah by the waist, turning him to face the lake. The vista looked completely different from this angle—different temples, different islands. "Say hello."

Ronoah didn't know what he was greeting, but he did it anyway, the words tumbling out of his mouth in timid Acharrioni. A flock of birds, too far away to identify, took off from an island. Something swelled up and spilled over from Hanéong, powerful enough to sting Ronoah's eyes with inexplicable tears.

"As you know by now," the creature said beside him, "Yanah and I made history whenever we could get our hands dirty in it. We caused as many problems as we fixed. We tried everything, in excess, in delight—but there is one thing we only ever did once." The sheen of its words hung on those seconds of silence like oil on water. "We had a child."

Ronoah glanced down at Hanéong. For all its apparent youth, the look on its face was timeless. Undying.

"Did you," he asked, after clearing his throat to dislodge the lump.

"Not a child of our own bodies, that would have been a disaster, we agreed from the start. A human child. We took one, or found one—don't ask me which it was, or where or who from, because it doesn't matter. He certainly didn't know; we told him something different every time he asked, a new origin story for him to toy with, to teethe on." Hanéong tilted its head, eyes roving the lake. "I think in the end we fooled ourselves into believing each other's legends, just as much as he did. One more reason the scholars can't agree on anything."

"What legends? What—scholars?" Even though he'd barely spoken all morning, Ronoah still felt short of breath. The almost-panic of a great secret made him nearly nauseous with instinct, with intuition. "Who was he?"

Hanéong drew in a breath, as if savouring the taste of everything in this moment. The long ached-for sweetness of saying these words. "You know that book we've been reading," it said, and it was so *not* what Ronoah was expecting that it made him blink hard as his hand went automatically to his empty hip searching for the weight of that tome, for the words inside it that would illuminate this clue: stories on stories about a young prophet caught between worlds, about a boy touched by magic who set himself loose on the world, trying and playing and sometimes failing, sometimes needing rescuing by—

"No." It came out of him hushed as moss, airless as the dream at the bottom of the world. "Hanéong, you—no."

"Yes." Hanéong's smile was apologetic, indestructible. "I promise we didn't try to make him a prophet. That happened all on its own."

Not a prophet. *The* Prophet. The original Chainbreaker, the bane of the ancient shalledrim, the saviour of North Berena. Ronoah had seen Hanéong in Chapter Eight—but he'd been looking the wrong way. He'd assumed incorrectly. Hanéong wasn't the dreamwalker.

It was Evin's father.

The creature could have told him it was also Genoveffa's aunt and he would have been less staggered. Gods—the *irony* of it. Like the monastery, the classic, Chiropolene irony. The so-called liberator of humanity from the shalledrim called a shalledra mother. The shalledra who had become the Soul of the Human Earth.

What were they standing on, exactly?

"Tell me," he heard himself say. He still felt underwater, but now suddenly he'd grown gills, could process what filtered through his system. He wanted to know. "Tell me about Evin."

And Hanéong obliged him, with a strange and buoyant urgency that thrilled in Ronoah's open heart. "We knew there was something odd about him from the start. Perhaps that's why we chose him—wouldn't that be typical of us, to claim such godly foresight. More likely we were lucky, or else being around us changed him, sprouted some seed in him that lies dormant in all of you." A soft sound, a scoff, incomparably fond. "Prophet or not, he had a knack, Ronoah. A way with the curtain between worlds, a sight for everything that lies unseen between the trees, beneath the river. Demons roamed the rattled earth aplenty in those days, and he reached his pudgy baby hands out to all of them. Nearly got them bit off at the wrists for it, I don't know how many times." A pinch on his wrist—Ronoah jumped, yelled, and Hanéong withdrew its hand, wiggling its fingers and grinning. "Sensitive child."

Ronoah regained his footing, hand cradled to his chest, exasperated glare firmly in place. He had no idea who Hanéong was referring to, him or Evin—

I think you very well could learn the art of interfacing with that affective plane. It has happened before.

—and he felt his face go slack as, for one blazing uncanny instant, he saw himself outside his own viewpoint. What he represented; what he resembled. Reminded of.

How long?

How long had it been—since the jungle? since the caves?—since Hanéong had decided to liken the two of them? Since this shrewd, amused, *nostalgic* force of nature had judged the new note of Ronoah Genoveffa Elizzi-denna Pilanovani against the old melody of its son, its son the Prophet Evin, and found that the two of them matched? Or—complemented. Activated each other, made each other ring, the way the right whistle pitch could bring the Chiropolene arch to life.

The Scybene play came back to him then. His birthday present, sitting side by side with this creature watching the heavily-edited legend of its child on stage. Facing Dephnos—facing Evin—across a pit of oblivion, an impossible divide, without knowing who he was really looking at, or what they meant to each other. What they both meant to Hanéong.

I need him more than you do.

There was no adequate response for that kind of appreciation, that kind of sea-deep care. It left him completely at a loss. Luckily, Hanéong didn't give him time to try. "To answer your original question," the creature said, hands on its hips as it surveyed the water like it was reading the sun glitter off the waves, "this is why Yanah keeps sticking her gold-tipped nose in your business. She likes you. She likes you like I do, like Evin would." An expression surfaced on its face, a familiar look—so very close, so very far away. "The mayhem you two would have caused—he would have got you into trouble, you would have got him out of it. You would have made excellent friends."

Vespasi wake, the pain. The *pull* he felt, like every bone was bending toward something—it was so tender it made Ronoah want to scream, roused some primal infant urge to rake at the wind and stomp on the boardwalk until his sandals frayed to shreds. To have a tantrum like the Maelstrom, ornery, demanding, until whatever was sitting so *wrong* was forced right, until all the wreckage was concealed beneath the waves. For once, he had no trouble identifying the emotions his porous spirit was absorbing, no problem labelling the face Hanéong was making. It was the same as Sophrastus, on a blue hill long ago.

It was love. The great plains of love, and the prairie fire of loss.

"Why did you only have one child?" he asked. He knew the answer before it came.

"Because life is biterminal: having begun, it ends. Is it not the human way, that parents should be spared the entombment of their children?" A current of scorn. A current of sympathy. Its voice was soft as the lullaby sands where his ancestors' bones were bundled. "When we took him back, when it was over—because humanity's needfulness had taken so much of him from us, from himself, right to the end—when we'd laid him in the ground and our arms were still smeared to the elbow with dirt, Yanah ordered through her tears that we never try anything like it again. I understood her horror. I obliged her. We let the House of Evin sprawl untended, found other adventures to claim our attention, to soften our heartache. We walked away."

Hanéong bent one knee to the boards, passed a palm across the lapping water like a lover's hair. "It never worked," it murmured. "Not completely. Of all our achievements, all our perfect crimes, Evin was Yanah's favourite—even though he never knew as much, and she herself only discovered it long after their time together had ended. So when her own time came, some five or six hundred years later, to choose her place to die, we came back to him."

This was something Ronoah knew about; it fluttered at the edge of his mind like a scrap of paper, a flyleaf lifted by the breeze. In the old days, said the logs, before the hunts cut so many shalledrim lifespans short, those elegant predators held an innate sense of their own mortality. When they felt it rising to meet them, they left their home—Empire, colony, solitary haunt—and began a pilgrimage of their own: a death walk, a procession of one, ending in whichever place they chose to contain the passionflower bloom of their blast radius.

Contrary to the last, Raphyanachel did not take this journey alone. "We walked—no magic, no cheating, just one foot in front of the other—down the ka-Khastan Alps to this land of lakes and maple, where our family hut once crouched among the moss, where we buried our son in the garden. We discussed her last wishes on the way—mostly she demanded things of me, in true Yanah style." Hanéong chuckled, reverent and irreverent and proud. "What demands she made. *One more novelty*, she said. One last bet. Don't you want to try something you've never tried before?"

Ronoah could have sworn its voice trembled.

"You've never seen so much ambition. If anyone in this world is unduly weak-willed, it's because she stole their fair share and hoarded it for herself. She reclined in the bower above our child, among the bleeding-heart and blueberry, and tried something she had never tried before, which was apologize." Ronoah's throat went tight; prickling pressure built between his brows. Hanéong rose from its crouch, wiping the water on its cheek. A mimicry of tears. "Then she died, and it was my turn for trying. I took everything that she was, everything that was escaping her, and *fixed it in place*. I grabbed that tumultuous unifying power of hers and I anchored it to the land, stitched it into the gossamer floating between worlds. You know the pent-up energy of a shalledra leaves an imprint once released from the confines of the body, but the shalledra itself—its essence, its personality—that dissipates, embarks on a journey back to the source it came from. It goes against everything nature intended to lash the two back together in death, but Yanah wasn't done with the world and I wasn't done with her, and so—we tried. We planted her like she had planted so much else. We never knew it would yield something so marvelous." Hanéong turned to Ronoah. Behind it, another cascade of dogwood petals blew across the water. "This is how the Pilgrim State was made; this is where it started. This lake, the crater of her grave. That island, there—that island, the garden where I stood."

Ronoah followed the arc of Hanéong's arm, laid eyes on the island. Evin was in that ground. In those trees, grown so wizened and gnarled now. In the bellies of the waxwings who ate from the blueberries. After nearly five thousand years, Evin *was* that island; Ronoah was laying eyes on the Prophet himself, cradled for eternity in the golden arms of his mother.

From this family plot, the greatest wonder of the human world stretched its tendrils. He understood now. The temples, the shrines, they weren't part of the Pilgrim State—they were *tributes* to it. Byproducts of what the Pilgrim State really was, which was raw connective power—Yanah's power—and the unstoppable urge to create something with it. To commune with something larger than the self.

"Chamya Bor." Hanéong cocked its head, and Ronoah realized he'd spoken aloud. He cleared the smoke from his throat and repeated, a little shy: "Chamya Bor. You said—that place, that land, it was marked by magic, by energy in the water and the hills and—you brought it back, or something like it. Like Yanah's seeds, like a transplant—you repotted that energy here. This ..." He turned a slow semi-circle, facing the temple at the lakeshore, the thousand more that lay beyond the trees. He lifted his hands, gently outstretched. "It's New Chamya Bor."

Between his hands something invisible nudged him, like an enormous lioness butting her head into his palms. His fingers curled on reflex.

"It was never mine to name," came Hanéong's voice behind him, "but if the opportunity had presented itself, that might have been my choice, too."

Ronoah felt a pair of arms encircle his waist, felt the slight weight of a forehead pressed to his back. A sigh that ruffled the lake beneath the boardwalk. A contentment as quiet as the first clear sky after the Shattering.

It makes it real again. It makes it mine. Even pseudo-gods were not immune to the loneliness of secretkeeping. Even forces of nature needed, once every hundred or thousand years, to tell a story.

Ronoah tried and failed to take it in stride, to find a response. Tried and failed to do anything but bask in glorious overwhelm, in the speechless afterglow of Truth patting the cushion beside her and asking him to tea. After so many gauntlets run, at last, she approved.

They stood together like that for a minute or an hour—it was impossible to tell. He had questions, he knew he did, but his soul was refusing further input, already full to the brim. Enough, it said. For now, this is enough.

But he was a fool, and ever in thrall to curiosity, and so he asked just one more.

FIFTY-FOUR

*I*T SEEMED LIKE AN INNOCENT QUESTION TO ASK, was the thing. It seemed improper *not* to ask it after everything he'd just heard. So, as delicately as he could, "Is this why you've been acting so strange? Because the Pilgrim State—because Yanah and Evin—this is difficult for you, isn't it? Being here."

The creature behind him let out a sharp exhale of a laugh, nuzzling its face into his back. "It is difficult, little one, but not in the way you're thinking. Sentiment isn't distracting me; exertion is."

Frowning, Ronoah squeezed Hanéong's arm between his elbow and his ribs, prodding it to elaborate. It took a long moment to consider its words. Ronoah swore he felt it set its feet, preparing.

"By force of will alone I planted what became the Pilgrim State—for all its beauty, it is an aberration. Whenever I return, it is by force of will alone that I refrain from pulling it free again. Now our situations are reversed, and it's my turn to want to eat her alive—loosely speaking." Hanéong shrugged its shoulders against Ronoah's sides. "As long as I don't, the Pilgrim State survives."

"You—!" Sharp pain bloomed along the inside of Ronoah's cheek, where he'd bit by accident. A moment later, blood. "You, you can *end* the Pilgrim State?" Silence; affirmative. "Wh—chuta ka saag, *how?* Why? Why do you want to—eat her?"

Hanéong inhaled. "Time's come," it said, mostly to itself, Ronoah thought. "Yanah is so many things to me. She is a wife and an enemy and an accomplice and a dear, dear friend, but in the cold and all-knowing joke of the Universe, she is a shalledra." A midnight silence, in full golden noon. "Which makes her a daughter, too."

That was when Ronoah's overstuffed mind tipped into dizzying light-headedness, into a woozy headrush like trying to stand up after one too many shots of rose liqueur with Ean-Bei. That was when his grip on himself slipped. His ego surrendered to pure molten processing power; for an instant, his consciousness' only purpose was to ransack the halls of memory for supporting evidence, for clues too long hidden, for the dozens and hundreds of ways Hanéong had said all along, had said without saying—

I don't like any of my children enough to let them actually succeed me.

"She's your …they *all* are," Ronoah said dazedly, because it was true, it wasn't just Yanah. Hanéong had made it explicit, she was a daughter *because* she was a shalledra, which meant it claimed the category as a whole, which— "The shalledrim—come from you?"

Hanéong's grip had gone slack. Ronoah stumbled around to face the child. It was looking across the lake, some unknown jumble of feeling trapped up in the fine creases by its eyes. "Indeed they do."

Ronoah stared at it, completely blank. Mounting pressure knocked on his chest for attention: he was forgetting to breathe. He choked on his inhale, coughing, and saw Hanéong's brows scrunch in one quick motion—the closest thing to a flinch he'd ever seen, *oh*, oh gods, that's what it was, Hanéong was *bracing*. Readying itself for Ronoah's judgement, because Ronoah was a human being and Hanéong was the originator of— "Have I said lately how much of an idiot I am?"

Hanéong wasn't expecting that. The creature forgot in its haste to express its reaction through words or body language; its perplexed attention just switchbacked and crashed into Ronoah like a dust squall. The force of it punched another breath from Ronoah, left the taste of mint in his mouth, tingling on his hard palate. "I should have—I should have seen this coming. It's obvious. It's obvious! You're—if you think you're hiding it, you're sort of not? Listen to you long enough and you say all kinds of incriminating things. Of course they come from you. Of course."

Hanéong opened its mouth—and then closed it again, taken aback. "Not everyone gets to *listen to me long enough*, little pilgrim," it eventually replied, like it had no idea what to do with him. "Not everyone follows me around recording every pithy thing out of my mouth and stashing it away in the perfectly-indexed library of their mind."

"I haven't been *following* you," Ronoah countered, "we're travel companions—we're fellow strangers."

Hanéong looked at him with such open disbelief that Ronoah realized belatedly he was responding very much besides the point. Then, beautifully, wonderfully—a smile, so wide it was silly, helplessly frustrated, helplessly in love.

"You fucking pedant," Hanéong said, with all the reverence it reserved for the great wonders of the world. "You will split hairs until the death of the Universe, won't you?"

Laughter overcame Ronoah. It left him winded, left dancing spots in his vision. The soles of his feet were prickling; the boardwalk felt like it was shifting with the lake. "You're the one who taught me over and over that the words you use matter, Ōzrek."

Recognition dawned on Hanéong's face. "Ah, now I see. You're in shock."

"And so what if I am," Ronoah retorted, and oh his voice *was* climbing higher wasn't it— "You just told me you *made* the shalledrim. Now I need to rethink every time we've ever talked about them, ever, I need to—" A glitter of apprehension under Hanéong's skin. Did it regret telling him? Was it reconsidering his capacity as an audience? Vespasi wake, it wasn't going to end the story *there*, was it? "I need to know *how*, you have to tell me the rest, I'll never sleep again if I don't find out, I won't, Hanéong, come *on*—"

Hanéong considered his increasingly giddy pleading. It was a bad idea, they both knew it—his fragile, hyperaroused human mind was already soaked in excess information, drunk off the revelations of Yanah and Evin and the Pilgrim State, and now this had come and set him completely on his side. He was overloaded; he was overwhelmed.

But what a *delicious* overwhelm. What an intensity, what a way to feel. Was he ever going to hold this much again? He felt as young as Hanéong looked, a child goading another into a risky game. Come on, he dared silently, through the empathic current between them—play with me here. Try something we haven't tried before.

Curiosity was Hanéong's biggest weakness, and Ronoah exploited it shamelessly, selfishly. And it worked—charmed by its overambitious friend and the desperate grin on his face, Hanéong finally discarded its restraint.

"I didn't make them alone," the creature started, low and slow, the glint of the game kindling in its eye. "They come from me, but they come from you, too. At least, from one of you, long ago."

Ronoah covered his mouth, ever the demonstrative listener. "We—?"

Hanéong inclined its head, pinned Ronoah with its sly black eye. "I told you that Yanah and I ruled out conceiving a child. But we were a pair of wicked little mavericks, and nothing ought to have got in the way of trying whatever we wanted. Nothing except a very good reason. Nothing except precedent. As of this century, the prevailing idea about the shalledrim seems to be that they came before you people—but the truth is, you precede them by tens of thousands of years. First me, then you. Then the shalledrim, volatile merger of the two.

"In the early days, when I wasn't yet used to being the only one of me, I befriended a human companion. That word is bereft of the heft it needs, the richness, the depth—I orbited them like a luminary, attuned myself to their rhythms and moods like a jellyfish to the oceanflow. They endured my youth, my ignorance, my insult and folly as I learned how to mirror your kind. They took me for a deity; they took my strangeness in stride, and I found them an inexhaustible source of wonder. They're the one who gave me this."

Hanéong hovered its hand over its heart. The tattoo. That dark crescent that never faded no matter how many bodies the creature sloughed away—that mark was human in origin. It had come from Ronoah's ancestors.

"Eventually, they wanted to bear something of mine, too." Hanéong's eyes narrowed in wistful relish. "Ink on skin wasn't enough for them. So we tried to procreate. I wasn't quite sure *how*, at first—we're not even close to the same sort of thing, it wasn't going to happen without a lot of tinkering—but they were determined, and I was curious. Eventually, I even let myself be invested. And then it worked, and a living thing was coming up to us, unfurling like a fern shoot in the womb. We were ecstatic. We couldn't wait to welcome it into the world.

"Of course, the very first thing the very first shalledra ever did was rupture the living cradle that had borne her." Ronoah's breath hitched; Hanéong gave him a weary, appreciative grin. "What did you expect? For everything to just work itself out, like we expected? No—not expected. Insisted. We'd simply allowed no room in our minds for an experiment to succeed and fail in the same breath that way. But it did, and she was born bright as magma, and likewise she burned her bearer—and the valley—to ashes. I held that tiny squalling star in my arms, surrounded on all sides by dead land, and what could I do but raise her? What could I do," the creature said musingly, foreboding lifting from its slim frame like sulfur, "but try again?"

It swayed Ronoah in its wake, the cruelty of it, the calculation. "Even though…?"

"Even so. I was young then, and lethal. Still volcanic with anger about my aloneness—that first magmic daughter was a simple stone in the explosion that was looking for a way out of me. I wanted family again. I tried to will one into existence." A cataclysm of colours flashed under its skin, a rainbow of regrets, a cataract of memories of the first shalledrim to walk the earth and their celestial, grieving parent. "It didn't much work how I'd've liked it to."

One star swanned brighter than the rest, miniscule nova circling the corner of Hanéong's jaw. It bobbed and spun through Hanéong's armature, to the palm of its outstretched hand. "That unique understanding of the Universe which empowers a shalledra—that comes from me. Bazzenine's voids; Jesprechel's insubstantiations. Raphyanachel's living forge. Each of these, one star of the vast galaxy of my knowing, bestowed. That energy, it's on loan—and the energy knows so, even if the shalledra doesn't. It knows where it came from, as you know you came from Genoveffa. And, as you anticipate upon your own passing, once that energy is no longer bound to the physical plane, it races back to its source." The star fizzed, flared, faded as Hanéong gestured at the golden land around them. "Most of the time. Exceptions are made, once in a while. But on the whole, I feel it every time a shalledra dies, because the fragment that made it what it is returns to me. That's why the Pilgrim State and I strain towards one another—because she belongs in my body. Because she is a piece of me."

It was only at this reminder of bodies that Ronoah remembered he had one. He felt weightless, dissolved—it was like a fever dream, so heady, so intense. None of this is real, part of him said absently; it can't be, it's too old, it's from a time that doesn't even exist. An equally significant part of him was so lost in the story it had all but forgotten he wasn't right there alongside Hanéong as the shalledrim burst to life. His heart was racing, his head was swimming—but it wasn't unpleasant. He could barely think straight but it didn't matter because Hanéong was sort of thinking for him, the creature's story pouring fulsome into his mind. It felt like he was being hand-fed morsels of the ripest most decadent food, leaving him equally nauseous and wanting. His own individuality was an afterthought.

"How did you do it?" he breathed. "You can't—can you? We're not compatible, are we?"

Hanéong huffed a laugh. "No, we are not. I tried to figure out how to do it your way—made considerable progress understanding your anatomy in the process, let me tell you—but my companion's monthly blood came nonetheless. No, in the end we did things a little closer to…my way."

It paused, dangling temptation. It knew full-well that Ronoah's impatience was undoing him, that he was fully seduced by this secret now. A fervent whine escaped Ronoah's teeth and Hanéong grinned, obliging.

"It was the symbolism of things, more than the science, that gave me the idea. When two of your kind—two of most kind, really—put together the ingredients to procreate, those ingredients talk to each other, make decisions together about what kind of walrus or mountain lion or Acharrioni they're going to cook. Each brings a bit of their source to the table, and they negotiate how those sources blend. So I bypassed the mechanics entirely and just talked to the egg myself. How, you ask?" Hanéong met his eyes and it was like every bell in the Pilgrim State a-pealing, every tender shoot in the earth unfurling its first leaf. "I told it my name."

Ronoah parted his lips, couldn't find anything to say. "Sorry, you—you told it—"

"My name. Not any moniker stripped or given from humankind, little

one. My *name*. The one from before. The one from the very beginning."
Hanéong—the thing conveniently known as Hanéong—planted a look
in him that bloomed like a whole meadow of lotus, smug and sweet and
secret. "There *is* some truth to summoning by speaking, after all—though
your people shouldn't worry so much about it, human language doesn't
work the same way. That name contains everything I have been and will
be; we transfigure in symmetry. I spoke it to the egg, brought a cosmic
pantry's worth of ingredients to the table, and she took what she liked.
It's why all shalledrim are different, even the children of shalledrim, and
their grandchildren: because the magic in them is endlessly recombinant.
And it's why they are all the same—because they are shards of the same
thing, and that thing is me."

Only one question mattered in the world, the only thing he needed
to learn ever again: "What's the name?"

Hanéong raised one eyebrow and Ronoah thought *it's going to tell me no,
it's going to keep this secret* and nearly succumbed to pleading again—but
then it said something that stopped him in his tracks: "You almost said
it once." In the stunned silence that followed, the child brought a hand
to its chin, musing. "Somehow."

Once…before? Ronoah's brow quirked, confused, and some secret
rustled deep within him, a flicker of light in the woods, a feeling like running
on water—but it ducked away before he could catch it, and Hanéong only
shrugged and let its hand drop, apparently settled on the matter.

"Why not," it said, to Ronoah and to itself and to Yanah and to the
whole sparkling spiralling world. "We've come this far. If you want to
know, Ronoah Genoveffa Elizzi-denna Pilanovani, then I'll tell you."

Ronoah wanted with every god-given cell of his body to know. He
yearned for it like he yearned for air and sunlight and life. He wanted it
like it was his job to know, like it was his destiny.

So without a fuss, it told him.

That name was not a sound, although the creature's mouth moved
and a sound came out. It was smell and colour and texture too, a ballistic
bouquet of impressionistic language. It was the endlessly recessing chambers of a nautilus shell, linden layered on clary sage layered on molten
syrupy amber, sunshowers and gunpowder and glee, all floating in a bath
of static hiss like a pentatonic sandstorm, a marbled blinding of sapphire
and magenta and bright alveolar hum. To hear it was wicked innocence,
pleasure and impetus, the moment before the heist began; to say it back
was mouthwatering promise, trickster's luck, infamy infamy infamy, the
very first newborn's very first gurgling laugh blown wide across eternity.

Ronoah couldn't resist. He opened his heart. He opened his mouth.

"—?" he tried.

The self-satisfied look on his friend's face vanished, replaced by slack surprise. "That's—very close. Closer than last time even, how are you managing that—?"

But *close* wasn't good enough, Ronoah couldn't stop at close, he wanted to get it *right*—especially because even saying it wrong felt amazing, felt like conducting lightning. He dug deeper, pulled it together, tried again—

And *saw* the creature twitch, not in body but in spirit, a reorientation towards his calling like a helichrysum turning grudgingly to the sun. "You can stop, I'm right here," it answered as it took his hand between its own, sounding nearly agitated, and Ronoah knew that this name could and would call this being from across a continent, across the world even, it wouldn't be able to ignore the summons because this was what summoning by speaking *meant*, because the name *was* the creature and saying it in a place where the thing itself *wasn't* simply defied the laws of physics.

But he still didn't have it quite right.

Almost, *almost.* And he didn't know if he'd ever get it this close again, didn't know if this was a once-in-a-lifetime chance, between his own power primed and hungry and Yanah's collaborative magic in the air and this creature's energetic defenses down—he might never get a better shot to learn the thing that could always call his friend back to him, *now or never, little empath*, so he slashed open another conduit between them, let the walls around his spirit splash to nothing, sluiced a whiplash of effort through the channel of their clasped hands and *articulated*—

And something popped, static shock, between their hands.

The creature yelped, letting go of Ronoah so fast one of his fingers sprained. Hands balled into fists at its sides, it—froze, staring with something akin to horror at Ronoah's hand.

Ronoah followed its astounded gaze just in time to see something blue-bleached and flickering, some tinnitic light dodging under his fingernail and darting like a dolphin up the gulf stream of his veins. It dipped beneath his tissue and was gone.

You called?

He had about ten seconds where they looked at his arm and each other—a sound started like crystal ringing, small but then swelling, a ringing report like a bell in reverse, sticking to his inner ear like sickness, like honey—before his knees gave out and his friend lunged to catch him with a loud and disparaging *fuck* and a laugh came out of Ronoah that did not feel fully his own, a weird and worldshaking thing that slammed him with more endorphins than all the nuam leaf in Khepsuong Phae.

And then he passed out.

*N*EBULAE SPREAD AROUND HIM, rippling, reactive. Different colours than usual—ochre, umber, ultramarine. Vermillion harsh as epiphany. Only one whistling comet trailed the aqua blue plumage he'd come to expect.

"Trust you to make the kind of rash decision that changes everything. Nice one."

It came from everywhere and nowhere, from every pore of negative space in the emberous membrane of firelight. Ronoah frowned. Had speaking the name transported him somewhere? Had it—gods, had it killed him? Was he dead?

Laughter shivered through the airwaves. "*Now* you start to worry about it? Still don't have much of a self-preservation instinct, do you?" Ronoah prickled, and it backtracked. "Not dead, no—far from it. But still. Yank the raw creative force of the Universe into your gooey mortal body, what did you think was going to happen? Good thing you're pliant, or we'd be in trouble."

"If it was that dangerous to say," he said, somewhat petulantly, "you shouldn't have told it to me. You should have known I'd try it back."

This laughter was tangible, slipped deliciously warm over his senses. "Who exactly do you think you're talking to?"

Before he could ask, Ronoah knew.

He knew the same way he knew what was really in Ol-Penh's ancient underground library, knew how to get from here to there in an instant— the folding points, the crinkles in the cloth of the Universe, the secret knock it took to get the door to open, to get all doors to open—the same way he understood the mysteries of his empathy, its origins, with pure and simple clarity, understood how all things really *did* happen in threes and in fives, especially when they pretended otherwise. The location of every shalledra that was still out there now, the profile of each and every one of their magics, the trick to literally making lemons from lychees—all of it, everything, he got it all. He knew what Acharrio tasted like before the Shattering charred the flavour, and he knew all eighteen tribal dialects of Shaipuri, and he knew who he faced in this place that was not a place but a perspective, but a soul.

"Now you're getting a hold of it," grinned the latest brick in the behavioural castle. "But don't be mad when you lose it all again. We've got some furniture to move around before we settle on a floorplan."

The thing that was and was not Ronoah breathed out, and as if they had all along been two parts of one organism, Ronoah breathed in. Circling each other, reciprocal already.

"Sometimes my lady's shining *and sometimes she's glowering grey*
sometimes she tantrums whitecaps and sometimes she's still as day
my lady be a changing one and changing she remain, but
I love her for the changing and she loves me just the—hey. You're awake."

Tycho leaned into view, peering down at him. Above her head, her
hurricane of a halo fluttered peach and pink, theatregoing gods elbowing for the best seat in the mezzanine of her mind's eye. Ronoah parted
parched lips to speak:

"That's a Chiropolene seasong," he croaked before anything else could
come out. "A shanty for keeping time."

"You bet." She smiled brightly, untucked her legs and hugged them
to her chest. "Feris brought it from the coast and Sophrastus taught us
all on harmonies."

"You sing it beautifully. Are you keeping time for something?"

Tycho shook her head, tinkling the tiny chimes of her hairpiece.
"Passing it. I told Ybh I'd watch you for a minute while he got dressed."

"People keep singing me awake," Ronoah commented with a winded
little huff. "I don't know how I earned such generous minders." Like
Nazum. Nazum Vashnarajandra, Beloved of Shaipuri, who even now was
leading the longboats down the Chasauga River, casting purifying spice
into the water, singing the opening verses of—wait, what verse? Nazum
was—what?

"What was ..." Ronoah sat up, scouting the sky, the pond, the half-fin-
ished shade of Genoveffa's shrine, settled on Tycho's patient face. "Awake.
Awake from *what*," he said slowly, his tone flattened by confusion. "What
am I—why am I here?"

He knew where he'd *been*, moments ago. The boardwalk, the lake, the
dogwoods and crabapples and their petals like sparks, the island and

547

Hanéong, and Hanéong's—that story, that *name*, that transcendence of smells and syllables and melody that started with—started, how did it start, no, no no *no*—

He had it, and then just like that, he lost it.

"Here." Ronoah lifted his face from his hands to see Tycho holding out a mug. "You look like you need it."

The water sloshed darkly as he accepted it. She was right, he did need it, so badly that every other thought retreated. He tried not to drain the mug all at once, but gods, the flowing sensation over his tongue was like the first sip of Pilgrim State water he'd ever had, like the first drink of Pilanova's oasis even, the first drops of water ever to land on his infant tongue. Was he that dehydrated? How long had he been under for? The light said it was late afternoon, but the cloud patterns, the wind, it said— "Is it tomorrow?" Ronoah asked, turning desperately puzzled eyes on Tycho. "How long have…when did you—?"

"I got here yesterday morning. There are a few days of rest during Phandalos, no rituals necessary, so I came to visit but I missed you while you were out. I put some extra cob on the shrine while I waited; I hope you don't mind." Ronoah shook his head. "That's what I was working on when Hanéong showed up carrying you. You were all right, but gosh, was he worried. He's been fretting over you ever since." She brought her fist to her mouth, a reflexive attempt to hide her giggle. "It's kind of cute. Like a clucking hen."

Hanéong? Worried? The creature had saved him from so much before, from slot canyons and snake jaws and his own self-destruction, all with nothing but a well-placed quip and a pinch on the cheek. Why the fretting *now*? He was fine, wasn't he? He'd probably gotten a little carried away with the naming, sure, but nothing had even…

Oh wait.

No, it *had*.

Because.

And then there was—

Compulsively he glanced at his hand. It seemed fine, didn't it? Perfectly normal functioning hand, holding an empty mug. Nothing obviously suggesting that a burning grain of whatever Hanéong was had plunged up his bloodstream and into his body, that he'd *taken* it— "Is Hanéong all right? Where did…?"

"He goes by Ybh now." Right, that's right, that name she'd said, that sound like a rounder *eve*, so it was Hanéong's—Ybh's? "Actually it's Azr-Ybh, but I was told I could get him to smile if I shortened it, and he looked like he needed the joke, whatever it is." Ronoah wondered which of Tycho's gods had tipped her off. Probably Roryx, with his penchant for good humour, for predicting storms. "He's at the edge of the State for a bit, I think just to cool down. He said he might come back different, so don't be surprised, okay?"

"Okay," Ronoah managed faintly, and then, "would you mind if—could I get some more water?"

With a rustle of leaf-green skirts, Tycho stood and gestured for the mug. He passed it to her, and watched her leave the shrine, and only when she was gone did he muster his bubbling courage for a closer examination of his arm.

Honestly, he could be forgiven for forgetting what happened: there wasn't a single flake of skin out of place, not a hair on his knuckles dislodged, not one dry line on his palm diverted. Tripping over a rock had marked him up more than this cosmic theft. And yet something in there called to him. Some richness in hue, some irresistible composition, had him lingering riveted over his own arm as if it were a scrying mirror, or a prayer fire, or a porthole. His body felt suddenly like the house of something set apart, the vaunted hall of some sprightly new guest. But not a guest; something come to stay. He caught the thread of it, glimmering iris blue, tried to follow it to source, to spool—and brushed shoulders with something that bristled with friendly lightning, something that shocked his eyes for one second into seeing the land's hidden mesh of energy like the long strands of Yanah's fireblond hair.

He spooked and the vision faded, trailed by a deep-inside snicker that sounded at once like it came from Genoveffa and from himself and from something that was neither of them. What the kulim putrash *was* that? He didn't have time to pry further; another ping was pulling his attention in the direction of the shrine's threshold, and the—*ocean?*—on the other side of it.

He looked up just as Tycho paraded back in, Tycho and the person she'd brought with her, the fiery thing who was bounding nearly over her head to come have a look at him.

"Azr-Ybh," Ronoah said, the moniker like volcanic glass in his mouth, as the creature swept down upon him. "Ybh?"

"Anything," it—he—said, hands hovering an inch above Ronoah's shoulders like he was palpating some auroral pulse. The gale of his wake raised all the hairs on Ronoah's arms; his voice was plush with harmonics, with multiples of fear and relief and delight. "Anything you like, little pilgrim, little star—oh, my—"

Azr-Ybh's fingers twitched like they'd come into contact with something. He drew in a gleeful, disbelieving gasp, and Ronoah was toppled over by the force of the man throwing his arms around him and squeez-ing like he hadn't since Marghat's villa, since the last time he'd needed assurance of Ronoah's survival—and after only the briefest flash of nerve-lessness Ronoah squeezed back hard as he could, burying his face in the crook of this old-new neck and inhaling the trace scent of gunpowder and lime.

"Azr-Ybh," he said, and his own voice flexed with choral complexity he'd never heard before, "what *happened* to me?"

"I don't know," the man blurted, drawing back and looking at him like a freshly-glazed pastry, "this has never happened before, I haven't the slightest idea, I'm *speechless*, I've been a wreck ever since just waiting to see what you'd be when you woke up, *if* you woke up, aha, this is *terrify-ing*—" A poisonous pastry, then? Was there something inedible within him? "Maybe, maybe not, we don't know. We don't know!" Azr-Ybh seized him and brought him back upright, pulsing a sort of lightless, affective glow. He'd never seen someone panic so eagerly, with such joy. "The only thing I'm even remotely certain of is that something *passed* from me to you when you invoked that name, some sentient transfusion that miracle of miracles did *not* burn you to a crisp, no, I think, I think it *took* to you—"

"Like a parasite?" Even before he finished, he was frowning. Wrong word; too harsh, too antagonistic. A different one suggested itself, floated to the top of his brain, and he grabbed it on instinct, said it even though he wasn't entirely sure what it meant: "A symbiote?"

Azr-Ybh pressed his fingers to his cheeks, staring fascinated at Ronoah. "ka-Khastan sounds good out of your mouth," the man said—wait, was that?— "Maybe you're right. Maybe you're two separate consciousnesses orbiting each other, or maybe you're just conceptualizing it that way, or maybe it's diffusing into you moment by moment until tomorrow or ten years from now it becomes indistinguishable from you—maybe anything. You'd be the one to ask. You're the expert. You're the only thing like you on earth."

The way he said it, so completely enchanted, made Ronoah's ears go warm. But before had time to get properly embarrassed, Azr-Ybh swerved subject in that rhizomatic way of his, scooting back and open-ing his arms like a gallery. "And I couldn't just let you be the *only* one to rearrange your atoms, could I, that's *my* trick, not yours, and besides I had to do something to shake off the nerves, would have paced a whole new maze into the Pilgrim State otherwise—so I went and sculpted *this*." Like a coloured lens sliding over his vision, Ronoah was suddenly aware not just of Azr-Ybh's emotive presence but his physical one, too. Azr-Ybh noticed; his smile widened. "Is it nice?"

Nice was true, but not the truth. The truth was that looking at Azr-Ybh made Ronoah want to cry. The urge welled up from an inexplicable sense of homesickness—he had never seen this body in his life, and yet he felt his affinity for it like a tide. The honey-red hair, already escaping its loose braid; the montane nut-butter Ol-Penher complexion, speckled with freckles like a corncrake's egg; the couple inches of height on Ronoah, taller without being tall. Azr-Ybh had forearms like dark marzipan, had the long fingers and wide nails of a Shaipurin heartlander, had an aquiline nose Amimna would be proud of, and not one piece of it did Ronoah remember with his mind but it panged off his heart like a favourite childhood toy. Only the eyes, wide-set and brilliant blue-hazel, bore any resemblance to previous incarnations—and the beauty mark to match. It sat alongside another, slightly smaller, like two moons together in the sky, like a nebula and its newborn young.

"Do—do I know you?" he asked, stumbling as he tried to orient his yearning on something that made sense. Of course he knew Azr-Ybh, he'd know the creature as a trace element on the wind by now, but this … "Where is it from?"

"From you." Azr-Ybh twisted back a lock of hair, fingers lingering on the milk-tea ridge of his ear. "From now—from this moment, this momentous occasion. From scratch."

Change of pace, change of face. You would not find this profile in any history book, no matter how far you searched; it was bespoke, custom-fit for a new era, a turn of the creature's personal Great Wheel. Built to mark this great and terrifying newness. Built in memoriam of the journey it had taken to achieve it. Every friend, every secret, every day of the last two years was in there, if you looked with a sharp enough eye. Ronoah gaped, and Azr-Ybh grinned like a desert at sunrise, fresh-made vessel turning this way and that, baking in the kiln of Ronoah's admiration. Basking in it.

Then came a cough that managed to be as delicate as it was sarcastic, and Ronoah was flooded with a feeling like he'd been caught reading bad poetry aloud. "Tycho—"

"Your water?" *Sketas naska,* but she could be every bit as taunting as Sophrastus when she wanted to be. At least she didn't look put out about being forgotten. She proffered the mug and Ronoah busied himself with drinking from it, as if he could hide his embarrassment behind the stiff upper lip of ceramic. No use; the snicker she leveled him with may as well have punted him right back to the caravans. "Now that you're awake, I have to head back. Everyone's probably worried where I got to—Phandalos is still happening," she said in response to Ronoah's furrowed brow, "and I *did* stay an extra day to make sure you two were okay. I missed out on

Fishing for Omens *and* Dancing in Blue and Green, and Magdalo was going to let me dance in center spot."

Ronoah's embarrassment spontaneously combusted into full-blown mortification.

"My infinite thanks for your sacrifice, little miss *sesoula*," Azr-Ybh said over the loud sounds of Ronoah coughing up water. "We'll have an offering for your pantheon set to match; you just tell us where to put it."

"Anywhere's fine," she answered breezily as she pushed off the wall where she was leaning. "But you still owe *me* treats, too."

"Tycho," spluttered Ronoah, having finally drawn enough breath to speak, "I'm so sorry, please tell them I, tell me how I can—we kept you from your ceremonies, you came so far for this ..." Tycho did not interrupt his rambling. She waited, as she always had, for him to tumble to a stop himself. Flexing his fingers around the mug, feeling the tendons in one hand crackle invisibly, he looked to her beseechingly. "I know we're important, but your gods are important, too. It isn't right for us to trespass on their sacred days."

Azr-Ybh was about to say something, but Tycho got there first. "You're not trespassing." She touched her fingers to the points of the lily petals Azr-Ybh had sculpted into the walls. "You're exactly where I needed to be. So many of Phandalos' ceremonies are supposed to invite the divine, to open the gate for it to come into our world. When the gods heed your prayers, it's okay to take a day to appreciate their handiwork." An unfamiliar mischief crept into her face as she clasped her hands behind her back, rocking up onto the balls of her feet. "Besides, I wanted to see it happen myself. Sometimes it's nice to confirm a dream with your own eyes."

A muscle in his thumb fluttered. Tycho smiled—smiled *at it*, and then readjusted her shawl and flounced out of the shrine, calling a see-you-soon behind her.

Save the sifting, shifting amber light of Yanah's afternoon, they were alone. After a moment, the tentative touch of Azr-Ybh's hands on Ronoah's knees alit like warm sand. "How is it?" he asked, like he was asking both Ronoah and the thing inside him, the thing that used to be Azr-Ybh's. "How do you feel?"

Ronoah swallowed, twisting the mug in his hands. "I ... don't know yet."

How *did* he feel? Not bad, that was for sure. Not like he'd felt waking up in Marghat's villa, or the monastery, no, it didn't feel like he needed to *recover* from anything. It felt like—what? Like there was something spreading roots in him? Like he took up more space than he occupied?

Like music was playing just out of earshot, like if he tilted his head to just the right angle he could catch the notes? Like he was so deeply seated in himself he could barely move but also so far outside himself he could see his own facial expression, the crease in his brow, the scar on his scalp you could usually never see, the indigo underglitter of his skull like Bazzenine's bones, that was new wasn't it, that wasn't always there?

"It certainly was not."

Ronoah startled, then squinted at Azr-Ybh as the realization crept up on him: "Are you reading my mind, or did I say all that out loud?"

Azr-Ybh heaved an exasperated sigh. "Who can tell?" he replied, morose and yet marvelling, it seemed, at his own inability to answer, and Ronoah did some marvelling of his own at the profoundly eldritch peculiarity of the two of them speaking half in word and half in thought for the rest of his life.

That's what awaited him, wasn't it? This wasn't temporary, some brief empathic rush of perspective or power—this was for good. Forever. Oh.

"I might throw up," he said, giddy and grinning, and no matter how nimble Azr-Ybh was, he was only barely quick enough out the door and back with a pail before Ronoah did, in fact, hurl those two precious cups of water right back out of his body. His body, light as a falcon's wing. His body, bright as molten glass, tensing all over with the voracious pucker of salt on a taste bud.

"Give it to me straight," he said once he'd pressed back against the blessed cool of the cob wall. "Am I a shalledra now?"

Now it was Azr-Ybh's turn to laugh, sharp as pine and a little hysterical around the edges. "If you *were* I could tell you what to expect from this transformation," he said, swatting the idea gone with a flick of his freckled wrist. "You can't grow shalledrim via *injection*, that's not how it works."

"And it's not that…*you're* in me, right?" He didn't need the man to answer this time; a scoff like a bloom of shrewd bluebells somewhere behind his left ear was answer enough. "Apparently not," he muttered, and the hypothesis confirmed itself when Azr-Ybh looked askance at him and then flared his nostrils when he realized Ronoah was talking to something that wasn't him. "But clearly I'm not just me anymore, either."

"You were never *just* anything," Azr-Ybh scolded, "don't diminish yourself, you were magnificent long before this, but—but *ecologically* speaking, no, I wouldn't say so. You are—it might—" Again that look, like the man couldn't make sense of what he was seeing, like it unnerved him even as he hungered for it. Despite his newly-augmented hearing, Ronoah almost didn't catch it when the man whispered, "Would that even be possible?"

Ronoah raised his eyebrows. Azr-Ybh didn't clarify. His gaze only flickered, nictitating membrane of starlight, as he sifted Ronoah's cells in search of evidence to support whatever theory he was patching together. *Maybe?* You certainly smell like one, but—I mean, put you back in the world and see, see if it treats you any different—but how will it *manifest*, how will it express itself, you're a human being, what's the fullness of your radius if you, god and gods alike, I don't know, I don't *know*—"

Concerned though Azr-Ybh was, he sure did seem to relish saying those words. Ronoah reached out and put a finger overtop the two beauty marks on the man's face. "Sorry, but can you tell me what you *do* know?" he asked, smiling apologetically. "Or even what you guess, honestly, because it's more than what I've got to work with."

"Of course, of course, it just—" It flooded Ronoah like monsoon season in Shaipuri, swept from his fingertip to his core: the ecstatic shock of a centuries-long monotony broken, shattered into chips of brilliant mystery. How it made this creature young again, how it left him so happily, horrendously helpless. They surged through it together until Azr-Ybh recovered himself. "The theory is simple. I've just never needed to explain it to anyone—to *apply* it to someone like this. It's unprecedented." He ran a hand through his hair, whistled another preparatory exhale. "Right. From the beginning.

"Chamya Bor, I told you, was a very special land. It is not the only one of its kind. That energy, the substance that gave Chamya Bor such unusual qualities, it swirls in currents all across the globe—usually far out of reach, miles underwater or up in the clouds, but sometimes it bubbles up, touches down, and we call the places where it does Wellsprings." *We.* Of all the fantastical things in that sentence, somehow it was that inclusive plural that struck Ronoah the hardest. There were people— beings—that knew about this, and with a sentence he had joined their ranks. "Wellsprings are the pockets and pouches tucked into the world where potential energy pools through all planes of existence, where knowledge from below and beside and beyond seeps and collects. Most of them are little things, bounded by or perhaps bounding nature's shape: this canyon, that grassy dell. There are very few widespread Wellsprings on this earth. Chamya Bor was one; the Pilgrim State is another. It's one reason beyond the sentimental that this place is so special, and so volatile—you can't really *make* a Wellspring. They're fixed to the land in some esoteric pattern, appearing and disappearing in different spots as the millennium arm of that potential energy slowly undulates.

"The thing is, I'm mostly made of that energy." For a moment, some great privacy settled about Azr-Ybh—his body lit up almost shyly, that jewel-toned flow flickering luminous beneath the sheath it bounded, was bounded by. He was looking at himself so unselfconsciously, so full of unsullied awe. Grateful, after all this time, to be what he was, to hold what he held. "Yanah knew it, as everything knows it who has the sensitivity to know these things. That's how she found me, how everything finds me who perseveres. I'm a conscious Wellspring." Azr-Ybh looked up, the stars in his eyes swayed by solar winds, stirred as the acknowledgement moved through him. "And now—unless I am very mistaken—in a round-about way, a little bit, so are you."

Ronoah would have scoffed, if not for the way Azr-Ybh said it: so jubilant, so grave. If not for the way the vertigo took him, so sudden, so sweet, like for one instant he could sense how impossibly quickly they were all moving as the planet whirled through space. Like he could see it from afar. Like he could see a lot of things.

So instead he laughed, a laugh that swooped open like the wings of the cranes off the pond, startling Azr-Ybh with the way it pulsed like nothing but Azr-Ybh ever had before. He laughed the dust up from the ground, doubled over in his mirth. It was just so *funny*, in the inside-joke way of the Universe, that— "A long, long time ago, I told you about *those people* and how desperately I wanted to be one and, and—!" At a loss for words, he seized Azr-Ybh's hands, placed them atop his heart, the better to feel the exultant fire burning there, the radical acceptance, the transcendent appetite.

No wonder that drip of Wellspring energy was bonding to him instead of destroying him—every heartbeat was like a cry of *come in!*, that emotive space he always held open inside of him ready to embrace it, to give it a home. To build it into the castle, no questions asked. At last, he was fully, unresistingly open to change—and in return, just this once, change itself came upon him effortlessly. Like destiny.

Are you with me? he asked Genoveffa. Are you seeing this? Not good, not bad, just—just big, really *really* big, like you wanted, ai?

And Genoveffa was fierce as a fire ant with her reply.

She came to him like raw ginger comes to the tongue, so piquant it was nearly painful, so full of rigor and spice that his sinuses cleared. She came like a tonic, like an arrow, like a shout. She grew in him with all the upright decisiveness of a desert lily stalk, and then she unfolded within him, took his breath away with the beauty and candour and conspiracy of her response. Firewalker; fountainhead. Freshly-lit beacon for the strange.

Did you ever think, glowed a garnet voice in his head, *that it would be any less than extraordinary, when you pulled it off?*

With the heels of his palms, he wiped warm, good tears from his eyes. Okay, he answered, you win. Wish granted. I hope you're happy.

"What you're telling me," he said to Azr-Ybh, with supreme humour, as he picked himself up to stand, "is that *I'm* the glorious unknown now."

He could sense the prelude to Azr-Ybh's laugh, like the drawback of the tide before the wave—but he ruined the moment when his legs buckled and he keeled sideways. Azr-Ybh leapt to catch him, a flurry of freckles and tangled auburn hair. "Are you all right?" he asked, cradling Ronoah like a precious child but also like he was possibly made of wasps. "What happened? Did something break?"

"No, no I just—can't use my legs right now? Nothing's broken, I think—actually, it feels, it feels like—" Like they were *reconnecting*, like they'd only ever been attached by a thin fray of muscle and nerve and now fresh new tissue was bonding them to the rest of him, springloaded and spry. He'd always been a quick sprint, but something told him he would be breaking his own records soon.

Azr-Ybh snorted with exquisite disdain, distraught and adoring every second of it. "It is *incomprehensible* that you're still alive. I know your porousness better than anyone, little empath, and there still aren't enough empty spaces inside you to let something like that nest without driving you completely out of your wits. No matter how internally flexible you are, there are some things the human animal simply will not accommodate—"

Ronoah squeaked as Azr-Ybh suddenly squeezed him, harder than he'd ever been squeezed in his life. "—unless something *helps it along*." The man's voice took on the revelatory tang of a pomegranate, the furious affection of oil splashed on fire: "*You* stuck your nose in, didn't you?"

In response, the Pilgrim State hummed under their feet, the land shifting like a shoulder shrugged. Ronoah had never heard her that clearly except in his dreams. Raphyanachel, disembodied but still very much alive, even after five thousand years—alive enough to harness her power, to alloy one more thing, marble one more set of disparate energies together.

"*Meddling* wife," Azr-Ybh shouted, as if it were a call to prayer, and in a way it was.

Ronoah chuckled, then gripped Azr-Ybh harder as his feet played another round of treachery beneath him; the shrine spun and glittered as he let the man leverage him back to the ground. He closed his eyes, leaned his head against the wall, swore he could taste the clay in his mouth. "Thank you," he said, to both of them—the creature whose name he had called and the one who'd prevented it from ending him. All this, from saying a name.

"Did I get it right?" he asked, reaching for Azr-Ybh's hands. He found them, pulsed once with what he remembered—a tender twist of sapphire, a whiff of amber, the prickle of sunbright rain. "When the Wellspring, when it—cleaved off, is it because I called it right?"

"That name hasn't been pronounced by any mouth but mine in millennia," was Azr-Ybh's reply—and he said it with such classic Azr-Ybh duality, such flippant triviality and such trembling conviction, that Ronoah had to smile. "It isn't possible for anything except what I am to do so. I don't even remember how it used to sound." That struck Ronoah as terribly sad, but the man was clearly viewing it from a different angle: "When the reference is made, the referent must attend. I remember that much. And you did call some tiny, restless piece of me out to play."

"So ...?"

"So in one way, you've given me a gift I can never repay, even if I oblige your whims for all the rest of your days. In another?" A heat radiated, pink and playful and smirking. "You *almost* got it."

Ronoah opened his eyes. Azr-Ybh was beholding him like the first sunrise after the Shattering, the first struggling ray of possibility after an unfathomable dark. "You never know," the creature said, hushed and young and in love with positively everything. "Maybe with practice. Maybe in time."

Ronoah leaned over and kissed his friend on the forehead. Genoveffa burned up his spine like a prizefighter, like a contender ready to run one more gauntlet.

"Practice sounds good," he said.

FIFTY-FIVE

WHEN ASKED ABOUT THE PILGRIM STATE, Ngoluydinh had praised it for its elusive transcendence, its mystical, mysterious essence. *So much worship all mosaiced together like that, it does something to you. I don't even know how to describe it.* Three journeys she had made, and all three had lingered in her, changing her subtly and forever.

She was one of countless others. The Pilgrim State had welcomed an untold number of seekers into its valleys, and all of them left this place altered, alloyed. All of them left feeling more connected to what they'd sought.

And yet, as the next days raced up to meet him, Ronoah could not help but wonder how many before him had experienced that transcendence quite so physically.

With that drop of Wellspring energy swirling the circuit of his veins, the divine was suddenly everywhere. He heard the lusty alto of Raphyanachel's laughter whenever the wind gusted right; on his jogs around the pond, he saw Genoveffa's fireshine flickering out the corner of his eye. Tiny enlightenments clung to his skin, lured by the electrostatic charge built on the friction of his soul against its new cohabitant. The more he explored—his self, his surroundings, everything—with his newfangled faculties, the more he discovered that the gods were suddenly, delightedly within reach.

Sometimes that reach was alarmingly literal.

Like the morning with the dragontails. It started like any other practice session—Ronoah had taken them pondside to try and split-time spirograph his brain into some focus. After all, he couldn't fret over knowing and unknowing the number of fish in the pond, or scratch at the niggling sense that his shrine was still a few degrees off of true east, or grasp for the trick to gripping and twisting the earth to correct it—he couldn't do all that when he was concentrating on not whacking himself in the face with a fireball. Amazing as all these new perceptions were, they were also overwhelming. An hour with his flaming meditation tools would do him good.

The first thirty minutes of that hour passed calmly enough. Then, presumably after hitting some critical threshold of boredom, the little blue comet in Ronoah decided to throw a surprise into his path with all the grace of throwing a cat in a bathtub. He was mid-weave when it yanked on his attention hard enough to send him actually sprawling, and whether it was Yanah's complicit wind blowing or Genoveffa's own coy kinetic energy that did it, the tethers miswrapped and the wicks whiplashed back on him and he threw his hands up on stupid idiot reflex and *caught* them.

Caught them on fire.

If he had any common sense left he would have just volleyed them away again before the fuel blistered his skin—but an uncommon sense took hold of him instead. Stop squinching your eyes shut, it said, and look what we have here. Despite the rational, human part of him wailing in protest, he gingerly obliged.

The burning bulbs of the tether weights prickled, parcels of cord and fire. No welts, no scorching, no char that he could see, just—just a rainshower of hot prickling, like scooping noontime sand into his palms. The longer he stared, the longer he held, the more certain he was that, whatever it was doing, it wasn't *hurting*.

"Dragon's tits," he breathed. The flame curled and snapped, a nod of agreement, a wink. Something way down in him was laughing.

After ten incredulous minutes holding the flames steady like two big ripe bolls of red cotton, he was forced to accept that he was, for all intents and purposes, fireproof now.

He looked at his own hands; imagined them smaller, chubbier, stubbornly waving through the flames in a baked clay hearth and insisting to his mother that it wouldn't hurt. I guess, he thought, you were just a little early. A little impatient. Typical.

A smile tugged at his face. He had a feeling this was one knack that was going to stick. He tossed the flaming dragontails from hand to hand a few times, secured the loose tethers around his forearm, and then made his way to the shrine to drop a clove in his palm—and to scare the living starlights out of Azr-Ybh with his new find.

Ever since Ronoah had become host to his new blue passenger, Azr-Ybh had been cheerfully inconsolable. The man hovered around him like an enormous nosey dragonfly, investigating even the most banal motions and choices. When Azr-Ybh wasn't physically present, Ronoah would still feel an insistent little poke of sapphire and clary sage when he was out scouring the Pilgrim State for decorative materials or practicing his inspin toss or trying—*trying*—to take a nap. Ngeome could only aspire to such levels of meddling.

"We just don't know," was the man's giddy refrain whenever Ronoah tried to dissuade him from this energetic espionage. "We don't know what it's doing to you, we don't know how it's going to manifest—will it fizzle out? Will it *multiply*? It could do anything, and I do mean *anything*, you don't understand little star, the whole world bunches up around Wellsprings, incredible things happen, incredible and unpredictable—you could live to two hundred or it could eat you up within the decade, we don't know!"

Azr-Ybh never seemed able to make up his mind on whether this new development was horrifying or the best thing that had happened to him this century. It was probably both. But Ronoah couldn't bring himself to join Azr-Ybh in this ontological angst. He couldn't even bring himself to be worried. Perhaps it was anticlimactic to believe, but he had a hunch he was going to stay more or less the same—if anything, he might just become *more himself*.

Because that was the thing with the Wellspring: it seemed to really like hyper-augmenting the wishes and talents he already had. While it was positively slamming him full of secrets and wisdom and eldritch odds and ends, most of that stuff sieved out of him before the next meal. The things that stuck were the ones that already had a firm handhold within him, in one way or another.

Like his empathy. He'd thought the Pilgrim State had elevated that sensitivity as high as it would go, but now he knew what Azr-Ybh meant when the man said he could *read the colour of the lightning storm in your brain*. When he passed the Fufori pagoda on the other side of the pond, he could tell by the taste in his mouth that one of the monks had woken up on the wrong side of bed, though he couldn't say which one. Sometimes he walked back through his own glittering emotional imprints, marks he'd left in the fabric of the shrine grounds in moments of heightened intensity—he whacked into the ghost of the first day so often he put a stone cairn there to remind himself. Marvelous as that explosion of triumph and belonging was, he could only go through it so many times in an afternoon.

His weren't the only imprints he could fully process now. The next time Yanah spoke to him in a dream, he startled so hard he actually jolted himself awake. She was still laughing by the time he fell asleep and got back to her—a real, solid, hear-it-with-his-ears-not-just-his-heart laugh, just as her voice was suddenly the voice of a woman and not of a spirit or a sentiment.

"Look who finally started paying attention," she said, with a haughtiness that was twice as strong as Pashangali Jau-Hasthasndra's and thrice as befitting. "I was starting to wonder if you were worth the trouble my dawdling one went through to get you here."

Ronoah took a second to gather his words from wherever they'd dropped on the floor; in the end, Yanah was a shalledra, and every bit as mesmerizing as the hunting logs had warned. "You—you mean Azr-Ybh?" he finally asked.

"Hmph." Yanah let her head loll back on her jasper stag, her glossy hair dripping through its antlers. "So it's Azr-Ybh again, is it. I was given that name, too, once." She cut her eyes Ronoah's way, a glance so lazy and yet so sharp he nearly jumped. "I suppose you are worth something."

Ronoah took the teasing on the chin, and for his trouble earned a smile that stole the breath from him. Yanah slipped from her steed like a mercury spill, brushed the seat of a tree stump and arranged herself on it as if it were her throne—given they were in the Pilgrim State, in a way, every stump was—and flourished with a swinging sleeve at the tea service steaming before her.

"So," she said as Ronoah took his place, "how grows my garden?"

They talked. He told her about Shaipuri; she hummed her approval at some parts, sucked her teeth at others, arched one impeccable eyebrow at the whole concept of the War of Heavenly Seeds in a way that felt disorientingly comforting. So went the playful disdain of the millennium toward the century. She had seen far greater tragedy before Shaipuri was so much as a banyan in the bog. She told him about Chamya Bor, when he asked; told him about Wellspring countryside, how fruitful and fulsome it was, how essential and sentient, how it metamorphosed everything into something good and right and aligned, how it *understood*. Told him about how Azr-Ybh told her long ago that even though Chamya Bor was gone, there still existed a few shreds of the energetic undertow that had made it possible.

"Even the collapse of the Empire isn't enough to wring that Wellspring dry," she said, sounding at once entirely contemptuous of the Empire in question and also unwilling to hear a word against it. Ronoah, wisely, did not speak one. He remembered Azr-Ybh's throwaway comment about brigadier generals.

Shyly, he asked about the Prophet Evin. He caught the way Yanah's chin tilted up as he said her son's name, that updraft of unbearable parental pride, the conscious choice to respond with joy and not with loss. She sipped mist from her cup, seemingly considering what pieces of that child she was willing to release from the dominion of her memory.

"He would have been horrified to see you shave your head like that," she finally pointed out, with a wrinkle of her nose. Taking pity on Ronoah's confused frown, she continued: "For him—for most humans then, but especially him—that was a sign of shalledrim rulership. Also, he was vain. Got it from Azr-Ybh, I'm sure."

Ronoah startled into a laugh; something deep down in the earth laughed along with him, something that made the tea in Yanah's half-full cup run over anew. She tisked and swiftly set the teacup down to shake droplets off her hand, and in that moment it hit Ronoah—they could actually talk about Azr-Ybh. Commiserate on the creature's faults, rejoice in its quirks. Its fullness, its richness. Together.

Yanah was the first person Ronoah had ever met who knew Azr-Ybh like he did. Who'd travelled with it, lived a life with it, linked elbows and jumped with it into the secret delights of the world. She was the only one who understood what the last two years had contained, what they meant to him.

There had been others in between the two of them, glittering links in the chain of Azr-Ybh's long life, there must have been—but Ronoah didn't need to know them all. One confidant was enough, no matter how many thousands of years split them apart. One more exiled elder sister.

Gathering his courage, he drained the last cornflower dregs from his cup and set it down in his palm, asking: "Tell me how you met. What was it like, in those days?"

A spark in Yanah's eye. "Oh, it's a story you want, is it? Some sweeping epic, some wonder-filled fairy tale about that thing and its capering—like the jaguar-faced creator god, or the warrior of Torrene, or whatever else you've heard, you want more, ah?"

A hunger they shared; he to listen, she to share. All the dream tea in the world couldn't keep Ronoah's mouth from going dry when he nodded.

The shalledra Raphyanachel reclined on her throne, yawned wide like a lion, lifted a hand to catch it, considered him leisurely through her splayed fingers. Useless performance, all of it. Ronoah had spent enough time with Shaipuri's proud wisewomen, with the granddaughters of Yanah's garden, to know when someone was playing coy. These ancient beings, sighed a blue crackling inside him; always so ready for dramatics.

He didn't mind. He let her have her fun. And after one more slow, elaborately casual blink, the shalledra Raphyanachel decided it was time. "I'm insulted you didn't ask sooner. A myth from the mouth of a myth, no?" She crossed one leg over the other and leaned forward, her long hair slipping over her shoulders in conspiratorial whispers. "Very well," she said. "Let me tell you the thousand ways I tried to kill the thing that saved the world."

And she told him.

As it turned out, landscapes were the best storytellers in all the world. Maybe even better than Azr-Ybh. The Pilgrim State made Ronoah laugh loud enough that the dogwood trees around them blossomed spontaneous; she made him weep with such abject tenderness that a new crop of bleeding-heart grew to consolingly nudge his thigh. She made him feel every instant of those centuries. She spun a vision of Azr-Ybh so true that Ronoah nearly remembered that name she referred to, nearly caught it once again under his tongue. It slipped his grip in the end, but perhaps that was for the best—he wasn't so sure how summoning a pseudo-god into his dreams would go.

"Do you know what it means?" he asked over another cup of tea. "Azr-Ybh. Who—?"

Yanah scoffed a scuff of gold dust up from the ground, regal in her distaste. "Of course I know what it means," she replied. "It's the first human name that thing was ever given. My *ancestor* bequeathed it, that one who bore my kind."

"Oh." Oh, wow. He was speaking a name that predated the shalledrim. No wonder it felt so potent.

"*Planetbound*," said the Pilgrim State, and there was nearly a sneer in her voice. "That's what it means. The fool is so terribly fond of it—you see that tattoo, that's what's written there—but personally I think it's a nasty, callous little joke." Ronoah frowned, and Yanah sighed like this was elementary knowledge. "They named it a fallen god. Imagine—every time you're called, you are reminded of your confines, your limitations. It's the height of rudeness."

Although he would never tell her so, he disagreed. *Planetbound* didn't seem rude to him at all. It sounded fond, and surefooted, and honest. A clear-eyed acknowledgement of what was, and a declaration to love what could come of it. Was it so bad, to be tied to your world?

Differences of opinion aside, Ronoah was deeply grateful for Yanah for another reason: she didn't bat an eye at his transformation. Of course she didn't—she was partially responsible. She found his fits and starts of magic positively adorable. Given Azr-Ybh was so cheerfully out of sorts about it, he found he really needed her steadying presence to bolster his sense of composure about the consequences of his new human-adjacent status.

Because the question had started asking itself again, gripping and ever-present: *what are you going to do, when you leave this place?*

That question had haunted him since the Iphigene Sea. It had changed valence over the course of a year and a half, from a panic-inducing intimidation to a grounded, curious inquiry to an ecstatic, ravenous possibility. Now it morphed one more time, unfolded the corners of its central verb into a whole new field of inquiry:

What are you going to *be*?

How was he going to take these newly planted abilities with him back out into the world? In the Pilgrim State, nobody looked at you strangely—everyone was just caught in the sway of Yanah's great creative intoxication, and knowing or doing strange and magical things registered differently. He was fairly certain he wasn't even the only fireproof person here; he felt twin pricklings like headwinds from different directions sometimes, the north, the south-east, beacons from others who could plunge with full abandon into the inferno.

But he couldn't imagine, say, going back to the academy in Padjenne and impressing his fellow students at a party with sticking his hands into live fire. That seemed more likely to make him into someone's research project than anything. And there was the ghost of the shalledrim to contend with, the suspicion alive in most of Berena's mind, that would work against him too. Kourannia had been ostracized simply for bright eyes and thick skin—how dangerous would it be, in the wrong place at the wrong time, to be as he was now? The wisewomen of Shaipuri might not blink twice—there goes Runa, doing weird shiyalshandr things again—but everyone else? His friends? His family?

How was he supposed to present himself to the people he cared about? How was he supposed to reconcile truth with responsibility?

The same old challenge. He'd circled it resentfully since he was a child. Now, though, he felt its impact with new resonance—and new humility. He was no longer the repressed young rebel of Pilanova, fighting for blunt honesty at all costs. There were more ways than one to be truthful.

He put this maturation of philosophy into practice when the time came to fulfil another promise: writing letters to Ean-Bei, and Ngodi, and Yengh-Sier. They had made him swear to send word once he'd settled in, and he did not intend to let them down. But he couldn't just write *The weather's great, the architecture is fascinating, oh and also I'm a really clumsy interdimensional being now, and did I mention the Pilgrim State is my friend's wife?* He had to gather the words to tell the story true without telling it factual.

Luckily, he knew a master in this art.

Azr-Ybh spent a solid hour playing hard to get when Ronoah asked him for help—"What? You want to tell a tale without upsetting the sacred harmony of the Universe? But you'll have to be sly! And cryptic! Gods in heaven, Ronoah, you might need to leave one or two things out, how will you ever!"—but once his point had been thoroughly made, Ybh agreed. Together, they crafted language flexible enough to hold the necessary tension between accuracy and authenticity, to satisfy the dual desires of communication and discretion.

"It's all in the poetry," Azr-Ybh instructed, while Ronoah crossed out another ill-fated phrase in his notes. "Who's to say whether or not the reality you're describing is reality exact or an elegant crabwalk around that reality? You don't have to tell them you mean it *literally*; you people love a good metaphor."

The test, ultimately, was to be content in knowingly sowing that misdirection, to focus on what was being shared and not what was being obscured. Ronoah had always admired poets their ability to write things that were at the same time imaginary and profoundly true—now he joined their ranks, stumblingly learned their outlet, that medium in which the truths of his heart could find a workable home.

I feel, he wrote, *as if some new space has opened up inside me, and a mystery has seeped into that space which I am only just beginning to comprehend.* To Yengh-Sier specifically, he added, *My firedancing has improved considerably since I got here.* To Ngodi, *It's all blue and gold, just like you said.*

Humour, he discovered, was also vital to this practice. Now he knew where so many of Azr-Ybh's inside jokes originated.

When he had them written—three plump envelopes, one for each wayward Ol-Penher friend, plus one more letter he'd been inspired to pen last-minute—he brought them to the one human exception to this new creed of secrecy.

"Tycho, I cannot thank you enough for this." They sat on the wide porch steps of the Chiropolene temple, out of the way of brisk steps chiming with the occasional belled anklet, as Ronoah gave Tycho the parcel. She was wearing a sturdy teal travelling shawl around her shoulders; inside the temple, the bustling of priestesses packing their sacred tools and instruments for the long road back to Aeonna. Phandalos was over, and it was time to say farewell.

"It's not hard to stop by the postal office on the way out," Tycho said with a giggle, but Ronoah was insistent in his gratitude.

"Everything I've been through here—ever since we first arrived—it's been easier and, and more *fun* because of you." That piqued her smiling attention; for such a serious girl carrying such a heavy responsibility, she cared a lot about fun. Maybe she valued it precisely because of the weight she shouldered, the weight of her peoples' pleas and futures, the weight of being a divine conduit. In a much realer way now, Ronoah could empathize. "Thank you for being here." A crackle at the nape of the neck, a blue ember, a suggestion: "Thank you for *being*."

Tycho took the parcel from his willing hands, smoothed it like a cat in her lap. "Being's harder than it sounds, isn't it," she said, and he nodded vigorously. "Complicated, even though it's supposed to be simple."

"You said once," Ronoah replied as the memory surfaced, "about how even simple things are so complicated that it's amazing anything even works. You said seeing that complexity makes everything shine brighter."

"Did I?"

"It was very wise of you."

"It's true." She searched him with that premonition of a look that was so unique to her, somehow ominous without being even a little frightening. "You see that complexity more now, and now everything shines when you look at it. Did you know? It puffs up and preens like a bird. Because it knows it's being recognized," she said to Ronoah's bewildered expression. "Because it feels you're paying attention in a way lots of people don't. I think it did that before, a little, but now it's really obvious. Your attention is a prayer; everyone can hear it."

Stare boldly enough and life itself will swoon for you. Ronoah felt the tendril of limeflower laughter that was Azr-Ybh, miles away at the shrine site, and batted it away.

Tycho ran her thumb along the corner of the parcel, then tilted her head and examined the letters in her lap more closely. "You said you had three you wanted to send," she said, one side of her mouth turning up as if she knew what was coming. "What's this last one for?"

"For you to hold onto." Anticipation swayed him, leaned him forward like a cattail on a breezy pond. "In case Kharoun and everyone come to pay a visit soon."

Tycho beamed. "I bet they'll really enjoy that, it'll be such an unexpected surprise."

"I hope it's not too much to ask you to keep it safe until then."

The little priestess sighed. "Stop worrying about imposing on my helpfulness, Ronoah. One day it'll be your turn to help us." She peered at his letters a moment longer, then shrugged. "Unrelated, but you should visit me next time. Aeonna's really pretty, I think you'd like it."

"…I think I will," Ronoah replied, letting it sweep through him like the premonition it was, the orienting force like one of Yanah's winds. The mirage of the Chiropolene city swam in his mind—reminded him of something. He rummaged around in his satchel. "Until then, have this as a token."

Tycho accepted the gauzy bag of sugared nuts with unadulterated delight. As much as she professed to love them, she ate them sparingly, savouringly, as they said their goodbyes. The bag was still more than half full when they hugged each other one final time and he took his leave.

"Say bye to Ybh for me, okay?" were her parting words, hollered at him when he was already halfway up the first hill. He turned and waved at her, waved like she had at him way back on the roof of the caravan. It took until he was down that hill and up the next before it came together in him.

The name. Ybh. *Planetbound*. Of course. That was the joke Tycho had been let in on, the secret to the shortened form. Even without the Wellspring guiding his morphological analysis, Ronoah could see it: there the resplendent noun, there the confining modifier. *Ybh* was an ancient word for planet. Calling the creature by that syllable was akin to calling him your world.

A laugh pushed out of him, small and determined as a wild violet. When he got back to the pond he tried it, so simple, so velveteen: "Ybh?"

A bright spike of surprise from inside the shrine caught him like a rock in the arch of his foot, enlivened, endeared. "Yes, little star?" came Ybh's voice floating out after it.

Ronoah's smile softened. He said it more cautious than he thought he would. More wistful. Like a rehearsal. "Tycho says goodbye."

FIFTY-SIX

*I*T IS THE NATURE OF A JOURNEY that you will meet friends and fellow strangers along the way. You will share campsites and swap stories and learn from each other how to weather your futures just a little more wisely. Then the sun will rise, or the signpost arrive, and you will go your separate ways. This, too, is the way of things: most of the souls you encounter will not go with you to the end. You have the time you have with them, and if you are skilled enough in pilgrimage, bittersweetened by your travels, you will learn to let that be enough.

Ronoah thought he had honed this skill. Since before he'd even set his sights on the Pilgrim State, he'd been practicing saying goodbye: to his family, to the desert, to Padjenne. He had left Hexiphines and Kourrania in a blur of determination, he had left the Tellers in a sting of regret, he had left Bazzenine and Jesprechel with a promise and a purpose. He had left Nazum with a hollowness that only later swelled into love; he had left Ean-Bei and Yengh-Sier and Ngodi full of hope and aspiration. The modulation changed, the timbre of abandonment, but the pattern was ironclad: he always walked away. He always said goodbye. He'd thought he was practiced enough to be composed about it by now.

But with Tycho's farewell in his mouth, he was reminded that there was one person no amount of practice would ever prepare him to leave with grace.

When they lit the brazier in the inner courtyard, when Genoveffa's clove-roasted fire painted the terracotta tangerine in approval, Ronoah knew his time with Azr-Ybh was running short.

The shrine's windows gleamed with scavenged stained glass, red as a garnet, blue as a star, so the light danced in sprites on the walls; Tycho's macrame tapestry added yet more richness, more warmth. The undu-lating curve of the roofline was shingled, spread with loam, sown with sedge grass and stonecrop. No pillows plumped the benches yet, no jars of seeds or spices on the shelves, but those were accoutrements. In the ways that mattered, Genoveffa's shrine was finished—and she was very happy with it.

But Ronoah wasn't. Or so it might seem, to an observer. One would be forgiven for reading dissatisfaction into the crease of his brows as he spent hours resculpting the second leaf on the lily bas-relief so it pointed a little more to the left, or trekking into the jungle to find precisely the right branch to strip and set up as a—purely decorative—support for the front awning. This place was the culmination of his pilgrimage, the testament to his devotion to his god. It made sense that he would want it perfect. It made sense that he was lingering over the tiniest, most incidental of details. It would be easy, should the need arise, for Ronoah to dismiss the notion that he was stalling.

Except he knew that's what he was doing.

Of course he was. He remembered doing just the same in the monastery, deep-cleaning stone facades and counting columns and taking (and re-taking) inventory of the kitchen storehouse in order to avoid getting out there and finding Özrek's great elusive something. He remembered three months of intentional distraction in Khepsuong Phae, learning circus and researching a thesis just to fend off someone else's apology. This was a habit. He always clambered down into the details of something when he struggled to face the uncomfortable whole.

Here was the whole of it: the shrine was complete. That meant his pilgrimage was over.

That meant he had to go home.

It was one thing to valiantly promise himself that he would return to Pilanova when the moment for it still dwelled in the fantasyland of the future—quite another thing when that moment had arrived in the hard land of now. Doubts were nibbling at his resolve, pecking holes in what seemed in hindsight like a very idealistic vision of things to come, revealing the turmoil beneath.

If Ronoah was being honest with himself, he was scared down to his bones of Pilanova's reaction to his return. Maybe *he* was proud of himself for making this pilgrimage, for building Genoveffa's shrine on the other side of the world, maybe he considered himself a better person now than he was when he left the desert—but would his people see it that way? Was his personal growth worth the pain and confusion he put everyone through? Would the priests in the temple recognize him as a wishgranter blazing Genoveffa's unconventional trail, or would he be rejected, dismissed as a heretic and a disappointment? Would his family forgive their greedy, dream-chasing son, or would they practice that punishing silence Pilanova was so notorious for, and act as if he no longer existed?

Maybe if he was more self-respecting he wouldn't care. He would walk back into his childhood home and present himself and if they didn't approve of him, well, that would be their problem, not his. But it *was* his problem. He was, after everything else, still soft at heart, and vulnerable to the opinions of those he loved. Susceptible to their judgement. Longing for their forgiveness. And maybe that wasn't actually a problem—maybe it was just part of loving people, worrying about what they thought. Not a weakness, but a bond. A sign that they mattered to you.

He wished Tycho were still here. He would ask her counsel, bring her an offering of apricots or more candied almonds and beseech her to peek into his future. Or at the very least, ask her opinion as his friend. There were other oracles, other soothsayers—this was the Pilgrim State after all—but he didn't trust anyone else enough to lay this dilemma at their feet. He didn't even quite trust the Pilgrim State itself: he could ask Yanah for her thoughts, but he expected he knew what her answer would be. After all, Raphyanachel the woman had once left Chamya Bor, only to have it destroyed by the Shattering. They had both abandoned their homes, but only Ronoah could open the doorway back. He worried she would urge him into doing it because she couldn't. He worried about dangling the possibility in front of her, about taunting her by accident.

And Ybh, Ybh was—hope leapt like a fish in Ronoah's heart at the prospect of confiding in Azr-Ybh about this. But it was hope in vain. He could talk to Azr-Ybh about almost anything, but he could not ask the creature to help convince Ronoah to leave. He could not task the originator of this adventure with cutting the adventure short. That was too twisted an irony for him to take.

What he needed was to be away from the shrine for a minute, to step back and gain some insight from afar. He needed someplace he could be quiet and reflect on family and obligation and doing the right thing even if it wasn't pleasant or easy. Somewhere to steel his resolve.

With no one left to turn to, he turned inward, tentatively nudging the drop of Wellspring energy coursing through his body. How about it, he asked—do you have any ideas?

A suggestion bubbled up, confident and crystalline. The crater, the cradle, the lake. The island.

Ybh and Raphyanachel won't do you much good, but their son will spare some sympathy for you.

Evin. He could visit Evin. Immediately it settled something in him, some helplessness quelled. It managed to feel implausible at the same time—of all the options at his disposal, petitioning ka-Khasta's beloved prophet was something Ronoah would never have considered. That was the Wellspring doing what it did best, though, wasn't it? Creating opportunities where Ronoah's mortal mind could find none.

So the next morning, he put down his procrastinating and set out on a journey.

He went alone, so it took most of the day to get there; without Azr-Ybh's celestial strides to condense the journey, the road to what he was calling Prophet's Isle was long and winding. He alternated between asking the Pilgrim State attendants for directions to the lake with the dogwood trees, and asking the glint of knowledge that was humming and stirring down in his marrow, allowing it to tug him magnetic toward his destination. By the time the landscape started to resemble what he was looking for, the sun was dipping her copper head beneath the treeline.

A twilight visit, then. Perfect timing for beneficent ghosts. He borrowed a rowboat from one of the shoreside temples and glided out onto the lake.

It took until moonrise to find the right island. Temples were lighting their lanterns on the coast; some had even sent them floating onto the water, distant clusters of fireflies weaving in the waves. He'd brought his own lantern, a clay one he'd made himself during one of his periods of distraction, but he left the candle quiet for now; Pao and Innos were nearly full tonight, tumbling light like silver mist upon the island's shore.

Ronoah had always considered himself good at showing appropriate respect to greater powers—banter with Ybh and Yanah aside—but as he moored the boat, he found himself at a loss. Evin wasn't a deity, but he was a hero, and this was his grave Ronoah was treading upon. He didn't know how Evin felt about that. Didn't know if Evin was around to feel anything about it at all. After all, he hadn't been affixed to the land the way the Pilgrim State had. Maybe there was no ghost, no imprint. Maybe when they'd buried him under the blueberries, Evin had finally gone down to the dream at the bottom of the world, and rolled the rock away, and stepped inside with nothing left to lose.

But just in case. "Hello," he called, his own voice vetiver smoke in his nostrils. "My name is Ronoah Genoveffa Elizzi-denna Pilanovani, and it makes my heart shy to meet you. I came here to—get some perspective. I hope it's okay if I walk around for a bit. Let me know if there's anywhere I shouldn't step."

No response but the wind, the quiet lapping of waves. He took it for permission and set to wandering, one hand rested on his satchel where *The Prophesier* nestled like a talisman. Like an offering.

Azr-Ybh had finished reading the novel to Ronoah last week, and in so doing had founded in Ronoah an almost embarrassingly ardent admiration for Ybh's son. The way Maril Bi-Jelsihad wrote it, Evin and his family had willed a better life for humanity by the force of their sheer stubbornness. The Prophet convinced local spirits to help safeguard early settlements against encroaching shalledrim. He foretold the worst of the wars, the earthquakes and forest fires, so that human communities had ample time to prepare. His wife—with some help from her mother-in-law—re-educated humanity in medicine, concocting tinctures and salves to heal the bruises of the body and the mind. They had over a dozen children, and when his youngest was kidnapped by a neighbouring shalledrim warlord and returned in pieces, Evin somehow found the grace in his grief not to go hunt it down. He could have—knowing Ybh and Yanah as Ronoah did, either one would have gladly taken care of it—but he didn't. That vengeance went to Evin's eldest daughter, who spent her life devoted to ending the shalledrim, and whose ideas and principles were passed down until the age of the Chainbreakers, her millennial legacy.

Evin was the reason they weren't all still slave to the shalledrim now. He was, tangentially, the reason the Pilgrim State existed, the source of generations of inspiration. After thousands of years, Evin was still a guiding light to people all across Berena.

"How heavy was it?" Ronoah asked the blueberry bushes. His voice hovered like a honeybee, tentative, freighted with pollen and awe. "That kind of responsibility. Did you know it had to be you? Did you hate that it was?"

The legends were all pomp and honour, but Maril Bi-Jelsihad's telling left space for ambiguity in Evin's life, left room for the reader to wonder: was it a work of love, or of loyalty? Evin had started as such a feral, impulsive child, twigs in his hair and amber in his eyes—and yet somehow he had grown up and given that away to be what humanity needed him to be.

Humanity's needfulness had taken so much of him from us, from himself, right to the end.

Ronoah was facing nothing so grandiose as this. His struggles were almost insultingly personal compared to the catastrophes Evin had averted, the calamities he'd endured. But, but still—

"How did you do it? Where did you draw the strength to give up what you wanted for what was right? Or the—the self-sacrifice." Evin was the child of Yanah and Azr-Ybh. He'd been suckled on selfishness. If he could do it, so could Ronoah. If Evin could walk away from the promise of endless woodland adventure to martyr himself for their species, Ronoah could damn well leave the Pilgrim State for Pilanova. Leave Azr-Ybh for his family.

He didn't want to choose. He wanted so desperately to have both. In fact it would—it would make everything easier, if Azr-Ybh could accompany him home. It would soothe his most atavistic fears if he could hold that creature's hand as he fulfilled this promise.

But a horrible sense of finality told him that wouldn't happen. He couldn't drag Azr-Ybh with him, no matter how much he wanted to. It wouldn't be fair—it wouldn't be kind. It was going to take three or four months just to *return* to Pilanova, depending on whether he could find a ship that sailed straight for Lavola and whether the Shattered Sea was in its ornery season by the time they got there, and then the weeks on camelback from Padjenne into Acharrioni lands, out to the oasis—and once he arrived, then what? Who could predict how long it would take for Ronoah to atone, to accept the judgement of his family, to restore himself as a good sibling, a grateful child? They might not—a shudder rippled through him, cold as the bottom of the lake—they might not even acknowledge him until a few weeks had passed. They might not speak to him for *months*. After all, he had abandoned them for years.

He'd be asking Azr-Ybh to throw away endless opportunities for mystery and escapade in order to—what, watch Ronoah flub a family reunion? Some thanks, for everything the man had given him. And on the slim chance it actually turned out all right...what if he decided he wanted to stay for a while? Reclaim his Pilanovani life, his role as a member of the community? No way Azr-Ybh would want to stick around while Ronoah picked figs and washed laundry and took Gengi out for morning walks. It would be ridiculous; it would be *boring*. It would be embarrassing even to raise the question.

It would be a side trip, a timid voice pointed out in his head. Azr-Ybh asked you to go on a side trip, and that ended up lasting a year and nearly killing you.

But that doesn't mean I'm allowed to *get it back*, Ronoah groaned internally. He couldn't use Shaipuri as an excuse to coerce Ybh into doing Ronoah a favour, that felt—disrespectful. To Azr-Ybh, and to Shaipuri. He couldn't even argue that they would enjoy the voyage back to Acharrio, because in all likelihood Ronoah was going to be an absolutely lousy travel companion. He was going to spend the whole thing sulking and worrying and in his own head, because of course he was, and that made for one supremely unpleasant trip. He'd already been unpleasant to Ybh—to Hanéong—and he really didn't want to put the creature through that nastiness again so soon.

He should just pluck up the courage to get it over with. The sooner he went home, the sooner he might come back. It wasn't like this would be goodbye forever; Ybh had made it perfectly clear that he was interested in watching Ronoah's Wellspring develop for years to come. That they were friends for life. With that blue ginger spark in his veins, Ronoah no longer worried about being left behind for the next most interesting thing.

He would just—like someone to talk to. On the lonesome road back. In Pilanova's shunning shadow. In the event he was ostracized. In the event he was cast out.

It was horrific to consider, but it was a possibility. As long as he didn't mention what happened in Khepsuong Phae, with Kauryingh, he was safe. But if he told anyone the truth, he'd be in trouble. He was kidding himself thinking he might stay for long in Pilanova—the pressure of that secretkeeping would poison him just like it had when he was a child.

Stop that, swished the Wellspring inside him. You're only spiralling now. No one is going to exile you.

There was a grove, an alcove of flat earth hugged by gneiss outcrops. The smell of fermented fruit swam inside like a ribbon eel in a jar. Ronoah lit his lantern: blueberry bushes lined a space no larger than his shrine's inner courtyard, spattering the rocks with smeared berries. With the stunted trees slinging their canopies low overhead, the magnolia, the mountain laurel, it felt nearly like a cocoon, every bit as cozy as the dream at the bottom of the world. He sat cross-legged, examined the berries bursting in drooping chandeliers off the branches. Found the firm ones to eat, so zesty, so bright. There—something else for his stomach to roll around.

"Help me," he murmured, as he ferried a seed out from between his teeth. "Help me find the nerve to risk this. Please."

Evin's grave was silent all around him, witnessing. Perhaps it had no reply, or perhaps the best response it had to offer was this wordless capacity, this petrichoral patience. Ronoah didn't think he felt Evin anywhere here, but he felt understood just the same.

He contemplated this until his candle drowned itself, until the waft of blueberry wind-wine made him lightheaded and droopy-eyed. Humming a prayer in the back of his mind, he let himself drift off on Prophet's Isle.

Yanah did not visit him that night. Perhaps she was disinclined to disturb her son's resting place, which was also, ultimately, her own. Instead Ronoah dreamt of chasing a brown-braided boy through gigantic oaken woods, climbing trees and dodging tossed acorns and laughing. One acorn hit the bone of his wrist and made him lose grip on a branch, and he fell. As he tumbled through the air, he worried he would snap his neck on impact, would begin the boy's long years of sadness—but he landed instead in a basket of figs. He was himself inside a fig, like the baby in the Pilanovani story, curled up where red pulp should be. A point of light incised the skin, sliced an opening, and he peered through the gap and saw Diadenna looking down at him, paring knife in one hand.

They stared at each other while the sands of time flowed upwards, flowed backwards. Eucalyptus rinsed the air clean. Then Diadenna leveled the knife, huge as a sail, and placed its tip to his chest.

"We need to talk," she said, and then, with love, she pushed.

Ronoah woke with a start, with a galloping heart. The dark before dawn rang metallic all around him; from the treetops, birdsong. He spent a minute just catching his breath, getting his bearings on where and when and who he was. The dream sat heavy as a hen in his lap, pointedly ignoring all his waking melodramatics. When he finally gave it a second look, he realized it had not been a nightmare. No.

It was a reason. It was a push.

We need to talk. The words that had scared Ronoah to the next country, that had set him running to the other side of the sea. Diadenna had needed to deliver something to her son—a judgement, a criticism, a disappointment—and tried to invoke the auspices of the mountain to do it, the bounding power of Sweetwood Day. It was bad enough that she'd given him that advance warning. It was that life-changing.

Ronoah didn't know what it was. Years of nighttime hypothesizing, of desperately trying to divine his wrongness through the shivering nausea of fear-beyond-fear, and he'd never come up with a theory that satisfied him. His mother's motivation remained a mystery.

And—oh, gods, that was it, wasn't it?—if he didn't go back to Pilanova, he would never, ever find out.

It shocked him to realize this was something he was willing to disgrace himself for: understanding a previous disgrace. It was almost perversely self-destructive. But also—it made sense. He'd spent years on this journey caught in the friction between running from and running to. He knew what he'd run toward now—the pride of Genoveffa, the glory of the Pilgrim State, the glee of Ybh's friendship. But he didn't know what he'd run from, not really, and without that context, that bookend, this pilgrimage would always feel slightly incomplete. Lopsided. It would feel not fully his, and that was unacceptable.

He needed the resolution, even if it was probably going to hurt. He couldn't live his life not knowing. He was—Vespasi wake, he was just too *curious*, in the end.

You are impossible, he admonished himself, lifting his eyes to the canopy in powerless exasperation. You are infuriating, and obscene, and absolutely ridiculous. You're going to throw this all to the wind for one painful truth.

But there it was. If he could uncover the secret to Diadenna's disappointment, he would go to Pilanova. He would even go alone.

Ronoah allowed himself one long, derisive sigh, startling the waxwings from the laurel trees. He picked a breakfast of blueberries, stored them in his lantern. He turned for the boat.

Azr-Ybh was on the roof of the shrine when Ronoah returned, crouched among the seedlings, telling them stories to encourage them to grow big and strong and strange. Once and always a mentor; once and always a trickster.

"Ybh," he called, and the man straightened, high noon like ruby in his auburn hair, arm raised to wave or to shield out the sun, and Dragon's tits, Ronoah wanted to burn this moment into his mind forever.

When Azr-Ybh joined him, the first thing Ronoah did was seize him in a big, tight hug, burying his face in the fabric of the man's tunic. He didn't explain himself, and Ybh did not ask—after an aqua-magenta blip of surprise, the man settled in, happily wrapping his freckled arms around Ronoah in turn. They swayed there, wordless, as the air glittered citrine satisfaction. Across the pond, from the Evnist church, the faint strains of singing.

Nose pressed to Azr-Ybh's collarbone, Ronoah breathed in. Limeflower, gunpowder, hay after rain. The smell of a maelstrom, the smell of the stars. All the perfumeries in Padjenne could never. "You are the most amazing thing that's ever happened to me," he insisted as he drew back, hands on his friend's shoulders. He willed his voice steady, willed it bright. "You are resplendent, and terrible, and preposterous, and you have made my life a legend worth telling."

True to style, Azr-Ybh didn't even blink at the praise. "I did say it would happen," it replied, sly and wise and unrepentant. It was going to be one sorry boat ride without this banter to distract him. But the decision was made.

Ronoah summoned the oasis inside him. He summoned his mother— both his mothers, flesh and faith, their restlessness, their determination. "I think I'm ready to go now."

Azr-Ybh lifted its chin. "Ah? Where to?"

"Home." It welled up on command, bright as dyed cotton: the heat dry as a snap, the tooth-keening sweet of preserved dates, the bruises from a baby goat's headbutts, *home*. The Land of Twenty Thousand Fig Trees, the House of Glass— "Pilanova. I promised myself I would go back after I made it, I vowed I would show them how I've changed." The Echo Chamber held that promise, rebounding silent and endless. He was going to live up to it. "I want to say sorry to my family. I want them to know I'm not—you know, dead or something. I've been gone for years, they're my family, they deserve to know what's happened to me—more or less. I'm not, I'm not exactly going to walk through fire in front of them, but I mean this journey, this pilgrimage, Genoveffa—" He was stalling again. Trust him to eke out even a second longer. He clamped down on his rambling, straightened his shoulders. Exhaled. It's okay, he told himself. Be brave. "The shrine is finished. So it's time to go home."

"Very thoughtful of you," said Azr-Ybh, "when are we leaving?"

"Honestly I was thinking today," Ronoah said on the rush of another pent-up exhale, the wave of a nervous laugh, "I don't do great with extended goodbyes, it'll get worse the longer I leave it, I'll just sigh around morosely all day—"

It pinged him belatedly. That pesky plural. Always showing up where he didn't expect it.

"…We?" he asked.

Azr-Ybh did not repeat itself. The silence protracted to embarrassing lengths.

With a deliberation so extremely serious it skipped serious and went straight to parody, Azr-Ybh took Ronoah's hands off its shoulders and held them in its own. "You know," it remarked, "you've intimated twice now that we should go our separate ways. Have you tired of me?"

Ronoah made an affronted wheeze somewhere between *what* and *no*, and Ybh inclined its head. "Thought not, but at this rate a less arrogant creature might be offended thinking you were *trying* to get rid of them. What's your angle?"

"It's not, I'm not trying to *rid* myself of you—" Ybh cocked an eyebrow. The tender, melancholy goodbye of Ronoah's hopes was rapidly dissolving into something much more flailing and obstinate. "I just don't want to *deprive* you of—"

"What could you possibly deprive me of?"

"Of life! Of freedom? Of the chance to be yourself, to move at your pace, to do what takes your fancy for a while, Ybh—"

Ybh. Planet. Affectionate nicknames aside, Ybh was not Ronoah's world, just like Ronoah wasn't Ybh's. The world was the world, teeming with wonder, enchanting and fascinating and full of whimsy. *Trouble to get into and out of again*. It was all out there, beckoning for the curious to come and play.

Ronoah's dull little family errand was positively stifling in comparison. It had to be. He'd already argued this with himself and no matter how much he wanted it to be true, it just didn't hold up that Azr-Ybh would be willing to waste its time on something so mundane. The creature had probably seen a hundred thousand children reconcile with their parents. No way it cared to watch one more.

"It's not like we'll never see each other again," Ronoah said, "I just, I have to go do this thing and it'll bore you to tears and I don't want to do that, I don't want to bore you and I don't want to have to worry about it being boring when it's so important to me, and I—it'll take so long, you'd miss out on so many opportunities, the world would miss out on *you*, I don't want to do that either, get in the way of someone's chance to meet you and change and—"

Azr-Ybh's mouth was crimped on one side, trying in vain to hide a patronizing smile. "Still thinking of yourself as separate from the world, I see," it interrupted, and Ronoah tumbled to a halt. "You're trying to *share* me."

Said like that, Ronoah heard how assumptive it was, how—almost proprietary?—and his ears burned even as he nodded.

"For heaven's sake, humble yourself, little star. You have power, but you don't have *authority*, not over anything but you." The creature gave a snort. "Certainly not over me."

"I just thought," Ronoah groaned, having exhausted all delicacy, "you would want to—I don't know, start another empire, end another war, visit the molewhales at the bottom of the sea while I was busy." These were placeholder aspirations. Ronoah didn't have anything concrete on-hand. Did Azr-Ybh have aspirations, goals? As far as Ronoah remembered, it had never expressed one.

"You thought," Azr-Ybh echoed, "but you did not ask." That was occurring to Ronoah now, with increasingly sheepish blatancy—but Ybh didn't give him time to self-castigate for it. It just released Ronoah's hands to cup his cheeks, to hold his gaze captive in that airless way it did, and said, quite simply, "Ask."

Ronoah stared steadily back. Nothing for it. "What do you want?"

"I want to learn from this sliver of the world a little longer." Ybh slid his palms from Ronoah's cheeks, across his chest, demonstrating the sliver in question. Ronoah shivered. "I want to dwell in your orbit. I want to see how you handle this next challenge. How you work—your stubbornness, your sincerity, and your new blue eldritch friend, all in concert. What will you achieve together, and how will those follies cascade? What more will your Genoveffa demand of you—and how will you exceed her expectations? How will you surprise me next?" A muscle twitched in Azr-Ybh's jaw. A hunger reflex. "I wish to know. I wouldn't want to miss it when it happens."

It made Ronoah tingle all over, this declaration and the eager, easy affection it rode on. It soaked him through like warm water. Azr-Ybh wanted to accompany him—not because they were going towards anything particularly interesting, but because it would be by Ronoah's side as they went. He was momentarily stumped for any appropriate response.

Azr-Ybh helped him get to one. "So," it said slowly, "you're going back to Pilanova."

Ronoah nodded. Ybh grinned its canniest, most conspiratorial grin. "Can I come with you?"

On the breeze, the scent of acrid coffee and sweet mint tea. God and gods alike, this creature and its patterns, its games—just like Azr-Ybh to cast them in the Chiropolene play of themselves and reverse their roles for fun. To take an exchange as old as their friendship and flip it to see if anything would change. To see if the magic of imposing yourself on an adventure still worked.

Ronoah grinned helplessly back. Of course it did. "All right," he said.

Ybh lifted a hand to its mouth, mock surprised. *"What?"*

Now Ronoah was laughing. "I said," he completed, "you can come with me."

Azr-Ybh swept him up in its own hug and Ronoah expected to be tossed or squeezed at least—but it was tender, calm, it diffused instead of intensifying, and after a few heartbeats passed, Ronoah's shoulders came down from the defensive hitch he hadn't even realized they were stuck in. The brittle shell of his courage softened, relaxed as he processed that there was no impossible decision to make after all. He could have both. He could have everything.

"Any unreasonable rules you want to lob at me, now's the time," Ybh whispered in his ear, and Ronoah whacked the creature on the arm, overcome with another fit of giggles.

"I might come up with one or two reasonable ones on the way," he said once he'd calmed down. "For now, we're good."

"It is a long haul," Ybh agreed. "Which route interests you more? The ka-Khastan Alps, faithful path of Tycho and her ensemble, or through Mahabur and around the cobalt coast?"

Ronoah had been envisioning a voyage by sea—but then an idea bubbled up, a third possibility, an option that his idiot self-absorbed brain hadn't even *acknowledged as an option*. It took the Wellspring poking him right in his creative thinking to get him to notice another way might exist. How had he gotten anything done before this mystical symbiosis?

"Neither," he said slowly, provoking a questioning shoulder-bump from Azr-Ybh. "I—I think I want the straight shot." He stepped back so he could face Azr-Ybh, assessing the creature, warming up to the notion.

It certainly would remove four months' worth of obsessive worrying, if they could do it this way. It would remove four months altogether. "If it's possible, if it's within your power, then I want the secret route. I want to move like you move."

Now his friend was catching on. "You want to cheat us out of a journey?" it asked, all teasing scandal. "How unprincipled."

"The faster we get there, the faster we can do something after," Ronoah countered. "Something fun. Come on, just this once. I don't want to make them wait longer than they already have."

At this, Azr-Ybh's mockery softened. "We do what we can," it conceded, and the other half echoed back across the years, from the other side of the *Tris Mantarinis'* tinkling door—*to show we care.* Ronoah nodded. "Fine. Sideways it is. Today, you said?"

Setten and Ibisca, he *did* say that, didn't he, back when he'd thought there would be a buffer— "Yeah. Today."

It wouldn't help, to give himself time to doubt. He was as ready as he would ever be. No more stalling. No more inertia.

"We did *just* finish building," Azr-Ybh said, turning to face the shrine. "You're sure you don't want to stay another week to bask in your accomplishment?"

Feeling the nerves welling in the crooks of his fingers, Ronoah approached the entrance, the lacquer-stencilled swell of the wall. "Where I'm from," he said, "we leave a new house to dry out and settle for a while before moving in. Give it a season to sit." He pressed a hand to the clay. "Let it rest."

It wasn't like he was never coming back. On the contrary—already he was wondering whether desert lilies would grow in the garden, whether he could coax a clove bush to take in the courtyard. Wondering about learning how to fix up the Mbazalzni sound bath, for his next visit. Wonder aplenty.

But for now? Destiny was calling, and its song spelled a homecoming.

"Very well," Azr-Ybh said, and held out his hand for Ronoah's. "We've met my family—let's call in on yours."

They strolled back out of the Pilgrim State. No magic, no cheating, just one deliciously slow final hike. They bid farewell to the churches and statues, the valleys and temples, the peacocks, the foxes, the cranes. They stole stonefruit from an altar, sated their appetites on the rich juices; at one of the welcome fountains, they waved thank you to a group of Pilgrim State attendants, thank you and goodbye. Ronoah removed his sandals, left them in the lap of a sandal tree. Put his outdoor shoes back on with a hitch in his chest.

It was time to do it. To keep his promise to himself; to return to Pilanova, and show the people he loved what it looked like when you granted a wish of Genoveffa, daughter of Pao. What it looked like when you became a world-shaker.

He took a step forward. Another. Said a last goodbye to Raphyanachel, humming reverent gratitude through the airwaves. Took a step forward. Another.

They crested the hill, and Azr-Ybh let out a deep, revitalizing sigh—

And Ronoah's own breath rushed out of him as he was struck by its meteoric force all over again.

He got positively dizzy with it, muddled and befuddled by the sheer sweeping *capacity* that rose from the creature like a tidal wave pulled up from some abyssal ocean depth. He'd forgotten—chuta ka saag, he'd *forgotten* that while he was riding high on Yanah's colluding power, Azr-Ybh had been forced to rein it in for fear of consuming her. He'd forgotten the intemperate taste of his companion, the actual gravity it possessed. In a way, thanks to his new sensitivities, he'd never felt it more intensely.

They descended the hill, Ronoah watching in awe as Azr-Ybh shook itself loose from its restraints and reseated itself fully sovereign. It was like watching something be born. It was like falling in love.

"*Right*," proclaimed his friend and fellow stranger, cracking its knuckles with a spasm of starshine like lightning branching up the tendons. "Fully operational again. Thank goodness for that, I do so enjoy my housecalls but they leave me *extravagantly* cramped—nothing like a brisk jaunt across the continent to warm up the muscles again." It laid eyes on Ronoah, all genial ease and canniness, refreshed and resplendent, a not-god resurrected from its own elective slumber. Ronoah nearly forgot to breathe; the Wellspring in him positively swooned, charmed beyond redemption. "Let's take this nice and slow. Make it instructive—who knows, maybe one day you'll be able to do it solo. Wouldn't that be a nifty trick." Again, it proffered its hand. Wiggled its fingers, tempting. "With me, my little star. Into sideways we go."

Ronoah grabbed that hand like a torch. Gripped tight enough to bruise any ordinary living thing. Flung his faith like a door wide open.

The creature stepped, and he stepped with it.

Part Seven

LIBEROSIS

*T*HE LITTLE ELEPHANT WAS FOLLOWING the Big Elephant into the west, baby trunk wrapped bashfully around its mother's tail; the Goatherd had taken his first brisk step over the eastern horizon, his goat still hidden beyond celestial sightlines; the Flywhisk was poised high overhead, ready to swat away stray meteorites.

It was still dark in the Acharrioni desert, and the stars were all out to play.

Their jaunt through sideways had taken a fraction of a second to complete—but what a fraction, what an otherworldly instant. Ronoah had thrown his whole self into paying attention to the jump, and he still had utterly no idea how to describe to himself what he'd just stepped through, or what had occurred in his body to make it possible. Nudging the Wellspring for assistance provided only a laugh like lapis beads clinking in a dish, and the vague intimation that the best teacher was practice.

"Are we—?" Ronoah clutched Azr-Ybh's hand tighter, taken by belated vertigo. For a disoriented moment he thought they might *still* be between locations—there were just as many stars below them as there were above. It sprawled beneath his feet, the drop into infinity.

He stumbled, and heard the high splash, and then he knew.

Not sideways. Landed after all. Landed in the Salt Flats.

It was *shoshoretta*, the wet season. The rains had just come. One inch deep, maybe two, a film of water coated the salt pan with a mirror glaze that spanned for miles. Despite this, the air was still dry enough that nothing obscured the view of the Great Smoke, that long and lurid plume of dusty starlight that wafted as if from a bonfire at the center of the Universe. Like the end of a rainbow, its origin point was impossible to locate, even by their best astronomers. Some stories said that the unknowable flame it came from was Genoveffa's hearth.

Gods, this. This. He used to come for this every year.

"Apologies, missed the mark a little," came Azr-Ybh's voice beside him. "Been a while since the last precision jump I made—I slungshot us in more or less the correct direction and let the Wellspring make up the difference. We magnetized to one of the shreds left from Chamya Bor."

"Don't apologize," Ronoah said, leaning into Ybh as he craned his face to the salt-scatter of stars, the billow of the Great Smoke. As he felt an old ritual slide into place inside him. "Not for this."

Like it always had, the vision of that limitless and glittering abyss quelled something in his heart. Which was useful, because when he pointed himself at the constellation of the Goatherd, oriented himself toward Pilanova, then the physicality of his whereabouts gripped him with such urgent terror he felt it like nausea. The inevitability of what he was about to do.

They were here. And it was there, right over that way, only a day's trek away. They would arrive before nightfall today if they started now. Everything he'd run from. Everyone he'd left behind.

They watched the theatre of the heavens together, humbled by a beauty they both reflected, in their own ways. Ronoah felt his own little star fizzing somewhere in his browbone, straining to get a better look.

Then Ronoah cowled his red wrap around his head and shoulders. Threadbare fabric caressed his cheek, ready to be pulled up over his nose when the wet wind burst down from the north and threw handfuls of stinging sand like it loved to this time of year. Now he was ready for daybreak. Ready to walk.

Genoveffa's presence wreathed around him, her hyena's cackle, her baboon's watchful stare. *Go on, already, go. You'll be all right. Make something happen. Change something.*

"Lead the way, little star," said Azr-Ybh, and Ronoah Genoveffa Elizzidenna Pilanovani did exactly that.

Three years hunting wonder and legend, and still there was nothing quite so starkly gorgeous as the desert. The dunes unveiled themselves like pulling a rug of shadow off a tile of light; all at once the morning sun struck their summits, painted their undulating sides. Even in the rainy season, the aridity was like nothing he'd breathed in all of North Berena; the air scratched like a cedar chip at the back of his throat, scoured his lungs clean.

From the sand to the savannah. The edges of the dunes nibbled at the scrub-covered hills, the rocky slopes, the acacias—but the bush won out, cumulated in tufts of tough grasses and ornery cacti and there, in that recess, a desert lily. Ronoah plucked one bloom, tucked it behind his ear.

Safe under the awning of his cowl, that flower whispered a welcome home, trumpet of velvet and nectar and spice. It embraced his return like only another child of Genoveffa could. It gave him courage to keep moving.

As they hiked the incline that marked the edge of the wilderness, an amorphous sort of intensity climbed alongside him, a tension between two rapidly oscillating responses. He couldn't tell whether he was growing more resolute or more fretful, whether the emotion filling him like water in a vase was determination or giddy panic. He had the firm sense that everything was going right—but he also had the sense it was going *wrong*, and moreover that neither of these intimations were fully contradicting each other. They did battle in him, jostling as he walked, but they also expressed a strange, undefined sort of unity, and he didn't know why.

The lip of the valley was within striking distance. The sun was behind them now, casting their shadows intrepid ahead of them; in an absent corner of Ronoah's mind it struck him as funny that his shadow, figuratively all the parts of himself he'd tried to neglect and repress for the sake of this city, would technically return before the rest of him. How very heretical of him indeed. They crested the ridge, and—

There it was.

Palm groves like a flock of green peacocks. Patios and ateliers crowning the rounded sandstone and clay. The crumbling tumbledown of the southern ruins, left standing after the Ravaging. Glazed windows glinting in the sun. Still here, still whole, bright as malachite: Pilanova, City by The Salt, Land of Twenty Thousand Fig Trees.

Ronoah beheld his home, one-fourth of his namesake, and that was when it hit. That was when those not-quite-contradictory feelings solved the equation between them, a sinking and a soaring in his stomach all at once:

If he was going to come home, he had to do it alone.

He couldn't actually hide behind the dazzling distraction of Azr-Ybh. Even if it wasn't someone as attention-grabbing as Azr-Ybh, even if it had been Yengh-Sier or Kharoun—he couldn't bring a friend into his family's house to diffuse the tension. The tension had to be faced. That was the point.

"Ybh." He used the diminutive to soften this; he didn't want it to come across as a third rejection after the man had shown such enthusiasm about coming with him. "I ..."

But if he'd thought he was being subtle in coming to this conclusion, he'd forgotten just how easily Azr-Ybh could pluck a thought from your head like a grape. Even more so now, with the Wellspring thinning the barrier between them. The creature already knew.

"To be truthful," Azr-Ybh said smoothly, "I was wondering if you'd disarm yourself of me at the threshold. I make a fine shield—goodness knows I can steal a show—but this isn't an encounter you want to walk into with your guard up, is it."

It wasn't. It couldn't be. "There's lots to explore here," Ronoah said, by way of apology. "Forges, glass workshops, the observatory on the northern edge in the eyes of the city. There's a few ruined houses we left standing to commemorate the Ravaging, I ran through one of them, it's still standing there. And there'll be plenty of rain dances and river watching picnics, and maybe the lily pan will bloom, and if you walk out east you can find the goatherds on their grazing trails and they always have interesting things to say—"

He gabbled on, detailing the myriad ways Azr-Ybh could amuse or divert or engage himself. He talked for a solid minute before he really heard himself, before it struck him how proud he was to have a chance at showing the city off. How proud he was to belong to it—how grateful he was to lay eyes on it again and not cringe back from its magnificence.

"Your people just love a mysterious trader," came a voice Ronoah hadn't heard in a while—he turned and there was Chashakva, working a kink out of her bony shoulder, mischief spelled plain on her Acharrioni face. "I'll make my fun, don't worry about me. Just call when you're ready." She tapped his nose; a good luck spark. "Off you go. Into the tender familiar."

With that, she turned on her heel and snapped out of sight before he could change his mind. She was probably already miles away.

Mirage lifted from the city in the afternoon heat, made all the buildings shimmer. Everything quavered with anticipation, just as nervously eager as he was. Already he was tracing his path home, eye scouting the backroads and palm groves that he used to slip through like a clove-scented shadow on his clandestine return from Genoveffa's patron day. He inhaled the scent of the lily at his ear.

Come, my Firewalker. Shall we see what happens next?

He descended, unguarded.

$\mathcal{T}$HE FIRST THING HE NOTICED was that something was different about the house.

What was it? The varnish was new, probably finished just before the rainy season started, but it wasn't the shine of the clay catching his attention. Were the designs altered? Had the foundations been shored up? Was the front courtyard shaped different, was it bigger?

He stepped over the high threshold to that courtyard, plonked down on the undulating bench smoothed into the wall, and stared with increasingly intense bafflement at the thick geometrics of the outer walls.

The wind blew a grasshopper into the yard. Slowly, it found its way to the far side, bounced up the front step, and sprang out of sight.

He should probably just. Go ask. Instead of lurking in the front like a surly *tupogla*, a house goblin kicked out with the sweeping. He should just go inside and find out. Every second he stayed slouched here was another second the rumours had to accumulate. He'd tried to be discrete making his way here, using all his old secret trails to keep out of the main trafficways, but half a dozen people still saw him and at least two recognized him under his cowl—or recognized Elizze's beadwork on his satchel—and were probably heading home to tell *their* families about it.

Eh, you see Ronoah come walking up from the south-west? Mave-la-lizzi-denna, that one? Like he used to on Genoveffa's day, nn? Long devotion on him, westing to meet his godmother before he even greets his blood one!

Classic Pilanovani gossip. It was inevitable. If he was bothering to come home at all, his family should at least be the first ones to know.

He touched a finger to the desert lily; an offering, a prayer. He went for the entrance.

The front room was empty. Everyone was elsewhere, either in the bedrooms behind the door flaps—those were new, nice colours, orange and indigo and a yellow that smiled even in the dim light—or else maybe in the inner courtyard, their workroom. He took a breath to call himself home, but it stuck in his chest, so somewhat dazedly he just wandered to the stacks of dishware nestled in their recess and grabbed one of their stippled tin cups and dipped it into the water pot someone had filled this morning. He didn't need to—his waterskin still sat half-heavy on his thigh. It was just what he'd always done, first thing when he came home.

He sipped from his cup as he drifted to the inner courtyard, feeling profoundly, preposterously awkward. Slipped out into the sunlight.

Saw his father bent to work at their loom, one elbow rested on knobbly knee as he fiddled with the back beam.

"Um," he said, just as the man looked up.

"Oh!" said Elizze.

They gawked at each other, two gazelles startled from their grazing. Azr-Ybh would have taken that silence and spread it on a pastry like apricot jam.

They both shifted at the same time—Elizze put weight on one foot as if to rise and the many anklets up his skinny leg clinked and Ronoah unwrapped the arm that was clenched like a python around his middle and raised it in half a salutation—and they both opened their mouths and who knows what mortifying joke his father was about to make, what absolutely inadequate version of *hi, Dad* was perched on Ronoah's own tongue, because before either of them could get a word in—

"Stezza, do you know where we put—*oh.*"

Behind Ronoah, that rich, mellifluous, familiar voice cut short in a strangled squawk. Ngeome's sense of indignance was clearly alive and well. Ronoah suppressed the urge to scrunch up his nose—this was the one time he could not afford to dismiss Ngeome's skirt-clutching, no, he had to face the inevitable upbraiding with grace and humility. He deserved that, he'd earned it.

So he turned around, and there was his older brother, disgustingly beautiful as always, radiant in red cotton trimmed with that same citrusy yellow. Bangles clanking on his arms as he brought both hands to his mouth, sea-green eyes instantly awash with disbelief, that flamboyant hairstyle pulled back in—wait, what had happened to his hair? Had Ngeome shaved his head recently too?

Then he saw the person standing in Ngeome's distraught shadow. That wasn't Lelos or Diadenna, was—was that Mamag? Magdaleza Setten Giamba-peleh, one of the girls Ngeome used to pine after?

Was she holding a *baby* in that sling?

"Did you get married?" was all he could think to say—almost accusingly—before Ngeome rushed up and collapsed on him in a sobbing, disconsolate heap.

Ronoah got the breath knocked out of him. A waft of rich shea butter engulfed him a second later, floating up from his brother's shining skin. Ngeome had never been particularly strong but he was absolutely crushing Ronoah now, his arms pinned to his sides so he couldn't even lift them to hug back. He stood there dumbstruck. Miracle that he didn't drop the cup.

"You—you're—you couldn't—I thought you—*I thought*—"

Ngeome gripped Ronoah's arms, twisted his fingers in that red threadbare cotton and *shook* him, something Ngeome would not do even if Vespasi himself flat-out commanded him to. Desperately, Ronoah met Mamag's glance over his brother's heaving shoulder. She only pressed her lips together, bemused and pitying.

"Ngeome, why don't you," Ronoah began uselessly, but the sound of his name from his long-lost brother's mouth was apparently too much for Ngeome, who made a keening clenched-teeth noise like he'd curse at the gods if propriety or his own upright moral character allowed for it. He abruptly relinquished Ronoah and swept back into the house, trailing his inconsolable moans all the way.

Ronoah stood there, thoroughly dishevelled. He looked again at Magdaleza, still leaning in the doorway. "Hi," he managed.

She shifted the baby—her child, *Ngeome's child*—in its sling, settled it snug against her chest. "Hi. Nice to see you."

"Yeah, um, yes, good to—be here." He squinted. "Welcome to the family?"

She smiled, but it might as well have been a wince. "Thank you." An excruciating pause while both of them looked for another polite thing to say. Mamag got there first: "So, I should probably see—"

"Of course! Of—of course. Thank you."

She turned and headed after her wreck of a husband. Ronoah stared with naked astonishment as she went. Belatedly, he noticed the Wellspring laughing, curled around his shoulders like a starlit vervet. Genoveffa was probably much the same. Figures.

He felt his father's hand close on his arm, offering a conciliatory squeeze. "Ah, my beautiful lily," Elizze said, "spicing our house's pilaf already?"

"I didn't even *do* anything," Ronoah protested, all his lofty notions of atonement gone in a flash of old-boned petulance.

Elizze only sighed. "You know Ngeyyo," he replied, lifting his hand to rub it over Ronoah's head like he was nine and not nearly twenty-three. "He is gentler than his brother. The baboon gobbles up the hare, nn?"

Meaning: *you scared him, Ronoah.* This time Ronoah did scrunch up his nose. "I'll try not to."

Elizze chuckled. "We'll see how trying goes." And then, tenderly, before Ronoah could so much as draw breath to note how it had taken all of three seconds to start making fun of him again: "Welcome back, *mave lai.*"

Whatever snippy Acharrioni thing he was going to say dissolved under a spring surge of tears, his own personal shoshoretta welling up and flooding his field of vision.

He was being teased, but he wasn't being shunned. The realization throbbed in his chest: he wasn't a ghost in this place just yet. Elizze—his father—his *stezza* was accepting him, right now, before a single word came out of Ronoah's mouth to apologize for what he'd done. That mercy trembled in him, that grace, astonishing, vertiginous, wide as the void of the underground monastery, clean as the cataracts of Sasaupta Falls.

There was still love for him here. It didn't even need to be earned.

"Hi, stezza." His voice wobbled, wonderstruck. He didn't know where to start. "Hello, oh, *hi.*"

"All his impressive schooling," Elizze said, laughing again as he folded his weeping, ungentle son into his lanky embrace, "and he can only greet his father with words his baby niece already knows. They're very smart, aren't they, them in Lavola."

*H*IS FIRST NIGHT HOME was a blessedly quiet one. Thunder in the distance; more rain was coming to sweep down the city. If Lelos were here, she would be out under the canopies with the other wishgranters of Moretto, preparing to welcome the godling's life-giving tears to the desert. But as Ronoah had discovered, Lelos wasn't here. Neither was Diadenna.

"I understand *kitta* being away," Ronoah was saying as he finished off the heart-and-kidney brochettes his father had brought back from the neighbourhood kitchens, "but Lele? What is she doing out west?"

"Her job," Elizze replied. "Your sister is a matchmaker now."

Ronoah nearly spat the chunk of heart he was chewing. "Lelos? A matchmaker? But she's—" The words faltered, foundered. Speaking plainly in Acharrioni—at least, to other Pilanovani—was difficult. He waved the skewer around while he dredged up the way to say it without saying it. All he could find was, "She's *Lelos.*"

"She's new to the work, and she has long success so far. We went to a wedding she arranged just last season: behold, there's a happy couple!"

"Did she make it work for Ngeome and Mamag?"

"I leave your sister's story in her mouth," Elizze said, grinning and shrugging at Ronoah's groan. "You ask her when she comes easting home."

So there it was, the thing that was different about the house. It had four people in it, but they were a different four than he'd expected. Their mingled auras took new shape, new marbled colour—the song, the chemistry, it had tugged on Ronoah's Wellspring-augmented empathy before he'd even walked inside.

To his immense and offended surprise, some things *had* actually changed in Pilanova since he left. So much for his righteous ranting about how the city refused to grow.

Even if he hadn't come to this conclusion on his own, Lelos made it abundantly clear to him when she returned. She came back a week later, gusting in from Sinsaccia or Uferenza or one of the other western cities, the sound of her singing announcing her down the street, loud as a bell and proud as a jay. That melody came crashing to a halt when she saw him in the front courtyard waiting for her. "*Ronoah?*"

"I missed your weird little songs," Ronoah said as he stood up—and that was as much brotherly ribbing as he could get in before Lelos scooped up a handful of dirt and flung it at him. He was still rubbing it out of his face when she flung herself at him for good measure. "I'm sorry Lele, I'm sorry, I shouldn't've—"

Whap. A stinging sensation, bright as grapefruit. She'd gone one step further than Ngeome and actually slapped him, right in the face. "You. Are. An. *Ass,*" she ground out, and all Ronoah could think in that moment was, well, at least you did your sister justice in the Echo Chamber.

She berated him for the next few minutes, saying-without-saying be damned, until she finally cooled down enough to plant a firm kiss on the cheek that was still warm from her smack. "I'm going inside to get changed," she announced, drawing back and yanking the end of her headscarf out from where it was stuck under the strap of her pack. "And then we're playing knives, and I will win."

And how could he do anything but concede? She went inside and he set the sandbags up, fetched the knives and tested their edges. Spared a thought for Kauryingh, a prayer and a regret, before his sister returned clad in sky-blue skirts, draped in ropes of red glass beads, kicking one sandal more firmly into place. With her travel scarf done away with, he saw the short halo of coils she was sporting. Gone were the elbow-length braids. Gone was the kid sister he'd known.

Or maybe not gone—maybe just grown. It took a second, but he noticed it, peeking clandestine from between the necklaces: a gerbil skull pendant, nestled between her breasts.

"You kept that?" he asked, voice gone just a little husky. "You still wear it?"

"Of course I do, it's a reminder to get out there and make my mark like you did. And to not do it like an emu in the glass shop, like you did."

The fond smile on his face vanished. "Right, because deciding who gets married and when is such a light touch."

"Don't give me that, Ronono, I'm good with people. You just don't count."

"What, I'm not people?"

"Are you looking to marry anyone any time soon? No, you're not. Only thing you'd start a family with is the books in the temple, and I can tell you it doesn't work that way."

He opened his mouth to retort—and instead all he could do was laugh, because it was true, because Lelos always had a knack for being funny even when she was nasty, because here they were throwing knives and arguing like nothing had changed but it had, it had. "You and Ngeome have both gone through your own transformations since I left, nn?"

"Ah, this one, he expects us to stay exactly the same, of course he does," Lelos huffed, taking two knives from Ronoah's waiting hands. "You always thought you were the only person in the world who was capable of learning anything new. You're not special!" Again, Ronoah felt the old urge to counter this complaint, or worse, to fester in it. He resisted, tried to stay with her line of reasoning all the way to the end. "I have friends in cities you've never seen—*kitta* even took me south to Mbazalza, and we're going back in the winter and you're not invited. Even Ngeome wanted something more for himself, and now you have a *baby niece* because of it. We all have interesting lives, Ronoah. It's your own problem if you can't take an interest in them."

Absurdly enough, of all people, in that moment she reminded Ronoah of Azr-Ybh. That confidence that everything could be fascinating, if you looked at it right. That insistence that the entire world could teach you something, if you were willing to absorb the lesson.

And she was right. After all the nuanced and complicated ways Ronoah had changed in the years he'd been away, he couldn't walk back in and expect his family not to have grown. *Life was transformation*, after all. This was the city that had given him that maxim, contradictory though it sometimes felt. His family could not fathom how he had transformed—but perhaps that fathomlessness went both ways. Perhaps he didn't know them as well as he thought. Perhaps he ought to find out.

"I want to take an interest in your lives," he said, and caught his scoffing sister off-guard.

There, the suspicious glance. There, the kernel of yearning hidden under all her bluster. Behind the pouting and the insults, Lelos cared what he thought, wanted his attention and his affection. He could taste that uncertain hope, sweet as an Ol-Penher fondant egg, and it softened his heart and hardened his resolve, because it shouldn't have been so uncertain, because his sister deserved to know that she was loved. That he loved her.

"I'm sorry I did such a bad job of it before," Ronoah said, and he meant it. "Can I try again?"

Lelos glared at him, sizing him up. Then she turned and threw the first of her knives into the sandbag, just shy of center ring. "You can start by playing with me," she harrumphed, and it was enough. It was more than enough.

They played into the afternoon, exchanging little jibes, comparing travel notes. Ronoah wasn't ready to tell the story yet, but he hinted at enough wide-open oceans and delectable rainforest feasts to make Lelos jealous. Her aim had improved remarkably; she hit the sandbag every time. She must have spent a lot of time honing her skills. Waiting for the opportunity to show him.

As for Ronoah—he felt like how he imagined Azr-Ybh must feel, when pulled into contests like this. With the Wellspring spreading mycelial up his muscles, he probably wouldn't miss even with his right hand. Even with his eyes closed. He let Lelos win by a slim margin anyway. It was a strange kind of repentance, but it was his.

*T*HAT WAS ONE SIBLING willing to forgive him. The other was proving more difficult.

Ngeome was not speaking to Ronoah. His brother had apparently decided that the only rebuke strong enough was some traditional Pilanovani shunning; after his initial emotional outburst, Ngeome hadn't done a thing to acknowledge his presence since, except the involuntary groans he emitted when he walked into a room Ronoah was already in, like the mere sight of him pained Ngeome too much to contain. It was annoying, and embarrassing given Ngeome was the only one doing it. Maybe a little hurtful too.

Ronoah did his best to distract himself from being bothered by it. He busied himself befriending his brother's wife instead—it turned out Mamag had just as much interest in architecture and design as he did, she'd done the house's new stencilling herself—and watching the misadventures of her daughter, his baby niece.

Seven seasons old, nearly a year; it would take another year before she got a given name, and then another yet for one of Obagli's oracles to divine her godling. For now, she was just *piki-Magdalezni*, little one of Magdaleza's. She was an intrepid explorer, crawling everywhere and picking up a rattle or an embroidery hoop or one of Ronoah's firedancing tethers and babbling enthusiastically about her find. Despite the fact that she had spent her entire tiny life not knowing him, she didn't seem anxious around Ronoah at all. And despite the fact that Ronoah's only intimate experience with newborns had been Lelos, a long time ago, still he felt like he knew how to handle piki. It came almost intuitively.

Of course, his interactions with piki were limited to when she was in Mamag's care. When the baby was with Ngeome—which was about half the time—Ronoah couldn't bring himself to even ask to hold her.

He was lucky only to be receiving this treatment from one direction, and he knew it. That's why he had been so relieved to discover Azr-Ybh wanted to accompany him, and so tense when he realized his friend could not cross the threshold. He supposed the only reason Elizze and Lelos were choosing not to shun him was because—well, it was counterintuitive, wasn't it? Ignoring someone because you were upset that they'd disappeared. It only prolonged the separation, the disconnect. It only made it harder for Ronoah to make amends.

Two weeks into his stay, Ronoah woke to a fresh cascade of rain and thought, enough. Lelos was right—he needed to actively take an interest in his loved ones' lives. And sometimes that interest had to look like interception; Lelos wouldn't have allowed this to drag on past a fortnight. She would have pestered Ngeome into relenting long ago.

It was time he became apprentice to his sister's impatience. After all, he didn't have forever to spend waiting.

"Hey." They were in their childhood bedroom. Ronoah had planted himself in front of Ngeome, cornered him where he couldn't slip away. "Hear me out."

Ngeome pointedly busied himself looking at his own hands, rubbing nonexistent dirt off his knuckles. It didn't matter. "The rains have brought the Jegnarecci river back," Ronoah said, "and I'm bringing piki-Magdalezni to watch it come down the escarpment. She's lucky to get to see her first river flow so early—like you were." He saw Ngeome's eyebrow twitch. "Mamag's visiting her parents this afternoon, so she's letting Uncle Ronoah take the little one. But I'm sure she'd feel more secure if she knew her husband was there too."

Ronoah sensed his brother drawing near to his words, to the sound of his smokeshot voice, even as he remained resolutely silent. "You can ignore me the whole time if you want," he added, knowing it was a real possibility. Such was the risk. "But come see the water with your kid, nn?"

He relented in the end. Still not on speaking terms, but at least cooperating, they bundled piki-Magdalezni into a sling around Ngeome's front, packed a basket of Lavolani apricots, and hopped aboard one of the ox carts transporting people to the Jegnarecci Escarpment for the viewing parties.

The river hadn't come yet. They chose a vantage point under an acacia on high ground, ideal for spotting the first brown trickle of water when it came to flood the pan. The sky was a rare pearly grey above them, the ground refreshingly cool, and Ngeome still wasn't talking. It wasn't as awkward as Ronoah had worried. Outdoors there was plenty to pique his interest, and he'd learned how to make silences companionable over the last couple years.

And it wasn't actually silent: there was piki-Magdalezni, who was shrieking and gurgling and occasionally saying *kiki*, which might either have been an attempt at her own pseudo-name or a call for her absent *kitta*. She got wriggly in the sling, twisting and reaching for Ronoah; ultimately, Ngeome's dignified silence was broken by an exasperated "Piki, no, *wait*—" as he unwrapped his daughter and handed her over. Ronoah let her explore him, picked a wildflower and tied it around her chubby wrist, responded to her gabbling like he would a respected scholar:

"Really? That's fascinating, tell me more. And then what? Eh, wow, you're joking, no? No?"

"I thought she was you."

"Now, piki, where's your evidence for—what?" Ronoah looked up at the comment—and then it registered that it was Ngeome who'd said it and *then* it registered what he'd actually said, and he echoed himself, twice as perplexed: "*What?*"

Ngeome just gestured helplessly at his infant daughter. There were already tears in his glass-green eyes.

"I was so sure. She's showing the same signs you did when you were new, kitta and stezza said so. I thought we would take her to the oracles in two years and they would pronounce her Genoveffa's child, and—and then I'd know for sure that—that you were, were—"

Abruptly the time for playing was over. Ronoah scrambled into a more attentive cross-legged seat, a hand to piki's back to keep her from toppling. "That isn't—" *How it works*, he wanted to say. Godlings didn't plant wishes into family lines that way. And besides, no matter what Elizze and Diadenna said, it was way too early to make guesses about that sort of thing.

But Ngeome knew that. Ronoah looked again at his brother; tentatively, he called up the Wellspring, reached a tendril of empathy out and touched something that nearly doubled him over, a grey pain like food poisoning, cramped deep in his gut. It told him everything Ngeome would never allow himself to say: *I thought you were lost. I thought you were dead. I thought my own daughter was the closest I would ever come to seeing you again.*

Gods, he must have grieved Ronoah so hard these past years. No wonder he was adjusting slowly.

A younger Ronoah would have condemned himself for putting his brother through this pain. He would have mistaken Ngeome's fear for his own, would have shrunk in or lashed out as that hurt wormed its way inside him. But three years and a drop of cosmic perspective had changed him. He reached out for Ngeome's hand, twined his brother's fingers with his own. The right hand. The giving hand.

"I'm here, Ngeyyo. I came back." The pain squirmed around his heart, but did not penetrate. A sad smile tugged at his mouth. "I'm sorry I did this to you."

Ngeome's handsome face creased with the particular heartache that comes of having your pain acknowledged after a long time sweeping it aside. He leaned his forehead into their clasped hands and just—cried. His low, melodious voice fractured on his stifled sobs, and piki sensed her father's distress and started fussing and mewling too, and *chuta ka saag*, Ronoah had *never* been the stoic one in the family, so they all three wound up having a good cleansing cry on each other, sniffling in the shade of the acacia.

Piki-Magdalezni was actually the one who noticed first: she stopped wailing so hard, her cries shifting from sad to confused to urgent, excited. By the time Ronoah had wiped his eyes to see, the Jegnarecci was flowing, growing its way down the dusty river pan and gaining with every second, first a trickle, then a tumble, then a sprawl. They had missed it appearing around the bend.

"Look," he breathed, nudging his brother in the arm. Other Pilanovani parties were cheering, or dumping pailfuls of yellow petals over the river to see them taken swift away; parents and children alike were making their way down to splash around. Ronoah watched the water, saw how it flowed past them all, bringing joy and exaltation but not pooling here, not ending here, pushing on determined to its own unknowable destination—and he knew he had to make something clear, right now.

"Ngeome," he said, eyes on the riverflow. Praying for courage. "I need you to know that—that I'm leaving again. I am," he repeated, over the despairing noise his brother made, "I'm going. Soon. After *kitta* comes northing home and we all spend some time together."

"Why didn't you tell me?"

"I just did—you wouldn't *speak* to me before—"

Oh, *putrash*. Now he understood. Ngeome Vespasi Elizzi-denna Pilanovani was counting on having a long, long time to reconnect with his brother. That's why he'd thought he could afford to spend two weeks in stony silence. Because there would be weeks, and months, and years after that. "Ngeome," he said consolingly, as his brother hid his face in his hands.

"Everyone in this family leaves. Kitta goes on her long walks in the desert, Lelos travels between cities for arrangements, you—you. Even stezza went to Mbazalza when he was young, when he was sorting out how to make the marriage work. Everyone *goes* places." He let his hands slip down his face. "Is it that tempting out there? Why do I have no desire to see any of it? Am I simple, Ronoah, am I—tedious, for being happy exactly where Vespasi put me?"

Ronoah took his time replying. He wanted to respect his brother's sincerity with a real answer. "It must be hard," he finally said, "being born into a family of travellers." Wordlessly, Ngeome nodded. "I have to be honest, I don't think I'd ever be happy staying in one place like you do. I've never understood how you do it. But there's—there's nothing *wrong* with it. Most people in Pilanova have never left Pilanova; we're pretty strange, all things considered."

"But you're my family." Mournful, morose, almost yearning. It cut through Ronoah like a fish through the river, the fresh realization of just how deeply this man loved them all, just how vital it was for him to live up to their peculiar standard.

"I don't think it makes you boring," Ronoah said, and discovered as he was saying it that it was true. He didn't, not anymore. "I think it makes you fortunate. The rest of us, we're restless—always going out there to try and find whatever's missing inside us. But you live life like your brothers the aloes: whole just as you are." A kink of a smile in the corner of his mouth. "You're at peace."

Despite himself, Ngeome laughed at the joke. "Vespasi wake," he said, invoking his own celestial father, patron of peace and harmony. Summoning some of that cosmic contentment for his own querulous doubts. "I thought I was meant to transform as I got older. From Innos to Pao, you know."

"That's probably why we're all here shaking you up and making you miserable," Ronoah pointed out reasonably. Ngeome sputtered another laugh. "Show you how *not* to do chaos, nn?"

Ngeome turned to Ronoah with that nearly paternal tenderness that could come across as so patronizing in the wrong moment, but it was the right moment then. "And you're supposed to mellow out. Imagine."

"I'm a slow learner," Ronoah replied, grinning. He leaned his shoulder against his brother's. "I won't disappear for three years again, I promise you that. I've—missed you. I wouldn't want to do it the same way again." He traced the contour of the Jegnarecci with his gaze, flowing in full force now. "Maybe I can come back for shoshoretta. I should be here for my patron day, after all. There's no one else to honour Genoveffa."

"Unless," Ngeome said tentatively, "piki grows up to be like her uncle."

"Don't count on it," Ronoah scoffed, but the funny thing was, he couldn't tell if he was being all the way serious. He had never known himself as a baby, so he obviously couldn't compare, but...but he did feel something when he looked at his niece's wide stray-toothed smile, her determined, greedy little grasp. A kinship that went beyond blood. He sure hoped she wouldn't be sticking her hands into the hearth any time soon, but it wouldn't come as a shock if she did, one day.

He bounced piki-Magdalezni on one knee, listened to her cooing join the other sounds of riverside revelry. Allowed himself to wonder. "It might be nice, to have someone new," he murmured, and the odd thought struck him that, once, somewhere, he'd said the words before.

*T*HE DAYS STRETCHED THEMSELVES OUT over the divan of Acharrioni life. Time was not brisk in the oasis; it draped and folded like honey, more like the Pilgrim State than Ronoah could have guessed. Except in Raphyanachel's domain he'd had nothing to worry about. Here there was still one test left to pass, one secret left to uncover.

Curious or not, Ronoah was still terrible at waiting for someone's judgement, still resorted to distraction when he needed soothing. He spent his spare hours scribbling notes about his pilgrimage, trying to find ways to fold the wild, vibrant fabric of his journey into the neat patterns of Pilanovani speech and still have it remain itself. He spent them sweeping the courtyard and milling flour for the house and fetching cured ostrich and redbush tea from the markets. He spent them engrossing himself in the concentrated study of his family, how they fared, how they'd changed. Anything he could muster to suppress the nervous jolt at the bottom of his stomach whenever his gaze strayed in the direction of the mountain. Whenever it strayed to the dunes. Her pathway home.

Five weeks in Pilanova, and finally Diadenna arrived.

The family was congregated in the inner courtyard, enjoying a supper of roast chicken with lentils and fenugreek, drinking melon juice and hot mint tea. Ronoah was sitting closest to the doorway, but even so, he never would have heard her entry. No, it was the smell that told him: sweatsalt and coriander, older than memory, sieved through the house by the cool wind and snatched up by the hound-snouted Wellspring. Instinctively he turned, still half-laughing from his father's old joke about the bricklayer—

Green eyes like two desert wells greeted him. Wise eyes, perched in a face evermore mottled by sun and wind—gods, nearly half her face was bleached by now, and her neck as she unwound her indigo headscarf, her arms splotched like two beautiful brown cows. She looked like a map of every place he ever wanted to visit.

"Hello, *kitta*," he called, and everyone behind him quit their playing to peer into the shadow of the house.

Diadenna's mouth twisted at the chorus of greetings, a smile like a thorn tree branch, a smile that hadn't seen much use in recent weeks. She was often like that when she came back, though Ronoah knew for a fact that she smiled at the dunes. Her sharp gaze roamed the faces of her family—husband, daughter, son and daughter-in-law, grandchild— and settled on him a second time, and that was when his heart skipped, that was when his mouth went dry, that was when he remembered fear. Because those eyes were so resigned, so resolute.

"Ronoah," she said softly, and that was a relief, that ruled out shunning, but then— "Come with me."

Diadenna remembered too. She wasn't wasting a second. He supposed that made sense, given how abruptly he'd run away the first time.

"Kitta, have some chicken first," Ngeome tried—perhaps sensing the possibility of danger and trying to smooth it over—but Diadenna simply turned her head to one side, ghost of a head shake, and waited for her middle child to attend her. She didn't need to wait long. Ronoah was already on his feet.

It wasn't the season for Sweetwood Day, but that hardly mattered to them now.

Outward, chasing the dusk. Out to the edge of the oasis, to the rim of the valley, nearly back out to the waste. They went, she in front, he behind, in silence. The stars congregated on the ledge of heaven to watch.

By the time they climbed the last outcrop and only flat scrubland lay before them, Ronoah was shaking. He couldn't help it; some young thing in him was weakened, wakened by this walk. His present self wasn't even that scared of what was coming—logically, he had survived and endured far worse than whatever criticism his mother had for him. He *wanted* to know what she had to say. It was quite literally what he had come back to receive. But logic didn't soothe the gut-low instinct, the sick tingle in his palms, the aura of fear-beyond-fear rising like the stench of hot copper.

Stay close for this one, he prayed to Genoveffa, *okay?*

Heat bloomed in the base of his spine, chased some of the fear away. Be brave.

Diadenna scouted a flat rock to sit on, gestured for her son to join her. The oasis draped velvet and volcanic in the dark, embroidered with the amber beads of bonfires. Timidly, Ronoah reached for Diadenna's hand. She let him take it.

Thunder on the plains, miles behind them, carried from the flatlands to their ears. The wind was westing tonight; that storm would not find them, but its waters would, eventually, trickling in rivulets and rivers like the Jegnarecci until they emptied themselves into the oasis. Ronoah thought about how it took so many disparate parts coming together across such a distance to feed a single ecosystem. He thought about water tables and saturation points and the impermeability of clay, about how even the most vicious of rainstorms were still considered by the Acharrioni to be Moretto's tears of joy. He thought about how fierce a thing joy could be. He thought any stray thought he could get a hold of, to avoid thinking about how his mother was staying silent so long.

In the glowing, gloaming dark, Diadenna made up her mind. He felt the impulse like a cold jolt, stirring as steel on the cheek. She inhaled— Ronoah braced for it, energy running electric up his blood, charging him fast as if he were back in the Lightning Room, ready for the arc, the spark—

"I'm sorry."

—and things flipped faster than one of Ean-Bei's handstands.

"Um," Ronoah said, stunned. "Sorry?" A tight nod. "What . . . for?"

Her face was inscrutable, in shadow. "For scaring you. For being a coward."

Beneath his shock, he felt it: the corrosive bite of anxiety. It was not his own. Numbly, it dawned upon him that this confrontation was just as hard—*harder*—for Diadenna. What—?

"I should have just taken you here from the start," his mother mused, "instead of hiding behind the mountain. I should have told you what I wanted to talk about straightaway instead of leaving so much room for it to fester. It must have been awful. It must have kept you up at night. Must have felt like poison."

It—had done all of these things. Ronoah was at a loss for what to say about them. This wasn't what he'd thought they would talk about. He had the catalogue of his mistakes prepared, the same neat folio he'd been compiling for years, and he'd primed himself to flip through it with her and earmark the elusive thing he'd done to make her so disappointed in him, so he could finally understand it. This was meant to be a criticism. Why did it sound so suspiciously like a confession instead?

Diadenna did not wait for his confirmation of her assessment; she looked like she was convinced already. Like she knew. "You were prone to making monsters out of things. You sponged up other people's anger and embarrassment until it went rancid in you. You must have thought whatever I needed to say was so bad that I needed protection to say it. Vespasi wake, you probably thought you had ruined something, or everything, only you didn't know how." That rueful twist of her mouth. "And the wait to find out consumed you."

She lifted her dry fingers to his wet cheek. He hadn't even realized he'd started crying.

"That is why you left, isn't it," she said. Her gaze so forlorn, so steady. So sorry.

What *was* this? What was she working her way towards? Why was she saying these things, these excruciatingly true things that lay at the heart of his anxiety, why was she pointing them out this way? So patiently, with such regret—was that the problem? Was it his sensitivity she took issue with? But she didn't seem disapproving, she just seemed—it was like she *appreciated* his struggles, like she found a desolate sort of satisfaction in them. But why? How had she even figured it out? He had never told anyone.

He didn't know how to respond. He was off-balance, vulnerable, the tempered husk of him shucked to reveal the delicate child underneath. When he dug deep inside himself and begged help from all the ethereal allies he had, what emerged from his mouth was, "How do you know this?"

"Because this is what I wanted to say on the mountain." Creases in the corners of her eyes; pain. "You get that monster-making tendency from *me*, dear one. I passed it down to you. And I'm sorry."

At first it simply refused to register. Ronoah stared at her, uncomprehending, this magnificent woman, this Indigo Queen who stalked the desert fearless as a lion and brought incense and silver and honest-to-gods *coral* to cities far and wide and who was his mother, who'd had the fortitude to bring him from Genoveffa's burning hands into the world. It didn't make sense. It didn't make sense.

But with the slow inevitability of clove buds pushing forth on the branch, it started to. It started making sense.

Not bad, chimed the Wellspring, *as far as secrets go, is it?*

"I saw you," Diadenna said as Ronoah crumpled weeping into her lap. "I saw you fearful and shaking, and I worried you had inherited my suffering. I hoped it wasn't true. Sometimes I hoped so hard I refused to acknowledge what was happening in my own home. It gave me my own shaking, my own long nights to fight." She drew the rough edge of her travelling shawl around him, blanketing him in canvas and the smell of coriander. Her words came roughened, thick with sorrow and honesty. "Eventually I couldn't avoid it. We chose *Solidarity* for your left foot, and there I was, abandoning you in anguish. It wasn't right. I wanted to tell you that I understood, teach you how to manage yourself in this city that is so brimming with unspoken fears and envies. But I ruined it, at the last moment, I drove you away and I have not forgiven myself, Ronoah, my little lily, my fireshine, I'm *sorry*—"

"That's three sorries." Ronoah sniffed, exhaled, pressed his forehead hard against his mother's thigh. Inhaled. "Three sorries is all you get, *kitta*."

Her hand faltered its smoothing motion along his back.

She hadn't expected that. She did not know that what lay upon her had learned to manage without her, did not even begrudge her for it. She did not know yet how her child had transformed.

Ronoah was not sorry to have sent Chashakva on her way, but if there was any moment he would have wanted her to see, it would be this next one. This one he was about to create, with his own will, his own words. From language, life.

He lifted himself from Diadenna's lap, sat tall. Rebelled. "Do you also feel other people's fear, and sorrow, and joy? Do you shelter it like a guest who won't leave?"

He had never seen her react that way, like the sting of hot beeswax had struck her. She swallowed, the map-patches of her throat shifting. Breaking new ground. "I do."

"I met someone like us," Ronoah said, scrubbing at his eyes with the heel of his hand, "in a jungle bigger and fiercer than even the Mbazalzni tropics. She saw a kiss and felt it on her lips; she heard a shout and it tore her own throat. She's the head of her tribe, and she's younger than I was when I left." Pashangali Jau-Hasthasndra, sweetest and meanest of the wisewomen. If you didn't count Nazum. "I met her, and I was tasked with teaching her to manage what we all three live through, and I succeeded."

Diadenna was looking at him like she had pulled him from a fire expecting burns, and found him happy and whole. Her hands lingered on his arms—and the thing she had borne, softhearted demon Runa, the Firewalker alive and ravenous, Ronoah Genoveffa Elizzi-denna Pilanovani flared under her touch. He crackled with a drop of the energy that used to fill their whole horizon with green. He saw it connect, saw it string itself like spidersilk between his mother's flinching fingers, saw it vanish.

"Other things happened, too," he said quietly to the disbelief on her face. "Come home with me, and I'll tell you about them."

It was fully dark when they crossed the threshold, kicking the sand from their sandals. "I'm pulling out the Lavolani coffee for everyone," Ronoah announced amid the noises of the family's welcome, "and then I'm building a fire."

"Sounds like you want us awake until daybreak," Elizze said, eyebrows raised. "Now why would you do this to us, little spark?"

As if he didn't know. As if they couldn't all tell just by looking at him, at the readiness glowing out of him like lamplight. "I have a story to tell you," Ronoah answered anyway. "And it's going to take a while."

He brewed the rich bittersweet concoction, poured it foaming into six tin demitasses, left five on the tray for the others to sip. The last he took with him into the courtyard, where he prepared his offering. Here the flint and firesteel, and here the infant flames, fed kindling right from his surreptitious fingers. Here the hand of salt, the bowl of clove. Spiced smoke prowled the edges of the courtyard by the time everyone wandered in cradling their cups; it coiled above the fire, transforming into endless shapes. Hyenas, Chiropolene steeds, a lighthouse, a crane, a plum-black face in profile. Innumerable, ephemeral, reminiscent. And totally out of order, but that was okay. Genoveffa wasn't telling the story.

"Okay," he said as Ngeome laid his head on Elizze's shoulder and Lelos finally stopped fussing with her cushion and Diadenna set one hand on Mamag's knee, watched Ronoah with a hunger he recognized. "I leave with barely a goodbye and it takes me three years to return and apologize. That's—kind of a long time, even for me, isn't it? I should have wested back long ago, I know that, and if things had gone differently I probably would have. But there was this—person I met. This friend I made. And this place I had to go. For myself—and my godling, my fate. For Genoveffa."

He was still cross-legged. That wouldn't do. He readjusted, shifted his cushion, tucked his legs underneath like a Teller. Crumpled notes in one hand, garnet smouldering in the other, he closed his eyes and breathed in.

The slightest trace of lime flowered in the air. He smiled to himself. Nosey as ever.

"Listen," he said.

And he told them.

*F*OUR NAMES, THE PILANOVANI ARE GIVEN. Four keystones, four ways of relating, of moving and seeing and being in the world. One for the ground, for the land they are born to; one for the human kin who love and prepare them; one for their gods, the divine impulse that wished them to life; and one for themselves, to honour that the rest mean nothing without a self and a soul to act on their behalf. They may be a mouthful to say, but there's nothing better to remind you of your destiny.

For the next few weeks, Ronoah's names folded into him. He was Ronoah Genoveffa Elizzi-denna, because nobody in Pilanova called each other Pilanovani, because why would they; he was Ronoah Genoveffa, because his parents and siblings and neighbours all knew from whose uncommon union he sprang. Sometimes, in moments of frustration or sheer unthinking glee, he was just Ronoah. He sensed his godling draw back in those moments, allowing him the space to simply be, to know himself important even without her.

He didn't worry. Like the summer, she always circled on back. Genoveffa was with him when he watched his father sketching, rapt in the capturing of life on canvas; she was with him when he taught Lelos the foundations of firedancing, correcting her grip on her unlit tethers, narrowly avoiding her overzealous swings. Genoveffa was with him the day he spent in the tattoo artist's atelier, crackling her approval inside him as he withstood the necessary pain of a new pair of family blessings. *Discernment* and *Composure* sat liquorice black on his feet, waiting to be walked into the soles.

And she was with him when he realized there was one last thing he had to do. One thing neither of them could allow to remain the same. Something he now had the power to change.

It was—kind of an ostentatious plan. It had to be, in order to work. But he didn't think he'd be able to just come home and drink melon juice in the courtyard afterwards. There was going to be talk, after a scene like that, especially if it got back to his family. It was going to be a good time to disappear for a while.

Luckily, he had places to be. And a friend to escape with.

But he took his time plotting. He took his time celebrating, savouring his tiny piece of Pilanovani life. He'd been right, in the end—staying too long would inevitably breed irritation within him, irritation and guilt. Every time he threw a round of knives with Lelos, he remembered Khepsuong Phae, and the fact that he could never be all the way honest here again, not without becoming unwelcome. He couldn't endure that friction forever. But he made the most of his stay. He let Ngeome fill him in on three years of neighbourhood gossip, the fencing dispute by the south-west ranch and the not-so-clandestine competition between two glass studios for superior materials and Ngeome's own tentative plans to apply as a councilman. He followed Lelos out to the eastern grazing pastures to see Gengi, chancing a pat on the now-adult goat's nose and receiving a friendly nip for his troubles. He taught his father how to play *aephelys* with a board drawn from memory in the dust. Elizze presented him with a new sarong—indigo, with wax-dyed waves of bright orange like sunset clouds, like firesmoke—and sent him into the city wearing it, to draw water and mill flour and to dispel any rumours about whether his family had received him with grace. He endured the variable teasing and cold-shouldering without complaint, with all the humour he could muster. More than once he caught sight of Chashakva amid the stalls, hawking seashells bright as boiled sweets or huddled around a gameboard drinking date juice and cackling with the other traders, regaling them with some tall tale. He let her be until it was time.

And then, when time came, he did it in a way to be glad of. To be proud of.

On the dawn of his departure, he packed light. A groundsheet, a water gourd, a spicebox of salt and clove, a pot of shea butter gifted to him by Ngeome after the man had bemoaned the state of Ronoah's dry, dark-scarred skin. His dragontails, neatly looped and tied; his flint and firesteel, wrapped in supple leather. A ball of waxy twine. A pair of throwing knives.

"That's *all* you're bringing?" Lelos demanded as she hovered over his preparations. Ronoah smiled at her confusion. One last chance to be her weird, mysterious older brother.

"There's a saying I learned," he said, "about the three kinds of travellers. Bad ones bring all their things with them; good ones look for what they need as they go."

Lelos squinted. "And the third kind?"

"The best don't go looking." Ronoah shrugged. "They just call, and their resources find them."

"Eh, he's long modest, him!"

"I didn't say anything about myself!" Regardless, Lelos poked her fun, and he let her. He even laughed along. This little dictum used to not make much sense to him either—but now, with the Wellspring brimming in his bones, that kind of mythic call didn't seem so out of reach.

Everyone was gathered in the front courtyard to send him off. It was nothing like his first departure; it made him want to weep for gratitude. Somehow, he held it in. He kissed everyone goodbye, even Mamag. He let piki-Magdalezni grasp his finger in solemn farewell, blessed her upcoming year. When he saw her again, she would have her own name. And the time after that—well, who could guess?

"Be safe, fireshine," Diadenna said when he reached her, last in line. She held his face in her wind-chapped hands, looked into his eyes so deeply, every shred as intense as the child she had borne. From one wayward empath to another: "Be well."

He promised he would try. He told her much the same. And then he shifted the shoulder strap of his satchel, embedded a pulse of garnet-red love in the ground beneath their feet, and set off in the direction of the temple.

Time to see how far his not-quite-humanity could take him. Time to put the Wellspring to use.

The temple façade still looked like something Chabra'i's bees would migrate the ocean to worship, honey-gold and many-combed and exuding oracular mystery. It still sent a shiver of pleasure up Ronoah's spine when he passed into the dense, incensed shade of the atrium. It still felt like it had his back. Good; he would need it.

Inside, the pressing sense of symmetry, of structure, of secrecy. All the things he loved about this place, all the things he could not bear to keep contained within it. And the priests—many of them would be further in the cloister studying at this hour, especially the younger ones, but some of the elders were arranging mint and tamarisk on the altar, and a flock of clergy walked briskly from one corridor and past him on their way to another, the hems of their rich robes billowing. Searching their faces, he recognized the priestess, child of Nataglio, who had taught him to read.

No better opportunity than this. With a thrill of anticipation, he approached the congregation with his appeal.

"I am Ronoah Genoveffa Elizzi-denna, and I have returned to honour my godling and her lineage." As if they didn't know who he was. They had sheltered his wayward passions and questions for over a year. But the formality of his address made it clear he was here with a mission, and the priesthood of Pilanova was trained to listen when it mattered. He'd got their attention; his old reading instructor opened her mouth, but closed it again, watching him keenly. "Her patron day is passed, and I shame myself for missing it, but I come with the hyena's coat of her blessing about me. I am here to redeem the name of my exiled elder sister, the one Genoveffa wished on this earth before me, and I will have the priesthood witness me."

Redemption rites were among the most opaque, enigmatic practices the Pilanovani priesthood enacted, in part because no two were alike. When a person was exiled from the city, it was because there was no safe or healthy choice left but to send them to reintegrate with their godling. It was technically not possible to know whether such a drastic measure had succeeded—unless the godling in question signalled so. Rarely, children of the same godling would call down some miracle from the divine in order to prove their misguided spiritual sibling had been absolved, to free them from a forever of besmirched memory. It was one of the kindest, most dangerous things you could do.

"I'm going to walk through the Great Fire," Ronoah said, to the sudden quiet of all who heard him. "And I'm doing it for the restored dignity of Genoveffa's nameless one. Attend me."

These were priests. They had seen miracles before. And everyone remembered fifteen-year-old Ronoah sprinting through the Ravaging. But they remembered the burns he had sustained, too, all too mortal, and so they followed him to the chamber that housed the Great Fire with fervent apprehension. A few tried to dissuade him. But when they reached the hall—ensconced deep in the temple, windowless except for the smokehole above—and Ronoah set his sights on the flames, even the most insistent of the congregation fell away.

This fire represented all fire. This fire had been going for decades, maybe centuries; part of his practice as a priest-in-training had been to tend to it, to *watch* it be tended, for he hadn't even been allowed to approach it as a neophyte. This fire was said to be hotter than lantern flame, hotter even than the glassblowers' furnaces. It growled with the power of the sun.

In front of half the priesthood, Ronoah slipped off his sandals, stripped out of his sarong, and walked right in.

It may not have hurt, may not even have felt that uncomfortably hot, but it sure was *loud*. He was pretty sure someone screamed, maybe a couple of someones, but that could just as easily be the howling laugh of the blaze. A molten cocoon, a Universe of gilt and glitter. For an instant, it felt almost like he was back in the Pilgrim State.

He felt the prickling sprint of the Wellspring through his bloodstream, lighting all his nerve endings like candles. He felt the terrified ecstasy of a body that remembered conflagration. He raised his head, searching through that eternity of burning like he had long ago, searching for a shade, a precious shape, for something to be saved. He couldn't see it when he found it, but he knew it was there all the same.

"I free you," he called, to the shadow of the exile who had stalked him all his life, "and I forgive you. I forgive us both."

And he let her go.

A strange giddiness overtook him then. He grinned irrepressibly at the fact that, wow, he was actually doing this, wasn't he? A real shiyalshandr at last; no tricks, no wiles, just pure magic. He twirled once or twice to feel the sweeping caress of fire skimming his wrists. He danced a silly, childish little dance behind his curtain of flame, ungraceful and unabashed, he and the Wellspring partnered arm-in-arm. Then, he reached for the composure he was meant to be building, inhaled that river of heat, emerged in a cloud of cinder and smoke to the starstruck faces of the laity.

"You will give me," he said, "her name."

And what choice did they have? They rushed to the archives and found it, recorded on some thrice-warded parchment of cursed things, and they struck it from the list, and then they gave it to him.

They did not give him what she had done. That was not the point. In this great act of faith, he had rendered her actions null; they no longer mattered. But they gave him her name, and that was everything.

"Thank you," he said as they laid reverent hands on him, feeling the heat of the Great Fire lift from his skin. He slid on his wrap, picked up his satchel. "For what you taught me, what you gave me—what you hold for all of us. Thank you from the bottom of everything."

And he made his exit, numinous, luminous, trailing awed whispers in his sizzling wake.

$\mathcal{N}$ow. as eminently suave as that just was, he probably had half an hour before everyone in this neighbourhood knew about it.

If he didn't want the temple's novices chasing him down the alleys chanting *Firewalker!*, a swift getaway was paramount. He lifted his eyes to the pearlescent sky, dug in himself for that snickering star orbiting his heart. Pulsed a summons through.

It took a few tries before he connected, before Azr-Ybh bounced that sapphire-amber spark back to him. Clearly he was out of practice.

Follow my lead, he called across the ether. My turn to show you something I love.

He chose the rendezvous for its ephemeral splendour, for its heart-stopping fantasy, for the fact that it was only here another couple of days. The south-east lily pan only bloomed for a week in shoshoretta, and some years the season simply didn't dump out enough water to reach the dormant bulbs. Some years they went without, the field fallow with dust.

Not this year. Ronoah arrived in the basin to a botanical dreamscape, to an infinity of orange and yellow and pink, to a perfume like a Shaipurin raincloud, so heavy, so heady, so sweet. Pashangali would have thrown up on the spot. It was magnificent.

He swished his way through calf-deep water, exclaiming at the beetles, the bees, the glory of short-lived beauty. He whistled to the swallows, waved at the children whooping and splashing in the shallows, was a child himself. Was happy.

"—goodness, *there* you are, my little star, this is a *feast* for hungry eyes—"

And there was Ybh, bounding towards him, snatching him up in its freckled arms and swinging him around until the blossoms all blurred into one long festive swirl.

"I'm bringing some with me," Ronoah said breathlessly when he was splashed back down. He patted his satchel, where among the other necessities a packet of dry lily bulbs awaited their beds. "For Yanah. For the shrine."

Azr-Ybh hummed, lifting a beetle from its perch. "If there's anything my Yanah approves of, it's planting seeds."

That reminded him. "I'm sorry I never actually—introduced you. To my family. There was so much to catch up on and sort through and I just—don't know if I was ready this time."

"No need. I took the liberty of meeting them myself. Your sister has *terrific* bargaining sense."

Ronoah cried out, equally affronted and amused, and Azr-Ybh did not even pretend to be sorry. The creature shrugged and stretched out its arm for the beetle to traverse, brave traveller on a strange and starry land. "You can have your time to yourself, this I do not begrudge you, but you can't keep me from being *curious*."

Curious, yes. Curiosity was what surged in them both now, more potent than the perfume of a hundred lily fields. Curiosity pulled him in a dozen directions at once: to Aeonna, to Ruppanteak, to Yengh-Sier's travelling show, to the great ka-Khastan library of Aç Sulsum—or back to Padjenne, to see if he'd been welcome there all along, to see if Kourrania ever came south, if his words had sparked a journey just as hers had done. To the other Wellsprings, to the shrine baking patiently in the Pilgrim State, to the edge of the ocean, to the other side. Up to snowy Svarok, down to the smokestrewn Ashlands. Back to the shadow of the monastery, to Bazzenine and Jesprechel. Out to the Shattering, if he could make it there. Everything, everywhere.

"Speaking of curious," Ronoah asked, as it rose in him like a galloping drumbeat, "where will the wind sweep us next?"

"I was thinking you could use a proper visit to the a-Meheyu isles, not the cringing little tour you self-conducted—you found a derelict shalle-drim temple but you didn't find the doorstep of the Splendid Multitude, they're a fantastic monastic order, I do so adore them. Their whole philosophy revolves around cutting free from a single self and exploring the far reaches of what one can be—they don't even *use* your singular pronoun, they say *we*, always we, always connected to a conch or an osprey or that star, there, the red one just on the horizon—" It was fully day, and cloudy besides, but Ronoah saw it anyway, glowing like a coal in the brazier of the sky. Maybe it was imagination. Maybe it was Ybh lending him its eyes, for but an instant, but a sight. "They've developed some scrumptious theory about the nature of things, allegedly from inhabiting those things and learning from the inside out, and they set it all down in the cleverest little morsels of poetry, mosaic, sculpture, horticulture—yes, even their *window gardens* are hiding clues about the Universe, I mean it when I say they're a favourite, definitely in my top hundred human-led exploratory ventures. Some of the most revered practitioners say they've projected themselves to other *planets*." Azr-Ybh blew a sigh like a mountain wind. "Now *that's* a glorious unknown."

Ronoah found himself smiling. He traced his fingers over the linen of Azr-Ybh's shirt, where the creature's tattoo slept upon its heart. "Maybe explore this planet with me first," he said to it, bittersweet and whimsical in one. "Before you go getting jealous."

"Fair enough." Azr-Ybh kissed above Ronoah's eyes. "Seeing it with someone new is almost like seeing it for the first time. Bring yourself to the experience and the experience will evolve, because you are part of it. I wonder how you will refresh the world. I wonder how you will transform it."

"I'll try not to disappoint you," Ronoah laughed, grabbing hold of Ybh's hands. It beheld him like he was an adventure all to himself, like he was the axis on which their next journey turned. In a way, he guessed he was.

"I do not think," said Azr-Ybh, "you will disappoint any of us, in the end."

The creature set its heel, ground it into the mud—the lilies shivered in anticipation—it called up the secret passage into sideways, into lemons and lychees, into the inferno—

And Ronoah dove in first, tugging his friend by the wrist, and didn't look back.

ACKNOWLEDGEMENTS

Another four and a half years; another doorstopper fantasy. For anyone keeping track, that's nearly a decade to bring the *Heretic's Guide to Homecoming* duology into the world. Some of that comes down to the plot twist that was 2020, but some of it is just because a story takes as long as it takes, and won't be rushed. It took those years of living to make *Heretic's Guide: Practice* what it is, and like Ronoah, it was only by the blessings of my friends, family, and co-conspirators that I made it to the end of the journey.

First, of course, Alex and Bex. Shale wouldn't be here without you, and neither would the delightful animal known as the molewhale. Thank you for the seeds of this magical world!

I am firmly convinced that this weird, highly-interior slowburn of a story would be way more obscure if it weren't for the tireless efforts of Carisa Van de Wetering and Cass Meehan. You two are a promotional force of nature.

To Claudie Arsenault, for geeking out about worldbuilding and queer representation with me, and to Joy Silvey, for doing the thing I am always secretly hoping people will do and sending me personal essays detailing thoughts on how Ronoah's trials and triumphs resonate in her own life. Thank you for always identifying exactly what I'm trying to reveal in my storytelling, and mirroring it back to me. To Maya Baumann, for inviting me to her island refuge and gracing me with the woods and the waterfalls, ideal places in which to put the final-final-*final* touches on a manuscript.

Huge gratitude to Haley Rose Szereszewski for pulling off yet another absolutely scrumptious cover—we did it again! Natalie Lythe was my personal print shop when time came to line edit 250,000+ words by hand, as well as a font of emotional support and encouragement; Elliott Dunstan provided thoughtful feedback on the disability representation in this story and helped me do justice to cultures and characters for which I had the ambition but lacked the experience. And of course, the Molewhales over at the Shale Patreon: thank you for being unabashed nerds about not just the stories but the *world* of Shale. I praise your exploratory spirit!

Brandon Crilly—you came in late but you came in swinging, my friend. I don't know if I'd have gotten this thing done if not for our regular three-hour writing talks. At the very least, I would not have had nearly so much fun.

My gratitude and admiration to the artists whose music inspired me, consoled me, and kept me company while I worked: Klô Pelgag, Darlingside, Kevin Penkin, Andrew Prahlow, Jeremy Dutcher, Zoe Keating, and dozens more. And to my writerly inspirations: Sofia Samatar, Rachel Hartman, Keith Miller, Tamsyn Muir—and Elizabeth Gilbert, whose work gave me the language to understand my own philosophy of creativity. This idea was clearly one of the patient ones.

To my given family, for encouraging my artistic streak since early childhood (and for indulging the ensuing introversion and general strangeness); to Mr. Kokko for always having another film or comic book recommendation to nourish my creative brain. And to the late Fred Torak, for "life is biterminal; having begun, it ends". I hope you're enjoying your glorious unknown.

To readers! Patient, thoughtful, open-hearted readers. You complete the story by bringing yourself to it; you dwell in this two-mooned world, you explore the ruins and the forests, you hold Ronoah's hand as he grows. Maybe you grow, too. Thank you for loaning some brainspace, some heartspace, and some precious time.

And of course, where would I be without Avi Silver? Editor, co-publisher, collaborative worldbuilder, best friend. In some ways this book began our partnership. I am thankful to you for it, but I am also thankful to it for *you*. You have steered *Heretic's Guide* right for nine years. Thank you. I love you. Ready for what comes next?

SIENNA TRISTEN,
Hamilton,
August 2022

Words on the Words

Didn't think I'd let a chance go by to geek out about linguistics, did you?

First of all, to the dozens of people who have asked me how to pronounce such-and-such's name—there is *finally* a pronunciation guide up on The Shale Project's website, complete with audio clips of yours truly. Enjoy!

In order of appearance: the Shaipurin language family is phonetically based on Hindi, with a three-vowel structure (plus phonological distinction in vowel length) borrowed from Inuktitut. Sanaat is pronounced with an extra-long 'ah' in the second syllable. Apostrophes represent glottal stops in Shaipurin languages: Chabra'i's name is pronounced (regionally) as /tchabra-ee/, with a distinction between the 'ah' and the 'ee'. Generally-speaking, Shapurin emphasis is on the final syllable, so we get Mar-*ghat* and Na-*zum*. But as we see, each regional language has its exceptions. As for where those regional languages—Subindr, Jau-Hasthasndr, Yacchatzndr, etc—falls on the spectrum of *language* to *dialect*, the answer is "it's complicated". You could probably divide Shaipurin into five or six "languages" (one for each of the four quadrants, one for Bhun Jivakta, one for Auyyid Gar) and then subdivide those into mutually-intelligible dialects. But the tribes wouldn't be very happy with you, and you don't want to mess with them.

Where Shaipurin has few vowels, Ol-Penher has lots, and diphthongs to match! Praise and gratitude go to the Tagalog and Khmer languages for inspiring the luscious inventory of phonemes here. Those final h's aren't for show: they signal a slight aspiration at the beginning of the syllable they're attached to. One example is the country's name itself, Ol-Penh. More accurately, notationally-speaking, you'd represent this as Ol-P^hen, with a breathy punch in the "penh" syllable. This three-way voiced/voiceless/aspirated consonant matrix is contrastive—meaning there's a difference between 'Ben', 'Pen' and 'Pʰen'—but we don't have the opportunity to enjoy an in-depth example on this particular visit. Ol-Penher is also the only language we've seen aside from Acharrioni that uses word-initial velar nasals, the /ng/ sound.

Those of you who have enjoyed Shale's *Sãoni Cycle* will recognize Qiao Sidhur as a language that was more fully explored on a different continent. Qiao Sidhur borrows phonetic inspiration from Norwegian and Mandarin. Its spelling is definitely the most confusing at first glance: 'hv' is pronounced /kv/, and accented vowels have a /y/ semivowel attached to them: á = /ya/, and so on. Hvanzhir Hanéong is therefore (more or less) pronounced /kvahn-djeer hahn-yaung/. That 'dh' in Sidhur is also pronounced somewhere between a /d/ and a /th/. If you've scoured the glossary at the end of *Three Seeking Stars*, you may notice that Hanéong's other appellation, Qøngemtøn, has some pretty significant cultural meaning back in the homeland. But I'll let you sniff that out for yourself.

As expected from a volume of *Heretic's Guide*, you've also encountered (been confronted by?) a bunch of my own playful experiments with English. Sometimes I like to verb nouns ('slingshotting'); most times I like to adjectivize them ('magmic', 'coralful', 'emberous', 'petrichoral'). Often I play fast and loose with the "is it two words or a hyphenated word or a compound word" dilemma English is always embroiled in—I'm largely in favour of compounds, as 'sunside' and 'smokeshot' and 'fireblond' will show you, but a good hyphen has its place for readability!

John Koenig gets another shoutout here for his volume of emotional neologisms, *The Dictionary of Obscure Sorrows*. Some words are loaned from his coinage, including 'agnosthesia', "the state of not knowing how you really feel about something", which got treated to an -ac suffix ("one affected with"), as in hemophiliac or insomniac, to form *The Agnosthesiac*. Énouement is another of Koenig's: "the bittersweetness of having arrived here in the future, where you can finally get the answers to how things turn out".

One of the core tenets of this story is that language is infinitely powerful and infinitely expansive. But most importantly, language *isn't finished yet*. It was built by people and continues to be shaped by people, and sometimes, to suit the moment, it needs an update. I've updated it for my purposes here; as always, I encourage you to mess around with it to more accurately describe your own life experience—if only to yourself. Have at it, my friends.

About the Author

Sienna Tristen is an author, poet, and literary organizer living in Treaty 3 territory who explores queer platonic partnership, the non-human world, and mythmaking in their work. Their award-winning duology *The Heretic's Guide to Homecoming* (*Theory*, 2018; *Practice*, 2022) is published through indie arts collective The Shale Project. You can find their poetry in *Augur Magazine* and *Plenitude*, and their chapbook *hortus animarum: a new herbal for the queer heart* is out with Frog Hollow Press. When the sun is up, they work with The Word On The Street Toronto to showcase the coolest Canadian & Indigenous literature.

🌐 siennatristen.com
🐦 @siennatristen

About the Project

The Shale Project is a multimedia storytelling initiative roughly in the shape of a planet. It's about three things: top-notch worldbuilding, daring and exploratory fiction, and the philosophy that art is medicine. You can discover what else it has to offer at www.welcometoshale.com

PATREON | THE SHALE PROJECT

A massive thank you to everybody who supports us on Patreon!
You make this work possible; we love you to the moons and back.

Beni	Nick Calow
Carisa Catherine	Rebecca Diem
Charlotte Ashley	Ryan Yu
Emily Colgan	Spenser Chicoine
Joy Silvey	Stephanie Elnomany
Laurence Dion	Cass Meehan
Maria Dominguez	Susan Meehan
Maryam R.	David Senft
Natalie Lythe	Yeli Cruz
Nicholas Mackenzie	

For access to essays, drawings, deleted scenes, discussions via
our Discord server, and sneak peeks at upcoming projects,
join our community for as little as $2 a month!

WWW.PATREON.COM/WELCOMETOSHALE

**Two Dark Moons
(Book One in the Sãoni Cycle)**

Avi Silver

ISBN 978-1-7752427-2-7
FROM MOLEWHALE PRESS

MORE FROM THE WORLD OF SHALE

**Three Seeking Stars
(Book Two in the Sãoni Cycle)**

Avi Silver

ISBN 978-1-7752427-4-1
FROM MOLEWHALE PRESS

MORE FROM THE WORLD OF SHALE

CPSIA information can be obtained
at www.ICGtesting.com
Printed in the USA
BVHW081126131022
649366BV00008B/569